Stephen Crane (November 1, 1871 – June 5, 1900) was an American poet, novelist, and short story writer. Prolific throughout his short life, he wrote notable works in the Realist tradition as well as early examples of American Naturalism and Impressionism. He is recognized by modern critics as one of the most innovative writers of his generation. The ninth surviving child of Methodist parents, Crane began writing at the age of four and had published several articles by the age of 16. Having little interest in university studies though he was active in a fraternity, he left Syracuse University in 1891 to work as a reporter and writer. Crane's first novel was the 1893 Bowery tale Maggie: A Girl of the Streets, generally considered by critics to be the first work of American literary Naturalism. He won international acclaim in 1895 for his Civil War novel The Red Badge of Courage, which he wrote without having any battle experience. (Source: Wikipedia)

Literary works:
Maggie: A Girl of the Streets (1893)
The Red Badge of Courage (1895)
The Black Riders and Other Lines (1895)
George's Mother (1896)
The Third Violet (1897)
The Open Boat and Other Tales of Adventure (1898)
War is Kind (1899)
Active Service (1899)
The Monster and Other Stories (1899)
Wounds in the Rain (1900)
Great Battles of the World
The O'Ruddy (1903)
The Monster. London
Last Words. London
Whilomville Stories

The Third Violet,
The Monster and Other Stories
&
The Little Regiment
and Other Episodes of the American Civil War
STEPHEN CRANE

PRINCE CLASSICS

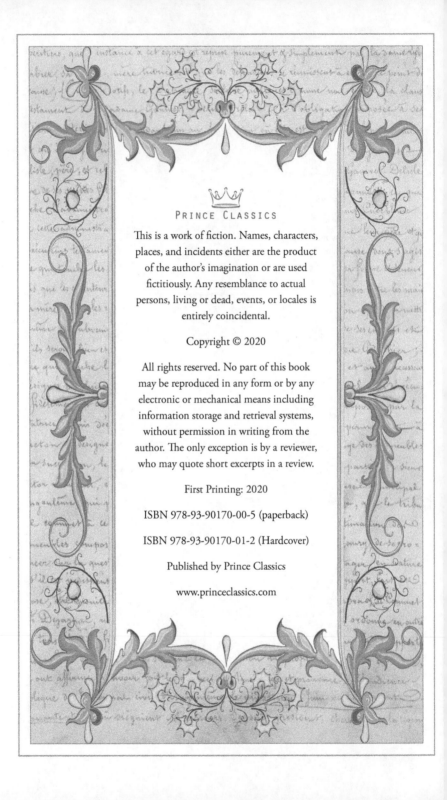

PRINCE CLASSICS

Copyright © 2020

First Printing: 2020

ISBN 978-93-90170-00-5 (paperback)

ISBN 978-93-90170-01-2 (Hardcover)

Published by Prince Classics

www.princeclassics.com

Contents

The Third Violet,
The Monster and Other Stories
&
The Little Regiment
and Other Episodes of the American Civil War

THE THIRD VIOLET

CHAPTER I.

The engine bellowed its way up the slanting, winding valley. Grey crags, and trees with roots fastened cleverly to the steeps looked down at the struggles of the black monster.

When the train finally released its passengers they burst forth with the enthusiasm of escaping convicts. A great bustle ensued on the platform of the little mountain station. The idlers and philosophers from the village were present to examine the consignment of people from the city. These latter, loaded with bundles and children, thronged at the stage drivers. The stage drivers thronged at the people from the city.

Hawker, with his clothes case, his paint-box, his easel, climbed awkwardly down the steps of the car. The easel swung uncontrolled and knocked against the head of a little boy who was disembarking backward with fine caution. "Hello, little man," said Hawker, "did it hurt?" The child regarded him in silence and with sudden interest, as if Hawker had called his attention to a phenomenon. The young painter was politely waiting until the little boy should conclude his examination, but a voice behind him cried, "Roger, go on down!" A nursemaid was conducting a little girl where she would probably be struck by the other end of the easel. The boy resumed his cautious descent.

The stage drivers made such great noise as a collection that as individuals their identities were lost. With a highly important air, as a man proud of being so busy, the baggageman of the train was thundering trunks at the other employees on the platform. Hawker, prowling through the crowd, heard a voice near his shoulder say, "Do you know where is the stage for Hemlock Inn?" Hawker turned and found a young woman regarding him. A wave of astonishment whirled into his hair, and he turned his eyes quickly for fear that she would think that he had looked at her. He said, "Yes, certainly, I think I can find it." At the same time he was crying to himself: "Wouldn't I like to paint her, though! What a glance—oh, murder! The—the—the distance in her eyes!"

He went fiercely from one driver to another. That obdurate stage for Hemlock Inn must appear at once. Finally he perceived a man who grinned expectantly at him. "Oh," said Hawker, "you drive the stage for Hemlock Inn?" The man admitted it. Hawker said, "Here is the stage." The young woman smiled.

The driver inserted Hawker and his luggage far into the end of the vehicle. He sat there, crooked forward so that his eyes should see the first coming of the girl into the frame of light at the other end of the stage. Presently she appeared there. She was bringing the little boy, the little girl, the nursemaid, and another young woman, who was at once to be known as the mother of the two children. The girl indicated the stage with a small gesture of triumph. When they were all seated uncomfortably in the huge covered vehicle the little boy gave Hawker a glance of recognition. "It hurted then, but it's all right now," he informed him cheerfully.

"Did it?" replied Hawker. "I'm sorry."

"Oh, I didn't mind it much," continued the little boy, swinging his long, red-leather leggings bravely to and fro. "I don't cry when I'm hurt, anyhow." He cast a meaning look at his tiny sister, whose soft lips set defensively.

The driver climbed into his seat, and after a scrutiny of the group in the gloom of the stage he chirped to his horses. They began a slow and thoughtful trotting. Dust streamed out behind the vehicle. In front, the green hills were still and serene in the evening air. A beam of gold struck them aslant, and on the sky was lemon and pink information of the sun's sinking. The driver knew many people along the road, and from time to time he conversed with them in yells.

The two children were opposite Hawker. They sat very correctly mucilaged to their seats, but their large eyes were always upon Hawker,

12

calmly valuing him.

"Do you think it nice to be in the country? I do," said the boy.

"I like it very well," answered Hawker.

"I shall go fishing, and hunting, and everything. Maybe I shall shoot a bears."

"I hope you may."

"Did you ever shoot a bears?"

"No."

"Well, I didn't, too, but maybe I will. Mister Hollanden, he said he'd look around for one. Where I live——"

"Roger," interrupted the mother from her seat at Hawker's side, "perhaps every one is not interested in your conversation." The boy seemed embarrassed at this interruption, for he leaned back in silence with an apologetic look at Hawker. Presently the stage began to climb the hills, and the two children were obliged to take grip upon the cushions for fear of being precipitated upon the nursemaid.

Fate had arranged it so that Hawker could not observe the girl with the—the—the distance in her eyes without leaning forward and discovering to her his interest. Secretly and impiously he wriggled in his seat, and as the bumping stage swung its passengers this way and that way, he obtained fleeting glances of a cheek, an arm, or a shoulder.

The driver's conversation tone to his passengers was also a yell. "Train was an hour late t'night," he said, addressing the interior. "It'll be nine o'clock before we git t' th' inn, an' it'll be perty dark travellin'."

Hawker waited decently, but at last he said, "Will it?"

"Yes. No moon." He turned to face Hawker, and roared, "You're ol' Jim Hawker's son, hain't yeh?"

"Yes."

"I thort I'd seen yeh b'fore. Live in the city now, don't yeh?"

"Yes."

"Want t' git off at th' cross-road?"

"Yes."

"Come up fer a little stay doorin' th' summer?"

"Yes."

"On'y charge yeh a quarter if yeh git off at cross-road. Useter charge 'em fifty cents, but I ses t' th' ol' man. 'Tain't no use. Goldern 'em, they'll walk ruther'n put up fifty cents.' Yep. On'y a quarter."

In the shadows Hawker's expression seemed assassinlike. He glanced furtively down the stage. She was apparently deep in talk with the mother of the children.

CHAPTER II.

When Hawker pushed at the old gate, it hesitated because of a broken hinge. A dog barked with loud ferocity and came headlong over the grass.

"Hello, Stanley, old man!" cried Hawker. The ardour for battle was instantly smitten from the dog, and his barking swallowed in a gurgle of delight. He was a large orange and white setter, and he partly expressed his emotion by twisting his body into a fantastic curve and then dancing over the ground with his head and his tail very near to each other. He gave vent to little sobs in a wild attempt to vocally describe his gladness. "Well, 'e was a dreat dod," said Hawker, and the setter, overwhelmed, contorted himself wonderfully.

There were lights in the kitchen, and at the first barking of the dog the door had been thrown open. Hawker saw his two sisters shading their eyes and peering down the yellow stream. Presently they shouted, "Here he is!" They flung themselves out and upon him. "Why, Will! why, Will!" they panted.

"We're awful glad to see you!" In a whirlwind of ejaculation and unanswerable interrogation they grappled the clothes case, the paint-box, the easel, and dragged him toward the house.

He saw his old mother seated in a rocking-chair by the table. She had laid aside her paper and was adjusting her glasses as she scanned the darkness. "Hello, mother!" cried Hawker, as he entered. His eyes were bright. The old mother reached her arms to his neck. She murmured soft and half-articulate words. Meanwhile the dog writhed from one to another. He raised his muzzle high to express his delight. He was always fully convinced that he was taking a principal part in this ceremony of welcome and that everybody was heeding him.

"Have you had your supper?" asked the old mother as soon as she recovered herself. The girls clamoured sentences at him. "Pa's out in the barn,

Will. What made you so late? He said maybe he'd go up to the cross-roads to see if he could see the stage. Maybe he's gone. What made you so late? And, oh, we got a new buggy!"

The old mother repeated anxiously, "Have you had your supper?"

"No," said Hawker, "but——"

The three women sprang to their feet. "Well, we'll git you something right away." They bustled about the kitchen and dove from time to time into the cellar. They called to each other in happy voices.

Steps sounded on the line of stones that led from the door toward the barn, and a shout came from the darkness. "Well, William, home again, hey?" Hawker's grey father came stamping genially into the room. "I thought maybe you got lost. I was comin' to hunt you," he said, grinning, as they stood with gripped hands. "What made you so late?"

While Hawker confronted the supper the family sat about and contemplated him with shining eyes. His sisters noted his tie and propounded some questions concerning it. His mother watched to make sure that he should consume a notable quantity of the preserved cherries. "He used to be so fond of 'em when he was little," she said.

"Oh, Will," cried the younger sister, "do you remember Lil' Johnson? Yeh? She's married. Married las' June."

"Is the boy's room all ready, mother?" asked the father.

"We fixed it this mornin'," she said.

"And do you remember Jeff Decker?" shouted the elder sister. "Well, he's dead. Yep. Drowned, pickerel fishin'—poor feller!"

"Well, how are you gitting along, William?" asked the father. "Sell many pictures?"

"An occasional one."

"Saw your illustrations in the May number of Perkinson's." The old man paused for a moment, and then added, quite weakly, "Pretty good."

"How's everything about the place?"

"Oh, just about the same—'bout the same. The colt run away with me last week, but didn't break nothin', though. I was scared, because I had out the new buggy—we got a new buggy—but it didn't break nothin'. I'm goin' to sell the oxen in the fall; I don't want to winter 'em. And then in the spring I'll get a good hoss team. I rented th' back five-acre to John Westfall. I had more'n I could handle with only one hired hand. Times is pickin' up a little, but not much—not much."

"And we got a new school-teacher," said one of the girls.

"Will, you never noticed my new rocker," said the old mother, pointing. "I set it right where I thought you'd see it, and you never took no notice. Ain't it nice? Father bought it at Monticello for my birthday. I thought you'd notice it first thing."

When Hawker had retired for the night, he raised a sash and sat by the window smoking. The odour of the woods and the fields came sweetly to his nostrils. The crickets chanted their hymn of the night. On the black brow of the mountain he could see two long rows of twinkling dots which marked the position of Hemlock Inn.

CHAPTER III.

Hawker had a writing friend named Hollanden. In New York Hollanden had announced his resolution to spend the summer at Hemlock Inn. "I don't like to see the world progressing," he had said; "I shall go to Sullivan County for a time."

In the morning Hawker took his painting equipment, and after manœuvring in the fields until he had proved to himself that he had no desire to go toward the inn, he went toward it. The time was only nine o'clock, and he knew that he could not hope to see Hollanden before eleven, as it was only through rumour that Hollanden was aware that there was a sunrise and an early morning.

Hawker encamped in front of some fields of vivid yellow stubble on which trees made olive shadows, and which was overhung by a china-blue sky and sundry little white clouds. He fiddled away perfunctorily at it. A spectator would have believed, probably, that he was sketching the pines on the hill where shone the red porches of Hemlock Inn.

Finally, a white-flannel young man walked into the landscape. Hawker waved a brush. "Hi, Hollie, get out of the colour-scheme!"

At this cry the white-flannel young man looked down at his feet apprehensively. Finally he came forward grinning. "Why, hello, Hawker, old boy! Glad to find you here." He perched on a boulder and began to study Hawker's canvas and the vivid yellow stubble with the olive shadows. He wheeled his eyes from one to the other. "Say, Hawker," he said suddenly, "why don't you marry Miss Fanhall?"

Hawker had a brush in his mouth, but he took it quickly out, and said, "Marry Miss Fanhall? Who the devil is Miss Fanhall?"

Hollanden clasped both hands about his knee and looked thoughtfully away. "Oh, she's a girl."

"She is?" said Hawker.

"Yes. She came to the inn last night with her sister-in-law and a small tribe of young Fanhalls. There's six of them, I think."

"Two," said Hawker, "a boy and a girl."

"How do you—oh, you must have come up with them. Of course. Why, then you saw her."

"Was that her?" asked Hawker listlessly.

"Was that her?" cried Hollanden, with indignation. "Was that her?"

"Oh!" said Hawker.

Hollanden mused again. "She's got lots of money," he said. "Loads of it. And I think she would be fool enough to have sympathy for you in your work. They are a tremendously wealthy crowd, although they treat it simply. It would be a good thing for you. I believe—yes, I am sure she could be fool enough to have sympathy for you in your work. And now, if you weren't such a hopeless chump——"

"Oh, shut up, Hollie," said the painter.

For a time Hollanden did as he was bid, but at last he talked again. "Can't think why they came up here. Must be her sister-in-law's health. Something like that. She——"

"Great heavens," said Hawker, "you speak of nothing else!"

"Well, you saw her, didn't you?" demanded Hollanden. "What can you expect, then, from a man of my sense? You—you old stick—you——"

"It was quite dark," protested the painter.

"Quite dark," repeated Hollanden, in a wrathful voice. "What if it was?"

"Well, that is bound to make a difference in a man's opinion, you know."

"No, it isn't. It was light down at the railroad station, anyhow. If you had any sand—thunder, but I did get up early this morning! Say, do you play

19

tennis?"

"After a fashion," said Hawker. "Why?"

"Oh, nothing," replied Hollanden sadly. "Only they are wearing me out at the game. I had to get up and play before breakfast this morning with the Worcester girls, and there is a lot more mad players who will be down on me before long. It's a terrible thing to be a tennis player."

"Why, you used to put yourself out so little for people," remarked Hawker.

"Yes, but up there"—Hollanden jerked his thumb in the direction of the inn—"they think I'm so amiable."

"Well, I'll come up and help you out."

"Do," Hollanden laughed; "you and Miss Fanhall can team it against the littlest Worcester girl and me." He regarded the landscape and meditated. Hawker struggled for a grip on the thought of the stubble.

"That colour of hair and eyes always knocks me kerplunk," observed Hollanden softly.

Hawker looked up irascibly. "What colour hair and eyes?" he demanded. "I believe you're crazy."

"What colour hair and eyes?" repeated Hollanden, with a savage gesture. "You've got no more appreciation than a post."

"They are good enough for me," muttered Hawker, turning again to his work. He scowled first at the canvas and then at the stubble. "Seems to me you had best take care of yourself, instead of planning for me," he said.

"Me!" cried Hollanden. "Me! Take care of myself! My boy, I've got a past of sorrow and gloom. I——"

"You're nothing but a kid," said Hawker, glaring at the other man.

"Oh, of course," said Hollanden, wagging his head with midnight wisdom. "Oh, of course."

20

"Well, Hollie," said Hawker, with sudden affability, "I didn't mean to be unpleasant, but then you are rather ridiculous, you know, sitting up there and howling about the colour of hair and eyes."

"I'm not ridiculous."

"Yes, you are, you know, Hollie."

The writer waved his hand despairingly. "And you rode in the train with her, and in the stage."

"I didn't see her in the train," said Hawker.

"Oh, then you saw her in the stage. Ha-ha, you old thief! I sat up here, and you sat down there and lied." He jumped from his perch and belaboured Hawker's shoulders.

"Stop that!" said the painter.

"Oh, you old thief, you lied to me! You lied—— Hold on—bless my life, here she comes now!"

CHAPTER IV.

One day Hollanden said: "There are forty-two people at Hemlock Inn, I think. Fifteen are middle-aged ladies of the most aggressive respectability. They have come here for no discernible purpose save to get where they can see people and be displeased at them. They sit in a large group on that porch and take measurements of character as importantly as if they constituted the jury of heaven. When I arrived at Hemlock Inn I at once cast my eye searchingly about me. Perceiving this assemblage, I cried, 'There they are!' Barely waiting to change my clothes, I made for this formidable body and endeavoured to conciliate it. Almost every day I sit down among them and lie like a machine. Privately I believe they should be hanged, but publicly I glisten with admiration. Do you know, there is one of 'em who I know has not moved from the inn in eight days, and this morning I said to her, 'These long walks in the clear mountain air are doing you a world of good.' And I keep continually saying, 'Your frankness is so charming!' Because of the great law of universal balance, I know that this illustrious corps will believe good of themselves with exactly the same readiness that they will believe ill of others. So I ply them with it. In consequence, the worst they ever say of me is, 'Isn't that Mr. Hollanden a peculiar man?' And you know, my boy, that's not so bad for a literary person." After some thought he added: "Good people, too. Good wives, good mothers, and everything of that kind, you know. But conservative, very conservative. Hate anything radical. Can not endure it. Were that way themselves once, you know. They hit the mark, too, sometimes. Such general volleyings can't fail to hit everything. May the devil fly away with them!"

Hawker regarded the group nervously, and at last propounded a great question: "Say, I wonder where they all are recruited? When you come to think that almost every summer hotel——"

"Certainly," said Hollanden, "almost every summer hotel. I've studied the question, and have nearly established the fact that almost every summer hotel is furnished with a full corps of——"

"To be sure," said Hawker; "and if you search for them in the winter, you can find barely a sign of them, until you examine the boarding houses, and then you observe——"

"Certainly," said Hollanden, "of course. By the way," he added, "you haven't got any obviously loose screws in your character, have you?"

"No," said Hawker, after consideration, "only general poverty—that's all."

"Of course, of course," said Hollanden. "But that's bad. They'll get on to you, sure. Particularly since you come up here to see Miss Fanhall so much."

Hawker glinted his eyes at his friend. "You've got a deuced open way of speaking," he observed.

"Deuced open, is it?" cried Hollanden. "It isn't near so open as your devotion to Miss Fanhall, which is as plain as a red petticoat hung on a hedge."

Hawker's face gloomed, and he said, "Well, it might be plain to you, you infernal cat, but that doesn't prove that all those old hens can see it."

"I tell you that if they look twice at you they can't fail to see it. And it's bad, too. Very bad. What's the matter with you? Haven't you ever been in love before?"

"None of your business," replied Hawker.

Hollanden thought upon this point for a time. "Well," he admitted finally, "that's true in a general way, but I hate to see you managing your affairs so stupidly."

Rage flamed into Hawker's face, and he cried passionately, "I tell you it is none of your business!" He suddenly confronted the other man.

Hollanden surveyed this outburst with a critical eye, and then slapped his knee with emphasis. "You certainly have got it—a million times worse than I thought. Why, you—you—you're heels over head."

"What if I am?" said Hawker, with a gesture of defiance and despair.

Hollanden saw a dramatic situation in the distance, and with a bright smile he studied it. "Say," he exclaimed, "suppose she should not go to the picnic to-morrow? She said this morning she did not know if she could go. Somebody was expected from New York, I think. Wouldn't it break you up, though! Eh?"

"You're so dev'lish clever!" said Hawker, with sullen irony.

Hollanden was still regarding the distant dramatic situation. "And rivals, too! The woods must be crowded with them. A girl like that, you know. And then all that money! Say, your rivals must number enough to make a brigade of militia. Imagine them swarming around! But then it doesn't matter so much," he went on cheerfully; "you've got a good play there. You must appreciate them to her—you understand?—appreciate them kindly, like a man in a watch-tower. You must laugh at them only about once a week, and then very tolerantly—you understand?—and kindly, and—and appreciatively."

"You're a colossal ass, Hollie!" said Hawker. "You———"

"Yes, yes, I know," replied the other peacefully; "a colossal ass. Of course." After looking into the distance again, he murmured: "I'm worried about that picnic. I wish I knew she was going. By heavens, as a matter of fact, she must be made to go!"

"What have you got to do with it?" cried the painter, in another sudden outburst.

"There! there!" said Hollanden, waving his hand. "You fool! Only a spectator, I assure you."

Hawker seemed overcome then with a deep dislike of himself. "Oh, well, you know, Hollie, this sort of thing———" He broke off and gazed at the trees. "This sort of thing——— It———"

"How?" asked Hollanden.

"Confound you for a meddling, gabbling idiot!" cried Hawker suddenly.

Hollanden replied, "What did you do with that violet she dropped at the side of the tennis court yesterday?"

CHAPTER V.

Mrs. Fanhall, with the two children, the Worcester girls, and Hollanden, clambered down the rocky path. Miss Fanhall and Hawker had remained on top of the ledge. Hollanden showed much zeal in conducting his contingent to the foot of the falls. Through the trees they could see the cataract, a great shimmering white thing, booming and thundering until all the leaves gently shuddered.

"I wonder where Miss Fanhall and Mr. Hawker have gone?" said the younger Miss Worcester. "I wonder where they've gone?"

"Millicent," said Hollander, looking at her fondly, "you always had such great thought for others."

"Well, I wonder where they've gone?"

At the foot of the falls, where the mist arose in silver clouds and the green water swept into the pool, Miss Worcester, the elder, seated on the moss, exclaimed, "Oh, Mr. Hollanden, what makes all literary men so peculiar?"

"And all that just because I said that I could have made better digestive organs than Providence, if it is true that he made mine," replied Hollanden, with reproach. "Here, Roger," he cried, as he dragged the child away from the brink, "don't fall in there, or you won't be the full-back at Yale in 1907, as you have planned. I'm sure I don't know how to answer you, Miss Worcester. I've inquired of innumerable literary men, and none of 'em know. I may say I have chased that problem for years. I might give you my personal history, and see if that would throw any light on the subject." He looked about him with chin high until his glance had noted the two vague figures at the top of the cliff. "I might give you my personal history——"

Mrs. Fanhall looked at him curiously, and the elder Worcester girl cried, "Oh, do!"

After another scanning of the figures at the top of the cliff, Hollanden established himself in an oratorical pose on a great weather-beaten stone. "Well—you must understand—I started my career—my career, you understand—with a determination to be a prophet, and, although I have ended in being an acrobat, a trained bear of the magazines, and a juggler of comic paragraphs, there was once carved upon my lips a smile which made many people detest me, for it hung before them like a banshee whenever they tried to be satisfied with themselves. I was informed from time to time that I was making no great holes in the universal plan, and I came to know that one person in every two thousand of the people I saw had heard of me, and that four out of five of these had forgotten it. And then one in every two of those who remembered that they had heard of me regarded the fact that I wrote as a great impertinence. I admitted these things, and in defence merely built a maxim that stated that each wise man in this world is concealed amid some twenty thousand fools. If you have eyes for mathematics, this conclusion should interest you. Meanwhile I created a gigantic dignity, and when men saw this dignity and heard that I was a literary man they respected me. I concluded that the simple campaign of existence for me was to delude the populace, or as much of it as would look at me. I did. I do. And now I can make myself quite happy concocting sneers about it. Others may do as they please, but as for me," he concluded ferociously, "I shall never disclose to anybody that an acrobat, a trained bear of the magazines, a juggler of comic paragraphs, is not a priceless pearl of art and philosophy."

"I don't believe a word of it is true," said Miss Worcester.

"What do you expect of autobiography?" demanded Hollanden, with asperity.

"Well, anyhow, Hollie," exclaimed the younger sister, "you didn't explain a thing about how literary men came to be so peculiar, and that's what you started out to do, you know."

"Well," said Hollanden crossly, "you must never expect a man to do what he starts to do, Millicent. And besides," he went on, with the gleam of a sudden idea in his eyes, "literary men are not peculiar, anyhow."

The elder Worcester girl looked angrily at him. "Indeed? Not you, of course, but the others."

"They are all asses," said Hollanden genially.

The elder Worcester girl reflected. "I believe you try to make us think and then just tangle us up purposely!"

The younger Worcester girl reflected. "You are an absurd old thing, you know, Hollie!"

Hollanden climbed offendedly from the great weather-beaten stone. "Well, I shall go and see that the men have not spilled the luncheon while breaking their necks over these rocks. Would you like to have it spread here, Mrs. Fanhall? Never mind consulting the girls. I assure you I shall spend a great deal of energy and temper in bullying them into doing just as they please. Why, when I was in Brussels——"

"Oh, come now, Hollie, you never were in Brussels, you know," said the younger Worcester girl.

"What of that, Millicent?" demanded Hollanden. "This is autobiography."

"Well, I don't care, Hollie. You tell such whoppers."

With a gesture of despair he again started away; whereupon the Worcester girls shouted in chorus, "Oh, I say, Hollie, come back! Don't be angry. We didn't mean to tease you, Hollie—really, we didn't!"

"Well, if you didn't," said Hollanden, "why did you——"

The elder Worcester girl was gazing fixedly at the top of the cliff. "Oh, there they are! I wonder why they don't come down?"

CHAPTER VI.

Stanley, the setter, walked to the edge of the precipice and, looking over at the falls, wagged his tail in friendly greeting. He was braced warily, so that if this howling white animal should reach up a hand for him he could flee in time.

The girl stared dreamily at the red-stained crags that projected from the pines of the hill across the stream. Hawker lazily aimed bits of moss at the oblivious dog and missed him.

"It must be fine to have something to think of beyond just living," said the girl to the crags.

"I suppose you mean art?" said Hawker.

"Yes, of course. It must be finer, at any rate, than the ordinary thing."

He mused for a time. "Yes. It is—it must be," he said. "But then—I'd rather just lie here."

The girl seemed aggrieved. "Oh, no, you wouldn't. You couldn't stop. It's dreadful to talk like that, isn't it? I always thought that painters were——"

"Of course. They should be. Maybe they are. I don't know. Sometimes I am. But not to-day."

"Well, I should think you ought to be so much more contented than just ordinary people. Now, I——"

"You!" he cried—"you are not 'just ordinary people.'"

"Well, but when I try to recall what I have thought about in my life, I can't remember, you know. That's what I mean."

"You shouldn't talk that way," he told her.

"But why do you insist that life should be so highly absorbing for me?"

"You have everything you wish for," he answered, in a voice of deep gloom.

"Certainly not. I am a woman."

"But——"

"A woman, to have everything she wishes for, would have to be Providence. There are some things that are not in the world."

"Well, what are they?" he asked of her.

"That's just it," she said, nodding her head, "no one knows. That's what makes the trouble."

"Well, you are very unreasonable."

"What?"

"You are very unreasonable. If I were you—an heiress——"

The girl flushed and turned upon him angrily.

"Well!" he glowered back at her. "You are, you know. You can't deny it."

She looked at the red-stained crags. At last she said, "You seemed really contemptuous."

"Well, I assure you that I do not feel contemptuous. On the contrary, I am filled with admiration. Thank Heaven, I am a man of the world. Whenever I meet heiresses I always have the deepest admiration." As he said this he wore a brave hang-dog expression. The girl surveyed him coldly from his chin to his eyebrows. "You have a handsome audacity, too."

He lay back in the long grass and contemplated the clouds.

"You should have been a Chinese soldier of fortune," she said.

He threw another little clod at Stanley and struck him on the head.

"You are the most scientifically unbearable person in the world," she said.

Stanley came back to see his master and to assure himself that the clump on the head was not intended as a sign of serious displeasure. Hawker took the dog's long ears and tried to tie them into a knot.

"And I don't see why you so delight in making people detest you," she continued.

Having failed to make a knot of the dog's ears, Hawker leaned back and surveyed his failure admiringly. "Well, I don't," he said.

"You do."

"No, I don't."

"Yes, you do. You just say the most terrible things as if you positively enjoyed saying them."

"Well, what did I say, now? What did I say?"

"Why, you said that you always had the most extraordinary admiration for heiresses whenever you met them."

"Well, what's wrong with that sentiment?" he said. "You can't find fault with that!"

"It is utterly detestable."

"Not at all," he answered sullenly. "I consider it a tribute—a graceful tribute."

Miss Fanhall arose and went forward to the edge of the cliff. She became absorbed in the falls. Far below her a bough of a hemlock drooped to the water, and each swirling, mad wave caught it and made it nod—nod—nod. Her back was half turned toward Hawker.

After a time Stanley, the dog, discovered some ants scurrying in the moss, and he at once began to watch them and wag his tail.

"Isn't it curious," observed Hawker, "how an animal as large as a dog will sometimes be so entertained by the very smallest things?"

Stanley pawed gently at the moss, and then thrust his head forward to see what the ants did under the circumstances.

"In the hunting season," continued Hawker, having waited a moment, "this dog knows nothing on earth but his master and the partridges. He is lost to all other sound and movement. He moves through the woods like a steel machine. And when he scents the bird—ah, it is beautiful! Shouldn't you like to see him then?"

Some of the ants had perhaps made war-like motions, and Stanley was pretending that this was a reason for excitement. He reared aback, and made grumbling noises in his throat.

After another pause Hawker went on: "And now see the precious old fool! He is deeply interested in the movements of the little ants, and as childish and ridiculous over them as if they were highly important.—There, you old blockhead, let them alone!"

Stanley could not be induced to end his investigations, and he told his master that the ants were the most thrilling and dramatic animals of his experience.

"Oh, by the way," said Hawker at last, as his glance caught upon the crags across the river, "did you ever hear the legend of those rocks yonder? Over there where I am pointing? Where I'm pointing? Did you ever hear it? What? Yes? No? Well, I shall tell it to you." He settled comfortably in the long grass.

CHAPTER VII.

"Once upon a time there was a beautiful Indian maiden, of course. And she was, of course, beloved by a youth from another tribe who was very handsome and stalwart and a mighty hunter, of course. But the maiden's father was, of course, a stern old chief, and when the question of his daughter's marriage came up, he, of course, declared that the maiden should be wedded only to a warrior of her tribe. And, of course, when the young man heard this he said that in such case he would, of course, fling himself headlong from that crag. The old chief was, of course, obdurate, and, of course, the youth did, of course, as he had said. And, of course, the maiden wept." After Hawker had waited for some time, he said with severity, "You seem to have no great appreciation of folklore."

The girl suddenly bent her head. "Listen," she said, "they're calling. Don't you hear Hollie's voice?"

They went to another place, and, looking down over the shimmering tree-tops, they saw Hollanden waving his arms. "It's luncheon," said Hawker. "Look how frantic he is!"

The path required that Hawker should assist the girl very often. His eyes shone at her whenever he held forth his hand to help her down a blessed steep place. She seemed rather pensive. The route to luncheon was very long. Suddenly he took a seat on an old tree, and said: "Oh, I don't know why it is, whenever I'm with you, I—I have no wits, nor good nature, nor anything. It's the worst luck!"

He had left her standing on a boulder, where she was provisionally helpless. "Hurry!" she said; "they're waiting for us."

Stanley, the setter, had been sliding down cautiously behind them. He now stood wagging his tail and waiting for the way to be cleared.

Hawker leaned his head on his hand and pondered dejectedly. "It's the worst luck!"

"Hurry!" she said; "they're waiting for us."

At luncheon the girl was for the most part silent. Hawker was superhumanly amiable. Somehow he gained the impression that they all quite fancied him, and it followed that being clever was very easy. Hollanden listened, and approved him with a benign countenance.

There was a little boat fastened to the willows at the edge of the black pool. After the spread, Hollanden navigated various parties around to where they could hear the great hollow roar of the falls beating against the sheer rocks. Stanley swam after sticks at the request of little Roger.

Once Hollanden succeeded in making the others so engrossed in being amused that Hawker and Miss Fanhall were left alone staring at the white bubbles that floated solemnly on the black water. After Hawker had stared at them a sufficient time, he said, "Well, you are an heiress, you know."

In return she chose to smile radiantly. Turning toward him, she said, "If you will be good now—always—perhaps I'll forgive you."

They drove home in the sombre shadows of the hills, with Stanley padding along under the wagon. The Worcester girls tried to induce Hollanden to sing, and in consequence there was quarrelling until the blinking lights of the inn appeared above them as if a great lantern hung there.

Hollanden conveyed his friend some distance on the way home from the inn to the farm. "Good time at the picnic?" said the writer.

"Yes."

"Picnics are mainly places where the jam gets on the dead leaves, and from thence to your trousers. But this was a good little picnic." He glanced at Hawker. "But you don't look as if you had such a swell time."

Hawker waved his hand tragically. "Yes—no—I don't know."

"What's wrong with you?" asked Hollanden.

"I tell you what it is, Hollie," said the painter darkly, "whenever I'm with that girl I'm such a blockhead. I'm not so stupid, Hollie. You know I'm not.

But when I'm with her I can't be clever to save my life."

Hollanden pulled contentedly at his pipe. "Maybe she don't notice it."

"Notice it!" muttered Hawker, scornfully; "of course she notices it. In conversation with her, I tell you, I am as interesting as an iron dog." His voice changed as he cried, "I don't know why it is. I don't know why it is."

Blowing a huge cloud of smoke into the air, Hollanden studied it thoughtfully. "Hits some fellows that way," he said. "And, of course, it must be deuced annoying. Strange thing, but now, under those circumstances, I'm very glib. Very glib, I assure you."

"I don't care what you are," answered Hawker. "All those confounded affairs of yours—they were not——"

"No," said Hollanden, stolidly puffing, "of course not. I understand that. But, look here, Billie," he added, with sudden brightness, "maybe you are not a blockhead, after all. You are on the inside, you know, and you can't see from there. Besides, you can't tell what a woman will think. You can't tell what a woman will think."

"No," said Hawker, grimly, "and you suppose that is my only chance?"

"Oh, don't be such a chump!" said Hollanden, in a tone of vast exasperation.

They strode for some time in silence. The mystic pines swaying over the narrow road made talk sibilantly to the wind. Stanley, the setter, took it upon himself to discover some menacing presence in the woods. He walked on his toes and with his eyes glinting sideways. He swore half under his breath.

"And work, too," burst out Hawker, at last. "I came up here this season to work, and I haven't done a thing that ought not be shot at."

"Don't you find that your love sets fire to your genius?" asked Hollanden gravely.

"No, I'm hanged if I do."

Hollanden sighed then with an air of relief. "I was afraid that a popular impression was true," he said, "but it's all right. You would rather sit still and moon, wouldn't you?"

"Moon—blast you! I couldn't moon to save my life."

"Oh, well, I didn't mean moon exactly."

CHAPTER VIII.

The blue night of the lake was embroidered with black tree forms. Silver drops sprinkled from the lifted oars. Somewhere in the gloom of the shore there was a dog, who from time to time raised his sad voice to the stars.

"But still, the life of the studios——" began the girl.

Hawker scoffed. "There were six of us. Mainly we smoked. Sometimes we played hearts and at other times poker—on credit, you know—credit. And when we had the materials and got something to do, we worked. Did you ever see these beautiful red and green designs that surround the common tomato can?"

"Yes."

"Well," he said proudly, "I have made them. Whenever you come upon tomatoes, remember that they might once have been encompassed in my design. When first I came back from Paris I began to paint, but nobody wanted me to paint. Later, I got into green corn and asparagus——"

"Truly?"

"Yes, indeed. It is true."

"But still, the life of the studios——"

"There were six of us. Fate ordained that only one in the crowd could have money at one time. The other five lived off him and despised themselves. We despised ourselves five times as long as we had admiration."

"And was this just because you had no money?"

"It was because we had no money in New York," said Hawker.

"Well, after a while something happened——"

"Oh, no, it didn't. Something impended always, but it never happened."

"In a case like that one's own people must be such a blessing. The sympathy——"

"One's own people!" said Hawker.

"Yes," she said, "one's own people and more intimate friends. The appreciation——"

"'The appreciation!'" said Hawker. "Yes, indeed!"

He seemed so ill-tempered that she became silent. The boat floated through the shadows of the trees and out to where the water was like a blue crystal. The dog on the shore thrashed about in the reeds and waded in the shallows, mourning his unhappy state in an occasional cry. Hawker stood up and sternly shouted. Thereafter silence was among the reeds. The moon slipped sharply through the little clouds.

The girl said, "I liked that last picture of yours."

"What?"

"At the last exhibition, you know, you had that one with the cows—and things—in the snow—and—and a haystack."

"Yes," he said, "of course. Did you like it, really? I thought it about my best. And you really remembered it? Oh," he cried, "Hollanden perhaps recalled it to you."

"Why, no," she said. "I remembered it, of course."

"Well, what made you remember it?" he demanded, as if he had cause to be indignant.

"Why—I just remembered it because—I liked it, and because—well, the people with me said—said it was about the best thing in the exhibit, and they talked about it a good deal. And then I remember that Hollie had spoken of you, and then I—I——"

"Never mind," he said. After a moment, he added, "The confounded picture was no good, anyhow!"

The girl started. "What makes you speak so of it? It was good. Of course, I don't know—I can't talk about pictures, but," she said in distress, "everybody said it was fine."

"It wasn't any good," he persisted, with dogged shakes of the head.

From off in the darkness they heard the sound of Hollanden's oars splashing in the water. Sometimes there was squealing by the Worcester girls, and at other times loud arguments on points of navigation.

"Oh," said the girl suddenly, "Mr. Oglethorpe is coming to-morrow!"

"Mr. Oglethorpe?" said Hawker. "Is he?"

"Yes." She gazed off at the water.

"He's an old friend of ours. He is always so good, and Roger and little Helen simply adore him. He was my brother's chum in college, and they were quite inseparable until Herbert's death. He always brings me violets. But I know you will like him."

"I shall expect to," said Hawker.

"I'm so glad he is coming. What time does that morning stage get here?"

"About eleven," said Hawker.

"He wrote that he would come then. I hope he won't disappoint us."

"Undoubtedly he will be here," said Hawker.

The wind swept from the ridge top, where some great bare pines stood in the moonlight. A loon called in its strange, unearthly note from the lakeshore. As Hawker turned the boat toward the dock, the flashing rays from the boat fell upon the head of the girl in the rear seat, and he rowed very slowly.

The girl was looking away somewhere with a mystic, shining glance. She leaned her chin in her hand. Hawker, facing her, merely paddled subconsciously. He seemed greatly impressed and expectant.

At last she spoke very slowly. "I wish I knew Mr. Oglethorpe was not going to disappoint us."

Hawker said, "Why, no, I imagine not."

"Well, he is a trifle uncertain in matters of time. The children—and all of us—shall be anxious. I know you will like him."

CHAPTER IX.

"Eh?" said Hollanden. "Oglethorpe? Oglethorpe? Why, he's that friend of the Fanhalls! Yes, of course, I know him! Deuced good fellow, too! What about him?"

"Oh, nothing, only he's coming here to-morrow," answered Hawker. "What kind of a fellow did you say he was?"

"Deuced good fellow! What are you so—— Say, by the nine mad blacksmiths of Donawhiroo, he's your rival! Why, of course! Glory, but I must be thick-headed to-night!"

Hawker said, "Where's your tobacco?"

"Yonder, in that jar. Got a pipe?"

"Yes. How do you know he's my rival?"

"Know it? Why, hasn't he been—— Say, this is getting thrilling!" Hollanden sprang to his feet and, filling a pipe, flung himself into the chair and began to rock himself madly to and fro. He puffed clouds of smoke.

Hawker stood with his face in shadow. At last he said, in tones of deep weariness, "Well, I think I'd better be going home and turning in."

"Hold on!" Hollanden exclaimed, turning his eyes from a prolonged stare at the ceiling, "don't go yet! Why, man, this is just the time when—— Say, who would ever think of Jem Oglethorpe's turning up to harrie you! Just at this time, too!"

"Oh," cried Hawker suddenly, filled with rage, "you remind me of an accursed duffer! Why can't you tell me something about the man, instead of sitting there and gibbering those crazy things at the ceiling?"

"By the piper——"

"Oh, shut up! Tell me something about Oglethorpe, can't you? I want to hear about him. Quit all that other business!"

"Why, Jem Oglethorpe, he—why, say, he's one of the best fellows going. If he were only an ass! If he were only an ass, now, you could feel easy in your mind. But he isn't. No, indeed. Why, blast him, there isn't a man that knows him who doesn't like Jem Oglethorpe! Excepting the chumps!"

The window of the little room was open, and the voices of the pines could be heard as they sang of their long sorrow. Hawker pulled a chair close and stared out into the darkness. The people on the porch of the inn were frequently calling, "Good-night! Good-night!"

Hawker said, "And of course he's got train loads of money?"

"You bet he has! He can pave streets with it. Lordie, but this is a situation!"

A heavy scowl settled upon Hawker's brow, and he kicked at the dressing case. "Say, Hollie, look here! Sometimes I think you regard me as a bug and like to see me wriggle. But——"

"Oh, don't be a fool!" said Hollanden, glaring through the smoke. "Under the circumstances, you are privileged to rave and ramp around like a wounded lunatic, but for heaven's sake don't swoop down on me like that! Especially when I'm—when I'm doing all I can for you."

"Doing all you can for me! Nobody asked you to. You talk as if I were an infant."

"There! That's right! Blaze up like a fire balloon just because I said that, will you? A man in your condition—why, confound you, you are an infant!"

Hawker seemed again overwhelmed in a great dislike of himself. "Oh, well, of course, Hollie, it——" He waved his hand. "A man feels like—like——"

"Certainly he does," said Hollanden. "That's all right, old man."

"And look now, Hollie, here's this Oglethorpe——"

"May the devil fly away with him!"

"Well, here he is, coming along when I thought maybe—after a while, you know—I might stand some show. And you are acquainted with him, so give me a line on him."

"Well, I should advise you to——"

"Blow your advice! I want to hear about Oglethorpe."

"Well, in the first place, he is a rattling good fellow, as I told you before, and this is what makes it so——"

"Oh, hang what it makes it! Go on."

"He is a rattling good fellow and he has stacks of money. Of course, in this case his having money doesn't affect the situation much. Miss Fanhall——"

"Say, can you keep to the thread of the story, you infernal literary man!"

"Well, he's popular. He don't talk money—ever. And if he's wicked, he's not sufficiently proud of it to be perpetually describing his sins. And then he is not so hideously brilliant, either. That's great credit to a man in these days. And then he—well, take it altogether, I should say Jem Oglethorpe was a smashing good fellow."

"I wonder how long he is going to stay?" murmured Hawker.

During this conversation his pipe had often died out. It was out at this time. He lit another match. Hollanden had watched the fingers of his friend as the match was scratched. "You're nervous, Billie," he said.

Hawker straightened in his chair. "No, I'm not."

"I saw your fingers tremble when you lit that match."

"Oh, you lie!"

Hollanden mused again. "He's popular with women, too," he said ultimately; "and often a woman will like a man and hunt his scalp just because she knows other women like him and want his scalp."

"Yes, but not——"

"Hold on! You were going to say that she was not like other women, weren't you?"

"Not exactly that, but——"

"Well, we will have all that understood."

After a period of silence Hawker said, "I must be going."

As the painter walked toward the door Hollanden cried to him: "Heavens! Of all pictures of a weary pilgrim!" His voice was very compassionate.

Hawker wheeled, and an oath spun through the smoke clouds.

CHAPTER X.

"Where's Mr. Hawker this morning?" asked the younger Miss Worcester. "I thought he was coming up to play tennis?"

"I don't know. Confound him! I don't see why he didn't come," said Hollanden, looking across the shining valley. He frowned questioningly at the landscape. "I wonder where in the mischief he is?"

The Worcester girls began also to stare at the great gleaming stretch of green and gold. "Didn't he tell you he was coming?" they demanded.

"He didn't say a word about it," answered Hollanden. "I supposed, of course, he was coming. We will have to postpone the mêlée."

Later he met Miss Fanhall. "You look as if you were going for a walk?"

"I am," she said, swinging her parasol. "To meet the stage. Have you seen Mr. Hawker to-day?"

"No," he said. "He is not coming up this morning. He is in a great fret about that field of stubble, and I suppose he is down there sketching the life out of it. These artists—they take such a fiendish interest in their work. I dare say we won't see much of him until he has finished it. Where did you say you were going to walk?"

"To meet the stage."

"Oh, well, I won't have to play tennis for an hour, and if you insist——"

"Of course."

As they strolled slowly in the shade of the trees Hollanden began, "Isn't that Hawker an ill-bred old thing?"

"No, he is not." Then after a time she said, "Why?"

"Oh, he gets so absorbed in a beastly smudge of paint that I really suppose he cares nothing for anything else in the world. Men who are really artists—I don't believe they are capable of deep human affections. So much of them is occupied by art. There's not much left over, you see."

"I don't believe it at all," she exclaimed.

"You don't, eh?" cried Hollanden scornfully. "Well, let me tell you, young woman, there is a great deal of truth in it. Now, there's Hawker—as good a fellow as ever lived, too, in a way, and yet he's an artist. Why, look how he treats—look how he treats that poor setter dog!"

"Why, he's as kind to him as he can be," she declared.

"And I tell you he is not!" cried Hollanden.

"He is, Hollie. You—you are unspeakable when you get in these moods."

"There—that's just you in an argument. I'm not in a mood at all. Now, look—the dog loves him with simple, unquestioning devotion that fairly brings tears to one's eyes——"

"Yes," she said.

"And he—why, he's as cold and stern——"

"He isn't. He isn't, Holly. You are awf'ly unfair."

"No, I'm not. I am simply a liberal observer. And Hawker, with his people, too," he went on darkly; "you can't tell—you don't know anything about it—but I tell you that what I have seen proves my assertion that the artistic mind has no space left for the human affections. And as for the dog——"

"I thought you were his friend, Hollie?"

"Whose?"

"No, not the dog's. And yet you—really, Hollie, there is something unnatural in you. You are so stupidly keen in looking at people that you do not possess common loyalty to your friends. It is because you are a writer, I suppose. That has to explain so many things. Some of your traits are very disagreeable."

"There! there!" plaintively cried Hollanden. "This is only about the treatment of a dog, mind you. Goodness, what an oration!"

"It wasn't about the treatment of a dog. It was about your treatment of your friends."

"Well," he said sagely, "it only goes to show that there is nothing impersonal in the mind of a woman. I undertook to discuss broadly——

"Oh, Hollie!"

"At any rate, it was rather below you to do such scoffing at me."

"Well, I didn't mean—not all of it, Hollie."

"Well, I didn't mean what I said about the dog and all that, either."

"You didn't?" She turned toward him, large-eyed.

"No. Not a single word of it."

"Well, what did you say it for, then?" she demanded indignantly.

"I said it," answered Hollanden placidly, "just to tease you." He looked abstractedly up to the trees.

Presently she said slowly, "Just to tease me?"

At this time Hollanden wore an unmistakable air of having a desire to turn up his coat collar. "Oh, come now——" he began nervously.

"George Hollanden," said the voice at his shoulder, "you are not only disagreeable, but you are hopelessly ridiculous. I—I wish you would never speak to me again!"

"Oh, come now, Grace, don't—don't—— Look! There's the stage coming, isn't it?"

"No, the stage is not coming. I wish—I wish you were at the bottom of the sea, George Hollanden. And—and Mr. Hawker, too. There!"

"Oh, bless my soul! And all about an infernal dog," wailed Hollanden.

"Look! Honest, now, there's the stage. See it? See it?"

"It isn't there at all," she said.

Gradually he seemed to recover his courage. "What made you so tremendously angry? I don't see why."

After consideration, she said decisively, "Well, because."

"That's why I teased you," he rejoined.

"Well, because—because——"

"Go on," he told her finally. "You are doing very well." He waited patiently.

"Well," she said, "it is dreadful to defend somebody so—so excitedly, and then have it turned out just a tease. I don't know what he would think."

"Who would think?"

"Why—he."

"What could he think? Now, what could he think? Why," said Hollanden, waxing eloquent, "he couldn't under any circumstances think—think anything at all. Now, could he?"

She made no reply.

"Could he?"

She was apparently reflecting.

"Under any circumstances," persisted Hollanden, "he couldn't think anything at all. Now, could he?"

"No," she said.

"Well, why are you angry at me, then?"

CHAPTER XI.

"John," said the old mother, from the profound mufflings of the pillow and quilts.

"What?" said the old man. He was tugging at his right boot, and his tone was very irascible.

"I think William's changed a good deal."

"Well, what if he has?" replied the father, in another burst of ill-temper. He was then tugging at his left boot.

"Yes, I'm afraid he's changed a good deal," said the muffled voice from the bed. "He's got a good many fine friends, now, John—folks what put on a good many airs; and he don't care for his home like he did."

"Oh, well, I don't guess he's changed very much," said the old man cheerfully. He was now free of both boots.

She raised herself on an elbow and looked out with a troubled face. "John, I think he likes that girl."

"What girl?" said he.

"What girl? Why, that awful handsome girl you see around—of course."

"Do you think he likes 'er?"

"I'm afraid so—I'm afraid so," murmured the mother mournfully.

"Oh, well," said the old man, without alarm, or grief, or pleasure in his tone.

He turned the lamp's wick very low and carried the lamp to the head of the stairs, where he perched it on the step. When he returned he said, "She's mighty good-look-in'!"

"Well, that ain't everything," she snapped. "How do we know she ain't proud, and selfish, and—everything?"

"How do you know she is?" returned the old man.

"And she may just be leading him on."

"Do him good, then," said he, with impregnable serenity. "Next time he'll know better."

"Well, I'm worried about it," she said, as she sank back on the pillow again. "I think William's changed a good deal. He don't seem to care about—us—like he did."

"Oh, go to sleep!" said the father drowsily.

She was silent for a time, and then she said, "John?"

"What?"

"Do you think I better speak to him about that girl?"

"No."

She grew silent again, but at last she demanded, "Why not?"

"'Cause it's none of your business. Go to sleep, will you?" And presently he did, but the old mother lay blinking wild-eyed into the darkness.

In the morning Hawker did not appear at the early breakfast, eaten when the blue glow of dawn shed its ghostly lights upon the valley. The old mother placed various dishes on the back part of the stove. At ten o'clock he came downstairs. His mother was sweeping busily in the parlour at the time, but she saw him and ran to the back part of the stove. She slid the various dishes on to the table. "Did you oversleep?" she asked.

"Yes. I don't feel very well this morning," he said. He pulled his chair close to the table and sat there staring.

She renewed her sweeping in the parlour. When she returned he sat still staring undeviatingly at nothing.

"Why don't you eat your breakfast?" she said anxiously.

"I tell you, mother, I don't feel very well this morning," he answered quite sharply.

"Well," she said meekly, "drink some coffee and you'll feel better."

Afterward he took his painting machinery and left the house. His younger sister was at the well. She looked at him with a little smile and a little sneer. "Going up to the inn this morning?" she said.

"I don't see how that concerns you, Mary?" he rejoined, with dignity.

"Oh, my!" she said airily.

"But since you are so interested, I don't mind telling you that I'm not going up to the inn this morning."

His sister fixed him with her eye. "She ain't mad at you, is she, Will?"

"I don't know what you mean, Mary." He glared hatefully at her and strode away.

Stanley saw him going through the fields and leaped a fence jubilantly in pursuit. In a wood the light sifted through the foliage and burned with a peculiar reddish lustre on the masses of dead leaves. He frowned at it for a while from different points. Presently he erected his easel and began to paint. After a time he threw down his brush and swore. Stanley, who had been solemnly staring at the scene as if he too was sketching it, looked up in surprise.

In wandering aimlessly through the fields and the forest Hawker once found himself near the road to Hemlock Inn. He shied away from it quickly as if it were a great snake.

While most of the family were at supper, Mary, the younger sister, came charging breathlessly into the kitchen. "Ma—sister," she cried, "I know why—why Will didn't go to the inn to-day. There's another fellow come. Another fellow."

"Who? Where? What do you mean?" exclaimed her mother and her sister.

"Why, another fellow up at the inn," she shouted, triumphant in her information. "Another fellow come up on the stage this morning. And she went out driving with him this afternoon."

"Well," exclaimed her mother and her sister.

"Yep. And he's an awful good-looking fellow, too. And she—oh, my—she looked as if she thought the world and all of him."

"Well," exclaimed her mother and her sister again.

"Sho!" said the old man. "You wimen leave William alone and quit your gabbling."

The three women made a combined assault upon him. "Well, we ain't a-hurting him, are we, pa? You needn't be so snifty. I guess we ain't a-hurting him much."

"Well," said the old man. And to this argument he added, "Sho!"

They kept him out of the subsequent consultations.

CHAPTER XII.

The next day, as little Roger was going toward the tennis court, a large orange and white setter ran effusively from around the corner of the inn and greeted him. Miss Fanhall, the Worcester girls, Hollanden, and Oglethorpe faced to the front like soldiers. Hollanden cried, "Why, Billie Hawker must be coming!" Hawker at that moment appeared, coming toward them with a smile which was not overconfident.

Little Roger went off to perform some festivities of his own on the brown carpet under a clump of pines. The dog, to join him, felt obliged to circle widely about the tennis court. He was much afraid of this tennis court, with its tiny round things that sometimes hit him. When near it he usually slunk along at a little sheep trot and with an eye of wariness upon it.

At her first opportunity the younger Worcester girl said, "You didn't come up yesterday, Mr. Hawker."

Hollanden seemed to think that Miss Fanhall turned her head as if she wished to hear the explanation of the painter's absence, so he engaged her in swift and fierce conversation.

"No," said Hawker. "I was resolved to finish a sketch of a stubble field which I began a good many days ago. You see, I was going to do such a great lot of work this summer, and I've done hardly a thing. I really ought to compel myself to do some, you know."

"There," said Hollanden, with a victorious nod, "just what I told you!"

"You didn't tell us anything of the kind," retorted the Worcester girls with one voice.

A middle-aged woman came upon the porch of the inn, and after scanning for a moment the group at the tennis court she hurriedly withdrew. Presently she appeared again, accompanied by five more middle-aged women. "You see," she said to the others, "it is as I said. He has come back."

The five surveyed the group at the tennis court, and then said: "So he has. I knew he would. Well, I declare! Did you ever?" Their voices were pitched at low keys and they moved with care, but their smiles were broad and full of a strange glee.

"I wonder how he feels," said one in subtle ecstasy.

Another laughed. "You know how you would feel, my dear, if you were him and saw yourself suddenly cut out by a man who was so hopelessly superior to you. Why, Oglethorpe's a thousand times better looking. And then think of his wealth and social position!"

One whispered dramatically, "They say he never came up here at all yesterday."

Another replied: "No more he did. That's what we've been talking about. Stayed down at the farm all day, poor fellow!"

"Do you really think she cares for Oglethorpe?"

"Care for him? Why, of course she does. Why, when they came up the path yesterday morning I never saw a girl's face so bright. I asked my husband how much of the Chambers Street Bank stock Oglethorpe owned, and he said that if Oglethorpe took his money out there wouldn't be enough left to buy a pie."

The youngest woman in the corps said: "Well, I don't care. I think it is too bad. I don't see anything so much in that Mr. Oglethorpe."

The others at once patronized her. "Oh, you don't, my dear? Well, let me tell you that bank stock waves in the air like a banner. You would see it if you were her."

"Well, she don't have to care for his money."

"Oh, no, of course she don't have to. But they are just the ones that do, my dear. They are just the ones that do."

"Well, it's a shame."

"Oh, of course it's a shame."

The woman who had assembled the corps said to one at her side: "Oh, the commonest kind of people, my dear, the commonest kind. The father is a regular farmer, you know. He drives oxen. Such language! You can really hear him miles away bellowing at those oxen. And the girls are shy, half-wild things—oh, you have no idea! I saw one of them yesterday when we were out driving. She dodged as we came along, for I suppose she was ashamed of her frock, poor child! And the mother—well, I wish you could see her! A little, old, dried-up thing. We saw her carrying a pail of water from the well, and, oh, she bent and staggered dreadfully, poor thing!"

"And the gate to their front yard, it has a broken hinge, you know. Of course, that's an awful bad sign. When people let their front gate hang on one hinge you know what that means."

After gazing again at the group at the court, the youngest member of the corps said, "Well, he's a good tennis player anyhow."

The others smiled indulgently. "Oh, yes, my dear, he's a good tennis player."

CHAPTER XIII.

One day Hollanden said, in greeting, to Hawker, "Well, he's gone."

"Who?" asked Hawker.

"Why, Oglethorpe, of course. Who did you think I meant?"

"How did I know?" said Hawker angrily.

"Well," retorted Hollanden, "your chief interest was in his movements, I thought."

"Why, of course not, hang you! Why should I be interested in his movements?"

"Well, you weren't, then. Does that suit you?"

After a period of silence Hawker asked, "What did he—what made him go?"

"Who?"

"Why—Oglethorpe."

"How was I to know you meant him? Well, he went because some important business affairs in New York demanded it, he said; but he is coming back again in a week. They had rather a late interview on the porch last evening."

"Indeed," said Hawker stiffly.

"Yes, and he went away this morning looking particularly elated. Aren't you glad?"

"I don't see how it concerns me," said Hawker, with still greater stiffness.

In a walk to the lake that afternoon Hawker and Miss Fanhall found themselves side by side and silent. The girl contemplated the distant purple hills as if Hawker were not at her side and silent. Hawker frowned at the roadway. Stanley, the setter, scouted the fields in a genial gallop.

At last the girl turned to him. "Seems to me," she said, "seems to me you are dreadfully quiet this afternoon."

"I am thinking about my wretched field of stubble," he answered, still frowning.

Her parasol swung about until the girl was looking up at his inscrutable profile. "Is it, then, so important that you haven't time to talk to me?" she asked with an air of what might have been timidity.

A smile swept the scowl from his face. "No, indeed," he said, instantly; "nothing is so important as that."

She seemed aggrieved then. "Hum—you didn't look so," she told him.

"Well, I didn't mean to look any other way," he said contritely. "You know what a bear I am sometimes. Hollanden says it is a fixed scowl from trying to see uproarious pinks, yellows, and blues."

A little brook, a brawling, ruffianly little brook, swaggered from side to side down the glade, swirling in white leaps over the great dark rocks and shouting challenge to the hillsides. Hollanden and the Worcester girls had halted in a place of ferns and wet moss. Their voices could be heard quarrelling above the clamour of the stream. Stanley, the setter, had soused himself in a pool and then gone and rolled in the dust of the road. He blissfully lolled there, with his coat now resembling an old door mat.

"Don't you think Jem is a wonderfully good fellow?" said the girl to the painter.

"Why, yes, of course," said Hawker.

"Well, he is," she retorted, suddenly defensive.

"Of course," he repeated loudly.

She said, "Well, I don't think you like him as well as I like him."

"Certainly not," said Hawker.

"You don't?" She looked at him in a kind of astonishment.

"Certainly not," said Hawker again, and very irritably. "How in the wide world do you expect me to like him as well as you like him?"

"I don't mean as well," she explained.

"Oh!" said Hawker.

"But I mean you don't like him the way I do at all—the way I expected you to like him. I thought men of a certain pattern always fancied their kind of men wherever they met them, don't you know? And I was so sure you and Jem would be friends."

"Oh!" cried Hawker. Presently he added, "But he isn't my kind of a man at all."

"He is. Jem is one of the best fellows in the world."

Again Hawker cried "Oh!"

They paused and looked down at the brook. Stanley sprawled panting in the dust and watched them. Hawker leaned against a hemlock. He sighed and frowned, and then finally coughed with great resolution. "I suppose, of course, that I am unjust to him. I care for you myself, you understand, and so it becomes——"

He paused for a moment because he heard a rustling of her skirts as if she had moved suddenly. Then he continued: "And so it becomes difficult for me to be fair to him. I am not able to see him with a true eye." He bitterly addressed the trees on the opposite side of the glen. "Oh, I care for you, of course. You might have expected it." He turned from the trees and strode toward the roadway. The uninformed and disreputable Stanley arose and wagged his tail.

As if the girl had cried out at a calamity, Hawker said again, "Well, you might have expected it."

CHAPTER XIV.

At the lake, Hollanden went pickerel fishing, lost his hook in a gaunt, gray stump, and earned much distinction by his skill in discovering words to express his emotion without resorting to the list ordinarily used in such cases. The younger Miss Worcester ruined a new pair of boots, and Stanley sat on the bank and howled the song of the forsaken. At the conclusion of the festivities Hollanden said, "Billie, you ought to take the boat back."

"Why had I? You borrowed it."

"Well, I borrowed it and it was a lot of trouble, and now you ought to take it back."

Ultimately Hawker said, "Oh, let's both go!"

On this journey Hawker made a long speech to his friend, and at the end of it he exclaimed: "And now do you think she cares so much for Oglethorpe? Why, she as good as told me that he was only a very great friend."

Hollanden wagged his head dubiously. "What a woman says doesn't amount to shucks. It's the way she says it—that's what counts. Besides," he cried in a brilliant afterthought, "she wouldn't tell you, anyhow, you fool!"

"You're an encouraging brute," said Hawker, with a rueful grin.

Later the Worcester girls seized upon Hollanden and piled him high with ferns and mosses. They dragged the long gray lichens from the chins of venerable pines, and ran with them to Hollanden, and dashed them into his arms. "Oh, hurry up, Hollie!" they cried, because with his great load he frequently fell behind them in the march. He once positively refused to carry these things another step. Some distance farther on the road he positively refused to carry this old truck another step. When almost to the inn he positively refused to carry this senseless rubbish another step. The Worcester girls had such vivid contempt for his expressed unwillingness that they neglected to tell him of any appreciation they might have had for his noble struggle.

As Hawker and Miss Fanhall proceeded slowly they heard a voice ringing through the foliage: "Whoa! Haw! Git-ap, blast you! Haw! Haw, drat your hides! Will you haw? Git-ap! Gee! Whoa!"

Hawker said, "The others are a good ways ahead. Hadn't we better hurry a little?"

The girl obediently mended her pace.

"Whoa! haw! git-ap!" shouted the voice in the distance. "Git over there, Red, git over! Gee! Git-ap!" And these cries pursued the man and the maid.

At last Hawker said, "That's my father."

"Where?" she asked, looking bewildered.

"Back there, driving those oxen."

The voice shouted: "Whoa! Git-ap! Gee! Red, git over there now, will you? I'll trim the shin off'n you in a minute. Whoa! Haw! Haw! Whoa! Git-ap!"

Hawker repeated, "Yes, that's my father."

"Oh, is it?" she said. "Let's wait for him."

"All right," said Hawker sullenly.

Presently a team of oxen waddled into view around the curve of the road. They swung their heads slowly from side to side, bent under the yoke, and looked out at the world with their great eyes, in which was a mystic note of their humble, submissive, toilsome lives. An old wagon creaked after them, and erect upon it was the tall and tattered figure of the farmer swinging his whip and yelling: "Whoa! Haw there! Git-ap!" The lash flicked and flew over the broad backs of the animals.

"Hello, father!" said Hawker.

"Whoa! Back! Whoa! Why, hello, William, what you doing here?"

"Oh, just taking a walk. Miss Fanhall, this is my father. Father——"

"How d' you do?" The old man balanced himself with care and then raised his straw hat from his head with a quick gesture and with what was perhaps a slightly apologetic air, as if he feared that he was rather over-doing the ceremonial part.

The girl later became very intent upon the oxen. "Aren't they nice old things?" she said, as she stood looking into the faces of the team. "But what makes their eyes so very sad?"

"I dunno," said the old man.

She was apparently unable to resist a desire to pat the nose of the nearest ox, and for that purpose she stretched forth a cautious hand. But the ox moved restlessly at the moment and the girl put her hand apprehensively behind herself and backed away. The old man on the wagon grinned. "They won't hurt you," he told her.

"They won't bite, will they?" she asked, casting a glance of inquiry at the old man and then turning her eyes again upon the fascinating animals.

"No," said the old man, still grinning, "just as gentle as kittens."

She approached them circuitously. "Sure?" she said.

"Sure," replied the old man. He climbed from the wagon and came to the heads of the oxen. With him as an ally, she finally succeeded in patting the nose of the nearest ox. "Aren't they solemn, kind old fellows? Don't you get to think a great deal of them?"

"Well, they're kind of aggravating beasts sometimes," he said. "But they're a good yoke—a good yoke. They can haul with anything in this region."

"It doesn't make them so terribly tired, does it?" she said hopefully. "They are such strong animals."

"No-o-o," he said. "I dunno. I never thought much about it."

With their heads close together they became so absorbed in their conversation that they seemed to forget the painter. He sat on a log and watched them.

Ultimately the girl said, "Won't you give us a ride?"

"Sure," said the old man. "Come on, and I'll help you up." He assisted her very painstakingly to the old board that usually served him as a seat, and he clambered to a place beside her. "Come on, William," he called. The painter climbed into the wagon and stood behind his father, putting his hand on the old man's shoulder to preserve his balance.

"Which is the near ox?" asked the girl with a serious frown.

"Git-ap! Haw! That one there," said the old man.

"And this one is the off ox?"

"Yep."

"Well, suppose you sat here where I do; would this one be the near ox and that one the off ox, then?"

"Nope. Be just same."

"Then the near ox isn't always the nearest one to a person, at all? That ox there is always the near ox?"

"Yep, always. 'Cause when you drive 'em a-foot you always walk on the left side."

"Well, I never knew that before."

After studying them in silence for a while, she said, "Do you think they are happy?"

"I dunno," said the old man. "I never thought." As the wagon creaked on they gravely discussed this problem, contemplating profoundly the backs of the animals. Hawker gazed in silence at the meditating two before him. Under the wagon Stanley, the setter, walked slowly, wagging his tail in placid contentment and ruminating upon his experiences.

At last the old man said cheerfully, "Shall I take you around by the inn?"

Hawker started and seemed to wince at the question. Perhaps he was about to interrupt, but the girl cried: "Oh, will you? Take us right to the door? Oh, that will be awfully good of you!"

"Why," began Hawker, "you don't want—you don't want to ride to the inn on an—on an ox wagon, do you?"

"Why, of course I do," she retorted, directing a withering glance at him.

"Well——" he protested.

"Let 'er be, William," interrupted the old man. "Let 'er do what she wants to. I guess everybody in th' world ain't even got an ox wagon to ride in. Have they?"

"No, indeed," she returned, while withering Hawker again.

"Gee! Gee! Whoa! Haw! Git-ap! Haw! Whoa! Back!"

After these two attacks Hawker became silent.

"Gee! Gee! Gee there, blast—s'cuse me. Gee! Whoa! Git-ap!"

All the boarders of the inn were upon its porches waiting for the dinner gong. There was a surge toward the railing as a middle-aged woman passed the word along her middle-aged friends that Miss Fanhall, accompanied by Mr. Hawker, had arrived on the ox cart of Mr. Hawker's father.

"Whoa! Ha! Git-ap!" said the old man in more subdued tones. "Whoa there, Red! Whoa, now! Wh-o-a!"

Hawker helped the girl to alight, and she paused for a moment conversing with the old man about the oxen. Then she ran smiling up the steps to meet the Worcester girls.

"Oh, such a lovely time! Those dear old oxen—you should have been with us!"

CHAPTER XV.

"Oh, Miss Fanhall!"

"What is it, Mrs. Truscot?"

"That was a great prank of yours last night, my dear. We all enjoyed the joke so much."

"Prank?"

"Yes, your riding on the ox cart with that old farmer and that young Mr. What's-his-name, you know. We all thought it delicious. Ah, my dear, after all—don't be offended—if we had your people's wealth and position we might do that sort of unconventional thing, too; but, ah, my dear, we can't, we can't! Isn't the young painter a charming man?"

Out on the porch Hollanden was haranguing his friends. He heard a step and glanced over his shoulder to see who was about to interrupt him. He suddenly ceased his oration, and said, "Hello! what's the matter with Grace?" The heads turned promptly.

As the girl came toward them it could be seen that her cheeks were very pink and her eyes were flashing general wrath and defiance.

The Worcester girls burst into eager interrogation. "Oh, nothing!" she replied at first, but later she added in an undertone, "That wretched Mrs. Truscot——"

"What did she say?" whispered the younger Worcester girl.

"Why, she said—oh, nothing!"

Both Hollanden and Hawker were industriously reflecting.

Later in the morning Hawker said privately to the girl, "I know what Mrs. Truscot talked to you about."

She turned upon him belligerently. "You do?"

"Yes," he answered with meekness. "It was undoubtedly some reference to your ride upon the ox wagon."

She hesitated a moment, and then said, "Well?"

With still greater meekness he said, "I am very sorry."

"Are you, indeed?" she inquired loftily. "Sorry for what? Sorry that I rode upon your father's ox wagon, or sorry that Mrs. Truscot was rude to me about it?"

"Well, in some ways it was my fault."

"Was it? I suppose you intend to apologize for your father's owning an ox wagon, don't you?"

"No, but——"

"Well, I am going to ride in the ox wagon whenever I choose. Your father, I know, will always be glad to have me. And if it so shocks you, there is not the slightest necessity of your coming with us."

They glowered at each other, and he said, "You have twisted the question with the usual ability of your sex."

She pondered as if seeking some particularly destructive retort. She ended by saying bluntly, "Did you know that we were going home next week?"

A flush came suddenly to his face. "No. Going home? Who? You?"

"Why, of course." And then with an indolent air she continued, "I meant to have told you before this, but somehow it quite escaped me."

He stammered, "Are—are you, honestly?"

She nodded. "Why, of course. Can't stay here forever, you know."

They were then silent for a long time.

At last Hawker said, "Do you remember what I told you yesterday?"

"No. What was it?"

He cried indignantly, "You know very well what I told you!"

"I do not."

"No," he sneered, "of course not! You never take the trouble to remember such things. Of course not! Of course not!"

"You are a very ridiculous person," she vouchsafed, after eying him coldly.

He arose abruptly. "I believe I am. By heavens, I believe I am!" he cried in a fury.

She laughed. "You are more ridiculous now than I have yet seen you."

After a pause he said magnificently, "Well, Miss Fanhall, you will doubtless find Mr. Hollanden's conversation to have a much greater interest than that of such a ridiculous person."

Hollanden approached them with the blithesome step of an untroubled man. "Hello, you two people, why don't you—oh—ahem! Hold on, Billie, where are you going?"

"I——" began Hawker.

"Oh, Hollie," cried the girl impetuously, "do tell me how to do that slam thing, you know. I've tried it so often, but I don't believe I hold my racket right. And you do it so beautifully."

"Oh, that," said Hollanden. "It's not so very difficult. I'll show it to you. You don't want to know this minute, do you?"

"Yes," she answered.

"Well, come over to the court, then. Come ahead, Billie!"

"No," said Hawker, without looking at his friend, "I can't this morning, Hollie. I've got to go to work. Good-bye!" He comprehended them both in a swift bow and stalked away.

Hollanden turned quickly to the girl. "What was the matter with Billie?

What was he grinding his teeth for? What was the matter with him?"

"Why, nothing—was there?" she asked in surprise.

"Why, he was grinding his teeth until he sounded like a stone crusher," said Hollanden in a severe tone. "What was the matter with him?"

"How should I know?" she retorted.

"You've been saying something to him."

"I! I didn't say a thing."

"Yes, you did."

"Hollie, don't be absurd."

Hollanden debated with himself for a time, and then observed, "Oh, well, I always said he was an ugly-tempered fellow——"

The girl flashed him a little glance.

"And now I am sure of it—as ugly-tempered a fellow as ever lived."

"I believe you," said the girl. Then she added: "All men are. I declare, I think you to be the most incomprehensible creatures. One never knows what to expect of you. And you explode and go into rages and make yourselves utterly detestable over the most trivial matters and at the most unexpected times. You are all mad, I think."

"I!" cried Hollanden wildly. "What in the mischief have I done?"

CHAPTER XVI.

"Look here," said Hollanden, at length, "I thought you were so wonderfully anxious to learn that stroke?"

"Well, I am," she said.

"Come on, then." As they walked toward the tennis court he seemed to be plunged into mournful thought. In his eyes was a singular expression, which perhaps denoted the woe of the optimist pushed suddenly from its height. He sighed. "Oh, well, I suppose all women, even the best of them, are that way."

"What way?" she said.

"My dear child," he answered, in a benevolent manner, "you have disappointed me, because I have discovered that you resemble the rest of your sex."

"Ah!" she remarked, maintaining a noncommittal attitude.

"Yes," continued Hollanden, with a sad but kindly smile, "even you, Grace, were not above fooling with the affections of a poor country swain, until he don't know his ear from the tooth he had pulled two years ago."

She laughed. "He would be furious if he heard you call him a country swain."

"Who would?" said Hollanden.

"Why, the country swain, of course," she rejoined.

Hollanden seemed plunged in mournful reflection again. "Well, it's a shame, Grace, anyhow," he observed, wagging his head dolefully. "It's a howling, wicked shame."

"Hollie, you have no brains at all," she said, "despite your opinion."

"No," he replied ironically, "not a bit."

"Well, you haven't, you know, Hollie."

"At any rate," he said in an angry voice, "I have some comprehension and sympathy for the feelings of others."

"Have you?" she asked. "How do you mean, Hollie? Do you mean you have feeling for them in their various sorrows? Or do you mean that you understand their minds?"

Hollanden ponderously began, "There have been people who have not questioned my ability to——"

"Oh, then, you mean that you both feel for them in their sorrows and comprehend the machinery of their minds. Well, let me tell you that in regard to the last thing you are wrong. You know nothing of anyone's mind. You know less about human nature than anybody I have met."

Hollanden looked at her in artless astonishment. He said, "Now, I wonder what made you say that?" This interrogation did not seem to be addressed to her, but was evidently a statement to himself of a problem. He meditated for some moments. Eventually he said, "I suppose you mean that I do not understand you?"

"Why do you suppose I mean that?"

"That's what a person usually means when he—or she—charges another with not understanding the entire world."

"Well, at any rate, it is not what I mean at all," she said. "I mean that you habitually blunder about other people's affairs, in the belief, I imagine, that you are a great philanthropist, when you are only making an extraordinary exhibition of yourself."

"The dev——" began Hollanden. Afterward he said, "Now, I wonder what in blue thunder you mean this time?"

"Mean this time? My meaning is very plain, Hollie. I supposed the words were clear enough."

"Yes," he said thoughtfully, "your words were clear enough, but then you were of course referring back to some event, or series of events, in which I had the singular ill fortune to displease you. Maybe you don't know yourself, and spoke only from the emotion generated by the event, or series of events, in which, as I have said, I had the singular ill fortune to displease you."

"How awf'ly clever!" she said.

"But I can't recall the event, or series of events, at all," he continued, musing with a scholarly air and disregarding her mockery. "I can't remember a thing about it. To be sure, it might have been that time when——"

"I think it very stupid of you to hunt for a meaning when I believe I made everything so perfectly clear," she said wrathfully.

"Well, you yourself might not be aware of what you really meant," he answered sagely. "Women often do that sort of thing, you know. Women often speak from motives which, if brought face to face with them, they wouldn't be able to distinguish from any other thing which they had never before seen."

"Hollie, if there is a disgusting person in the world it is he who pretends to know so much concerning a woman's mind."

"Well, that's because they who know, or pretend to know, so much about a woman's mind are invariably satirical, you understand," said Hollanden cheerfully.

A dog ran frantically across the lawn, his nose high in the air and his countenance expressing vast perturbation and alarm. "Why, Billie forgot to whistle for his dog when he started for home," said Hollanden. "Come here, old man! Well, 'e was a nice dog!" The girl also gave invitation, but the setter would not heed them. He spun wildly about the lawn until he seemed to strike his master's trail, and then, with his nose near to the ground, went down the road at an eager gallop. They stood and watched him.

"Stanley's a nice dog," said Hollanden.

"Indeed he is!" replied the girl fervently.

Presently Hollanden remarked: "Well, don't let's fight any more, particularly since we can't decide what we're fighting about. I can't discover the reason, and you don't know it, so——"

"I do know it. I told you very plainly."

"Well, all right. Now, this is the way to work that slam: You give the ball a sort of a lift—see!—underhanded and with your arm crooked and stiff. Here, you smash this other ball into the net. Hi! Look out! If you hit it that way you'll knock it over the hotel. Let the ball drop nearer to the ground. Oh, heavens, not on the ground! Well, it's hard to do it from the serve, anyhow. I'll go over to the other court and bat you some easy ones."

Afterward, when they were going toward the inn, the girl suddenly began to laugh.

"What are you giggling at?" said Hollanden.

"I was thinking how furious he would be if he heard you call him a country swain," she rejoined.

"Who?" asked Hollanden.

CHAPTER XVII.

Oglethorpe contended that the men who made the most money from books were the best authors. Hollanden contended that they were the worst. Oglethorpe said that such a question should be left to the people. Hollanden said that the people habitually made wrong decisions on questions that were left to them. "That is the most odiously aristocratic belief," said Oglethorpe.

"No," said Hollanden, "I like the people. But, considered generally, they are a collection of ingenious blockheads."

"But they read your books," said Oglethorpe, grinning.

"That is through a mistake," replied Hollanden.

As the discussion grew in size it incited the close attention of the Worcester girls, but Miss Fanhall did not seem to hear it. Hawker, too, was staring into the darkness with a gloomy and preoccupied air.

"Are you sorry that this is your last evening at Hemlock Inn?" said the painter at last, in a low tone.

"Why, yes—certainly," said the girl.

Under the sloping porch of the inn the vague orange light from the parlours drifted to the black wall of the night.

"I shall miss you," said the painter.

"Oh, I dare say," said the girl.

Hollanden was lecturing at length and wonderfully. In the mystic spaces of the night the pines could be heard in their weird monotone, as they softly smote branch and branch, as if moving in some solemn and sorrowful dance.

"This has been quite the most delightful summer of my experience," said the painter.

"I have found it very pleasant," said the girl.

From time to time Hawker glanced furtively at Oglethorpe, Hollanden, and the Worcester girl. This glance expressed no desire for their well-being.

"I shall miss you," he said to the girl again. His manner was rather desperate. She made no reply, and, after leaning toward her, he subsided with an air of defeat.

Eventually he remarked: "It will be very lonely here again. I dare say I shall return to New York myself in a few weeks."

"I hope you will call," she said.

"I shall be delighted," he answered stiffly, and with a dissatisfied look at her.

"Oh, Mr. Hawker," cried the younger Worcester girl, suddenly emerging from the cloud of argument which Hollanden and Oglethorpe kept in the air, "won't it be sad to lose Grace? Indeed, I don't know what we shall do. Sha'n't we miss her dreadfully?"

"Yes," said Hawker, "we shall of course miss her dreadfully."

"Yes, won't it be frightful?" said the elder Worcester girl. "I can't imagine what we will do without her. And Hollie is only going to spend ten more days. Oh, dear! mamma, I believe, will insist on staying the entire summer. It was papa's orders, you know, and I really think she is going to obey them. He said he wanted her to have one period of rest at any rate. She is such a busy woman in town, you know."

"Here," said Hollanden, wheeling to them suddenly, "you all look as if you were badgering Hawker, and he looks badgered. What are you saying to him?"

"Why," answered the younger Worcester girl, "we were only saying to him how lonely it would be without Grace."

"Oh!" said Hollanden.

As the evening grew old, the mother of the Worcester girls joined the group. This was a sign that the girls were not to long delay the vanishing time.

She sat almost upon the edge of her chair, as if she expected to be called upon at any moment to arise and bow "Good-night," and she repaid Hollanden's eloquent attention with the placid and absent-minded smiles of the chaperon who waits.

Once the younger Worcester girl shrugged her shoulders and turned to say, "Mamma, you make me nervous!" Her mother merely smiled in a still more placid and absent-minded manner.

Oglethorpe arose to drag his chair nearer to the railing, and when he stood the Worcester mother moved and looked around expectantly, but Oglethorpe took seat again. Hawker kept an anxious eye upon her.

Presently Miss Fanhall arose.

"Why, you are not going in already, are you?" said Hawker and Hollanden and Oglethorpe. The Worcester mother moved toward the door followed by her daughters, who were protesting in muffled tones. Hollanden pitched violently upon Oglethorpe. "Well, at any rate——" he said. He picked the thread of a past argument with great agility.

Hawker said to the girl, "I—I—I shall miss you dreadfully."

She turned to look at him and smiled. "Shall you?" she said in a low voice.

"Yes," he said. Thereafter he stood before her awkwardly and in silence. She scrutinized the boards of the floor. Suddenly she drew a violet from a cluster of them upon her gown and thrust it out to him as she turned toward the approaching Oglethorpe.

"Good-night, Mr. Hawker," said the latter. "I am very glad to have met you, I'm sure. Hope to see you in town. Good-night."

He stood near when the girl said to Hawker: "Good-bye. You have given us such a charming summer. We shall be delighted to see you in town. You must come some time when the children can see you, too. Good-bye."

"Good-bye," replied Hawker, eagerly and feverishly, trying to interpret the inscrutable feminine face before him. "I shall come at my first opportunity."

"Good-bye."

"Good-bye."

Down at the farmhouse, in the black quiet of the night, a dog lay curled on the door-mat. Of a sudden the tail of this dog began to thump, thump, on the boards. It began as a lazy movement, but it passed into a state of gentle enthusiasm, and then into one of curiously loud and joyful celebration. At last the gate clicked. The dog uncurled, and went to the edge of the steps to greet his master. He gave adoring, tremulous welcome with his clear eyes shining in the darkness. "Well, Stan, old boy," said Hawker, stooping to stroke the dog's head. After his master had entered the house the dog went forward and sniffed at something that lay on the top step. Apparently it did not interest him greatly, for he returned in a moment to the door-mat.

But he was again obliged to uncurl himself, for his master came out of the house with a lighted lamp and made search of the door-mat, the steps, and the walk, swearing meanwhile in an undertone. The dog wagged his tail and sleepily watched this ceremony. When his master had again entered the house the dog went forward and sniffed at the top step, but the thing that had lain there was gone.

CHAPTER XVIII.

It was evident at breakfast that Hawker's sisters had achieved information. "What's the matter with you this morning?" asked one. "You look as if you hadn't slep' well."

"There is nothing the matter with me," he rejoined, looking glumly at his plate.

"Well, you look kind of broke up."

"How I look is of no consequence. I tell you there is nothing the matter with me."

"Oh!" said his sister. She exchanged meaning glances with the other feminine members of the family. Presently the other sister observed, "I heard she was going home to-day."

"Who?" said Hawker, with a challenge in his tone.

"Why, that New York girl—Miss What's-her-name," replied the sister, with an undaunted smile.

"Did you, indeed? Well, perhaps she is."

"Oh, you don't know for sure, I s'pose."

Hawker arose from the table, and, taking his hat, went away.

"Mary!" said the mother, in the sepulchral tone of belated but conscientious reproof.

"Well, I don't care. He needn't be so grand. I didn't go to tease him. I don't care."

"Well, you ought to care," said the old man suddenly. "There's no sense in you wimen folks pestering the boy all the time. Let him alone with his own business, can't you?"

"Well, ain't we leaving him alone?"

"No, you ain't—'cept when he ain't here. I don't wonder the boy grabs his hat and skips out when you git to going."

"Well, what did we say to him now? Tell us what we said to him that was so dreadful."

"Aw, thunder an' lightnin'!" cried the old man with a sudden great snarl. They seemed to know by this ejaculation that he had emerged in an instant from that place where man endures, and they ended the discussion. The old man continued his breakfast.

During his walk that morning Hawker visited a certain cascade, a certain lake, and some roads, paths, groves, nooks. Later in the day he made a sketch, choosing an hour when the atmosphere was of a dark blue, like powder smoke in the shade of trees, and the western sky was burning in strips of red. He painted with a wild face, like a man who is killing.

After supper he and his father strolled under the apple boughs in the orchard and smoked. Once he gestured wearily. "Oh, I guess I'll go back to New York in a few days."

"Um," replied his father calmly. "All right, William."

Several days later Hawker accosted his father in the barnyard. "I suppose you think sometimes I don't care so much about you and the folks and the old place any more; but I do."

"Um," said the old man. "When you goin'?"

"Where?" asked Hawker, flushing.

"Back to New York."

"Why—I hadn't thought much about—— Oh, next week, I guess."

"Well, do as you like, William. You know how glad me an' mother and the girls are to have you come home with us whenever you can come. You know that. But you must do as you think best, and if you ought to go back to

New York now, William, why—do as you think best."

"Well, my work——" said Hawker.

From time to time the mother made wondering speech to the sisters. "How much nicer William is now! He's just as good as he can be. There for a while he was so cross and out of sorts. I don't see what could have come over him. But now he's just as good as he can be."

Hollanden told him, "Come up to the inn more, you fool."

"I was up there yesterday."

"Yesterday! What of that? I've seen the time when the farm couldn't hold you for two hours during the day."

"Go to blazes!"

"Millicent got a letter from Grace Fanhall the other day."

"That so?"

"Yes, she did. Grace wrote—— Say, does that shadow look pure purple to you?"

"Certainly it does, or I wouldn't paint it so, duffer. What did she write?"

"Well, if that shadow is pure purple my eyes are liars. It looks a kind of slate colour to me. Lord! if what you fellows say in your pictures is true, the whole earth must be blazing and burning and glowing and——"

Hawker went into a rage. "Oh, you don't know anything about colour, Hollie. For heaven's sake, shut up, or I'll smash you with the easel."

"Well, I was going to tell you what Grace wrote in her letter. She said——"

"Go on."

"Gimme time, can't you? She said that town was stupid, and that she wished she was back at Hemlock Inn."

"Oh! Is that all?"

"Is that all? I wonder what you expected? Well, and she asked to be recalled to you."

"Yes? Thanks."

"And that's all. 'Gad, for such a devoted man as you were, your enthusiasm and interest is stupendous."

The father said to the mother, "Well, William's going back to New York next week."

"Is he? Why, he ain't said nothing to me about it."

"Well, he is, anyhow."

"I declare! What do you s'pose he's going back before September for, John?"

"How do I know?"

"Well, it's funny, John. I bet—I bet he's going back so's he can see that girl."

"He says it's his work."

CHAPTER XIX.

Wrinkles had been peering into the little dry-goods box that acted as a cupboard. "There are only two eggs and half a loaf of bread left," he announced brutally.

"Heavens!" said Warwickson from where he lay smoking on the bed. He spoke in a dismal voice. This tone, it is said, had earned him his popular name of Great Grief.

From different points of the compass Wrinkles looked at the little cupboard with a tremendous scowl, as if he intended thus to frighten the eggs into becoming more than two, and the bread into becoming a loaf. "Plague take it!" he exclaimed.

"Oh, shut up, Wrinkles!" said Grief from the bed.

Wrinkles sat down with an air austere and virtuous. "Well, what are we going to do?" he demanded of the others.

Grief, after swearing, said: "There, that's right! Now you're happy. The holy office of the inquisition! Blast your buttons, Wrinkles, you always try to keep us from starving peacefully! It is two hours before dinner, anyhow, and——"

"Well, but what are you going to do?" persisted Wrinkles.

Pennoyer, with his head afar down, had been busily scratching at a pen-and-ink drawing. He looked up from his board to utter a plaintive optimism. "The Monthly Amazement will pay me to-morrow. They ought to. I've waited over three months now. I'm going down there to-morrow, and perhaps I'll get it."

His friends listened with airs of tolerance. "Oh, no doubt, Penny, old man." But at last Wrinkles giggled pityingly. Over on the bed Grief croaked deep down in his throat. Nothing was said for a long time thereafter.

The crash of the New York streets came faintly to this room.

Occasionally one could hear the tramp of feet in the intricate corridors of the begrimed building which squatted, slumbering, and old, between two exalted commercial structures which would have had to bend afar down to perceive it. The northward march of the city's progress had happened not to overturn this aged structure, and it huddled there, lost and forgotten, while the cloud-veering towers strode on.

Meanwhile the first shadows of dusk came in at the blurred windows of the room. Pennoyer threw down his pen and tossed his drawing over on the wonderful heap of stuff that hid the table. "It's too dark to work." He lit a pipe and walked about, stretching his shoulders like a man whose labour was valuable.

When the dusk came fully the youths grew apparently sad. The solemnity of the gloom seemed to make them ponder. "Light the gas, Wrinkles," said Grief fretfully.

The flood of orange light showed clearly the dull walls lined with sketches, the tousled bed in one corner, the masses of boxes and trunks in another, a little dead stove, and the wonderful table. Moreover, there were wine-coloured draperies flung in some places, and on a shelf, high up, there were plaster casts, with dust in the creases. A long stove-pipe wandered off in the wrong direction and then turned impulsively toward a hole in the wall. There were some elaborate cobwebs on the ceiling.

"Well, let's eat," said Grief.

"Eat," said Wrinkles, with a jeer; "I told you there was only two eggs and a little bread left. How are we going to eat?"

Again brought face to face with this problem, and at the hour for dinner, Pennoyer and Grief thought profoundly. "Thunder and turf!" Grief finally announced as the result of his deliberations.

"Well, if Billie Hawker was only home——" began Pennoyer.

"But he isn't," objected Wrinkles, "and that settles that."

Grief and Pennoyer thought more. Ultimately Grief said, "Oh, well, let's eat what we've got." The others at once agreed to this suggestion, as if it had been in their minds.

Later there came a quick step in the passage and a confident little thunder upon the door. Wrinkles arranging the tin pail on the gas stove, Pennoyer engaged in slicing the bread, and Great Grief affixing the rubber tube to the gas stove, yelled, "Come in!"

The door opened, and Miss Florinda O'Connor, the model, dashed into the room like a gale of obstreperous autumn leaves.

"Why, hello, Splutter!" they cried.

"Oh, boys, I've come to dine with you."

It was like a squall striking a fleet of yachts.

Grief spoke first. "Yes, you have?" he said incredulously.

"Why, certainly I have. What's the matter?"

They grinned. "Well, old lady," responded Grief, "you've hit us at the wrong time. We are, in fact, all out of everything. No dinner, to mention, and, what's more, we haven't got a sou."

"What? Again?" cried Florinda.

"Yes, again. You'd better dine home to-night."

"But I'll—I'll stake you," said the girl eagerly. "Oh, you poor old idiots! It's a shame! Say, I'll stake you."

"Certainly not," said Pennoyer sternly.

"What are you talking about, Splutter?" demanded Wrinkles in an angry voice.

"No, that won't go down," said Grief, in a resolute yet wistful tone.

Florinda divested herself of her hat, jacket, and gloves, and put them where she pleased. "Got coffee, haven't you? Well, I'm not going to stir a step.

You're a fine lot of birds!" she added bitterly, "You've all pulled me out of a whole lot of scrape—oh, any number of times—and now you're broke, you go acting like a set of dudes."

Great Grief had fixed the coffee to boil on the gas stove, but he had to watch it closely, for the rubber tube was short, and a chair was balanced on a trunk, and two bundles of kindling was balanced on the chair, and the gas stove was balanced on the kindling. Coffee-making was here accounted a feat.

Pennoyer dropped a piece of bread to the floor. "There! I'll have to go shy one."

Wrinkles sat playing serenades on his guitar and staring with a frown at the table, as if he was applying some strange method of clearing it of its litter.

Florinda assaulted Great Grief. "Here, that's not the way to make coffee!"

"What ain't?"

"Why, the way you're making it. You want to take——" She explained some way to him which he couldn't understand.

"For heaven's sake, Wrinkles, tackle that table! Don't sit there like a music box," said Pennoyer, grappling the eggs and starting for the gas stove.

Later, as they sat around the board, Wrinkles said with satisfaction, "Well, the coffee's good, anyhow."

"'Tis good," said Florinda, "but it isn't made right. I'll show you how, Penny. You first——"

"Oh, dry up, Splutter," said Grief. "Here, take an egg."

"I don't like eggs," said Florinda.

"Take an egg," said the three hosts menacingly.

"I tell you I don't like eggs."

"Take—an—egg!" they said again.

"Oh, well," said Florinda, "I'll take one, then; but you needn't act like such a set of dudes—and, oh, maybe you didn't have much lunch. I had such a daisy lunch! Up at Pontiac's studio. He's got a lovely studio."

The three looked to be oppressed. Grief said sullenly, "I saw some of his things over in Stencil's gallery, and they're rotten."

"Yes—rotten," said Pennoyer.

"Rotten," said Grief.

"Oh, well," retorted Florinda, "if a man has a swell studio and dresses— oh, sort of like a Willie, you know, you fellows sit here like owls in a cave and say rotten—rotten—rotten. You're away off. Pontiac's landscapes——"

"Landscapes be blowed! Put any of his work alongside of Billie Hawker's and see how it looks."

"Oh, well, Billie Hawker's," said Florinda. "Oh, well."

At the mention of Hawker's name they had all turned to scan her face.

CHAPTER XX.

"He wrote that he was coming home this week," said Pennoyer.

"Did he?" asked Florinda indifferently.

"Yes. Aren't you glad?"

They were still watching her face.

"Yes, of course I'm glad. Why shouldn't I be glad?" cried the girl with defiance.

They grinned.

"Oh, certainly. Billie Hawker is a good fellow, Splutter. You have a particular right to be glad."

"You people make me tired," Florinda retorted. "Billie Hawker doesn't give a rap about me, and he never tried to make out that he did."

"No," said Grief. "But that isn't saying that you don't care a rap about Billie Hawker. Ah, Florinda!"

It seemed that the girl's throat suffered a slight contraction. "Well, and what if I do?" she demanded finally.

"Have a cigarette?" answered Grief.

Florinda took a cigarette, lit it, and, perching herself on a divan, which was secretly a coal box, she smoked fiercely.

"What if I do?" she again demanded. "It's better than liking one of you dubs, anyhow."

"Oh, Splutter, you poor little outspoken kid!" said Wrinkle in a sad voice.

Grief searched among the pipes until he found the best one. "Yes, Splutter, don't you know that when you are so frank you defy every law of your sex, and wild eyes will take your trail?"

"Oh, you talk through your hat," replied Florinda. "Billie don't care whether I like him or whether I don't. And if he should hear me now, he wouldn't be glad or give a hang, either way. I know that." The girl paused and looked at the row of plaster casts. "Still, you needn't be throwing it at me all the time."

"We didn't," said Wrinkles indignantly. "You threw it at yourself."

"Well," continued Florinda, "it's better than liking one of you dubs, anyhow. He makes money and———"

"There," said Grief, "now you've hit it! Bedad, you've reached a point in eulogy where if you move again you will have to go backward."

"Of course I don't care anything about a fellow's having money———"

"No, indeed you don't, Splutter," said Pennoyer.

"But then, you know what I mean. A fellow isn't a man and doesn't stand up straight unless he has some money. And Billie Hawker makes enough so that you feel that nobody could walk over him, don't you know? And there isn't anything jay about him, either. He's a thoroughbred, don't you know?"

After reflection, Pennoyer said, "It's pretty hard on the rest of us, Splutter."

"Well, of course I like him, but—but———"

"What?" said Pennoyer.

"I don't know," said Florinda.

Purple Sanderson lived in this room, but he usually dined out. At a certain time in his life, before he came to be a great artist, he had learned the gas-fitter's trade, and when his opinions were not identical with the opinions of the art managers of the greater number of New York publications he went to see a friend who was a plumber, and the opinions of this man he was thereafter said to respect. He frequented a very neat restaurant on Twenty-third Street. It was known that on Saturday nights Wrinkles, Grief, and Pennoyer frequently quarreled with him.

As Florinda ceased speaking Purple entered. "Hello, there, Splutter!" As he was neatly hanging up his coat, he said to the others, "Well, the rent will be due in four days."

"Will it?" asked Pennoyer, astounded.

"Certainly it will," responded Purple, with the air of a superior financial man.

"My soul!" said Wrinkles.

"Oh, shut up, Purple!" said Grief. "You make me weary, coming around here with your chin about rent. I was just getting happy."

"Well, how are we going to pay it? That's the point," said Sanderson.

Wrinkles sank deeper in his chair and played despondently on his guitar. Grief cast a look of rage at Sanderson, and then stared at the wall. Pennoyer said, "Well, we might borrow it from Billie Hawker."

Florinda laughed then.

"Oh," continued Pennoyer hastily, "if those Amazement people pay me when they said they would I'll have the money."

"So you will," said Grief. "You will have money to burn. Did the Amazement people ever pay you when they said they would? You are wonderfully important all of a sudden, it seems to me. You talk like an artist."

Wrinkles, too, smiled at Pennoyer. "The Eminent Magazine people wanted Penny to hire models and make a try for them, too. It would only cost him a stack of blues. By the time he has invested all his money he hasn't got, and the rent is three weeks overdue, he will be able to tell the landlord to wait seven months until the Monday morning after the day of publication. Go ahead, Penny."

After a period of silence, Sanderson, in an obstinate manner, said, "Well, what's to be done? The rent has got to be paid."

Wrinkles played more sad music. Grief frowned deeper. Pennoyer was evidently searching his mind for a plan.

Florinda took the cigarette from between her lips that she might grin with greater freedom.

"We might throw Purple out," said Grief, with an inspired air. "That would stop all this discussion."

"You!" said Sanderson furiously. "You can't keep serious a minute. If you didn't have us to take care of you, you wouldn't even know when they threw you out into the street."

"Wouldn't I?" said Grief.

"Well, look here," interposed Florinda, "I'm going home unless you can be more interesting. I am dead sorry about the rent, but I can't help it, and——"

"Here! Sit down! Hold on, Splutter!" they shouted. Grief turned to Sanderson: "Purple, you shut up!"

Florinda curled again on the divan and lit another cigarette. The talk waged about the names of other and more successful painters, whose work they usually pronounced "rotten."

CHAPTER XXI.

Pennoyer, coming home one morning with two gigantic cakes to accompany the coffee at the breakfast in the den, saw a young man bounce from a horse car. He gave a shout. "Hello, there, Billie! Hello!"

"Hello, Penny!" said Hawker. "What are you doing out so early?" It was somewhat after nine o'clock.

"Out to get breakfast," said Pennoyer, waving the cakes. "Have a good time, old man?"

"Great."

"Do much work?"

"No. Not so much. How are all the people?"

"Oh, pretty good. Come in and see us eat breakfast," said Pennoyer, throwing open the door of the den. Wrinkles, in his shirt, was making coffee. Grief sat in a chair trying to loosen the grasp of sleep. "Why, Billie Hawker, b'ginger!" they cried.

"How's the wolf, boys? At the door yet?"

"'At the door yet?' He's halfway up the back stairs, and coming fast. He and the landlord will be here to-morrow. 'Mr. Landlord, allow me to present Mr. F. Wolf, of Hunger, N. J. Mr. Wolf—Mr. Landlord.'"

"Bad as that?" said Hawker.

"You bet it is! Easy Street is somewhere in heaven, for all we know. Have some breakfast?—coffee and cake, I mean."

"No, thanks, boys. Had breakfast."

Wrinkles added to the shirt, Grief aroused himself, and Pennoyer brought the coffee. Cheerfully throwing some drawings from the table to the floor, they thus made room for the breakfast, and grouped themselves with beaming smiles at the board.

"Well, Billie, come back to the old gang again, eh? How did the country seem? Do much work?"

"Not very much. A few things. How's everybody?"

"Splutter was in last night. Looking out of sight. Seemed glad to hear that you were coming back soon."

"Did she? Penny, did anybody call wanting me to do a ten-thousand-dollar portrait for them?"

"No. That frame-maker, though, was here with a bill. I told him——"

Afterward Hawker crossed the corridor and threw open the door of his own large studio. The great skylight, far above his head, shed its clear rays upon a scene which appeared to indicate that some one had very recently ceased work here and started for the country. A distant closet door was open, and the interior showed the effects of a sudden pillage.

There was an unfinished "Girl in Apple Orchard" upon the tall Dutch easel, and sketches and studies were thick upon the floor. Hawker took a pipe and filled it from his friend the tan and gold jar. He cast himself into a chair and, taking an envelope from his pocket, emptied two violets from it to the palm of his hand and stared long at them. Upon the walls of the studio various labours of his life, in heavy gilt frames, contemplated him and the violets.

At last Pennoyer burst impetuously in upon him. "Hi, Billie! come over and—— What's the matter?"

Hawker had hastily placed the violets in the envelope and hurried it to his pocket. "Nothing," he answered.

"Why, I thought—" said Pennoyer, "I thought you looked rather rattled. Didn't you have—I thought I saw something in your hand."

"Nothing, I tell you!" cried Hawker.

"Er—oh, I beg your pardon," said Pennoyer. "Why, I was going to tell you that Splutter is over in our place, and she wants to see you."

"Wants to see me? What for?" demanded Hawker. "Why don't she come over here, then?"

"I'm sure I don't know," replied Pennoyer. "She sent me to call you."

"Well, do you think I'm going to—— Oh, well, I suppose she wants to be unpleasant, and knows she loses a certain mental position if she comes over here, but if she meets me in your place she can be as infernally disagreeable as she—— That's it, I'll bet."

When they entered the den Florinda was gazing from the window. Her back was toward the door.

At last she turned to them, holding herself very straight. "Well, Billie Hawker," she said grimly, "you don't seem very glad to see a fellow."

"Why, heavens, did you think I was going to turn somersaults in the air?"

"Well, you didn't come out when you heard me pass your door," said Florinda, with gloomy resentment.

Hawker appeared to be ruffled and vexed. "Oh, great Scott!" he said, making a gesture of despair.

Florinda returned to the window. In the ensuing conversation she took no part, save when there was an opportunity to harry some speech of Hawker's, which she did in short contemptuous sentences. Hawker made no reply save to glare in her direction. At last he said, "Well, I must go over and do some work." Florinda did not turn from the window. "Well, so-long, boys," said Hawker, "I'll see you later."

As the door slammed Pennoyer apologetically said, "Billie is a trifle off his feed this morning."

"What about?" asked Grief.

"I don't know; but when I went to call him he was sitting deep in his chair staring at some——" He looked at Florinda and became silent.

"Staring at what?" asked Florinda, turning then from the window.

Pennoyer seemed embarrassed. "Why, I don't know—nothing, I guess—I couldn't see very well. I was only fooling."

Florinda scanned his face suspiciously. "Staring at what?" she demanded imperatively.

"Nothing, I tell you!" shouted Pennoyer.

Florinda looked at him, and wavered and debated. Presently she said, softly: "Ah, go on, Penny. Tell me."

"It wasn't anything at all, I say!" cried Pennoyer stoutly. "I was only giving you a jolly. Sit down, Splutter, and hit a cigarette."

She obeyed, but she continued to cast the dubious eye at Pennoyer. Once she said to him privately: "Go on, Penny, tell me. I know it was something from the way you are acting."

"Oh, let up, Splutter, for heaven's sake!"

"Tell me," beseeched Florinda.

"No."

"Tell me."

"No."

"Pl-e-a-se tell me."

"No."

"Oh, go on."

"No."

"Ah, what makes you so mean, Penny? You know I'd tell you, if it was the other way about."

"But it's none of my business, Splutter. I can't tell you something which is Billie Hawker's private affair. If I did I would be a chump."

"But I'll never say you told me. Go on."

"No."

"Pl-e-a-se tell me."

"No."

CHAPTER XXII.

When Florinda had gone, Grief said, "Well, what was it?" Wrinkles looked curiously from his drawing-board.

Pennoyer lit his pipe and held it at the side of his mouth in the manner of a deliberate man. At last he said, "It was two violets."

"You don't say!" ejaculated Wrinkles.

"Well, I'm hanged!" cried Grief. "Holding them in his hand and moping over them, eh?"

"Yes," responded Pennoyer. "Rather that way."

"Well, I'm hanged!" said both Grief and Wrinkles. They grinned in a pleased, urchin-like manner. "Say, who do you suppose she is? Somebody he met this summer, no doubt. Would you ever think old Billie would get into that sort of a thing? Well, I'll be gol-durned!"

Ultimately Wrinkles said, "Well, it's his own business." This was spoken in a tone of duty.

"Of course it's his own business," retorted Grief. "But who would ever think——" Again they grinned.

When Hawker entered the den some minutes later he might have noticed something unusual in the general demeanour. "Say, Grief, will you loan me your—— What's up?" he asked.

For answer they grinned at each other, and then grinned at him.

"You look like a lot of Chessy cats," he told them.

They grinned on.

Apparently feeling unable to deal with these phenomena, he went at last to the door. "Well, this is a fine exhibition," he said, standing with his hand on the knob and regarding them. "Won election bets? Some good old auntie just died? Found something new to pawn? No? Well, I can't stand this. You resemble those fish they discover at deep sea. Good-bye!"

As he opened the door they cried out: "Hold on, Billie! Billie, look here! Say, who is she?"

"What?"

"Who is she?"

"Who is who?"

They laughed and nodded. "Why, you know. She. Don't you understand? She."

"You talk like a lot of crazy men," said Hawker. "I don't know what you mean."

"Oh, you don't, eh? You don't? Oh, no! How about those violets you were moping over this morning? Eh, old man! Oh, no, you don't know what we mean! Oh, no! How about those violets, eh? How about 'em?"

Hawker, with flushed and wrathful face, looked at Pennoyer. "Penny——" But Grief and Wrinkles roared an interruption. "Oh, ho, Mr. Hawker! so it's true, is it? It's true. You are a nice bird, you are. Well, you old rascal! Durn your picture!"

Hawker, menacing them once with his eyes, went away. They sat cackling.

At noon, when he met Wrinkles in the corridor, he said: "Hey, Wrinkles, come here for a minute, will you? Say, old man, I—I——"

"What?" said Wrinkles.

"Well, you know, I—I—of course, every man is likely to make an accursed idiot of himself once in a while, and I——"

"And you what?" asked Wrinkles.

"Well, we are a kind of a band of hoodlums, you know, and I'm just

94

enough idiot to feel that I don't care to hear—don't care to hear—well, her name used, you know."

"Bless your heart," replied Wrinkles, "we haven't used her name. We don't know her name. How could we use it?"

"Well, I know," said Hawker. "But you understand what I mean, Wrinkles."

"Yes, I understand what you mean," said Wrinkles, with dignity. "I don't suppose you are any worse of a stuff than common. Still, I didn't know that we were such outlaws."

"Of course, I have overdone the thing," responded Hawker hastily. "But—you ought to understand how I mean it, Wrinkles."

After Wrinkles had thought for a time, he said: "Well, I guess I do. All right. That goes."

Upon entering the den, Wrinkles said, "You fellows have got to quit guying Billie, do you hear?"

"We?" cried Grief. "We've got to quit? What do you do?"

"Well, I quit too."

Pennoyer said: "Ah, ha! Billie has been jumping on you."

"No, he didn't," maintained Wrinkles; "but he let me know it was— well, rather a—rather a—sacred subject." Wrinkles blushed when the others snickered.

In the afternoon, as Hawker was going slowly down the stairs, he was almost impaled upon the feather of a hat which, upon the head of a lithe and rather slight girl, charged up at him through the gloom.

"Hello, Splutter!" he cried. "You are in a hurry."

"That you, Billie?" said the girl, peering, for the hallways of this old building remained always in a dungeonlike darkness.

"Yes, it is. Where are you going at such a headlong gait?"

"Up to see the boys. I've got a bottle of wine and some—some pickles, you know. I'm going to make them let me dine with them to-night. Coming back, Billie?"

"Why, no, I don't expect to."

He moved then accidentally in front of the light that sifted through the dull, gray panes of a little window.

"Oh, cracky!" cried the girl; "how fine you are, Billie! Going to a coronation?"

"No," said Hawker, looking seriously over his collar and down at his clothes. "Fact is—er—well, I've got to make a call."

"A call—bless us! And are you really going to wear those gray gloves you're holding there, Billie? Say, wait until you get around the corner. They won't stand 'em on this street."

"Oh, well," said Hawker, depreciating the gloves—"oh, well."

The girl looked up at him. "Who you going to call on?"

"Oh," said Hawker, "a friend."

"Must be somebody most extraordinary, you look so dreadfully correct. Come back, Billie, won't you? Come back and dine with us."

"Why, I—I don't believe I can."

"Oh, come on! It's fun when we all dine together. Won't you, Billie?"

"Well, I——"

"Oh, don't be so stupid!" The girl stamped her foot and flashed her eyes at him angrily.

"Well, I'll see—I will if I can—I can't tell——" He left her rather precipitately.

Hawker eventually appeared at a certain austere house where he rang the bell with quite nervous fingers.

96

But she was not at home. As he went down the steps his eyes were as those of a man whose fortunes have tumbled upon him. As he walked down the street he wore in some subtle way the air of a man who has been grievously wronged. When he rounded the corner, his lips were set strangely, as if he were a man seeking revenge.

CHAPTER XXIII.

"It's just right," said Grief.

"It isn't quite cool enough," said Wrinkles.

"Well, I guess I know the proper temperature for claret."

"Well, I guess you don't. If it was buttermilk, now, you would know, but you can't tell anything about claret."

Florinda ultimately decided the question. "It isn't quite cool enough," she said, laying her hand on the bottle. "Put it on the window ledge, Grief."

"Hum! Splutter, I thought you knew more than——"

"Oh, shut up!" interposed the busy Pennoyer from a remote corner. "Who is going after the potato salad? That's what I want to know. Who is going?"

"Wrinkles," said Grief.

"Grief," said Wrinkles.

"There," said Pennoyer, coming forward and scanning a late work with an eye of satisfaction. "There's the three glasses and the little tumbler; and then, Grief, you will have to drink out of a mug."

"I'll be double-dyed black if I will!" cried Grief. "I wouldn't drink claret out of a mug to save my soul from being pinched!"

"You duffer, you talk like a bloomin' British chump on whom the sun never sets! What do you want?"

"Well, there's enough without that—what's the matter with you? Three glasses and the little tumbler."

"Yes, but if Billie Hawker comes——"

"Well, let him drink out of the mug, then. He——"

"No, he won't," said Florinda suddenly. "I'll take the mug myself."

"All right, Splutter," rejoined Grief meekly. "I'll keep the mug. But, still, I don't see why Billie Hawker——"

"I shall take the mug," reiterated Florinda firmly.

"But I don't see why——"

"Let her alone, Grief," said Wrinkles. "She has decided that it is heroic. You can't move her now."

"Well, who is going for the potato salad?" cried Pennoyer again. "That's what I want to know."

"Wrinkles," said Grief.

"Grief," said Wrinkles.

"Do you know," remarked Florinda, raising her head from where she had been toiling over the spaghetti, "I don't care so much for Billie Hawker as I did once?" Her sleeves were rolled above the elbows of her wonderful arms, and she turned from the stove and poised a fork as if she had been smitten at her task with this inspiration.

There was a short silence, and then Wrinkles said politely, "No."

"No," continued Florinda, "I really don't believe I do." She suddenly started. "Listen! Isn't that him coming now?"

The dull trample of a step could be heard in some distant corridor, but it died slowly to silence.

"I thought that might be him," she said, turning to the spaghetti again.

"I hope the old Indian comes," said Pennoyer, "but I don't believe he will. Seems to me he must be going to see——"

"Who?" asked Florinda.

"Well, you know, Hollanden and he usually dine together when they are both in town."

Florinda looked at Pennoyer. "I know, Penny. You must have thought I was remarkably clever not to understand all your blundering. But I don't care so much. Really I don't."

"Of course not," assented Pennoyer.

"Really I don't."

"Of course not."

"Listen!" exclaimed Grief, who was near the door. "There he comes now." Somebody approached, whistling an air from "Traviata," which rang loud and clear, and low and muffled, as the whistler wound among the intricate hallways. This air was as much a part of Hawker as his coat. The spaghetti had arrived at a critical stage. Florinda gave it her complete attention.

When Hawker opened the door he ceased whistling and said gruffly, "Hello!"

"Just the man!" said Grief. "Go after the potato salad, will you, Billie? There's a good boy! Wrinkles has refused."

"He can't carry the salad with those gloves," interrupted Florinda, raising her eyes from her work and contemplating them with displeasure.

"Hang the gloves!" cried Hawker, dragging them from his hands and hurling them at the divan. "What's the matter with you, Splutter?"

Pennoyer said, "My, what a temper you are in, Billie!"

"I am," replied Hawker. "I feel like an Apache. Where do you get this accursed potato salad?"

"In Second Avenue. You know where. At the old place."

"No, I don't!" snapped Hawker.

"Why——"

"Here," said Florinda, "I'll go." She had already rolled down her sleeves and was arraying herself in her hat and jacket.

100

"No, you won't," said Hawker, filled with wrath. "I'll go myself."

"We can both go, Billie, if you are so bent," replied the girl in a conciliatory voice.

"Well, come on, then. What are you standing there for?"

When these two had departed, Wrinkles said: "Lordie! What's wrong with Billie?"

"He's been discussing art with some pot-boiler," said Grief, speaking as if this was the final condition of human misery.

"No, sir," said Pennoyer. "It's something connected with the now celebrated violets."

Out in the corridor Florinda said, "What—what makes you so ugly, Billie?"

"Why, I am not ugly, am I?"

"Yes, you are—ugly as anything."

Probably he saw a grievance in her eyes, for he said, "Well, I don't want to be ugly." His tone seemed tender. The halls were intensely dark, and the girl placed her hand on his arm. As they rounded a turn in the stairs a straying lock of her hair brushed against his temple. "Oh!" said Florinda, in a low voice.

"We'll get some more claret," observed Hawker musingly. "And some cognac for the coffee. And some cigarettes. Do you think of anything more, Splutter?"

As they came from the shop of the illustrious purveyors of potato salad in Second Avenue, Florinda cried anxiously, "Here, Billie, you let me carry that!"

"What infernal nonsense!" said Hawker, flushing. "Certainly not!"

"Well," protested Florinda, "it might soil your gloves somehow."

"In heaven's name, what if it does? Say, young woman, do you think I am one of these cholly boys?"

"No, Billie; but then, you know———"

"Well, if you don't take me for some kind of a Willie, give us peace on this blasted glove business!"

"I didn't mean———"

"Well, you've been intimating that I've got the only pair of gray gloves in the universe, but you are wrong. There are several pairs, and these need not be preserved as unique in history."

"They're not gray. They're———"

"They are gray! I suppose your distinguished ancestors in Ireland did not educate their families in the matter of gloves, and so you are not expected to———"

"Billie!"

"You are not expected to believe that people wear gloves only in cold weather, and then you expect to see mittens."

On the stairs, in the darkness, he suddenly exclaimed, "Here, look out, or you'll fall!" He reached for her arm, but she evaded him. Later he said again: "Look out, girl! What makes you stumble around so? Here, give me the bottle of wine. I can carry it all right. There—now can you manage?"

CHAPTER XXIV.

"Penny," said Grief, looking across the table at his friend, "if a man thinks a heap of two violets, how much would he think of a thousand violets?"

"Two into a thousand goes five hundred times, you fool!" said Pennoyer. "I would answer your question if it were not upon a forbidden subject."

In the distance Wrinkles and Florinda were making Welsh rarebits.

"Hold your tongues!" said Hawker. "Barbarians!"

"Grief," said Pennoyer, "if a man loves a woman better than the whole universe, how much does he love the whole universe?"

"Gawd knows," said Grief piously. "Although it ill befits me to answer your question."

Wrinkles and Florinda came with the Welsh rarebits, very triumphant. "There," said Florinda, "soon as these are finished I must go home. It is after eleven o'clock.—Pour the ale, Grief."

At a later time, Purple Sanderson entered from the world. He hung up his hat and cast a look of proper financial dissatisfaction at the remnants of the feast. "Who has been——"

"Before you breathe, Purple, you graceless scum, let me tell you that we will stand no reference to the two violets here," said Pennoyer.

"What the——"

"Oh, that's all right, Purple," said Grief, "but you were going to say something about the two violets, right then. Weren't you, now, you old bat?"

Sanderson grinned expectantly. "What's the row?" said he.

"No row at all," they told him. "Just an agreement to keep you from chattering obstinately about the two violets."

"What two violets?"

"Have a rarebit, Purple," advised Wrinkles, "and never mind those maniacs."

"Well, what is this business about two violets?"

"Oh, it's just some dream. They gibber at anything."

"I think I know," said Florinda, nodding. "It is something that concerns Billie Hawker."

Grief and Pennoyer scoffed, and Wrinkles said: "You know nothing about it, Splutter. It doesn't concern Billie Hawker at all."

"Well, then, what is he looking sideways for?" cried Florinda.

Wrinkles reached for his guitar, and played a serenade, "The silver moon is shining——"

"Dry up!" said Pennoyer.

Then Florinda cried again, "What does he look sideways for?"

Pennoyer and Grief giggled at the imperturbable Hawker, who destroyed rarebit in silence.

"It's you, is it, Billie?" said Sanderson. "You are in this two-violet business?"

"I don't know what they're talking about," replied Hawker.

"Don't you, honestly?" asked Florinda.

"Well, only a little."

"There!" said Florinda, nodding again. "I knew he was in it."

"He isn't in it at all," said Pennoyer and Grief.

Later, when the cigarettes had become exhausted, Hawker volunteered to go after a further supply, and as he arose, a question seemed to come to the edge of Florinda's lips and pend there. The moment that the door was closed upon him she demanded, "What is that about the two violets?"

"Nothing at all," answered Pennoyer, apparently much aggrieved. He sat back with an air of being a fortress of reticence.

"Oh, go on—tell me! Penny, I think you are very mean.—Grief, you tell me!"

"The silver moon is shining;

Oh, come, my love, to me!

My heart——"

"Be still, Wrinkles, will you?—What was it, Grief? Oh, go ahead and tell me!"

"What do you want to know for?" cried Grief, vastly exasperated. "You've got more blamed curiosity—— It isn't anything at all, I keep saying to you."

"Well, I know it is," said Florinda sullenly, "or you would tell me."

When Hawker brought the cigarettes, Florinda smoked one, and then announced, "Well, I must go now."

"Who is going to take you home, Splutter?"

"Oh, anyone," replied Florinda.

"I tell you what," said Grief, "we'll throw some poker hands, and the one who wins will have the distinguished honour of conveying Miss Splutter to her home and mother."

Pennoyer and Wrinkles speedily routed the dishes to one end of the table. Grief's fingers spun the halves of a pack of cards together with the pleased eagerness of a good player. The faces grew solemn with the gambling solemnity. "Now, you Indians," said Grief, dealing, "a draw, you understand, and then a show-down."

Florinda leaned forward in her chair until it was poised on two legs. The cards of Purple Sanderson and of Hawker were faced toward her. Sanderson was gravely regarding two pair—aces and queens. Hawker scanned a little pair of sevens. "They draw, don't they?" she said to Grief.

"Certainly," said Grief. "How many, Wrink?"

"Four," replied Wrinkles, plaintively.

"Gimme three," said Pennoyer.

"Gimme one," said Sanderson.

"Gimme three," said Hawker. When he picked up his hand again Florinda's chair was tilted perilously. She saw another seven added to the little pair. Sanderson's draw had not assisted him.

"Same to the dealer," said Grief. "What you got, Wrink?"

"Nothing," said Wrinkles, exhibiting it face upward on the table. "Good-bye, Florinda."

"Well, I've got two small pair," ventured Pennoyer hopefully. "Beat 'em?"

"No good," said Sanderson. "Two pair—aces up."

"No good," said Hawker. "Three sevens."

"Beats me," said Grief. "Billie, you are the fortunate man. Heaven guide you in Third Avenue!"

Florinda had gone to the window. "Who won?" she asked, wheeling about carelessly.

"Billie Hawker."

"What! Did he?" she said in surprise.

"Never mind, Splutter. I'll win sometime," said Pennoyer. "Me too," cried Grief. "Good night, old girl!" said Wrinkles. They crowded in the doorway. "Hold on to Billie. Remember the two steps going up," Pennoyer called intelligently into the Stygian blackness. "Can you see all right?"

Florinda lived in a flat with fire-escapes written all over the front of it.

The street in front was being repaired. It had been said by imbecile residents of the vicinity that the paving was never allowed to remain down for a sufficient time to be invalided by the tramping millions, but that it was kept perpetually stacked in little mountains through the unceasing vigilance of a virtuous and heroic city government, which insisted that everything should be repaired. The alderman for the district had sometimes asked indignantly of his fellow-members why this street had not been repaired, and they, aroused, had at once ordered it to be repaired. Moreover, shopkeepers, whose stables were adjacent, placed trucks and other vehicles strategically in the darkness. Into this tangled midnight Hawker conducted Florinda. The great avenue behind them was no more than a level stream of yellow light, and the distant merry bells might have been boats floating down it. Grim loneliness hung over the uncouth shapes in the street which was being repaired.

"Billie," said the girl suddenly, "what makes you so mean to me?"

A peaceful citizen emerged from behind a pile of débris, but he might not have been a peaceful citizen, so the girl clung to Hawker.

"Why, I'm not mean to you, am I?"

"Yes," she answered. As they stood on the steps of the flat of innumerable fire-escapes she slowly turned and looked up at him. Her face was of a strange pallour in this darkness, and her eyes were as when the moon shines in a lake of the hills.

He returned her glance. "Florinda!" he cried, as if enlightened, and gulping suddenly at something in his throat. The girl studied the steps and moved from side to side, as do the guilty ones in country schoolhouses. Then she went slowly into the flat.

There was a little red lamp hanging on a pile of stones to warn people that the street was being repaired.

CHAPTER XXV.

"I'll get my check from the Gamin on Saturday," said Grief. "They bought that string of comics."

"Well, then, we'll arrange the present funds to last until Saturday noon," said Wrinkles. "That gives us quite a lot. We can have a table d'hôte on Friday night."

However, the cashier of the Gamin office looked under his respectable brass wiring and said: "Very sorry, Mr.—er—Warwickson, but our pay-day is Monday. Come around any time after ten."

"Oh, it doesn't matter," said Grief.

When he plunged into the den his visage flamed with rage. "Don't get my check until Monday morning, any time after ten!" he yelled, and flung a portfolio of mottled green into the danger zone of the casts.

"Thunder!" said Pennoyer, sinking at once into a profound despair

"Monday morning, any time after ten," murmured Wrinkles, in astonishment and sorrow.

While Grief marched to and fro threatening the furniture, Pennoyer and Wrinkles allowed their under jaws to fall, and remained as men smitten between the eyes by the god of calamity.

"Singular thing!" muttered Pennoyer at last. "You get so frightfully hungry as soon as you learn that there are no more meals coming."

"Oh, well——" said Wrinkles. He took up his guitar.

Oh, some folks say dat a niggah won' steal,

'Way down yondeh in d' cohn'-fiel';

But Ah caught two in my cohn'-fiel',

Way down yondeh in d' cohn'-fiel'.

"Oh, let up!" said Grief, as if unwilling to be moved from his despair.

"Oh, let up!" said Pennoyer, as if he disliked the voice and the ballad.

In his studio, Hawker sat braced nervously forward on a little stool before his tall Dutch easel. Three sketches lay on the floor near him, and he glared at them constantly while painting at the large canvas on the easel.

He seemed engaged in some kind of a duel. His hair dishevelled, his eyes gleaming, he was in a deadly scuffle. In the sketches was the landscape of heavy blue, as if seen through powder-smoke, and all the skies burned red. There was in these notes a sinister quality of hopelessness, eloquent of a defeat, as if the scene represented the last hour on a field of disastrous battle. Hawker seemed attacking with this picture something fair and beautiful of his own life, a possession of his mind, and he did it fiercely, mercilessly, formidably. His arm moved with the energy of a strange wrath. He might have been thrusting with a sword.

There was a knock at the door. "Come in." Pennoyer entered sheepishly. "Well?" cried Hawker, with an echo of savagery in his voice. He turned from the canvas precisely as one might emerge from a fight. "Oh!" he said, perceiving Pennoyer. The glow in his eyes slowly changed. "What is it, Penny?"

"Billie," said Pennoyer, "Grief was to get his check to-day, but they put him off until Monday, and so, you know—er—well——"

"Oh!" said Hawker again.

When Pennoyer had gone Hawker sat motionless before his work. He stared at the canvas in a meditation so profound that it was probably unconscious of itself.

The light from above his head slanted more and more toward the east.

Once he arose and lighted a pipe. He returned to the easel and stood staring with his hands in his pockets. He moved like one in a sleep. Suddenly the gleam shot into his eyes again. He dropped to the stool and grabbed a brush. At the end of a certain long, tumultuous period he clinched his pipe more firmly in his teeth and puffed strongly. The thought might have occurred to him that it was not alight, for he looked at it with a vague, questioning glance. There came another knock at the door. "Go to the devil!" he shouted, without turning his head.

Hollanden crossed the corridor then to the den.

"Hi, there, Hollie! Hello, boy! Just the fellow we want to see. Come in—sit down—hit a pipe. Say, who was the girl Billie Hawker went mad over this summer?"

"Blazes!" said Hollanden, recovering slowly from this onslaught. "Who—what—how did you Indians find it out?"

"Oh, we tumbled!" they cried in delight, "we tumbled."

"There!" said Hollanden, reproaching himself. "And I thought you were such a lot of blockheads."

"Oh, we tumbled!" they cried again in their ecstasy. "But who is she? That's the point."

"Well, she was a girl."

"Yes, go on."

"A New York girl."

"Yes."

"A perfectly stunning New York girl."

"Yes. Go ahead."

"A perfectly stunning New York girl of a very wealthy and rather old-fashioned family."

"Well, I'll be shot! You don't mean it! She is practically seated on top of the Matterhorn. Poor old Billie!"

"Not at all," said Hollanden composedly.

110

It was a common habit of Purple Sanderson to call attention at night to the resemblance of the den to some little ward in a hospital. Upon this night, when Sanderson and Grief were buried in slumber, Pennoyer moved restlessly. "Wrink!" he called softly into the darkness in the direction of the divan which was secretly a coal-box.

"What?" said Wrinkles in a surly voice. His mind had evidently been caught at the threshold of sleep.

"Do you think Florinda cares much for Billie Hawker?"

Wrinkles fretted through some oaths. "How in thunder do I know?" The divan creaked as he turned his face to the wall.

"Well——" muttered Pennoyer.

CHAPTER XXVI.

The harmony of summer sunlight on leaf and blade of green was not known to the two windows, which looked forth at an obviously endless building of brownstone about which there was the poetry of a prison. Inside, great folds of lace swept down in orderly cascades, as water trained to fall mathematically. The colossal chandelier, gleaming like a Siamese headdress, caught the subtle flashes from unknown places.

Hawker heard a step and the soft swishing of a woman's dress. He turned toward the door swiftly, with a certain dramatic impulsiveness. But when she entered the room he said, "How delighted I am to see you again!"

She had said, "Why, Mr. Hawker, it was so charming in you to come!"

It did not appear that Hawker's tongue could wag to his purpose. The girl seemed in her mind to be frantically shuffling her pack of social receipts and finding none of them made to meet this situation. Finally, Hawker said that he thought Hearts at War was a very good play.

"Did you?" she said in surprise. "I thought it much like the others."

"Well, so did I," he cried hastily—"the same figures moving around in the mud of modern confusion. I really didn't intend to say that I liked it. Fact is, meeting you rather moved me out of my mental track."

"Mental track?" she said. "I didn't know clever people had mental tracks. I thought it was a privilege of the theologians."

"Who told you I was clever?" he demanded.

"Why," she said, opening her eyes wider, "nobody."

Hawker smiled and looked upon her with gratitude. "Of course, nobody. There couldn't be such an idiot. I am sure you should be astonished to learn that I believed such an imbecile existed. But——"

"Oh!" she said.

"But I think you might have spoken less bluntly."

"Well," she said, after wavering for a time, "you are clever, aren't you?"

"Certainly," he answered reassuringly.

"Well, then?" she retorted, with triumph in her tone. And this interrogation was apparently to her the final victorious argument.

At his discomfiture Hawker grinned.

"You haven't asked news of Stanley," he said. "Why don't you ask news of Stanley?"

"Oh! and how was he?"

"The last I saw of him he stood down at the end of the pasture—the pasture, you know—wagging his tail in blissful anticipation of an invitation to come with me, and when it finally dawned upon him that he was not to receive it, he turned and went back toward the house 'like a man suddenly stricken with age,' as the story-tellers eloquently say. Poor old dog!"

"And you left him?" she said reproachfully. Then she asked, "Do you remember how he amused you playing with the ants at the falls?"

"No."

"Why, he did. He pawed at the moss, and you sat there laughing. I remember it distinctly."

"You remember distinctly? Why, I thought—well, your back was turned, you know. Your gaze was fixed upon something before you, and you were utterly lost to the rest of the world. You could not have known if Stanley pawed the moss and I laughed. So, you see, you are mistaken. As a matter of fact, I utterly deny that Stanley pawed the moss or that I laughed, or that any ants appeared at the falls at all."

"I have always said that you should have been a Chinese soldier of fortune," she observed musingly. "Your daring and ingenuity would be prized by the Chinese."

"There are innumerable tobacco jars in China," he said, measuring the advantages. "Moreover, there is no perspective. You don't have to walk two miles to see a friend. No. He is always there near you, so that you can't move a chair without hitting your distant friend. You——"

"Did Hollie remain as attentive as ever to the Worcester girls?"

"Yes, of course, as attentive as ever. He dragged me into all manner of tennis games——"

"Why, I thought you loved to play tennis?"

"Oh, well," said Hawker, "I did until you left."

"My sister has gone to the park with the children. I know she will be vexed when she finds that you have called."

Ultimately Hawker said, "Do you remember our ride behind my father's oxen?"

"No," she answered; "I had forgotten it completely. Did we ride behind your father's oxen?"

After a moment he said: "That remark would be prized by the Chinese. We did. And you most graciously professed to enjoy it, which earned my deep gratitude and admiration. For no one knows better than I," he added meekly, "that it is no great comfort or pleasure to ride behind my father's oxen."

She smiled retrospectively. "Do you remember how the people on the porch hurried to the railing?"

CHAPTER XXVII.

Near the door the stout proprietress sat intrenched behind the cash-box in a Parisian manner. She looked with practical amiability at her guests, who dined noisily and with great fire, discussing momentous problems furiously, making wide, maniacal gestures through the cigarette smoke. Meanwhile the little handful of waiters ran to and fro wildly. Imperious and importunate cries rang at them from all directions. "Gustave! Adolphe!" Their faces expressed a settled despair. They answered calls, commands, oaths in a semi-distraction, fleeting among the tables as if pursued by some dodging animal. Their breaths came in gasps. If they had been convict labourers they could not have surveyed their positions with countenances of more unspeakable injury. Withal, they carried incredible masses of dishes and threaded their ways with skill. They served people with such speed and violence that it often resembled a personal assault. They struck two blows at a table and left there a knife and fork. Then came the viands in a volley. The clatter of this business was loud and bewilderingly rapid, like the gallop of a thousand horses.

In a remote corner a band of mandolins and guitars played the long, sweeping, mad melody of a Spanish waltz. It seemed to go tingling to the hearts of many of the diners. Their eyes glittered with enthusiasm, with abandon, with deviltry. They swung their heads from side to side in rhythmic movement. High in air curled the smoke from the innumerable cigarettes. The long, black claret bottles were in clusters upon the tables. At an end of the hall two men with maudlin grins sang the waltz uproariously, but always a trifle belated.

An unsteady person, leaning back in his chair to murmur swift compliments to a woman at another table, suddenly sprawled out upon the floor. He scrambled to his feet, and, turning to the escort of the woman, heatedly blamed him for the accident. They exchanged a series of tense, bitter insults, which spatted back and forth between them like pellets. People arose from their chairs and stretched their necks. The musicians stood in a body, their faces turned with expressions of keen excitement toward this quarrel, but their fingers still twinkling over their instruments, sending into the middle of this turmoil the passionate, mad, Spanish music. The proprietor of the place came in agitation and plunged headlong into the argument, where he thereafter appeared as a frantic creature harried to the point of insanity, for they buried him at once in long, vociferous threats, explanations, charges, every form of declamation known to their voices. The music, the noise of the galloping horses, the voices of the brawlers, gave the whole thing the quality of war.

There were two men in the café who seemed to be tranquil. Hollanden carefully stacked one lump of sugar upon another in the middle of his saucer and poured cognac over them. He touched a match to the cognac and the blue and yellow flames eddied in the saucer. "I wonder what those two fools are bellowing at?" he said, turning about irritably.

"Hanged if I know!" muttered Hawker in reply. "This place makes me weary, anyhow. Hear the blooming din!"

"What's the matter?" said Hollanden. "You used to say this was the one natural, the one truly Bohemian, resort in the city. You swore by it."

"Well, I don't like it so much any more."

"Ho!" cried Hollanden, "you're getting correct—that's it exactly. You will become one of these intensely—— Look, Billie, the little one is going to punch him!"

"No, he isn't. They never do," said Hawker morosely. "Why did you bring me here to-night, Hollie?"

"I? I bring you? Good heavens, I came as a concession to you! What are you talking about?—Hi! the little one is going to punch him, sure!"

He gave the scene his undivided attention for a moment; then he turned again: "You will become correct. I know you will. I have been watching. You are about to achieve a respectability that will make a stone saint blush for himself. What's the matter with you? You act as if you thought falling in love with a girl was a most extraordinary circumstance.—I wish they would put those people out.—Of course I know that you—— There! The little one has swiped at him at last!"

After a time he resumed his oration. "Of course, I know that you are not reformed in the matter of this uproar and this remarkable consumption of bad wine. It is not that. It is a fact that there are indications that some other citizen was fortunate enough to possess your napkin before you; and, moreover, you are sure that you would hate to be caught by your correct friends with any such consommé in front of you as we had to-night. You have got an eye suddenly for all kinds of gilt. You are in the way of becoming a most unbearable person.—Oh, look! the little one and the proprietor are having it now.—You are in the way of becoming a most unbearable person. Presently many of your friends will not be fine enough.—In heaven's name, why don't they throw him out? Are you going to howl and gesticulate there all night?"

"Well," said Hawker, "a man would be a fool if he did like this dinner."

"Certainly. But what an immaterial part in the glory of this joint is the dinner! Who cares about dinner? No one comes here to eat; that's what you always claimed.—Well, there, at last they are throwing him out. I hope he lands on his head.—Really, you know, Billie, it is such a fine thing being in love that one is sure to be detestable to the rest of the world, and that is the reason they created a proverb to the other effect. You want to look out."

"You talk like a blasted old granny!" said Hawker. "Haven't changed at all. This place is all right, only——"

"You are gone," interrupted Hollanden in a sad voice. "It is very plain— you are gone."

CHAPTER XXVIII.

The proprietor of the place, having pushed to the street the little man, who may have been the most vehement, came again and resumed the discussion with the remainder of the men of war. Many of these had volunteered, and they were very enduring.

"Yes, you are gone," said Hollanden, with the sobriety of graves in his voice. "You are gone.—Hi!" he cried, "there is Lucian Pontiac.—Hi, Pontiac! Sit down here."

A man with a tangle of hair, and with that about his mouth which showed that he had spent many years in manufacturing a proper modesty with which to bear his greatness, came toward them, smiling.

"Hello, Pontiac!" said Hollanden. "Here's another great painter. Do you know Mr. Hawker?—Mr. William Hawker—Mr. Pontiac."

"Mr. Hawker—delighted," said Pontiac. "Although I have not known you personally, I can assure you that I have long been a great admirer of your abilities."

The proprietor of the place and the men of war had at length agreed to come to an amicable understanding. They drank liquors, while each firmly, but now silently, upheld his dignity.

"Charming place," said Pontiac. "So thoroughly Parisian in spirit. And from time to time, Mr. Hawker, I use one of your models. Must say she has the best arm and wrist in the universe. Stunning figure—stunning!"

"You mean Florinda?" said Hawker.

"Yes, that's the name. Very fine girl. Lunches with me from time to time and chatters so volubly. That's how I learned you posed her occasionally. If the models didn't gossip we would never know what painters were addicted to profanity. Now that old Thorndike—he told me you swore like a drill-sergeant if the model winked a finger at the critical time. Very fine girl, Florinda.

And honest, too—honest as the devil. Very curious thing. Of course honesty among the girl models is very common, very common—quite universal thing, you know—but then it always strikes me as being very curious, very curious. I've been much attracted by your girl Florinda."

"My girl?" said Hawker.

"Well, she always speaks of you in a proprietary way, you know. And then she considers that she owes you some kind of obedience and allegiance and devotion. I remember last week I said to her: 'You can go now. Come again Friday.' But she said: 'I don't think I can come on Friday. Billie Hawker is home now, and he may want me then.' Said I: 'The devil take Billie Hawker! He hasn't engaged you for Friday, has he? Well, then, I engage you now.' But she shook her head. No, she couldn't come on Friday. Billie Hawker was home, and he might want her any day. 'Well, then,' said I, 'you have my permission to do as you please, since you are resolved upon it anyway. Go to your Billie Hawker.' Did you need her on Friday?"

"No," said Hawker.

"Well, then, the minx, I shall scold her. Stunning figure—stunning! It was only last week that old Charley Master said to me mournfully: 'There are no more good models. Great Scott! not a one.' 'You're 'way off, my boy,' I said; 'there is one good model,' and then I named your girl. I mean the girl who claims to be yours."

"Poor little beggar!" said Hollanden.

"Who?" said Pontiac.

"Florinda," answered Hollanden. "I suppose——"

Pontiac interrupted. "Oh, of course, it is too bad. Everything is too bad. My dear sir, nothing is so much to be regretted as the universe. But this Florinda is such a sturdy young soul! The world is against her, but, bless your heart, she is equal to the battle. She is strong in the manner of a little child. Why, you don't know her. She——"

"I know her very well."

"Well, perhaps you do, but for my part I think you don't appreciate her formidable character and stunning figure—stunning!"

"Damn it!" said Hawker to his coffee cup, which he had accidentally overturned.

"Well," resumed Pontiac, "she is a stunning model, and I think, Mr. Hawker, you are to be envied."

"Eh?" said Hawker.

"I wish I could inspire my models with such obedience and devotion. Then I would not be obliged to rail at them for being late, and have to badger them for not showing up at all. She has a beautiful figure—beautiful."

CHAPTER XXIX.

When Hawker went again to the house of the great window he looked first at the colossal chandelier, and, perceiving that it had not moved, he smiled in a certain friendly and familiar way.

"It must be a fine thing," said the girl dreamily. "I always feel envious of that sort of life."

"What sort of life?"

"Why—I don't know exactly; but there must be a great deal of freedom about it. I went to a studio tea once, and——"

"A studio tea! Merciful heavens—— Go on."

"Yes, a studio tea. Don't you like them? To be sure, we didn't know whether the man could paint very well, and I suppose you think it is an imposition for anyone who is not a great painter to give a tea."

"Go on."

"Well, he had the dearest little Japanese servants, and some of the cups came from Algiers, and some from Turkey, and some from—— What's the matter?"

"Go on. I'm not interrupting you."

"Well, that's all; excepting that everything was charming in colour, and I thought what a lazy, beautiful life the man must lead, lounging in such a studio, smoking monogrammed cigarettes, and remarking how badly all the other men painted."

"Very fascinating. But——"

"Oh! you are going to ask if he could draw. I'm sure I don't know, but the tea that he gave was charming."

"I was on the verge of telling you something about artist life, but if you have seen a lot of draperies and drunk from a cup of Algiers, you know all about it."

"You, then, were going to make it something very terrible, and tell how young painters struggled, and all that."

"No, not exactly. But listen: I suppose there is an aristocracy who, whether they paint well or paint ill, certainly do give charming teas, as you say, and all other kinds of charming affairs too; but when I hear people talk as if that was the whole life, it makes my hair rise, you know, because I am sure that as they get to know me better and better they will see how I fall short of that kind of an existence, and I shall probably take a great tumble in their estimation. They might even conclude that I can not paint, which would be very unfair, because I can paint, you know."

"Well, proceed to arrange my point of view, so that you sha'n't tumble in my estimation when I discover that you don't lounge in a studio, smoke monogrammed cigarettes, and remark how badly the other men paint."

"That's it. That's precisely what I wish to do."

"Begin."

"Well, in the first place——"

"In the first place—what?"

"Well, I started to study when I was very poor, you understand. Look here! I'm telling you these things because I want you to know, somehow. It isn't that I'm not ashamed of it. Well, I began very poor, and I—as a matter of fact—I—well, I earned myself over half the money for my studying, and the other half I bullied and badgered and beat out of my poor old dad. I worked pretty hard in Paris, and I returned here expecting to become a great painter at once. I didn't, though. In fact, I had my worst moments then. It lasted for some years. Of course, the faith and endurance of my father were by this time worn to a shadow—this time, when I needed him the most. However, things got a little better and a little better, until I found that by working quite hard I could make what was to me a fair income. That's where I am now, too."

"Why are you so ashamed of this story?"

"The poverty."

"Poverty isn't anything to be ashamed of."

"Great heavens! Have you the temerity to get off that old nonsensical remark? Poverty is everything to be ashamed of. Did you ever see a person not ashamed of his poverty? Certainly not. Of course, when a man gets very rich he will brag so loudly of the poverty of his youth that one would never suppose that he was once ashamed of it. But he was."

"Well, anyhow, you shouldn't be ashamed of the story you have just told me."

"Why not? Do you refuse to allow me the great right of being like other men?"

"I think it was—brave, you know."

"Brave? Nonsense! Those things are not brave. Impression to that effect created by the men who have been through the mill for the greater glory of the men who have been through the mill."

"I don't like to hear you talk that way. It sounds wicked, you know."

"Well, it certainly wasn't heroic. I can remember distinctly that there was not one heroic moment."

"No, but it was—it was——"

"It was what?"

"Well, somehow I like it, you know."

CHAPTER XXX.

"There's three of them," said Grief in a hoarse whisper.

"Four, I tell you!" said Wrinkles in a low, excited tone.

"Four," breathed Pennoyer with decision.

They held fierce pantomimic argument. From the corridor came sounds of rustling dresses and rapid feminine conversation.

Grief had kept his ear to the panel of the door. His hand was stretched back, warning the others to silence. Presently he turned his head and whispered, "Three."

"Four," whispered Pennoyer and Wrinkles.

"Hollie is there, too," whispered Grief. "Billie is unlocking the door. Now they're going in. Hear them cry out, 'Oh, isn't it lovely!' Jinks!" He began a noiseless dance about the room. "Jinks! Don't I wish I had a big studio and a little reputation! Wouldn't I have my swell friends come to see me, and wouldn't I entertain 'em!" He adopted a descriptive manner, and with his forefinger indicated various spaces of the wall. "Here is a little thing I did in Brittany. Peasant woman in sabots. This brown spot here is the peasant woman, and those two white things are the sabots. Peasant woman in sabots, don't you see? Women in Brittany, of course, all wear sabots, you understand. Convenience of the painters. I see you are looking at that little thing I did in Morocco. Ah, you admire it? Well, not so bad—not so bad. Arab smoking pipe, squatting in doorway. This long streak here is the pipe. Clever, you say? Oh, thanks! You are too kind. Well, all Arabs do that, you know. Sole occupation. Convenience of the painters. Now, this little thing here I did in Venice. Grand Canal, you know. Gondolier leaning on his oar. Convenience of the painters. Oh, yes, American subjects are well enough, but hard to find, you know—hard to find. Morocco, Venice, Brittany, Holland—all oblige with colour, you know—quaint form—all that. We are so hideously modern over here; and, besides, nobody has painted us much. How the devil can I paint America when nobody has done it before me? My dear sir, are you aware that that would be originality? Good heavens! we are not æsthetic, you understand. Oh, yes, some good mind comes along and understands a thing and does it, and after that it is æsthetic. Yes, of course, but then—well——Now, here is a little Holland thing of mine; it——"

The others had evidently not been heeding him. "Shut up!" said Wrinkles suddenly. "Listen!" Grief paused his harangue and they sat in silence, their lips apart, their eyes from time to time exchanging eloquent messages. A dulled melodious babble came from Hawker's studio.

At length Pennoyer murmured wistfully, "I would like to see her."

Wrinkles started noiselessly to his feet. "Well, I tell you she's a peach. I was going up the steps, you know, with a loaf of bread under my arm, when I chanced to look up the street and saw Billie and Hollanden coming with four of them."

"Three," said Grief.

"Four; and I tell you I scattered. One of the two with Billie was a peach—a peach."

"O, Lord!" groaned the others enviously. "Billie's in luck."

"How do you know?" said Wrinkles. "Billie is a blamed good fellow, but that doesn't say she will care for him—more likely that she won't."

They sat again in silence, grinning, and listening to the murmur of voices.

There came the sound of a step in the hallway. It ceased at a point opposite the door of Hawker's studio. Presently it was heard again. Florinda entered the den. "Hello!" she cried, "who is over in Billie's place? I was just going to knock——"

They motioned at her violently. "Sh!" they whispered. Their countenances were very impressive.

"What's the matter with you fellows?" asked Florinda in her ordinary

125

tone; whereupon they made gestures of still greater wildness. "S-s-sh!"

Florinda lowered her voice properly. "Who is over there?"

"Some swells," they whispered.

Florinda bent her head. Presently she gave a little start. "Who is over there?" Her voice became a tone of deep awe. "She?"

Wrinkles and Grief exchanged a swift glance. Pennoyer said gruffly, "Who do you mean?"

"Why," said Florinda, "you know. She. The—the girl that Billie likes."

Pennoyer hesitated for a moment and then said wrathfully: "Of course she is! Who do you suppose?"

"Oh!" said Florinda. She took a seat upon the divan, which was privately a coal-box, and unbuttoned her jacket at the throat. "Is she—is she—very handsome, Wrink?"

Wrinkles replied stoutly, "No."

Grief said: "Let's make a sneak down the hall to the little unoccupied room at the front of the building and look from the window there. When they go out we can pipe 'em off."

"Come on!" they exclaimed, accepting this plan with glee.

Wrinkles opened the door and seemed about to glide away, when he suddenly turned and shook his head. "It's dead wrong," he said, ashamed.

"Oh, go on!" eagerly whispered the others. Presently they stole pattering down the corridor, grinning, exclaiming, and cautioning each other.

At the window Pennoyer said: "Now, for heaven's sake, don't let them see you!—Be careful, Grief, you'll tumble.—Don't lean on me that way, Wrink; think I'm a barn door? Here they come. Keep back. Don't let them see you."

"O-o-oh!" said Grief. "Talk about a peach! Well, I should say so."

Florinda's fingers tore at Wrinkle's coat sleeve. "Wrink, Wrink, is that her? Is that her? On the left of Billie? Is that her, Wrink?"

"What? Yes. Stop punching me! Yes, I tell you! That's her. Are you deaf?"

CHAPTER XXXI.

In the evening Pennoyer conducted Florinda to the flat of many fire-escapes. After a period of silent tramping through the great golden avenue and the street that was being repaired, she said, "Penny, you are very good to me."

"Why?" said Pennoyer.

"Oh, because you are. You—you are very good to me, Penny."

"Well, I guess I'm not killing myself."

"There isn't many fellows like you."

"No?"

"No. There isn't many fellows like you, Penny. I tell you 'most everything, and you just listen, and don't argue with me and tell me I'm a fool, because you know that it—because you know that it can't be helped, anyhow."

"Oh, nonsense, you kid! Almost anybody would be glad to——"

"Penny, do you think she is very beautiful?" Florinda's voice had a singular quality of awe in it.

"Well," replied Pennoyer, "I don't know."

"Yes, you do, Penny. Go ahead and tell me."

"Well——"

"Go ahead."

"Well, she is rather handsome, you know."

"Yes," said Florinda, dejectedly, "I suppose she is." After a time she cleared her throat and remarked indifferently, "I suppose Billie cares a lot for her?"

"Oh, I imagine that he does—in a way."

"Why, of course he does," insisted Florinda. "What do you mean by 'in a way'? You know very well that Billie thinks his eyes of her."

"No, I don't."

"Yes, you do. You know you do. You are talking in that way just to brace me up. You know you are."

"No, I'm not."

"Penny," said Florinda thankfully, "what makes you so good to me?"

"Oh, I guess I'm not so astonishingly good to you. Don't be silly."

"But you are good to me, Penny. You don't make fun of me the way—the way the other boys would. You are just as good as you can be.—But you do think she is beautiful, don't you?"

"They wouldn't make fun of you," said Pennoyer.

"But do you think she is beautiful?"

"Look here, Splutter, let up on that, will you? You keep harping on one string all the time. Don't bother me!"

"But, honest now, Penny, you do think she is beautiful?"

"Well, then, confound it—no! no! no!"

"Oh, yes, you do, Penny. Go ahead now. Don't deny it just because you are talking to me. Own up, now, Penny. You do think she is beautiful?"

"Well," said Pennoyer, in a dull roar of irritation, "do you?"

Florinda walked in silence, her eyes upon the yellow flashes which lights sent to the pavement. In the end she said, "Yes."

"Yes, what?" asked Pennoyer sharply.

"Yes, she—yes, she is—beautiful."

"Well, then?" cried Pennoyer, abruptly closing the discussion.

Florinda announced something as a fact. "Billie thinks his eyes of her."

"How do you know he does?"

"Don't scold at me, Penny. You—you——"

"I'm not scolding at you. There! What a goose you are, Splutter! Don't, for heaven's sake, go to whimpering on the street! I didn't say anything to make you feel that way. Come, pull yourself together."

"I'm not whimpering."

"No, of course not; but then you look as if you were on the edge of it. What a little idiot!"

CHAPTER XXXII.

When the snow fell upon the clashing life of the city, the exiled stones, beaten by myriad strange feet, were told of the dark, silent forests where the flakes swept through the hemlocks and swished softly against the boulders.

In his studio Hawker smoked a pipe, clasping his knee with thoughtful, interlocked fingers. He was gazing sourly at his finished picture. Once he started to his feet with a cry of vexation. Looking back over his shoulder, he swore an insult into the face of the picture. He paced to and fro, smoking belligerently and from time to time eying it. The helpless thing remained upon the easel, facing him.

Hollanden entered and stopped abruptly at sight of the great scowl. "What's wrong now?" he said.

Hawker gestured at the picture. "That dunce of a thing. It makes me tired. It isn't worth a hang. Blame it!"

"What?" Hollanden strode forward and stood before the painting with legs apart, in a properly critical manner. "What? Why, you said it was your best thing."

"Aw!" said Hawker, waving his arms, "it's no good! I abominate it! I didn't get what I wanted, I tell you. I didn't get what I wanted. That?" he shouted, pointing thrust-way at it—"that? It's vile! Aw! it makes me weary."

"You're in a nice state," said Hollanden, turning to take a critical view of the painter. "What has got into you now? I swear, you are more kinds of a chump!"

Hawker crooned dismally: "I can't paint! I can't paint for a damn! I'm no good. What in thunder was I invented for, anyhow, Hollie?"

"You're a fool," said Hollanden. "I hope to die if I ever saw such a complete idiot! You give me a pain. Just because she don't——"

"It isn't that. She has nothing to do with it, although I know well enough—I know well enough——"

"What?"

"I know well enough she doesn't care a hang for me. It isn't that. It is because—it is because I can't paint. Look at that thing over there! Remember the thought and energy I—— Damn the thing!"

"Why, did you have a row with her?" asked Hollanden, perplexed. "I didn't know——"

"No, of course you didn't know," cried Hawker, sneering; "because I had no row. It isn't that, I tell you. But I know well enough"—he shook his fist vaguely—"that she don't care an old tomato can for me. Why should she?" he demanded with a curious defiance. "In the name of Heaven, why should she?"

"I don't know," said Hollanden; "I don't know, I'm sure. But, then, women have no social logic. This is the great blessing of the world. There is only one thing which is superior to the multiplicity of social forms, and that is a woman's mind—a young woman's mind. Oh, of course, sometimes they are logical, but let a woman be so once, and she will repent of it to the end of her days. The safety of the world's balance lies in woman's illogical mind. I think——"

"Go to blazes!" said Hawker. "I don't care what you think. I am sure of one thing, and that is that she doesn't care a hang for me!"

"I think," Hollanden continued, "that society is doing very well in its work of bravely lawing away at Nature; but there is one immovable thing—a woman's illogical mind. That is our safety. Thank Heaven, it——"

"Go to blazes!" said Hawker again.

CHAPTER XXXIII.

As Hawker again entered the room of the great windows he glanced in sidelong bitterness at the chandelier. When he was seated he looked at it in open defiance and hatred.

Men in the street were shovelling at the snow. The noise of their instruments scraping on the stones came plainly to Hawker's ears in a harsh chorus, and this sound at this time was perhaps to him a miserere.

"I came to tell you," he began, "I came to tell you that perhaps I am going away."

"Going away!" she cried. "Where?"

"Well, I don't know—quite. You see, I am rather indefinite as yet. I thought of going for the winter somewhere in the Southern States. I am decided merely this much, you know—I am going somewhere. But I don't know where. 'Way off, anyhow."

"We shall be very sorry to lose you," she remarked. "We——"

"And I thought," he continued, "that I would come and say 'adios' now for fear that I might leave very suddenly. I do that sometimes. I'm afraid you will forget me very soon, but I want to tell you that——"

"Why," said the girl in some surprise, "you speak as if you were going away for all time. You surely do not mean to utterly desert New York?"

"I think you misunderstand me," he said. "I give this important air to my farewell to you because to me it is a very important event. Perhaps you recollect that once I told you that I cared for you. Well, I still care for you, and so I can only go away somewhere—some place 'way off—where—where—— See?"

"New York is a very large place," she observed.

"Yes, New York is a very large—— How good of you to remind me! But then you don't understand. You can't understand. I know I can find no place where I will cease to remember you, but then I can find some place where I can cease to remember in a way that I am myself. I shall never try to forget you. Those two violets, you know—one I found near the tennis court and the other you gave me, you remember—I shall take them with me."

"Here," said the girl, tugging at her gown for a moment—"Here! Here's a third one." She thrust a violet toward him.

"If you were not so serenely insolent," said Hawker, "I would think that you felt sorry for me. I don't wish you to feel sorry for me. And I don't wish to be melodramatic. I know it is all commonplace enough, and I didn't mean to act like a tenor. Please don't pity me."

"I don't," she replied. She gave the violet a little fling.

Hawker lifted his head suddenly and glowered at her. "No, you don't," he at last said slowly, "you don't. Moreover, there is no reason why you should take the trouble. But——"

He paused when the girl leaned and peered over the arm of her chair precisely in the manner of a child at the brink of a fountain. "There's my violet on the floor," she said. "You treated it quite contemptuously, didn't you?"

"Yes."

Together they stared at the violet. Finally he stooped and took it in his fingers. "I feel as if this third one was pelted at me, but I shall keep it. You are rather a cruel person, but, Heaven guard us! that only fastens a man's love the more upon a woman."

She laughed. "That is not a very good thing to tell a woman."

"No," he said gravely, "it is not, but then I fancy that somebody may have told you previously."

She stared at him, and then said, "I think you are revenged for my serene insolence."

134

"Great heavens, what an armour!" he cried. "I suppose, after all, I did feel a trifle like a tenor when I first came here, but you have chilled it all out of me. Let's talk upon indifferent topics." But he started abruptly to his feet. "No," he said, "let us not talk upon indifferent topics. I am not brave, I assure you, and it—it might be too much for me." He held out his hand. "Good-bye."

"You are going?"

"Yes, I am going. Really I didn't think how it would bore you for me to come around here and croak in this fashion."

"And you are not coming back for a long, long time?"

"Not for a long, long time." He mimicked her tone. "I have the three violets now, you know, and you must remember that I took the third one even when you flung it at my head. That will remind you how submissive I was in my devotion. When you recall the two others it will remind you of what a fool I was. Dare say you won't miss three violets."

"No," she said.

"Particularly the one you flung at my head. That violet was certainly freely—given."

"I didn't fling it at your head." She pondered for a time with her eyes upon the floor. Then she murmured, "No more freely—given than the one I gave you that night—that night at the inn."

"So very good of you to tell me so!"

Her eyes were still upon the floor.

"Do you know," said Hawker, "it is very hard to go away and leave an impression in your mind that I am a fool? That is very hard. Now, you do think I am a fool, don't you?"

She remained silent. Once she lifted her eyes and gave him a swift look with much indignation in it.

"Now you are enraged. Well, what have I done?"

It seemed that some tumult was in her mind, for she cried out to him at last in sudden tearfulness: "Oh, do go! Go! Please! I want you to go!"

Under this swift change Hawker appeared as a man struck from the sky. He sprang to his feet, took two steps forward, and spoke a word which was an explosion of delight and amazement. He said, "What?"

With heroic effort she slowly raised her eyes until, alight with anger, defiance, unhappiness, they met his eyes.

Later, she told him that he was perfectly ridiculous.

THE MONSTER AND OTHER STORIES

THE MONSTER

I

Little Jim was, for the time, engine Number 36, and he was making the run between Syracuse and Rochester. He was fourteen minutes behind time, and the throttle was wide open. In consequence, when he swung around the curve at the flower-bed, a wheel of his cart destroyed a peony. Number 36 slowed down at once and looked guiltily at his father, who was mowing the lawn. The doctor had his back to this accident, and he continued to pace slowly to and fro, pushing the mower.

Jim dropped the tongue of the cart. He looked at his father and at the broken flower. Finally he went to the peony and tried to stand it on its pins, resuscitated, but the spine of it was hurt, and it would only hang limply from his hand. Jim could do no reparation. He looked again towards his father.

He went on to the lawn, very slowly, and kicking wretchedly at the turf. Presently his father came along with the whirring machine, while the sweet, new grass blades spun from the knives. In a low voice, Jim said, "Pa!"

The doctor was shaving this lawn as if it were a priest's chin. All during the season he had worked at it in the coolness and peace of the evenings after supper. Even in the shadow of the cherry-trees the grass was strong and healthy. Jim raised his voice a trifle. "Pa!"

The doctor paused, and with the howl of the machine no longer occupying the sense, one could hear the robins in the cherry-trees arranging their affairs. Jim's hands were behind his back, and sometimes his fingers clasped and unclasped. Again he said, "Pa!" The child's fresh and rosy lip was lowered.

The doctor stared down at his son, thrusting his head forward and frowning attentively. "What is it, Jimmie?"

"Pa!" repeated the child at length. Then he raised his finger and pointed at the flowerbed. "There!"

"What?" said the doctor, frowning more. "What is it, Jim?"

After a period of silence, during which the child may have undergone a severe mental tumult, he raised his finger and repeated his former word—"There!" The father had respected this silence with perfect courtesy. Afterwards his glance carefully followed the direction indicated by the child's finger, but he could see nothing which explained to him. "I don't understand what you mean, Jimmie," he said.

It seemed that the importance of the whole thing had taken away the boy's vocabulary, He could only reiterate, "There!"

The doctor mused upon the situation, but he could make nothing of it. At last he said, "Come, show me."

Together they crossed the lawn towards the flower-bed. At some yards from the broken peony Jimmie began to lag. "There!" The word came almost breathlessly.

"Where?" said the doctor.

Jimmie kicked at the grass. "There!" he replied.

The doctor was obliged to go forward alone. After some trouble he found the subject of the incident, the broken flower. Turning then, he saw the child lurking at the rear and scanning his countenance.

The father reflected. After a time he said, "Jimmie, come here." With an infinite modesty of demeanor the child came forward. "Jimmie, how did this happen?"

The child answered, "Now—I was playin' train—and—now—I runned over it."

"You were doing what?"

"I was playin' train."

The father reflected again. "Well, Jimmie," he said, slowly, "I guess you had better not play train any more to-day. Do you think you had better?"

"No, sir," said Jimmie.

During the delivery of the judgment the child had not faced his father, and afterwards he went away, with his head lowered, shuffling his feet.

II

It was apparent from Jimmie's manner that he felt some kind of desire to efface himself. He went down to the stable. Henry Johnson, the negro who cared for the doctor's horses, was sponging the buggy. He grinned fraternally when he saw Jimmie coming. These two were pals. In regard to almost everything in life they seemed to have minds precisely alike. Of course there were points of emphatic divergence. For instance, it was plain from Henry's talk that he was a very handsome negro, and he was known to be a light, a weight, and an eminence in the suburb of the town, where lived the larger number of the negroes, and obviously this glory was over Jimmie's horizon; but he vaguely appreciated it and paid deference to Henry for it mainly because Henry appreciated it and deferred to himself. However, on all points of conduct as related to the doctor, who was the moon, they were in complete but unexpressed understanding. Whenever Jimmie became the victim of an eclipse he went to the stable to solace himself with Henry's crimes. Henry, with the elasticity of his race, could usually provide a sin to place himself on a footing with the disgraced one. Perhaps he would remember that he had forgotten to put the hitching-strap in the back of the buggy on some recent occasion, and had been reprimanded by the doctor. Then these two would commune subtly and without words concerning their moon, holding themselves sympathetically as people who had committed similar treasons. On the other hand, Henry would sometimes choose to absolutely repudiate this idea, and when Jimmie appeared in his shame would bully him most virtuously, preaching with assurance the precepts of the doctor's creed, and pointing out to Jimmie all his abominations. Jimmie did not discover that this was odious in his comrade. He accepted it and lived in its shadow with humility, merely trying to conciliate the saintly Henry with acts of deference.

Won by this attitude, Henry would sometimes allow the child to enjoy the felicity of squeezing the sponge over a buggy-wheel, even when Jimmie was still gory from unspeakable deeds.

Whenever Henry dwelt for a time in sackcloth, Jimmie did not patronize him at all. This was a justice of his age, his condition. He did not know. Besides, Henry could drive a horse, and Jimmie had a full sense of this sublimity. Henry personally conducted the moon during the splendid journeys through the country roads, where farms spread on all sides, with sheep, cows, and other marvels abounding.

"Hello, Jim!" said Henry, poising his sponge. Water was dripping from the buggy. Sometimes the horses in the stalls stamped thunderingly on the pine floor. There was an atmosphere of hay and of harness.

For a minute Jimmie refused to take an interest in anything. He was very downcast. He could not even feel the wonders of wagon washing. Henry, while at his work, narrowly observed him.

"Your pop done wallop yer, didn't he?" he said at last.

"No," said Jimmie, defensively; "he didn't."

After this casual remark Henry continued his labor, with a scowl of occupation. Presently he said: "I done tol' yer many's th' time not to go a-foolin' an' a-projjeckin' with them flowers. Yer pop don' like it nohow." As a matter of fact, Henry had never mentioned flowers to the boy.

Jimmie preserved a gloomy silence, so Henry began to use seductive wiles in this affair of washing a wagon. It was not until he began to spin a wheel on the tree, and the sprinkling water flew everywhere, that the boy was visibly moved. He had been seated on the sill of the carriage-house door, but at the beginning of this ceremony he arose and circled towards the buggy, with an interest that slowly consumed the remembrance of a late disgrace.

Johnson could then display all the dignity of a man whose duty it was to protect Jimmie from a splashing. "Look out, boy! look out! You done gwi' spile yer pants. I raikon your mommer don' 'low this foolishness, she know it. I ain't gwi' have you round yere spilin' yer pants, an' have Mis' Trescott light on me pressen'ly. 'Deed I ain't." He spoke with an air of great irritation, but he was not annoyed at all. This tone was merely a part of his importance. In reality he was always delighted to have the child there to witness the business of the stable. For one thing, Jimmie was invariably overcome with reverence when he was told how beautifully a harness was polished or a horse groomed. Henry explained each detail of this kind with unction, procuring great joy from the child's admiration.

III

After Johnson had taken his supper in the kitchen, he went to his loft in the carriage house and dressed himself with much care. No belle of a court circle could bestow more mind on a toilet than did Johnson. On second thought, he was more like a priest arraying himself for some parade of the church. As he emerged from his room and sauntered down the carriage-drive, no one would have suspected him of ever having washed a buggy.

It was not altogether a matter of the lavender trousers, nor yet the straw hat with its bright silk band. The change was somewhere, far in the interior of Henry. But there was no cake-walk hyperbole in it. He was simply a quiet, well-bred gentleman of position, wealth, and other necessary achievements out for an evening stroll, and he had never washed a wagon in his life.

In the morning, when in his working-clothes, he had met a friend— "Hello, Pete!" "Hello, Henry!" Now, in his effulgence, he encountered this same friend. His bow was not at all haughty. If it expressed anything, it expressed consummate generosity—"Good-evenin', Misteh Washington." Pete, who was very dirty, being at work in a potato-patch, responded in a mixture of abasement and appreciation—Good-evenin', Misteh Johnsing."

The shimmering blue of the electric arc lamps was strong in the main street of the town. At numerous points it was conquered by the orange glare of the outnumbering gaslights in the windows of shops. Through this radiant lane moved a crowd, which culminated in a throng before the post-office, awaiting the distribution of the evening mails. Occasionally there came into it a shrill electric street-car, the motor singing like a cageful of grasshoppers, and possessing a great gong that clanged forth both warnings and simple noise. At the little theatre, which was a varnish and red plush miniature of one of the famous New York theatres, a company of strollers was to play "East Lynne." The young men of the town were mainly gathered at the corners, in distinctive groups, which expressed various shades and lines of chumship, and had little to do with any social gradations. There they discussed everything with critical insight, passing the whole town in review as it swarmed in the street. When the gongs of the electric cars ceased for a moment to harry the ears, there could be heard the sound of the feet of the leisurely crowd on the bluestone pavement, and it was like the peaceful evening lashing at the shore of a lake. At the foot of the hill, where two lines of maples sentinelled the way, an electric lamp glowed high among the embowering branches, and made most wonderful shadow-etchings on the road below it.

When Johnson appeared amid the throng a member of one of the profane groups at a corner instantly telegraphed news of this extraordinary arrival to his companions. They hailed him. "Hello, Henry! Going to walk for a cake to-night?"

"Ain't he smooth?"

"Why, you've got that cake right in your pocket, Henry!"

"Throw out your chest a little more."

Henry was not ruffled in any way by these quiet admonitions and compliments. In reply he laughed a supremely good-natured, chuckling laugh, which nevertheless expressed an underground complacency of superior metal.

Young Griscom, the lawyer, was just emerging from Reifsnyder's barber shop, rubbing his chin contentedly. On the steps he dropped his hand and looked with wide eyes into the crowd. Suddenly he bolted back into the shop. "Wow!" he cried to the parliament; "you ought to see the coon that's coming!"

Reifsnyder and his assistant instantly poised their razors high and turned towards the window. Two belathered heads reared from the chairs. The electric shine in the street caused an effect like water to them who looked through the glass from the yellow glamour of Reifsnyder's shop. In fact, the people without resembled the inhabitants of a great aquarium that here had a square pane in it. Presently into this frame swam the graceful form of Henry Johnson.

"Chee!" said Reifsnyder. He and his assistant with one accord threw their obligations to the winds, and leaving their lathered victims helpless, advanced to the window. "Ain't he a taisy?" said Reifsnyder, marvelling.

But the man in the first chair, with a grievance in his mind, had found a weapon. "Why, that's only Henry Johnson, you blamed idiots! Come on now, Reif, and shave me. What do you think I am—a mummy?"

Reifsnyder turned, in a great excitement. "I bait you any money that vas not Henry Johnson! Henry Johnson! Rats!" The scorn put into this last word made it an explosion. "That man was a Pullman-car porter or someding. How could that be Henry Johnson?" he demanded, turbulently. "You vas crazy."

The man in the first chair faced the barber in a storm of indignation. "Didn't I give him those lavender trousers?" he roared.

And young Griscom, who had remained attentively at the window, said: "Yes, I guess that was Henry. It looked like him."

"Oh, vell," said Reifsnyder, returning to his business, "if you think so! Oh, vell!" He implied that he was submitting for the sake of amiability.

Finally the man in the second chair, mumbling from a mouth made timid by adjacent lather, said: "That was Henry Johnson all right. Why, he always dresses like that when he wants to make a front! He's the biggest dude in town—anybody knows that."

"Chinger!" said Reifsnyder.

Henry was not at all oblivious of the wake of wondering ejaculation that streamed out behind him. On other occasions he had reaped this same joy, and he always had an eye for the demonstration. With a face beaming with happiness he turned away from the scene of his victories into a narrow side street, where the electric light still hung high, but only to exhibit a row of tumble-down houses leaning together like paralytics.

The saffron Miss Bella Farragut, in a calico frock, had been crouched on the front stoop, gossiping at long range, but she espied her approaching caller at a distance. She dashed around the corner of the house, galloping like a horse. Henry saw it all, but he preserved the polite demeanor of a guest when a waiter spills claret down his cuff. In this awkward situation he was simply perfect.

The duty of receiving Mr. Johnson fell upon Mrs. Farragut, because Bella, in another room, was scrambling wildly into her best gown. The fat old woman met him with a great ivory smile, sweeping back with the door, and bowing low. "Walk in, Misteh Johnson, walk in. How is you dis ebenin', Misteh Johnson—how is you?"

Henry's face showed like a reflector as he bowed and bowed, bending almost from his head to his ankles, "Good-evenin', Mis' Fa'gut; good-evenin'. How is you dis evenin'? Is all you' folks well, Mis' Fa'gut?"

After a great deal of kowtow, they were planted in two chairs opposite each other in the living-room. Here they exchanged the most tremendous civilities, until Miss Bella swept into the room, when there was more kowtow on all sides, and a smiling show of teeth that was like an illumination.

The cooking-stove was of course in this drawing-room, and on the fire was some kind of a long-winded stew. Mrs. Farragut was obliged to arise and attend to it from time to time. Also young Sim came in and went to bed on his pallet in the corner. But to all these domesticities the three maintained an absolute dumbness. They bowed and smiled and ignored and imitated until a late hour, and if they had been the occupants of the most gorgeous salon in the world they could not have been more like three monkeys.

After Henry had gone, Bella, who encouraged herself in the appropriation of phrases, said, "Oh, ma, isn't he divine?"

IV

A Saturday evening was a sign always for a larger crowd to parade the thoroughfare. In summer the band played until ten o'clock in the little park. Most of the young men of the town affected to be superior to this band, even to despise it; but in the still and fragrant evenings they invariably turned out in force, because the girls were sure to attend this concert, strolling slowly over the grass, linked closely in pairs, or preferably in threes, in the curious public dependence upon one another which was their inheritance. There was no particular social aspect to this gathering, save that group regarded group with interest, but mainly in silence. Perhaps one girl would nudge another girl and suddenly say, "Look! there goes Gertie Hodgson and her sister!" And they would appear to regard this as an event of importance.

On a particular evening a rather large company of young men were gathered on the sidewalk that edged the park. They remained thus beyond the borders of the festivities because of their dignity, which would not exactly allow them to appear in anything which was so much fun for the younger lads. These latter were careering madly through the crowd, precipitating minor accidents from time to time, but usually fleeing like mist swept by the wind before retribution could lay hands upon them.

The band played a waltz which involved a gift of prominence to the bass horn, and one of the young men on the sidewalk said that the music reminded him of the new engines on the hill pumping water into the reservoir. A similarity of this kind was not inconceivable, but the young man did not say it because he disliked the band's playing. He said it because it was fashionable to say that manner of thing concerning the band. However, over in the stand, Billie Harris, who played the snare-drum, was always surrounded by a throng of boys, who adored his every whack.

After the mails from New York and Rochester had been finally distributed, the crowd from the post-office added to the mass already in the park. The wind waved the leaves of the maples, and, high in the air, the blue-burning globes of the arc lamps caused the wonderful traceries of leaf shadows on the ground. When the light fell upon the upturned face of a girl, it caused it to glow with a wonderful pallor. A policeman came suddenly from the darkness and chased a gang of obstreperous little boys. They hooted him from a distance. The leader of the band had some of the mannerisms of the great musicians, and during a period of silence the crowd smiled when they saw him raise his hand to his brow, stroke it sentimentally, and glance upward with a look of poetic anguish. In the shivering light, which gave to the park an effect like a great vaulted hall, the throng swarmed, with a gentle murmur of dresses switching the turf, and with a steady hum of voices.

Suddenly, without preliminary bars, there arose from afar the great hoarse roar of a factory whistle. It raised and swelled to a sinister note, and then it sang on the night wind one long call that held the crowd in the park immovable, speechless. The band-master had been about to vehemently let fall his hand to start the band on a thundering career through a popular march, but, smitten by this giant voice from the night, his hand dropped slowly to his knee, and, his mouth agape, he looked at his men in silence. The cry died away to a wail and then to stillness. It released the muscles of the company of young men on the sidewalk, who had been like statues, posed eagerly, lithely, their ears turned. And then they wheeled upon each other simultaneously, and, in a single explosion, they shouted, "One!"

Again the sound swelled in the night and roared its long ominous cry, and as it died away the crowd of young men wheeled upon each other and, in chorus, yelled, "Two!"

There was a moment of breathless waiting. Then they bawled, "Second district!" In a flash the company of indolent and cynical young men had vanished like a snowball disrupted by dynamite.

V

Jake Rogers was the first man to reach the home of Tuscarora Hose Company Number Six. He had wrenched his key from his pocket as he tore down the street, and he jumped at the spring-lock like a demon. As the doors flew back before his hands he leaped and kicked the wedges from a pair of wheels, loosened a tongue from its clasp, and in the glare of the electric light which the town placed before each of its hose-houses the next comers beheld the spectacle of Jake Rogers bent like hickory in the manfulness of his pulling, and the heavy cart was moving slowly towards the doors. Four men joined him at the time, and as they swung with the cart out into the street, dark figures sped towards them from the ponderous shadows back of the electric lamps. Some set up the inevitable question, "What district?"

"Second," was replied to them in a compact howl. Tuscarora Hose Company Number Six swept on a perilous wheel into Niagara Avenue, and as the men, attached to the cart by the rope which had been paid out from the windlass under the tongue, pulled madly in their fervor and abandon, the gong under the axle clanged incitingly. And sometimes the same cry was heard, "What district?"

"Second."

On a grade Johnnie Thorpe fell, and exercising a singular muscular ability, rolled out in time from the track of the on-coming wheel, and arose, dishevelled and aggrieved, casting a look of mournful disenchantment upon the black crowd that poured after the machine. The cart seemed to be the apex of a dark wave that was whirling as if it had been a broken dam. Back of the lad were stretches of lawn, and in that direction front-doors were banged by men who hoarsely shouted out into the clamorous avenue, "What district?"

At one of these houses a woman came to the door bearing a lamp, shielding her face from its rays with her hands. Across the cropped grass the avenue represented to her a kind of black torrent, upon which, nevertheless, fled numerous miraculous figures upon bicycles. She did not know that the towering light at the corner was continuing its nightly whine.

Suddenly a little boy somersaulted around the corner of the house as if he had been projected down a flight of stairs by a catapultian boot. He halted himself in front of the house by dint of a rather extraordinary evolution with his legs. "Oh, ma," he gasped, "can I go? Can I, ma?"

She straightened with the coldness of the exterior mother-judgment, although the hand that held the lamp trembled slightly. "No, Willie; you had better come to bed."

Instantly he began to buck and fume like a mustang. "Oh, ma," he cried, contorting himself—"oh, ma, can't I go? Please, ma, can't I go? Can't I go, ma?"

"It's half-past nine now, Willie."

He ended by wailing out a compromise: "Well, just down to the corner, ma? Just down to the corner?"

From the avenue came the sound of rushing men who wildly shouted. Somebody had grappled the bell-rope in the Methodist church, and now over the town rang this solemn and terrible voice, speaking from the clouds. Moved from its peaceful business, this bell gained a new spirit in the portentous night, and it swung the heart to and fro, up and down, with each peal of it.

"Just down to the corner, ma?"

"Willie, it's half-past nine now."

VI

The outlines of the house of Dr. Trescott had faded quietly into the evening, hiding a shape such as we call Queen Anne against the pall of the blackened sky. The neighborhood was at this time so quiet, and seemed so devoid of obstructions, that Hannigan's dog thought it a good opportunity to prowl in forbidden precincts, and so came and pawed Trescott's lawn, growling, and considering himself a formidable beast. Later, Peter Washington strolled past the house and whistled, but there was no dim light shining from Henry's loft, and presently Peter went his way. The rays from the street, creeping in silvery waves over the grass, caused the row of shrubs along the drive to throw a clear, bold shade.

A wisp of smoke came from one of the windows at the end of the house and drifted quietly into the branches of a cherry-tree. Its companions followed it in slowly increasing numbers, and finally there was a current controlled by invisible banks which poured into the fruit-laden boughs of the cherry-tree. It was no more to be noted than if a troop of dim and silent gray monkeys had been climbing a grapevine into the clouds.

After a moment the window brightened as if the four panes of it had been stained with blood, and a quick ear might have been led to imagine the fire-imps calling and calling, clan joining clan, gathering to the colors. From the street, however, the house maintained its dark quiet, insisting to a passer-by that it was the safe dwelling of people who chose to retire early to tranquil dreams. No one could have heard this low droning of the gathering clans.

150

Suddenly the panes of the red window tinkled and crashed to the ground, and at other windows there suddenly reared other flames, like bloody spectres at the apertures of a haunted house. This outbreak had been well planned, as if by professional revolutionists.

A man's voice suddenly shouted: "Fire! Fire! Fire!" Hannigan had flung his pipe frenziedly from him because his lungs demanded room. He tumbled down from his perch, swung over the fence, and ran shouting towards the front-door of the Trescotts'. Then he hammered on the door, using his fists as if they were mallets. Mrs. Trescott instantly came to one of the windows on the second floor. Afterwards she knew she had been about to say, "The doctor is not at home, but if you will leave your name, I will let him know as soon as he comes."

Hannigan's bawling was for a minute incoherent, but she understood that it was not about croup.

"What?" she said, raising the window swiftly.

"Your house is on fire! You're all ablaze! Move quick if—" His cries were resounding, in the street as if it were a cave of echoes. Many feet pattered swiftly on the stones. There was one man who ran with an almost fabulous speed. He wore lavender trousers. A straw hat with a bright silk band was held half crumpled in his hand.

As Henry reached the front-door, Hannigan had just broken the lock with a kick. A thick cloud of smoke poured over them, and Henry, ducking his head, rushed into it. From Hannigan's clamor he knew only one thing, but it turned him blue with horror. In the hall a lick of flame had found the cord that supported "Signing the Declaration." The engraving slumped suddenly down at one end, and then dropped to the floor, where it burst with the sound of a bomb. The fire was already roaring like a winter wind among the pines.

At the head of the stairs Mrs. Trescott was waving her arms as if they were two reeds.

"Jimmie! Save Jimmie!" she screamed in Henry's face. He plunged past

151

her and disappeared, taking the long-familiar routes among these upper chambers, where he had once held office as a sort of second assistant house-maid.

Hannigan had followed him up the stairs, and grappled the arm of the maniacal woman there. His face was black with rage. "You must come down," he bellowed.

She would only scream at him in reply: "Jimmie! Jimmie! Save Jimmie!" But he dragged her forth while she babbled at him.

As they swung out into the open air a man ran across the lawn, and seizing a shutter, pulled it from its hinges and flung it far out upon the grass. Then he frantically attacked the other shutters one by one. It was a kind of temporary insanity.

"Here, you," howled Hannigan, "hold Mrs. Trescott—And stop—"

The news had been telegraphed by a twist of the wrist of a neighbor who had gone to the fire-box at the corner, and the time when Hannigan and his charge struggled out of the house was the time when the whistle roared its hoarse night call, smiting the crowd in the park, causing the leader of the band, who was about to order the first triumphal clang of a military march, to let his hand drop slowly to his knees.

VII

Henry pawed awkwardly through the smoke in the upper halls. He had attempted to guide himself by the walls, but they were too hot. The paper was crimpling, and he expected at any moment to have a flame burst from under his hands.

"Jimmie!"

He did not call very loud, as if in fear that the humming flames below would overhear him.

"Jimmie! Oh, Jimmie!"

Stumbling and panting, he speedily reached the entrance to Jimmie's room and flung open the door. The little chamber had no smoke in it at all. It was faintly illuminated by a beautiful rosy light reflected circuitously from the flames that were consuming the house. The boy had apparently just been aroused by the noise. He sat in his bed, his lips apart, his eyes wide, while upon his little white-robed figure played caressingly the light from the fire. As the door flew open he had before him this apparition of his pal, a terror-stricken negro, all tousled and with wool scorching, who leaped upon him and bore him up in a blanket as if the whole affair were a case of kidnapping by a dreadful robber chief. Without waiting to go through the usual short but complete process of wrinkling up his face, Jimmie let out a gorgeous bawl, which resembled the expression of a calf's deepest terror. As Johnson, bearing him, reeled into the smoke of the hall, he flung his arms about his neck and buried his face in the blanket. He called twice in muffled tones: "Mam-ma! Mam-ma!" When Johnson came to the top of the stairs with his burden, he took a quick step backward. Through the smoke that rolled to him he could see that the lower hall was all ablaze. He cried out then in a howl that resembled Jimmie's former achievement. His legs gained a frightful faculty of bending sideways. Swinging about precariously on these reedy legs, he made his way back slowly, back along the upper hall. From the way of him then, he had given up almost all idea of escaping from the burning house, and with it the desire. He was submitting, submitting because of his fathers, bending his mind in a most perfect slavery to this conflagration.

He now clutched Jimmie as unconsciously as when, running toward the house, he had clutched the hat with the bright silk band.

Suddenly he remembered a little private staircase which led from a bedroom to an apartment which the doctor had fitted up as a laboratory and work-house, where he used some of his leisure, and also hours when he might have been sleeping, in devoting himself to experiments which came in the way of his study and interest.

When Johnson recalled this stairway the submission to the blaze departed instantly. He had been perfectly familiar with it, but his confusion had destroyed the memory of it.

In his sudden momentary apathy there had been little that resembled

153

fear, but now, as a way of safety came to him, the old frantic terror caught him. He was no longer creature to the flames, and he was afraid of the battle with them. It was a singular and swift set of alternations in which he feared twice without submission, and submitted once without fear.

"Jimmie!" he wailed, as he staggered on his way. He wished this little inanimate body at his breast to participate in his tremblings. But the child had lain limp and still during these headlong charges and countercharges, and no sign came from him.

Johnson passed through two rooms and came to the head of the stairs. As he opened the door great billows of smoke poured out, but gripping Jimmie closer, he plunged down through them. All manner of odors assailed him during this flight. They seemed to be alive with envy, hatred, and malice. At the entrance to the laboratory he confronted a strange spectacle. The room was like a garden in the region where might be burning flowers. Flames of violet, crimson, green, blue, orange, and purple were blooming everywhere. There was one blaze that was precisely the hue of a delicate coral. In another place was a mass that lay merely in phosphorescent inaction like a pile of emeralds. But all these marvels were to be seen dimly through clouds of heaving, turning, deadly smoke.

Johnson halted for a moment on the threshold. He cried out again in the negro wail that had in it the sadness of the swamps. Then he rushed across the room. An orange-colored flame leaped like a panther at the lavender trousers. This animal bit deeply into Johnson. There was an explosion at one side, and suddenly before him there reared a delicate, trembling sapphire shape like a fairy lady. With a quiet smile she blocked his path and doomed him and Jimmie. Johnson shrieked, and then ducked in the manner of his race in fights. He aimed to pass under the left guard of the sapphire lady. But she was swifter than eagles, and her talons caught in him as he plunged past her. Bowing his head as if his neck had been struck, Johnson lurched forward, twisting this way and that way. He fell on his back. The still form in the blanket flung from his arms, rolled to the edge of the floor and beneath the window.

Johnson had fallen with his head at the base of an old-fashioned desk.

There was a row of jars upon the top of this desk. For the most part, they were silent amid this rioting, but there was one which seemed to hold a scintillant and writhing serpent.

Suddenly the glass splintered, and a ruby-red snakelike thing poured its thick length out upon the top of the old desk. It coiled and hesitated, and then began to swim a languorous way down the mahogany slant. At the angle it waved its sizzling molten head to and fro over the closed eyes of the man beneath it. Then, in a moment, with a mystic impulse, it moved again, and the red snake flowed directly down into Johnson's upturned face.

Afterwards the trail of this creature seemed to reek, and amid flames and low explosions drops like red-hot jewels pattered softly down it at leisurely intervals.

VIII

Suddenly all roads led to Dr. Trescott's. The whole town flowed towards one point. Chippeway Hose Company Number One toiled desperately up Bridge Street Hill even as the Tuscaroras came in an impetuous sweep down Niagara Avenue. Meanwhile the machine of the hook-and-ladder experts from across the creek was spinning on its way. The chief of the fire department had been playing poker in the rear room of Whiteley's cigar-store, but at the first breath of the alarm he sprang through the door like a man escaping with the kitty.

In Whilomville, on these occasions, there was always a number of people who instantly turned their attention to the bells in the churches and school-houses. The bells not only emphasized the alarm, but it was the habit to send these sounds rolling across the sky in a stirring brazen uproar until the flames were practically vanquished. There was also a kind of rivalry as to which bell should be made to produce the greatest din. Even the Valley Church, four miles away among the farms, had heard the voices of its brethren, and immediately added a quaint little yelp.

Dr. Trescott had been driving homeward, slowly smoking a cigar, and feeling glad that this last case was now in complete obedience to him, like a wild animal that he had subdued, when he heard the long whistle, and chirped to his horse under the unlicensed but perfectly distinct impression that a fire had broken out in Oakhurst, a new and rather high-flying suburb of the town which was at least two miles from his own home. But in the second blast and in the ensuing silence he read the designation of his own district. He was then only a few blocks from his house. He took out the whip and laid it lightly on the mare. Surprised and frightened at this extraordinary action, she leaped forward, and as the reins straightened like steel bands, the doctor leaned backward a trifle. When the mare whirled him up to the closed gate he was wondering whose house could be afire. The man who had rung the signal-box yelled something at him, but he already knew. He left the mare to her will.

In front of his door was a maniacal woman in a wrapper. "Ned!" she screamed at sight of him. "Jimmie! Save Jimmie!"

Trescott had grown hard and chill. "Where?" he said. "Where?"

Mrs. Trescott's voice began to bubble. "Up—up—up—" She pointed at the second-story windows.

Hannigan was already shouting: "Don't go in that way! You can't go in that way!"

Trescott ran around the corner of the house and disappeared from them. He knew from the view he had taken of the main hall that it would be impossible to ascend from there. His hopes were fastened now to the stairway which led from the laboratory. The door which opened from this room out upon the lawn was fastened with a bolt and lock, but he kicked close to the lock and then close to the bolt. The door with a loud crash flew back. The doctor recoiled from the roll of smoke, and then bending low, he stepped into the garden of burning flowers. On the floor his stinging eyes could make out a form in a smouldering blanket near the window. Then, as he carried his son towards the door, he saw that the whole lawn seemed now alive with men and boys, the leaders in the great charge that the whole town was making. They seized him and his burden, and overpowered him in wet blankets and water.

But Hannigan was howling: "Johnson is in there yet! Henry Johnson is in there yet! He went in after the kid! Johnson is in there yet!"

These cries penetrated to the sleepy senses of Trescott, and he struggled with his captors, swearing, unknown to him and to them, all the deep blasphemies of his medical-student days. He rose to his feet and went again towards the door of the laboratory. They endeavored to restrain him, although they were much affrighted at him.

But a young man who was a brakeman on the railway, and lived in one of the rear streets near the Trescotts, had gone into the laboratory and brought forth a thing which he laid on the grass.

IX

There were hoarse commands from in front of the house. "Turn on your water, Five!" "Let 'er go, One!" The gathering crowd swayed this way and that way. The flames, towering high, cast a wild red light on their faces. There came the clangor of a gong from along some adjacent street. The crowd exclaimed at it. "Here comes Number Three!" "That's Three a-comin'!" A panting and irregular mob dashed into view, dragging a hose-cart. A cry of exultation arose from the little boys. "Here's Three!" The lads welcomed Never-Die Hose Company Number Three as if it was composed of a chariot dragged by a band of gods. The perspiring citizens flung themselves into the fray. The boys danced in impish joy at the displays of prowess. They acclaimed the approach of Number Two. They welcomed Number Four with cheers. They were so deeply moved by this whole affair that they bitterly guyed the late appearance of the hook and ladder company, whose heavy apparatus had almost stalled them on the Bridge Street hill. The lads hated and feared a fire, of course. They did not particularly want to have anybody's house burn, but still it was fine to see the gathering of the companies, and amid a great noise to watch their heroes perform all manner of prodigies.

They were divided into parties over the worth of different companies, and supported their creeds with no small violence. For instance, in that part of the little city where Number Four had its home it would be most daring for a boy to contend the superiority of any other company. Likewise, in another quarter, where a strange boy was asked which fire company was the best in

Whilomville, he was expected to answer "Number One." Feuds, which the boys forgot and remembered according to chance or the importance of some recent event, existed all through the town.

They did not care much for John Shipley, the chief of the department. It was true that he went to a fire with the speed of a falling angel, but when there he invariably lapsed into a certain still mood, which was almost a preoccupation, moving leisurely around the burning structure and surveying it, putting meanwhile at a cigar. This quiet man, who even when life was in danger seldom raised his voice, was not much to their fancy. Now old Sykes Huntington, when he was chief, used to bellow continually like a bull and gesticulate in a sort of delirium. He was much finer as a spectacle than this Shipley, who viewed a fire with the same steadiness that he viewed a raise in a large jack-pot. The greater number of the boys could never understand why the members of these companies persisted in re-electing Shipley, although they often pretended to understand it, because "My father says" was a very formidable phrase in argument, and the fathers seemed almost unanimous in advocating Shipley.

At this time there was considerable discussion as to which company had gotten the first stream of water on the fire. Most of the boys claimed that Number Five owned that distinction, but there was a determined minority who contended for Number One. Boys who were the blood adherents of other companies were obliged to choose between the two on this occasion, and the talk waxed warm.

But a great rumor went among the crowds. It was told with hushed voices. Afterwards a reverent silence fell even upon the boys. Jimmie Trescott and Henry Johnson had been burned to death, and Dr. Trescott himself had been most savagely hurt. The crowd did not even feel the police pushing at them. They raised their eyes, shining now with awe, towards the high flames.

The man who had information was at his best. In low tones he described the whole affair. "That was the kid's room—in the corner there. He had measles or somethin', and this coon—Johnson—was a-settin' up with 'im, and Johnson got sleepy or somethin' and upset the lamp, and the doctor he

158

was down in his office, and he came running up, and they all got burned together till they dragged 'em out."

Another man, always preserved for the deliverance of the final judgment, was saying: "Oh, they'll die sure. Burned to flinders. No chance. Hull lot of 'em. Anybody can see." The crowd concentrated its gaze still more closely upon these flags of fire which waved joyfully against the black sky. The bells of the town were clashing unceasingly.

A little procession moved across the lawn and towards the street. There were three cots, borne by twelve of the firemen. The police moved sternly, but it needed no effort of theirs to open a lane for this slow cortege. The men who bore the cots were well known to the crowd, but in this solemn parade during the ringing of the bells and the shouting, and with the red glare upon the sky, they seemed utterly foreign, and Whilomville paid them a deep respect. Each man in this stretcher party had gained a reflected majesty. They were footmen to death, and the crowd made subtle obeisance to this august dignity derived from three prospective graves. One woman turned away with a shriek at sight of the covered body on the first stretcher, and people faced her suddenly in silent and mournful indignation. Otherwise there was barely a sound as these twelve important men with measured tread carried their burdens through the throng.

The little boys no longer discussed the merits of the different fire companies. For the greater part they had been routed. Only the more courageous viewed closely the three figures veiled in yellow blankets.

X

Old Judge Denning Hagenthorpe, who lived nearly opposite the Trescotts, had thrown his door wide open to receive the afflicted family. When it was publicly learned that the doctor and his son and the negro were still alive, it required a specially detailed policeman to prevent people from scaling the front porch and interviewing these sorely wounded. One old lady appeared with a miraculous poultice, and she quoted most damning Scripture to the officer when he said that she could not pass him. Throughout the night some lads old enough to be given privileges or to compel them from their mothers remained vigilantly upon the kerb in anticipation of a death or some such event. The reporter of the Morning Tribune rode thither on his bicycle every hour until three o'clock.

Six of the ten doctors in Whilomville attended at Judge Hagenthorpe's house.

Almost at once they were able to know that Trescott's burns were not vitally important. The child would possibly be scarred badly, but his life was undoubtedly safe. As for the negro Henry Johnson, he could not live. His body was frightfully seared, but more than that, he now had no face. His face had simply been burned away.

Trescott was always asking news of the two other patients. In the morning he seemed fresh and strong, so they told him that Johnson was doomed. They then saw him stir on the bed, and sprang quickly to see if the bandages needed readjusting. In the sudden glance he threw from one to another he impressed them as being both leonine and impracticable.

The morning paper announced the death of Henry Johnson. It contained a long interview with Edward J. Hannigan, in which the latter described in full the performance of Johnson at the fire. There was also an editorial built from all the best words in the vocabulary of the staff. The town halted in its accustomed road of thought, and turned a reverent attention to the memory of this hostler. In the breasts of many people was the regret that they had not known enough to give him a hand and a lift when he was alive, and they judged themselves stupid and ungenerous for this failure.

The name of Henry Johnson became suddenly the title of a saint to the little boys. The one who thought of it first could, by quoting it in an argument, at once overthrow his antagonist, whether it applied to the subject or whether it did not.

"*Nigger, nigger, never die.*

Black face and shiny eye."

Boys who had called this odious couplet in the rear of Johnson's march buried the fact at the bottom of their hearts.

Later in the day Miss Bella Farragut, of No. 7 Watermelon Alley, announced that she had been engaged to marry Mr. Henry Johnson.

XI

The old judge had a cane with an ivory head. He could never think at his best until he was leaning slightly on this stick and smoothing the white top with slow movements of his hands. It was also to him a kind of narcotic. If by any chance he mislaid it, he grew at once very irritable, and was likely to speak sharply to his sister, whose mental incapacity he had patiently endured for thirty years in the old mansion on Ontario Street. She was not at all aware of her brother's opinion of her endowments, and so it might be said that the judge had successfully dissembled for more than a quarter of a century, only risking the truth at the times when his cane was lost.

On a particular day the judge sat in his armchair on the porch. The sunshine sprinkled through the lilac-bushes and poured great coins on the boards. The sparrows disputed in the trees that lined the pavements. The judge mused deeply, while his hands gently caressed the ivory head of his cane.

Finally he arose and entered the house, his brow still furrowed in a thoughtful frown. His stick thumped solemnly in regular beats. On the second floor he entered a room where Dr. Trescott was working about the bedside of Henry Johnson. The bandages on the negro's head allowed only one thing to appear, an eye, which unwinkingly stared at the judge. The later spoke to Trescott on the condition of the patient. Afterward he evidently had something further to say, but he seemed to be kept from it by the scrutiny of the unwinking eye, at which he furtively glanced from time to time.

When Jimmie Trescott was sufficiently recovered, his mother had taken him to pay a visit to his grandparents in Connecticut. The doctor had remained to take care of his patients, but as a matter of truth he spent most of his time at Judge Hagenthorpe's house, where lay Henry Johnson. Here he slept and ate almost every meal in the long nights and days of his vigil.

At dinner, and away from the magic of the unwinking eye, the judge said, suddenly, "Trescott, do you think it is—" As Trescott paused expectantly, the judge fingered his knife. He said, thoughtfully, "No one wants to advance such ideas, but somehow I think that that poor fellow ought to die."

There was in Trescott's face at once a look of recognition, as if in this tangent of the judge he saw an old problem. He merely sighed and answered, "Who knows?" The words were spoken in a deep tone that gave them an elusive kind of significance.

The judge retreated to the cold manner of the bench. "Perhaps we may not talk with propriety of this kind of action, but I am induced to say that you are performing a questionable charity in preserving this negro's life. As near as I can understand, he will hereafter be a monster, a perfect monster, and probably with an affected brain. No man can observe you as I have observed you and not know that it was a matter of conscience with you, but I am afraid, my friend, that it is one of the blunders of virtue." The judge had delivered his views with his habitual oratory. The last three words he spoke with a particular emphasis, as if the phrase was his discovery.

The doctor made a weary gesture. "He saved my boy's life."

"Yes," said the judge, swiftly—"yes, I know!"

"And what am I to do?" said Trescott, his eyes suddenly lighting like an outburst from smouldering peat. "What am I to do? He gave himself for—for Jimmie. What am I to do for him?"

The judge abased himself completely before these words. He lowered his eyes for a moment. He picked at his cucumbers.

Presently he braced himself straightly in his chair. "He will be your creation, you understand. He is purely your creation. Nature has very evidently given him up. He is dead. You are restoring him to life. You are making him, and he will be a monster, and with no mind.

"He will be what you like, judge," cried Trescott, in sudden, polite fury. "He will be anything, but, by God! he saved my boy."

The judge interrupted in a voice trembling with emotion: "Trescott!

Trescott! Don't I know?"

Trescott had subsided to a sullen mood. "Yes, you know," he answered, acidly; "but you don't know all about your own boy being saved from death." This was a perfectly childish allusion to the judge's bachelorhood. Trescott knew that the remark was infantile, but he seemed to take desperate delight in it.

But it passed the judge completely. It was not his spot.

"I am puzzled," said he, in profound thought. "I don't know what to say."

Trescott had become repentant. "Don't think I don't appreciate what you say, judge. But—"

"Of course!" responded the judge, quickly. "Of course."

"It—" began Trescott.

"Of course," said the judge.

In silence they resumed their dinner.

"Well," said the judge, ultimately, "it is hard for a man to know what to do."

"It is," said the doctor, fervidly.

There was another silence. It was broken by the judge:

"Look here, Trescott; I don't want you to think—"

"No, certainly not," answered the doctor, earnestly.

"Well, I don't want you to think I would say anything to—It was only that I thought that I might be able to suggest to you that—perhaps—the affair was a little dubious."

With an appearance of suddenly disclosing his real mental perturbation, the doctor said: "Well, what would you do? Would you kill him?" he asked, abruptly and sternly.

"Trescott, you fool," said the old man, gently.

"Oh, well, I know, judge, but then—" He turned red, and spoke with new violence: "Say, he saved my boy—do you see? He saved my boy."

"You bet he did," cried the judge, with enthusiasm. "You bet he did." And they remained for a time gazing at each other, their faces illuminated with memories of a certain deed.

After another silence, the judge said, "It is hard for a man to know what to do."

XII

Late one evening Trescott, returning from a professional call, paused his buggy at the Hagenthorpe gate. He tied the mare to the old tin-covered post, and entered the house. Ultimately he appeared with a companion—a man who walked slowly and carefully, as if he were learning. He was wrapped to the heels in an old-fashioned ulster. They entered the buggy and drove away.

After a silence only broken by the swift and musical humming of the wheels on the smooth road, Trescott spoke. "Henry," he said, "I've got you a home here with old Alek Williams. You will have everything you want to eat and a good place to sleep, and I hope you will get along there all right. I will pay all your expenses, and come to see you as often as I can. If you don't get along, I want you to let me know as soon as possible, and then we will do what we can to make it better."

The dark figure at the doctor's side answered with a cheerful laugh. "These buggy wheels don' look like I washed 'em yesterday, docteh," he said.

Trescott hesitated for a moment, and then went on insistently, "I am taking you to Alek Williams, Henry, and I—"

The figure chuckled again. "No, 'deed! No, seh! Alek Williams don' know a hoss! 'Deed he don't. He don' know a hoss from a pig." The laugh that followed was like the rattle of pebbles.

Trescott turned and looked sternly and coldly at the dim form in the gloom from the buggy-top. "Henry," he said, "I didn't say anything about horses. I was saying—"

"Hoss? Hoss?" said the quavering voice from these near shadows. "Hoss? 'Deed I don' know all erbout a boss! 'Deed I don't." There was a satirical chuckle.

At the end of three miles the mare slackened and the doctor leaned forward, peering, while holding tight reins. The wheels of the buggy bumped often over out-cropping bowlders. A window shone forth, a simple square of topaz on a great black hill-side. Four dogs charged the buggy with ferocity, and when it did not promptly retreat, they circled courageously around the flanks, baying. A door opened near the window in the hill-side, and a man came and stood on a beach of yellow light.

"Yah! yah! You Roveh! You Susie! Come yah! Come yah this minit!"

Trescott called across the dark sea of grass, "Hello, Alek!"

"Hello!"

"Come down here and show me where to drive."

The man plunged from the beach into the surf, and Trescott could then only trace his course by the fervid and polite ejaculations of a host who was somewhere approaching. Presently Williams took the mare by the head, and uttering cries of welcome and scolding the swarming dogs, led the equipage towards the lights. When they halted at the door and Trescott was climbing out, Williams cried, "Will she stand, docteh?"

"She'll stand all right, but you better hold her for a minute. Now, Henry." The doctor turned and held both arms to the dark figure. It crawled to him painfully like a man going down a ladder. Williams took the mare away to be tied to a little tree, and when he returned he found them awaiting him in the gloom beyond the rays from the door.

He burst out then like a siphon pressed by a nervous thumb. "Hennery! Hennery, ma ol' frien'. Well, if I ain' glade. If I ain' glade!"

Trescott had taken the silent shape by the arm and led it forward into the full revelation of the light. "Well, now, Alek, you can take Henry and put him to bed, and in the morning I will—"

Near the end of this sentence old Williams had come front to front with Johnson. He gasped for a second, and then yelled the yell of a man stabbed in the heart.

For a fraction of a moment Trescott seemed to be looking for epithets. Then he roared: "You old black chump! You old black—Shut up! Shut up! Do you hear?"

Williams obeyed instantly in the matter of his screams, but he continued in a lowered voice: "Ma Lode amassy! Who'd ever think? Ma Lode amassy!"

Trescott spoke again in the manner of a commander of a battalion. "Alek!"

The old negro again surrendered, but to himself he repeated in a whisper, "Ma Lode!" He was aghast and trembling.

As these three points of widening shadows approached the golden doorway a hale old negress appeared there, bowing. "Good-evenin', docteh! Good-evenin'! Come in! come in!" She had evidently just retired from a tempestuous struggle to place the room in order, but she was now bowing rapidly. She made the effort of a person swimming.

"Don't trouble yourself, Mary," said Trescott, entering. "I've brought Henry for you to take care of, and all you've got to do is to carry out what I tell you." Learning that he was not followed, he faced the door, and said, "Come in, Henry."

Johnson entered. "Whee!" shrieked Mrs. Williams. She almost achieved a back somersault. Six young members of the tribe of Williams made a simultaneous plunge for a position behind the stove, and formed a wailing heap.

XIII

"You know very well that you and your family lived usually on less than three dollars a week, and now that Dr. Trescott pays you five dollars a week

166

for Johnson's board, you live like millionaires. You haven't done a stroke of work since Johnson began to board with you—everybody knows that—and so what are you kicking about?"

The judge sat in his chair on the porch, fondling his cane, and gazing down at old Williams, who stood under the lilac-bushes. "Yes, I know, jedge," said the negro, wagging his head in a puzzled manner. "Tain't like as if I didn't 'preciate what the docteh done, but—but—well, yeh see, jedge," he added, gaining a new impetus, "it's—it's hard wuk. This ol' man nev' did wuk so hard. Lode, no."

"Don't talk such nonsense, Alek," spoke the judge, sharply. "You have never really worked in your life—anyhow, enough to support a family of sparrows, and now when you are in a more prosperous condition than ever before, you come around talking like an old fool."

The negro began to scratch his head. "Yeh see, jedge," he said at last, "my ol' 'ooman she cain't 'ceive no lady callahs, nohow."

"Hang lady callers'" said the judge, irascibly. "If you have flour in the barrel and meat in the pot, your wife can get along without receiving lady callers, can't she?"

"But they won't come ainyhow, jedge," replied Williams, with an air of still deeper stupefaction. "Noner ma wife's frien's ner noner ma frien's 'll come near ma res'dence."

"Well, let them stay home if they are such silly people."

The old negro seemed to be seeking a way to elude this argument, but evidently finding none, he was about to shuffle meekly off. He halted, however. "Jedge," said he, "ma ol' 'ooman's near driv' abstracted."

"Your old woman is an idiot," responded the judge.

Williams came very close and peered solemnly through a branch of lilac. "Judge," he whispered, "the chillens."

"What about them?"

167

Dropping his voice to funereal depths, Williams said, "They—they cain't eat."

"Can't eat!" scoffed the judge, loudly. "Can't eat! You must think I am as big an old fool as you are. Can't eat—the little rascals! What's to prevent them from eating?"

In answer, Williams said, with mournful emphasis, "Hennery." Moved with a kind of satisfaction at his tragic use of the name, he remained staring at the judge for a sign of its effect.

The judge made a gesture of irritation. "Come, now, you old scoundrel, don't beat around the bush any more. What are you up to? What do you want? Speak out like a man, and don't give me any more of this tiresome rigamarole."

"I ain't er-beatin' round 'bout nuffin, jedge," replied Williams, indignantly. "No, seh; I say whatter got to say right out. 'Deed I do."

"Well, say it, then."

"Jedge," began the negro, taking off his hat and switching his knee with it, "Lode knows I'd do jes 'bout as much fer five dollehs er week as ainy cul'd man, but—but this yere business is awful, jedge. I raikon 'ain't been no sleep in—in my house sence docteh done fetch 'im."

"Well, what do you propose to do about it?"

Williams lifted his eyes from the ground and gazed off through the trees. "Raikon I got good appetite, an' sleep jes like er dog, but he—he's done broke me all up. 'Tain't no good, nohow. I wake up in the night; I hear 'im, mebbe, er-whimperin' an' er-whimperin', an' I sneak an' I sneak until I try th' do' to see if he locked in. An' he keep me er-puzzlin' an' er-quakin' all night long. Don't know how'll do in th' winter. Can't let 'im out where th' chillen is. He'll done freeze where he is now." Williams spoke these sentences as if he were talking to himself. After a silence of deep reflection he continued: "Folks go round sayin' he ain't Hennery Johnson at all. They say he's er devil!"

"What?" cried the judge.

"Yesseh," repeated Williams, in tones of injury, as if his veracity had been challenged. "Yesseh. I'm er-tellin' it to yeh straight, jedge. Plenty cul'd people folks up my way say it is a devil."

"Well, you don't think so yourself, do you?"

"No. 'Tain't no devil. It's Hennery Johnson."

"Well, then, what is the matter with you? You don't care what a lot of foolish people say. Go on 'tending to your business, and pay no attention to such idle nonsense."

"'Tis nonsense, jedge; but he looks like er devil."

"What do you care what he looks like?" demanded the judge.

"Ma rent is two dollehs and er half er month," said Williams, slowly.

"It might just as well be ten thousand dollars a month," responded the judge. "You never pay it, anyhow."

"Then, anoth' thing," continued Williams, in his reflective tone. "If he was all right in his haid I could stan' it; but, jedge, he's crazier 'n er loon. Then when he looks like er devil, an' done skears all ma frien's away, an' ma chillens cain't eat, an' ma ole 'ooman jes raisin' Cain all the time, an' ma rent two dollehs an' er half er month, an' him not right in his haid, it seems like five dollehs er week—"

The judge's stick came down sharply and suddenly upon the floor of the porch. "There," he said, "I thought that was what you were driving at."

Williams began swinging his head from side to side in the strange racial mannerism. "Now hol' on a minnet, jedge," he said, defensively. "'Tain't like as if I didn't 'preciate what the docteh done. 'Tain't that. Docteh Trescott is er kind man, an' 'tain't like as if I didn't 'preciate what he done; but—but—"

"But what? You are getting painful, Alek. Now tell me this: did you ever have five dollars a week regularly before in your life?"

Williams at once drew himself up with great dignity, but in the pause after that question he drooped gradually to another attitude. In the end he answered, heroically: "No, jedge, I 'ain't. An' 'tain't like as if I was er-sayin' five dollehs wasn't er lot er money for a man like me. But, jedge, what er man oughter git fer this kinder wuk is er salary. Yesseh, jedge," he repeated, with a great impressive gesture; "fer this kinder wuk er man oughter git er Salary." He laid a terrible emphasis upon the final word.

The judge laughed. "I know Dr. Trescott's mind concerning this affair, Alek; and if you are dissatisfied with your boarder, he is quite ready to move him to some other place; so, if you care to leave word with me that you are tired of the arrangement and wish it changed, he will come and take Johnson away."

Williams scratched his head again in deep perplexity. "Five dollehs is er big price fer bo'd, but 'tain't no big price fer the bo'd of er crazy man," he said, finally.

"What do you think you ought to get?" asked the judge.

"Well," answered Alek, in the manner of one deep in a balancing of the scales, "he looks like er devil, an' done skears e'rybody, an' ma chillens cain't eat, an' I cain't sleep, an' he ain't right in his haid, an'—"

"You told me all those things."

After scratching his wool, and beating his knee with his hat, and gazing off through the trees and down at the ground, Williams said, as he kicked nervously at the gravel, "Well, jedge, I think it is wuth—" He stuttered.

"Worth what?"

"Six dollehs," answered Williams, in a desperate outburst.

The judge lay back in his great arm-chair and went through all the motions of a man laughing heartily, but he made no sound save a slight cough. Williams had been watching him with apprehension.

"Well," said the judge, "do you call six dollars a salary?"

"No, seh," promptly responded Williams. "'Tain't a salary. No, 'deed!

'Tain't a salary." He looked with some anger upon the man who questioned his intelligence in this way.

"Well, supposing your children can't eat?"

"I—"

"And supposing he looks like a devil? And supposing all those things continue? Would you be satisfied with six dollars a week?"

Recollections seemed to throng in Williams's mind at these interrogations, and he answered dubiously. "Of co'se a man who ain't right in his haid, an' looks like er devil—But six dollehs—" After these two attempts at a sentence Williams suddenly appeared as an orator, with a great shiny palm waving in the air. "I tell yeh, jedge, six dollehs is six dollehs, but if I git six dollehs for bo'ding Hennery Johnson, I uhns it! I uhns it!"

"I don't doubt that you earn six dollars for every week's work you do," said the judge.

"Well, if I bo'd Hennery Johnson fer six dollehs er week, I uhns it! I uhns it!" cried Williams, wildly.

XIV

Reifsnyder's assistant had gone to his supper, and the owner of the shop was trying to placate four men who wished to be shaved at once. Reifsnyder was very garrulous—a fact which made him rather remarkable among barbers, who, as a class, are austerely speechless, having been taught silence by the hammering reiteration of a tradition. It is the customers who talk in the ordinary event.

As Reifsnyder waved his razor down the cheek of a man in the chair, he turned often to cool the impatience of the others with pleasant talk, which they did not particularly heed.

"Oh, he should have let him die," said Bainbridge, a railway engineer, finally replying to one of the barber's orations. "Shut up, Reif, and go on with your business!"

Instead, Reifsnyder paused shaving entirely, and turned to front the

171

speaker. "Let him die?" he demanded. "How vas that? How can you let a man die?"

"By letting him die, you chump," said the engineer. The others laughed a little, and Reifsnyder turned at once to his work, sullenly, as a man overwhelmed by the derision of numbers.

"How vas that?" he grumbled later. "How can you let a man die when he vas done so much for you?"

"'When he vas done so much for you?'" repeated Bainbridge. "You better shave some people. How vas that? Maybe this ain't a barber shop?"

A man hitherto silent now said, "If I had been the doctor, I would have done the same thing."

"Of course," said Reifsnyder. "Any man could do it. Any man that vas not like you, you—old—flint-hearted—fish." He had sought the final words with painful care, and he delivered the collection triumphantly at Bainbridge. The engineer laughed.

The man in the chair now lifted himself higher, while Reifsnyder began an elaborate ceremony of anointing and combing his hair. Now free to join comfortably in the talk, the man said: "They say he is the most terrible thing in the world. Young Johnnie Bernard—that drives the grocery wagon—saw him up at Alek Williams's shanty, and he says he couldn't eat anything for two days."

"Chee!" said Reifsnyder.

"Well, what makes him so terrible?" asked another.

"Because he hasn't got any face," replied the barber and the engineer in duct.

"Hasn't got any face!" repeated the man. "How can he do without any face?"

"He has no face in the front of his head.

In the place where his face ought to grow."

Bainbridge sang these lines pathetically as he arose and hung his hat on a hook. The man in the chair was about to abdicate in his favor. "Get a gait on you now," he said to Reifsnyder. "I go out at 7.31."

As the barber foamed the lather on the cheeks of the engineer he seemed to be thinking heavily. Then suddenly he burst out. "How would you like to be with no face?" he cried to the assemblage.

"Oh, if I had to have a face like yours—" answered one customer.

Bainbridge's voice came from a sea of lather. "You're kicking because if losing faces became popular, you'd have to go out of business."

"I don't think it will become so much popular," said Reifsnyder.

"Not if it's got to be taken off in the way his was taken off," said another man. "I'd rather keep mine, if you don't mind."

"I guess so!" cried the barber. "Just think!"

The shaving of Bainbridge had arrived at a time of comparative liberty for him. "I wonder what the doctor says to himself?" he observed. "He may be sorry he made him live."

"It was the only thing he could do," replied a man. The others seemed to agree with him.

"Supposing you were in his place," said one, "and Johnson had saved your kid. What would you do?"

"Certainly!"

"Of course! You would do anything on earth for him. You'd take all the trouble in the world for him. And spend your last dollar on him. Well, then?"

"I wonder how it feels to be without any face?" said Reifsnyder, musingly.

The man who had previously spoken, feeling that he had expressed himself well, repeated the whole thing. "You would do anything on earth for him. You'd take all the trouble in the world for him. And spend your last dollar on him. Well, then?"

"No, but look," said Reifsnyder; "supposing you don't got a face!"

<u>XV</u>

As soon as Williams was hidden from the view of the old judge he began to gesture and talk to himself. An elation had evidently penetrated to his vitals, and caused him to dilate as if he had been filled with gas. He snapped his fingers in the air, and whistled fragments of triumphal music. At times, in his progress towards his shanty, he indulged in a shuffling movement that was really a dance. It was to be learned from the intermediate monologue that he had emerged from his trials laurelled and proud. He was the unconquerable Alexander Williams. Nothing could exceed the bold self-reliance of his manner. His kingly stride, his heroic song, the derisive flourish of his hands— all betokened a man who had successfully defied the world.

On his way he saw Zeke Paterson coming to town. They hailed each other at a distance of fifty yards.

"How do, Broth' Paterson?"

"How do, Broth' Williams?"

They were both deacons.

"Is you' folks well, Broth' Paterson?"

"Middlin', middlin'. How's you' folks, Broth' Williams?"

Neither of them had slowed his pace in the smallest degree. They had simply begun this talk when a considerable space separated them, continued it as they passed, and added polite questions as they drifted steadily apart. Williams's mind seemed to be a balloon. He had been so inflated that he had not noticed that Paterson had definitely shied into the dry ditch as they came to the point of ordinary contact.

Afterwards, as he went a lonely way, he burst out again in song and pantomimic celebration of his estate. His feet moved in prancing steps.

When he came in sight of his cabin, the fields were bathed in a blue dusk, and the light in the window was pale. Cavorting and gesticulating, he gazed joyfully for some moments upon this light. Then suddenly another idea seemed to attack his mind, and he stopped, with an air of being suddenly dampened. In the end he approached his home as if it were the fortress of an enemy.

Some dogs disputed his advance for a loud moment, and then discovering their lord, slunk away embarrassed. His reproaches were addressed to them in muffled tones.

Arriving at the door, he pushed it open with the timidity of a new thief. He thrust his head cautiously sideways, and his eyes met the eyes of his wife, who sat by the table, the lamp-light defining a half of her face. "'Sh!" he said, uselessly. His glance travelled swiftly to the inner door which shielded the one bed-chamber. The pickaninnies, strewn upon the floor of the living-room, were softly snoring. After a hearty meal they had promptly dispersed themselves about the place and gone to sleep. "'Sh!" said Williams again to his motionless and silent wife. He had allowed only his head to appear. His wife, with one hand upon the edge of the table and the other at her knee, was regarding him with wide eyes and parted lips as if he were a spectre. She looked to be one who was living in terror, and even the familiar face at the door had thrilled her because it had come suddenly.

Williams broke the tense silence. "Is he all right?" he whispered, waving his eyes towards the inner door. Following his glance timorously, his wife nodded, and in a low tone answered:

"I raikon he's done gone t' sleep."

Williams then slunk noiselessly across his threshold.

He lifted a chair, and with infinite care placed it so that it faced the dreaded inner door. His wife moved slightly, so as to also squarely face it. A silence came upon them in which they seemed to be waiting for a calamity, pealing and deadly.

Williams finally coughed behind his hand. His wife started, and looked upon him in alarm. "Pears like he done gwine keep quiet ternight," he breathed. They continually pointed their speech and their looks at the inner door, paying it the homage due to a corpse or a phantom. Another long stillness followed this sentence. Their eyes shone white and wide. A wagon rattled down the distant road. From their chairs they looked at the window, and the effect of the light in the cabin was a presentation of an intensely black and solemn night. The old woman adopted the attitude used always in church at funerals. At times she seemed to be upon the point of breaking out in prayer.

"He mighty quiet ter-night," whispered Williams. "Was he good ter-day?" For answer his wife raised her eyes to the ceiling in the supplication of Job. Williams moved restlessly. Finally he tiptoed to the door. He knelt slowly and without a sound, and placed his ear near the key-hole. Hearing a noise behind him, he turned quickly. His wife was staring at him aghast. She stood in front of the stove, and her arms were spread out in the natural movement to protect all her sleeping ducklings.

But Williams arose without having touched the door. "I raikon he er-sleep," he said, fingering his wool. He debated with himself for some time. During this interval his wife remained, a great fat statue of a mother shielding her children.

It was plain that his mind was swept suddenly by a wave of temerity. With a sounding step he moved towards the door. His fingers were almost upon the knob when he swiftly ducked and dodged away, clapping his hands to the back of his head. It was as if the portal had threatened him. There was a little tumult near the stove, where Mrs. Williams's desperate retreat had involved her feet with the prostrate children.

After the panic Williams bore traces of a feeling of shame. He returned to the charge. He firmly grasped the knob with his left hand, and with his other hand turned the key in the lock. He pushed the door, and as it swung portentously open he sprang nimbly to one side like the fearful slave liberating the lion. Near the stove a group had formed, the terror stricken mother, with her arms stretched, and the aroused children clinging frenziedly to her skirts.

The light streamed after the swinging door, and disclosed a room six feet one way and six feet the other way. It was small enough to enable the radiance to lay it plain. Williams peered warily around the corner made by the door-post.

Suddenly he advanced, retired, and advanced again with a howl. His palsied family had expected him to spring backward, and at his howl they heaped themselves wondrously. But Williams simply stood in the little room emitting his howls before an open window. "He's gone! He's gone! He's gone!" His eye and his hand had speedily proved the fact. He had even thrown open a little cupboard.

Presently he came flying out. He grabbed his hat, and hurled the outer door back upon its hinges. Then he tumbled headlong into the night. He was yelling: "Docteh Trescott! Docteh Trescott!" He ran wildly through the fields, and galloped in the direction of town. He continued to call to Trescott, as if the latter was within easy hearing. It was as if Trescott was poised in the contemplative sky over the running negro, and could heed this reaching voice—"Docteh Trescott!"

In the cabin, Mrs. Williams, supported by relays from the battalion of children, stood quaking watch until the truth of daylight came as a reinforcement and made the arrogant, strutting, swashbuckler children, and a mother who proclaimed her illimitable courage.

XVI

Theresa Page was giving a party. It was the outcome of a long series of arguments addressed to her mother, which had been overheard in part by her father. He had at last said five words, "Oh, let her have it." The mother had then gladly capitulated.

Theresa had written nineteen invitations, and distributed them at recess to her schoolmates. Later her mother had composed five large cakes, and still later a vast amount of lemonade.

So the nine little girls and the ten little boys sat quite primly in the dining-room, while Theresa and her mother plied them with cake and lemonade, and also with ice-cream. This primness sat now quite strangely upon them. It was owing to the presence of Mrs. Page. Previously in the parlor alone with their games they had overturned a chair; the boys had let more or less of their hoodlum spirit shine forth. But when circumstances could be possibly magnified to warrant it, the girls made the boys victims of an insufferable pride, snubbing them mercilessly. So in the dining-room they resembled a class at Sunday-school, if it were not for the subterranean smiles, gestures, rebuffs, and poutings which stamped the affair as a children's party.

Two little girls of this subdued gathering were planted in a settle with their backs to the broad window. They were beaming lovingly upon each other with an effect of scorning the boys.

Hearing a noise behind her at the window, one little girl turned to face it. Instantly she screamed and sprang away, covering her face with her hands. "What was it? What was it?" cried every one in a roar. Some slight movement of the eyes of the weeping and shuddering child informed the company that she had been frightened by an appearance at the window. At once they all faced the imperturbable window, and for a moment there was a silence. An astute lad made an immediate census of the other lads. The prank of slipping out and looming spectrally at a window was too venerable. But the little boys were all present and astonished.

As they recovered their minds they uttered warlike cries, and through a side door sallied rapidly out against the terror. They vied with each other in daring.

None wished particularly to encounter a dragon in the darkness of the garden, but there could be no faltering when the fair ones in the dining-room were present. Calling to each other in stern voices, they went dragooning over the lawn, attacking the shadows with ferocity, but still with the caution of reasonable beings. They found, however, nothing new to the peace of the night. Of course there was a lad who told a great lie. He described a grim figure, bending low and slinking off along the fence. He gave a number of details, rendering his lie more splendid by a repetition of certain forms which he recalled from romances. For instance, he insisted that he had heard the creature emit a hollow laugh.

Inside the house the little girl who had raised the alarm was still shuddering and weeping. With the utmost difficulty was she brought to a state approximating calmness by Mrs. Page. Then she wanted to go home at once.

Page entered the house at this time. He had exiled himself until he concluded that this children's party was finished and gone. He was obliged to escort the little girl home because she screamed again when they opened the door and she saw the night.

She was not coherent even to her mother. Was it a man? She didn't know. It was simply a thing, a dreadful thing.

XVII

In Watermelon Alley the Farraguts were spending their evening as usual on the little rickety porch. Sometimes they howled gossip to other people on other rickety porches. The thin wail of a baby arose from a near house. A man had a terrific altercation with his wife, to which the alley paid no attention at all.

There appeared suddenly before the Farraguts a monster making a low and sweeping bow. There was an instant's pause, and then occurred something that resembled the effect of an upheaval of the earth's surface. The old woman hurled herself backward with a dreadful cry. Young Sim had been perched gracefully on a railing. At sight of the monster he simply fell over it to the ground. He made no sound, his eyes stuck out, his nerveless hands tried to grapple the rail to prevent a tumble, and then he vanished. Bella, blubbering, and with her hair suddenly and mysteriously dishevelled, was crawling on her hands and knees fearsomely up the steps.

Standing before this wreck of a family gathering, the monster continued to bow. It even raised a deprecatory claw. "Doh' make no botheration 'bout me, Miss Fa'gut," it said, politely. "No, 'deed. I jes drap in ter ax if yer well this evenin', Miss Fa'gut. Don' make no botheration. No, 'deed. I gwine ax you to go to er daince with me, Miss Fa'gut. I ax you if I can have the magnifercent gratitude of you' company on that 'casion, Miss Fa'gut."

The girl cast a miserable glance behind her. She was still crawling away. On the ground beside the porch young Sim raised a strange bleat, which expressed both his fright and his lack of wind. Presently the monster, with a fashionable amble, ascended the steps after the girl.

She grovelled in a corner of the room as the creature took a chair. It seated itself very elegantly on the edge. It held an old cap in both hands. "Don' make no botheration, Miss Fa'gut. Don' make no botherations. No, 'deed. I jes drap in ter ax you if you won' do me the proud of acceptin' ma humble invitation to er daince, Miss Fa'gut."

She shielded her eyes with her arms and tried to crawl past it, but the genial monster blocked the way. "I jes drap in ter ax you 'bout er daince, Miss Fa'gut. I ax you if I kin have the magnifercent gratitude of you' company on that 'casion, Miss Fa'gut."

In a last outbreak of despair, the girl, shuddering and wailing, threw herself face downward on the floor, while the monster sat on the edge of the chair gabbling courteous invitations, and holding the old hat daintily to his stomach.

At the back of the house, Mrs. Farragut, who was of enormous weight, and who for eight years had done little more than sit in an armchair and describe her various ailments, had with speed and agility scaled a high board fence.

XVIII

The black mass in the middle of Trescott's property was hardly allowed to cool before the builders were at work on another house. It had sprung upward at a fabulous rate. It was like a magical composition born of the ashes. The doctor's office was the first part to be completed, and he had already moved in his new books and instruments and medicines.

Trescott sat before his desk when the chief of police arrived. "Well, we found him," said the latter.

"Did you?" cried the doctor. "Where?"

"Shambling around the streets at daylight this morning. I'll be blamed if I can figure on where he passed the night."

180

"Where is he now?"

"Oh, we jugged him. I didn't know what else to do with him. That's what I want you to tell me. Of course we can't keep him. No charge could be made, you know."

"I'll come down and get him."

The official grinned retrospectively. "Must say he had a fine career while he was out. First thing he did was to break up a children's party at Page's. Then he went to Watermelon Alley. Whoo! He stampeded the whole outfit. Men, women, and children running pell-mell, and yelling. They say one old woman broke her leg, or something, shinning over a fence. Then he went right out on the main street, and an Irish girl threw a fit, and there was a sort of a riot. He began to run, and a big crowd chased him, firing rocks. But he gave them the slip somehow down there by the foundry and in the railroad yard. We looked for him all night, but couldn't find him."

"Was he hurt any? Did anybody hit him with a stone?"

"Guess there isn't much of him to hurt any more, is there? Guess he's been hurt up to the limit. No. They never touched him. Of course nobody really wanted to hit him, but you know how a crowd gets. It's like—it's like—"

"Yes, I know."

For a moment the chief of the police looked reflectively at the floor. Then he spoke hesitatingly. "You know Jake Winter's little girl was the one that he scared at the party. She is pretty sick, they say."

"Is she? Why, they didn't call me. I always attend the Winter family."

"No? Didn't they?" asked the chief, slowly. "Well—you know—Winter is—well, Winter has gone clean crazy over this business. He wanted—he wanted to have you arrested."

"Have me arrested? The idiot! What in the name of wonder could he have me arrested for?"

"Of course. He is a fool. I told him to keep his trap shut. But then you know how he'll go all over town yapping about the thing. I thought I'd better tip you."

"Oh, he is of no consequence; but then, of course, I'm obliged to you, Sam."

"That's all right. Well, you'll be down tonight and take him out, eh? You'll get a good welcome from the jailer. He don't like his job for a cent. He says you can have your man whenever you want him. He's got no use for him."

"But what is this business of Winter's about having me arrested?"

"Oh, it's a lot of chin about your having no right to allow this—this—this man to be at large. But I told him to tend to his own business. Only I thought I'd better let you know. And I might as well say right now, doctor, that there is a good deal of talk about this thing. If I were you, I'd come to the jail pretty late at night, because there is likely to be a crowd around the door, and I'd bring a—er—mask, or some kind of a veil, anyhow."

XIX

Martha Goodwin was single, and well along into the thin years. She lived with her married sister in Whilomville. She performed nearly all the house-work in exchange for the privilege of existence. Every one tacitly recognized her labor as a form of penance for the early end of her betrothed, who had died of small-pox, which he had not caught from her.

But despite the strenuous and unceasing workaday of her life, she was a woman of great mind. She had adamantine opinions upon the situation in Armenia, the condition of women in China, the flirtation between Mrs. Minster of Niagara Avenue and young Griscom, the conflict in the Bible class of the Baptist Sunday-school, the duty of the United States towards the Cuban insurgents, and many other colossal matters. Her fullest experience of violence was gained on an occasion when she had seen a hound clubbed, but in the plan which she had made for the reform of the world she advocated drastic measures. For instance, she contended that all the Turks should be pushed into the sea and drowned, and that Mrs. Minster and young Griscom should be hanged side by side on twin gallows. In fact, this woman of peace, who had seen only peace, argued constantly for a creed of illimitable ferocity. She was invulnerable on these questions, because eventually she overrode all opponents with a sniff. This sniff was an active force. It was to her antagonists like a bang over the head, and none was known to recover from this expression of exalted contempt. It left them windless and conquered. They never again came forward as candidates for suppression. And Martha walked her kitchen with a stern brow, an invincible being like Napoleon.

Nevertheless her acquaintances, from the pain of their defeats, had been long in secret revolt. It was in no wise a conspiracy, because they did not care to state their open rebellion, but nevertheless it was understood that any woman who could not coincide with one of Martha's contentions was entitled to the support of others in the small circle. It amounted to an arrangement by which all were required to disbelieve any theory for which Martha fought. This, however, did not prevent them from speaking of her mind with profound respect.

Two people bore the brunt of her ability. Her sister Kate was visibly afraid of her, while Carrie Dungen sailed across from her kitchen to sit respectfully at Martha's feet and learn the business of the world. To be sure, afterwards, under another sun, she always laughed at Martha and pretended to deride her ideas, but in the presence of the sovereign she always remained silent or admiring. Kate, the sister, was of no consequence at all. Her principal delusion was that she did all the work in the up-stairs rooms of the house, while Martha did it down-stairs. The truth was seen only by the husband, who treated Martha with a kindness that was half banter, half deference. Martha herself had no suspicion that she was the only pillar of the domestic edifice. The situation was without definitions. Martha made definitions, but she devoted them entirely to the Armenians and Griscom and the Chinese and other subjects. Her dreams, which in early days had been of love of meadows and the shade of trees, of the face of a man, were now involved otherwise, and they were companioned in the kitchen curiously, Cuba, the hot-water kettle, Armenia, the washing of the dishes, and the whole thing being jumbled. In regard to social misdemeanors, she who was simply the mausoleum of a dead passion was probably the most savage critic in town. This unknown woman, hidden in a kitchen as in a well, was sure to have a considerable effect of the one kind or the other in the life of the town. Every time it moved a yard, she had personally contributed an inch. She could hammer so stoutly upon the door of a proposition that it would break from its hinges and fall upon her, but at any rate it moved. She was an engine, and the fact that she did not know that she was an engine contributed largely to the effect. One reason that she was formidable was that she did not even imagine that she was formidable. She remained a weak, innocent, and pig-headed creature, who alone would defy the universe if she thought the universe merited this proceeding.

One day Carrie Dungen came across from her kitchen with speed. She had a great deal of grist. "Oh," she cried, "Henry Johnson got away from where they was keeping him, and came to town last night, and scared everybody almost to death."

Martha was shining a dish-pan, polishing madly. No reasonable person could see cause for this operation, because the pan already glistened like silver. "Well!" she ejaculated. She imparted to the word a deep meaning. "This, my prophecy, has come to pass." It was a habit.

The overplus of information was choking Carrie. Before she could go on she was obliged to struggle for a moment. "And, oh, little Sadie Winter is awful sick, and they say Jake Winter was around this morning trying to get Doctor Trescott arrested. And poor old Mrs. Farragut sprained her ankle in trying to climb a fence. And there's a crowd around the jail all the time. They put Henry in jail because they didn't know what else to do with him, I guess. They say he is perfectly terrible."

Martha finally released the dish-pan and confronted the headlong speaker. "Well!" she said again, poising a great brown rag. Kate had heard the excited new-comer, and drifted down from the novel in her room. She was a shivery little woman. Her shoulder-blades seemed to be two panes of ice, for she was constantly shrugging and shrugging. "Serves him right if he was to lose all his patients," she said suddenly, in blood-thirsty tones. She snipped her words out as if her lips were scissors.

"Well, he's likely to," shouted Carrie Dungen. "Don't a lot of people say that they won't have him any more? If you're sick and nervous, Doctor Trescott would scare the life out of you, wouldn't he? He would me. I'd keep thinking."

Martha, stalking to and fro, sometimes surveyed the two other women with a contemplative frown.

XX

After the return from Connecticut, little Jimmie was at first much afraid of the monster who lived in the room over the carriage-house. He could not identify it in any way. Gradually, however, his fear dwindled under the influence of a weird fascination. He sidled into closer and closer relations with it.

One time the monster was seated on a box behind the stable basking in the rays of the afternoon sun. A heavy crepe veil was swathed about its head.

Little Jimmie and many companions came around the corner of the stable. They were all in what was popularly known as the baby class, and consequently escaped from school a half-hour before the other children. They halted abruptly at sight of the figure on the box. Jimmie waved his hand with the air of a proprietor.

"There he is," he said.

"O-o-o!" murmured all the little boys—"o-o-o!" They shrank back, and grouped according to courage or experience, as at the sound the monster slowly turned its head. Jimmie had remained in the van alone. "Don't be afraid! I won't let him hurt you," he said, delighted.

"Huh!" they replied, contemptuously. "We ain't afraid."

Jimmie seemed to reap all the joys of the owner and exhibitor of one of the world's marvels, while his audience remained at a distance—awed and entranced, fearful and envious.

One of them addressed Jimmie gloomily. "Bet you dassent walk right up to him." He was an older boy than Jimmie, and habitually oppressed him to a small degree. This new social elevation of the smaller lad probably seemed revolutionary to him.

"Huh!" said Jimmie, with deep scorn. "Dassent I? Dassent I, hey? Dassent I?"

The group was immensely excited. It turned its eyes upon the boy that Jimmie addressed. "No, you dassent," he said, stolidly, facing a moral defeat. He could see that Jimmie was resolved. "No, you dassent," he repeated, doggedly.

"Ho?" cried Jimmie. "You just watch!—you just watch!"

Amid a silence he turned and marched towards the monster. But possibly the palpable wariness of his companions had an effect upon him that weighed more than his previous experience, for suddenly, when near to the monster, he halted dubiously. But his playmates immediately uttered a derisive shout, and it seemed to force him forward. He went to the monster and laid his hand delicately on its shoulder. "Hello, Henry," he said, in a voice that trembled a trifle. The monster was crooning a weird line of negro melody that was scarcely more than a thread of sound, and it paid no heed to the boy.

Jimmie: strutted back to his companions. They acclaimed him and hooted his opponent. Amid this clamor the larger boy with difficulty preserved a dignified attitude.

"I dassent, dassent I?" said Jimmie to him.

"Now, you're so smart, let's see you do it!"

This challenge brought forth renewed taunts from the others. The larger boy puffed out his checks. "Well, I ain't afraid," he explained, sullenly. He had made a mistake in diplomacy, and now his small enemies were tumbling his prestige all about his ears. They crowed like roosters and bleated like lambs, and made many other noises which were supposed to bury him in ridicule and dishonor. "Well, I ain't afraid," he continued to explain through the din.

Jimmie, the hero of the mob, was pitiless. "You ain't afraid, hey?" he sneered. "If you ain't afraid, go do it, then."

"Well, I would if I wanted to," the other retorted. His eyes wore an expression of profound misery, but he preserved steadily other portions of a pot-valiant air. He suddenly faced one of his persecutors. "If you're so smart, why don't you go do it?" This persecutor sank promptly through the group to the rear. The incident gave the badgered one a breathing-spell, and for a moment even turned the derision in another direction. He took advantage of his interval. "I'll do it if anybody else will," he announced, swaggering to and fro.

Candidates for the adventure did not come forward. To defend themselves from this counter-charge, the other boys again set up their crowing and bleating. For a while they would hear nothing from him. Each time he opened his lips their chorus of noises made oratory impossible. But at last he was able to repeat that he would volunteer to dare as much in the affair as any other boy.

"Well, you go first," they shouted.

But Jimmie intervened to once more lead the populace against the large boy. "You're mighty brave, ain't you?" he said to him. "You dared me to do it, and I did—didn't I? Now who's afraid?" The others cheered this view loudly, and they instantly resumed the baiting of the large boy.

He shamefacedly scratched his left shin with his right foot. "Well, I ain't afraid." He cast an eye at the monster. "Well, I ain't afraid." With a glare of hatred at his squalling tormentors, he finally announced a grim intention. "Well, I'll do it, then, since you're so fresh. Now!"

The mob subsided as with a formidable countenance he turned towards the impassive figure on the box. The advance was also a regular progression from high daring to craven hesitation. At last, when some yards from the monster, the lad came to a full halt, as if he had encountered a stone wall. The observant little boys in the distance promptly hooted. Stung again by these cries, the lad sneaked two yards forward. He was crouched like a young cat ready for a backward spring. The crowd at the rear, beginning to respect this display, uttered some encouraging cries. Suddenly the lad gathered himself together, made a white and desperate rush forward, touched the monster's shoulder with a far-outstretched finger, and sped away, while his laughter rang out wild, shrill, and exultant.

The crowd of boys reverenced him at once, and began to throng into his camp, and look at him, and be his admirers. Jimmie was discomfited for a moment, but he and the larger boy, without agreement or word of any kind, seemed to recognize a truce, and they swiftly combined and began to parade before the others.

"Why, it's just as easy as nothing," puffed the larger boy. "Ain't it, Jim?"

"Course," blew Jimmie. "Why, it's as e-e-easy."

They were people of another class. If they had been decorated for courage on twelve battle-fields, they could not have made the other boys more ashamed of the situation.

Meanwhile they condescended to explain the emotions of the excursion, expressing unqualified contempt for any one who could hang back. "Why, it ain't nothin'. He won't do nothin' to you," they told the others, in tones of exasperation.

One of the very smallest boys in the party showed signs of a wistful desire to distinguish himself, and they turned their attention to him, pushing at his shoulders while he swung away from them, and hesitated dreamily. He was eventually induced to make furtive expedition, but it was only for a few yards. Then he paused, motionless, gazing with open mouth. The vociferous entreaties of Jimmie and the large boy had no power over him.

Mrs. Hannigan had come out on her back porch with a pail of water. From this coign she had a view of the secluded portion of the Trescott grounds that was behind the stable. She perceived the group of boys, and the monster on the box. She shaded her eyes with her hand to benefit her vision. She screeched then as if she was being murdered. "Eddie! Eddie! You come home this minute!"

Her son querulously demanded, "Aw, what for?"

"You come home this minute. Do you hear?"

The other boys seemed to think this visitation upon one of their number required them to preserve for a time the hang-dog air of a collection of culprits, and they remained in guilty silence until the little Hannigan, wrathfully protesting, was pushed through the door of his home. Mrs. Hannigan cast a piercing glance over the group, stared with a bitter face at the Trescott house, as if this new and handsome edifice was insulting her, and then followed her son.

There was wavering in the party. An inroad by one mother always caused them to carefully sweep the horizon to see if there were more coming. "This is my yard," said Jimmie, proudly. "We don't have to go home."

The monster on the box had turned its black crepe countenance towards the sky, and was waving its arms in time to a religious chant. "Look at him now," cried a little boy. They turned, and were transfixed by the solemnity and mystery of the indefinable gestures. The wail of the melody was mournful and slow. They drew back. It seemed to spellbind them with the power of a funeral. They were so absorbed that they did not hear the doctor's buggy drive up to the stable. Trescott got out, tied his horse, and approached the group. Jimmie saw him first, and at his look of dismay the others wheeled.

"What's all this, Jimmie?" asked Trescott, in surprise.

The lad advanced to the front of his companions, halted, and said nothing. Trescott's face gloomed slightly as he scanned the scene.

"What were you doing, Jimmie?"

"We was playin'," answered Jimmie, huskily.

"Playing at what?"

"Just playin'."

Trescott looked gravely at the other boys, and asked them to please go home. They proceeded to the street much in the manner of frustrated and revealed assassins. The crime of trespass on another boy's place was still a crime when they had only accepted the other boy's cordial invitation, and they were used to being sent out of all manner of gardens upon the sudden appearance

189

of a father or a mother. Jimmie had wretchedly watched the departure of his companions. It involved the loss of his position as a lad who controlled the privileges of his father's grounds, but then he knew that in the beginning he had no right to ask so many boys to be his guests.

Once on the sidewalk, however, they speedily forgot their shame as trespassers, and the large boy launched forth in a description of his success in the late trial of courage. As they went rapidly up the street, the little boy who had made the furtive expedition cried out confidently from the rear, "Yes, and I went almost up to him, didn't I, Willie?"

The large boy crushed him in a few words. "Huh!" he scoffed. "You only went a little way. I went clear up to him."

The pace of the other boys was so manly that the tiny thing had to trot, and he remained at the rear, getting entangled in their legs in his attempts to reach the front rank and become of some importance, dodging this way and that way, and always piping out his little claim to glory.

XXI

"By-the-way, Grace," said Trescott, looking into the dining-room from his office door, "I wish you would send Jimmie to me before school-time."

When Jimmie came, he advanced so quietly that Trescott did not at first note him. "Oh," he said, wheeling from a cabinet, "here you are, young man."

"Yes, sir."

Trescott dropped into his chair and tapped the desk with a thoughtful finger. "Jimmie, what were you doing in the back garden yesterday—you and the other boys—to Henry?"

"We weren't doing anything, pa."

Trescott looked sternly into the raised eyes of his son. "Are you sure you were not annoying him in any way? Now what were you doing, exactly?"

"Why, we—why, we—now—Willie Dalzel said I dassent go right up to him, and I did; and then he did; and then—the other boys were 'fraid; and

190

then—you comed."

Trescott groaned deeply. His countenance was so clouded in sorrow that the lad, bewildered by the mystery of it, burst suddenly forth in dismal lamentations. "There, there. Don't cry, Jim," said Trescott, going round the desk. "Only—" He sat in a great leather reading-chair, and took the boy on his knee. "Only I want to explain to you—"

After Jimmie had gone to school, and as Trescott was about to start on his round of morning calls, a message arrived from Doctor Moser. It set forth that the latter's sister was dying in the old homestead, twenty miles away up the valley, and asked Trescott to care for his patients for the day at least. There was also in the envelope a little history of each case and of what had already been done. Trescott replied to the messenger that he would gladly assent to the arrangement.

He noted that the first name on Moser's list was Winter, but this did not seem to strike him as an important fact. When its turn came, he rang the Winter bell. "Good-morning, Mrs. Winter," he said, cheerfully, as the door was opened. "Doctor Moser has been obliged to leave town to-day, and he has asked me to come in his stead. How is the little girl this morning?"

Mrs. Winter had regarded him in stony surprise. At last she said: "Come in! I'll see my husband." She bolted into the house. Trescott entered the hall, and turned to the left into the sitting-room.

Presently Winter shuffled through the door. His eyes flashed towards Trescott. He did not betray any desire to advance far into the room. "What do you want?" he said.

"What do I want? What do I want?" repeated Trescott, lifting his head suddenly. He had heard an utterly new challenge in the night of the jungle.

"Yes, that's what I want to know," snapped Winter. "What do you want?"

Trescott was silent for a moment. He consulted Moser's memoranda. "I see that your little girl's case is a trifle serious," he remarked. "I would advise you to call a physician soon. I will leave you a copy of Dr. Moser's record to give to any one you may call." He paused to transcribe the record on a page of his note-book. Tearing out the leaf, he extended it to Winter as he moved towards the door. The latter shrunk against the wall. His head was hanging as he reached for the paper. This caused him to grasp air, and so Trescott simply let the paper flutter to the feet of the other man.

"Good-morning," said Trescott from the hall. This placid retreat seemed to suddenly arouse Winter to ferocity. It was as if he had then recalled all the truths which he had formulated to hurl at Trescott. So he followed him into the hall, and down the hall to the door, and through the door to the porch, barking in fiery rage from a respectful distance. As Trescott imperturbably turned the mare's head down the road, Winter stood on the porch, still yelping. He was like a little dog.

XXII

"Have you heard the news?" cried Carrie Dungen as she sped towards Martha's kitchen. "Have you heard the news?" Her eyes were shining with delight.

"No," answered Martha's sister Kate, bending forward eagerly. "What was it? What was it?"

Carrie appeared triumphantly in the open door. "Oh, there's been an awful scene between Doctor Trescott and Jake Winter. I never thought that Jake Winter had any pluck at all, but this morning he told the doctor just what he thought of him."

"Well, what did he think of him?" asked Martha.

"Oh, he called him everything. Mrs. Howarth heard it through her front blinds. It was terrible, she says. It's all over town now. Everybody knows it."

"Didn't the doctor answer back?"

"No! Mrs. Howarth—she says he never said a word. He just walked down to his buggy and got in, and drove off as co-o-o-l. But Jake gave him jinks, by all accounts."

"But what did he say?" cried Kate, shrill and excited. She was evidently at some kind of a feast.

"Oh, he told him that Sadie had never been well since that night Henry Johnson frightened her at Theresa Page's party, and he held him responsible, and how dared he cross his threshold—and—and—and—"

"And what?" said Martha.

"Did he swear at him?" said Kate, in fearsome glee.

"No—not much. He did swear at him a little, but not more than a man does anyhow when he is real mad, Mrs. Howarth says."

"O-oh!" breathed Kate. "And did he call him any names?"

Martha, at her work, had been for a time in deep thought. She now interrupted the others. "It don't seem as if Sadie Winter had been sick since that time Henry Johnson got loose. She's been to school almost the whole time since then, hasn't she?"

They combined upon her in immediate indignation. "School? School? I should say not. Don't think for a moment. School!"

Martha wheeled from the sink. She held an iron spoon, and it seemed as if she was going to attack them. "Sadie Winter has passed here many a morning since then carrying her schoolbag. Where was she going? To a wedding?"

The others, long accustomed to a mental tyranny, speedily surrendered.

"Did she?" stammered Kate. "I never saw her."

Carrie Dungen made a weak gesture.

"If I had been Doctor Trescott," exclaimed Martha, loudly, "I'd have knocked that miserable Jake Winter's head off."

Kate and Carrie, exchanging glances, made an alliance in the air. "I don't see why you say that, Martha," replied Carrie, with considerable boldness, gaining support and sympathy from Kate's smile. "I don't see how anybody can be blamed for getting angry when their little girl gets almost scared to death and gets sick from it, and all that. Besides, everybody says—"

"Oh, I don't care what everybody says," said Martha.

"Well, you can't go against the whole town," answered Carrie, in sudden sharp defiance.

"No, Martha, you can't go against the whole town," piped Kate, following her leader rapidly.

"'The whole town,'" cried Martha. "I'd like to know what you call 'the whole town.' Do you call these silly people who are scared of Henry Johnson 'the whole town'?"

"Why, Martha," said Carrie, in a reasoning tone, "you talk as if you wouldn't be scared of him!"

"No more would I," retorted Martha.

"O-oh, Martha, how you talk!" said Kate. "Why, the idea! Everybody's afraid of him."

Carrie was grinning. "You've never seen him, have you?" she asked, seductively.

"No," admitted Martha.

"Well, then, how do you know that you wouldn't be scared?"

Martha confronted her. "Have you ever seen him? No? Well, then, how do you know you would be scared?"

The allied forces broke out in chorus: "But, Martha, everybody says so. Everybody says so."

"Everybody says what?"

"Everybody that's seen him say they were frightened almost to death. Tisn't only women, but it's men too. It's awful."

Martha wagged her head solemnly. "I'd try not to be afraid of him."

"But supposing you could not help it?" said Kate.

"Yes, and look here," cried Carrie. "I'll tell you another thing. The Hannigans are going to move out of the house next door."

"On account of him?" demanded Martha.

Carrie nodded. "Mrs. Hannigan says so herself."

"Well, of all things!" ejaculated Martha. "Going to move, eh? You don't say so! Where they going to move to?"

"Down on Orchard Avenue."

"Well, of all things! Nice house?"

"I don't know about that. I haven't heard. But there's lots of nice houses on Orchard."

"Yes, but they're all taken," said Kate. "There isn't a vacant house on Orchard Avenue."

"Oh yes, there is," said Martha. "The old Hampstead house is vacant."

"Oh, of course," said Kate. "But then I don't believe Mrs. Hannigan would like it there. I wonder where they can be going to move to?"

"I'm sure I don't know," sighed Martha. "It must be to some place we don't know about."

"Well." said Carrie Dungen, after a general reflective silence, "it's easy enough to find out, anyhow."

"Who knows—around here?" asked Kate.

"Why, Mrs. Smith, and there she is in her garden," said Carrie, jumping to her feet. As she dashed out of the door, Kate and Martha crowded at the window. Carrie's voice rang out from near the steps. "Mrs. Smith! Mrs. Smith! Do you know where the Hannigans are going to move to?"

XXIII

The autumn smote the leaves, and the trees of Whilomville were panoplied in crimson and yellow. The winds grew stronger, and in the melancholy purple of the nights the home shine of a window became a finer thing. The little boys, watching the sear and sorrowful leaves drifting down from the maples, dreamed of the near time when they could heap bushels in the streets and burn them during the abrupt evenings.

Three men walked down the Niagara Avenue. As they approached Judge Hagenthorpe's house he came down his walk to meet them in the manner of one who has been waiting.

"Are you ready, judge?" one said.

"All ready," he answered.

The four then walked to Trescott's house. He received them in his office, where he had been reading. He seemed surprised at this visit of four very active and influential citizens, but he had nothing to say of it.

After they were all seated, Trescott looked expectantly from one face to another. There was a little silence. It was broken by John Twelve, the wholesale grocer, who was worth $400,000, and reported to be worth over a million.

"Well, doctor," he said, with a short laugh, "I suppose we might as well admit at once that we've come to interfere in something which is none of our business."

"Why, what is it?" asked Trescott, again looking from one face to another. He seemed to appeal particularly to Judge Hagenthorpe, but the old man had his chin lowered musingly to his cane, and would not look at him.

"It's about what nobody talks of—much," said Twelve. "It's about Henry Johnson."

Trescott squared himself in his chair. "Yes?" he said.

Having delivered himself of the title, Twelve seemed to become more easy. "Yes," he answered, blandly, "we wanted to talk to you about it."

"Yes?" said Trescott.

Twelve abruptly advanced on the main attack. "Now see here, Trescott, we like you, and we have come to talk right out about this business. It may be none of our affairs and all that, and as for me, I don't mind if you tell me so; but I am not going to keep quiet and see you ruin yourself. And that's how we all feel."

"I am not ruining myself," answered Trescott.

"No, maybe you are not exactly ruining yourself," said Twelve, slowly, "but you are doing yourself a great deal of harm. You have changed from being the leading doctor in town to about the last one. It is mainly because there are always a large number of people who are very thoughtless fools, of course, but then that doesn't change the condition."

A man who had not heretofore spoken said, solemnly, "It's the women."

"Well, what I want to say is this," resumed Twelve: "Even if there are a lot of fools in the world, we can't see any reason why you should ruin yourself by opposing them. You can't teach them anything, you know."

"I am not trying to teach them anything." Trescott smiled wearily. "I— It is a matter of—well—"

"And there are a good many of us that admire you for it immensely," interrupted Twelve; "but that isn't going to change the minds of all those ninnies."

"It's the women," stated the advocate of this view again.

"Well, what I want to say is this," said Twelve. "We want you to get out of this trouble and strike your old gait again. You are simply killing your practice through your infernal pigheadedness. Now this thing is out of the ordinary, but there must be ways to—to beat the game somehow, you see. So we've talked it over—about a dozen of us—and, as I say, if you want to tell us to mind our own business, why, go ahead; but we've talked it over, and we've come to the conclusion that the only way to do is to get Johnson a place somewhere off up the valley, and—"

Trescott wearily gestured. "You don't know, my friend. Everybody is so afraid of him, they can't even give him good care. Nobody can attend to him as I do myself."

197

"But I have a little no-good farm up beyond Clarence Mountain that I was going to give to Henry," cried Twelve, aggrieved. "And if you—and if you—if you—through your house burning down, or anything—why, all the boys were prepared to take him right off your hands, and—and—"

Trescott arose and went to the window. He turned his back upon them. They sat waiting in silence. When he returned he kept his face in the shadow. "No, John Twelve," he said, "it can't be done."

There was another stillness. Suddenly a man stirred on his chair.

"Well, then, a public institution—" he began.

"No," said Trescott; "public institutions are all very good, but he is not going to one."

In the background of the group old Judge Hagenthorpe was thoughtfully smoothing the polished ivory head of his cane.

XXIV

Trescott loudly stamped the snow from his feet and shook the flakes from his shoulders. When he entered the house he went at once to the dining-room, and then to the sitting-room. Jimmie was there, reading painfully in a large book concerning giraffes and tigers and crocodiles.

"Where is your mother, Jimmie?" asked Trescott.

"I don't know, pa," answered the boy. "I think she is up-stairs."

Trescott went to the foot of the stairs and called, but there came no answer. Seeing that the door of the little drawing-room was open, he entered. The room was bathed in the half-light that came from the four dull panes of mica in the front of the great stove. As his eyes grew used to the shadows he saw his wife curled in an arm-chair. He went to her. "Why, Grace." he said, "didn't you hear me calling you?"

She made no answer, and as he bent over the chair he heard her trying to smother a sob in the cushion.

"Grace!" he cried. "You're crying!"

She raised her face. "I've got a headache, a dreadful headache, Ned."

"A headache?" he repeated, in surprise and incredulity.

He pulled a chair close to hers. Later, as he cast his eye over the zone of light shed by the dull red panes, he saw that a low table had been drawn close to the stove, and that it was burdened with many small cups and plates of uncut tea-cake. He remembered that the day was Wednesday, and that his wife received on Wednesdays.

"Who was here to-day, Gracie?" he asked.

From his shoulder there came a mumble, "Mrs. Twelve."

"Was she—um," he said. "Why—didn't Anna Hagenthorpe come over?"

The mumble from his shoulder continued, "She wasn't well enough."

Glancing down at the cups, Trescott mechanically counted them. There were fifteen of them. "There, there," he said. "Don't cry, Grace. Don't cry."

The wind was whining round the house, and the snow beat aslant upon the windows. Sometimes the coal in the stove settled with a crumbling sound, and the four panes of mica flashed a sudden new crimson. As he sat holding her head on his shoulder, Trescott found himself occasionally trying to count the cups. There were fifteen of them.

THE BLUE HOTEL

I

The Palace Hotel at Fort Romper was painted a light blue, a shade that is on the legs of a kind of heron, causing the bird to declare its position against any background. The Palace Hotel, then, was always screaming and howling in a way that made the dazzling winter landscape of Nebraska seem only a gray swampish hush. It stood alone on the prairie, and when the snow was falling the town two hundred yards away was not visible. But when the traveller alighted at the railway station he was obliged to pass the Palace Hotel before he could come upon the company of low clapboard houses which composed Fort Romper, and it was not to be thought that any traveller could pass the Palace Hotel without looking at it. Pat Scully, the proprietor, had proved himself a master of strategy when he chose his paints. It is true that on clear days, when the great trans-continental expresses, long lines of swaying Pullmans, swept through Fort Romper, passengers were overcome at the sight, and the cult that knows the brown-reds and the subdivisions of the dark greens of the East expressed shame, pity, horror, in a laugh. But to the citizens of this prairie town and to the people who would naturally stop there, Pat Scully had performed a feat. With this opulence and splendor, these creeds, classes, egotisms, that streamed through Romper on the rails day after day, they had no color in common.

As if the displayed delights of such a blue hotel were not sufficiently enticing, it was Scully's habit to go every morning and evening to meet the leisurely trains that stopped at Romper and work his seductions upon any man that he might see wavering, gripsack in hand.

One morning, when a snow-crusted engine dragged its long string of freight cars and its one passenger coach to the station, Scully performed the marvel of catching three men. One was a shaky and quick-eyed Swede, with a great shining cheap valise; one was a tall bronzed cowboy, who was on his way to a ranch near the Dakota line; one was a little silent man from the East, who didn't look it, and didn't announce it. Scully practically made them prisoners. He was so nimble and merry and kindly that each probably felt it would be the height of brutality to try to escape. They trudged off over the creaking board sidewalks in the wake of the eager little Irishman. He wore a heavy fur cap squeezed tightly down on his head. It caused his two red ears to stick out stiffly, as if they were made of tin.

At last, Scully, elaborately, with boisterous hospitality, conducted them through the portals of the blue hotel. The room which they entered was small. It seemed to be merely a proper temple for an enormous stove, which, in the centre, was humming with godlike violence. At various points on its surface the iron had become luminous and glowed yellow from the heat. Beside the stove Scully's son Johnnie was playing High-Five with an old farmer who had whiskers both gray and sandy. They were quarrelling. Frequently the old farmer turned his face towards a box of sawdust—colored brown from tobacco juice—that was behind the stove, and spat with an air of great impatience and irritation. With a loud flourish of words Scully destroyed the game of cards, and bustled his son up-stairs with part of the baggage of the new guests. He himself conducted them to three basins of the coldest water in the world. The cowboy and the Easterner burnished themselves fiery-red with this water, until it seemed to be some kind of a metal polish. The Swede, however, merely dipped his fingers gingerly and with trepidation. It was notable that throughout this series of small ceremonies the three travellers were made to feel that Scully was very benevolent. He was conferring great favors upon them. He handed the towel from one to the other with an air of philanthropic impulse.

Afterwards they went to the first room, and, sitting about the stove, listened to Scully's officious clamor at his daughters, who were preparing the mid-day meal. They reflected in the silence of experienced men who tread carefully amid new people. Nevertheless, the old farmer, stationary, invincible in his chair near the warmest part of the stove, turned his face from the sawdust box frequently and addressed a glowing commonplace to the strangers. Usually he was answered in short but adequate sentences by either the cowboy or the Easterner. The Swede said nothing. He seemed to be occupied in making furtive estimates of each man in the room. One might have thought that he had the sense of silly suspicion which comes to guilt. He resembled a badly frightened man.

Later, at dinner, he spoke a little, addressing his conversation entirely to Scully. He volunteered that he had come from New York, where for ten years he had worked as a tailor. These facts seemed to strike Scully as fascinating, and afterwards he volunteered that he had lived at Romper for fourteen years. The Swede asked about the crops and the price of labor. He seemed barely to listen to Scully's extended replies. His eyes continued to rove from man to man.

Finally, with a laugh and a wink, he said that some of these Western communities were very dangerous; and after his statement he straightened his legs under the table, tilted his head, and laughed again, loudly. It was plain that the demonstration had no meaning to the others. They looked at him wondering and in silence.

II

As the men trooped heavily back into the front-room, the two little windows presented views of a turmoiling sea of snow. The huge arms of the wind were making attempts—mighty, circular, futile—to embrace the flakes as they sped. A gate-post like a still man with a blanched face stood aghast amid this profligate fury. In a hearty voice Scully announced the presence of a blizzard. The guests of the blue hotel, lighting their pipes, assented with grunts of lazy masculine contentment. No island of the sea could be exempt in the degree of this little room with its humming stove. Johnnie, son of Scully, in a tone which defined his opinion of his ability as a card-player, challenged the old farmer of both gray and sandy whiskers to a game of High-Five. The farmer agreed with a contemptuous and bitter scoff. They sat close to the stove, and squared their knees under a wide board. The cowboy and the Easterner watched the game with interest. The Swede remained near the window, aloof, but with a countenance that showed signs of an inexplicable excitement.

The play of Johnnie and the gray-beard was suddenly ended by another quarrel. The old man arose while casting a look of heated scorn at his adversary. He slowly buttoned his coat, and then stalked with fabulous dignity from the room. In the discreet silence of all other men the Swede laughed. His laughter rang somehow childish. Men by this time had begun to look at him askance, as if they wished to inquire what ailed him.

A new game was formed jocosely. The cowboy volunteered to become the partner of Johnnie, and they all then turned to ask the Swede to throw in his lot with the little Easterner, He asked some questions about the game, and, learning that it wore many names, and that he had played it when it was under an alias, he accepted the invitation. He strode towards the men nervously, as if he expected to be assaulted. Finally, seated, he gazed from face to face and laughed shrilly. This laugh was so strange that the Easterner looked up quickly, the cowboy sat intent and with his mouth open, and Johnnie paused, holding the cards with still fingers.

Afterwards there was a short silence. Then Johnnie said, "Well, let's get at it. Come on now!" They pulled their chairs forward until their knees were bunched under the board. They began to play, and their interest in the game caused the others to forget the manner of the Swede.

The cowboy was a board-whacker. Each time that he held superior cards he whanged them, one by one, with exceeding force, down upon the improvised table, and took the tricks with a glowing air of prowess and pride that sent thrills of indignation into the hearts of his opponents. A game with a board-whacker in it is sure to become intense. The countenances of the Easterner and the Swede were miserable whenever the cowboy thundered down his aces and kings, while Johnnie, his eyes gleaming with joy, chuckled and chuckled.

Because of the absorbing play none considered the strange ways of the Swede. They paid strict heed to the game. Finally, during a lull caused by a new deal, the Swede suddenly addressed Johnnie: "I suppose there have been a good many men killed in this room." The jaws of the others dropped and they looked at him.

"What in hell are you talking about?" said Johnnie.

The Swede laughed again his blatant laugh, full of a kind of false courage and defiance. "Oh, you know what I mean all right," he answered.

"I'm a liar if I do!" Johnnie protested. The card was halted, and the men stared at the Swede. Johnnie evidently felt that as the son of the proprietor he should make a direct inquiry. "Now, what might you be drivin' at, mister?" he asked. The Swede winked at him. It was a wink full of cunning. His fingers shook on the edge of the board. "Oh, maybe you think I have been to nowheres. Maybe you think I'm a tenderfoot?"

"I don't know nothin' about you," answered Johnnie, "and I don't give a damn where you've been. All I got to say is that I don't know what you're driving at. There hain't never been nobody killed in this room."

The cowboy, who had been steadily gazing at the Swede, then spoke: "What's wrong with you, mister?"

Apparently it seemed to the Swede that he was formidably menaced. He shivered and turned white near the corners of his mouth. He sent an appealing glance in the direction of the little Easterner. During these moments he did not forget to wear his air of advanced pot-valor. "They say they don't know what I mean," he remarked mockingly to the Easterner.

The latter answered after prolonged and cautious reflection. "I don't understand you," he said, impassively.

The Swede made a movement then which announced that he thought he had encountered treachery from the only quarter where he had expected sympathy, if not help. "Oh, I see you are all against me. I see—"

The cowboy was in a state of deep stupefaction. "Say." he cried, as he tumbled the deck violently down upon the board "—say, what are you gittin' at, hey?"

The Swede sprang up with the celerity of a man escaping from a snake on the floor. "I don't want to fight!" he shouted. "I don't want to fight!"

The cowboy stretched his long legs indolently and deliberately. His hands were in his pockets. He spat into the sawdust box. "Well, who the hell thought you did?" he inquired.

The Swede backed rapidly towards a corner of the room. His hands were out protectingly in front of his chest, but he was making an obvious struggle to control his fright. "Gentlemen," he quavered, "I suppose I am going to be killed before I can leave this house! I suppose I am going to be killed before I can leave this house!" In his eyes was the dying-swan look. Through the windows could be seen the snow turning blue in the shadow of dusk. The wind tore at the house and some loose thing beat regularly against the clapboards like a spirit tapping.

A door opened, and Scully himself entered. He paused in surprise as he noted the tragic attitude of the Swede. Then he said, "What's the matter here?"

The Swede answered him swiftly and eagerly: "These men are going to kill me."

"Kill you!" ejaculated Scully. "Kill you! What are you talkin'?"

The Swede made the gesture of a martyr.

Scully wheeled sternly upon his son. "What is this, Johnnie?"

The lad had grown sullen. "Damned if I know," he answered. "I can't make no sense to it." He began to shuffle the cards, fluttering them together with an angry snap. "He says a good many men have been killed in this room, or something like that. And he says he's goin' to be killed here too. I don't know what ails him. He's crazy, I shouldn't wonder."

Scully then looked for explanation to the cowboy, but the cowboy simply shrugged his shoulders.

"Kill you?" said Scully again to the Swede. "Kill you? Man, you're off your nut."

"Oh, I know." burst out the Swede. "I know what will happen. Yes, I'm crazy—yes. Yes, of course, I'm crazy—yes. But I know one thing—" There was a sort of sweat of misery and terror upon his face. "I know I won't get out of here alive."

The cowboy drew a deep breath, as if his mind was passing into the last stages of dissolution. "Well, I'm dog-goned," he whispered to himself.

Scully wheeled suddenly and faced his son. "You've been troublin' this man!"

Johnnie's voice was loud with its burden of grievance. "Why, good Gawd, I ain't done nothin' to 'im."

The Swede broke in. "Gentlemen, do not disturb yourselves. I will leave this house. I will go away because"—he accused them dramatically with his glance—"because I do not want to be killed."

Scully was furious with his son. "Will you tell me what is the matter, you young divil? What's the matter, anyhow? Speak out!"

"Blame it!" cried Johnnie in despair, "don't I tell you I don't know. He—he says we want to kill him, and that's all I know. I can't tell what ails him."

The Swede continued to repeat: "Never mind, Mr. Scully; nevermind. I will leave this house. I will go away, because I do not wish to be killed. Yes, of course, I am crazy—yes. But I know one thing! I will go away. I will leave this house. Never mind, Mr. Scully; never mind. I will go away."

"You will not go 'way," said Scully. "You will not go 'way until I hear the reason of this business. If anybody has troubled you I will take care of him. This is my house. You are under my roof, and I will not allow any peaceable man to be troubled here." He cast a terrible eye upon Johnnie, the cowboy, and the Easterner.

"Never mind, Mr. Scully; never mind. I will go away. I do not wish to be killed." The Swede moved towards the door, which opened upon the stairs. It was evidently his intention to go at once for his baggage.

"No, no," shouted Scully peremptorily; but the white-faced man slid by him and disappeared. "Now," said Scully severely, "what does this mane?"

Johnnie and the cowboy cried together: "Why, we didn't do nothin' to 'im!"

Scully's eyes were cold. "No," he said, "you didn't?"

Johnnie swore a deep oath. "Why this is the wildest loon I ever see. We didn't do nothin' at all. We were jest sittin' here playin' cards, and he—"

The father suddenly spoke to the Easterner. "Mr. Blanc," he asked, "what has these boys been doin'?"

The Easterner reflected again. "I didn't see anything wrong at all," he said at last, slowly.

Scully began to howl. "But what does it mane?" He stared ferociously at his son. "I have a mind to lather you for this, me boy."

Johnnie was frantic. "Well, what have I done?" he bawled at his father.

III

"I think you are tongue-tied," said Scully finally to his son, the cowboy, and the Easterner; and at the end of this scornful sentence he left the room.

Up-stairs the Swede was swiftly fastening the straps of his great valise. Once his back happened to be half turned towards the door, and, hearing a noise there, he wheeled and sprang up, uttering a loud cry. Scully's wrinkled visage showed grimly in the light of the small lamp he carried. This yellow effulgence, streaming upward, colored only his prominent features, and left his eyes, for instance, in mysterious shadow. He resembled a murderer.

"Man! man!" he exclaimed, "have you gone daffy?"

"Oh, no! Oh, no!" rejoined the other. "There are people in this world who know pretty nearly as much as you do—understand?"

For a moment they stood gazing at each other. Upon the Swede's deathly pale checks were two spots brightly crimson and sharply edged, as if they had been carefully painted. Scully placed the light on the table and sat himself on the edge of the bed. He spoke ruminatively. "By cracky, I never heard of such a thing in my life. It's a complete muddle. I can't, for the soul of me, think how you ever got this idea into your head." Presently he lifted his eyes and asked: "And did you sure think they were going to kill you?"

The Swede scanned the old man as if he wished to see into his mind. "I did," he said at last. He obviously suspected that this answer might precipitate an outbreak. As he pulled on a strap his whole arm shook, the elbow wavering like a bit of paper.

Scully banged his hand impressively on the foot-board of the bed. "Why, man, we're goin' to have a line of ilictric street-cars in this town next spring."

"'A line of electric street-cars,'" repeated the Swede, stupidly.

"And," said Scully, "there's a new railroad goin' to be built down from Broken Arm to here. Not to mintion the four churches and the smashin' big brick school-house. Then there's the big factory, too. Why, in two years Romper 'll be a metropolis."

Having finished the preparation of his baggage, the Swede straightened himself. "Mr. Scully," he said, with sudden hardihood, "how much do I owe you?"

"You don't owe me anythin'," said the old man, angrily.

"Yes, I do," retorted the Swede. He took seventy-five cents from his pocket and tendered it to Scully; but the latter snapped his fingers in disdainful refusal. However, it happened that they both stood gazing in a strange fashion at three silver pieces on the Swede's open palm.

"I'll not take your money," said Scully at last. "Not after what's been goin' on here." Then a plan seemed to strike him. "Here," he cried, picking up his lamp and moving towards the door. "Here! Come with me a minute."

"No," said the Swede, in overwhelming alarm.

"Yes," urged the old man. "Come on! I want you to come and see a picter—just across the hall—in my room."

The Swede must have concluded that his hour was come. His jaw dropped and his teeth showed like a dead man's. He ultimately followed Scully across the corridor, but he had the step of one hung in chains.

Scully flashed the light high on the wall of his own chamber. There was revealed a ridiculous photograph of a little girl. She was leaning against a balustrade of gorgeous decoration, and the formidable bang to her hair was prominent. The figure was as graceful as an upright sled-stake, and, withal, it was of the hue of lead. "There," said Scully, tenderly, "that's the picter of my little girl that died. Her name was Carrie. She had the purtiest hair you ever saw! I was that fond of her, she—"

Turning then, he saw that the Swede was not contemplating the picture at all, but, instead, was keeping keen watch on the gloom in the rear.

"Look, man!" cried Scully, heartily. "That's the picter of my little gal that died. Her name was Carrie. And then here's the picter of my oldest boy, Michael. He's a lawyer in Lincoln, an' doin' well. I gave that boy a grand eddycation, and I'm glad for it now. He's a fine boy. Look at 'im now. Ain't he bold as blazes, him there in Lincoln, an honored an' respicted gintleman. An honored an' respicted gintleman," concluded Scully with a flourish. And, so saying, he smote the Swede jovially on the back.

The Swede faintly smiled.

"Now," said the old man, "there's only one more thing." He dropped suddenly to the floor and thrust his head beneath the bed. The Swede could hear his muffled voice. "I'd keep it under me piller if it wasn't for that boy Johnnie. Then there's the old woman—Where is it now? I never put it twice in the same place. Ah, now come out with you!"

Presently he backed clumsily from under the bed, dragging with him an old coat rolled into a bundle. "I've fetched him," he muttered. Kneeling on the floor, he unrolled the coat and extracted from its heart a large yellow-brown whiskey bottle.

His first maneuver was to hold the bottle up to the light. Reassured, apparently, that nobody had been tampering with it, he thrust it with a generous movement towards the Swede.

The weak-kneed Swede was about to eagerly clutch this element of strength, but he suddenly jerked his hand away and cast a look of horror upon Scully.

"Drink," said the old man affectionately. He had risen to his feet, and now stood facing the Swede.

There was a silence. Then again Scully said: "Drink!"

The Swede laughed wildly. He grabbed the bottle, put it to his mouth, and as his lips curled absurdly around the opening and his throat worked, he kept his glance, burning with hatred, upon the old man's face.

IV

After the departure of Scully the three men, with the card-board still upon their knees, preserved for a long time an astounded silence. Then Johnnie said: "That's the dod-dangest Swede I ever see."

"He ain't no Swede," said the cowboy, scornfully.

"Well, what is he then?" cried Johnnie. "What is he then?"

"It's my opinion," replied the cowboy deliberately, "he's some kind of a Dutchman." It was a venerable custom of the country to entitle as Swedes all light-haired men who spoke with a heavy tongue. In consequence the idea of the cowboy was not without its daring. "Yes, sir," he repeated. "It's my opinion this feller is some kind of a Dutchman."

"Well, he says he's a Swede, anyhow," muttered Johnnie, sulkily. He turned to the Easterner: "What do you think, Mr. Blanc?"

"Oh, I don't know," replied the Easterner.

"Well, what do you think makes him act that way?" asked the cowboy.

"Why, he's frightened." The Easterner knocked his pipe against a rim of the stove. "He's clear frightened out of his boots."

"What at?" cried Johnnie and cowboy together.

The Easterner reflected over his answer.

"What at?" cried the others again.

210

"Oh, I don't know, but it seems to me this man has been reading dime-novels, and he thinks he's right out in the middle of it—the shootin' and stabbin' and all."

"But," said the cowboy, deeply scandalized, "this ain't Wyoming, ner none of them places. This is Nebrasker."

"Yes," added Johnnie, "an' why don't he wait till he gits out West?"

The travelled Easterner laughed. "It isn't different there even—not in these days. But he thinks he's right in the middle of hell."

Johnnie and the cowboy mused long.

"It's awful funny," remarked Johnnie at last.

"Yes," said the cowboy. "This is a queer game. I hope we don't git snowed in, because then we'd have to stand this here man bein' around with us all the time. That wouldn't be no good."

"I wish pop would throw him out," said Johnnie.

Presently they heard a loud stamping on the stairs, accompanied by ringing jokes in the voice of old Scully, and laughter, evidently from the Swede. The men around the stove stared vacantly at each other. "Gosh!" said the cowboy. The door flew open, and old Scully, flushed and anecdotal, came into the room. He was jabbering at the Swede, who followed him, laughing bravely. It was the entry of two roisterers from a banquet-hall.

"Come now," said Scully sharply to the three seated men, "move up and give us a chance at the stove." The cowboy and the Easterner obediently sidled their chairs to make room for the new-comers. Johnnie, however, simply arranged himself in a more indolent attitude, and then remained motionless.

"Come! Git over, there," said Scully.

"Plenty of room on the other side of the stove," said Johnnie.

"Do you think we want to sit in the draught?" roared the father.

But the Swede here interposed with a grandeur of confidence. "No, no.

211

Let the boy sit where he likes," he cried in a bullying voice to the father.

"All right! All right!" said Scully, deferentially. The cowboy and the Easterner exchanged glances of wonder.

The five chairs were formed in a crescent about one side of the stove. The Swede began to talk; he talked arrogantly, profanely, angrily. Johnnie, the cowboy, and the Easterner maintained a morose silence, while old Scully appeared to be receptive and eager, breaking in constantly with sympathetic ejaculations.

Finally the Swede announced that he was thirsty. He moved in his chair, and said that he would go for a drink of water.

"I'll git it for you," cried Scully at once.

"No," said the Swede, contemptuously. "I'll get it for myself." He arose and stalked with the air of an owner off into the executive parts of the hotel.

As soon as the Swede was out of hearing Scully sprang to his feet and whispered intensely to the others: "Up-stairs he thought I was tryin' to poison 'im.'"

"Say," said Johnnie, "this makes me sick. Why don't you throw 'im out in the snow?"

"Why, he's all right now," declared Scully. "It was only that he was from the East, and he thought this was a tough place. That's all. He's all right now."

The cowboy looked with admiration upon the Easterner. "You were straight," he said. "You were on to that there Dutchman."

"Well," said Johnnie to his father, "he may be all right now, but I don't see it. Other time he was scared, but now he's too fresh."

Scully's speech was always a combination of Irish brogue and idiom, Western twang and idiom, and scraps of curiously formal diction taken from the story-books and newspapers, He now hurled a strange mass of language at the head of his son. "What do I keep? What do I keep? What do I keep?" he demanded, in a voice of thunder. He slapped his knee impressively, to indicate that he himself was going to make reply, and that all should heed. "I keep a hotel," he shouted. "A hotel, do you mind? A guest under my roof has sacred privileges. He is to be intimidated by none. Not one word shall he hear that would prejudice him in favor of goin' away. I'll not have it. There's no place in this here town where they can say they iver took in a guest of mine because he was afraid to stay here." He wheeled suddenly upon the cowboy and the Easterner. "Am I right?"

"Yes, Mr. Scully," said the cowboy, "I think you're right."

"Yes, Mr. Scully," said the Easterner, "I think you're right."

V

At six-o'clock supper, the Swede fizzed like a fire-wheel. He sometimes seemed on the point of bursting into riotous song, and in all his madness he was encouraged by old Scully. The Easterner was incased in reserve; the cowboy sat in wide-mouthed amazement, forgetting to eat, while Johnnie wrathily demolished great plates of food. The daughters of the house, when they were obliged to replenish the biscuits, approached as warily as Indians, and, having succeeded in their purpose, fled with ill-concealed trepidation. The Swede domineered the whole feast, and he gave it the appearance of a cruel bacchanal. He seemed to have grown suddenly taller; he gazed, brutally disdainful, into every face. His voice rang through the room. Once when he jabbed out harpoon-fashion with his fork to pinion a biscuit, the weapon nearly impaled the hand of the Easterner which had been stretched quietly out for the same biscuit.

After supper, as the men filed towards the other room, the Swede smote Scully ruthlessly on the shoulder. "Well, old boy, that was a good, square meal." Johnnie looked hopefully at his father; he knew that shoulder was tender from an old fall; and, indeed, it appeared for a moment as if Scully was going to flame out over the matter, but in the end he smiled a sickly smile and remained silent. The others understood from his manner that he was admitting his responsibility for the Swede's new view-point.

Johnnie, however, addressed his parent in an aside. "Why don't you license somebody to kick you down-stairs?" Scully scowled darkly by way of reply.

When they were gathered about the stove, the Swede insisted on another game of High Five. Scully gently deprecated the plan at first, but the Swede turned a wolfish glare upon him. The old man subsided, and the Swede canvassed the others. In his tone there was always a great threat. The cowboy and the Easterner both remarked indifferently that they would play. Scully said that he would presently have to go to meet the 6.58 train, and so the Swede turned menacingly upon Johnnie. For a moment their glances crossed like blades, and then Johnnie smiled and said, "Yes, I'll play."

They formed a square, with the little board on their knees. The Easterner and the Swede were again partners. As the play went on, it was noticeable that the cowboy was not board-whacking as usual. Meanwhile, Scully, near the lamp, had put on his spectacles and, with an appearance curiously like an old priest, was reading a newspaper. In time he went out to meet the 6.58 train, and, despite his precautions, a gust of polar wind whirled into the room as he opened the door. Besides scattering the cards, it dulled the players to the marrow. The Swede cursed frightfully. When Scully returned, his entrance disturbed a cosey and friendly scene. The Swede again cursed. But presently they were once more intent, their heads bent forward and their hands moving swiftly. The Swede had adopted the fashion of board-whacking.

Scully took up his paper and for a long time remained immersed in matters which were extraordinarily remote from him. The lamp burned badly, and once he stopped to adjust the wick. The newspaper, as he turned from page to page, rustled with a slow and comfortable sound. Then suddenly he heard three terrible words: "You are cheatin'!"

Such scenes often prove that there can be little of dramatic import in environment. Any room can present a tragic front; any room can be comic. This little den was now hideous as a torture-chamber. The new faces of the men themselves had changed it upon the instant. The Swede held a huge fist in front of Johnnie's face, while the latter looked steadily over it into the blazing orbs of his accuser. The Easterner had grown pallid; the cowboy's jaw had dropped in that expression of bovine amazement which was one of his important mannerisms. After the three words, the first sound in the room was made by Scully's paper as it floated forgotten to his feet. His spectacles had also fallen from his nose, but by a clutch he had saved them in air. His hand, grasping the spectacles, now remained poised awkwardly and near his shoulder. He stared at the card-players.

Probably the silence was while a second elapsed. Then, if the floor had been suddenly twitched out from under the men they could not have moved quicker. The five had projected themselves headlong towards a common point. It happened that Johnnie, in rising to hurl himself upon the Swede, had stumbled slightly because of his curiously instinctive care for the cards and the board. The loss of the moment allowed time for the arrival of Scully, and also allowed the cowboy time to give the Swede a great push which sent him staggering back. The men found tongue together, and hoarse shouts of rage, appeal, or fear burst from every throat. The cowboy pushed and jostled feverishly at the Swede, and the Easterner and Scully clung wildly to Johnnie; but, through the smoky air, above the swaying bodies of the peace-compellers, the eyes of the two warriors ever sought each other in glances of challenge that were at once hot and steely.

Of course the board had been overturned, and now the whole company of cards was scattered over the floor, where the boots of the men trampled the fat and painted kings and queens as they gazed with their silly eyes at the war that was waging above them.

Scully's voice was dominating the yells. "Stop now? Stop, I say! Stop, now—"

Johnnie, as he struggled to burst through the rank formed by Scully and the Easterner, was crying, "Well, he says I cheated! He says I cheated! I won't allow no man to say I cheated! If he says I cheated, he's a ——— ———!"

The cowboy was telling the Swede, "Quit, now! Quit, d'ye hear—"

The screams of the Swede never ceased: "He did cheat! I saw him! I saw him—"

As for the Easterner, he was importuning in a voice that was not heeded:

215

"Wait a moment, can't you? Oh, wait a moment. What's the good of a fight over a game of cards? Wait a moment—"

In this tumult no complete sentences were clear. "Cheat"—"Quit"—"He says"—these fragments pierced the uproar and rang out sharply. It was remarkable that, whereas Scully undoubtedly made the most noise, he was the least heard of any of the riotous band.

Then suddenly there was a great cessation. It was as if each man had paused for breath; and although the room was still lighted with the anger of men, it could be seen that there was no danger of immediate conflict, and at once Johnnie, shouldering his way forward, almost succeeded in confronting the Swede. "What did you say I cheated for? What did you say I cheated for? I don't cheat, and I won't let no man say I do!"

The Swede said, "I saw you! I saw you!"

"Well," cried Johnnie, "I'll fight any man what says I cheat!"

"No, you won't," said the cowboy. "Not here."

"Ah, be still, can't you?" said Scully, coming between them.

The quiet was sufficient to allow the Easterner's voice to be heard. He was repealing, "Oh, wait a moment, can't you? What's the good of a fight over a game of cards? Wait a moment!"

Johnnie, his red face appearing above his father's shoulder, hailed the Swede again. "Did you say I cheated?"

The Swede showed his teeth. "Yes."

"Then," said Johnnie, "we must fight."

"Yes, fight," roared the Swede. He was like a demoniac. "Yes, fight! I'll show you what kind of a man I am! I'll show you who you want to fight! Maybe you think I can't fight! Maybe you think I can't! I'll show you, you skin, you card-sharp! Yes, you cheated! You cheated! You cheated!"

"Well, let's go at it, then, mister," said Johnnie, coolly.

216

The cowboy's brow was beaded with sweat from his efforts in intercepting all sorts of raids. He turned in despair to Scully. "What are you goin' to do now?"

A change had come over the Celtic visage of the old man. He now seemed all eagerness; his eyes glowed.

"We'll let them fight," he answered, stalwartly. "I can't put up with it any longer. I've stood this damned Swede till I'm sick. We'll let them fight."

VI

The men prepared to go out-of-doors. The Easterner was so nervous that he had great difficulty in getting his arms into the sleeves of his new leather coat. As the cowboy drew his fur cap down over his ears his hands trembled. In fact, Johnnie and old Scully were the only ones who displayed no agitation. These preliminaries were conducted without words.

Scully threw open the door. "Well, come on," he said. Instantly a terrific wind caused the flame of the lamp to struggle at its wick, while a puff of black smoke sprang from the chimney-top. The stove was in mid-current of the blast, and its voice swelled to equal the roar of the storm. Some of the scarred and bedabbled cards were caught up from the floor and dashed helplessly against the farther wall. The men lowered their heads and plunged into the tempest as into a sea.

No snow was falling, but great whirls and clouds of flakes, swept up from the ground by the frantic winds, were streaming southward with the speed of bullets. The covered land was blue with the sheen of an unearthly satin, and there was no other hue save where, at the low, black railway station—which seemed incredibly distant—one light gleamed like a tiny jewel. As the men floundered into a thigh deep drift, it was known that the Swede was bawling out something. Scully went to him, put a hand on his shoulder and projected an ear. "What's that you say?" he shouted.

"I say," bawled the Swede again, "I won't stand much show against this gang. I know you'll all pitch on me."

Scully smote him reproachfully on the arm. "Tut, man!" he yelled. The wind tore the words from Scully's lips and scattered them far alee.

"You are all a gang of—" boomed the Swede, but the storm also seized the remainder of this sentence.

Immediately turning their backs upon the wind, the men had swung around a corner to the sheltered side of the hotel. It was the function of the little house to preserve here, amid this great devastation of snow, an irregular V-shape of heavily incrusted grass, which crackled beneath the feet. One could imagine the great drifts piled against the windward side. When the party reached the comparative peace of this spot it was found that the Swede was still bellowing.

"Oh, I know what kind of a thing this is! I know you'll all pitch on me. I can't lick you all!"

Scully turned upon him panther fashion. "You'll not have to whip all of us. You'll have to whip my son Johnnie. An' the man what troubles you durin' that time will have me to dale with."

The arrangements were swiftly made. The two men faced each other, obedient to the harsh commands of Scully, whose face, in the subtly luminous gloom, could be seen set in the austere impersonal lines that are pictured on the countenances of the Roman veterans. The Easterner's teeth were chattering, and he was hopping up and down like a mechanical toy. The cowboy stood rock-like.

The contestants had not stripped off any clothing. Each was in his ordinary attire. Their fists were up, and they eyed each other in a calm that had the elements of leonine cruelty in it.

During this pause, the Easterner's mind, like a film, took lasting impressions of three men—the iron-nerved master of the ceremony; the Swede, pale, motionless, terrible; and Johnnie, serene yet ferocious, brutish yet heroic. The entire prelude had in it a tragedy greater than the tragedy of action, and this aspect was accentuated by the long, mellow cry of the blizzard, as it sped the tumbling and wailing flakes into the black abyss of the south.

218

"Now!" said Scully.

The two combatants leaped forward and crashed together like bullocks. There was heard the cushioned sound of blows, and of a curse squeezing out from between the tight teeth of one.

As for the spectators, the Easterner's pent-up breath exploded from him with a pop of relief, absolute relief from the tension of the preliminaries. The cowboy bounded into the air with a yowl. Scully was immovable as from supreme amazement and fear at the fury of the fight which he himself had permitted and arranged.

For a time the encounter in the darkness was such a perplexity of flying arms that it presented no more detail than would a swiftly revolving wheel. Occasionally a face, as if illumined by a flash of light, would shine out, ghastly and marked with pink spots. A moment later, the men might have been known as shadows, if it were not for the involuntary utterance of oaths that came from them in whispers.

Suddenly a holocaust of warlike desire caught the cowboy, and he bolted forward with the speed of a broncho. "Go it, Johnnie! go it! Kill him! Kill him!"

Scully confronted him. "Kape back," he said; and by his glance the cowboy could tell that this man was Johnnie's father.

To the Easterner there was a monotony of unchangeable fighting that was an abomination. This confused mingling was eternal to his sense, which was concentrated in a longing for the end, the priceless end. Once the fighters lurched near him, and as he scrambled hastily backward he heard them breathe like men on the rack.

"Kill him, Johnnie! Kill him! Kill him! Kill him!" The cowboy's face was contorted like one of those agony masks in museums.

"Keep still," said Scully, icily.

Then there was a sudden loud grunt, incomplete, cut short, and Johnnie's body swung away from the Swede and fell with sickening heaviness to the grass. The cowboy was barely in time to prevent the mad Swede from flinging himself upon his prone adversary. "No, you don't," said the cowboy, interposing an arm. "Wait a second."

Scully was at his son's side. "Johnnie! Johnnie, me boy!" His voice had a quality of melancholy tenderness. "Johnnie! Can you go on with it?" He looked anxiously down into the bloody, pulpy face of his son.

There was a moment of silence, and then Johnnie answered in his ordinary voice, "Yes, I—it—yes."

Assisted by his father he struggled to his feet. "Wait a bit now till you git your wind," said the old man.

A few paces away the cowboy was lecturing the Swede. "No, you don't! Wait a second!"

The Easterner was plucking at Scully's sleeve. "Oh, this is enough," he pleaded. "This is enough! Let it go as it stands. This is enough!"

"Bill," said Scully, "git out of the road." The cowboy stepped aside. "Now." The combatants were actuated by a new caution as they advanced towards collision. They glared at each other, and then the Swede aimed a lightning blow that carried with it his entire weight. Johnnie was evidently half stupid from weakness, but he miraculously dodged, and his fist sent the over-balanced Swede sprawling.

The cowboy, Scully, and the Easterner burst into a cheer that was like a chorus of triumphant soldiery, but before its conclusion the Swede had scuffled agilely to his feet and come in berserk abandon at his foe. There was another perplexity of flying arms, and Johnnie's body again swung away and fell, even as a bundle might fall from a roof. The Swede instantly staggered to a little wind-waved tree and leaned upon it, breathing like an engine, while his savage and flame-lit eyes roamed from face to face as the men bent over Johnnie. There was a splendor of isolation in his situation at this time which the Easterner felt once when, lifting his eyes from the man on the ground, he beheld that mysterious and lonely figure, waiting.

"Arc you any good yet, Johnnie?" asked Scully in a broken voice.

The son gasped and opened his eyes languidly. After a moment he answered, "No—I ain't—any good—any—more." Then, from shame and bodily ill he began to weep, the tears furrowing down through the blood-stains on his face. "He was too—too—too heavy for me."

Scully straightened and addressed the waiting figure. "Stranger," he said, evenly, "it's all up with our side." Then his voice changed into that vibrant huskiness which is commonly the tone of the most simple and deadly announcements. "Johnnie is whipped."

Without replying, the victor moved off on the route to the front door of the hotel.

The cowboy was formulating new and un-spellable blasphemies. The Easterner was startled to find that they were out in a wind that seemed to come direct from the shadowed arctic floes. He heard again the wail of the snow as it was flung to its grave in the south. He knew now that all this time the cold had been sinking into him deeper and deeper, and he wondered that he had not perished. He felt indifferent to the condition of the vanquished man.

"Johnnie, can you walk?" asked Scully.

"Did I hurt—hurt him any?" asked the son.

"Can you walk, boy? Can you walk?"

Johnnie's voice was suddenly strong. There was a robust impatience in it. "I asked you whether I hurt him any!"

"Yes, yes, Johnnie," answered the cowboy, consolingly; "he's hurt a good deal."

They raised him from the ground, and as soon as he was on his feet he went tottering off, rebuffing all attempts at assistance. When the party rounded the corner they were fairly blinded by the pelting of the snow. It burned their faces like fire. The cowboy carried Johnnie through the drift to the door. As they entered some cards again rose from the floor and beat against the wall.

The Easterner rushed to the stove. He was so profoundly chilled that he almost dared to embrace the glowing iron. The Swede was not in the room. Johnnie sank into a chair, and, folding his arms on his knees, buried his face in them. Scully, warming one foot and then the other at a rim of the stove, muttered to himself with Celtic mournfulness. The cowboy had removed his fur cap, and with a dazed and rueful air he was running one hand through his tousled locks. From overhead they could hear the creaking of boards, as the Swede tramped here and there in his room.

The sad quiet was broken by the sudden flinging open of a door that led towards the kitchen. It was instantly followed by an inrush of women. They precipitated themselves upon Johnnie amid a chorus of lamentation. Before they carried their prey off to the kitchen, there to be bathed and harangued with that mixture of sympathy and abuse which is a feat of their sex, the mother straightened herself and fixed old Scully with an eye of stern reproach. "Shame be upon you, Patrick Scully!" she cried. "Your own son, too. Shame be upon you!"

"There, now! Be quiet, now!" said the old man, weakly.

"Shame be upon you, Patrick Scully!" The girls, rallying to this slogan, sniffed disdainfully in the direction of those trembling accomplices, the cowboy and the Easterner. Presently they bore Johnnie away, and left the three men to dismal reflection.

VII

"I'd like to fight this here Dutchman myself," said the cowboy, breaking a long silence.

Scully wagged his head sadly. "No, that wouldn't do. It wouldn't be right. It wouldn't be right."

"Well, why wouldn't it?" argued the cowboy. "I don't see no harm in it."

"No," answered Scully, with mournful heroism. "It wouldn't be right. It was Johnnie's fight, and now we mustn't whip the man just because he whipped Johnnie."

"Yes, that's true enough," said the cowboy; "but—he better not get fresh with me, because I couldn't stand no more of it."

"You'll not say a word to him," commanded Scully, and even then they heard the tread of the Swede on the stairs. His entrance was made theatric. He swept the door back with a bang and swaggered to the middle of the room. No one looked at him. "Well," he cried, insolently, at Scully, "I s'pose you'll tell me now how much I owe you?"

The old man remained stolid. "You don't owe me nothin'."

"Huh!" said the Swede, "huh! Don't owe 'im nothin'."

The cowboy addressed the Swede. "Stranger, I don't see how you come to be so gay around here."

Old Scully was instantly alert. "Stop!" he shouted, holding his hand forth, fingers upward. "Bill, you shut up!"

The cowboy spat carelessly into the sawdust box. "I didn't say a word, did I?" he asked.

"Mr. Scully," called the Swede, "how much do I owe you?" It was seen that he was attired for departure, and that he had his valise in his hand.

"You don't owe me nothin'," repeated Scully in his same imperturbable way.

"Huh!" said the Swede. "I guess you're right. I guess if it was any way at all, you'd owe me somethin'. That's what I guess." He turned to the cowboy. "'Kill him! Kill him! Kill him!'" he mimicked, and then guffawed victoriously. "'Kill him!'" He was convulsed with ironical humor.

But he might have been jeering the dead. The three men were immovable and silent, staring with glassy eyes at the stove.

The Swede opened the door and passed into the storm, giving one derisive glance backward at the still group.

As soon as the door was closed, Scully and the cowboy leaped to their feet and began to curse. They trampled to and fro, waving their arms and smashing into the air with their fists. "Oh, but that was a hard minute!" wailed Scully. "That was a hard minute! Him there leerin' and scoffin'! One bang at his nose was worth forty dollars to me that minute! How did you stand it, Bill?"

"How did I stand it?" cried the cowboy in a quivering voice. "How did I stand it? Oh!"

The old man burst into sudden brogue. "I'd loike to take that Swade," he wailed, "and hould 'im down on a shtone flure and bate 'im to a jelly wid a shtick!"

The cowboy groaned in sympathy. "I'd like to git him by the neck and ha-ammer him "—he brought his hand down on a chair with a noise like a pistol-shot—"hammer that there Dutchman until he couldn't tell himself from a dead coyote!"

"I'd bate 'im until he—"

"I'd show him some things—"

And then together they raised a yearning, fanatic cry—"Oh-o-oh! if we only could—"

"Yes!"

"Yes!"

"And then I'd—"

"O-o-oh!"

VIII

The Swede, tightly gripping his valise, tacked across the face of the storm as if he carried sails. He was following a line of little naked, gasping trees, which he knew must mark the way of the road. His face, fresh from the pounding of Johnnie's fists, felt more pleasure than pain in the wind and the driving snow. A number of square shapes loomed upon him finally, and he knew them as the houses of the main body of the town. He found a street and made travel along it, leaning heavily upon the wind whenever, at a corner, a terrific blast caught him.

He might have been in a deserted village. We picture the world as thick with conquering and elate humanity, but here, with the bugles of the tempest pealing, it was hard to imagine a peopled earth. One viewed the existence of man then as a marvel, and conceded a glamour of wonder to these lice which were caused to cling to a whirling, fire-smote, ice-locked, disease-stricken, space-lost bulb. The conceit of man was explained by this storm to be the very engine of life. One was a coxcomb not to die in it. However, the Swede found a saloon.

In front of it an indomitable red light was burning, and the snow-flakes were made blood color as they flew through the circumscribed territory of the lamp's shining. The Swede pushed open the door of the saloon and entered. A sanded expanse was before him, and at the end of it four men sat about a table drinking. Down one side of the room extended a radiant bar, and its guardian was leaning upon his elbows listening to the talk of the men at the table. The Swede dropped his valise upon the floor, and, smiling fraternally upon the barkeeper, said, "Gimme some whiskey, will you?" The man placed a bottle, a whiskey-glass, and a glass of ice-thick water upon the bar. The Swede poured himself an abnormal portion of whiskey and drank it in three gulps. "Pretty bad night," remarked the bartender, indifferently. He was making the pretension of blindness which is usually a distinction of his class; but it could have been seen that he was furtively studying the half-erased blood-stains on the face of the Swede. "Bad night," he said again.

"Oh, it's good enough for me," replied the Swede, hardily, as he poured himself some more whiskey. The barkeeper took his coin and maneuvered it through its reception by the highly nickelled cash-machine. A bell rang; a card labelled "20 cts." had appeared.

"No," continued the Swede, "this isn't too bad weather. It's good enough for me."

"So?" murmured the barkeeper, languidly.

The copious drams made the Swede's eyes swim, and he breathed a trifle heavier. "Yes, I like this weather. I like it. It suits me." It was apparently his design to impart a deep significance to these words.

"So?" murmured the bartender again. He turned to gaze dreamily at the scroll-like birds and bird-like scrolls which had been drawn with soap upon the mirrors back of the bar.

"Well, I guess I'll take another drink," said the Swede, presently. "Have something?"

"No, thanks; I'm not drinkin'," answered the bartender. Afterwards he asked, "How did you hurt your face?"

The Swede immediately began to boast loudly. "Why, in a fight. I thumped the soul out of a man down here at Scully's hotel."

The interest of the four men at the table was at last aroused.

"Who was it?" said one.

"Johnnie Scully," blustered the Swede. "Son of the man what runs it. He will be pretty near dead for some weeks, I can tell you. I made a nice thing of him, I did. He couldn't get up. They carried him in the house. Have a drink?"

Instantly the men in some subtle way incased themselves in reserve. "No, thanks," said one. The group was of curious formation. Two were prominent local business men; one was the district-attorney; and one was a professional gambler of the kind known as "square." But a scrutiny of the group would not have enabled an observer to pick the gambler from the men of more reputable pursuits. He was, in fact, a man so delicate in manner, when among people of fair class, and so judicious in his choice of victims, that in the strictly masculine part of the town's life he had come to be explicitly trusted and admired. People called him a thoroughbred. The fear and contempt with which his craft was regarded was undoubtedly the reason that his quiet dignity shone conspicuous above the quiet dignity of men who might be merely hatters, billiard markers, or grocery-clerks. Beyond an occasional unwary traveller, who came by rail, this gambler was supposed to prey solely upon reckless and senile farmers, who, when flush with good crops, drove into town in all

226

the pride and confidence of an absolutely invulnerable stupidity. Hearing at times in circuitous fashion of the despoilment of such a farmer, the important men of Romper invariably laughed in contempt of the victim, and, if they thought of the wolf at all, it was with a kind of pride at the knowledge that he would never dare think of attacking their wisdom and courage. Besides, it was popular that this gambler had a real wife and two real children in a neat cottage in a suburb, where he led an exemplary home life; and when any one even suggested a discrepancy in his character, the crowd immediately vociferated descriptions of this virtuous family circle. Then men who led exemplary home lives, and men who did not lead exemplary home lives, all subsided in a bunch, remarking that there was nothing more to be said.

However, when a restriction was placed upon him—as, for instance, when a strong clique of members of the new Pollywog Club refused to permit him, even as a spectator, to appear in the rooms of the organization—the candor and gentleness with which he accepted the judgment disarmed many of his foes and made his friends more desperately partisan. He invariably distinguished between himself and a respectable Romper man so quickly and frankly that his manner actually appeared to be a continual broadcast compliment.

And one must not forget to declare the fundamental fact of his entire position in Romper. It is irrefutable that in all affairs outside of his business, in all matters that occur eternally and commonly between man and man, this thieving card-player was so generous, so just, so moral, that, in a contest, he could have put to flight the consciences of nine-tenths of the citizens of Romper.

And so it happened that he was seated in this saloon with the two prominent local merchants and the district-attorney.

The Swede continued to drink raw whiskey, meanwhile babbling at the barkeeper and trying to induce him to indulge in potations. "Come on. Have a drink. Come on. What—no? Well, have a little one, then. By gawd, I've whipped a man to-night, and I want to celebrate. I whipped him good, too. Gentlemen," the Swede cried to the men at the table, "have a drink?"

"Ssh!" said the barkeeper.

The group at the table, although furtively attentive, had been pretending to be deep in talk, but now a man lifted his eyes towards the Swede and said, shortly, "Thanks. We don't want any more."

At this reply the Swede ruffled out his chest like a rooster. "Well," he exploded, "it seems I can't get anybody to drink with me in this town. Seems so, don't it? Well!"

"Ssh!" said the barkeeper.

"Say," snarled the Swede, "don't you try to shut me up. I won't have it. I'm a gentleman, and I want people to drink with me. And I want 'em to drink with me now. Now—do you understand?" He rapped the bar with his knuckles.

Years of experience had calloused the bartender. He merely grew sulky. "I hear you," he answered.

"Well," cried the Swede, "listen hard then. See those men over there? Well, they're going to drink with me, and don't you forget it. Now you watch."

"Hi!" yelled the barkeeper, "this won't do!"

"Why won't it?" demanded the Swede. He stalked over to the table, and by chance laid his hand upon the shoulder of the gambler. "How about this?" he asked, wrathfully. "I asked you to drink with me."

The gambler simply twisted his head and spoke over his shoulder. "My friend, I don't know you."

"Oh, hell!" answered the Swede, "come and have a drink."

"Now, my boy," advised the gambler, kindly, "take your hand off my shoulder and go 'way and mind your own business." He was a little, slim man, and it seemed strange to hear him use this tone of heroic patronage to the burly Swede. The other men at the table said nothing.

"What! You won't drink with me, you little dude? I'll make you then! I'll

228

make you!" The Swede had grasped the gambler frenziedly at the throat, and was dragging him from his chair. The other men sprang up. The barkeeper dashed around the corner of his bar. There was a great tumult, and then was seen a long blade in the hand of the gambler. It shot forward, and a human body, this citadel of virtue, wisdom, power, was pierced as easily as if it had been a melon. The Swede fell with a cry of supreme astonishment.

The prominent merchants and the district attorney must have at once tumbled out of the place backward. The bartender found himself hanging limply to the arm of a chair and gazing into the eyes of a murderer.

"Henry," said the latter, as he wiped his knife on one of the towels that hung beneath the bar-rail, "you tell 'em where to find me. I'll be home, waiting for 'em." Then he vanished. A moment afterwards the barkeeper was in the street dinning through the storm for help, and, moreover, companionship.

The corpse of the Swede, alone in the saloon, had its eyes fixed upon a dreadful legend that dwelt atop of the cash-machine: "This registers the amount of your purchase."

IX

Months later, the cowboy was frying pork over the stove of a little ranch near the Dakota line, when there was a quick thud of hoofs outside, and presently the Easterner entered with the letters and the papers.

"Well," said the Easterner at once, "the chap that killed the Swede has got three years. Wasn't much, was it?"

"He has? Three years?" The cowboy poised his pan of pork, while he ruminated upon the news. "Three years. That ain't much."

"No. It was a light sentence," replied the Easterner as he unbuckled his spurs. "Seems there was a good deal of sympathy for him in Romper."

"If the bartender had been any good," observed the cowboy, thoughtfully, "he would have gone in and cracked that there Dutchman on the head with a bottle in the beginnin' of it and stopped all this here murderin'."

"Yes, a thousand things might have happened," said the Easterner, tartly.

The cowboy returned his pan of pork to the fire, but his philosophy continued. "It's funny, ain't it? If he hadn't said Johnnie was cheatin' he'd be alive this minute. He was an awful fool. Game played for fun, too. Not for money. I believe he was crazy."

"I feel sorry for that gambler," said the Easterner.

"Oh, so do I," said the cowboy. "He don't deserve none of it for killin' who he did."

"The Swede might not have been killed if everything had been square."

"Might not have been killed?" exclaimed the cowboy. "Everythin' square? Why, when he said that Johnnie was cheatin' and acted like such a jackass? And then in the saloon he fairly walked up to git hurt?" With these arguments the cowboy browbeat the Easterner and reduced him to rage.

"You're a fool!" cried the Easterner, viciously. "You're a bigger jackass than the Swede by a million majority. Now let me tell you one thing. Let me tell you something. Listen! Johnnie was cheating!"

"'Johnnie,'" said the cowboy, blankly. There was a minute of silence, and then he said, robustly, "Why, no. The game was only for fun."

"Fun or not," said the Easterner, "Johnnie was cheating. I saw him. I know it. I saw him. And I refused to stand up and be a man. I let the Swede fight it out alone. And you—you were simply puffing around the place and wanting to fight. And then old Scully himself! We are all in it! This poor gambler isn't even a noun. He is kind of an adverb. Every sin is the result of a collaboration. We, five of us, have collaborated in the murder of this Swede. Usually there are from a dozen to forty women really involved in every murder, but in this case it seems to be only five men—you, I, Johnnie, old Scully, and that fool of an unfortunate gambler came merely as a culmination, the apex of a human movement, and gets all the punishment."

The cowboy, injured and rebellious, cried out blindly into this fog of mysterious theory: "Well, I didn't do anythin', did I?"

HIS NEW MITTENS

I

Little Horace was walking home from school, brilliantly decorated by a pair of new red mittens. A number of boys were snowballing gleefully in a field. They hailed him. "Come on, Horace! We're having a battle."

Horace was sad. "No," he said, "I can't. I've got to go home." At noon his mother had admonished him: "Now, Horace, you come straight home as soon as school is out. Do you hear? And don't you get them nice new mittens all wet, either. Do you hear?" Also his aunt had said: "I declare, Emily, it's a shame the way you allow that child to ruin his things." She had meant mittens. To his mother, Horace had dutifully replied, "Yes'm." But he now loitered in the vicinity of the group of uproarious boys, who were yelling like hawks as the white balls flew.

Some of them immediately analyzed this extraordinary hesitancy. "Hah!" they paused to scoff, "afraid of your new mittens, ain't you?" Some smaller boys, who were not yet so wise in discerning motives, applauded this attack with unreasonable vehemence. "A-fray-ed of his mit-tens! A-fray-ed of his mit-tens." They sang these lines to cruel and monotonous music which is as old perhaps as American childhood, and which it is the privilege of the emancipated adult to completely forget. "Afray-ed of his mit-tens!"

Horace cast a tortured glance towards his playmates, and then dropped his eyes to the snow at his feet. Presently he turned to the trunk of one of the great maple-trees that lined the curb. He made a pretence of closely examining the rough and virile bark. To his mind, this familiar street of Whilomville seemed to grow dark in the thick shadow of shame. The trees and the houses were now palled in purple.

"A-fray-ed of his mit-tens!" The terrible music had in it a meaning from the moonlit war-drums of chanting cannibals.

At last Horace, with supreme effort, raised his head. "'Tain't them I care about," he said, gruffly. "I've got to go home. That's all."

Whereupon each boy held his left forefinger as if it were a pencil and began to sharpen it derisively with his right forefinger. They came closer, and sang like a trained chorus, "A-fray-ed of his mittens!"

When he raised his voice to deny the charge it was simply lost in the screams of the mob. He was alone, fronting all the traditions of boyhood held before him by inexorable representatives. To such a low state had he fallen that one lad, a mere baby, outflanked him and then struck him in the cheek with a heavy snowball. The act was acclaimed with loud jeers. Horace turned to dart at his assailant, but there was an immediate demonstration on the other flank, and he found himself obliged to keep his face towards the hilarious crew of tormentors. The baby retreated in safety to the rear of the crowd, where he was received with fulsome compliments upon his daring. Horace retreated slowly up the walk. He continually tried to make them heed him, but the only sound was the chant, "A-fray-ed of his mit-tens!" In this desperate withdrawal the beset and haggard boy suffered more than is the common lot of man.

Being a boy himself, he did not understand boys at all. He had, of course, the dismal conviction that they were going to dog him to his grave. But near the corner of the field they suddenly seemed to forget all about it. Indeed, they possessed only the malevolence of so many flitter-headed sparrows. The interest had swung capriciously to some other matter. In a moment they were off in the field again, carousing amid the snow. Some authoritative boy had probably said, "Aw, come on!"

As the pursuit ceased, Horace ceased his retreat. He spent some time in what was evidently an attempt to adjust his self respect, and then began to wander furtively down towards the group. He, too, had undergone an important change. Perhaps his sharp agony was only as durable as the malevolence of the others. In this boyish life obedience to some unformulated creed of manners was enforced with capricious but merciless rigor. However, they were, after all, his comrades, his friends.

They did not heed his return. They were engaged in an altercation. It had evidently been planned that this battle was between Indians and soldiers. The smaller and weaker boys had been induced to appear as Indians in the initial skirmish, but they were now very sick of it, and were reluctantly but steadfastly, affirming their desire for a change of caste. The larger boys had all won great distinction, devastating Indians materially, and they wished the war to go on as planned. They explained vociferously that it was proper for the soldiers always to thrash the Indians. The little boys did not pretend to deny the truth of this argument; they confined themselves to the simple statement that, in that case, they wished to be soldiers. Each little boy willingly appealed to the others to remain Indians, but as for himself he reiterated his desire to enlist as a soldier. The larger boys were in despair over this dearth of enthusiasm in the small Indians. They alternately wheedled and bullied, but they could not persuade the little boys, who were really suffering dreadful humiliation rather than submit to another onslaught of soldiers. They were called all the baby names that had the power of stinging deep into their pride, but they remained firm.

Then a formidable lad, a leader of reputation, one who could whip many boys that wore long trousers, suddenly blew out his cheeks and shouted, "Well, all right then. I'll be an Indian myself. Now." The little boys greeted with cheers this addition to their wearied ranks, and seemed then content. But matters were not mended in the least, because all of the personal following of the formidable lad, with the addition of every outsider, spontaneously forsook the flag and declared themselves Indians. There were now no soldiers. The Indians had carried everything unanimously. The formidable lad used his influence, but his influence could not shake the loyalty of his friends, who refused to fight under any colors but his colors.

Plainly there was nothing for it but to coerce the little ones. The formidable lad again became a soldier, and then graciously permitted to join him all the real fighting strength of the crowd, leaving behind a most forlorn band of little Indians. Then the soldiers attacked the Indians, exhorting them to opposition at the same time.

The Indians at first adopted a policy of hurried surrender, but this had no success, as none of the surrenders were accepted. They then turned to flee, bawling out protests. The ferocious soldiers pursued them amid shouts. The battle widened, developing all manner of marvellous detail.

Horace had turned towards home several times, but, as a matter of fact, this scene held him in a spell. It was fascinating beyond anything which the grown man understands. He had always in the back of his head a sense of guilt, even a sense of impending punishment for disobedience, but they could not weigh with the delirium of this snow-battle.

II

One of the raiding soldiers, espying Horace, called out in passing, "A-fray-ed of his mit-tens!" Horace flinched at this renewal, and the other lad paused to taunt him again. Horace scooped some snow, moulded it into a ball, and flung it at the other. "Ho!" cried the boy, "you're an Indian, are you? Hey, fellers, here's an Indian that ain't been killed yet." He and Horace engaged in a duel in which both were in such haste to mould snowballs that they had little time for aiming.

Horace once struck his opponent squarely in the chest. "Hey," he shouted, "you're dead. You can't fight any more, Pete. I killed you. You're dead."

The other boy flushed red, but he continued frantically to make ammunition. "You never touched me!" he retorted, glowering. "You never touched me! Where, now?" he added, defiantly. "Where did you hit me?"

"On the coat! Right on your breast! You can't fight any more! You're dead!"

"You never!"

"I did, too! Hey, fellers, ain't he dead? I hit 'im square!"

"He never!"

Nobody had seen the affair, but some of the boys took sides in absolute accordance with their friendship for one of the concerned parties. Horace's opponent went about contending, "He never touched me! He never came near me! He never came near me!"

The formidable leader now came forward and accosted Horace. "What was you? An Indian? Well, then, you're dead—that's all. He hit you. I saw him."

"Me?" shrieked Horace. "He never came within a mile of me——"

At that moment he heard his name called in a certain familiar tune of two notes, with the last note shrill and prolonged. He looked towards the sidewalk, and saw his mother standing there in her widow's weeds, with two brown paper parcels under her arm. A silence had fallen upon all the boys. Horace moved slowly towards his mother. She did not seem to note his approach; she was gazing austerely off through the naked branches of the maples where two crimson sunset bars lay on the deep blue sky.

At a distance of ten paces Horace made a desperate venture. "Oh, ma," he whined, "can't I stay out for a while?"

"No," she answered solemnly, "you come with me." Horace knew that profile; it was the inexorable profile. But he continued to plead, because it was not beyond his mind that a great show of suffering now might diminish his suffering later.

He did not dare to look back at his playmates. It was already a public scandal that he could not stay out as late as other boys, and he could imagine his standing now that he had been again dragged off by his mother in sight of the whole world. He was a profoundly miserable human being.

Aunt Martha opened the door for them. Light streamed about her straight skirt. "Oh," she said, "so you found him on the road, eh? Well, I declare! It was about time!"

Horace slunk into the kitchen. The stove, straddling out on its four iron legs, was gently humming. Aunt Martha had evidently just lighted the lamp, for she went to it and began to twist the wick experimentally.

"Now," said the mother, "let's see them mittens."

Horace's chin sank. The aspiration of the criminal, the passionate desire for an asylum from retribution, from justice, was aflame in his heart. "I—I—

235

don't—don't know where they are." he gasped finally, as he passed his hand over his pockets.

"Horace," intoned his mother, "you are tellin' me a story!"

"'Tain't a story," he answered, just above his breath. He looked like a sheep-stealer.

His mother held him by the arm, and began to search his pockets. Almost at once she was able to bring forth a pair of very wet mittens. "Well, I declare!" cried Aunt Martha. The two women went close to the lamp, and minutely examined the mittens, turning them over and over. Afterwards, when Horace looked up, his mother's sad-lined, homely face was turned towards him. He burst into tears.

His mother drew a chair near the stove. "Just you sit there now, until I tell you to git off." He sidled meekly into the chair. His mother and his aunt went briskly about the business of preparing supper. They did not display a knowledge of his existence; they carried an effect of oblivion so far that they even did not speak to each other. Presently they went into the dining and living room; Horace could hear the dishes rattling. His Aunt Martha brought a plate of food, placed it on a chair near him, and went away without a word.

Horace instantly decided that he would not touch a morsel of the food. He had often used this ruse in dealing with his mother. He did not know why it brought her to terms, but certainly it sometimes did.

The mother looked up when the aunt returned to the other room. "Is he eatin' his supper?" she asked.

The maiden aunt, fortified in ignorance, gazed with pity and contempt upon this interest. "Well, now, Emily, how do I know?" she queried. "Was I goin' to stand over 'im? Of all the worryin' you do about that child! It's a shame the way you're bringin' up that child."

"Well, he ought to eat somethin'. It won't do fer him to go without eatin'," the mother retorted, weakly.

Aunt Martha, profoundly scorning the policy of concession which these words meant, uttered a long, contemptuous sigh.

III

Alone in the kitchen, Horace stared with sombre eyes at the plate of food. For a long time he betrayed no sign of yielding. His mood was adamantine. He was resolved not to sell his vengeance for bread, cold ham, and a pickle, and yet it must be known that the sight of them affected him powerfully. The pickle in particular was notable for its seductive charm. He surveyed it darkly.

But at last, unable to longer endure his state, his attitude in the presence of the pickle, he put out an inquisitive finger and touched it, and it was cool and green and plump. Then a full conception of the cruel woe of his situation swept upon him suddenly, and his eyes filled with tears, which began to move down his cheeks. He sniffled. His heart was black with hatred. He painted in his mind scenes of deadly retribution. His mother would be taught that he was not one to endure persecution meekly, without raising an arm in his defence. And so his dreams were of a slaughter of feelings, and near the end of them his mother was pictured as coming, bowed with pain, to his feet. Weeping, she implored his charity. Would he forgive her? No; his once tender heart had been turned to stone by her injustice. He could not forgive her. She must pay the inexorable penalty.

The first item in this horrible plan was the refusal of the food. This he knew by experience would work havoc in his mother's heart. And so he grimly waited.

But suddenly it occurred to him that the first part of his revenge was in danger of failing. The thought struck him that his mother might not capitulate in the usual way. According to his recollection, the time was more than due when she should come in, worried, sadly affectionate, and ask him if he was ill. It had then been his custom to hint in a resigned voice that he was the victim of secret disease, but that he preferred to suffer in silence and alone. If she was obdurate in her anxiety, he always asked her in a gloomy, low voice to go away and leave him to suffer in silence and alone in the darkness without food. He had known this maneuvering to result even in pie.

But what was the meaning of the long pause and the stillness? Had his old and valued ruse betrayed him? As the truth sank into his mind, he supremely loathed life, the world, his mother. Her heart was beating back the besiegers; he was a defeated child.

He wept for a time before deciding upon the final stroke. He would run away. In a remote corner of the world he would become some sort of bloody-handed person driven to a life of crime by the barbarity of his mother. She should never know his fate. He would torture her for years with doubts and doubts, and drive her implacably to a repentant grave. Nor would Aunt Martha escape. Some day, a century hence, when his mother was dead, he would write to his Aunt Martha, and point out her part in the blighting of his life. For one blow against him now he would, in time, deal back a thousand—aye, ten thousand.

He arose and took his coat and cap. As he moved stealthily towards the door he cast a glance backward at the pickle. He was tempted to take it, but he knew that if he left the plate inviolate his mother would feel even worse.

A blue snow was falling. People, bowed forward, were moving briskly along the walks. The electric lamps hummed amid showers of flakes. As Horace emerged from the kitchen, a shrill squall drove the flakes around the corner of the house. He cowered away from it, and its violence illumined his mind vaguely in new directions. He deliberated upon a choice of remote corners of the globe. He found that he had no plans which were definite enough in a geographical way, but without much loss of time he decided upon California. He moved briskly as far as his mother's front gate on the road to California. He was off at last. His success was a trifle dreadful; his throat choked.

But at the gate he paused. He did not know if his journey to California would be shorter if he went down Niagara Avenue or off through Hogan Street. As the storm was very cold and the point was very important, he decided to withdraw for reflection to the wood-shed. He entered the dark shanty, and took seat upon the old chopping-block upon which he was supposed to perform for a few minutes every afternoon when he returned from school. The wind screamed and shouted at the loose boards, and there was a rift of snow on the floor to leeward of a crack.

Here the idea of starting for California on such a night departed from his mind, leaving him ruminating miserably upon his martyrdom. He saw nothing for it but to sleep all night in the wood-shed and start for California in the morning bright and early. Thinking of his bed, he kicked over the floor and found that the innumerable chips were all frozen tightly, bedded in ice.

Later he viewed with joy some signs of excitement in the house. The flare of a lamp moved rapidly from window to window. Then the kitchen door slammed loudly and a shawled figure sped towards the gate. At last he was making them feel his power. The shivering child's face was lit with saturnine glee as in the darkness of the wood-shed he gloated over the evidences of consternation in his home. The shawled figure had been his Aunt Martha dashing with the alarm to the neighbors.

The cold of the wood-shed was tormenting him. He endured only because of the terror he was causing. But then it occurred to him that, if they instituted a search for him, they would probably examine the wood-shed. He knew that it would not be manful to be caught so soon. He was not positive now that he was going to remain away forever, but at any rate he was bound to inflict some more damage before allowing himself to be captured. If he merely succeeded in making his mother angry, she would thrash him on sight. He must prolong the time in order to be safe. If he held out properly, he was sure of a welcome of love, even though he should drip with crimes.

Evidently the storm had increased, for when he went out it swung him violently with its rough and merciless strength. Panting, stung, half blinded with the driving flakes, he was now a waif, exiled, friendless, and poor. With a bursting heart, he thought of his home and his mother. To his forlorn vision they were as far away as heaven.

IV

Horace was undergoing changes of feeling so rapidly that he was merely moved hither and then thither like a kite. He was now aghast at the merciless ferocity of his mother. It was she who had thrust him into this wild storm, and she was perfectly indifferent to his fate, perfectly indifferent. The forlorn wanderer could no longer weep. The strong sobs caught at his throat, making his breath come in short, quick snuffles. All in him was conquered save the enigmatical childish ideal of form, manner. This principle still held out, and it was the only thing between him and submission. When he surrendered, he must surrender in a way that deferred to the undefined code. He longed simply to go to the kitchen and stumble in, but his unfathomable sense of fitness forbade him.

Presently he found himself at the head of Niagara Avenue, staring through the snow into the blazing windows of Stickney's butcher-shop. Stickney was the family butcher, not so much because of a superiority to other Whilomville butchers as because he lived next door and had been an intimate friend of the father of Horace. Rows of glowing pigs hung head downward back of the tables, which bore huge pieces of red beef. Clumps of attenuated turkeys were suspended here and there. Stickney, hale and smiling, was bantering with a woman in a cloak, who, with a monster basket on her arm, was dickering for eight cents' worth of some thing. Horace watched them through a crusted pane. When the woman came out and passed him, he went towards the door. He touched the latch with his finger, but withdrew again suddenly to the sidewalk. Inside Stickney was whistling cheerily and assorting his knives.

Finally Horace went desperately forward, opened the door, and entered the shop. His head hung low. Stickney stopped whistling. "Hello, young man," he cried, "what brings you here?"

Horace halted, but said nothing. He swung one foot to and fro over the saw-dust floor.

Stickney had placed his two fat hands palms downward and wide apart on the table, in the attitude of a butcher facing a customer, but now he straightened.

"Here," he said, "what's wrong? What's wrong, kid?"

"Nothin'," answered Horace, huskily. He labored for a moment with something in his throat, and afterwards added, "O'ny——I've——I've run away, and—"

"Run away!" shouted Stickney. "Run away from what? Who?"

"From——home," answered Horace. "I don't like it there any more. I——" He had arranged an oration to win the sympathy of the butcher; he had prepared a table setting forth the merits of his case in the most logical fashion, but it was as if the wind had been knocked out of his mind. "I've run away. I——"

Stickney reached an enormous hand over the array of beef, and firmly grappled the emigrant. Then he swung himself to Horace's side. His face was stretched with laughter, and he playfully shook his prisoner. "Come——come——come. What dashed nonsense is this? Run away, hey? Run away?" Whereupon the child's long-tried spirit found vent in howls.

"Come, come," said Stickney, busily. "Never mind now, never mind. You just come along with me. It'll be all right. I'll fix it. Never you mind."

Five minutes later the butcher, with a great ulster over his apron, was leading the boy homeward.

At the very threshold, Horace raised his last flag of pride. "No——no," he sobbed. "I don't want to. I don't want to go in there." He braced his foot against the step and made a very respectable resistance.

"Now, Horace," cried the butcher. He thrust open the door with a bang. "Hello there!" Across the dark kitchen the door to the living-room opened and Aunt Martha appeared. "You've found him!" she screamed.

"We've come to make a call," roared the butcher. At the entrance to the living-room a silence fell upon them all. Upon a couch Horace saw his mother lying limp, pale as death, her eyes gleaming with pain. There was an electric pause before she swung a waxen hand towards Horace. "My child," she murmured, tremulously. Whereupon the sinister person addressed, with a prolonged wail of grief and joy, ran to her with speed. "Mam-ma! Mam-ma! Oh, mam-ma!" She was not able to speak in a known tongue as she folded him in her weak arms.

Aunt Martha turned defiantly upon the butcher because her face betrayed her. She was crying. She made a gesture half military, half feminine. "Won't you have a glass of our root-beer, Mr. Stickney? We make it ourselves."

THE LITTLE REGIMENT, AND OTHER EPISODES OF THE AMERICAN CIVIL WAR

THE LITTLE REGIMENT.

I.

The fog made the clothes of the men of the column in the roadway seem of a luminous quality. It imparted to the heavy infantry overcoats a new colour, a kind of blue which was so pale that a regiment might have been merely a long, low shadow in the mist. However, a muttering, one part grumble, three parts joke, hovered in the air above the thick ranks, and blended in an undertoned roar, which was the voice of the column.

The town on the southern shore of the little river loomed spectrally, a faint etching upon the gray cloud-masses which were shifting with oily languor. A long row of guns upon the northern bank had been pitiless in their hatred, but a little battered belfry could be dimly seen still pointing with invincible resolution toward the heavens.

The enclouded air vibrated with noises made by hidden colossal things. The infantry tramplings, the heavy rumbling of the artillery, made the earth speak of gigantic preparation. Guns on distant heights thundered from time to time with sudden, nervous roar, as if unable to endure in silence a knowledge of hostile troops massing, other guns going to position. These sounds, near and remote, defined an immense battle-ground, described the tremendous width of the stage of the prospective drama. The voices of the guns, slightly casual, unexcited in their challenges and warnings, could not destroy the unutterable eloquence of the word in the air, a meaning of impending struggle which made the breath halt at the lips.

The column in the roadway was ankle-deep in mud. The men swore piously at the rain which drizzled upon them, compelling them to stand always very erect in fear of the drops that would sweep in under their coat-collars. The fog was as cold as wet cloths. The men stuffed their hands deep in their pockets, and huddled their muskets in their arms. The machinery of orders had rooted these soldiers deeply into the mud precisely as almighty nature roots mullein stalks.

They listened and speculated when a tumult of fighting came from the dim town across the river. When the noise lulled for a time they resumed their descriptions of the mud and graphically exaggerated the number of hours they had been kept waiting. The general commanding their division rode along the ranks, and they cheered admiringly, affectionately, crying out to him gleeful prophecies of the coming battle. Each man scanned him with a peculiarly keen personal interest, and afterward spoke of him with unquestioning devotion and confidence, narrating anecdotes which were mainly untrue.

When the jokers lifted the shrill voices which invariably belonged to them, flinging witticisms at their comrades, a loud laugh would sweep from rank to rank, and soldiers who had not heard would lean forward and demand repetition. When were borne past them some wounded men with gray and blood-smeared faces, and eyes that rolled in that helpless beseeching for assistance from the sky which comes with supreme pain, the soldiers in the mud watched intently, and from time to time asked of the bearers an account of the affair. Frequently they bragged of their corps, their division, their brigade, their regiment. Anon they referred to the mud and the cold drizzle. Upon this threshold of a wild scene of death they, in short, defied the proportion of events with that splendour of heedlessness which belongs only to veterans.

"Like a lot of wooden soldiers," swore Billie Dempster, moving his feet in the thick mass, and casting a vindictive glance indefinitely; "standing in the mud for a hundred years."

"Oh, shut up!" murmured his brother Dan. The manner of his words implied that this fraternal voice near him was an indescribable bore.

"Why should I shut up?" demanded Billie.

244

"Because you're a fool," cried Dan, taking no time to debate it; "the biggest fool in the regiment."

There was but one man between them, and he was habituated. These insults from brother to brother had swept across his chest, flown past his face, many times during two long campaigns. Upon this occasion he simply grinned first at one, then at the other.

The way of these brothers was not an unknown topic in regimental gossip. They had enlisted simultaneously, with each sneering loudly at the other for doing it. They left their little town, and went forward with the flag, exchanging protestations of undying suspicion. In the camp life they so openly despised each other that, when entertaining quarrels were lacking, their companions often contrived situations calculated to bring forth display of this fraternal dislike.

Both were large-limbed, strong young men, and often fought with friends in camp unless one was near to interfere with the other. This latter happened rather frequently, because Dan, preposterously willing for any manner of combat, had a very great horror of seeing Billie in a fight; and Billie, almost odiously ready himself, simply refused to see Dan stripped to his shirt and with his fists aloft. This sat queerly upon them, and made them the objects of plots.

When Dan jumped through a ring of eager soldiers and dragged forth his raving brother by the arm, a thing often predicted would almost come to pass. When Billie performed the same office for Dan, the prediction would again miss fulfilment by an inch. But indeed they never fought together, although they were perpetually upon the verge.

They expressed longing for such conflict. As a matter of truth, they had at one time made full arrangement for it, but even with the encouragement and interest of half of the regiment they somehow failed to achieve collision.

If Dan became a victim of police duty, no jeering was so destructive to the feelings as Billie's comment. If Billie got a call to appear at the headquarters, none would so genially prophesy his complete undoing as Dan. Small misfortunes to one were, in truth, invariably greeted with hilarity by the other, who seemed to see in them great re-enforcement of his opinion.

As soldiers, they expressed each for each a scorn intense and blasting. After a certain battle, Billie was promoted to corporal. When Dan was told of it, he seemed smitten dumb with astonishment and patriotic indignation. He stared in silence, while the dark blood rushed to Billie's forehead, and he shifted his weight from foot to foot. Dan at last found his tongue, and said: "Well, I'm durned!" If he had heard that an army mule had been appointed to the post of corps commander, his tone could not have had more derision in it. Afterward, he adopted a fervid insubordination, an almost religious reluctance to obey the new corporal's orders, which came near to developing the desired strife.

It is here finally to be recorded also that Dan, most ferociously profane in speech, very rarely swore in the presence of his brother; and that Billie, whose oaths came from his lips with the grace of falling pebbles, was seldom known to express himself in this manner when near his brother Dan.

At last the afternoon contained a suggestion of evening. Metallic cries rang suddenly from end to end of the column. They inspired at once a quick, business-like adjustment. The long thing stirred in the mud. The men had hushed, and were looking across the river. A moment later the shadowy mass of pale blue figures was moving steadily toward the stream. There could be heard from the town a clash of swift fighting and cheering. The noise of the shooting coming through the heavy air had its sharpness taken from it, and sounded in thuds.

There was a halt upon the bank above the pontoons. When the column went winding down the incline, and streamed out upon the bridge, the fog had faded to a great degree, and in the clearer dusk the guns on a distant ridge were enabled to perceive the crossing. The long whirling outcries of the shells came into the air above the men. An occasional solid shot struck the surface of the river, and dashed into view a sudden vertical jet. The distance was subtly illuminated by the lightning from the deep-booming guns. One by one the batteries on the northern shore aroused, the innumerable guns bellowing in angry oration at the distant ridge. The rolling thunder crashed and reverberated as a wild surf sounds on a still night, and to this music the column marched across the pontoons.

The waters of the grim river curled away in a smile from the ends of the great boats, and slid swiftly beneath the planking. The dark, riddled walls of the town upreared before the troops, and from a region hidden by these hammered and tumbled houses came incessantly the yells and firings of a prolonged and close skirmish.

When Dan had called his brother a fool, his voice had been so decisive, so brightly assured, that many men had laughed, considering it to be great humour under the circumstances. The incident happened to rankle deep in Billie. It was not any strange thing that his brother had called him a fool. In fact, he often called him a fool with exactly the same amount of cheerful and prompt conviction, and before large audiences, too. Billie wondered in his own mind why he took such profound offence in this case; but, at any rate, as he slid down the bank and on to the bridge with his regiment, he was searching his knowledge for something that would pierce Dan's blithesome spirit. But he could contrive nothing at this time, and his impotency made the glance which he was once able to give his brother still more malignant.

The guns far and near were roaring a fearful and grand introduction for this column which was marching upon the stage of death. Billie felt it, but only in a numb way. His heart was cased in that curious dissonant metal which covers a man's emotions at such times. The terrible voices from the hills told him that in this wide conflict his life was an insignificant fact, and that his death would be an insignificant fact. They portended the whirlwind to which he would be as necessary as a butterfly's waved wing. The solemnity, the sadness of it came near enough to make him wonder why he was neither solemn nor sad. When his mind vaguely adjusted events according to their importance to him, it appeared that the uppermost thing was the fact that upon the eve of battle, and before many comrades, his brother had called him a fool.

Dan was in a particularly happy mood. "Hurray! Look at 'em shoot," he said, when the long witches' croon of the shells came into the air. It enraged Billie when he felt the little thorn in him, and saw at the same time that his brother had completely forgotten it.

The column went from the bridge into more mud. At this southern end there was a chaos of hoarse directions and commands. Darkness was coming upon the earth, and regiments were being hurried up the slippery bank. As Billie floundered in the black mud, amid the swearing, sliding crowd, he suddenly resolved that, in the absence of other means of hurting Dan, he would avoid looking at him, refrain from speaking to him, pay absolutely no heed to his existence; and this done skilfully would, he imagined, soon reduce his brother to a poignant sensitiveness.

At the top of the bank the column again halted and rearranged itself, as a man after a climb rearranges his clothing. Presently the great steel-backed brigade, an infinitely graceful thing in the rhythm and ease of its veteran movement, swung up a little narrow, slanting street.

Evening had come so swiftly that the fighting on the remote borders of the town was indicated by thin flashes of flame. Some building was on fire, and its reflection upon the clouds was an oval of delicate pink.

II.

All demeanour of rural serenity had been wrenched violently from the little town by the guns and by the waves of men which had surged through it. The hand of war laid upon this village had in an instant changed it to a thing of remnants. It resembled the place of a monstrous shaking of the earth itself. The windows, now mere unsightly holes, made the tumbled and blackened dwellings seem skeletons. Doors lay splintered to fragments. Chimneys had flung their bricks everywhere. The artillery fire had not neglected the rows of gentle shade-trees which had lined the streets. Branches and heavy trunks cluttered the mud in drift-wood tangles, while a few shattered forms had contrived to remain dejectedly, mournfully upright. They expressed an innocence, a helplessness, which perforce created a pity for their happening into this cauldron of battle. Furthermore, there was under foot a vast collection of odd things reminiscent of the charge, the fight, the retreat. There were boxes and barrels filled with earth, behind which riflemen had lain snugly, and in these little trenches were the dead in blue with the dead in gray, the poses eloquent of the struggles for possession of the town until the history of the whole conflict was written plainly in the streets.

And yet the spirit of this little city, its quaint individuality, poised in the air above the ruins, defying the guns, the sweeping volleys; holding in contempt those avaricious blazes which had attacked many dwellings. The hard earthen sidewalks proclaimed the games that had been played there during long lazy days, in the careful shadows of the trees. "General Merchandise," in faint letters upon a long board, had to be read with a slanted glance, for the sign dangled by one end; but the porch of the old store was a palpable legend of wide-hatted men, smoking.

This subtle essence, this soul of the life that had been, brushed like invisible wings the thoughts of the men in the swift columns that came up from the river.

In the darkness a loud and endless humming arose from the great blue crowds bivouacked in the streets. From time to time a sharp spatter of firing from far picket lines entered this bass chorus. The smell from the smouldering ruins floated on the cold night breeze.

Dan, seated ruefully upon the doorstep of a shot-pierced house, was proclaiming the campaign badly managed. Orders had been issued forbidding camp-fires.

Suddenly he ceased his oration, and scanning the group of his comrades, said: "Where's Billie? Do you know?"

"Gone on picket."

"Get out! Has he?" said Dan. "No business to go on picket. Why don't some of them other corporals take their turn?"

A bearded private was smoking his pipe of confiscated tobacco, seated comfortably upon a horse-hair trunk which he had dragged from the house. He observed: "Was his turn."

"No such thing," cried Dan. He and the man on the horse-hair trunk held discussion in which Dan stoutly maintained that if his brother had been sent on picket it was an injustice. He ceased his argument when another soldier, upon whose arms could faintly be seen the two stripes of a corporal, entered the circle. "Humph," said Dan, "where you been?"

The corporal made no answer. Presently Dan said: "Billie, where you been?"

His brother did not seem to hear these inquiries. He glanced at the house which towered above them, and remarked casually to the man on the horse-hair trunk: "Funny, ain't it? After the pelting this town got, you'd think there wouldn't be one brick left on another."

"Oh," said Dan, glowering at his brother's back. "Getting mighty smart, ain't you?"

The absence of camp-fires allowed the evening to make apparent its quality of faint silver light in which the blue clothes of the throng became black, and the faces became white expanses, void of expression. There was considerable excitement a short distance from the group around the doorstep. A soldier had chanced upon a hoop-skirt, and arrayed in it he was performing a dance amid the applause of his companions. Billie and a greater part of the men immediately poured over there to witness the exhibition.

"What's the matter with Billie?" demanded Dan of the man upon the horse-hair trunk.

"How do I know?" rejoined the other in mild resentment. He arose and walked away. When he returned he said briefly, in a weather-wise tone, that it would rain during the night.

Dan took a seat upon one end of the horse-hair trunk. He was facing the crowd around the dancer, which in its hilarity swung this way and that way. At times he imagined that he could recognise his brother's face.

He and the man on the other end of the trunk thoughtfully talked of the army's position. To their minds, infantry and artillery were in a most precarious jumble in the streets of the town; but they did not grow nervous over it, for they were used to having the army appear in a precarious jumble to their minds. They had learned to accept such puzzling situations as a consequence of their position in the ranks, and were now usually in possession of a simple but perfectly immovable faith that somebody understood the jumble. Even if they had been convinced that the army was a headless monster, they would merely have nodded with the veteran's singular cynicism. It was none of their business as soldiers. Their duty was to grab sleep and food when occasion permitted, and cheerfully fight wherever their feet were planted until more orders came. This was a task sufficiently absorbing.

They spoke of other corps, and this talk being confidential, their voices dropped to tones of awe. "The Ninth"—"The First"—"The Fifth"—"The Sixth"—"The Third"—the simple numerals rang with eloquence, each having a meaning which was to float through many years as no intangible arithmetical mist, but as pregnant with individuality as the names of cities.

Of their own corps they spoke with a deep veneration, an idolatry, a supreme confidence which apparently would not blanch to see it match against everything.

It was as if their respect for other corps was due partly to a wonder that organizations not blessed with their own famous numeral could take such an interest in war. They could prove that their division was the best in the corps, and that their brigade was the best in the division. And their regiment—it was plain that no fortune of life was equal to the chance which caused a man to be born, so to speak, into this command, the keystone of the defending arch.

At times Dan covered with insults the character of a vague, unnamed general to whose petulance and busy-body spirit he ascribed the order which made hot coffee impossible.

Dan said that victory was certain in the coming battle. The other man seemed rather dubious. He remarked upon the fortified line of hills, which had impressed him even from the other side of the river. "Shucks," said Dan. "Why, we—" He pictured a splendid overflowing of these hills by the sea of men in blue. During the period of this conversation Dan's glance searched the merry throng about the dancer. Above the babble of voices in the street a far-away thunder could sometimes be heard—evidently from the very edge of the horizon—the boom-boom of restless guns.

III.

Ultimately the night deepened to the tone of black velvet. The outlines of the fireless camp were like the faint drawings upon ancient tapestry. The glint of a rifle, the shine of a button, might have been of threads of silver and gold sewn upon the fabric of the night. There was little presented to the vision, but to a sense more subtle there was discernible in the atmosphere something like a pulse; a mystic beating which would have told a stranger of the presence of a giant thing—the slumbering mass of regiments and batteries.

With fires forbidden, the floor of a dry old kitchen was thought to be a good exchange for the cold earth of December, even if a shell had exploded in it and knocked it so out of shape that when a man lay curled in his blanket his last waking thought was likely to be of the wall that bellied out above him as if strongly anxious to topple upon the score of soldiers.

Billie looked at the bricks ever about to descend in a shower upon his face, listened to the industrious pickets plying their rifles on the border of the town, imagined some measure of the din of the coming battle, thought of Dan and Dan's chagrin, and rolling over in his blanket went to sleep with satisfaction.

At an unknown hour he was aroused by the creaking of boards. Lifting himself upon his elbow, he saw a sergeant prowling among the sleeping forms. The sergeant carried a candle in an old brass candle-stick. He would have resembled some old farmer on an unusual midnight tour if it were not for the significance of his gleaming buttons and striped sleeves.

Billie blinked stupidly at the light until his mind returned from the journeys of slumber. The sergeant stooped among the unconscious soldiers, holding the candle close, and peering into each face.

"Hello, Haines," said Billie. "Relief?"

"Hello, Billie," said the sergeant. "Special duty."

"Dan got to go?"

"Jameson, Hunter, McCormack, D. Dempster. Yes. Where is he?"

"Over there by the winder," said Billie, gesturing. "What is it for, Haines?"

"You don't think I know, do you?" demanded the sergeant. He began to pipe sharply but cheerily at men upon the floor. "Come, Mac, get up here. Here's a special for you. Wake up, Jameson. Come along, Dannie, me boy."

Each man at once took this call to duty as a personal affront. They pulled themselves out of their blankets, rubbed their eyes, and swore at whoever was responsible. "Them's orders," cried the sergeant. "Come! Get out of here." An undetailed head with dishevelled hair thrust out from a blanket, and a sleepy voice said: "Shut up, Haines, and go home."

When the detail clanked out of the kitchen, all but one of the remaining men seemed to be again asleep. Billie, leaning on his elbow, was gazing into darkness. When the footsteps died to silence, he curled himself into his blanket.

At the first cool lavender lights of daybreak he aroused again, and scanned his recumbent companions. Seeing a wakeful one he asked: "Is Dan back yet?"

The man said: "Hain't seen 'im."

Billie put both hands behind his head, and scowled into the air. "Can't see the use of these cussed details in the night-time," he muttered in his most unreasonable tones. "Darn nuisances. Why can't they—" He grumbled at length and graphically.

When Dan entered with the squad, however, Billie was convincingly asleep.

IV.

The regiment trotted in double time along the street, and the colonel seemed to quarrel over the right of way with many artillery officers. Batteries were waiting in the mud, and the men of them, exasperated by the bustle of this ambitious infantry, shook their fists from saddle and caisson, exchanging all manner of taunts and jests. The slanted guns continued to look reflectively

253

at the ground.

On the outskirts of the crumbled town a fringe of blue figures were firing into the fog. The regiment swung out into skirmish lines, and the fringe of blue figures departed, turning their backs and going joyfully around the flank.

The bullets began a low moan off toward a ridge which loomed faintly in the heavy mist. When the swift crescendo had reached its climax, the missiles zipped just overhead, as if piercing an invisible curtain. A battery on the hill was crashing with such tumult that it was as if the guns had quarrelled and had fallen pell-mell and snarling upon each other. The shells howled on their journey toward the town. From short range distance there came a spatter of musketry, sweeping along an invisible line and making faint sheets of orange light.

Some in the new skirmish lines were beginning to fire at various shadows discerned in the vapour, forms of men suddenly revealed by some humour of the laggard masses of clouds. The crackle of musketry began to dominate the purring of the hostile bullets. Dan, in the front rank, held his rifle poised, and looked into the fog keenly, coldly, with the air of a sportsman. His nerves were so steady that it was as if they had been drawn from his body, leaving him merely a muscular machine; but his numb heart was somehow beating to the pealing march of the fight.

The waving skirmish line went backward and forward, ran this way and that way. Men got lost in the fog, and men were found again. Once they got too close to the formidable ridge, and the thing burst out as if repulsing a general attack. Once another blue regiment was apprehended on the very edge of firing into them. Once a friendly battery began an elaborate and scientific process of extermination. Always as busy as brokers, the men slid here and there over the plain, fighting their foes, escaping from their friends, leaving a history of many movements in the wet yellow turf, cursing the atmosphere, blazing away every time they could identify the enemy.

In one mystic changing of the fog, as if the fingers of spirits were drawing aside these draperies, a small group of the gray skirmishers, silent, statuesque, were suddenly disclosed to Dan and those about him. So vivid and near were they that there was something uncanny in the revelation.

There might have been a second of mutual staring. Then each rifle in each group was at the shoulder. As Dan's glance flashed along the barrel of his weapon, the figure of a man suddenly loomed as if the musket had been a telescope. The short black beard, the slouch hat, the pose of the man as he sighted to shoot, made a quick picture in Dan's mind. The same moment, it would seem, he pulled his own trigger, and the man, smitten, lurched forward, while his exploding rifle made a slanting crimson streak in the air, and the slouch hat fell before the body. The billows of the fog, governed by singular impulses, rolled between.

"You got that feller sure enough," said a comrade to Dan. Dan looked at him absent-mindedly.

V.

When the next morning calmly displayed another fog, the men of the regiment exchanged eloquent comments; but they did not abuse it at length, because the streets of the town now contained enough galloping aides to make three troops of cavalry, and they knew that they had come to the verge of the great fight.

Dan conversed with the man who had once possessed a horse-hair trunk; but they did not mention the line of hills which had furnished them in more careless moments with an agreeable topic. They avoided it now as condemned men do the subject of death, and yet the thought of it stayed in their eyes as they looked at each other and talked gravely of other things.

The expectant regiment heaved a long sigh of relief when the sharp call: "Fall in," repeated indefinitely, arose in the streets. It was inevitable that a bloody battle was to be fought, and they wanted to get it off their minds. They were, however, doomed again to spend a long period planted firmly in the mud. They craned their necks, and wondered where some of the other regiments were going.

At last the mists rolled carelessly away. Nature made at this time all provisions to enable foes to see each other, and immediately the roar of guns resounded from every hill. The endless cracking of the skirmishers swelled to rolling crashes of musketry. Shells screamed with panther-like noises at the houses. Dan looked at the man of the horse-hair trunk, and the man said: "Well, here she comes!"

The tenor voices of younger officers and the deep and hoarse voices of the older ones rang in the streets. These cries pricked like spurs. The masses of men vibrated from the suddenness with which they were plunged into the situation of troops about to fight. That the orders were long-expected did not concern the emotion.

Simultaneous movement was imparted to all these thick bodies of men and horses that lay in the town. Regiment after regiment swung rapidly into the streets that faced the sinister ridge.

This exodus was theatrical. The little sober-hued village had been like the cloak which disguises the king of drama. It was now put aside, and an army, splendid thing of steel and blue, stood forth in the sunlight.

Even the soldiers in the heavy columns drew deep breaths at the sight, more majestic than they had dreamed. The heights of the enemy's position were crowded with men who resembled people come to witness some mighty pageant. But as the column moved steadily to their positions, the guns, matter-of-fact warriors, doubled their number, and shells burst with red thrilling tumult on the crowded plain. One came into the ranks of the regiment, and after the smoke and the wrath of it had faded, leaving motionless figures, everyone stormed according to the limits of his vocabulary, for veterans detest being killed when they are not busy.

The regiment sometimes looked sideways at its brigade companions composed of men who had never been in battle; but no frozen blood could withstand the heat of the splendour of this army before the eyes on the plain, these lines so long that the flanks were little streaks, this mass of men of one intention. The recruits carried themselves heedlessly. At the rear was an idle battery, and three artillery men in a foolish row on a caisson nudged each other and grinned at the recruits. "You'll catch it pretty soon," they called out.

They were impersonally gleeful, as if they themselves were not also likely to catch it pretty soon. But with this picture of an army in their hearts, the new men perhaps felt the devotion which the drops may feel for the wave; they were of its power and glory; they smiled jauntily at the foolish row of gunners, and told them to go to blazes.

The column trotted across some little bridges, and spread quickly into lines of battle. Before them was a bit of plain, and back of the plain was the ridge. There was no time left for considerations. The men were staring at the plain, mightily wondering how it would feel to be out there, when a brigade in advance yelled and charged. The hill was all gray smoke and fire-points.

That fierce elation in the terrors of war, catching a man's heart and making it burn with such ardour that he becomes capable of dying, flashed in the faces of the men like coloured lights, and made them resemble leashed animals, eager, ferocious, daunting at nothing. The line was really in its first leap before the wild, hoarse crying of the orders.

The greed for close quarters which is the emotion of a bayonet charge, came then into the minds of the men and developed until it was a madness. The field, with its faded grass of a Southern winter, seemed to this fury miles in width.

High, slow-moving masses of smoke, with an odour of burning cotton, engulfed the line until the men might have been swimmers. Before them the ridge, the shore of this gray sea, was outlined, crossed, and re-crossed by sheets of flame. The howl of the battle arose to the noise of innumerable wind demons.

The line, galloping, scrambling, plunging like a herd of wounded horses, went over a field that was sown with corpses, the records of other charges.

Directly in front of the black-faced, whooping Dan, carousing in this onward sweep like a new kind of fiend, a wounded man appeared, raising his shattered body, and staring at this rush of men down upon him. It seemed to occur to him that he was to be trampled; he made a desperate, piteous effort to escape; then finally huddled in a waiting heap. Dan and the soldier near him widened the interval between them without looking down, without appearing to heed the wounded man. This little clump of blue seemed to reel past them as boulders reel past a train.

Bursting through a smoke-wave, the scampering, unformed bunches came upon the wreck of the brigade that had preceded them, a floundering mass stopped afar from the hill by the swirling volleys.

It was as if a necromancer had suddenly shown them a picture of the fate which awaited them; but the line with muscular spasm hurled itself over this wreckage and onward, until men were stumbling amid the relics of other assaults, the point where the fire from the ridge consumed.

The men, panting, perspiring, with crazed faces, tried to push against it; but it was as if they had come to a wall. The wave halted, shuddered in an agony from the quick struggle of its two desires, then toppled, and broke into a fragmentary thing which has no name.

Veterans could now at last be distinguished from recruits. The new regiments were instantly gone, lost, scattered, as if they never had been. But the sweeping failure of the charge, the battle, could not make the veterans forget their business. With a last throe, the band of maniacs drew itself up and blazed a volley at the hill, insignificant to those iron intrenchments, but nevertheless expressing that singular final despair which enables men coolly to defy the walls of a city of death.

After this episode the men renamed their command. They called it the Little Regiment.

VI.

"I seen Dan shoot a feller yesterday. Yes sir. I'm sure it was him that done it. And maybe he thinks about that feller now, and wonders if he tumbled down just about the same way. Them things come up in a man's mind."

Bivouac fires upon the sidewalks, in the streets, in the yards, threw high their wavering reflections, which examined, like slim, red fingers, the dingy, scarred walls and the piles of tumbled brick. The droning of voices again arose from great blue crowds.

258

The odour of frying bacon, the fragrance from countless little coffee-pails floated among the ruins. The rifles, stacked in the shadows, emitted flashes of steely light. Wherever a flag lay horizontally from one stack to another was the bed of an eagle which had led men into the mystic smoke.

The men about a particular fire were engaged in holding in check their jovial spirits. They moved whispering around the blaze, although they looked at it with a certain fine contentment, like labourers after a day's hard work.

There was one who sat apart. They did not address him save in tones suddenly changed. They did not regard him directly, but always in little sidelong glances.

At last a soldier from a distant fire came into this circle of light. He studied for a time the man who sat apart. Then he hesitatingly stepped closer, and said: "Got any news, Dan?"

"No," said Dan.

The new-comer shifted his feet. He looked at the fire, at the sky, at the other men, at Dan. His face expressed a curious despair; his tongue was plainly in rebellion. Finally, however, he contrived to say: "Well, there's some chance yet, Dan. Lots of the wounded are still lying out there, you know. There's some chance yet."

"Yes," said Dan.

The soldier shifted his feet again, and looked miserably into the air. After another struggle he said: "Well, there's some chance yet, Dan." He moved hastily away.

One of the men of the squad, perhaps encouraged by this example, now approached the still figure. "No news yet, hey?" he said, after coughing behind his hand.

"No," said Dan.

"Well," said the man, "I've been thinking of how he was fretting about you the night you went on special duty. You recollect? Well, sir, I was surprised.

He couldn't say enough about it. I swan, I don't believe he slep' a wink after you left, but just lay awake cussing special duty and worrying. I was surprised. But there he lay cussing. He——"

Dan made a curious sound, as if a stone had wedged in his throat. He said: "Shut up, will you?"

Afterward the men would not allow this moody contemplation of the fire to be interrupted.

"Oh, let him alone, can't you?"

"Come away from there, Casey!"

"Say, can't you leave him be?"

They moved with reverence about the immovable figure, with its countenance of mask-like invulnerability.

VII.

After the red round eye of the sun had stared long at the little plain and its burden, darkness, a sable mercy, came heavily upon it, and the wan hands of the dead were no longer seen in strange frozen gestures.

The heights in front of the plain shone with tiny camp-fires, and from the town in the rear, small shimmerings ascended from the blazes of the bivouac. The plain was a black expanse upon which, from time to time, dots of light, lanterns, floated slowly here and there. These fields were long steeped in grim mystery.

Suddenly, upon one dark spot, there was a resurrection. A strange thing had been groaning there, prostrate. Then it suddenly dragged itself to a sitting posture, and became a man.

The man stared stupidly for a moment at the lights on the hill, then turned and contemplated the faint colouring over the town. For some moments he remained thus, staring with dull eyes, his face unemotional, wooden.

Finally he looked around him at the corpses dimly to be seen. No change flashed into his face upon viewing these men. They seemed to suggest merely that his information concerning himself was not too complete. He ran his fingers over his arms and chest, bearing always the air of an idiot upon a bench at an almshouse door.

Finding no wound in his arms nor in his chest, he raised his hand to his head, and the fingers came away with some dark liquid upon them. Holding these fingers close to his eyes, he scanned them in the same stupid fashion, while his body gently swayed.

The soldier rolled his eyes again toward the town. When he arose, his clothing peeled from the frozen ground like wet paper. Hearing the sound of it, he seemed to see reason for deliberation. He paused and looked at the ground, then at his trousers, then at the ground.

Finally he went slowly off toward the faint reflection, holding his hands palm outward before him, and walking in the manner of a blind man.

VIII.

The immovable Dan again sat unaddressed in the midst of comrades, who did not joke aloud. The dampness of the usual morning fog seemed to make the little camp-fires furious.

Suddenly a cry arose in the streets, a shout of amazement and delight. The men making breakfast at the fire looked up quickly. They broke forth in clamorous exclamation: "Well! Of all things! Dan! Dan! Look who's coming! Oh, Dan!"

Dan the silent raised his eyes and saw a man, with a bandage of the size of a helmet about his head, receiving a furious demonstration from the company. He was shaking hands, and explaining, and haranguing to a high degree.

Dan started. His face of bronze flushed to his temples. He seemed about to leap from the ground, but then suddenly he sank back, and resumed his impassive gazing.

The men were in a flurry. They looked from one to the other. "Dan!

Look! See who's coming!" some cried again. "Dan! Look!"

He scowled at last, and moved his shoulders sullenly. "Well, don't I know it?"

But they could not be convinced that his eyes were in service. "Dan! Why can't you look? See who's coming!"

He made a gesture then of irritation and rage. "Curse it! Don't I know it?"

The man with a bandage of the size of a helmet moved forward, always shaking hands and explaining. At times his glance wandered to Dan, who saw with his eyes riveted.

After a series of shiftings, it occurred naturally that the man with the bandage was very near to the man who saw the flames. He paused, and there was a little silence. Finally he said: "Hello, Dan."

"Hello, Billie."

THREE MIRACULOUS SOLDIERS.

I.

The girl was in the front room on the second floor, peering through the blinds. It was the "best room." There was a very new rag carpet on the floor. The edges of it had been dyed with alternate stripes of red and green. Upon the wooden mantel there were two little puffy figures in clay—a shepherd and a shepherdess probably. A triangle of pink and white wool hung carefully over the edge of this shelf. Upon the bureau there was nothing at all save a spread newspaper, with edges folded to make it into a mat. The quilts and sheets had been removed from the bed and were stacked upon a chair. The pillows and the great feather mattress were muffled and tumbled until they resembled great dumplings. The picture of a man terribly leaden in complexion hung in an oval frame on one white wall and steadily confronted the bureau.

From between the slats of the blinds she had a view of the road as it wended across the meadow to the woods, and again where it reappeared crossing the hill, half a mile away. It lay yellow and warm in the summer sunshine. From the long grasses of the meadow came the rhythmic click of the insects. Occasional frogs in the hidden brook made a peculiar chug-chug sound, as if somebody throttled them. The leaves of the wood swung in gentle winds. Through the dark-green branches of the pines that grew in the front yard could be seen the mountains, far to the southeast, and inexpressibly blue.

Mary's eyes were fastened upon the little streak of road that appeared on the distant hill. Her face was flushed with excitement, and the hand which stretched in a strained pose on the sill trembled because of the nervous shaking of the wrist. The pines whisked their green needles with a soft, hissing sound against the house.

At last the girl turned from the window and went to the head of the stairs. "Well, I just know they're coming, anyhow," she cried argumentatively to the depths.

A voice from below called to her angrily: "They ain't. We've never seen one yet. They never come into this neighbourhood. You just come down here and 'tend to your work insteader watching for soldiers."

"Well, ma, I just know they're coming."

A voice retorted with the shrillness and mechanical violence of occasional housewives. The girl swished her skirts defiantly and returned to the window.

Upon the yellow streak of road that lay across the hillside there now was a handful of black dots—horsemen. A cloud of dust floated away. The girl flew to the head of the stairs and whirled down into the kitchen.

"They're coming! They're coming!"

It was as if she had cried "Fire!" Her mother had been peeling potatoes while seated comfortably at the table. She sprang to her feet. "No—it can't be—how you know it's them—where?" The stubby knife fell from her hand, and two or three curls of potato skin dropped from her apron to the floor.

The girl turned and dashed upstairs. Her mother followed, gasping for breath, and yet contriving to fill the air with questions, reproach, and remonstrance. The girl was already at the window, eagerly pointing. "There! There! See 'em! See 'em!"

Rushing to the window, the mother scanned for an instant the road on the hill. She crouched back with a groan. "It's them, sure as the world! It's them!" She waved her hands in despairing gestures.

The black dots vanished into the wood. The girl at the window was quivering and her eyes were shining like water when the sun flashes. "Hush! They're in the woods! They'll be here directly." She bent down and intently watched the green archway whence the road emerged. "Hush! I hear 'em coming," she swiftly whispered to her mother, for the elder woman had dropped dolefully upon the mattress and was sobbing. And indeed the girl could hear the quick, dull trample of horses. She stepped aside with sudden apprehension, but she bent her head forward in order to still scan the road.

"Here they are!"

There was something very theatrical in the sudden appearance of these men to the eyes of the girl. It was as if a scene had been shifted. The forest suddenly disclosed them—a dozen brown-faced troopers in blue—galloping.

"Oh, look!" breathed the girl. Her mouth was puckered into an expression of strange fascination as if she had expected to see the troopers change into demons and gloat at her. She was at last looking upon those curious beings who rode down from the North—those men of legend and colossal tale—they who were possessed of such marvellous hallucinations.

The little troop rode in silence. At its head was a youthful fellow with some dim yellow stripes upon his arm. In his right hand he held his carbine, slanting upward, with the stock resting upon his knee. He was absorbed in a scrutiny of the country before him.

At the heels of the sergeant the rest of the squad rode in thin column, with creak of leather and tinkle of steel and tin. The girl scanned the faces of the horsemen, seeming astonished vaguely to find them of the type she knew.

The lad at the head of the troop comprehended the house and its environments in two glances. He did not check the long, swinging stride of his horse. The troopers glanced for a moment like casual tourists, and then returned to their study of the region in front. The heavy thudding of the hoofs became a small noise. The dust, hanging in sheets, slowly sank.

The sobs of the woman on the bed took form in words which, while strong in their note of calamity, yet expressed a querulous mental reaching for some near thing to blame. "And it'll be lucky fer us if we ain't both butchered in our sleep—plundering and running off horses—old Santo's gone—you see if he ain't—plundering——"

"But, ma," said the girl, perplexed and terrified in the same moment, "they've gone."

"Oh, but they'll come back!" cried the mother, without pausing her wail. "They'll come back—trust them for that—running off horses. O John,

John! why did you, why did you?" She suddenly lifted herself and sat rigid, staring at her daughter. "Mary," she said in tragic whisper, "the kitchen door isn't locked!" Already she was bended forward to listen, her mouth agape, her eyes fixed upon her daughter.

"Mother," faltered the girl.

Her mother again whispered, "The kitchen door isn't locked."

Motionless and mute they stared into each other's eyes.

At last the girl quavered, "We better—we better go and lock it." The mother nodded. Hanging arm in arm they stole across the floor toward the head of the stairs. A board of the floor creaked. They halted and exchanged a look of dumb agony.

At last they reached the head of the stairs. From the kitchen came the bass humming of the kettle and frequent sputterings and cracklings from the fire. These sounds were sinister. The mother and the girl stood incapable of movement. "There's somebody down there!" whispered the elder woman.

Finally, the girl made a gesture of resolution. She twisted her arm from her mother's hands and went two steps downward. She addressed the kitchen: "Who's there?" Her tone was intended to be dauntless. It rang so dramatically in the silence that a sudden new panic seized them as if the suspected presence in the kitchen had cried out to them. But the girl ventured again: "Is there anybody there?" No reply was made save by the kettle and the fire.

With a stealthy tread the girl continued her journey. As she neared the last step the fire crackled explosively and the girl screamed. But the mystic presence had not swept around the corner to grab her, so she dropped to a seat on the step and laughed. "It was—was only the—the fire," she said, stammering hysterically.

Then she arose with sudden fortitude and cried: "Why, there isn't anybody there! I know there isn't." She marched down into the kitchen. In her face was dread, as if she half expected to confront something, but the room was empty. She cried joyously: "There's nobody here! Come on down, ma." She ran to the kitchen door and locked it.

The mother came down to the kitchen. "Oh, dear, what a fright I've had! It's given me the sick headache. I know it has."

"Oh, ma," said the girl.

"I know it has—I know it. Oh, if your father was only here! He'd settle those Yankees mighty quick—he'd settle 'em! Two poor helpless women———"

"Why, ma, what makes you act so? The Yankees haven't———"

"Oh, they'll be back—they'll be back. Two poor helpless women! Your father and your uncle Asa and Bill off galavanting around and fighting when they ought to be protecting their home! That's the kind of men they are. Didn't I say to your father just before he left———"

"Ma," said the girl, coming suddenly from the window, "the barn door is open. I wonder if they took old Santo?"

"Oh, of course they have—of course———Mary, I don't see what we are going to do—I don't see what we are going to do."

The girl said, "Ma, I'm going to see if they took old Santo."

"Mary," cried the mother, "don't you dare!"

"But think of poor old Sant, ma."

"Never you mind old Santo. We're lucky to be safe ourselves, I tell you. Never mind old Santo. Don't you dare to go out there, Mary—Mary!"

The girl had unlocked the door and stepped out upon the porch. The mother cried in despair, "Mary!"

"Why, there isn't anybody out here," the girl called in response. She stood for a moment with a curious smile upon her face as of gleeful satisfaction at her daring.

The breeze was waving the boughs of the apple trees. A rooster with an air importantly courteous was conducting three hens upon a foraging tour.

On the hillside at the rear of the gray old barn the red leaves of a creeper flamed amid the summer foliage. High in the sky clouds rolled toward the north. The girl swung impulsively from the little stoop and ran toward the barn.

The great door was open, and the carved peg which usually performed the office of a catch lay on the ground. The girl could not see into the barn because of the heavy shadows. She paused in a listening attitude and heard a horse munching placidly. She gave a cry of delight and sprang across the threshold. Then she suddenly shrank back and gasped. She had confronted three men in gray seated upon the floor with their legs stretched out and their backs against Santo's manger. Their dust-covered countenances were expanded in grins.

II.

As Mary sprang backward and screamed, one of the calm men in gray, still grinning, announced, "I knowed you'd holler." Sitting there comfortably the three surveyed her with amusement.

Mary caught her breath, throwing her hand up to her throat. "Oh!" she said, "you—you frightened me!"

"We're sorry, lady, but couldn't help it no way," cheerfully responded another. "I knowed you'd holler when I seen you coming yere, but I raikoned we couldn't help it no way. We hain't a-troubling this yere barn, I don't guess. We been doing some mighty tall sleeping yere. We done woke when them Yanks loped past."

"Where did you come from? Did—did you escape from the—the Yankees?" The girl still stammered and trembled. The three soldiers laughed. "No, m'm. No, m'm. They never cotch us. We was in a muss down the road yere about two mile. And Bill yere they gin it to him in the arm, kehplunk. And they pasted me thar, too. Curious. And Sim yere, he didn't get nothing, but they chased us all quite a little piece, and we done lose track of our boys."

"Was it—was it those who passed here just now? Did they chase you?"

The men in gray laughed again. "What—them? No, indeedee! There was a mighty big swarm of Yanks and a mighty big swarm of our boys, too. What—that little passel? No, m'm."

She became calm enough to scan them more attentively. They were much begrimed and very dusty. Their gray clothes were tattered. Splashed mud had dried upon them in reddish spots. It appeared, too, that the men had not shaved in many days. In the hats there was a singular diversity. One soldier wore the little blue cap of the Northern infantry, with corps emblem and regimental number; one wore a great slouch hat with a wide hole in the crown; and the other wore no hat at all. The left sleeve of one man and the right sleeve of another had been slit and the arms were neatly bandaged with clean cloth. "These hain't no more than two little cuts," explained one. "We stopped up yere to Mis' Leavitts—she said her name was—and she bind them for us. Bill yere, he had the thirst come on him. And the fever too. We——"

"Did you ever see my father in the army?" asked Mary. "John Hinckson—his name is."

The three soldiers grinned again, but they replied kindly: "No, m'm. No, m'm, we hain't never. What is he—in the cavalry?"

"No," said the girl. "He and my uncle Asa and my cousin—his name is Bill Parker—they are all with Longstreet—they call him."

"Oh," said the soldiers. "Longstreet? Oh, they're a good smart ways from yere. 'Way off up nawtheast. There hain't nothing but cavalry down yere. They're in the infantry, probably."

"We haven't heard anything from them for days and days," said Mary.

"Oh, they're all right in the infantry," said one man, to be consoling. "The infantry don't do much fighting. They go bellering out in a big swarm and only a few of 'em get hurt. But if they was in the cavalry—the cavalry——"

Mary interrupted him without intention. "Are you hungry?" she asked.

The soldiers looked at each other, struck by some sudden and singular shame. They hung their heads. "No, m'm," replied one at last.

Santo, in his stall, was tranquilly chewing and chewing. Sometimes he looked benevolently over at them. He was an old horse and there was something about his eyes and his forelock which created the impression that he wore spectacles. Mary went and patted his nose. "Well, if you are hungry, I can get you something," she told the men. "Or you might come to the house."

"We wouldn't dast go to the house," said one. "That passel of Yanks was only a scouting crowd, most like. Just an advance. More coming, likely."

"Well, I can bring you something," cried the girl eagerly. "Won't you let me bring you something?"

"Well," said a soldier with embarrassment, "we hain't had much. If you could bring us a little snack-like—just a snack—we'd——"

Without waiting for him to cease, the girl turned toward the door. But before she had reached it she stopped abruptly. "Listen!" she whispered. Her form was bent forward, her head turned and lowered, her hand extended toward the men in a command for silence.

They could faintly hear the thudding of many hoofs, the clank of arms, and frequent calling voices.

"By cracky, it's the Yanks!" The soldiers scrambled to their feet and came toward the door. "I knowed that first crowd was only an advance."

The girl and the three men peered from the shadows of the barn. The view of the road was intersected by tree trunks and a little henhouse. However, they could see many horsemen streaming down the road. The horsemen were in blue. "Oh, hide—hide—hide!" cried the girl, with a sob in her voice.

"Wait a minute," whispered a gray soldier excitedly. "Maybe they're going along by. No, by thunder, they hain't! They're halting. Scoot, boys!"

They made a noiseless dash into the dark end of the barn. The girl, standing by the door, heard them break forth an instant later in clamorous whispers. "Where'll we hide? Where'll we hide? There hain't a place to hide!" The girl turned and glanced wildly about the barn. It seemed true. The stock of hay had grown low under Santo's endless munching, and from occasional levyings by passing troopers in gray. The poles of the mow were barely covered, save in one corner where there was a little bunch.

The girl espied the great feed box. She ran to it and lifted the lid. "Here! here!" she called. "Get in here."

They had been tearing noiselessly around the rear part of the barn. At her low call they came and plunged at the box. They did not all get in at the same moment without a good deal of a tangle. The wounded men gasped and muttered, but they at last were flopped down on the layer of feed which covered the bottom. Swiftly and softly the girl lowered the lid and then turned like a flash toward the door.

No one appeared there, so she went close to survey the situation. The troopers had dismounted and stood in silence by their horses. A gray-bearded man, whose red cheeks and nose shone vividly above the whiskers, was strolling about with two or three others. They wore double-breasted coats, and faded yellow sashes were wound under their black leather sword belts. The gray-bearded soldier was apparently giving orders, pointing here and there.

Mary tiptoed to the feed box. "They've all got off their horses," she said to it. A finger projected from a knothole near the top and said to her very plainly, "Come closer." She obeyed, and then a muffled voice could be heard: "Scoot for the house, lady, and if we don't see you again, why, much obliged for what you done."

"Good-bye," she said to the feed box.

She made two attempts to walk dauntlessly from the barn, but each time she faltered and failed just before she reached the point where she could have been seen by the blue-coated troopers. At last, however, she made a sort of a rush forward and went out into the bright sunshine.

The group of men in double-breasted coats wheeled in her direction at the instant. The gray-bearded officer forgot to lower his arm which had been stretched forth in giving an order.

She felt that her feet were touching the ground in a most unnatural manner. Her bearing, she believed, was suddenly grown awkward and ungainly. Upon her face she thought that this sentence was plainly written: "There are three men hidden in the feed box."

The gray-bearded soldier came toward her. She stopped; she seemed about to run away. But the soldier doffed his little blue cap and looked amiable. "You live here, I presume?" he said.

"Yes," she answered.

"Well, we are obliged to camp here for the night, and as we've got two wounded men with us I don't suppose you'd mind if we put them in the barn."

"In—in the barn?"

He became aware that she was agitated. He smiled assuringly. "You needn't be frightened. We won't hurt anything around here. You'll all be safe enough."

The girl balanced on one foot and swung the other to and fro in the grass. She was looking down at it. "But—but I don't think ma would like it if—if you took the barn."

The old officer laughed. "Wouldn't she?" said he. "That's so. Maybe she wouldn't." He reflected for a time and then decided cheerfully: "Well, we will have to go ask her, anyhow. Where is she? In the house?"

"Yes," replied the girl, "she's in the house. She—she'll be scared to death when she sees you!"

"Well, you go and ask her then," said the soldier, always wearing a benign smile. "You go ask her and then come and tell me."

When the girl pushed open the door and entered the kitchen, she found it empty. "Ma!" she called softly. There was no answer. The kettle still was humming its low song. The knife and the curl of potato skin lay on the floor.

She went to her mother's room and entered timidly. The new, lonely aspect of the house shook her nerves. Upon the bed was a confusion of

272

coverings. "Ma!" called the girl, quaking in fear that her mother was not there to reply. But there was a sudden turmoil of the quilts, and her mother's head was thrust forth. "Mary!" she cried, in what seemed to be a supreme astonishment, "I thought—I thought——"

"Oh, ma," blurted the girl, "there's over a thousand Yankees in the yard, and I've hidden three of our men in the feed box!"

The elder woman, however, upon the appearance of her daughter had begun to thrash hysterically about on the bed and wail.

"Ma," the girl exclaimed, "and now they want to use the barn—and our men in the feed box! What shall I do, ma? What shall I do?"

Her mother did not seem to hear, so absorbed was she in her grievous flounderings and tears. "Ma!" appealed the girl. "Ma!"

For a moment Mary stood silently debating, her lips apart, her eyes fixed. Then she went to the kitchen window and peeked.

The old officer and the others were staring up the road. She went to another window in order to get a proper view of the road, and saw that they were gazing at a small body of horsemen approaching at a trot and raising much dust. Presently she recognised them as the squad that had passed the house earlier, for the young man with the dim yellow chevron still rode at their head. An unarmed horseman in gray was receiving their close attention.

As they came very near to the house she darted to the first window again. The gray-bearded officer was smiling a fine broad smile of satisfaction. "So you got him?" he called out. The young sergeant sprang from his horse and his brown hand moved in a salute. The girl could not hear his reply. She saw the unarmed horseman in gray stroking a very black mustache and looking about him coolly and with an interested air. He appeared so indifferent that she did not understand he was a prisoner until she heard the graybeard call out: "Well, put him in the barn. He'll be safe there, I guess." A party of troopers moved with the prisoner toward the barn.

The girl made a sudden gesture of horror, remembering the three men in the feed box.

III.

The busy troopers in blue scurried about the long lines of stamping horses. Men crooked their backs and perspired in order to rub with cloths or bunches of grass these slim equine legs, upon whose splendid machinery they depended so greatly. The lips of the horses were still wet and frothy from the steel bars which had wrenched at their mouths all day. Over their backs and about their noses sped the talk of the men.

"Moind where yer plug is steppin', Finerty! Keep 'im aff me!"

"An ould elephant! He shtrides like a schoolhouse."

"Bill's little mar—she was plum beat when she come in with Crawford's crowd."

"Crawford's the hardest-ridin' cavalryman in the army. An he don't use up a horse, neither—much. They stay fresh when the others are most a-droppin'."

"Finerty, will yeh moind that cow a yours?"

Amid a bustle of gossip and banter, the horses retained their air of solemn rumination, twisting their lower jaws from side to side and sometimes rubbing noses dreamfully.

Over in front of the barn three troopers sat talking comfortably. Their carbines were leaned against the wall. At their side and outlined in the black of the open door stood a sentry, his weapon resting in the hollow of his arm. Four horses, saddled and accoutred, were conferring with their heads close together. The four bridle reins were flung over a post.

Upon the calm green of the land, typical in every way of peace, the hues of war brought thither by the troops shone strangely. Mary, gazing curiously, did not feel that she was contemplating a familiar scene. It was no longer the home acres. The new blue, steel, and faded yellow thoroughly dominated the old green and brown. She could hear the voices of the men, and it seemed from their tone that they had camped there for years. Everything with them was usual. They had taken possession of the landscape in such a way that even the old marks appeared strange and formidable to the girl.

Mary had intended to go and tell the commander in blue that her mother did not wish his men to use the barn at all, but she paused when she heard him speak to the sergeant. She thought she perceived then that it mattered little to him what her mother wished, and that an objection by her or by anybody would be futile. She saw the soldiers conduct the prisoner in gray into the barn, and for a long time she watched the three chatting guards and the pondering sentry. Upon her mind in desolate weight was the recollection of the three men in the feed box.

It seemed to her that in a case of this description it was her duty to be a heroine. In all the stories she had read when at boarding school in Pennsylvania, the girl characters, confronted with such difficulties, invariably did hair breadth things. True, they were usually bent upon rescuing and recovering their lovers, and neither the calm man in gray nor any of the three in the feed box was lover of hers, but then a real heroine would not pause over this minor question. Plainly a heroine would take measures to rescue the four men. If she did not at least make the attempt, she would be false to those carefully constructed ideals which were the accumulation of years of dreaming.

But the situation puzzled her. There was the barn with only one door, and with four armed troopers in front of this door, one of them with his back to the rest of the world, engaged, no doubt, in a steadfast contemplation of the calm man and, incidentally, of the feed box. She knew, too, that even if she should open the kitchen door, three heads and perhaps four would turn casually in her direction. Their ears were real ears.

Heroines, she knew, conducted these matters with infinite precision and despatch. They severed the hero's bonds, cried a dramatic sentence, and stood between him and his enemies until he had run far enough away. She saw well, however, that even should she achieve all things up to the point where she might take glorious stand between the escaping and the pursuers, those grim troopers in blue would not pause. They would run around her, make a circuit. One by one she saw the gorgeous contrivances and expedients of fiction fall before the plain, homely difficulties of this situation. They were of no service. Sadly, ruefully, she thought of the calm man and of the contents of the feed box.

The sum of her invention was that she could sally forth to the commander of the blue cavalry, and confessing to him that there were three of her friends and his enemies secreted in the feed box, pray him to let them depart unmolested. But she was beginning to believe the old graybeard to be a bear. It was hardly probable that he would give this plan his support. It was more probable that he and some of his men would at once descend upon the feed box and confiscate her three friends. The difficulty with her idea was that she could not learn its value without trying it, and then in case of failure it would be too late for remedies and other plans. She reflected that war made men very unreasonable.

All that she could do was to stand at the window and mournfully regard the barn. She admitted this to herself with a sense of deep humiliation. She was not, then, made of that fine stuff, that mental satin, which enabled some other beings to be of such mighty service to the distressed. She was defeated by a barn with one door, by four men with eight eyes and eight ears—trivialities that would not impede the real heroine.

The vivid white light of broad day began slowly to fade. Tones of gray came upon the fields, and the shadows were of lead. In this more sombre atmosphere the fires built by the troops down in the far end of the orchard grew more brilliant, becoming spots of crimson colour in the dark grove.

The girl heard a fretting voice from her mother's room. "Mary!" She hastily obeyed the call. She perceived that she had quite forgotten her mother's existence in this time of excitement.

The elder woman still lay upon the bed. Her face was flushed and perspiration stood amid new wrinkles upon her forehead. Weaving wild glances from side to side, she began to whimper. "Oh, I'm just sick—I'm just sick! Have those men gone yet? Have they gone?"

The girl smoothed a pillow carefully for her mother's head. "No, ma.

They're here yet. But they haven't hurt anything—it doesn't seem. Will I get you something to eat?"

Her mother gestured her away with the impatience of the ill. "No—no—just don't bother me. My head is splitting, and you know very well that nothing can be done for me when I get one of these spells. It's trouble—that's what makes them. When are those men going? Look here, don't you go 'way. You stick close to the house now."

"I'll stay right here," said the girl. She sat in the gloom and listened to her mother's incessant moaning. When she attempted to move, her mother cried out at her. When she desired to ask if she might try to alleviate the pain, she was interrupted shortly. Somehow her sitting in passive silence within hearing of this illness seemed to contribute to her mother's relief. She assumed a posture of submission. Sometimes her mother projected questions concerning the local condition, and although she laboured to be graphic and at the same time soothing, unalarming, her form of reply was always displeasing to the sick woman, and brought forth ejaculations of angry impatience.

Eventually the woman slept in the manner of one worn from terrible labour. The girl went slowly and softly to the kitchen. When she looked from the window, she saw the four soldiers still at the barn door. In the west, the sky was yellow. Some tree trunks intersecting it appeared black as streaks of ink. Soldiers hovered in blue clouds about the bright splendour of the fires in the orchard. There were glimmers of steel.

The girl sat in the new gloom of the kitchen and watched. The soldiers lit a lantern and hung it in the barn. Its rays made the form of the sentry seem gigantic. Horses whinnied from the orchard. There was a low hum of human voices. Sometimes small detachments of troopers rode past the front of the house. The girl heard the abrupt calls of sentries. She fetched some food and ate it from her hand, standing by the window. She was so afraid that something would occur that she barely left her post for an instant.

A picture of the interior of the barn hung vividly in her mind. She recalled the knot-holes in the boards at the rear, but she admitted that the prisoners could not escape through them. She remembered some inadequacies of the roof, but these also counted for nothing. When confronting the problem, she felt her ambitions, her ideals tumbling headlong like cottages of straw.

Once she felt that she had decided to reconnoitre at any rate. It was night; the lantern at the barn and the camp fires made everything without their circle into masses of heavy mystic blackness. She took two steps toward the door. But there she paused. Innumerable possibilities of danger had assailed her mind. She returned to the window and stood wavering. At last, she went swiftly to the door, opened it, and slid noiselessly into the darkness.

For a moment she regarded the shadows. Down in the orchard the camp fires of the troops appeared precisely like a great painting, all in reds upon a black cloth. The voices of the troopers still hummed. The girl started slowly off in the opposite direction. Her eyes were fixed in a stare; she studied the darkness in front for a moment, before she ventured upon a forward step. Unconsciously, her throat was arranged for a sudden shrill scream. High in the tree branches she could hear the voice of the wind, a melody of the night, low and sad, the plaint of an endless, incommunicable sorrow. Her own distress, the plight of the men in gray—these near matters as well as all she had known or imagined of grief—everything was expressed in this soft mourning of the wind in the trees. At first she felt like weeping. This sound told her of human impotency and doom. Then later the trees and the wind breathed strength to her, sang of sacrifice, of dauntless effort, of hard carven faces that did not blanch when Duty came at midnight or at noon.

She turned often to scan the shadowy figures that moved from time to time in the light at the barn door. Once she trod upon a stick, and it flopped, crackling in the intolerable manner of all sticks. At this noise, however, the guards at the barn made no sign. Finally, she was where she could see the knot-holes in the rear of the structure gleaming like pieces of metal from the effect of the light within. Scarcely breathing in her excitement she glided close and applied an eye to a knothole. She had barely achieved one glance at the interior before she sprang back shuddering.

For the unconscious and cheerful sentry at the door was swearing away in flaming sentences, heaping one gorgeous oath upon another, making a conflagration of his description of his troop horse.

"Why," he was declaring to the calm prisoner in gray, "you ain't got a horse in your hull —— army that can run forty rod with that there little mar'!"

As in the outer darkness Mary cautiously returned to the knothole, the three guards in front suddenly called in low tones: "S-s-s-h!"

"Quit, Pete; here comes the lieutenant." The sentry had apparently been about to resume his declamation, but at these warnings he suddenly posed in a soldierly manner.

A tall and lean officer with a smooth face entered the barn. The sentry saluted primly. The officer flashed a comprehensive glance about him. "Everything all right?"

"All right, sir."

This officer had eyes like the points of stilettos. The lines from his nose to the corners of his mouth were deep and gave him a slightly disagreeable aspect, but somewhere in his face there was a quality of singular thoughtfulness, as of the absorbed student dealing in generalities, which was utterly in opposition to the rapacious keenness of the eyes which saw everything.

Suddenly he lifted a long finger and pointed. "What's that?"

"That? That's a feed box, I suppose."

"What's in it?"

"I don't know. I——"

"You ought to know," said the officer sharply. He walked over to the feed box and flung up the lid. With a sweeping gesture, he reached down and scooped a handful of feed. "You ought to know what's in everything when you have prisoners in your care," he added, scowling.

During the time of this incident, the girl had nearly swooned. Her hands searched weakly over the boards for something to which to cling. With the pallor of the dying she had watched the downward sweep of the officer's arm, which after all had only brought forth a handful of feed. The result was a stupefaction of her mind. She was astonished out of her senses at this spectacle of three large men metamorphosed into a handful of feed.

IV.

It is perhaps a singular thing that this absence of the three men from the feed box at the time of the sharp lieutenant's investigation should terrify the girl more than it should joy her. That for which she had prayed had come to pass. Apparently the escape of these men in the face of every improbability had been granted her, but her dominating emotion was fright. The feed box was a mystic and terrible machine, like some dark magician's trap. She felt it almost possible that she should see the three weird men floating spectrally away through the air. She glanced with swift apprehension behind her, and when the dazzle from the lantern's light had left her eyes, saw only the dim hillside stretched in solemn silence.

The interior of the barn possessed for her another fascination because it was now uncanny. It contained that extraordinary feed box. When she peeped again at the knothole, the calm, gray prisoner was seated upon the feed box, thumping it with his dangling, careless heels as if it were in nowise his conception of a remarkable feed-box. The sentry also stood facing it. His carbine he held in the hollow of his arm. His legs were spread apart, and he mused. From without came the low mumble of the three other troopers. The sharp lieutenant had vanished.

The trembling yellow light of the lantern caused the figures of the men to cast monstrous wavering shadows. There were spaces of gloom which shrouded ordinary things in impressive garb. The roof presented an inscrutable blackness, save where small rifts in the shingles glowed phosphorescently. Frequently old Santo put down a thunderous hoof. The heels of the prisoner made a sound like the booming of a wild kind of drum. When the men moved their heads, their eyes shone with ghoulish whiteness, and their complexions were always waxen and unreal. And there was that profoundly strange feed box, imperturbable with its burden of fantastic mystery.

Suddenly from down near her feet the girl heard a crunching sound, a sort of a nibbling, as if some silent and very discreet terrier was at work upon the turf. She faltered back; here was no doubt another grotesque detail of this most unnatural episode. She did not run, because physically she was in the power of these events. Her feet chained her to the ground in submission to this march of terror after terror. As she stared at the spot from which this sound seemed to come, there floated through her mind a vague, sweet vision—a vision of her safe little room, in which at this hour she usually was sleeping.

The scratching continued faintly and with frequent pauses, as if the terrier was then listening. When the girl first removed her eyes from the knothole the scene appeared of one velvet blackness; then gradually objects loomed with a dim lustre. She could see now where the tops of the trees joined the sky and the form of the barn was before her dyed in heavy purple. She was ever about to shriek, but no sound came from her constricted throat. She gazed at the ground with the expression of countenance of one who watches the sinister-moving grass where a serpent approaches.

Dimly she saw a piece of sod wrenched free and drawn under the great foundation beam of the barn. Once she imagined that she saw human hands, not outlined at all, but sufficient in colour, form, or movement to make subtle suggestion.

Then suddenly a thought that illuminated the entire situation flashed in her mind like a light. The three men, late of the feed box, were beneath the floor of the barn and were now scraping their way under this beam. She did not consider for a moment how they could come there. They were marvellous creatures. The supernatural was to be expected of them. She no longer trembled, for she was possessed upon this instant of the most unchangeable species of conviction. The evidence before her amounted to no evidence at all, but nevertheless her opinion grew in an instant from an irresponsible acorn to a rooted and immovable tree. It was as if she was on a jury.

She stooped down hastily and scanned the ground. There she indeed saw a pair of hands hauling at the dirt where the sod had been displaced. Softly, in a whisper like a breath, she said, "Hey!"

The dim hands were drawn hastily under the barn. The girl reflected for a moment. Then she stooped and whispered: "Hey! It's me!"

After a time there was a resumption of the digging. The ghostly hands began once more their cautious mining. She waited. In hollow reverberations from the interior of the barn came the frequent sounds of old Santo's lazy movements. The sentry conversed with the prisoner.

At last the girl saw a head thrust slowly from under the beam. She perceived the face of one of the miraculous soldiers from the feed box. A pair of eyes glintered and wavered, then finally settled upon her, a pale statue of a girl. The eyes became lit with a kind of humorous greeting. An arm gestured at her.

Stooping, she breathed, "All right." The man drew himself silently back under the beam. A moment later the pair of hands resumed their cautious task. Ultimately the head and arms of the man were thrust strangely from the earth. He was lying on his back. The girl thought of the dirt in his hair. Wriggling slowly and pushing at the beam above him he forced his way out of the curious little passage. He twisted his body and raised himself upon his hands. He grinned at the girl and drew his feet carefully from under the beam. When he at last stood erect beside her, he at once began mechanically to brush the dirt from his clothes with his hands. In the barn the sentry and his prisoner were evidently engaged in an argument.

The girl and the first miraculous soldier signalled warily. It seemed that they feared that their arms would make noises in passing through the air. Their lips moved, conveying dim meanings.

In this sign language the girl described the situation in the barn. With guarded motions, she told him of the importance of absolute stillness. He nodded, and then in the same manner he told her of his two companions under the barn floor. He informed her again of their wounded state, and wagged his head to express his despair. He contorted his face, to tell how sore were their arms; and jabbed the air mournfully, to express their remote geographical position.

This signalling was interrupted by the sound of a body being dragged or dragging itself with slow, swishing sound under the barn. The sound was too loud for safety. They rushed to the hole and began to semaphore until a shaggy head appeared with rolling eyes and quick grin.

With frantic downward motions of their arms they suppressed this grin and with it the swishing noise. In dramatic pantomime they informed this head of the terrible consequences of so much noise. The head nodded, and painfully but with extreme care the second man pushed and pulled himself from the hole.

In a faint whisper the first man said, "Where's Sim?"

The second man made low reply. "He's right here." He motioned reassuringly toward the hole.

When the third head appeared, a soft smile of glee came upon each face, and the mute group exchanged expressive glances.

When they all stood together, free from this tragic barn, they breathed a long sigh that was contemporaneous with another smile and another exchange of glances.

One of the men tiptoed to a knothole and peered into the barn. The sentry was at that moment speaking. "Yes, we know 'em all. There isn't a house in this region that we don't know who is in it most of the time. We collar 'em once in a while—like we did you. Now, that house out yonder, we——"

The man suddenly left the knothole and returned to the others. Upon his face, dimly discerned, there was an indication that he had made an astonishing discovery. The others questioned him with their eyes, but he simply waved an arm to express his inability to speak at that spot. He led them back toward the hill, prowling carefully. At a safe distance from the barn he halted and as they grouped eagerly about him, he exploded in an intense undertone: "Why, that—that's Cap'n Sawyer they got in yonder."

"Cap'n Sawyer!" incredulously whispered the other men.

But the girl had something to ask. "How did you get out of that feed box?" He smiled. "Well, when you put us in there, we was just in a minute when we allowed it wasn't a mighty safe place, and we allowed we'd get out. And we did. We skedaddled 'round and 'round until it 'peared like we was going to get cotched, and then we flung ourselves down in the cow stalls where it's low-like—just dirt floor—and then we just naturally went a-whooping under the barn floor when the Yanks come. And we didn't know Cap'n Sawyer by his voice nohow. We heard 'im discoursing, and we allowed it was a mighty pert man, but we didn't know that it was him. No, m'm."

These three men, so recently from a situation of peril, seemed suddenly to have dropped all thought of it. They stood with sad faces looking at the barn. They seemed to be making no plans at all to reach a place of more complete safety. They were halted and stupefied by some unknown calamity.

"How do you raikon they cotch him, Sim?" one whispered mournfully.

"I don't know," replied another, in the same tone.

Another with a low snarl expressed in two words his opinion of the methods of Fate: "Oh, hell!"

The three men started then as if simultaneously stung and gazed at the young girl who stood silently near them. The man who had sworn began to make agitated apology: "Pardon, miss! 'Pon my soul I clean forgot you was by. 'Deed, and I wouldn't swear like that if I had knowed. 'Deed, I wouldn't."

The girl did not seem to hear him. She was staring at the barn. Suddenly she turned and whispered, "Who is he?"

"He's Cap'n Sawyer, m'm," they told her sorrowfully. "He's our own cap'n. He's been in command of us yere since a long time. He's got folks about yere. Raikon they cotch him while he was a-visiting."

She was still for a time and then, awed, she said, "Will they—will they hang him?"

"No, m'm. Oh, no, m'm. Don't raikon no such thing. No, m'm."

The group became absorbed in a contemplation of the barn. For a time no one moved nor spoke. At last the girl was aroused by slight sounds, and turning, she perceived that the three men who had so recently escaped from the barn were now advancing toward it.

V.

The girl, waiting in the darkness, expected to hear the sudden crash and uproar of a fight as soon as the three creeping men should reach the barn. She reflected in an agony upon the swift disaster that would befall any enterprise so desperate. She had an impulse to beg them to come away. The grass rustled in silken movements as she sped toward the barn.

When she arrived, however, she gazed about her bewildered. The men were gone. She searched with her eyes, trying to detect some moving thing, but she could see nothing.

Left alone again, she began to be afraid of the night. The great stretches of darkness could hide crawling dangers. From sheer desire to see a human, she was obliged to peep again at the knothole. The sentry had apparently wearied of talking. Instead, he was reflecting. The prisoner still sat on the feed box, moodily staring at the floor. The girl felt in one way that she was looking at a ghastly group in wax. She started when the old horse put down an echoing hoof. She wished the men would speak; their silence re-enforced the strange aspect. They might have been two dead men.

The girl felt impelled to look at the corner of the interior where were the cow stalls. There was no light there save the appearance of peculiar gray haze which marked the track of the dimming rays of the lantern. All else was sombre shadow. At last she saw something move there. It might have been as small as a rat, or it might have been a part of something as large as a man. At any rate, it proclaimed that something in that spot was alive. At one time she saw it plainly and at other times it vanished, because her fixture of gaze caused her occasionally to greatly tangle and blur those peculiar shadows and faint lights. At last, however, she perceived a human head. It was monstrously dishevelled and wild. It moved slowly forward until its glance could fall upon the prisoner and then upon the sentry. The wandering rays caused the eyes to glitter like silver. The girl's heart pounded so that she put her hand over it.

The sentry and the prisoner remained immovably waxen, and over in the gloom the head thrust from the floor watched them with its silver eyes.

Finally, the prisoner slipped from the feed box, and, raising his arms, yawned at great length. "Oh, well," he remarked, "you boys will get a good licking if you fool around here much longer. That's some satisfaction, anyhow, even if you did bag me. You'll get a good walloping." He reflected for a moment, and decided: "I'm sort of willing to be captured if you fellows only get a d——d good licking for being so smart."

The sentry looked up and smiled a superior smile. "Licking, hey? Nixey!" He winked exasperatingly at the prisoner. "You fellows are not fast enough, my boy. Why didn't you lick us at ——? and at ——? and at ----?" He named some of the great battles.

To this the captive officer blurted in angry astonishment, "Why, we did!"

The sentry winked again in profound irony. "Yes—I know you did. Of course. You whipped us, didn't you? Fine kind of whipping that was! Why, we——"

He suddenly ceased, smitten mute by a sound that broke the stillness of the night. It was the sharp crack of a distant shot that made wild echoes among the hills. It was instantly followed by the hoarse cry of a human voice, a far-away yell of warning, singing of surprise, peril, fear of death. A moment later there was a distant, fierce spattering of shots. The sentry and the prisoner stood facing each other, their lips apart, listening.

The orchard at that instant awoke to sudden tumult. There were the thud and scramble and scamper of feet, the mellow, swift clash of arms, men's voices in question, oath, command, hurried and unhurried, resolute and frantic. A horse sped along the road at a raging gallop. A loud voice shouted, "What is it, Ferguson?" Another voice yelled something incoherent. There was a sharp, discordant chorus of command. An uproarious volley suddenly rang from the orchard. The prisoner in gray moved from his intent, listening attitude. Instantly the eyes of the sentry blazed, and he said with a new and

286

terrible sternness, "Stand where you are!"

The prisoner trembled in his excitement. Expressions of delight and triumph bubbled to his lips. "A surprise, by Gawd! Now—now, you'll see!"

The sentry stolidly swung his carbine to his shoulder. He sighted carefully along the barrel until it pointed at the prisoner's head, about at his nose. "Well, I've got you, anyhow. Remember that! Don't move!"

The prisoner could not keep his arms from nervously gesturing. "I won't; but——"

"And shut your mouth!"

The three comrades of the sentry flung themselves into view. "Pete—devil of a row!—can you——"

"I've got him," said the sentry calmly and without moving. It was as if the barrel of the carbine rested on piers of stone. The three comrades turned and plunged into the darkness.

In the orchard it seemed as if two gigantic animals were engaged in a mad, floundering encounter, snarling, howling in a whirling chaos of noise and motion. In the barn the prisoner and his guard faced each other in silence.

As for the girl at the knothole, the sky had fallen at the beginning of this clamour. She would not have been astonished to see the stars swinging from their abodes, and the vegetation, the barn, all blow away. It was the end of everything, the grand universal murder. When two of the three miraculous soldiers who formed the original feed-box corps emerged in detail from the hole under the beam and slid away into the darkness, she did no more than glance at them.

Suddenly she recollected the head with silver eyes. She started forward and again applied her eyes to the knothole. Even with the din resounding from the orchard, from up the road and down the road, from the heavens and from the deep earth, the central fascination was this mystic head. There, to her, was the dark god of the tragedy.

The prisoner in gray at this moment burst into a laugh that was no more than a hysterical gurgle. "Well, you can't hold that gun out forever! Pretty soon you'll have to lower it."

The sentry's voice sounded slightly muffled, for his cheek was pressed against the weapon. "I won't be tired for some time yet."

The girl saw the head slowly rise, the eyes fixed upon the sentry's face. A tall, black figure slunk across the cow stalls and vanished back of old Santo's quarters. She knew what was to come to pass. She knew this grim thing was upon a terrible mission, and that it would reappear again at the head of the little passage between Santo's stall and the wall, almost at the sentry's elbow; and yet when she saw a faint indication as of a form crouching there, a scream from an utterly new alarm almost escaped her.

The sentry's arms, after all, were not of granite. He moved restively. At last he spoke in his even, unchanging tone: "Well, I guess you'll have to climb into that feed box. Step back and lift the lid."

"Why, you don't mean——"

"Step back!"

The girl felt a cry of warning arising to her lips as she gazed at this sentry. She noted every detail of his facial expression. She saw, moreover, his mass of brown hair bunching disgracefully about his ears, his clear eyes lit now with a hard, cold light, his forehead puckered in a mighty scowl, the ring upon the third finger of the left hand. "Oh, they won't kill him! Surely they won't kill him!" The noise of the fight in the orchard was the loud music, the thunder and lightning, the rioting of the tempest which people love during the critical scene of a tragedy.

When the prisoner moved back in reluctant obedience, he faced for an instant the entrance of the little passage, and what he saw there must have been written swiftly, graphically in his eyes. And the sentry read it and knew then that he was upon the threshold of his death. In a fraction of time, certain information went from the grim thing in the passage to the prisoner, and from the prisoner to the sentry. But at that instant the black formidable figure arose, towered, and made its leap. A new shadow flashed across the floor when the blow was struck.

As for the girl at the knothole, when she returned to sense she found herself standing with clinched hands and screaming with her might.

As if her reason had again departed from her, she ran around the barn, in at the door, and flung herself sobbing beside the body of the soldier in blue.

The uproar of the fight became at last coherent, inasmuch as one party was giving shouts of supreme exultation. The firing no longer sounded in crashes; it was now expressed in spiteful crackles, the last words of the combat, spoken with feminine vindictiveness.

Presently there was a thud of flying feet. A grimy panting, red-faced mob of troopers in blue plunged into the barn, became instantly frozen to attitudes of amazement and rage, and then roared in one great chorus, "He's gone!"

The girl who knelt beside the body upon the floor turned toward them her lamenting eyes and cried: "He's not dead, is he? He can't be dead?"

They thronged forward. The sharp lieutenant who had been so particular about the feed box knelt by the side of the girl and laid his head against the chest of the prostrate soldier. "Why, no," he said, rising and looking at the man. "He's all right. Some of you boys throw some water on him."

"Are you sure?" demanded the girl, feverishly.

"Of course! He'll be better after awhile."

"Oh!" said she softly, and then looked down at the sentry. She started to arise, and the lieutenant reached down and hoisted rather awkwardly at her arm.

"Don't you worry about him. He's all right."

She turned her face with its curving lips and shining eyes once more toward the unconscious soldier upon the floor. The troopers made a lane to the door, the lieutenant bowed, the girl vanished.

"Queer," said a young officer. "Girl very clearly worst kind of rebel,

289

and yet she falls to weeping and wailing like mad over one of her enemies. Be around in the morning with all sorts of doctoring—you see if she ain't. Queer."

The sharp lieutenant shrugged his shoulders. After reflection he shrugged his shoulders again. He said: "War changes many things; but it doesn't change everything, thank God!"

A MYSTERY OF HEROISM.

The dark uniforms of the men were so coated with dust from the incessant wrestling of the two armies that the regiment almost seemed a part of the clay bank which shielded them from the shells. On the top of the hill a battery was arguing in tremendous roars with some other guns, and to the eye of the infantry, the artillerymen, the guns, the caissons, the horses, were distinctly outlined upon the blue sky. When a piece was fired, a red streak as round as a log flashed low in the heavens, like a monstrous bolt of lightning. The men of the battery wore white duck trousers, which somehow emphasized their legs; and when they ran and crowded in little groups at the bidding of the shouting officers, it was more impressive than usual to the infantry.

Fred Collins, of A Company, was saying: "Thunder! I wisht I had a drink. Ain't there any water round here?" Then somebody yelled, "There goes th' bugler!"

As the eyes of half the regiment swept in one machinelike movement there was an instant's picture of a horse in a great convulsive leap of a death wound and a rider leaning back with a crooked arm and spread fingers before his face. On the ground was the crimson terror of an exploding shell, with fibres of flame that seemed like lances. A glittering bugle swung clear of the rider's back as fell headlong the horse and the man. In the air was an odour as from a conflagration.

Sometimes they of the infantry looked down at a fair little meadow which spread at their feet. Its long, green grass was rippling gently in a breeze. Beyond it was the gray form of a house half torn to pieces by shells and by the busy axes of soldiers who had pursued firewood. The line of an old fence was now dimly marked by long weeds and by an occasional post. A shell had blown the well-house to fragments. Little lines of gray smoke ribboning upward from some embers indicated the place where had stood the barn.

From beyond a curtain of green woods there came the sound of some stupendous scuffle, as if two animals of the size of islands were fighting. At a distance there were occasional appearances of swift-moving men, horses, batteries, flags, and, with the crashing of infantry volleys were heard, often, wild and frenzied cheers. In the midst of it all Smith and Ferguson, two privates of A Company, were engaged in a heated discussion, which involved the greatest questions of the national existence.

The battery on the hill presently engaged in a frightful duel. The white legs of the gunners scampered this way and that way, and the officers redoubled their shouts. The guns, with their demeanours of stolidity and courage, were typical of something infinitely self-possessed in this clamour of death that swirled around the hill.

One of a "swing" team was suddenly smitten quivering to the ground, and his maddened brethren dragged his torn body in their struggle to escape from this turmoil and danger. A young soldier astride one of the leaders swore and fumed in his saddle, and furiously jerked at the bridle. An officer screamed out an order so violently that his voice broke and ended the sentence in a falsetto shriek.

The leading company of the infantry regiment was somewhat exposed, and the colonel ordered it moved more fully under the shelter of the hill. There was the clank of steel against steel.

A lieutenant of the battery rode down and passed them, holding his right arm carefully in his left hand. And it was as if this arm was not at all a part of him, but belonged to another man. His sober and reflective charger went slowly. The officer's face was grimy and perspiring, and his uniform was tousled as if he had been in direct grapple with an enemy. He smiled grimly when the men stared at him. He turned his horse toward the meadow.

Collins, of A Company, said: "I wisht I had a drink. I bet there's water in that there ol' well yonder!"

"Yes; but how you goin' to git it?"

For the little meadow which intervened was now suffering a terrible onslaught of shells. Its green and beautiful calm had vanished utterly. Brown earth was being flung in monstrous handfuls. And there was a massacre of the young blades of grass. They were being torn, burned, obliterated. Some curious fortune of the battle had made this gentle little meadow the object of the red hate of the shells, and each one as it exploded seemed like an imprecation in the face of a maiden.

The wounded officer who was riding across this expanse said to himself, "Why, they couldn't shoot any harder if the whole army was massed here!"

A shell struck the gray ruins of the house, and as, after the roar, the shattered wall fell in fragments, there was a noise which resembled the flapping of shutters during a wild gale of winter. Indeed, the infantry paused in the shelter of the bank appeared as men standing upon a shore contemplating a madness of the sea. The angel of calamity had under its glance the battery upon the hill. Fewer white-legged men laboured about the guns. A shell had smitten one of the pieces, and after the flare, the smoke, the dust, the wrath of this blow were gone, it was possible to see white legs stretched horizontally upon the ground. And at that interval to the rear, where it is the business of battery horses to stand with their noses to the fight awaiting the command to drag their guns out of the destruction or into it or wheresoever these incomprehensible humans demanded with whip and spur—in this line of passive and dumb spectators, whose fluttering hearts yet would not let them forget the iron laws of man's control of them—in this rank of brute-soldiers there had been relentless and hideous carnage. From the ruck of bleeding and prostrate horses, the men of the infantry could see one animal raising its stricken body with its fore legs, and turning its nose with mystic and profound eloquence toward the sky.

Some comrades joked Collins about his thirst. "Well, if yeh want a drink so bad, why don't yeh go git it!"

"Well, I will in a minnet, if yeh don't shut up!"

A lieutenant of artillery floundered his horse straight down the hill with as great concern as if it were level ground. As he galloped past the colonel of the infantry, he threw up his hand in swift salute. "We've got to get out of that," he roared angrily. He was a black-bearded officer, and his eyes, which resembled beads, sparkled like those of an insane man. His jumping horse sped along the column of infantry.

The fat major, standing carelessly with his sword held horizontally behind him and with his legs far apart, looked after the receding horseman and laughed. "He wants to get back with orders pretty quick, or there'll be no batt'ry left," he observed.

The wise young captain of the second company hazarded to the lieutenant colonel that the enemy's infantry would probably soon attack the hill, and the lieutenant colonel snubbed him.

A private in one of the rear companies looked out over the meadow, and then turned to a companion and said, "Look there, Jim!" It was the wounded officer from the battery, who some time before had started to ride across the meadow, supporting his right arm carefully with his left hand. This man had encountered a shell apparently at a time when no one perceived him, and he could now be seen lying face downward with a stirruped foot stretched across the body of his dead horse. A leg of the charger extended slantingly upward precisely as stiff as a stake. Around this motionless pair the shells still howled.

There was a quarrel in A Company. Collins was shaking his fist in the faces of some laughing comrades. "Dern yeh! I ain't afraid t' go. If yeh say much, I will go!"

"Of course, yeh will! You'll run through that there medder, won't yeh?"

Collins said, in a terrible voice, "You see now!" At this ominous threat his comrades broke into renewed jeers.

Collins gave them a dark scowl and went to find his captain. The latter was conversing with the colonel of the regiment.

"Captain," said Collins, saluting and standing at attention—in those days all trousers bagged at the knees—"captain, I want t' get permission to go git some water from that there well over yonder!"

The colonel and the captain swung about simultaneously and stared across the meadow. The captain laughed. "You must be pretty thirsty, Collins?"

"Yes, sir, I am."

"Well—ah," said the captain. After a moment, he asked, "Can't you wait?"

"No, sir."

The colonel was watching Collins's face. "Look here, my lad," he said, in a pious sort of a voice—"look here, my lad"—Collins was not a lad—"don't you think that's taking pretty big risks for a little drink of water?"

"I dunno," said Collins uncomfortably. Some of the resentment toward his companions, which perhaps had forced him into this affair, was beginning to fade. "I dunno wether 'tis."

The colonel and the captain contemplated him for a time.

"Well," said the captain finally.

"Well," said the colonel, "if you want to go, why, go."

Collins saluted. "Much obliged t' yeh."

As he moved away the colonel called after him. "Take some of the other boys' canteens with you an' hurry back now."

"Yes, sir, I will."

The colonel and the captain looked at each other then, for it had suddenly occurred that they could not for the life of them tell whether Collins wanted to go or whether he did not.

They turned to regard Collins, and as they perceived him surrounded by gesticulating comrades, the colonel said: "Well, by thunder! I guess he's going."

Collins appeared as a man dreaming. In the midst of the questions, the advice, the warnings, all the excited talk of his company mates, he maintained a curious silence.

They were very busy in preparing him for his ordeal. When they inspected him carefully it was somewhat like the examination that grooms give a horse before a race; and they were amazed, staggered by the whole affair. Their astonishment found vent in strange repetitions.

"Are yeh sure a-goin'?" they demanded again and again.

"Certainly I am," cried Collins, at last furiously.

He strode sullenly away from them. He was swinging five or six canteens by their cords. It seemed that his cap would not remain firmly on his head, and often he reached and pulled it down over his brow.

There was a general movement in the compact column. The long animal-like thing moved slightly. Its four hundred eyes were turned upon the figure of Collins.

"Well, sir, if that ain't th' derndest thing! I never thought Fred Collins had the blood in him for that kind of business."

"What's he goin' to do, anyhow?"

"He's goin' to that well there after water."

"We ain't dyin' of thirst, are we? That's foolishness."

"Well, somebody put him up to it, an' he's doin' it."

"Say, he must be a desperate cuss."

When Collins faced the meadow and walked away from the regiment, he was vaguely conscious that a chasm, the deep valley of all prides, was suddenly between him and his comrades. It was provisional, but the provision was that he return as a victor. He had blindly been led by quaint emotions, and laid himself under an obligation to walk squarely up to the face of death.

But he was not sure that he wished to make a retraction, even if he could do so without shame. As a matter of truth, he was sure of very little. He was mainly surprised.

It seemed to him supernaturally strange that he had allowed his mind to man[oe]uvre his body into such a situation. He understood that it might be called dramatically great.

However, he had no full appreciation of anything, excepting that he was actually conscious of being dazed. He could feel his dulled mind groping after the form and colour of this incident. He wondered why he did not feel some keen agony of fear cutting his sense like a knife. He wondered at this, because human expression had said loudly for centuries that men should feel afraid of certain things, and that all men who did not feel this fear were phenomena—heroes.

He was, then, a hero. He suffered that disappointment which we would all have if we discovered that we were ourselves capable of those deeds which we most admire in history and legend. This, then, was a hero. After all, heroes were not much.

No, it could not be true. He was not a hero. Heroes had no shames in their lives, and, as for him, he remembered borrowing fifteen dollars from a friend and promising to pay it back the next day, and then avoiding that friend for ten months. When at home his mother had aroused him for the early labour of his life on the farm, it had often been his fashion to be irritable, childish, diabolical; and his mother had died since he had come to the war.

He saw that, in this matter of the well, the canteens, the shells, he was an intruder in the land of fine deeds.

He was now about thirty paces from his comrades. The regiment had just turned its many faces toward him.

From the forest of terrific noises there suddenly emerged a little uneven line of men. They fired fiercely and rapidly at distant foliage on which appeared little puffs of white smoke. The spatter of skirmish firing was added to the thunder of the guns on the hill. The little line of men ran forward. A colour sergeant fell flat with his flag as if he had slipped on ice. There was hoarse cheering from this distant field.

Collins suddenly felt that two demon fingers were pressed into his ears. He could see nothing but flying arrows, flaming red. He lurched from the shock of this explosion, but he made a mad rush for the house, which he viewed as a man submerged to the neck in a boiling surf might view the shore. In the air, little pieces of shell howled and the earthquake explosions drove him insane with the menace of their roar. As he ran the canteens knocked together with a rhythmical tinkling.

As he neared the house, each detail of the scene became vivid to him. He was aware of some bricks of the vanished chimney lying on the sod. There was a door which hung by one hinge.

Rifle bullets called forth by the insistent skirmishers came from the far-off bank of foliage. They mingled with the shells and the pieces of shells until the air was torn in all directions by hootings, yells, howls. The sky was full of fiends who directed all their wild rage at his head.

When he came to the well, he flung himself face downward and peered into its darkness. There were furtive silver glintings some feet from the surface. He grabbed one of the canteens and, unfastening its cap, swung it down by the cord. The water flowed slowly in with an indolent gurgle.

And now as he lay with his face turned away he was suddenly smitten with the terror. It came upon his heart like the grasp of claws. All the power faded from his muscles. For an instant he was no more than a dead man.

The canteen filled with a maddening slowness, in the manner of all bottles. Presently he recovered his strength and addressed a screaming oath to it. He leaned over until it seemed as if he intended to try to push water into it with his hands. His eyes as he gazed down into the well shone like two pieces of metal and in their expression was a great appeal and a great curse. The stupid water derided him.

There was the blaring thunder of a shell. Crimson light shone through the swift-boiling smoke and made a pink reflection on part of the wall of the well. Collins jerked out his arm and canteen with the same motion that a man would use in withdrawing his head from a furnace.

He scrambled erect and glared and hesitated. On the ground near him lay the old well bucket, with a length of rusty chain. He lowered it swiftly into the well. The bucket struck the water and then, turning lazily over,

298

sank. When, with hand reaching tremblingly over hand, he hauled it out, it knocked often against the walls of the well and spilled some of its contents.

In running with a filled bucket, a man can adopt but one kind of gait. So through this terrible field over which screamed practical angels of death Collins ran in the manner of a farmer chased out of a dairy by a bull.

His face went staring white with anticipation—anticipation of a blow that would whirl him around and down. He would fall as he had seen other men fall, the life knocked out of them so suddenly that their knees were no more quick to touch the ground than their heads. He saw the long blue line of the regiment, but his comrades were standing looking at him from the edge of an impossible star. He was aware of some deep wheel ruts and hoofprints in the sod beneath his feet.

The artillery officer who had fallen in this meadow had been making groans in the teeth of the tempest of sound. These futile cries, wrenched from him by his agony, were heard only by shells, bullets. When wild-eyed Collins came running, this officer raised himself. His face contorted and blanched from pain, he was about to utter some great beseeching cry. But suddenly his face straightened and he called: "Say, young man, give me a drink of water, will you?"

Collins had no room amid his emotions for surprise. He was mad from the threats of destruction.

"I can't!" he screamed, and in his reply was a full description of his quaking apprehension. His cap was gone and his hair was riotous. His clothes made it appear that he had been dragged over the ground by the heels. He ran on.

The officer's head sank down and one elbow crooked. His foot in its brass-bound stirrup still stretched over the body of his horse and the other leg was under the steed.

But Collins turned. He came dashing back. His face had now turned gray and in his eyes was all terror. "Here it is! here it is!"

The officer was as a man gone in drink. His arm bent like a twig. His

299

head drooped as if his neck were of willow. He was sinking to the ground, to lie face downward.

Collins grabbed him by the shoulder. "Here it is. Here's your drink. Turn over. Turn over, man, for God's sake!"

With Collins hauling at his shoulder, the officer twisted his body and fell with his face turned toward that region where lived the unspeakable noises of the swirling missiles. There was the faintest shadow of a smile on his lips as he looked at Collins. He gave a sigh, a little primitive breath like that from a child.

Collins tried to hold the bucket steadily, but his shaking hands caused the water to splash all over the face of the dying man. Then he jerked it away and ran on.

The regiment gave him a welcoming roar. The grimed faces were wrinkled in laughter.

His captain waved the bucket away. "Give it to the men!"

The two genial, skylarking young lieutenants were the first to gain possession of it. They played over it in their fashion.

When one tried to drink the other teasingly knocked his elbow. "Don't, Billie! You'll make me spill it," said the one. The other laughed.

Suddenly there was an oath, the thud of wood on the ground, and a swift murmur of astonishment among the ranks. The two lieutenants glared at each other. The bucket lay on the ground empty.

AN INDIANA CAMPAIGN.

I.

When the able-bodied citizens of the village formed a company and marched away to the war, Major Tom Boldin assumed in a manner the burden of the village cares. Everybody ran to him when they felt obliged to discuss their affairs. The sorrows of the town were dragged before him. His little bench at the sunny side of Migglesville tavern became a sort of an open court where people came to speak resentfully of their grievances. He accepted his position and struggled manfully under the load. It behooved him, as a man who had seen the sky red over the quaint, low cities of Mexico, and the compact Northern bayonets gleaming on the narrow roads.

One warm summer day the major sat asleep on his little bench. There was a lull in the tempest of discussion which usually enveloped him. His cane, by use of which he could make the most tremendous and impressive gestures, reposed beside him. His hat lay upon the bench, and his old bald head had swung far forward until his nose actually touched the first button of his waistcoat.

The sparrows wrangled desperately in the road, defying perspiration. Once a team went jangling and creaking past, raising a yellow blur of dust before the soft tones of the field and sky. In the long grass of the meadow across the road the insects chirped and clacked eternally.

Suddenly a frouzy-headed boy appeared in the roadway, his bare feet pattering rapidly. He was extremely excited. He gave a shrill whoop as he discovered the sleeping major and rushed toward him. He created a terrific panic among some chickens who had been scratching intently near the major's feet. They clamoured in an insanity of fear, and rushed hither and thither seeking a way of escape, whereas in reality all ways lay plainly open to them.

This tumult caused the major to arouse with a sudden little jump of amazement and apprehension. He rubbed his eyes and gazed about him. Meanwhile, some clever chicken had discovered a passage to safety and led the flock into the garden, where they squawked in sustained alarm.

Panting from his run and choked with terror, the little boy stood before the major, struggling with a tale that was ever upon the tip of his tongue.

"Major—now—major——"

The old man, roused from a delicious slumber, glared impatiently at the little boy. "Come, come! What's th' matter with yeh?" he demanded. "What's th' matter? Don't stand there shaking! Speak up!"

"Lots is th' matter!" the little boy shouted valiantly, with a courage born of the importance of his tale. "My ma's chickens 'uz all stole, an'—now—he's over in th' woods!"

"Who is? Who is over in the woods? Go ahead!"

"Now—th' rebel is!"

"What?" roared the major.

"Th' rebel!" cried the little boy, with the last of his breath.

The major pounced from his bench in tempestuous excitement. He seized the little boy by the collar and gave him a great jerk. "Where? Are yeh sure? Who saw 'im? How long ago? Where is he now? Did you see 'im?"

The little boy, frightened at the major's fury, began to sob. After a moment he managed to stammer: "He—now—he's in the woods. I saw 'im. He looks uglier'n anythin'."

The major released his hold upon the boy, and, pausing for a time, indulged in a glorious dream. Then he said: "By thunder! we'll ketch th' cuss. You wait here," he told the boy, "an' don't say a word t' anybody. Do yeh hear?"

The boy, still weeping, nodded, and the major hurriedly entered the inn. He took down from its pegs an awkward, smoothbore rifle and

302

carefully examined the enormous percussion cap that was fitted over the nipple. Mistrusting the cap, he removed it and replaced it with a new one. He scrutinized the gun keenly, as if he could judge in this manner of the condition of the load. All his movements were deliberate and deadly.

When he arrived upon the porch of the tavern he beheld the yard filled with people. Peter Witheby, sooty-faced and grinning, was in the van. He looked at the major. "Well?" he said.

"Well?" returned the major, bridling.

"Well, what's 'che got?" said old Peter.

"'Got?' Got a rebel over in th' woods!" roared the major.

At this sentence the women and boys, who had gathered eagerly about him, gave vent to startled cries. The women had come from adjacent houses, but the little boys represented the entire village. They had miraculously heard the first whisper of rumour, and they performed wonders in getting to the spot. They clustered around the important figure of the major and gazed in silent awe. The women, however, burst forth. At the word "rebel," which represented to them all terrible things, they deluged the major with questions which were obviously unanswerable.

He shook them off with violent impatience. Meanwhile Peter Witheby was trying to force exasperating interrogations through the tumult to the major's ears. "What? No! Yes! How d' I know?" the maddened veteran snarled as he struggled with his friends. "No! Yes! What? How in thunder d' I know?" Upon the steps of the tavern the landlady sat, weeping forlornly.

At last the major burst through the crowd, and went to the roadway. There, as they all streamed after him, he turned and faced them. "Now, look a' here, I don't know any more about this than you do," he told them forcibly. "All that I know is that there's a rebel over in Smith's woods, an' all I know is that I'm agoin' after 'im."

"But hol' on a minnet," said old Peter. "How do yeh know he's a rebel?"

"I know he is!" cried the major. "Don't yeh think I know what a rebel is?"

Then, with a gesture of disdain at the babbling crowd, he marched determinedly away, his rifle held in the hollow of his arm. At this heroic moment a new clamour arose, half admiration, half dismay. Old Peter hobbled after the major, continually repeating, "Hol' on a minnet."

The little boy who had given the alarm was the centre of a throng of lads who gazed with envy and awe, discovering in him a new quality. He held forth to them eloquently. The women stared after the figure of the major and old Peter, his pursuer. Jerozel Bronson, a half-witted lad who comprehended nothing save an occasional genial word, leaned against the fence and grinned like a skull. The major and the pursuer passed out of view around the turn in the road where the great maples lazily shook the dust that lay on their leaves.

For a moment the little group of women listened intently as if they expected to hear a sudden shot and cries from the distance. They looked at each other, their lips a little ways apart. The trees sighed softly in the heat of the summer sun. The insects in the meadow continued their monotonous humming, and, somewhere, a hen had been stricken with fear and was cackling loudly.

Finally, Mrs. Goodwin said, "Well, I'm goin' up to th' turn a' th' road, anyhow." Mrs. Willets and Mrs. Joe Petersen, her particular friends, cried out at this temerity, but she said, "Well, I'm goin', anyhow."

She called Bronson. "Come on, Jerozel. You're a man, an' if he should chase us, why, you mus' pitch inteh 'im. Hey?"

Bronson always obeyed everybody. He grinned an assent, and went with her down the road.

A little boy attempted to follow them, but a shrill scream from his mother made him halt.

The remaining women stood motionless, their eyes fixed upon Mrs. Goodwin and Jerozel. Then at last one gave a laugh of triumph at her conquest of caution and fear, and cried, "Well, I'm goin' too!"

Another instantly said, "So am I." There began a general movement. Some of the little boys had already ventured a hundred feet away from the main body, and at this unanimous advance they spread out ahead in little groups. Some recounted terrible stories of rebel ferocity. Their eyes were large with excitement. The whole thing with its possible dangers had for them a delicious element. Johnnie Peterson, who could whip any boy present, explained what he would do in case the enemy should happen to pounce out at him.

The familiar scene suddenly assumed a new aspect. The field of corn which met the road upon the left was no longer a mere field of corn. It was a darkly mystic place whose recesses could contain all manner of dangers. The long green leaves, waving in the breeze, rustled from the passing of men. In the song of the insects there were now omens, threats.

There was a warning in the enamel blue of the sky, in the stretch of yellow road, in the very atmosphere. Above the tops of the corn loomed the distant foliage of Smith's woods, curtaining the silent action of a tragedy whose horrors they imagined.

The women and the little boys came to a halt, overwhelmed by the impressiveness of the landscape. They waited silently.

Mrs. Goodwin suddenly said, "I'm goin' back." The others, who all wished to return, cried at once disdainfully:

"Well, go back, if yeh want to!"

A cricket at the roadside exploded suddenly in his shrill song, and a woman who had been standing near shrieked in startled terror. An electric movement went through the group of women. They jumped and gave vent to sudden screams. With the fears still upon their agitated faces, they turned to berate the one who had shrieked. "My! what a goose you are, Sallie! Why, it took my breath away. Goodness sakes, don't holler like that again!"

II.

"Hol' on a minnet!" Peter Witheby was crying to the major, as the latter, full of the importance and dignity of his position as protector of Migglesville, paced forward swiftly. The veteran already felt upon his brow a wreath formed of the flowers of gratitude, and as he strode he was absorbed in planning a calm and self-contained manner of wearing it. "Hol' on a minnet!" piped old Peter in the rear.

At last the major, aroused from his dream of triumph, turned about wrathfully. "Well, what?"

"Now, look a' here," said Peter. "What 'che goin' t' do?"

The major, with a gesture of supreme exasperation, wheeled again and went on. When he arrived at the cornfield he halted and waited for Peter. He had suddenly felt that indefinable menace in the landscape.

"Well?" demanded Peter, panting.

The major's eyes wavered a trifle. "Well," he repeated—"well, I'm goin' in there an' bring out that there rebel."

They both paused and studied the gently swaying masses of corn, and behind them the looming woods, sinister with possible secrets.

"Well," said old Peter.

The major moved uneasily and put his hand to his brow. Peter waited in obvious expectation.

The major crossed through the grass at the roadside and climbed the fence. He put both legs over the topmost rail and then sat perched there, facing the woods. Once he turned his head and asked, "What?"

"I hain't said anythin'," answered Peter.

The major clambered down from the fence and went slowly into the corn, his gun held in readiness. Peter stood in the road.

Presently the major returned and said, in a cautious whisper, "If yeh hear anythin', you come a-runnin', will yeh?"

"Well, I hain't got no gun nor nuthin'," said Peter, in the same low tone; "what good 'ud I do?"

306

"Well, yeh might come along with me an' watch," said the major. "Four eyes is better'n two."

"If I had a gun——" began Peter.

"Oh, yeh don't need no gun," interrupted the major, waving his hand. "All I'm afraid of is that I won't find 'im. My eyes ain't so good as they was."

"Well——"

"Come along," whispered the major. "Yeh hain't afraid, are yeh?"

"No, but——"

"Well, come along, then. What's th' matter with yeh?"

Peter climbed the fence. He paused on the top rail and took a prolonged stare at the inscrutable woods. When he joined the major in the cornfield he said, with a touch of anger:

"Well, you got the gun. Remember that. If he comes for me, I hain't got a blame thing!"

"Shucks!" answered the major. "He ain't agoin' t' come for yeh."

The two then began a wary journey through the corn. One by one the long aisles between the rows appeared. As they glanced along each of them it seemed as if some gruesome thing had just previously vacated it. Old Peter halted once and whispered: "Say, look a' here; supposin'—supposin'——"

"Supposin' what?" demanded the major.

"Supposin'——" said Peter. "Well, remember you got th' gun, an' I hain't got anythin'."

"Thunder!" said the major.

When they got to where the stalks were very short because of the shade cast by the trees of the wood, they halted again. The leaves were gently swishing in the breeze. Before them stretched the mystic green wall of the forest, and there seemed to be in it eyes which followed each of their movements.

Peter at last said, "I don't believe there's anybody in there."

"Yes, there is, too," said the major. "I'll bet anythin' he's in there."

"How d' yeh know?" asked Peter. "I'll bet he ain't within a mile o' here."

The major suddenly ejaculated, "Listen!"

They bent forward, scarce breathing, their mouths agape, their eyes glinting. Finally, the major turned his head. "Did yeh hear that?" he said hoarsely.

"No," said Peter, in a low voice. "What was it?"

The major listened for a moment. Then he turned again. "I thought I heered somebody holler!" he explained cautiously.

They both bent forward and listened once more. Peter in the intentness of his attitude lost his balance and was obliged to lift his foot hastily and with noise. "S-s-sh!" hissed the major.

After a minute Peter spoke quite loudly, "Oh, shucks! I don't believe yeh heered anythin'."

The major made a frantic downward gesture with his hand. "Shet up, will yeh!" he said, in an angry undertone.

Peter became silent for a moment, but presently he said again, "Oh, yeh didn't hear anythin'."

The major turned to glare at his companion in despair and wrath.

"What's th' matter with yeh? Can't yeh shet up?"

"Oh, this here ain't no use. If you're goin' in after 'im, why don't yeh go in after 'im?"

"Well, gimme time, can't yeh?" said the major, in a growl. And, as if to add more to this reproach, he climbed the fence that compassed the woods, looking resentfully back at his companion.

"Well," said Peter, when the major paused.

308

The major stepped down upon the thick carpet of brown leaves that stretched under the trees. He turned then to whisper, "You wait here, will yeh?" His face was red with determination.

"Well, hol' on a minnet!" said Peter. "You—I—we'd better——"

"No," said the major. "You wait here."

He went stealthily into the thickets. Peter watched him until he grew to be a vague, slow-moving shadow. From time to time he could hear the leaves crackle and twigs snap under the major's awkward tread. Peter, intent, breathless, waited for the peal of sudden tragedy. Finally, the woods grew silent in a solemn and impressive hush that caused Peter to feel the thumping of his heart. He began to look about him to make sure that nothing should spring upon him from the sombre shadows. He scrutinized this cool gloom before him, and at times he thought he could perceive the moving of swift silent shapes. He concluded that he had better go back and try to muster some assistance to the major.

As Peter came through the corn, the women in the road caught sight of the glittering figure and screamed. Many of them began to run. The little boys, with all their valour, scurried away in clouds. Mrs. Joe Peterson, however, cast a glance over her shoulders as she, with her skirts gathered up, was running as best she could. She instantly stopped and, in tones of deepest scorn, called out to the others, "Why, it's on'y Pete Witheby!" They came faltering back then, those who had been naturally swiftest in the race avoiding the eyes of those whose limbs had enabled them to flee a short distance.

Peter came rapidly, appreciating the glances of vivid interest in the eyes of the women. To their lightning-like questions, which hit all sides of the episode, he opposed a new tranquillity gained from his sudden ascent in importance. He made no answer to their clamour. When he had reached the top of the fence, he called out commandingly: "Here you, Johnnie, you and George, run an' git my gun! It's hangin' on th' pegs over th' bench in th' shop."

At this terrible sentence, a shuddering cry broke from the women. The boys named sped down the road, accompanied by a retinue of envious companions.

Peter swung his legs over the rail and faced the woods again. He twisted his head once to say: "Keep still, can't yeh? Quit scufflin' aroun'!" They could see by his manner that this was a supreme moment. The group became motionless and still. Later, Peter turned to say, "S-s-sh!" to a restless boy, and the air with which he said it smote them all with awe.

The little boys who had gone after the gun came pattering along hurriedly, the weapon borne in the midst of them. Each was anxious to share in the honour. The one who had been delegated to bring it was bullying and directing his comrades.

Peter said, "S-s-sh!" He took the gun and poised it in readiness to sweep the cornfield. He scowled at the boys and whispered angrily: "Why didn't yeh bring th' powder horn an' th' thing with th' bullets in? I told yeh t' bring 'em. I'll send somebody else next time."

"Yeh didn't tell us!" cried the two boys shrilly.

"S-s-sh! Quit yeh noise," said Peter, with a violent gesture.

However, this reproof enabled other boys to recover that peace of mind which they had lost when seeing their friends loaded with honours.

The women had cautiously approached the fence and, from time to time, whispered feverish questions; but Peter repulsed them savagely, with an air of being infinitely bothered by their interference in his intent watch. They were forced to listen again in silence to the weird and prophetic chanting of the insects and the mystic silken rustling of the corn.

At last the thud of hurrying feet in the soft soil of the field came to their ears. A dark form sped toward them. A wave of a mighty fear swept over the group, and the screams of the women came hoarsely from their choked throats. Peter swung madly from his perch, and turned to use the fence as a rampart.

But it was the major. His face was inflamed and his eyes were glaring. He clutched his rifle by the middle and swung it wildly. He was bounding at a great speed for his fat, short body.

"It's all right! it's all right!" he began to yell, some distance away. "It's all right! It's on'y ol' Milt' Jacoby!"

When he arrived at the top of the fence, he paused and mopped his brow.

"What?" they thundered, in an agony of sudden unreasoning disappointment.

Mrs. Joe Petersen, who was a distant connection of Milton Jacoby, thought to forestall any damage to her social position by saying at once disdainfully, "Drunk, I s'pose!"

"Yep," said the major, still on the fence, and mopped his brow. "Drunk as a fool. Thunder! I was surprised. I—I—thought it was a rebel, sure."

The thoughts of all these women wavered for a time. They were at a loss for precise expression of their emotion. At last, however, they hurled this superior sentence at the major:

"Well, yeh might have known."

A GRAY SLEEVE.

I.

"It looks as if it might rain this afternoon," remarked the lieutenant of artillery.

"So it does," the infantry captain assented. He glanced casually at the sky. When his eyes had lowered to the green-shadowed landscape before him, he said fretfully: "I wish those fellows out yonder would quit pelting at us. They've been at it since noon."

At the edge of a grove of maples, across wide fields, there occasionally appeared little puffs of smoke of a dull hue in this gloom of sky which expressed an impending rain. The long wave of blue and steel in the field moved uneasily at the eternal barking of the far-away sharpshooters, and the men, leaning upon their rifles, stared at the grove of maples. Once a private turned to borrow some tobacco from a comrade in the rear rank, but, with his hand still stretched out, he continued to twist his head and glance at the distant trees. He was afraid the enemy would shoot him at a time when he was not looking.

Suddenly the artillery officer said, "See what's coming!"

Along the rear of the brigade of infantry a column of cavalry was sweeping at a hard gallop. A lieutenant, riding some yards to the right of the column, bawled furiously at the four troopers just at the rear of the colours. They had lost distance and made a little gap, but at the shouts of the lieutenant they urged their horses forward. The bugler, careering along behind the captain of the troop, fought and tugged like a wrestler to keep his frantic animal from bolting far ahead of the column.

On the springy turf the innumerable hoofs thundered in a swift storm of sound. In the brown faces of the troopers their eyes were set like bits of flashing steel.

The long line of the infantry regiments standing at ease underwent a sudden movement at the rush of the passing squadron. The foot soldiers turned their heads to gaze at the torrent of horses and men.

The yellow folds of the flag fluttered back in silken, shuddering waves as if it were a reluctant thing. Occasionally a giant spring of a charger would rear the firm and sturdy figure of a soldier suddenly head and shoulders above his comrades. Over the noise of the scudding hoofs could be heard the creaking of leather trappings, the jingle and clank of steel, and the tense, low-toned commands or appeals of the men to their horses. And the horses were mad with the headlong sweep of this movement. Powerful under jaws bent back and straightened so that the bits were clamped as rigidly as vices upon the teeth, and glistening necks arched in desperate resistance to the hands at the bridles. Swinging their heads in rage at the granite laws of their lives, which compelled even their angers and their ardours to chosen directions and chosen faces, their flight was as a flight of harnessed demons.

The captain's bay kept its pace at the head of the squadron with the lithe bounds of a thoroughbred, and this horse was proud as a chief at the roaring trample of his fellows behind him. The captain's glance was calmly upon the grove of maples whence the sharpshooters of the enemy had been picking at the blue line. He seemed to be reflecting. He stolidly rose and fell with the plunges of his horse in all the indifference of a deacon's figure seated plumply in church. And it occurred to many of the watching infantry to wonder why this officer could remain imperturbable and reflective when his squadron was thundering and swarming behind him like the rushing of a flood.

The column swung in a sabre-curve toward a break in a fence, and dashed into a roadway. Once a little plank bridge was encountered, and the sound of the hoofs upon it was like the long roll of many drums. An old captain in the infantry turned to his first lieutenant and made a remark which was a compound of bitter disparagement of cavalry in general and soldiery admiration of this particular troop.

Suddenly the bugle sounded, and the column halted with a jolting upheaval amid sharp, brief cries. A moment later the men had tumbled from their horses, and, carbines in hand, were running in a swarm toward the grove of maples. In the road one of every four of the troopers was standing with braced legs, and pulling and hauling at the bridles of four frenzied horses.

The captain was running awkwardly in his boots. He held his sabre low so that the point often threatened to catch in the turf. His yellow hair ruffled out from under his faded cap. "Go in hard now!" he roared, in a voice of hoarse fury. His face was violently red.

The troopers threw themselves upon the grove like wolves upon a great animal. Along the whole front of woods there was the dry, crackling of musketry, with bitter, swift flashes and smoke that writhed like stung phantoms. The troopers yelled shrilly and spanged bullets low into the foliage.

For a moment, when near the woods, the line almost halted. The men struggled and fought for a time like swimmers encountering a powerful current. Then with a supreme effort they went on again. They dashed madly at the grove, whose foliage from the high light of the field was as inscrutable as a wall.

Then suddenly each detail of the calm trees became apparent, and with a few more frantic leaps the men were in the cool gloom of the woods. There was a heavy odour as from burned paper. Wisps of gray smoke wound upward. The men halted and, grimy, perspiring, and puffing, they searched the recesses of the woods with eager, fierce glances. Figures could be seen flitting afar off. A dozen carbines rattled at them in an angry volley.

During this pause the captain strode along the line, his face lit with a broad smile of contentment. "When he sends this crowd to do anything, I guess he'll find we do it pretty sharp," he said to the grinning lieutenant.

"Say, they didn't stand that rush a minute, did they?" said the subaltern. Both officers were profoundly dusty in their uniforms, and their faces were soiled like those of two urchins.

Out in the grass behind them were three tumbled and silent forms.

Presently the line moved forward again. The men went from tree to tree like hunters stalking game. Some at the left of the line fired occasionally, and those at the right gazed curiously in that direction. The men still breathed heavily from their scramble across the field.

Of a sudden a trooper halted and said: "Hello! there's a house!" Every one paused. The men turned to look at their leader.

The captain stretched his neck and swung his head from side to side. "By George, it is a house!" he said.

Through the wealth of leaves there vaguely loomed the form of a large, white house. These troopers, brown-faced from many days of campaigning, each feature of them telling of their placid confidence and courage, were stopped abruptly by the appearance of this house. There was some subtle suggestion—some tale of an unknown thing—which watched them from they knew not what part of it.

A rail fence girded a wide lawn of tangled grass. Seven pines stood along a drive-way which led from two distant posts of a vanished gate. The blue-clothed troopers moved forward until they stood at the fence peering over it.

The captain put one hand on the top rail and seemed to be about to climb the fence, when suddenly he hesitated, and said in a low voice, "Watson, what do you think of it?"

The lieutenant stared at the house. "Derned if I know!" he replied.

The captain pondered. It happened that the whole company had turned a gaze of profound awe and doubt upon this edifice which confronted them. The men were very silent.

At last the captain swore and said: "We are certainly a pack of fools. Derned old deserted house halting a company of Union cavalry, and making us gape like babies!"

"Yes, but there's something—something——" insisted the subaltern in a half stammer.

"Well, if there's 'something—something' in there, I'll get it out," said the captain. "Send Sharpe clean around to the other side with about twelve men, so we will sure bag your 'something—something,' and I'll take a few of the boys and find out what's in the d——d old thing!"

He chose the nearest eight men for his "storming party," as the lieutenant called it. After he had waited some minutes for the others to get into position, he said "Come ahead" to his eight men, and climbed the fence.

The brighter light of the tangled lawn made him suddenly feel tremendously apparent, and he wondered if there could be some mystic thing in the house which was regarding this approach. His men trudged silently at his back. They stared at the windows and lost themselves in deep speculations as to the probability of there being, perhaps, eyes behind the blinds—malignant eyes, piercing eyes.

Suddenly a corporal in the party gave vent to a startled exclamation, and half threw his carbine into position. The captain turned quickly, and the corporal said: "I saw an arm move the blinds. An arm with a gray sleeve!"

"Don't be a fool, Jones, now!" said the captain sharply.

"I swear t'——" began the corporal, but the captain silenced him.

When they arrived at the front of the house, the troopers paused, while the captain went softly up the front steps. He stood before the large front door and studied it. Some crickets chirped in the long grass, and the nearest pine could be heard in its endless sighs. One of the privates moved uneasily, and his foot crunched the gravel. Suddenly the captain swore angrily and kicked the door with a loud crash. It flew open.

II.

The bright lights of the day flashed into the old house when the captain angrily kicked open the door. He was aware of a wide hallway carpeted with matting and extending deep into the dwelling. There was also an old walnut hatrack and a little marble-topped table with a vase and two books upon it. Farther back was a great, venerable fireplace containing dreary ashes.

But directly in front of the captain was a young girl. The flying open of the door had obviously been an utter astonishment to her, and she remained transfixed there in the middle of the floor, staring at the captain with wide eyes.

She was like a child caught at the time of a raid upon the cake. She wavered to and fro upon her feet, and held her hands behind her. There were two little points of terror in her eyes, as she gazed up at the young captain in dusty blue, with his reddish, bronze complexion, his yellow hair, his bright sabre held threateningly.

These two remained motionless and silent, simply staring at each other for some moments.

The captain felt his rage fade out of him and leave his mind limp. He had been violently angry, because this house had made him feel hesitant, wary. He did not like to be wary. He liked to feel confident, sure. So he had kicked the door open, and had been prepared to march in like a soldier of wrath.

But now he began, for one thing, to wonder if his uniform was so dusty and old in appearance. Moreover, he had a feeling that his face was covered with a compound of dust, grime, and perspiration. He took a step forward and said, "I didn't mean to frighten you." But his voice was coarse from his battle-howling. It seemed to him to have hempen fibres in it.

The girl's breath came in little, quick gasps, and she looked at him as she would have looked at a serpent.

"I didn't mean to frighten you," he said again.

The girl, still with her hands behind her, began to back away.

"Is there any one else in the house?" he went on, while slowly following her. "I don't wish to disturb you, but we had a fight with some rebel skirmishers in the woods, and I thought maybe some of them might have come in here. In fact, I was pretty sure of it. Are there any of them here?"

The girl looked at him and said, "No!" He wondered why extreme agitation made the eyes of some women so limpid and bright.

317

"Who is here besides yourself?"

By this time his pursuit had driven her to the end of the hall, and she remained there with her back to the wall and her hands still behind her. When she answered this question, she did not look at him but down at the floor. She cleared her voice and then said, "There is no one here."

"No one?"

She lifted her eyes to him in that appeal that the human being must make even to falling trees, crashing bowlders, the sea in a storm, and said, "No, no, there is no one here." He could plainly see her tremble.

Of a sudden he bethought him that she continually kept her hands behind her. As he recalled her air when first discovered, he remembered she appeared precisely as a child detected at one of the crimes of childhood. Moreover, she had always backed away from him. He thought now that she was concealing something which was an evidence of the presence of the enemy in the house.

"What are you holding behind you?" he said suddenly.

She gave a little quick moan, as if some grim hand had throttled her.

"What are you holding behind you?"

"Oh, nothing—please. I am not holding anything behind me; indeed I'm not."

"Very well. Hold your hands out in front of you, then."

"Oh, indeed, I'm not holding anything behind me. Indeed, I'm not."

"Well," he began. Then he paused, and remained for a moment dubious. Finally, he laughed. "Well, I shall have my men search the house, anyhow. I'm sorry to trouble you, but I feel sure that there is some one here whom we want." He turned to the corporal, who with the other men was gaping quietly in at the door, and said, "Jones, go through the house."

As for himself, he remained planted in front of the girl, for she evidently did not dare to move and allow him to see what she held so carefully behind her back. So she was his prisoner.

The men rummaged around on the ground floor of the house. Sometimes the captain called to them, "Try that closet," "Is there any cellar?" But they found no one, and at last they went trooping toward the stairs which led to the second floor.

But at this movement on the part of the men the girl uttered a cry—a cry of such fright and appeal that the men paused. "Oh, don't go up there! Please don't go up there!—ple—ease! There is no one there! Indeed—indeed there is not! Oh, ple—ease!"

"Go on, Jones," said the captain calmly.

The obedient corporal made a preliminary step, and the girl bounded toward the stairs with another cry.

As she passed him, the captain caught sight of that which she had concealed behind her back, and which she had forgotten in this supreme moment. It was a pistol.

She ran to the first step, and standing there, faced the men, one hand extended with perpendicular palm, and the other holding the pistol at her side. "Oh, please, don't go up there! Nobody is there—indeed, there is not! P-l-e-a-s-e!" Then suddenly she sank swiftly down upon the step, and, huddling forlornly, began to weep in the agony and with the convulsive tremors of an infant. The pistol fell from her fingers and rattled down to the floor.

The astonished troopers looked at their astonished captain. There was a short silence.

Finally, the captain stooped and picked up the pistol. It was a heavy weapon of the army pattern. He ascertained that it was empty.

He leaned toward the shaking girl, and said gently, "Will you tell me what you were going to do with this pistol?"

He had to repeat the question a number of times, but at last a muffled voice said, "Nothing."

"Nothing!" He insisted quietly upon a further answer. At the tender tones of the captain's voice, the phlegmatic corporal turned and winked gravely at the man next to him.

"Won't you tell me?"

The girl shook her head.

"Please tell me!"

The silent privates were moving their feet uneasily and wondering how long they were to wait.

The captain said, "Please won't you tell me?"

Then this girl's voice began in stricken tones half coherent, and amid violent sobbing: "It was grandpa's. He—he—he said he was going to shoot anybody who came in here—he didn't care if there were thousands of 'em. And—and I know he would, and I was afraid they'd kill him. And so—and—so I stole away his pistol—and I was going to hide it when you—you—you kicked open the door."

The men straightened up and looked at each other. The girl began to weep again.

The captain mopped his brow. He peered down at the girl. He mopped his brow again. Suddenly he said, "Ah, don't cry like that."

He moved restlessly and looked down at his boots. He mopped his brow again.

Then he gripped the corporal by the arm and dragged him some yards back from the others. "Jones," he said, in an intensely earnest voice, "will you tell me what in the devil I am going to do?"

The corporal's countenance became illuminated with satisfaction at being thus requested to advise his superior officer. He adopted an air of great thought, and finally said: "Well, of course, the feller with the gray sleeve must be upstairs, and we must get past the girl and up there somehow. Suppose I take her by the arm and lead her——"

"What!" interrupted the captain from between his clinched teeth. As he turned away from the corporal, he said fiercely over his shoulder, "You touch that girl and I'll split your skull!"

III.

The corporal looked after his captain with an expression of mingled amazement, grief, and philosophy. He seemed to be saying to himself that there unfortunately were times, after all, when one could not rely upon the most reliable of men. When he returned to the group he found the captain bending over the girl and saying, "Why is it that you don't want us to search upstairs?"

The girl's head was buried in her crossed arms. Locks of her hair had escaped from their fastenings and these fell upon her shoulder.

"Won't you tell me?"

The corporal here winked again at the man next to him.

"Because," the girl moaned—"because—there isn't anybody up there."

The captain at last said timidly, "Well, I'm afraid—I'm afraid we'll have to——"

The girl sprang to her feet again, and implored him with her hands. She looked deep into his eyes with her glance, which was at this time like that of the fawn when it says to the hunter, "Have mercy upon me!"

These two stood regarding each other. The captain's foot was on the bottom step, but he seemed to be shrinking. He wore an air of being deeply wretched and ashamed. There was a silence.

Suddenly the corporal said in a quick, low tone, "Look out, captain!"

All turned their eyes swiftly toward the head of the stairs. There had appeared there a youth in a gray uniform. He stood looking coolly down at them. No word was said by the troopers. The girl gave vent to a little wail of desolation, "O Harry!"

He began slowly to descend the stairs. His right arm was in a white sling, and there were some fresh blood stains upon the cloth. His face was rigid and deathly pale, but his eyes flashed like lights. The girl was again moaning in an utterly dreary fashion, as the youth came slowly down toward the silent men in blue.

Six steps from the bottom of the flight he halted and said, "I reckon it's me you're looking for."

The troopers had crowded forward a trifle and, posed in lithe, nervous attitudes, were watching him like cats. The captain remained unmoved. At the youth's question he merely nodded his head and said, "Yes."

The young man in gray looked down at the girl, and then, in the same even tone which now, however, seemed to vibrate with suppressed fury, he said, "And is that any reason why you should insult my sister?"

At this sentence, the girl intervened, desperately, between the young man in gray and the officer in blue. "Oh, don't, Harry, don't! He was good to me! He was good to me, Harry—indeed he was!"

The youth came on in his quiet, erect fashion until the girl could have touched either of the men with her hand, for the captain still remained with his foot upon the first step. She continually repeated: "O Harry! O Harry!"

The youth in gray man[oe]uvred to glare into the captain's face, first over one shoulder of the girl and then over the other. In a voice that rang like metal, he said: "You are armed and unwounded, while I have no weapons and am wounded; but——"

The captain had stepped back and sheathed his sabre. The eyes of these two men were gleaming fire, but otherwise the captain's countenance was imperturbable. He said: "You are mistaken. You have no reason to——"

"You lie!"

All save the captain and the youth in gray started in an electric movement.

These two words crackled in the air like shattered glass. There was a breathless silence.

The captain cleared his throat. His look at the youth contained a quality of singular and terrible ferocity, but he said in his stolid tone, "I don't suppose you mean what you say now."

Upon his arm he had felt the pressure of some unconscious little fingers. The girl was leaning against the wall as if she no longer knew how to keep her balance, but those fingers—he held his arm very still. She murmured: "O Harry, don't! He was good to me—indeed he was!"

The corporal had come forward until he in a measure confronted the youth in gray, for he saw those fingers upon the captain's arm, and he knew that sometimes very strong men were not able to move hand nor foot under such conditions.

The youth had suddenly seemed to become weak. He breathed heavily and clung to the rail. He was glaring at the captain, and apparently summoning all his will power to combat his weakness. The corporal addressed him with profound straightforwardness, "Don't you be a derned fool!" The youth turned toward him so fiercely that the corporal threw up a knee and an elbow like a boy who expects to be cuffed.

The girl pleaded with the captain. "You won't hurt him, will you? He don't know what he's saying. He's wounded, you know. Please don't mind him!"

"I won't touch him," said the captain, with rather extraordinary earnestness; "don't you worry about him at all. I won't touch him!"

Then he looked at her, and the girl suddenly withdrew her fingers from his arm.

The corporal contemplated the top of the stairs, and remarked without surprise, "There's another of 'em coming!"

An old man was clambering down the stairs with much speed. He waved a cane wildly. "Get out of my house, you thieves! Get out! I won't have you cross my threshold! Get out!" He mumbled and wagged his head in an old man's fury. It was plainly his intention to assault them.

And so it occurred that a young girl became engaged in protecting a stalwart captain, fully armed, and with eight grim troopers at his back, from the attack of an old man with a walking-stick!

A blush passed over the temples and brow of the captain, and he looked particularly savage and weary. Despite the girl's efforts, he suddenly faced the old man.

"Look here," he said distinctly, "we came in because we had been fighting in the woods yonder, and we concluded that some of the enemy were in this house, especially when we saw a gray sleeve at the window. But this young man is wounded, and I have nothing to say to him. I will even take it for granted that there are no others like him upstairs. We will go away, leaving your d——d old house just as we found it! And we are no more thieves and rascals than you are!"

The old man simply roared: "I haven't got a cow nor a pig nor a chicken on the place! Your soldiers have stolen everything they could carry away. They have torn down half my fences for firewood. This afternoon some of your accursed bullets even broke my window panes!"

The girl had been faltering: "Grandpa! O grandpa!"

The captain looked at the girl. She returned his glance from the shadow of the old man's shoulder. After studying her face a moment, he said, "Well, we will go now." He strode toward the door and his men clanked docilely after him.

At this time there was the sound of harsh cries and rushing footsteps from without. The door flew open, and a whirlwind composed of blue-coated troopers came in with a swoop. It was headed by the lieutenant. "Oh, here you are!" he cried, catching his breath. "We thought——Oh, look at the girl!"

The captain said intensely, "Shut up, you fool!"

The men settled to a halt with a clash and a bang. There could be heard the dulled sound of many hoofs outside of the house.

"Did you order up the horses?" inquired the captain.

"Yes. We thought——"

"Well, then, let's get out of here," interrupted the captain morosely.

The men began to filter out into the open air. The youth in gray had been hanging dismally to the railing of the stairway. He now was climbing slowly up to the second floor. The old man was addressing himself directly to the serene corporal.

"Not a chicken on the place!" he cried.

"Well, I didn't take your chickens, did I?"

"No, maybe you didn't, but——"

The captain crossed the hall and stood before the girl in rather a culprit's fashion. "You are not angry at me, are you?" he asked timidly.

"No," she said. She hesitated a moment, and then suddenly held out her hand. "You were good to me—and I'm—much obliged."

The captain took her hand, and then he blushed, for he found himself unable to formulate a sentence that applied in any way to the situation.

She did not seem to heed that hand for a time.

He loosened his grasp presently, for he was ashamed to hold it so long without saying anything clever. At last, with an air of charging an intrenched brigade, he contrived to say, "I would rather do anything than frighten or trouble you."

His brow was warmly perspiring. He had a sense of being hideous in his dusty uniform and with his grimy face.

She said, "Oh, I'm so glad it was you instead of somebody who might have—might have hurt brother Harry and grandpa!"

He told her, "I wouldn't have hurt 'em for anything!"

There was a little silence.

"Well, good-bye!" he said at last.

"Good-bye!"

He walked toward the door past the old man, who was scolding at the vanishing figure of the corporal. The captain looked back. She had remained there watching him.

At the bugle's order, the troopers standing beside their horses swung briskly into the saddle. The lieutenant said to the first sergeant:

"Williams, did they ever meet before?"

"Hanged if I know!"

"Well, say——"

The captain saw a curtain move at one of the windows. He cantered from his position at the head of the column and steered his horse between two flower beds.

"Well, good-bye!"

The squadron trampled slowly past.

"Good-bye!"

They shook hands.

He evidently had something enormously important to say to her, but it seems that he could not manage it. He struggled heroically. The bay charger, with his great mystically solemn eyes, looked around the corner of his shoulder at the girl.

The captain studied a pine tree. The girl inspected the grass beneath the window. The captain said hoarsely, "I don't suppose—I don't suppose—I'll ever see you again!"

She looked at him affrightedly and shrank back from the window. He seemed to have woefully expected a reception of this kind for his question. He gave her instantly a glance of appeal.

She said, "Why, no, I don't suppose we will."

"Never?"

"Why, no, 'tain't possible. You—you are a—Yankee!"

"Oh, I know it, but——" Eventually he continued, "Well, some day, you know, when there's no more fighting, we might——" He observed that she had again withdrawn suddenly into the shadow, so he said, "Well, good-bye!"

When he held her fingers she bowed her head, and he saw a pink blush steal over the curves of her cheek and neck.

"Am I never going to see you again?"

She made no reply.

"Never?" he repeated.

After a long time, he bent over to hear a faint reply: "Sometimes—when there are no troops in the neighbourhood—grandpa don't mind if I—walk over as far as that old oak tree yonder—in the afternoons."

It appeared that the captain's grip was very strong, for she uttered an exclamation and looked at her fingers as if she expected to find them mere fragments. He rode away.

The bay horse leaped a flower bed. They were almost to the drive, when the girl uttered a panic-stricken cry.

The captain wheeled his horse violently and upon his return journey went straight through a flower bed.

The girl had clasped her hands. She beseeched him wildly with her eyes. "Oh, please, don't believe it! I never walk to the old oak tree. Indeed, I don't! I never—never—never walk there."

The bridle drooped on the bay charger's neck. The captain's figure seemed limp. With an expression of profound dejection and gloom he stared off at where the leaden sky met the dark green line of the woods. The long-impending rain began to fall with a mournful patter, drop and drop. There was a silence.

At last a low voice said, "Well—I might—sometimes I might—perhaps—but only once in a great while—I might walk to the old tree—in the afternoons."

THE VETERAN.

Out of the low window could be seen three hickory trees placed irregularly in a meadow that was resplendent in springtime green. Farther away, the old, dismal belfry of the village church loomed over the pines. A horse meditating in the shade of one of the hickories lazily swished his tail. The warm sunshine made an oblong of vivid yellow on the floor of the grocery.

"Could you see the whites of their eyes?" said the man who was seated on a soap box.

"Nothing of the kind," replied old Henry warmly. "Just a lot of flitting figures, and I let go at where they 'peared to be the thickest. Bang!"

"Mr. Fleming," said the grocer—his deferential voice expressed somehow the old man's exact social weight—"Mr. Fleming, you never was frightened much in them battles, was you?"

The veteran looked down and grinned. Observing his manner, the entire group tittered. "Well, I guess I was," he answered finally. "Pretty well scared, sometimes. Why, in my first battle I thought the sky was falling down. I thought the world was coming to an end. You bet I was scared."

Every one laughed. Perhaps it seemed strange and rather wonderful to them that a man should admit the thing, and in the tone of their laughter there was probably more admiration than if old Fleming had declared that he had always been a lion. Moreover, they knew that he had ranked as an orderly sergeant, and so their opinion of his heroism was fixed. None, to be sure, knew how an orderly sergeant ranked, but then it was understood to be somewhere just shy of a major general's stars. So, when old Henry admitted that he had been frightened, there was a laugh.

"The trouble was," said the old man, "I thought they were all shooting at me. Yes, sir, I thought every man in the other army was aiming at me in particular, and only me. And it seemed so darned unreasonable, you know. I wanted to explain to 'em what an almighty good fellow I was, because I thought then they might quit all trying to hit me. But I couldn't explain, and they kept on being unreasonable—blim!—blam!—bang! So I run!"

Two little triangles of wrinkles appeared at the corners of his eyes. Evidently he appreciated some comedy in this recital. Down near his feet, however, little Jim, his grandson, was visibly horror-stricken. His hands were clasped nervously, and his eyes were wide with astonishment at this terrible scandal, his most magnificent grandfather telling such a thing.

"That was at Chancellorsville. Of course, afterward I got kind of used to it. A man does. Lots of men, though, seem to feel all right from the start. I did, as soon as I 'got on to it,' as they say now; but at first I was pretty well flustered. Now, there was young Jim Conklin, old Si Conklin's son—that used to keep the tannery—you none of you recollect him—well, he went into it from the start just as if he was born to it. But with me it was different. I had to get used to it."

When little Jim walked with his grandfather he was in the habit of skipping along on the stone pavement in front of the three stores and the hotel of the town and betting that he could avoid the cracks. But upon this day he walked soberly, with his hand gripping two of his grandfather's fingers. Sometimes he kicked abstractedly at dandelions that curved over the walk. Any one could see that he was much troubled.

"There's Sickles's colt over in the medder, Jimmie," said the old man. "Don't you wish you owned one like him?"

"Um," said the boy, with a strange lack of interest. He continued his reflections. Then finally he ventured, "Grandpa—now—was that true what you was telling those men?"

"What?" asked the grandfather. "What was I telling them?"

"Oh, about your running."

"Why, yes, that was true enough, Jimmie. It was my first fight, and there was an awful lot of noise, you know."

Jimmie seemed dazed that this idol, of its own will, should so totter. His

330

stout boyish idealism was injured.

Presently the grandfather said: "Sickles's colt is going for a drink. Don't you wish you owned Sickles's colt, Jimmie?"

The boy merely answered, "He ain't as nice as our'n." He lapsed then into another moody silence.

One of the hired men, a Swede, desired to drive to the county seat for purposes of his own. The old man loaned a horse and an unwashed buggy. It appeared later that one of the purposes of the Swede was to get drunk.

After quelling some boisterous frolic of the farm hands and boys in the garret, the old man had that night gone peacefully to sleep, when he was aroused by clamouring at the kitchen door. He grabbed his trousers, and they waved out behind as he dashed forward. He could hear the voice of the Swede, screaming and blubbering. He pushed the wooden button, and, as the door flew open, the Swede, a maniac, stumbled inward, chattering, weeping, still screaming: "De barn fire! Fire! Fire! De barn fire! Fire! Fire! Fire!"

There was a swift and indescribable change in the old man. His face ceased instantly to be a face; it became a mask, a gray thing, with horror written about the mouth and eyes. He hoarsely shouted at the foot of the little rickety stairs, and immediately, it seemed, there came down an avalanche of men. No one knew that during this time the old lady had been standing in her night clothes at the bedroom door, yelling: "What's th' matter? What's th' matter? What's th' matter?"

When they dashed toward the barn it presented to their eyes its usual appearance, solemn, rather mystic in the black night. The Swede's lantern was overturned at a point some yards in front of the barn doors. It contained a wild little conflagration of its own, and even in their excitement some of those who ran felt a gentle secondary vibration of the thrifty part of their minds at sight of this overturned lantern. Under ordinary circumstances it would have been a calamity.

But the cattle in the barn were trampling, trampling, trampling, and above this noise could be heard a humming like the song of innumerable bees. The old man hurled aside the great doors, and a yellow flame leaped out at one corner and sped and wavered frantically up the old gray wall. It was glad, terrible, this single flame, like the wild banner of deadly and triumphant foes.

The motley crowd from the garret had come with all the pails of the farm. They flung themselves upon the well. It was a leisurely old machine, long dwelling in indolence. It was in the habit of giving out water with a sort of reluctance. The men stormed at it, cursed it; but it continued to allow the buckets to be filled only after the wheezy windlass had howled many protests at the mad-handed men.

With his opened knife in his hand old Fleming himself had gone headlong into the barn, where the stifling smoke swirled with the air currents, and where could be heard in its fulness the terrible chorus of the flames, laden with tones of hate and death, a hymn of wonderful ferocity.

He flung a blanket over an old mare's head, cut the halter close to the manger, led the mare to the door, and fairly kicked her out to safety. He returned with the same blanket, and rescued one of the work horses. He took five horses out, and then came out himself, with his clothes bravely on fire. He had no whiskers, and very little hair on his head. They soused five pailfuls of water on him. His eldest son made a clean miss with the sixth pailful, because the old man had turned and was running down the decline and around to the basement of the barn, where were the stanchions of the cows. Some one noticed at the time that he ran very lamely, as if one of the frenzied horses had smashed his hip.

The cows, with their heads held in the heavy stanchions, had thrown themselves, strangled themselves, tangled themselves: done everything which the ingenuity of their exuberant fear could suggest to them.

Here, as at the well, the same thing happened to every man save one. Their hands went mad. They became incapable of everything save the power to rush into dangerous situations.

The old man released the cow nearest the door, and she, blind drunk with terror, crashed into the Swede. The Swede had been running to and fro babbling. He carried an empty milk pail, to which he clung with an unconscious, fierce enthusiasm. He shrieked like one lost as he went under the cow's hoofs, and the milk pail, rolling across the floor, made a flash of silver in the gloom.

Old Fleming took a fork, beat off the cow, and dragged the paralyzed Swede to the open air. When they had rescued all the cows save one, which had so fastened herself that she could not be moved an inch, they returned to the front of the barn and stood sadly, breathing like men who had reached the final point of human effort.

Many people had come running. Some one had even gone to the church, and now, from the distance, rang the tocsin note of the old bell. There was a long flare of crimson on the sky, which made remote people speculate as to the whereabouts of the fire.

The long flames sang their drumming chorus in voices of the heaviest bass. The wind whirled clouds of smoke and cinders into the faces of the spectators. The form of the old barn was outlined in black amid these masses of orange-hued flames.

And then came this Swede again, crying as one who is the weapon of the sinister fates. "De colts! De colts! You have forgot de colts!"

Old Fleming staggered. It was true; they had forgotten the two colts in the box stalls at the back of the barn. "Boys," he said, "I must try to get 'em out." They clamoured about him then, afraid for him, afraid of what they should see. Then they talked wildly each to each. "Why, it's sure death!" "He would never get out!" "Why, it's suicide for a man to go in there!" Old Fleming stared absent-mindedly at the open doors. "The poor little things!" he said. He rushed into the barn.

When the roof fell in, a great funnel of smoke swarmed toward the sky, as if the old man's mighty spirit, released from its body—a little bottle— had swelled like the genie of fable. The smoke was tinted rose-hue from the flames, and perhaps the unutterable midnights of the universe will have no power to daunt the colour of this soul.

THE END.

About Author

Stephen Crane (November 1, 1871 – June 5, 1900) was an American poet, novelist, and short story writer. Prolific throughout his short life, he wrote notable works in the Realist tradition as well as early examples of American Naturalism and Impressionism. He is recognized by modern critics as one of the most innovative writers of his generation.

The ninth surviving child of Methodist parents, Crane began writing at the age of four and had published several articles by the age of 16. Having little interest in university studies though he was active in a fraternity, he left Syracuse University in 1891 to work as a reporter and writer. Crane's first novel was the 1893 Bowery tale Maggie: A Girl of the Streets, generally considered by critics to be the first work of American literary Naturalism. He won international acclaim in 1895 for his Civil War novel The Red Badge of Courage, which he wrote without having any battle experience.

In 1896, Crane endured a highly publicized scandal after appearing as a witness in the trial of a suspected prostitute, an acquaintance named Dora Clark. Late that year he accepted an offer to travel to Cuba as a war correspondent. As he waited in Jacksonville, Florida for passage, he met Cora Taylor, with whom he began a lasting relationship. En route to Cuba, Crane's vessel the SS Commodore sank off the coast of Florida, leaving him and others adrift for 30 hours in a dinghy. Crane described the ordeal in "The Open Boat". During the final years of his life, he covered conflicts in Greece (accompanied by Cora, recognized as the first woman war correspondent) and later lived in England with her. He was befriended by writers such as Joseph Conrad and H. G. Wells. Plagued by financial difficulties and ill health, Crane died of tuberculosis in a Black Forest sanatorium in Germany at the age of 28.

At the time of his death, Crane was considered an important figure in American literature. After he was nearly forgotten for two decades, critics revived interest in his life and work. Crane's writing is characterized by vivid intensity, distinctive dialects, and irony. Common themes involve fear, spiritual crises and social isolation. Although recognized primarily for The Red Badge of Courage, which has become an American classic, Crane is also known for his poetry, journalism, and short stories such as "The Open Boat", "The Blue Hotel", "The Bride Comes to Yellow Sky", and The Monster. His writing made a deep impression on 20th-century writers, most prominent among them Ernest Hemingway, and is thought to have inspired the Modernists and the Imagists.

Biography

Early years

Stephen Crane was born on November 1, 1871, in Newark, New Jersey, to Jonathan Townley Crane, a minister in the Methodist Episcopal church, and Mary Helen Peck Crane, daughter of a clergyman, George Peck. He was the fourteenth and last child born to the couple. At 45, Helen Crane had suffered the early deaths of her previous four children, each of whom died within one year of birth. Nicknamed "Stevie" by the family, he joined eight surviving brothers and sisters—Mary Helen, George Peck, Jonathan Townley, William Howe, Agnes Elizabeth, Edmund Byran, Wilbur Fiske, and Luther.

The Cranes were descended from Jaspar Crane, a founder of New Haven Colony, who had migrated there from England in 1639. Stephen was named for a putative founder of Elizabethtown, New Jersey, who had, according to family tradition, come from England or Wales in 1665, as well as his great-great-grandfather Stephen Crane (1709–1780), a Revolutionary War patriot who served as New Jersey delegate to the First Continental Congress in Philadelphia. Crane later wrote that his father, Dr. Crane, "was a great, fine, simple mind," who had written numerous tracts on theology. Although his mother was a popular spokeswoman for the Woman's Christian Temperance Union and a highly religious woman, Crane wrote that he did not believe "she was as narrow as most of her friends or family." The young Stephen was raised primarily by his sister Agnes, who was 15 years his senior. The family moved to Port Jervis, New York, in 1876, where Dr. Crane became the pastor of Drew Methodist Church, a position that he retained until his death.

As a child, Stephen was often sickly and afflicted by constant colds.

When the boy was almost two, his father wrote in his diary that his youngest son became "so sick that we are anxious about him." Despite his fragile nature, Crane was an intelligent child who taught himself to read before the age of four. His first known inquiry, recorded by his father, dealt with writing; at the age of three, while imitating his brother Townley's writing, he asked his mother, "how do you spell O?" In December 1879, Crane wrote a poem about wanting a dog for Christmas. Entitled "I'd Rather Have –", it is his first surviving poem. Stephen was not regularly enrolled in school until January 1880, but he had no difficulty in completing two grades in six weeks. Recalling this feat, he wrote that it "sounds like the lie of a fond mother at a teaparty, but I do remember that I got ahead very fast and that father was very pleased with me."

Dr. Crane died on February 16, 1880, at the age of 60; Stephen was eight years old. Some 1,400 people mourned Dr. Crane at his funeral, more than double the size of his congregation. After her husband's death, Mrs. Crane moved to Roseville, near Newark, leaving Stephen in the care of his older brother Edmund, with whom the young boy lived with cousins in Sussex County. He next lived with his brother William, a lawyer, in Port Jervis for several years.

His older sister Helen took him to Asbury Park to be with their brother Townley and his wife, Fannie. Townley was a professional journalist; he headed the Long Branch department of both the New-York Tribune and the Associated Press, and also served as editor of the Asbury Park Shore Press. Agnes, another Crane sister, joined the siblings in New Jersey. She took a position at Asbury Park's intermediate school and moved in with Helen to care for the young Stephen.

Within a couple of years, the Crane family suffered more losses. First, Townley and his wife lost their two young children. His wife Fannie died of Bright's disease in November 1883. Agnes Crane became ill and died on June 10, 1884, of meningitis at the age of 28.

Schooling

Crane wrote his first known story, "Uncle Jake and the Bell Handle", when he was 14. In late 1885, he enrolled at Pennington Seminary, a ministry-focused coeducational boarding school 7 miles (11 km) north of Trenton. His father had been principal there from 1849 to 1858. Soon after her youngest son left for school, Mrs. Crane began suffering what the Asbury Park Shore Press reported as "a temporary aberration of the mind." She had apparently recovered by early 1886, but later that year, her son, 23-year-old Luther Crane, died after falling in front of an oncoming train while working as a flagman for the Erie Railroad. It was the fourth death in six years among Stephen's immediate family.

After two years, Crane left Pennington for Claverack College, a quasi-military school. He later looked back on his time at Claverack as "the happiest period of my life although I was not aware of it." A classmate remembered him as a highly literate but erratic student, lucky to pass examinations in math and science, and yet "far in advance of his fellow students in his knowledge of History and Literature", his favorite subjects. While he held an impressive record on the drill field and baseball diamond, Crane generally did not excel in the classroom. Not having a middle name, as was customary among other students, he took to signing his name "Stephen T. Crane" in order "to win recognition as a regular fellow". Crane was seen as friendly, but also moody and rebellious. He sometimes skipped class in order to play baseball, a game in which he starred as catcher. He was also greatly interested in the school's military training program. He rose rapidly in the ranks of the student battalion. One classmate described him as "indeed physically attractive without being handsome", but he was aloof, reserved and not generally popular at Claverack. Although academically weak, Crane gained experience at Claverack that provided background (and likely some anecdotes from the Civil War veterans on the staff) that proved useful when he came to write The Red Badge of Courage.

In mid-1888, Crane became his brother Townley's assistant at a New Jersey shore news bureau, working there every summer until 1892. Crane's first publication under his byline was an article on the explorer Henry M. Stanley's famous quest to find the Scottish missionary David Livingstone in Africa. It appeared in the February 1890 Claverack College Vidette. Within a few months, Crane was persuaded by his family to forgo a military career and transfer to Lafayette College in Easton, Pennsylvania, in order to pursue a mining engineering degree. He registered at Lafayette on September 12, and promptly became involved in extracurricular activities; he took up baseball again and joined the largest fraternity, Delta Upsilon. He also joined both rival literary societies, named for (George) Washington and (Benjamin) Franklin. Crane infrequently attended classes and ended the semester with grades for four of the seven courses he had taken.

After one semester, Crane transferred to Syracuse University, where he enrolled as a non-degree candidate in the College of Liberal Arts. He roomed in the Delta Upsilon fraternity house and joined the baseball team. Attending just one class (English Literature) during the middle trimester, he remained in residence while taking no courses in the third semester.

Concentrating on his writing, Crane began to experiment with tone and style while trying out different subjects. He published his fictional story, "Great Bugs of Onondaga," simultaneously in the Syracuse Daily Standard and the New York Tribune. Declaring college "a waste of time", Crane decided to become a full-time writer and reporter. He attended a Delta Upsilon chapter meeting on June 12, 1891, but shortly afterward left college for good.

Full-time writer

In the summer of 1891, Crane often camped with friends in the nearby area of Sullivan County, New York, where his brother Edmund occupied a house obtained as part of their brother William's Hartwood Club (Association) land dealings. He used this area as the geographic setting for several short stories, which were posthumously published in a collection under the title Stephen Crane: Sullivan County Tales and Sketches. Crane showed two of these works to Tribune editor Willis Fletcher Johnson, a friend of the family, who accepted them for the publication. "Hunting Wild Dogs" and "The Last of the Mohicans" were the first of fourteen unsigned Sullivan County sketches and tales that were published in the Tribune between February and July 1892. Crane also showed Johnson an early draft of his first novel, Maggie: A Girl of the Streets.

Later that summer, Crane met and befriended author Hamlin Garland, who had been lecturing locally on American literature and the expressive arts; on August 17 he gave a talk on novelist William Dean Howells, which Crane wrote up for the Tribune. Garland became a mentor for and champion of the young writer, whose intellectual honesty impressed him. Their relationship suffered in later years, however, because Garland disapproved of Crane's alleged immorality, related to his living with a woman married to another man.

Stephen moved into his brother Edmund's house in Lakeview, a suburb of Paterson, New Jersey, in the fall of 1891. From here he made frequent trips into New York City, writing and reporting particularly on its impoverished tenement districts. Crane focused particularly on The Bowery, a small and once prosperous neighborhood in the southern part of Manhattan. After the Civil War, Bowery shops and mansions had given way to saloons, dance halls, brothels and flophouses, all of which Crane frequented. He later said he did so for research. He was attracted to the human nature found in the slums, considering it "open and plain, with nothing hidden". Believing nothing honest and unsentimental had been written about the Bowery, Crane became determined to do so himself; this was the setting of his first novel. On December 7, 1891, Crane's mother died at the age of 64, and the 20-year-old appointed Edmund as his guardian.

Despite being frail, undernourished and suffering from a hacking cough, which did not prevent him from smoking cigarettes, in the spring of 1892 Crane began a romance with Lily Brandon Munroe, a married woman who was estranged from her husband. Although Munroe later said Crane "was not a handsome man", she admired his "remarkable almond-shaped gray eyes." He begged her to elope with him, but her family opposed the match because Crane lacked money and prospects, and she declined. Their last meeting likely occurred in April 1898, when he again asked her to run away with him and she again refused.

Between July 2 and September 11, 1892, Crane published at least ten news reports on Asbury Park affairs. Although a Tribune colleague stated that Crane "was not highly distinguished above any other boy of twenty who had gained a reputation for saying and writing bright things," that summer his reporting took on a more skeptical, hypocrisy-deflating tone. A storm of controversy erupted over a report he wrote on the Junior Order of United American Mechanics' American Day Parade, entitled "Parades and Entertainments". Published on August 21, the report juxtaposes the "bronzed, slope-shouldered, uncouth" marching men "begrimed with dust" and the spectators dressed in "summer gowns, lace parasols, tennis trousers, straw hats and indifferent smiles". Believing they were being ridiculed, some JOUAM marchers were outraged and wrote to the editor. The owner of the Tribune, Whitelaw Reid, was that year's Republican vice-presidential candidate, and this likely increased the sensitivity of the paper's management to the issue. Although Townley wrote a piece for the Asbury Park Daily Press in his brother's defense, the Tribune quickly apologized to its readers, calling Stephen Crane's piece "a bit of random correspondence, passed inadvertently by the copy editor". Hamlin Garland and biographer John Barry attested that Crane told them he had been dismissed by the Tribune, although Willis Fletcher Johnson later denied this. The paper did not publish any of Crane's work after 1892.

> Such an assemblage of the spraddle-legged men of the middle class, whose hands were bent and shoulders stooped from delving and constructing, had never appeared to an Asbury Park summer crowd, and the latter was vaguely amused.

> — Stephen Crane, account of the JOUAM parade as it appeared in the Tribune.

Life in New York

Crane struggled to make a living as a free-lance writer, contributing sketches and feature articles to various New York newspapers. In October 1892, he moved into a rooming house in Manhattan whose boarders were a group of medical students. During this time, he expanded or entirely reworked Maggie: A Girl of the Streets, which is about a girl who "blossoms in a mud-puddle" and becomes a pitiful victim of circumstance. In the winter of 1893, Crane took the manuscript of Maggie to Richard Watson Gilder, who rejected it for publication in The Century Magazine.

Crane decided to publish it privately, with money he had inherited from his mother. The novel was published in late February or early March 1893 by a small printing shop that usually printed medical books and religious tracts. The typewritten title page for the Library of Congress copyright application read simply: "A Girl of the Streets, / A Story of New York. / —By—/Stephen Crane." The name "Maggie" was added to the title later. Crane used the pseudonym "Johnston Smith" for the novel's initial publication, later telling friend and artist Corwin Knapp Linson that the nom de plume was the "commonest name I could think of. I had an editor friend named Johnson, and put in the "t", and no one could find me in the mob of Smiths." Hamlin Garland reviewed the work in the June 1893 issue of The Arena, calling it "the most truthful and unhackneyed study of the slums I have yet read, fragment though it is." Despite this early praise, Crane became depressed and destitute from having spent $869 for 1,100 copies of a novel that did not sell; he ended up giving a hundred copies away. He would later remember "how I looked forward to publication and pictured the sensation I thought it would make. It fell flat. Nobody seemed to notice it or care for it... Poor Maggie! She was one of my first loves."

In March 1893, Crane spent hours lounging in Linson's studio while having his portrait painted. He became fascinated with issues of the Century that were largely devoted to famous battles and military leaders from the Civil War. Frustrated with the dryly written stories, Crane stated, "I wonder that some of those fellows don't tell how they felt in those scraps. They spout enough of what they did, but they're as emotionless as rocks." Crane returned to these magazines during subsequent visits to Linson's studio, and eventually the idea of writing a war novel overtook him. He would later state that he "had been unconsciously working the detail of the story out through most of his boyhood" and had imagined "war stories ever since he was out of knickerbockers." This novel would ultimately become The Red Badge of Courage.

A river, amber-tinted in the shadow of its banks, purled at the army's feet; and at night, when the stream had become of a sorrowful blackness, one could see across it the red, eyelike gleam of hostile camp-fires set in the low brows of distant hills.

— Stephen Crane, The Red Badge of Courage

From the beginning, Crane wished to show how it felt to be in a war by writing "a psychological portrayal of fear." Conceiving his story from the point of view of a young private who is at first filled with boyish dreams of the glory of war and then quickly becomes disillusioned by war's reality, Crane borrowed the private's surname, "Fleming", from his sister-in-law's maiden name. He later said that the first paragraphs came to him with "every word in place, every comma, every period fixed." Working mostly nights, he wrote from around midnight until four or five in the morning. Because he could not afford a typewriter, he wrote carefully in ink on legal-sized paper, seldom crossing through or interlining a word. If he did change something, he would rewrite the whole page.

While working on his second novel, Crane remained prolific, concentrating on publishing stories to stave off poverty; "An Experiment in Misery", based on Crane's experiences in the Bowery, was printed by the New York Press. He also wrote five or six poems a day. In early 1894, he showed some of his poems or "lines" as he called them, to Hamlin Garland, who said he read "some thirty in all" with "growing wonder." Although Garland and William Dean Howells encouraged him to submit his poetry for publication, Crane's free verse was too unconventional for most. After brief wrangling between poet and publisher, Copeland & Day accepted Crane's first book of poems, The Black Riders and Other Lines, although it would not be published until after The Red Badge of Courage. He received a 10 percent royalty and the publisher assured him that the book would be in a form "more severely classic than any book ever yet issued in America."

In the spring of 1894, Crane offered the finished manuscript of The Red Badge of Courage to McClure's Magazine, which had become the foremost magazine for Civil War literature. While McClure's delayed giving him an answer on his novel, they offered him an assignment writing about the Pennsylvania coal mines. "In the Depths of a Coal Mine", a story with pictures by Linson, was syndicated by McClure's in a number of newspapers, heavily edited. Crane was reportedly disgusted by the cuts, asking Linson: "Why the hell did they send me up there then? Do they want the public to think the coal mines gilded ball-rooms with the miners eating ice-cream in boiled shirt-fronts?"

Sources report that following an encounter with a male prostitute that spring, Crane began a novel on the subject entitled Flowers of Asphalt, which he later abandoned. The manuscript has never been recovered.

After discovering that McClure's could not afford to pay him, Crane took his war novel to Irving Bacheller of the Bacheller-Johnson Newspaper Syndicate, which agreed to publish The Red Badge of Courage in serial form. Between the third and the ninth of December 1894, The Red Badge of Courage was published in some half-dozen newspapers in the United States. Although it was greatly cut for syndication, Bacheller attested to its causing a stir, saying "its quality [was] immediately felt and recognized." The lead editorial in the Philadelphia Press of December 7 said that Crane "is a new name now and unknown, but everybody will be talking about him if he goes on as he has begun".

Travels and fame

At the end of January 1895, Crane left on what he called "a very long and circuitous newspaper trip" to the west. While writing feature articles for the Bacheller syndicate, he traveled to Saint Louis, Missouri, Nebraska, New Orleans, Galveston, Texas and then Mexico City. Irving Bacheller would later state that he "sent Crane to Mexico for new color", which the author found in the form of Mexican slum life. Whereas he found the lower class in New York pitiful, he was impressed by the "superiority" of the Mexican peasants' contentment and "even refuse[d] to pity them."

Returning to New York five months later, Crane joined the Lantern (alternately spelled "Lanthom" or "Lanthorne") Club organized by a group of young writers and journalists. The Club, located on the roof of an old house on William Street near the Brooklyn Bridge, served as a drinking establishment of sorts and was decorated to look like a ship's cabin. There Crane ate one good meal a day, although friends were troubled by his "constant smoking,

344

too much coffee, lack of food and poor teeth", as Nelson Greene put it. Living in near-poverty and greatly anticipating the publication of his books, Crane began work on two more novels: The Third Violet and George's Mother.

The Black Riders was published by Copeland & Day shortly before his return to New York in May, but it received mostly criticism, if not abuse, for the poems' unconventional style and use of free verse. A piece in the Bookman called Crane "the Aubrey Beardsley of poetry," and a commentator from the Chicago Daily Inter-Ocean stated that "there is not a line of poetry from the opening to the closing page. Whitman's Leaves of Grass were luminous in comparison. Poetic lunacy would be a better name for the book." In June, the New York Tribune dismissed the book as "so much trash." Crane was pleased that the book was "making some stir".

In contrast to the reception for Crane's poetry, The Red Badge of Courage was welcomed with acclaim after its publication by Appleton in September 1895. For the next four months, the book was in the top six on various bestseller lists around the country. It arrived on the literary scene "like a flash of lightning out of a clear winter sky", according to H. L. Mencken, who was about 15 at the time. The novel also became popular in Britain; Joseph Conrad, a future friend of Crane, wrote that the novel "detonated... with the impact and force of a twelve-inch shell charged with a very high explosive." Appleton published two, possibly three, printings in 1895 and as many as eleven more in 1896. Although some critics considered the work overly graphic and profane, it was widely heralded for its realistic portrayal of war and unique writing style. The Detroit Free Press declared that The Red Badge would give readers "so vivid a picture of the emotions and the horrors of the battlefield that you will pray your eyes may never look upon the reality."

Wanting to capitalize on the success of The Red Badge, McClure Syndicate offered Crane a contract to write a series on Civil War battlefields. Because it was a wish of his to "visit the battlefield—which I was to describe— at the time of year when it was fought", Crane agreed to take the assignment. Visiting battlefields in Northern Virginia, including Fredericksburg, he would later produce five more Civil War tales: "Three Miraculous Soldiers",

"The Veteran", "An Indiana Campaign", "An Episode of War" and The Little Regiment.

Scandal

At the age of 24, Crane, who was reveling in his success, became involved in a highly publicized case involving a suspected prostitute named Dora Clark. At 2 a.m. on September 16, 1896, he escorted two chorus girls and Clark from New York City's Broadway Garden, a popular "resort" where he had interviewed the women for a series he was writing. As Crane saw one woman safely to a streetcar, a plainclothes policeman named Charles Becker arrested the other two for solicitation; Crane was threatened with arrest when he tried to interfere. One of the women was released after Crane confirmed her erroneous claim that she was his wife, but Clark was charged and taken to the precinct. Against the advice of the arresting sergeant, Crane made a statement confirming Dora Clark's innocence, stating that "I only know that while with me she acted respectably, and that the policeman's charge was false." On the basis of Crane's testimony, Clark was discharged. The media seized upon the story; news spread to Philadelphia, Boston and beyond, with papers focusing on Crane's courage. The Stephen Crane story, as it became known, soon became a source for ridicule; the Chicago Dispatch in particular quipped that "Stephen Crane is respectfully informed that association with women in scarlet is not necessarily a 'Red Badge of Courage' ".

A couple of weeks after her trial, Clark pressed charges of false arrest against the officer who had arrested her. The next day, the officer physically attacked Clark in the presence of witnesses for having brought charges against him. Crane, who initially went briefly to Philadelphia to escape the pressure of publicity, returned to New York to give testimony at Becker's trial despite advice given to him from Theodore Roosevelt, who was Police Commissioner at the time and a new acquaintance of Crane. The defense targeted Crane: police raided his apartment and interviewed people who knew him, trying to find incriminating evidence in order to lessen the effect of his testimony. A vigorous cross-examination took place that sought to portray Crane as a man of dubious morals; while the prosecution proved that he frequented brothels, Crane claimed this was merely for research purposes. After the trial ended on

346

October 16, the arresting officer was exonerated, and Crane's reputation was ruined.

Cora Taylor and the Commodore shipwreck

None of them knew the color of the sky. Their eyes glanced level and were fastened upon the waves that swept toward them. These waves were of the hue of slate, save for the tops, which were of foaming white, and all of the men knew the colors of the sea.

— Stephen Crane, "The Open Boat"

Given $700 in Spanish gold by the Bacheller-Johnson syndicate to work as a war correspondent in Cuba as the Spanish–American War was pending, the 25-year-old Crane left New York on November 27, 1896, on a train bound for Jacksonville, Florida. Upon arrival in Jacksonville, he registered at the St. James Hotel under the alias of Samuel Carleton to maintain anonymity while seeking passage to Cuba. While waiting for a boat, he toured the city and visited the local brothels. Within days he met 31-year-old Cora Taylor, proprietor of the downtown bawdy house Hotel de Dream. Born into a respectable Boston family, Taylor (whose legal name was Cora Ethel Stewart) had already had two brief marriages; her first husband, Vinton Murphy, divorced her on grounds of adultery. In 1889, she had married British Captain Donald William Stewart. She left him in 1892 for another man, but was still legally married. By the time Crane arrived, Taylor had been in Jacksonville for two years. She lived a bohemian lifestyle, owned a hotel of assignation, and was a well-known and respected local figure. The two spent much time together while Crane awaited his departure. He was finally cleared to leave for the Cuban port of Cienfuegos on New Year's Eve aboard the SS Commodore.

The ship sailed from Jacksonville with 27 or 28 men and a cargo of supplies and ammunition for the Cuban rebels. On the St. Johns River and less than 2 miles (3.2 km) from Jacksonville, Commodore struck a sandbar in a dense fog and damaged its hull. Although towed off the sandbar the following day, it was beached again in Mayport and again damaged. A leak began in the boiler room that evening and, as a result of malfunctioning water pumps, the ship came to a standstill about 16 miles (26 km) from Mosquito Inlet. As the ship took on more water, Crane described the engine room as resembling "a scene at this time taken from the middle kitchen of hades." Commodore's lifeboats were lowered in the early hours of the morning on January 2, 1897 and the ship ultimately sank at 7 a.m. Crane was one of the last to leave the ship in a 10-foot (3.0 m) dinghy. In an ordeal that he recounted in the short story "The Open Boat", Crane and three other men (including the ship's Captain) foundered off the coast of Florida for a day and a half before trying to land the dinghy at Daytona Beach. The small boat overturned in the surf, forcing the exhausted men to swim to shore; one of them died. Having lost the gold given to him for his journey, Crane wired Cora Taylor for help. She traveled to Daytona and returned to Jacksonville with Crane the next day, only four days after he had left on the Commodore.

The disaster was reported on the front pages of newspapers across the country. Rumors that the ship had been sabotaged were widely circulated but never substantiated. Portrayed favorably and heroically by the press, Crane emerged from the ordeal with his reputation enhanced, if not restored, after the battering he had received in the Dora Clark affair. Meanwhile, Crane's affair with Taylor blossomed.

Three seasons of archaeological investigation were conducted in 2002-04 to examine and document the exposed remains of a wreck near Ponce Inlet, FL conjectured to be that of the SS Commodore. The collected data, and other accumulated evidence, finally substantiated the identification of the Commodore beyond a reasonable doubt.

Greco-Turkish War

Despite contentment in Jacksonville and the need for rest after his ordeal, Crane became restless. He left Jacksonville on January 11 for New York City, where he applied for a passport to Cuba, Mexico and the West Indies. Spending three weeks in New York, he completed "The Open Boat" and periodically visited Port Jervis to see family. By this time, however, blockades had formed along the Florida coast as tensions rose with Spain, and Crane concluded that he would never be able to travel to Cuba. He sold "The Open

Boat" to Scribner's for $300 in early March. Determined to work as a war correspondent, Crane signed on with William Randolph Hearst's New York Journal to cover the impending Greco-Turkish conflict. He brought along Taylor, who had sold the Hotel de Dream in order to follow him.

On March 20, they sailed first to England, where Crane was warmly received. They arrived in Athens in early April; between April 17 (when Turkey declared war on Greece) and April 22, Crane wrote his first published report of the war, "An Impression of the 'Concert' ". When he left for Epirus in the northwest, Taylor remained in Athens, where she became the Greek war's first woman war correspondent. She wrote under the pseudonym "Imogene Carter" for the New York Journal, a job that Crane had secured for her. They wrote frequently, traveling throughout the country separately and together. The first large battle that Crane witnessed was the Turks' assault on General Constantine Smolenski's Greek forces at Velestino. Crane wrote, "It is a great thing to survey the army of the enemy. Just where and how it takes hold upon the heart is difficult of description." During this battle, Crane encountered "a fat waddling puppy" that he immediately claimed, dubbing it "Velestino, the Journal dog". Greece and Turkey signed an armistice on May 20, ending the 30-day war; Crane and Taylor left Greece for England, taking two Greek brothers as servants and Velestino the dog with them.

Spanish–American War

After staying in Limpsfield, Surrey, for a few days, Crane and Taylor settled in Ravensbrook, a plain brick villa in Oxted. Referring to themselves as Mr. and Mrs. Crane, the couple lived openly in England, but Crane concealed the relationship from his friends and family in the United States. Admired in England, Crane thought himself attacked back home: "There seem so many of them in America who want to kill, bury and forget me purely out of unkindness and envy and—my unworthiness, if you choose", he wrote. Velestino the dog sickened and died soon after their arrival in England, on August 1. Crane, who had a great love for dogs, wrote an emotional letter to a friend an hour after the dog's death, stating that "for eleven days we fought death for him, thinking nothing of anything but his life." The Limpsfield-Oxted area was home to members of the socialist Fabian

Society and a magnet for writers such as Edmund Gosse, Ford Madox Ford and Edward Garnett. Crane also met the Polish-born novelist Joseph Conrad in October 1897, with whom he would have what Crane called a "warm and endless friendship".

Although Crane was confident among peers, strong negative reviews of the recently published The Third Violet were causing his literary reputation to dwindle. Reviewers were also highly critical of Crane's war letters, deeming them self-centered. Although The Red Badge of Courage had by this time gone through fourteen printings in the United States and six in England, Crane was running out of money. To survive financially, he worked at a feverish pitch, writing prolifically for both the English and the American markets. He wrote in quick succession stories such as The Monster, "The Bride Comes to Yellow Sky", "Death and the Child" and "The Blue Hotel". Crane began to attach price tags to his new works of fiction, hoping that "The Bride", for example, would fetch $175.

As 1897 ended, Crane's money crisis worsened. Amy Leslie, a reporter from Chicago and a former lover, sued him for $550. The New York Times reported that Leslie gave him $800 in November 1896 but that he'd repaid only a quarter of the sum. In February he was summoned to answer Leslie's claim. The claim was apparently settled out of court, because no record of adjudication exists. Meanwhile, Crane felt "heavy with troubles" and "chased to the wall" by expenses. He confided to his agent that he was $2,000 in debt but that he would "beat it" with more literary output.

Soon after the USS Maine exploded in Havana Harbor on February 15, 1898, under suspicious circumstances, Crane was offered a £60 advance by Blackwood's Magazine for articles "from the seat of war in the event of a war breaking out" between the United States and Spain. His health was failing, and it is believed that signs of his pulmonary tuberculosis, which he may have contracted in childhood, became apparent.With almost no money coming in from his finished stories, Crane accepted the assignment and left Oxted for New York. Taylor and the rest of the household stayed behind to fend off local creditors. Crane applied for a passport and left New York for Key West two days before Congress declared war. While the war idled, he interviewed people and produced occasional copy.

In early June, he observed the establishment of an American base in Cuba when Marines seized Guantánamo Bay. He went ashore with the Marines, planning "to gather impressions and write them as the spirit moved." Although he wrote honestly about his fear in battle, others observed his calmness and composure. He would later recall "this prolonged tragedy of the night" in the war tale "Marines Signaling Under Fire at Guantanamo". After showing a willingness to serve during fighting at Cuzco, Cuba, by carrying messages to company commanders, Crane was officially cited for his "material aid during the action".

He continued to report upon various battles and the worsening military conditions and praised Theodore Roosevelt's Rough Riders, despite past tensions with the Commissioner. In early July, Crane was sent to the United States for medical treatment for a high fever. He was diagnosed with yellow fever, then malaria. Upon arrival in Old Point Comfort, Virginia, he spent a few weeks resting in a hotel. Although Crane had filed more than twenty dispatches in the three months he had covered the war, the World's business manager believed that the paper had not received its money's worth and fired him. In retaliation, Crane signed with Hearst's New York Journal with the wish to return to Cuba. He traveled first to Puerto Rico and then to Havana. In September, rumors began to spread that Crane, who was working anonymously, had either been killed or disappeared. He sporadically sent out dispatches and stories; he wrote about the mood in Havana, the crowded city sidewalks, and other topics, but he was soon desperate for money again. Taylor, left alone in England, was also penniless. She became frantic with worry over her lover's whereabouts; they were not in direct communication until the end of the year. Crane left Havana and arrived in England on January 11, 1899.

Death

Rent on Ravensbrook had not been paid for a year. Upon returning to England, Crane secured a solicitor to act as guarantor for their debts, after which Crane and Taylor relocated to Brede Place. This manor in Sussex, which dated to the 14th century and had neither electricity nor indoor plumbing, was offered to them by friends at a modest rent. The relocation appeared to give hope to Crane, but his money problems continued. Deciding that he could no longer afford to write for American publications, he concentrated on publishing in English magazines.

Crane pushed himself to write feverishly during the first months at Brede; he told his publisher that he was "doing more work now than I have at any other period in my life". His health worsened, and by late 1899 he was asking friends about health resorts. The Monster and Other Stories was in production and War Is Kind, his second collection of poems, was published in the United States in May. None of his books after The Red Badge of Courage had sold well, and he bought a typewriter to spur output. Active Service, a novella based on Crane's correspondence experience, was published in October. The New York Times reviewer questioned "whether the author of 'Active Service' himself really sees anything remarkable in his newspapery hero."

In December, the couple held an elaborate Christmas party at Brede, attended by Conrad, Henry James, H. G. Wells and other friends; it lasted several days. On December 29 Crane suffered a severe pulmonary hemorrhage. In January 1900 he'd recovered sufficiently to work on a new novel, The O'Ruddy, completing 25 of the 33 chapters. Plans were made for him to travel as a correspondent to Gibraltar to write sketches from Saint Helena, the site of a Boer prison, but at the end of March and in early April he suffered two more hemorrhages. Taylor took over most of Crane's correspondence while he was ill, writing to friends for monetary aid. The couple planned to travel on the continent, but Conrad, upon visiting Crane for the last time, remarked that his friend's "wasted face was enough to tell me that it was the most forlorn of all hopes."

On May 28, the couple arrived at Badenweiler, Germany, a health spa on the edge of the Black Forest. Despite his weakened condition, Crane continued to dictate fragmentary episodes for the completion of The O'Ruddy. He died on June 5, 1900, at the age of 28. In his will he left everything to Taylor, who took his body to New Jersey for burial. Crane was interred in Evergreen Cemetery in what is now Hillside, New Jersey.

Fiction and poetry

Style and technique

Stephen Crane's fiction is typically categorized as representative of Naturalism, American realism, Impressionism or a mixture of the three. Critic Sergio Perosa, for example, wrote in his essay, "Stephen Crane fra naturalismo e impressionismo," that the work presents a "symbiosis" of Naturalistic ideals and Impressionistic methods. When asked whether or not he would write an autobiography in 1896, Crane responded that he "dare not say that I am honest. I merely say that I am as nearly honest as a weak mental machinery will allow." Similarities between the stylistic techniques in Crane's writing and Impressionist painting—including the use of color and chiaroscuro—are often cited to support the theory that Crane was not only an Impressionist but also influenced by the movement. H. G. Wells remarked upon "the great influence of the studio" on Crane's work, quoting a passage from The Red Badge of Courage as an example: "At nightfall the column broke into regimental pieces, and the fragments went into the fields to camp. Tents sprang up like strange plants. Camp fires, like red, peculiar blossoms, dotted the night.... From this little distance the many fires, with the black forms of men passing to and fro before the crimson rays, made weird and satanic effects." Although no direct evidence exists that Crane formulated a precise theory of his craft, he vehemently rejected sentimentality, asserting that "a story should be logical in its action and faithful to character. Truth to life itself was the only test, the greatest artists were the simplest, and simple because they were true."

Poet and biographer John Berryman suggested that there were three basic variations, or "norms", of Crane's narrative style. The first, being "flexible, swift, abrupt and nervous", is best exemplified in The Red Badge of Courage, while the second ("supple majesty") is believed to relate to "The Open Boat", and the third ("much more closed, circumstantial and 'normal' in feeling and syntax") to later works such as The Monster. Crane's work, however, cannot be determined by style solely on chronology. Not only does his fiction not take place in any particular region with similar characters, but it varies from serious in tone to reportorial writing and light fiction. Crane's writing, both fiction and nonfiction, is consistently driven by immediacy and is at once concentrated, vivid and intense. The novels and short stories contain poetic characteristics such as shorthand prose, suggestibility, shifts in perspective and ellipses between and within sentences. Similarly, omission plays a large part in Crane's work; the names of his protagonists are not commonly used and sometimes they are not named at all.

Crane was often criticized by early reviewers for his frequent incorporation of everyday speech into dialogue, mimicking the regional accents of his characters with colloquial stylization. This is apparent in his first novel, in which Crane ignored the romantic, sentimental approach of slum fiction; he instead concentrated on the cruelty and sordid aspects of poverty, expressed by the brashness of the Bowery's crude dialect and profanity, which he used lavishly. The distinct dialect of his Bowery characters is apparent at the beginning of the text; the title character admonishes her brother saying: "Yeh knows it puts mudder out when yes comes home half dead, an' it's like we'll all get a poundin'."

Major themes

Crane's work is often thematically driven by Naturalistic and Realistic concerns, including ideals versus realities, spiritual crises and fear. These themes are particularly evident in Crane's first three novels, Maggie: A Girl of the Streets, The Red Badge of Courage and George's Mother. The three main characters search for a way to make their dreams come true, but ultimately suffer from crises of identity. Crane was fascinated by war and death, as well as fire, disfigurement, fear and courage, all of which inspired him to write many works based on these concepts. In The Red Badge of Courage, the main character both longs for the heroics of battle but ultimately fears it, demonstrating the dichotomy of courage and cowardice. He experiences the threat of death, misery and a loss of self.

Extreme isolation from society and community is also apparent in Crane's work. During the most intense battle scenes in The Red Badge of Courage, for example, the story's focus is mainly "on the inner responses of a self unaware of others". In "The Open Boat", "An Experiment in Misery" and other stories, Crane uses light, motion and color to express degrees of epistemological uncertainty. Similar to other Naturalistic writers, Crane scrutinizes the position of man, who has been isolated not only from society, but also from God and nature. "The Open Boat", for example, distances itself from Romantic optimism and affirmation of man's place in the world by concentrating on the characters' isolation.

While he lived, Stephen Crane was denominated by critical readers a realist, a naturalist, an impressionist, symbolist, Symboliste, expressionist and ironist; his posthumous life was enriched by critics who read him as nihilistic, existentialist, a neo-Romantic, a sentimentalist, protomodernist, pointilliste, visionist, imagist and, by his most recent biographer, a "bleak naturalist." At midcentury he was a "predisciple of the New Criticism"; by its end he was "a proto-deconstructionist anti-artist hero" who had "leapfrogged modernism, landing on postmodernist ground." Or, as Sergio Perosa wrote in 1964, "The critic wanders in a labyrinth of possibilities, which every new turn taken by Crane's fiction seems to explode or deny."

One undeniable fact about Crane's work, as Anthony Splendora noted in 2015, is that Death haunts it; like a threatening eclipse it overshadows his best efforts, each of which features the signal demise of a main character. Allegorically, "The Blue Hotel," at the pinnacle of the short story form, may even be an autothanatography, the author's intentional exteriorization or objectification, in this case for the purpose of purgation, of his own impending death. Crane's "Swede" in that story can be taken, following current psychoanalytical theory, as a surrogative, sacrificial victim, ritually to be purged.

Transcending this "dark circumstance of composition," Crane had a particular telos and impetus for his creation: beyond the tautologies that all art is alterity and to some formal extent mimesis, Crane sought and obviously found "a form of catharsis" in writing. This view accounts for his uniqueness, especially as operative through his notorious "disgust" with his family's religion, their "vacuous, futile psalm-singing". His favorite book, for example, was Mark Twain's Life on the Mississippi, in which God is mentioned only twice—once as irony and once as "a swindle." Not only did Crane call out God specifically with the lines "Well then I hate thee / righteous image" in "The Black Riders" (1895), but even his most hopeful tropes, such as the "comradeship" of his "Open Boat" survivors, make no mention of deity, specifying only "indifferent nature." His antitheism is most evident in his characterization of the human race as "lice clinging to a space-lost bulb," a climax-nearing speech in "The Blue Hotel," Ch. VI. It is possible that Crane utilized religion's formal psychic space, now suddenly available resulting from the recent "Death of God", as a milieu for his compensative art.

Novels

Beginning with the publication of Maggie: A Girl of the Streets in 1893, Crane was recognized by critics mainly as a novelist. Maggie was initially rejected by numerous publishers because of its atypical and true-to-life depictions of class warfare, which clashed with the sentimental tales of that time. Rather than focusing on the very rich or middle class, the novel's characters are lower-class denizens of New York's Bowery. The main character, Maggie, descends into prostitution after being led astray by her lover. Although the novel's plot is simple, its dramatic mood, quick pace and portrayal of Bowery life have made it memorable. Maggie is not merely an account of slum life, but also represents eternal symbols. In his first draft, Crane did not give his characters proper names. Instead, they were identified by epithets: Maggie, for example, was the girl who "blossomed in a mud-puddle" and Pete, her seducer, was a "knight". The novel is dominated by bitter irony and anger, as well as destructive morality and treacherous sentiment. Critics would later call the novel "the first dark flower of American Naturalism" for its distinctive elements of naturalistic fiction.

Written thirty years after the end of the Civil War and before Crane had any experience of battle, The Red Badge of Courage was innovative stylistically as well as psychologically. Often described as a war novel, it focuses less on battle and more on the main character's psyche and his reactions and responses in war. It is believed that Crane based the fictional battle in the novel on that of Chancellorsville; he may also have interviewed veterans of the 124th New York Volunteer Infantry Regiment, commonly known as the Orange Blossoms, in Port Jervis, New York. Told in a third-person limited point of view, it reflects the private experience of Henry Fleming, a young soldier who flees from combat. The Red Badge of Courage is notable in its vivid descriptions and well-cadenced prose, both of which help create suspense within the story. Similarly, by substituting epithets for characters' names ("the youth", "the tattered soldier"), Crane injects an allegorical quality into his work, making his characters point to a specific characteristic of man. Like Crane's first novel, The Red Badge of Courage has a deeply ironic tone which increases in severity as the novel progresses. The title of the work is ironic; Henry wishes "that he, too, had a wound, a red badge of courage", echoing a wish to have been wounded in battle. The wound he does receive (from the rifle butt of a fleeing Union soldier) is not a badge of courage but a badge of shame.

The novel expresses a strong connection between humankind and nature, a frequent and prominent concern in Crane's fiction and poetry throughout his career. Whereas contemporary writers (Ralph Waldo Emerson, Nathaniel Hawthorne, Henry David Thoreau) focused on a sympathetic bond on the two elements, Crane wrote from the perspective that human consciousness distanced humans from nature. In The Red Badge of Courage, this distance is paired with a great number of references to animals, and men with animalistic characteristics: people "howl", "squawk", "growl", or "snarl".

Since the resurgence of Crane's popularity in the 1920s, The Red Badge of Courage has been deemed a major American text. The novel has been anthologized numerous times, including in the 1942 collection Men at War: The Best War Stories of All Time, edited by Ernest Hemingway. In the introduction, Hemingway wrote that the novel "is one of the finest books of our literature, and I include it entire because it is all as much of a piece as a great poem is."

Crane's later novels have not received as much critical praise. After the success of The Red Badge of Courage, Crane wrote another tale set in the Bowery. George's Mother is less allegorical and more personal than his two previous novels, and it focuses on the conflict between a church-going, temperance-adhering woman (thought to be based on Crane's mother) and her single remaining offspring, who is a naive dreamer. Critical response to the novel was mixed. The Third Violet, a romance that he wrote quickly after publishing The Red Badge of Courage, is typically considered as Crane's attempt to appeal to popular audiences. Crane considered it a "quiet little story." Although it contained autobiographical details, the characters have been deemed inauthentic and stereotypical. Crane's second to last novel, Active Service, revolves around the Greco-Turkish War of 1897, with which the author was familiar. Although noted for its satirical take on the melodramatic and highly passionate works that were popular of the nineteenth century, the novel was not successful. It is generally accepted by critics that Crane's work suffered at this point due to the speed which he wrote in order to meet his high expenses. His last novel, a suspenseful and picaresque work entitled The O'Ruddy, was finished posthumously by Robert Barr and published in 1903.

Short fiction

Crane wrote many different types of fictional pieces while indiscriminately applying to them terms such as "story", "tale" and "sketch". For this reason, critics have found clear-cut classification of Crane's work problematic. While "The Open Boat" and "The Bride Comes to Yellow Sky" are often considered short stories, others are variously identified.

In an 1896 interview with Herbert P. Williams, a reporter for the Boston Herald, Crane said that he did "not find that short stories are utterly different in character from other fiction. It seems to me that short stories are the easiest things we write." During his brief literary career, he wrote more than a hundred short stories and fictional sketches. Crane's early fiction was based in camping expeditions in his teen years; these stories eventually became known as The Sullivan County Tales and Sketches. He considered these "sketches", which are mostly humorous and not of the same caliber of work as his later fiction, to be "articles of many kinds," in that they are part fiction and part journalism.

The subject matter for his stories varied extensively. His early New York City sketches and Bowery tales accurately described the results of industrialization, immigration and the growth of cities and their slums. His collection of six short stories, The Little Regiment, covered familiar ground with the American Civil War, a subject for which he became famous with The Red Badge of Courage. Although similar to Crane's noted novel, The Little Regiment was believed to lack vigor and originality. Realizing the limitations of these tales, Crane wrote: "I have invented the sum of my invention with regard to war and this story keeps me in internal despair."

The Open Boat and Other Tales of Adventure (1898) contains thirteen short stories that deal with three periods in Crane's life: his Asbury Park boyhood, his trip to the West and Mexico in 1895, and his Cuban adventure in 1897. This collection was well received and included several of his most critically successful works. His 1899 collection, The Monster and Other Stories, was similarly well received.

Two posthumously published collections were not as successful. In August 1900 The Whilomville Stories were published, a collection of thirteen stories that Crane wrote during the last year of his life. The work deals almost exclusively with boyhood, and the stories are drawn from events occurring in Port Jervis, where Crane lived from the age of six to eleven. Focusing on small-town America, the stories tend toward sentimentality, but remain perceptive of the lives of children. Wounds in the Rain, published in September 1900, contains fictional tales based on Crane's reports for the World and the Journal during the Spanish–American War. These stories, which Crane wrote while desperately ill, include "The Price of the Harness" and "The Lone Charge of William B. Perkins" and are dramatic, ironic and sometimes humorous.

Despite Crane's prolific output, only four stories--"The Open Boat", "The Blue Hotel", "The Bride Comes to Yellow Sky", and The Monster— have received extensive attention from scholars. H. G. Wells considered "The Open Boat" to be "beyond all question, the crown of all his work", and it is one of the most frequently discussed of Crane's works.

Poetry

Many red devils ran from my heart

And out upon the page.

They were so tiny

The pen could mash them.

And many struggled in the ink.

It was strange

To write in this red muck

Of things from my heart.

— Stephen Crane

Crane's poems, which he preferred to call "lines", are typically not given as much scholarly attention as his fiction; no anthology contained Crane's verse until 1926. Although it is not certain when Crane began to write poetry seriously, he once said that his overall poetic aim was "to give my ideas of life as a whole, so far as I know it". The poetic style used in both of his books of poetry, The Black Riders and Other Lines and War is Kind, was unconventional for the time in that it was written in free verse without rhyme, meter, or even titles for individual works. They are typically short in length; although several poems, such as "Do not weep, maiden, for war is kind", use stanzas and refrains, most do not. Crane also differed from his peers and poets of later generations in that his work contains allegory, dialectic and narrative situations.

Critic Ruth Miller claimed that Crane wrote "an intellectual poetry rather than a poetry that evokes feeling, a poetry that stimulates the mind rather than arouses the heart". In the most complexly organized poems, the significance of the states of mind or feelings is ambiguous, but Crane's poems tend to affirm certain elemental attitudes, beliefs, opinions and stances toward God, man and the universe. The Black Riders in particular is essentially a dramatic concept and the poems provide continuity within the dramatic structure. There is also a dramatic interplay in which there is frequently a major voice reporting an incident seen ("In the desert / I saw a creature, naked, bestial") or experienced ("A learned man came to me once"). The second voice or additional voices represent a point of view which is revealed to be inferior; when these clash, a dominant attitude emerges.

Legacy

In four years, Crane published five novels, two volumes of poetry, three short story collections, two books of war stories, and numerous works of short fiction and reporting. Today he is mainly remembered for The Red Badge of Courage, which is regarded as an American classic. The novel has been adapted several times for the screen, including John Huston's 1951 version. By the time of his death, Crane had become one of the best known writers of his generation. His eccentric lifestyle, frequent newspaper reporting, association with other famous authors, and expatriate status made him somewhat of an international celebrity. Although most stories about his life tended toward the romantic, rumors about his alleged drug use and alcoholism persisted long after his death.

By the early 1920s, Crane and his work were nearly forgotten. It was not until Thomas Beer published his biography in 1923, which was followed by editor Wilson Follett's The Work of Stephen Crane (1925–1927), that Crane's writing came to the attention of a scholarly audience. Crane's reputation was then enhanced by faithful support from writer friends such as Joseph Conrad, H. G. Wells and Ford Madox Ford, all of whom either published recollections or commented upon their time with Crane. John Berryman's 1950 biography of Crane further established him as an important American author. Since 1951 there has been a steady outpouring of articles, monographs and reprints in Crane scholarship.

Today, Crane is considered one of the most innovative writers of the 1890s. His peers, including Conrad and James, as well as later writers such as Robert Frost, Ezra Pound and Willa Cather, hailed Crane as one of the finest creative spirits of his time. His work was described by Wells as "the first expression of the opening mind of a new period, or, at least, the early emphatic phase of a new initiative." Wells said that "beyond dispute", Crane was "the best writer of our generation, and his untimely death was an irreparable loss to our literature." Conrad wrote that Crane was an "artist" and "a seer with a gift for rendering the significant on the surface of things and with an incomparable insight into primitive emotions". Crane's work has proved inspirational for future writers; not only have scholars drawn similarities between Hemingway's A Farewell to Arms and The Red Badge of Courage, but Crane's fiction is thought to have been an important inspiration for Hemingway and his fellow Modernists. In 1936, Hemingway wrote in The Green Hills of Africa that "The good writers are Henry James, Stephen Crane, and Mark Twain. That's not the order they're good in. There is no order for good writers." Crane's poetry is thought to have been a precursor to the Imagist movement, and his short fiction has also influenced American literature. "The Open Boat", "The Blue Hotel", The Monster and "The Bride Comes to Yellow Sky" are generally considered by critics to be examples of Crane's best work.

Several institutions and places have endeavored to keep Crane's legacy alive. Badenweiler and the house where he died became something of a tourist attraction for its fleeting association with the American author; Alexander Woollcott attested to the fact that, long after Crane's death, tourists would be directed to the room where he died. Columbia University Rare Book and Manuscript Library has a collection of Crane and Taylor's personal correspondence dating from 1895 to 1908. Near his brother Edmund's Sullivan County home in New York, where Crane stayed for a short time, a pond is named after him. The Stephen Crane House in Asbury Park, New Jersey, where the author lived with his siblings for nine years, is operated as a museum dedicated to his life and work. Syracuse University has an annual Stephen Crane Lecture Series which is sponsored by the Dikaia Foundation.

Columbia University purchased much of the Stephen Crane materials held by Cora Crane at her death. The Crane Collection is one of the largest in the nation of his materials. Columbia University had an exhibit: 'The Tall Swift Shadow of a Ship at Night': Stephen and Cora Crane, November 2, 1995 through February 16, 1996, about the lives of the couple, featuring letters and other documents and memorabilia. (Source : Wikipedia)

NOTABLE WORKS

NOVELS

Maggie: A Girl of the Streets, 1893.

The Red Badge of Courage, 1895.

George's Mother, 1896.

The Third Violet, 1897.

Active Service, 1899.

Crane, Stephen and Robert Barr. The O'Ruddy, 1903.

The Black Riders and Other Lines, 1895.

The Open Boat and Other Tales of Adventure, 1898

War is Kind, 1899

The Monster and Other Stories, 1899

Wounds in the Rain, 1900

Great Battles of the World, 1901

The O'Ruddy, 1903

SHORT STORY COLLECTIONS

The Little Regiment and Other Episodes from the American Civil War, 1896.

The Open Boat and Other Tales of Adventure, 1898.

The Monster and Other Stories, 1899.

Whilomville Stories, 1900.

Wounds in the Rain: War Stories, 1900.

Great Battles of the World, 1901.

The Monster,1901.

Last Words, 1902.

POETRY COLLECTIONS

The Black Riders and Other Lines, 1895.

War is Kind, 1899.

UNFINISHED WORKS

Sources report that following an encounter with a male prostitute in the spring of 1894, Crane began a novel on the subject entitled Flowers of Asphalt. He reportedly abandoned the project and the manuscript has never been recovered.

CPSIA information can be obtained
at www.ICGtesting.com
Printed in the USA
LVHW091555230620
658719LV00002B/296

Tony Davis-Patrick

GLOBETROTTER'S QUEST

A worldwide search for carp and other giant fish

A carp leaps to the top of a raging waterfall on a wild Canadian river.

First published by Westerlaan Publishers in 2004.©
www.westerlaan-publisher.com

Text and photographs copyright© Tony Davies-Patrick

ISBN No. 90-808453-1-0

CONTENTS

'Globetrotter' searching for carp in the stunning
wilderness regions of the Colorado River, USA.

INTRODUCTION

When things become too easy and knowledge has swallowed all mystery, life becomes boring. Boredom feeds off repetition. Excitement feeds off the unknown.

All of my life I have been drawn to the unknown, unexplored areas in search of adventure. As a boy - in dark corners of woods or across gently rolling hills beyond the protective boundaries of my garden; and as a man - to snow-capped peaks or wild interiors of rainforests in far-flung regions of this planet. But when I climb over the mountains and through those forests, sunbeams light up the darkest, unexplored corners. The untouched becomes known, all my trepidation, excitement and fears vanish; the search is over. Yet water, whether it is a still and silent pool or rushing torrents, always holds on to some of its secrets. No matter how far I search into the deepest corners of rivers, lakes or oceans, their treasures remain hidden in mystery.

Fishing has always meant more to me than catching. It takes me to the edges of water and calls at my heart to cast a line, so as to tempt the unknown. It surrounds me for hours, days, weeks or months in beautiful landscapes, until the moving hands of my watch are forgotten and time loses all meaning. It shows me wonders of nature that are rarely seen by others. It bites at repetition and hooks me into excitement!

Although I enjoy fishing for most species of fish, carp fishing has always remained my first love. I am sure that most people who read this book will also hold a passion for carp. It is for these reasons that a large portion of this book, including the majority of photos, concentrates on carp fishing.

Fishing, especially for carp, has brought me in contact with thousands of wonderful people and helped establish many friendships. Some of these friends are outstanding anglers and I could have filled the book with guest writers, but it would have made the book just too big to publish within financial boundaries. Most of my fishing expeditions tend to revolve around personal experience because they are solitary affairs and I enjoy my own company. However, on the rare occasions when I travel with others to wild or exotic locations, it is invariably with my good friend Jens Bursell.

Jens is a Danish biologist and lives with his girlfriend in Copenhagen. I first met him in 1988, when he fished with me as a guest near my home on the beautiful island of Fyn in Denmark. I only knew his face from a photo published in a fishing magazine, so my first sight of him as he climbed off the bus gave me quite a shock. A scruffy, Punk rocker with orange hair and a half shaven head, jumped on to the pavement at the bus stop. I began to wonder where Jens was, but when the Punk rocker started unloading a mountain of carp fishing gear off the bus, I realised with horror that this must be him! Those early impressions and fears were soon to fall like autumn leaves in a wind, and that first carp fishing trip is locked in my vault of fondest memories. Since that day, we have had many trips together in search of carp and other species; first in Scandinavia, and later to exotic waters located around the World.

Even though 10 years my younger, Jens' love of fishing in wilderness areas echoed my own, and our friendship grew and grew. Since this book's inception, I have wanted Jens to write some chapters covering a few of his most memorable fishing trips. Many of those sessions were spent with me in foreign waters all over the Globe, but I wanted him to write about other exploratory searches for big fish, in places even I had yet to visit. Jens has chosen to detail his recent incredible expeditions in search of gigantic fish in New Zealand's south island, China and Kazakhstan. Of these three chapters, my favourite is a splendid account of his quest for 'black'carp (a sub-species of Cyprinus carpio) in the vast, remote regions of China. It strongly emphasises that in fishing, as in most things, the experiences gathered en-route to your goal, often mean more than the goal itself.

The true Black Carp is actually not the common carp sub-species that Jens searched for in China, but a separate species similar in appearance to the grass carp. Very little is known about this incredible fish, that can exceed 150lb in weight, so I have asked Steven Sands – one of the few anglers to seriously spend time in the pursuit of Black Carp – to write a special chapter detailing his search for 'blue giants' in the land of the rising sun.

While I was on a fishing expedition to Africa during Autumn 2002, my mobile phone received a text message from one of my close friends in Germany. The simple text mentioned that he had just landed a monster-sized carp from a north German water. I leave Andreas Philip to tell the full story of his amazing carp fishing session in the chapter Reward For Effort.

The Siamese Carp is the World's largest species of carp – able to grow to over 200lb, and occasionally 400lb in weight. For the Siamese Giants chapter, I have included two anglers who have both caught carp exceeding 100lb: Stuart Brewster - a veteran of many Thailand fishing expeditions, and Jean-Francois Helias – manager of Fishing Adventures Thailand, and probably the most experienced Siamese Carp expert on this planet.

In the end, all we are left with is our memories. During the past 20 years of travel and fishing expeditions, I have striven to capture some of those golden memories in photos and words. I cannot possibly transform each magical moment and transfer them on to paper, only when I close my eyes and think of past events do they truly come 'alive' again. But I hope this book reflects some of the excitement, atmosphere and emotions experienced during my worldwide quest for adventure.

> 'And yet, there is only one great thing,
> The only thing;
> To live to see on journeys
> The great day that dawns
> And the light that fills the world.' (Old Inuit poem)

I dedicate this book:

To my incredible Mother, who rarely seems to understand me, yet knows me so well
To my wonderful sister, Linda, who's successful career has made me so proud
To my beautiful daughter, Amber, who rarely ceases to amaze me
To Chez (Cheryl) who has grabbed my heart and shares my passion
My love for them all just grows with every passing year
And to the greatest man who ever touched the deepest corners of my soul -
.... my Father.

Also to Gallen & Barbera Rowell – true wilderness photographers and authors, who tragically died in a plane crash on August 11th 2002, during their return home to California after completing a circumnavigation of the Bering Sea. The mountains will miss your tread, and the sunlight will no longer paint your shadows, but the love you both shared for each other and the 'magic' you spread to others hearts, will linger in the high peaks and crisp clear air... forever....

Tony with a big winter mirror carp from a lake in northern Germany.

A spectacular sky over a 13.800-acre lake in Arkansas.

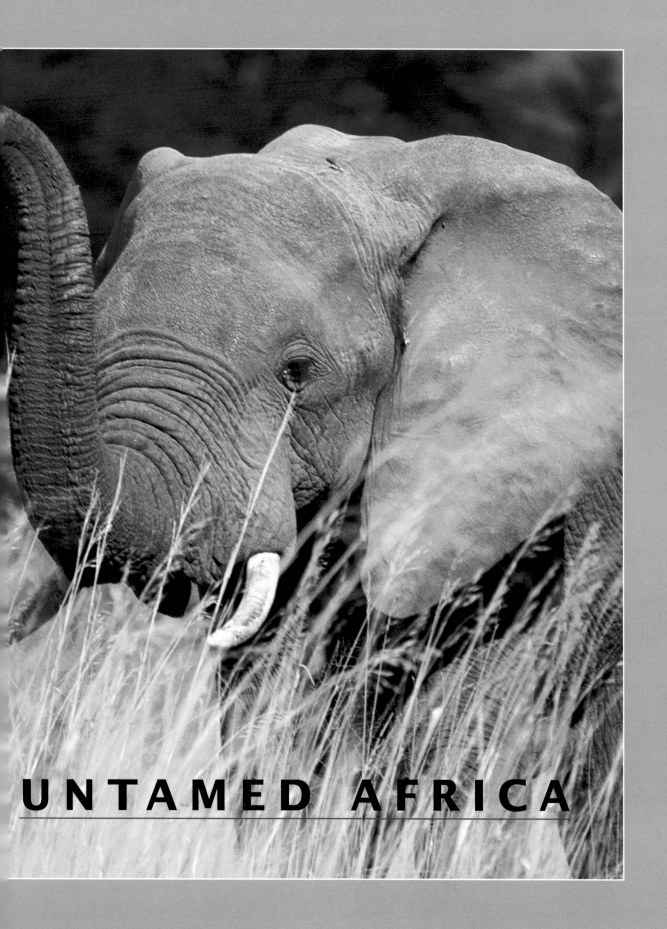

UNTAMED AFRICA

...From the bowels of Earth, a deep bellowing noise sweeps across the lake as the king of the jungle calls to his pride. The mighty lions roar shakes through the trees and the forest answers him - jackals howl and hyenas laugh, baboons bark and monkeys shriek - screams that echo within the darkest corners of my mind....

The day wears on, and the sun rises high in a white-hot sky then slowly descends towards the opposite horizon until it bursts into flames and sets the waters of Klaserie on fire. Reflections beneath my rod tips turn orange and indigo, as they spiral on the waves and softly lap against the bank. The kaleidoscope of fantastic colours are short-lived, soon to be replaced by monotonous shades of monochrome. The earth continues to spin, causing a black shadow to slowly unroll like a carpet across the water. Silent fingers quench all colours in their path as they reach into the heart of darkness. As the last colours fade, it signals the first chorus of chirping cicada wings, until eventually the air is filled with the constant whine of insects.

Large African bullfrogs join the cacophony of sound as my ears begin to ache with the constant bombardment of voices. These massive bullfrogs (Pyxicephalus adspersus) have extremely large mouths with three internal projections, like teeth, and aggressively hunt insects, other frogs, rodents and even birds. But predatory instincts are no match for the huge Nile Monitor (Varanus niloticus). These beautiful yellow and black striped lizards can grow to lengths exceeding 8ft (and occasionally 10ft!). They are very strong swimmers and will often...

...Wallop! Just now, as I am speaking notes into the Sanyo micro recorder, a 6ft monitor lizard that has remained hidden in the rushes only inches from my rodpod, decides to pounce on some unsuspecting amphibian. There is a sudden squelch as the frog's croaks are abruptly cut off in mid call, and I can now hear the horrible slap of powerful jaws on slimy skin. A single Delkim bleeps in time with a long, thick reptilian tail that gently knocks against the pod while the lizard enjoys its slimy meal. I watch in fascination as the blue diode casts a strange, unearthly light over the macabre scene.

Four 13ft lengths of carbon sit on the Solar Globetrotter Pod, pointing at the stars of the Southern Cross. The drags on the big spools of the Ultegra XT 14000's are adjusted to give line out smoothly and under gentle pressure. A mixed bucket of maize, peanuts and tigernuts is placed in position then I quietly slip the fibreglass canoe into the lukewarm water and climb inside. Four hookbaits hang suspended from the rod tips. I reach up to grab one of the 4oz leads and drop the rig inside the bait bucket, then close the lid. The canoe glides away from the bank and the revolving spool begins to mimic the clicking sounds of crickets.

I reach 150 metres from shore and the distance muffles the loud hum of insects. All I can hear is my own breathing and the heavy "slap" of paddle hitting water. After travelling 350 metres, my ears begin to pick up the whirring sounds of crickets on the opposite bank, so I slow down the pace of my strokes and switch on the head torch. A strong beam of light cuts through a gentle mist that drifts out from the margins. The canoe glides across the oily water and nudges its nose into the thick mass of tangled roots and lily fronds that grow in profusion. I open the bucket lid, and am about to lift out the hookbait, when my head torch catches something in its beam. The light reflects off two eyes that stare from within the ancient heart of the forest. They shine like diamonds in coal

dust. "Impala, or Bushbuck" I think to myself; so I ignore it and continue to lower the lead so that the hookbait lies in position tight to the lily stems.

I hear a twig snap, then a movement in the trees. My head lifts up and the torchlight once again reflects off the diamonds; but this time they are dancing through the darkness as the animal moves closer to the edges of the reeds. Suddenly, a coarse, grinding sound rumbles through the ground, then carries across the water and vibrates through the canoe. My muscles tense and the hairs begin to rise at the back of my neck. The animal is now less than 4 metres in front of me and the strong torch beam paints a giant shadow behind it. He lifts his head and sniffs the air, and I watch in awe as the spotted fur ripples beneath those powerful muscles. A leopard!

I am tempted to panic, but a lifetime of close encounters with wild animals around the World has wizened me to the wonders of nature. My racing heartbeat begins to quiet and the pounding blood eases in my brain.

Five handfuls of free offerings are quickly scattered around the hookbait. The big cat watches me with interest. He takes two steps forward. The torchlight reflects off those massive pads and sharp claws that grip the moist soil at the very edges of the water. He is not afraid of me; although I realise that leopards sometimes swim across the lake, they rarely attack something in the water. These facts fail to boost my confidence! He is so close now. So close that I can hear the strong purring sound rising up his throat and hissing through those pointed teeth. The hair on my scalp begins to rise again, and the heavy thudding sound is my own heartbeat.

"Calm down, calm down Tony." I say to myself, and it somehow reassures me. I manoeuvre the canoe away from the bank and swing it round. I know he's still watching me, and those piercing eyes seem

An orange sun rises above the mists of Klaserie.

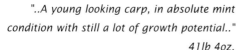

"..A young looking carp, in absolute mint condition with still a lot of growth potential.."
41lb 4oz.

to be drilling into the back of my head. The gentle sounds of blades slicing through water seem to comfort me, and I try to concentrate on keeping the canoe pointed towards the opposite shoreline. My bivvy is hidden in the darkness, so I must head for a certain prominent tree on the skyline. The big cat watches in silence as droplets of water spin off my paddles...and the canoe fades into darkness.

The bow eventually nudges the reeds at the edges of my swim, so I climb out of the canoe and walk over to the freshly baited rod. My fingers gently spin the reel spool so as to take up the slack then I wedge the line tightly in the clip and switch back on the Delkim alarm. The same procedure is carried out with the remaining three baits. Mounting fatigue from a long, hot day has finally caught up with me and the comfort of the bedchair beckons my tired body to rest. Soon, I am fast asleep. The earth continues to spin and the stars of the galaxy move slowly across a black sky. I travel within my dreams, enclosed within the comfort of the bivvy. The doors are closed (to prevent insects and other African wildlife entering while I sleep!), but the window flaps are down so as to allow air to circulate through the mosquito netting. Outside, the air beats to the croak of frogs and whirr of cricket; but inside are only the soft sounds of my breathing.

'The JUNGLE'

Since yesterday, huge carp have been crashing at the very edges of a big bed of reeds, about 200 metres along the bank to my left, called the 'Jungle'. I want to place some baits there, but another reed bed stretching out from the near margins blocks my path. A cut out section of the reeds further along the bank gives more direct access to where I want to fish, but I would not be able to apply any side pressure on the rod to prevent a big carp from ploughing straight through the dense rushes.

I decide to go out in the canoe to take a closer look. Once my canoe reaches the very edges of the big reed bed, I look back across towards my rodpod. I cannot see the rods; in fact I can't even see the bivvy from this position! However, if I adjust the Globetrotter Pod to it's highest position and cut some of the outer rushes that block my path, I might just be able to place one hookbait in the desired spot.

The peanut/tigernut combination hookbaits have been working quite well, but I decide to drop the peanuts and try only tigers. One large tigernut and a small piece of shaped cork are threaded on to a hair that extends from the hook knot; and a second tigernut is threaded on to a separate, shorter hair tied to the eye of the hook.

'..The fish looks absolutely stunning in this soft, morning light..' Ready to return the wonderful 48lb mirror.

It takes me about 20 minutes to paddle out the left-hand hookbait, drop it in position only inches from the rushes, scatter half a bucket of freebies over it, then slowly back-track along the taught line and breaking off overlapping reed stems by hand, until everything is clear.

Satisfied that everything is perfect, I finally sit down in front of the rods and begin tying new rigs, then placing them in my Terry Eustace Rig Wallet. Repeatedly, I lift my head up from the pile of swivels, hooks and braid lying on my lap, to watch in wonder at the multitude of colourful life that constantly surrounds me. Noisy flocks of Glossy Ibis' fly low overhead, calling repeatedly to each other. A Darter perches on a short branch sticking out of the water then stretches its wings like a phoenix to dry damp feathers in the warm air. On the far bank, an Impala stretches a long, delicate neck and begins to quench its thirst from the waters of Klaserie. The Fish Eagle screeches out a haunting cry, before swooping through the trees on outstretched wings. It's mirror image speeds across the surface of the lake, until the twin images collide as sharp talons crash through the sparkling waters.

A sudden movement catches my eye as the tip of the left-hand rod taps once then slowly begins to bend over. My reactions are instantaneous, and before the line is pulled out of the run clip I sweep the rod hard over my shoulder and make positive contact with the fish. I must now run along the bank and assert heavy side strain to prevent the carp from entering the rushes. But I am fishing from a small peninsular and there is no more bank space to my right - so I just jump straight into the water and lean hard in to the Globetrotter Supreme. Once the powerful rod reaches full flex and takes out the stretch in the nylon line, the carp has nowhere to go and is stopped in its tracks.

The rod is rated at around 3.5 lb test curve, but once full parabolic curve is reached, it asserts a pressure of 4-5lb. This immense power will stop almost any carp, and as long as you use strong, reliable hooks, no problems will present themselves. The Gold Label size 2 Penetrator hook matches the strength of my rod and I feel a big fish rolling frantically at the very edges of the weeds, until the constant pressure gradually pulls it clear.

As soon as the carp is pulled well clear of the reed bed, I begin to wade back to the peninsular, reeling and pumping steadily, to keep constant pressure on the fish. There is another dense bed of weeds and lilies between the fish, and myself, so I must now jump off the left side of the peninsular and wade through the weeds for 50 metres, dragging the landing net behind me, until I reach open water. The carp turns and swims straight towards me, so I need to make a mad dash to get there before it burrows itself in the weeds. With only moments to spare, my chest breaks through the last strands of lily roots and the carp boils under my rod tip, then powers off into open water again.

There are no shakes or judders transmitted down the rod as I play the fish; just a slow, steady force, so I know that it is a big carp. Eventually a broad back breaks the surface and I ease the carp over the outstretched landing net. My fingers grasp tightly around the mesh above the fish, and then I turn around and make the long journey back to shore.

The carp swings the pointer on the weighing scales round to 40lb 4ozs. It is a beautiful, pink-tinted mirror, which has obviously been feeding heavily on the natural larder of crabs and crayfish. I decide to phone Martin on my mobile to let him know the news, but before I can inform him about the forty, he tells me that he's fishing at Goldmire and has just landed a 37lb common, 37lb mirror brace, including a 34lb+ common! He also informs me that Simon Carder has just returned from a session on Rushmere Lake and landed five thirties up to 39lb. We congratulate each other on our

Fighting a big carp at sunset.

*Martin Davidson with a
beautifully scaled big African
mirror.*

recent catches, but Martin pleads for me to land a fifty. My confidence is now sky high and I'm certain of meeting such an order as long as I keep working at it; so I relay down the phone that a fifty will eventually come my way, and maybe a sixty is on the cards!

The night passes by very quietly, and it is not until 16:00 hrs that one of my Delkims registers a take on the long distance rod, which results in a 28lb+ mirror. Jason also enjoys some action and lands a lovely mirror carp weighing 30lb 4oz. At 17:30 hrs, another big fish picks up the double tigernut pop-up presented close to the margin reed bed, but it gets me in a snag. Jason brings round the big dinghy and we both go out to try and free it, but the fish eventually sheds the hook in the snag. I pull on the line with all my strength until a forked branch appears on the surface. I grab this before it sinks again, only to eventually realise that it is attached to a giant tree. I'd been fishing with my line directly through this huge sunken tree all the time! How I'd managed to pull the forty straight through it without snagging up is a complete mystery - or sheer luck.

I cannot possibly continue to fish this swim with such a snag, so we try to remove it. The tree is bigger and heavier than we first imagine and the outboard motor is taxed to overload in trying to pull it to shore. At one point, the propeller catches on a branch and Jason is unable to control the motor as I hold on to the tree with all my strength. Then the retaining pin breaks and the prop spins straight off the shaft and sinks to the bottom of the lake! I have no choice but to let go of the heavy tree and watch it slowly sink back to the lakebed. I'm still left with a massive unwanted snag in my swim, but at least it is now far enough away from the rushes to allow me to continue fishing in the hotspot.

At 17:45 hrs, a 27lb Mirror picks up a hookbait presented in the entrance to a small bay at the far bank, called Leopard Bay. At 19:30 hrs, a high-pitched tone signals another take to one of my rods. I am just finishing off a tasty meal of Impala steaks cooked by Lowe at Base Camp; so I set down the plate, and then strike in to a fast moving fish. It has picked up the bait presented tight to a dense bed of margin reeds situated 400 metres away. This is the exact position from where I lost the 50lb+ earlier in the week, but this time I'm lucky and the carp bolts straight towards me after taking the tigernuts.

The fish makes many powerful runs, but most of this is in the relative safety of open water, until finally it is only about 40 metres out and I begin to wade out with the landing net until I am beyond the marginal weedbeds. Suddenly, something shows on the surface then as I gain more line, a large clump of weed stems begins to hang out of the water. I'm horrified, and immediately wade back to

'The untamed heart of Africa...'a baboon looks across at the awesome sight of the Victoria Falls - 'The Smoke That Thunders'.

A huge elephant wades across the waters.   *A crocodile sunbathes on a rock in mid-river.*

shore and lower the rod tip so that Jason can untangle the weeds. With the carp still moving towards the bank, it becomes difficult to maintain a tight line, so I ask Jason politely to 'bloody well get it sorted!' He seems to be having great difficulty untangling the weed stems and tries to break them off the line, but is unable to. I'm frightened of him breaking the line, and tell him so - but Jason is also terrified of making a mistake and I hear him muttering to himself - "Oh God, please don't let me break it!' Slack begins to form, and I place my free hand on the line beneath the rod tip so as to maintain pressure on the hookhold. Then the carp rolls close to the marginal weeds, so I decide to go straight out and play it by hand lining until Jason can untangle the mess at the rod tip. But he's still having problems, so I shout for him to chuck me the landing net, and I gently continue hand lining the carp until it is eventually swallowed inside the deep mesh.

The carp looks very big as I stare down at the fish in the water, but once I check the girth, I realise that it's just a long, lean specimen. As I lower the carp on to the unhooking mat and unfurl the mesh from it's flank, the true beauty of this fish presents itself.

"Wow! What a fabulous fish!" gasps Jason; and my words echo his own.

On the scales it shows a weight of 41lb 4oz. This time it's a young looking mirror carp, in absolute mint condition with still a lot of growth potential.

The rest of the night passes by quietly, and it is not until the early pre-dawn light that I get another take, which results in a 22lb+ mirror. At 11:05 hrs, I hook but eventually loose a big mirror around 40lb, due to a speedboat going through my line. This is just the beginning of a stream of bad luck over the next two days where I have eight more runs, but only manage to land one carp of 30lb 6oz. Two of the takes are missed drop-backs, three carp are lost due to line breaking or hook pulls in dense weeds, and the rest are due to boats going through my lines. It is rare to see boats in the Bushcamp section of the lake during weekdays, but the weekend boat traffic is becoming a nightmare for me. Martin and Norman are working hard with the local authorities to alleviate the problem, but at the moment it is driving me mad (The problem with boat traffic is eventually sorted and the tranquil calm of Klaserie has now been restored).

It's just before midday and a bright sun hangs in a cloudless, sapphire coloured sky. I'm half-naked, lazing on the chair and soaking in the warm rays. I want to fetch some things from Base Camp, but I'm loathed to leave my swim, so I stay put and watch my skin changing to a darker shade of brown.

Two single 'bleeps' shake me out of my trance and I manage to hit the take before the fish swims more than a few feet with the hookbait. The rod takes up its battle curve, and I begin to feel tremors vibrating down the line as the fish burrows its head through the tangle of lily stems. But as the rod locks in to full power, it halts the carp's progress and forces it to crash on the surface in a sheet of spray and foam.

Constant, unrelenting pressure on the 13ft of carbon slowly drags the carp clear of the weeds, then the rod tip abruptly changes direction as the carp bolts away from the rushes and heads for open water. I take this opportunity to gain some line on to the spool, then jump in to the margins and wade towards the fish, dragging the big landing net behind me. For the next fifteen minutes I stand in the water up to my waist, battling with some unseen leviathan. The fish has incredible power and continues to go on slow, almost unstoppable runs and I need to use the full extent of my tackle to prevent it from entering the profusion of weed beds that surround me. With persistent side strain, and delicate finger control on the madly spinning spool, I manage to gradually sap the strength from the fish.

Suddenly, the rod tip locks in to one position, then everything goes solid - the fish has found an unknown snag in the open water, only 5 metres in front of me. I can't believe my bad luck and begin to shiver as a grating sensation vibrates down the line and tingles under my fingers. I try gentle persuasions by softly plucking the rod tip, but to no avail; then I try opposite tactics by submerging the complete rod under water and applying full pressure. This works and I feel the line ping free of a tree branch, then the carp erupts on the surface, before screaming line against the clutch as it powers off on another run. I quickly seize this opportunity to wade away from the unseen snag, and then sink the landing net in front of me. Suddenly the carp changes direction again, and before I can stop it, the carp is back in the snag. Five short seconds pass by, then the rod jerks back in my hands.... the line has broken.

For a full minute I stand motionless up to my chest in the water, just staring at vacant space. My mind keeps throwing up visions of the carp when it had rolled on the surface in front of me. I have no doubts that it weighed well in excess of 60lb. Heavy feet drag me back towards shore and I swear and curse at everything and nothing, before eventually throwing my rod at the rushes in anger. But it doesn't help my growing fever, because half an hour later I am sitting in the chair, still shaking like a leaf in the wind.

Finally, I calm down and begin the tasks of tying up a new rig then paddling the hookbait back out to the marginal rushes. I am not happy using nylon when I'm fishing so close to snags and weedbeds, because it's inherent stretch qualities allows the carp to travel too far before being stopped, and abrasion resistance doesn't match that of the top braids. The 60lb+ mirror broke 20lb Nash Power Plus nylon, and although it is a partially pre-stretched line with superior abrasion qualities than the Berkley nylon I had tried earlier, it is just not coping with all the problems. I decide to change the spool of Power Plus on the Ultegra and replace it with a spool of 50lb PowerPro. This high-tech Braided line is thinner than 15lb nylon, has zero stretch, and incredible abrasion resistance qualities. I would like to change all my reels to PowerPro, but unfortunately I just don't have enough with me to fill all four big spools. There are some bulk spools of Terry Eustace's green coloured 20lb test Pro Gold nylon in my bag. I've already tested the 15lb version of this nylon in France and it helped me land some very big carp in difficult conditions. Without a second thought, I quickly reel in the remaining hookbaits and re-spool the 3 big Ultegra XT's with 20lb Pro Gold. However, I still waver on the side of caution, and decide to use the remaining PowerPro left in my tackle bag to tie up as 10 metre long rubbing leaders.

The carp activity in Leopard Bay has eased off over the past 24 hours, but big fish are still crashing at intervals close to 'The Jungle'. I continue to regularly paddle out for 400 metres to scatter freebies directly over the hookbaits positioned around Leopard Bay, but step up my baiting campaign at the edge of The Jungle. I brought only two Globetrotter Supreme rods with me from England and have been using one of these to fish the distant shoreline of Leopard Bay, so I decide at this point to reel in that hookbait and re-position it about 4 metres away from the Jungle hookbait. The other two rods I'm using are 12ft Rod Hutchinson Dream Makers of 3lb 4oz and 3lb 8oz test curves. I find these rods a little stiff, as well as too short to keep the line clear of marginal rushes; so I've opted only to use them when fishing outside the difficult Jungle area.

All week I have been pouring buckets full of peanuts, maize, and tigernuts mix into the swims; but I'm slowly running out of peanuts and tigers, so I've asked Peter to get a giant pan of maples on the boil so that I can add it to the mixes tomorrow.

The sun races it's path across the southern sky and falls behind the forest, turning the far bank a warm shade of orange. A flock of six pearl white Cattle Egrets skim silently over the water, their wing tips brushing the surface as they fly upriver. Jackals roaming the dark interiors of the forest begin to call to each other. Near the Dam wall, a lone Hyena, hunting through desolate bushland of the northern bank, sends a hideous mixture of grunts and laughter to echo across the lake. Then from behind me, I hear the deep, bellowing sounds of a Lion's roar.

Carp occasionally crash over my baited areas during the night, but I have to wait until the faint shades of dawn show above the treetops before a Delkim registers a short drop-back. I fail to make contact on the strike, so immediately paddle out the hookbait again to the edge of the Jungle and heavily spray the area with freebies from the bait bucket.

I still feel that carp are present in the baited areas, and ask Peter to bring breakfast down to my swim so that I can remain close to the rods. But I have to wait until 16:00 hrs before the bait positioned closest to the Jungle reedbed tempts a hungry carp. The powerful Globetrotter rod combined with the zero-stretch of PowerPro line proves their outstanding capabilities and stop the fish in its tracks immediately after setting the hook. After a short but very exciting fight, I'm able to bring another lovely looking specimen over the landing net. The length of this mirror carp indicates that it could easily carry more than it's present 39lb 6oz. Two hours later, a hard fighting common of around 25lb+ picks up one of the Leopard Bay tigernut hookbaits; and I return it immediately to the water without weighing.

Jason, in the next swim to my right, has yet to land a carp since his 30lb 4oz mirror, although he's lost two good specimens. But he seems to have the same problem that David had and is now plagued with catfish. Some of the cats have weighed over 20lb, but he's getting sick of them, and so spent the whole morning sitting in a boat at the wild river entrance, trying to tempt a big carp to pick up his float-fished tigernuts - which resulted in a total of 5 catfish to 17lb! I think the main problem is that he's been presenting his baits on the bottom. The catfish seem to feed with their bodies tight to the bottom and move slowly along the lakebed, hoovering up items with their large mouths. A bait popped up with foam or cork a few inches off the bottom results in far fewer catfish hook-ups. They love boilies, which is why I've stopped using them at Klaserie; but they also seem to prefer peanuts than tigernuts, which is why I am now only using tigers for hookbaits. I persuade Jason to do the same, and also advise him to move one of his hookbaits to a new position, tight to the far bank and closer to my baited swim, about 80 metres from the entrance to Leopard Bay.

Just as I'm returning the 25lb common, Peter comes down to my swim and tells me that Lowe is ready to serve the evening meal. Lowe and his friend have cooked up a special treat for Jason and me tonight; something we've never tried before - Giraffe steaks!

The last few nights were quite cool, but this evening is quite mild and the heat from the campfire adds extra warmth to the air. Lowe stands beside the soft light of a gas lamp and serves out the large portions of Giraffe meat, garnished with potatoes and fresh salad. I am the first to bring this strange new flesh to my lips, but as soon as my tongue touches the delicate meat I lose all apprehension. The meat is succulent, tender and similar to veal, but 10 times better. In fact, it must surely be the best meat I've ever tasted, and Jason is quick to agree with me. We sit around the fire, munching, chewing, swallowing and licking our lips until our hunger is satisfied, and then refill the plates with extra helpings of our over indulgence. Finally, our greed is satisfied and we pop a few cans of beer, and then sit like greased pigs around the campfire and stare in fascination at the flickering flames.

There is nothing quite like the atmosphere provided by a campfire, and as I watch the glowing sparks lifting off the tongues of dancing flames, then rising up towards a galaxy of white stars, I am reminded of nights spent around campfires in the Indian jungle. The constant hum of crickets acts as gentle background music to our conversations. A series of wonderful, deep, rumbling growls from a Leopard hunting along the distant shoreline, begins to carry across the water and reaches our ears. I recognise the tone of those calls and am sure that it is the big Leopard that I saw at close quarters from the canoe. This particular cat must live in one of the trees surrounding Leopard Bay,

Scanning the calm waters of Rushmere for signs of carp.

because I hear it calling across the lake every night. I begin to talk in detail to everyone sitting around the campfire about this exciting close encounter, when a sudden harsh growl stops me mid-sentence. All our heads spin towards a noise that emanates from the deep darkness just beyond the orange light of the campfire. Lowe flicks on his torch and I watch the beam cutting through the tangled growth of long grasses, bushes and trees that lay behind us.

"Leopard!' remarks Lowe. 'And judging by the depth and power of that growl, it's a big male."

Lowe is a qualified Big Game Guide and has spent a lifetime in the wilds of the Kruger National Park, so I'm not going to argue with those facts. The torch beam carves holes in the darkness as it searches for spotted fur, but the deep African Bush hides it's secrets. Then a twig snaps amongst the forest about 50 metres to our left, followed by another, nerve tingling growl.

Lowe looks a little concerned, as he continues to talk and hunts with the torch beam from left to right.

"It can smell our meat. Leopards don't normally come so close to humans, but this one is obviously attracted by our nightly barbecues. It should be OK, but we'll have to keep an eye on it to make sure that it does not become too confident with our presence. I think this one is a particularly large animal, so be extra careful."

I've known about this particular Leopard for the last two nights, so I take this opportunity to take Lowe down the muddy track that leads from the Base Camp to my swim, and show him a set of giant tracks left in the soft mud. My own torch lights the way, until we reach a water-filled rut in the track left by LandRover tyres. I then kneel down and point to a single, deeply imprinted form in the mud. " Wow! He's a big specimen. A huge adult male by the look of it." Declares Lowe.

We then walk back to the seemingly safe environment provided by the glow of the campfire and Lowe begins to talk of true incidents of Leopard attacks on humans.

"Lions definitely attack people, but even big Leopards rarely bring down a human; although there have been several incidents with big, rogue cats. I remember one incident where two guys were sitting round a campfire when a huge wild Leopard jumped out of the darkness and sank it's teeth into one of their necks. The other guy tried to help his friend, but somehow it eventually managed to kill both men. This was a very rare event and attacks usually occur only when most of the small game - the Leopards prime food source - is killed off through over hunting or poaching. Here at Klaserie and Kruger, there are no such problems and the Leopards have an abundance of Bushbuck and Impala to satisfy their hunger."

Jason's, Peter's, and my own eyebrows lift in surprise as Lowe mentions the attack, and the whites of our eyes reflect the flickering images of fire.

One hour later, Lowe drives home and Peter retires to the comfort of the Caravan, leaving Jason and I to continue chatting and swilling cold beers in front of the warm, orange flames. Finally, we both begin to yawn and I say goodnight to Jason, then turn away from the red glowing embers and walk alone down the dark, forest track. My torch throws a narrow beam in front of me, and every so often I stop walking and swing the light erratically away from the track, just to check out the occasional sources of sounds that drift out of the forest. I can hear something moving to my left, and I stop breathing so as to attune my ears to every sound. Nothing stirs, just the constant and gentle whirr from crickets. But when I continue to walk, a glimpse of moving black shadow warns me that something else is also walking in the same direction, but my torchlight fails to locate it. A sixth sense tells me that I'm being watched...Then a deep purring sound makes my head twist towards the nearby rushes. There is a sudden movement amongst the grasses then a huge animal crosses the track in front of me and melts in to the darkest heart of the forest. There is a tingling sensation as the fine hairs of my body rise stiffly on their follicles as I fight to hold my breath and listen for sounds amongst the dry leaves. But the Leopard leaves no sound as it hunts through the night; only fresh tracks in the mud that now show up in my torchlight...

The rest of the night passes without incident and I have to wait until the sun rises and reaches it's zenith, before a 33lb 4oz mirror carp finally picks up one of my tigernut hook baits placed tight to the Jungle. A fresh bait is paddled back out then dropped in position, and I scatter five handfuls of free offerings directly over it. Two more carp follow in quick succession to the same rod, weighing 27lb+ and 22lb, then the swim goes dead. This prompts me to paddle back out and drop almost a full bucket of mix over the side.

During the next four hours, I listen to the occasional big lumps of skin and flesh pounding the surface directly over the heavily baited area; but the Delkims remain silent. I think to myself - are the carp already growing wise to my rig set-up? Finally, after a further hour with no movements to my rod tips, I decide to reel in and change some of the presentations. The baits positioned across the far side of the lake near the edges of Leopard Bay, are double tigernuts popped up 3 inches above a 4oz lead. I leave these two rigs in position unchanged, but alter the other two rigs positioned at the edge of the margin Jungle, simply by sliding a small Solar Depth Charge on to the

Spiderwire Spectra hooklink about 1/2 inch above the eye of the hook. This will pin-down the buoyant hookbaits and hold the last few inches of hooklink tighter to the lakebed. Obviously this can also invite problems with the small catfish, but I think if I continue to pile in the buckets of mix, it will attract large numbers of very big carp to move in on the bait, and they invariably push the catfish to the outer perimeters.

I remain close to my rods for the rest of the day, but Cormorants, Fish Eagles, Pied or Malachite Kingfishers, and giant Monitor Lizards are the only living things that disturb the tranquil waters of Klaserie. Then just as the last rays of sunlight disappear beyond the horizon, I hear the first heavy slap of fins and flesh smacking the surface. This first crash of a carp is followed shortly after by two more heavy thumps. From where I sit, it's difficult to gage their exact location, but it seems that they have begun feeding at the edges of the densest part of the Jungle rushes, about 700 metres past my baits.

At dusk, I move in to my bivvy and zip up the doors to keep out the mosquitoes; but August is the tail end of winter in South Africa and there are still very few mosquitoes about. Within an hour the cooler air has chased them away, so I move back out and sit beside my rodpod beneath a canopy of stars. The frogs are extremely noisy tonight and their constant croaking is beginning to give me a headache. Lowe brought up the subject of frogs during our conversations around the campfire during this evenings meal. He owns a small, private pool near Bushcamp and he rarely caught carp from there, but when he did, it was always a night when the frogs were loudly calling to each other. Re-counting all our previous carp catches at Klaserie Bush Camp brings us to the same conclusion, so we're looking forward to some action tonight!

Two hours later, I can still hear the regular crashing of fish, but this time they seem to be slightly closer, maybe 500 metres. This has become a regular occurrence over the last few days and judging by the sounds, I'm sure that it is a shoal of extra large specimens. The moist night air finally stops the frogs croaking and I retire back inside the bivvy to escape the cold.

At precisely 04:30 hrs, a single 'bleep' shatters my dreams and I lift my head off the pillow to stare through the mosquito mesh towards a red diode that lights up the pod. The four rods point like javelins straight at the stars; but as I squint through the mesh, the tip of the left-hand rod begins to bend towards the rushes. I pounce off the bedchair and unzip the door, but before I reach the rod, the spool is rapidly revolving and the Delkim lets out a constant, high-pitched tone.

A solid strike makes good contact, but even at 200 metres the line gives not an inch of stretch and I'm immediately able to stop the carp in it's tracks, then pull it clear of the tangle of roots in the Jungle. Jason must be deep in sleep, because three loud shouts fail to wake him; so I continue to awkwardly slip in to the chest waders and strap on the Pexel Head Torch, while at the same time maintaining pressure on a fast-moving fish. Then I jump straight in to the water and wade quickly through the 50 metres of marginal weeds in an attempt to reach the outer fringes before the carp does. But I'm too late, and the taught braid begins to transmit horrible tremors down the line as the carp burrows through the root systems.

With amazing strength, more line screams off the spool as it heads straight for one of two sunken trees that poke their gnarled branches above the water. My hand clamps on the spool to stop it revolving, until the carp suddenly erupts in a sheet of spray just inches from the branches. Slowly, I manage to drag the fish away from the branches, but I'm now standing almost to the limit of the chest waders and in the centre of the weeds. The carp is so powerful that I'm afraid to ease off the pressure, as it will quickly snag the line amongst the tangle of thick lily roots and reed stems. My fingers shift to the drag nut and tighten it with one turn, and then I just hold on! The water surrounding me suddenly turns into a cauldron of churning white-water as the carp goes ballistic, but it's brute strength is matched by the rod's progressive power, and it finally crashes inside the landing net rim. But before I'm able to adjust the clutch to allow the carp to sink inside the mesh, a violent flap of its huge tail sends it powering back out of the net! My heart almost stops at this moment, but with luck, the hook remains firmly bedded in those thick, rubbery lips as I lean hard back on the rod and guide the carp back inside the landing net.

This time my fingers manage to loosen the drag nut, then I pull out some slack line and watch the carp sink down to safety. Slowly I wade back to shore with the net then lay it down on the unhooking mat. It is a very long, spectacular looking mirror carp with a perfect, unbroken dorsal fin and massive tail. The landing net is quickly collapsed and removed from the pole, then hooked on to the scales. I have no doubts that it weighs over forty, but when my eyes watch the needle swing round past 50lbs, I let out a whoop for joy! After deducting the weight of the net, I settle for a weight of 48lb+.

The faint light of pre-dawn begins to show in the eastern sky, but it is still too dark for good photos without the aid of a flash, so I sack the fish and then paddle out a fresh bait to the same area. Within an hour, a 20lb mirror screams off with the other hookbait positioned in deeper water, about three rod lengths away from the Jungle reeds. The take coincides with Peter bringing breakfast to my swim (the luxury of being an African Gold customer!), and I ask him to take a quick returning shot with my camera, for although small, it is a stunning looking young carp.

The sun finally lifts it's head above the Drakenburg Mountains and sends warm shafts of golden light over Klaserie; so I take this opportunity to remove the 48lb mirror from the sack for a photo session. The fish looks absolutely stunning in this soft, morning light, so I instruct Jason to keep the motor drive purring on my Pentax cameras. After some land shots over the unhooking mat, I ask Jason to take some returning shots; but just as I begin lowering this beautiful carp in to the water, the left-hand Delkim signals another take! Peter rushes in to the water by my side and takes the 48lber in his arms so that I can strike the rod. As I play the fish, I instruct Jason to help Peter lift the forty back on to the mat, then slip it gently inside a sack and back in to the water. The carp I'm fighting turns out to be a 31lb 12oz mirror, and is released immediately after a few photos. I then wade over to the sacked 48lb mirror and get Jason to join me in the water, to blast off a series of photo-shots using the motordrive, as I let the carp swim from my open hands.

As soon as the photo session is over, I paddle back out to the Jungle with a fresh hookbait and pour an extra half-bucket of mix directly over both rigs. I'm running short on film and now only have 5 shots left on each camera, so if I continue catching whackers I'm going to be in trouble. Lowe is driving in to town today, so I ask him to buy some more Fuji transparency films.

At 09:15 hrs, another monster Klaserie mirror feeding at the edge of the Jungle reeds is seduced by one of the 'pin-down' double tigernut rigs. Sitting tight to the rodpod proves it's worth again, and I'm able to immediately halt the carp's onward rush. But this very strong and fast swimming fish manages to get inside the large marginal weed bed before I can reach it. I quickly wade up to my chest through the thick tangle of lily roots until I'm level with the fish; then pull the rod in to it's full power curve. The rest of the fight is spent with the carp ploughing through the weeds on a short line beneath the rod tip. No carp can maintain strength against such unrelenting pressure, and moments later it rolls inside my landing net, along with a mountain of weed. Part of the hook point is protruding through the outside of the lip and somehow it catches on the inside of the mesh. I just can't believe this and begin to swear and curse at my bad luck.

The snagged hook is holding the carp's head close to the inner rim of the net and preventing the fish from sliding down inside. I try to free the hook from the mesh, but the barb is well and truly snagged. Suddenly the carp shakes it's head and rips the hook point off the mesh, but the full weight of the fish is now on the short length of braid in my hands, and one extra kick from it's tail breaks the line instantly. The carp continues thrashing its huge tail and manages to swim straight back over the cord to freedom! My utter panic sets me into jet-speed mode, as I drop the rod in panic and grab the landing net with both hands, then scoop the carp back inside the mesh for a second time.

As I wade back with my prize, I know it is a good specimen, but it is not until the scales show me a weight of 51lb+ (after deducting the weight of the net), do I finally realise just how heavy it is.

I ask Jason to click off a few photos of the fifty before sacking it in the margins, then quickly paddle back out with the hookbait and pile in some fresh mix from the bucket. I don't have to wait long, and within an hour, another big mirror carp picks up the same bait. After a very exciting fight, I'm finally able to swallow a 46lb+ fish with my landing net. I just cannot believe my luck and just sit on the chair staring at the two full sacks in the margins with a big grin on my face! Lowe has not yet returned with fresh film, so I use up the remaining 10 exposures left in the cameras on brace shots.

There are still some fish crashing over my heavily baited swims, but I have no further action for the remainder of the afternoon. So, after Lowe has brought some fresh film, I spend my time photographing brightly coloured dragonflies hovering low over the rushes, or butterflies settling beside my sandals to suck moisture from the damp sand; or kingfishers plunging head first into shoals of minute fish that constantly dapple the surface beneath my rod tips, until I eventually sit back on the comfy chair to soak in the last hot rays of sunshine.

As yet another glorious sunset paints the waters of Klaserie in warm shades of red and gold, I quietly sit next to my rods and reflect on the recent action - 2 twenties, a thirty, 2 forties and a fifty in the same day!

The soft, golden light of evening begins to slowly ebb and is replaced by monochrome shades of dusk. The last flocks of Hadeda Ibis and African Spoonbills fly noisily overhead in the fading gloom. Whitebreasted Cormorants skim across the lake on their own reflections on a journey back to their night roosts in the dead branches of a large, half submerged tree. The dark silhouette of a Crowned Eagle perches proudly amongst the highest branches of forest canopy, and the shadow of a Fierynecked Nightjar sweeps over the rushes. Behind me, a Bush pig snuffles noisily amongst the long grasses at the base of a Tree Fern in its search for underground rhizomes. A troop of Samango Monkeys walks quietly down the track; each individual eyeing with interest the plastic waste bag hanging from a branch next to my bivvy. They won't attempt to look inside the bag while I'm sitting here, but the more confident Chacma Baboons sometimes raid my gear while I sleep.

By 19:00 hrs, most daylight fauna has quietly disappeared to be replaced by a cacophony of nocturnal creatures. I have noticed that each evening is warmer than the last, as winter season slowly transforms in to spring. The rising daytime temperatures are waking more insects and reptiles form hibernation and attracting rising numbers of colourful migrant birds. Tonight, the sub-tropical air literally hums to the constant sounds of thousands of frogs and crickets.

At 17:15hrs, a 25lb+ common carp picks up the tigernut rig positioned closest the Jungle rushes and I return it to the water after a short, but strong fight. Half an hour later, another carp sucks up two tigernuts from the same place, but unfortunately I'm in the next swim at the time, helping Jason re-position a long distance hookbait. I manage to run quickly back to my own swim and strike in to a strong fish, but the hook pulls after only a few seconds.

Jason and myself normally leave the rod in the rests, then paddle out long distances with a hookbait. But the revolving spool causes excessive line twist and if a strong wind is blowing, too much line is pulled off the reel and a large bow is formed between rod and bait. To alleviate these problems, it is best to get someone to hold the rod and open the bail-arm of the reel, then control the line tension with forefinger and thumb as it is pulled off the spool, while you paddle out with the hookbait. This also means that should a take occur on another of your rods while you're paddling out a bait, the other person can strike and play the fish - Just hope that it isn't a monster and he doesn't land it before you paddle madly back to shore! The only other down side to this is that you are forced to occasionally walk away from your rods to help each other re-place fresh baits. Twice we have had takes while we've been helping each other get the baits back out. But this last loss of a good carp has caused us to re-think the situation, so we have finally decided to revert back to re-baiting on our own and putting up with the dreaded line twist!

I've just returned to shore after re-baiting with a mixed bucket of peanuts, maples, maize and tigernuts. A big carp suddenly crashes out near the far bank, close to Jason's left-hand rig. I hope it soon picks up his hookbait, because he deserves to land a forty after his long run of bad luck. Time is quickly running out for him, as this is our second to last night on the water. Jason has also booked a weeks fishing on the superb Rushmere Lake and is looking forward to it, but I know that he's secretly wishing for another Klaserie monster to pick up one of his hookbaits before this session ends.

Shadows of carnivores continue to hunt for meat throughout the night. While I sleep - barks, yelps, shrieks and roars echo through the darkest corridors of my dreams. The alarms remain silent, and the rods continue pointing directly at the distant stars of the Southern Cross.

Very gradually, a faint purple; then orange; then yellow begins to rim the western sky, until the sun eventually peeps over the lips of Drakenburg peaks to send sparks in to the darkest heart of the forest. Clouds gather on the high rocky plateaux, then roll off the cliffs and sweep down on Klaserie. Mist streams out of the rushes to mingle with the clouds, until a giant fog bank hangs low over the lake. Solid objects suck moisture from its grey heart and form droplets on their surfaces, until the margins ring to the gentle sounds of dripping water.

The sun slowly rises and arcs through the sapphire sky, to stretch its warm fingers over Africa. Fog twists and slides across the tranquil waters of Klaserie, then curls up in great clouds of vapour, before being sucked off the surface and vanishing in a blue void. Within two hours, the sun has baked the rushes dry and only a few lingering droplets remain on the cool, carbon surfaces of my rods or within the lingering shadows of my canvas bivvy.

At 11.25 hrs, I hook in to a very strong and fast swimming fish, but the powerful rod keeps it away from any dangerous snags, although I just cannot believe my luck when yet another forty rolls over the landing net. On the scales, this gorgeous looking mirror carp pulls the pointer round to 40lb 4oz, my sixth forty in a week!

At 16:45 hrs, I hook in to yet another very big carp. This time it comes to one of the extreme distance hookbaits positioned at the edge of Leopard Bay - my first take from this area in almost 3 days! The carp ploughs through the far margin lilies, but heavy pressure finally pulls it clear and back into open water. The carp then begins swimming at ultra high speed to my right and I need to pump the rod and churn the reel like mad to maintain contact. Suddenly the pounding rod tip shudders to a halt and I stop gaining line - the carp has found a snag, and it's still over 250 metres from shore. While I'm trying to free this big carp from a snag, I get a take on another rod, and to cut a long story short, the hook eventually pulls free and the other line parts close to the swivel. I'm well chuffed!

I'm angry at loosing both carp and to take my mind off it, I quickly get back to the task of tying new rigs and getting fresh baits out. Soon I'm able to push away from shore and the paddle cleanly cuts through the warm waters of Klaserie. It's strange, but the water in this lake seems to remain fairly warm even during winter; which is a welcome change from the ice-cold waters of Goldmire and Rushmere lakes located hundreds of miles to the south. When the canoe drifts over the baited area close to the Jungle rushes, I'm amazed to see the water bubbling and fizzing like a boiling kettle, as carp continue to search frantically for free offerings amongst the bottom debris. I gently lower the hookbait in to position and pour the remainder of my bait-mix over the side. That should keep them interested!

The day quickly draws to a close as we enter the final night of the session. I'm happy with my results so far, but still feel very confident of continued action from the Jungle area. A 24lb+ common answers my predictions at 19:45 hrs, and 2 hours 40 minutes later I am back up to my waist in the lilies, battling it out with a spectacular looking 34lb 2oz mirror carp.

Dawn eventually breaks over Klaserie and the sun's warm rays light up my bivvy for the final time. Before breakfast, I begin to slowly pack away the mountain of gear and by 07:30 hrs, the only remaining items of tackle is a single rod sitting on the pod. Then suddenly it begins to bend and the alarm lets out a high-pitched scream - a 27lb 2oz mirror wants to say goodbye!

What an absolutely mind blowing session this has turned out to be. Over the past seven days I've landed twenty carp, including six over forty. I should have landed twice this number of fish and experienced a great deal of losses during the early days due partly to using inadequate tackle in difficult, heavily weeded areas. Changing to more appropriate rods and line definitely helped reverse the odds in my favour. During the most hectic 7 hours of action I managed to land five carp, topped by giant mirrors weighing 46lb+, 48lb and 51lb. Those incredible hours of supreme joy will live inside my memories forever...

Tony with a spectacular brace of 46lb+ mirror carp
(holding), and 51lb mirror carp (on mat).

Extreme low temperatures of a misty winter's dawn, paint the rods in a thick layer of frost.

FROZEN DREAMS

"..30lb 6oz of awesome looking barbel.."

The golden sun rises slowly above the ridges of La Mancha. Yellow beams spread throughout the valley and squeeze through the window shutters until they fall softly across my pillow. I awake from deep sleep and slowly open my eyes. No alarm has woken me, just the natural cycle of an internal body clock and my eardrums vibrate only to the gentle sound of moving water. I slide out of bed and walk over to the window, then pull open the shutters. In the distance, sheets of fine spray mingle with the morning mist, as the River Ruidera cascades over Hundiemento waterfall and crashes onto the moss-covered boulders. The river rushes onwards through the valley, until it is swallowed in the blue-green waters of Cueva Morenilla Lake; then overfills into Coladilla Pool, before finally spewing out across the marshes of Cenegosa. At the bottom of my garden I can hear the songs of fast water, as it ripples through the dense reed beds between the two lakes.

I just stand at the bedroom window for a few minutes, scanning the glorious vistas and sucking in lungs full of fresh air. A Marsh Harrier is hovering over the reeds in search of mice, and a vulture is spiralling above the highest crests of hills in search of warm thermals. A gold-scaled carp crashes out of the tranquil waters at the southern end of Coladilla Pool. Three more carp roll on the surface in the same area over the next few minutes, and then a heavier, deep-bodied mirror crashes near the outflow of Morenilla Lake. Almost every second evening during the past few weeks, I have walked down to the sandy beach and baited up this part of Morenilla with the aid of a boat or cobra stick. My numerous night sessions from the beach swim have rewarded me with plenty of carp, but

I have yet to land one of the few, but giant barbel that I have occasionally seen roll over the pre-baited area. I will continue to try for one of the elusive Morenilla monsters, but not today. Instead, I will drive to Tommeloso to stock up on food supplies, then spend most of the afternoon searching for likely looking areas to fish on some of the other lakes in the valley.

The Vado Blanco and Ruidera streams run through more than 15 lakes and small pools before they reach the Cenogosa marshes. Running water that seeps through porous rock strata, underground caverns or natural springs, also help swell the volume of these natural stillwaters. All of these small, but incredibly beautiful lakes are joined to each other by a tier of cascading waterfalls, and forms a green belt of forested landscape surrounded by the drier, high plateaux of La Mancha. The northwestern section of this stunning water-filled terrain comes under the protective wings of a nature park, known as: 'Parqu Natural de las Lagunas de Ruidera'.

Soon after returning from Tommeloso, I take a drive and walking tour to various lakes – called 'lagunas' – located in the upper valley. These are lakes: Bolana, Santo Morillo, Salvadora, Lengua, Redondilla, San Pedro, Tinajas, Tomilla, Concejo, and Blanca.

The Laguna Lengua and Laguna Concejo show the best potential of these lakes, but after a lot of consideration I finally choose to concentrate on two central lakes in the lower valley – Laguna de la Colgada and Lagunas del Rey. I have already fished some parts of Colgada, which is the largest natural lake in the complex. My first session from the central peninsular drew a blank, but this was followed by a succession of spectacularly successful sessions from swims located in a small bay on the eastern arm. Even though I have caught many carp up to 30lb 8oz and a stack of big barbel up to 31lb+ from the eastern peninsular, I do not want to continue to plug at the same area. These two waters are the deepest in the complex and offer the best chance of contacting the biggest fish, but my love for pioneering new swims means that I need to search out virgin areas if I am to stay one step ahead.

By renting a house on the shores of Morenilla, it is giving me the opportunity to not only search all the different waters within the Nature Park, but also allows me to get to know the locals in the surrounding community and glean information from them. By piecing together these snippets of information and combining this with my own increasing knowledge of the various waters, it is helping me fit vitally important pieces to the jigsaw.

The sun is low in the western sky as I pull off the 430 road and drive slowly down a small dirt track that skirts the west side of Lagunas del Rey. The track crosses the small Carros stream that feeds the southern fringes of Lake Rey, passes Casa del Cerro then joins the western arm of Lake Colgada. For the next kilometre, the track hugs the western arm, and then turns south along the edges of the southern arm, which terminates in a large, square-shaped bay. 5-7 metres wide strip of reeds fringes both lakes, but there are cutouts at varying intervals along the banks used by local fishermen. Some of the places where the reeds have been cut back are wider and more open than others, indicating their use for launching small boats. During the peak of summer this may be a problem, but in the depths of winter, hardly a soul visits these quiet waters.

I analyse the positive and negative aspects of each swim in turn, before finally opting to fish two separate swims. One swim is located half way along the western shoreline of Lake Rey, and the other is at the entrance to the bay on the southern arm of Lake Colgada. By the time the headlights of the car are lighting a passage homeward, my left arm is sore from the constant strain of expelling hundreds of Shellfish flavoured boilies with the throwing stick.

Over the next fortnight, I spend a lot of time writing articles or editing photos back at the house, but still allocate some of my time to fish short but very productive sessions on Lake Rey, the beach swim at Morenilla and the eastern arm of Colgada. I choose not fish the southern arm of Lake Colgada during this period, but still force myself to drive down it every few days to bait up a virgin swim. Before I finally decide to fish this particular swim, I bait the area very heavily, and then leave it for 48 hours.

Up until now, most of my big winter barbel and carp have fallen to baits presented in depths ranging between 25ft – 40ft. My good friend, Jose Luis, has caught many big barbel from the relatively shallower water of the marginal shelf, but these have fallen mainly to float tackle techniques during daylight in mild weather. Float tackle or ultra-light ledgering techniques have accounted for almost 100% of all big barbel previously caught by local Spanish fishermen. The

This fabulous brace of 30lb+ mirror and common carp were caught from extremely deep water and ice-cold December conditions.

A scarred warrior, but still a tremendous fighter.

deepest parts of the lakes just have not received any serious pressure, which has resulted in a slow and very inconsistent pattern to their catch rates. I strongly believe that outside the springtime spawning migrations (when both barbel and carp migrate to either shallow or fast and oxygenated waters), most of the fish move to deeper water. When the temperatures plummet well below zero, the largest barbel will move to the very deepest troughs of the river/lake systems and spend most of their time feeding through the hours of darkness. These areas also seem to attract big carp, and both species will often feed in similar extreme depths. My knowledge gained from fishing very deep waters around the World, combined with the previous outstanding success fishing baits in this river & lake system at a depth of 40ft, has given me confidence to try to fish even deeper.

Yet another glorious blue sky greets me as I step out of the house to load up the car for my first single-night session on the southern arm. The clear, starlit night has left frost amongst the shadows, and as the car moves slowly past the margins of Lakes Rey and Colgada, the tyres break through thick ice formed in puddles along the long and winding track.

The large bay that covers most of the southern arm is quite shallow, but I have chosen to fish a very deep trench opposite a long peninsular jutting into the central part of the lake. The tip of this peninsular forms a large tree-covered island, which is the same place from where I blanked during that first session. I had watched numerous carp crashing beyond casting distance when I fished there, but am now easily able to cast to that particular area from this southwestern bank. The dense reed beds grow on a clay bottom covered by shallow water and the marginal shelf that drops steeply from the edges of this is hard-bottom and clean for the next 7 metres. But beyond this, a dense underwater forest of weed grows up from the bottom to a height of more than 5 metres. This thick and vibrant strain of weed stays evergreen throughout the year, and in this particular part of the lake it stretches in a wide belt horizontal to the bank, in water ranging from 3, to as much as 15 metres deep (10ft – 40ft+)! The shelf beyond the massive weed bed continues to slope downwards in to extremely deep, dark water where it levels off at around 65ft deep. I must cast more than 100 metres to reach this clear area, but it also means that each hooked fish will need to be coaxed almost to the surface to enable it to be brought over the weeds. My long rods and fishing position atop a high bank will help a little, but it's not going to be easy.

I park the car under a tree and walk to the swim where I have been baiting up over the past weeks. A high bank slopes steeply down to a gap cut in the marginal reed beds. The gap in the reeds is just wide enough to accommodate my rodpod, but there is no room for anything else. I will not be erecting a bivvy, but need somewhere to place the bedchair and the top of the slope provides the only stable platform. I like to be quick to hit a take, so eventually select to place the pod on the brim of the slope and position the bedchair very close to it.

An umbrella is erected above the bedchair and I begin to set up the three rods. A small white church is pinpointed on the far horizon, which has been used as a marker to aid the baiting campaign during the past weeks, and I now throw out 100 free baits towards that same area. Using the big Cobra stick, I try to keep the baiting pattern as tight as possible then cast each hookbait very accurately over the freebies. Two of the hookbaits are double-balanced boilies on the same hair (one sinker + one floater), and the third hookbait is a single sinking boilie. These baits now lie in the darkness of almost 60ft deep water.

At about 22:00hrs during this first night in the new swim, a good common picks up one of the

Fully-scaled carp + huge barbel -
an incredible looking brace.

Amazing brace of 29lb 12oz Barbel & 30lb+ Mirror carp!

Jens Bursell cradles a Spanish monster-sized barbel weighing 29lb+.

double-boilie hookbaits. I estimate it to be around 28lb, and decide to quickly return the fish without weighing or photographing. The rest of the night is very quiet and a new dawn breaks over the frost-covered landscape of Castilla La Mancha, with dry sacks still hidden inside my rucksack. I certainly hoped for more action, but at least the capture of this one carp on a particularly cold night at extreme depths, has given me confidence enough to try again. Once the sun has raised enough to disperse the moisture from my gear, I pack up, and then chuck plenty of freebies into the swim before driving home.

I drive back down the same desolate track twice over the next four days to bait up very heavily with 20mm Shellfish boilies. The swim is then left to settle for a further 48hrs before I return to try a second short overnight session lasting around 18 hours.

I am still a little apprehensive when I arrive at the same swim to begin my second session. 'Was the carp caught during the last trip just an isolated wanderer, or are the fish moving down to 60ft in numbers' I think to myself. But my uncertainty is quickly dispelled when, shortly after topping up the swim with around 100 boilies, a big mirror crashes over the baited area.

Nothing pulls line out of the line clips for the rest of the evening and I have to wait until well into darkness before the first carp picks up one of the baits and goes on a blistering run. This is just the beginning of a glorious night of action and by midnight, I have landed two 26lb+ commons, a 27lb+ mirror, and a superb barbel in immaculate condition that swung the scales pointer round to just a few ounces short of 30lb. I am ecstatic and my confidence climbs skyward.

My confidence continues to soar towards the stratosphere when my third short night session produces a 23lb common, another colossal barbel weighing 29lb 12oz, and a heavily scaled 30lb+ mirror carp. I'm on a roll, and decide to extend my next session over two nights.

It is seven days before Christmas. I've arrived much earlier this time, around 15:00hrs. My past sessions have passed beneath cold and crisp starlit skies, but the blue is already beginning to cloud over while I set up the rods, so I decide to bait up twice as heavily as normal, in anticipation of a warm and active night. The wind feels quite mild, and judging by the dark grey bank of clouds that are already blocking out sun, it could bring rain. A carp crashes out about 80 metres to the left of the baited area. Two more carp disturb the surface during the next fifteen minutes and each one is closer to my baits. Then a big barbel rolls on the surface right above my baits. There is usually a marked difference between the way a big barbel rolls on the surface compared to a carp. The barbel rarely lifts its head above the surface as high as a carp does, and instead prefers to almost slide over on its flanks. This seems to form a small pocket of air between skin and water, like two cupped palms squeezed together, which produces a recognisable 'clop' sound. So unusual is this sound, that I can often detect the difference between a barbel and carp crashing during the hours of pitch darkness.

Suddenly a Delkim lights up as a powerful common decides it doesn't like the boilie attached to a 4oz lead! The carp speeds off into the middle of the lake and begins to rise to the upper layers of water. By maintaining intense and steady force on the tackle, I am able to stop the first run and keep it within a few feet of the surface while I regain line. I lever back hard with the powerful rod until the carp crashes on the surface, and keep it rolling until I am sure it is clear of the subsurface weeds, then release pressure slightly to allow the fish to fight once again in relatively clear water. By wading to the edge of the marginal shelf, I am able to stretch the 13ft rod out over clear water and so prevent the fish from ploughing through marginal rushes. Soon the carp is swimming in the gin clear water beneath the rod tip and I can sea that it is a superb common. It finally rolls into the landing net and I wade back to shore and lower my prize onto the unhooking mat. The size No.2 Penetrator hook is removed and I transfer the fish into the weigh sling and then on to the zeroed scales. The pointer shows a weight of 31lb 12oz. The carp has a notch in the upper caudal lobe which seems familiar, but it is not until I check through my photos that I realise it is the very same common that I caught a month previous, from a bay about 1km away in the eastern arm. Just as I am tying off the cord on the sacked carp, the blue Delkim signals another take. This results in a 28lb+ common. There is now only one hookbait left in the swim, so I thread fresh boilies and tie PVA stringers to the other two rigs, then cast them back out. Within 2 hours, both baits are sucked inside the huge mouths of monster-sized barbel. One is a 26lb 10oz specimen with silver-tinged scales. The other barbel, a bronze coloured 28lb 12oz beauty, comes in easily at first, but then wakes up and fights an incredible battle in the deep, clear water beneath my rod tip.

As dusk descends over Colgada on the second evening, a strong wind pushes the last grey clouds overhead and a thin line of deep blue begins to appear on the far horizon. The wind turns into a gentle breeze, which changes the waves to ripples that gradually fade away until the surface is like a sheet of glass. By nightfall, high above my head is a black canopy, studded with shining stars. The warm air rises and escapes through the upper atmosphere, causing the mercury level to plummet. The vapour of each exhaled breath can already be seen hanging in the cooling air, and soon I am encased within several layers of clothes and a thermal winter under-suit to fight off the cold. A pair of waterproof & breathable (Touch 9 Aquamax) salopettes is slipped over the top to keep me dry if I need to unhook a fish in the middle of the night.

Some large fish begin topping about 30 metres to the right of my baited area during the next few hours, so I decide to recast the right hand rod. Before I am able to lower the rod back in the rests, it is almost ripped out of my hands by a 28lb+ barbel! I recast a fresh boilie to the same area and

Tony with an immaculate common caught in extreme conditions.

Another carp & barbel brace caught from very deep water.

within 30 minutes a 29lb carp sucks it in.

The rods remain still on the pod for a while, until just shortly before midnight, the right hand rod taps twice, then jerks wildly as the spool begins to spin. Something has yet again fallen to the newly positioned bait, but this time things don't go so smoothly. Up until now I have not lost a single fish in this difficult swim. If a big fish did manage to bury it's head in the dense tangle of weed, I would simply bend the Globetrotter Supreme rod until it took up its full power curve and walk back slowly. This immense pressure would always free the fish and there would be no problems as long as I kept things moving. But it seems that the weed bed is more densely packed and grows closer to the surface where I have repositioned the right hand bait.

To compound my problem, this last fish picks up the bait in 59ft of water then swims directly towards me at incredible speed. I just don't have enough time to apply full pressure so as to lift the heavy fish into the upper layers of water, and enable me to bully it over the high ridge of thick weed. The fish is still in extremely deep water before it reaches the far side of the weeds and buries its nose inside the tangle of fronds. No amount of pressure will shift it, and I suddenly feel the sickening jolt of a hook pull.

The temperature continues to drop and freezes the soft mud until it becomes rock hard and resonates beneath the soles of my Gore-Tex boots. Already the landscape is covered in a thick layer of white frost that sparkles beneath a full moon. My umbrella looks like a giant silver mushroom, but at least it keeps the cold fingers of frost from coating the upper half of the bedchair. The landing net is sunk in the margins to prevent from freezing solid. For the same reason, the spare sacks are placed beneath the large unhooking mat. I climb back up the steep bank then pour hot coffee from the flask and as I drink it my head envelops in a cloud of vapour and steam. I remove both boots and place them next to the bedchair legs so that I can jump into them if I get a take. The laces are pushed inside the boots so that they don't trip me up and also enable a quick change into the thermal wellingtons, just in case I need to wade out in deeper water to land a fish. A groundsheet is wrapped over the bottom half of the bedchair to keep frost off the sleeping bag then I climb inside its thick layer of warmth and zip out the cold. A dog fox on the far side of the bay suddenly lets out a series of gruff barks. Its calls carry across the waters until they drift and disperse amongst the marshes. A vixen answers him. Her strange and eerie calls ride like ghosts on the crisp, knife-edged air, until their echoes fade into silence. Slowly I drift into deep sleep whilst ice begins to form in the margins and air temperatures sink to minus 10° Centigrade.

Two short bleeps shake me from my dreams at about 04:00hrs. I sit bolt upright on the bedchair and notice the right hand rod begin to bend sharply downwards. The line is already out of the clip, but even though I slackened off the Baitrunner knob earlier tonight in anticipation of the frost, it is not moving at all. The rod then starts to lift from the back rest, so without further hesitation I fling open the sleeping bag and grab the rod, just in time to stop it from being wrenched straight off the pod. The spool is encrusted in a sheet of thick frost and all rod rings a clogged with ice. I place the butt on the hard ground and frantically try to chip most of the ice from the rings, then lift the rod back up and try to turn the reel handle, but it won't budge an inch! The rod tip is bucking and I must do something quick before the fish breaks the line. In desperation I start bashing the Baitrunner with the palm of my hand. Thankfully, the third hard smack gets everything moving again and I feel the ice particles hitting my cheeks as they spin off a revolving spool!

Tony with a gigantic 31lb+ barbel from the eastern peninsular.

As the rod handle begins to curve beneath my palm I can feel the skin sticking like glue. The metal parts of the reel hold on like Velcrose to my fingers. Thankfully it is a short fight and I soon engulf the fish inside my landing net. At around 19lb, it is my first ever Comiza barbel under 21lb. The hook is removed from its rubbery lip while it is still in the water to prevent any danger from frost damaging its delicate gill membranes. Without lifting it from the water, I lower the rim of the landing net and gently release it again. The barbel seems unimpressed by my concern for its well being, and just as I open both hands it decides to give a last slap of its huge tail on the surface and covers me in spray. Within moments of walking back up the slope the outer layer of my clothes turn into a sheet of solid ice!

Finally the sun once again lifts above the Palomas Forest and sends shafts of light to shimmer across the waters. But I wait for it to rise higher in the sky and vaporise most of the frost, before attempting to remove the two fish sacked in the deep margins. The carp is a pristine common with classic form, so I decide to take a few photos of it beside my rods. Just as I am about to lift the carp gently from the mat, it flaps wildly so I quickly cover the carp with my chest. This immediately calms down the fish and prevents any damage to its sovereign scales. As I begin to release my grip and slowly rise, the carp decides to give one more flap and as it does so, a sudden violent pain jolts my head back. Somehow the erect and jagged, primary ray of the carp's dorsal fin stabbed its sharp point into my throat and cut my neck wide open! I call an abrupt halt to the photo session, quickly slide the carp back inside the sack and lower it into the margins, then with one hand clamped round my neck in an attempt to ebb the flow, I rush back up the bank to attend to my wounds...

Blood is gushing everywhere, and I can't find a cloth amongst my tackle bags to wipe away the blood, so begin to walk over to the car. Eventually some rags are found in the boot, but just as I am standing beside the car, with the rag held against my throbbing neck wound and bemoaning my bad luck, I suddenly notice that one of the car tyres is flat!

'At least I can get some nice photos in this soft morning light', I think to myself. I switch the camera onto its triple-self timer mode, and then go to pick up the fish, only to realise that there is just one exposure left on the roll of film and I've inadvertently left all the spare films back at the house.

In a sulk, I turn back to the swim and go about packing up my gear. All the tackle is finally packed away, but I leave one remaining rod on the pod, while I get down to the enjoyable business of jacking up the car and changing the wheel in ice-cold, slimy mud. Just as I am swearing at a particularly obstinate wheel nut, two short 'bleeps' emit from one of the Delkims behind me, then a rod begins to bounce on the pod!

I run over to the pod and strike into a very strong swimming fish that feels very much like a big barbel, but soon it becomes bogged down at the very base of the weed bed. I try everything to budge it, but in the end, have to resort to pointing the rod tip at the water and walking backwards. The line stretches to its limits, until a loud 'crack' as it parts. I then realise just how close the car is behind me, because the sudden jolt of the line parting pushes me back, to send the rod butt smacking against the car and leaves a lovely groove in the paint-work. What a wonderful morning! I'd better get back to the house before my good luck continues and somebody decides to shoot me in the head again...

I still have a lot of writing left to do for many different European magazines, so I decide to give the fishing a break, but will return to the same swim after Christmas. It is good to get back to the house and cook some warm food and sit in front of a roaring log fire. My next session will be my last chance to fish in Spain before I make the long drive back to England in the New Year. Peter Staggs, who I have fished with on many different waters all over Spain, wants to say farewell before I leave, so what better place to say goodbye than on the beautiful banks of lake Colgada? Over the phone, we finalise plans to meet each other at the lake and fish for three nights between the 27th and 29th December. In the meantime, I get down to writing some more articles, but still make sure to drive down a few times to bait up the swim with plenty of shellfish boilies.

On the 27th, Pete arrives and we load all our gear into his big 4WD Pajero. The Zodiac inflatable is parked on a trailer in the garden and up until now I have only used it for baiting up the swims on Lake Morenilla. I discuss with Pete my earlier problems with the big weed bed and that the only reason that I did not use it on Colgada was the problem of manoeuvring the vessel alone while fighting a big fish. With two of us, there should be no such problems, so we decide to clip it on to the tow bar.

We soon return to the southern arm and look down from the high bank into the crystal clear waters. As I've already enjoyed tremendous success over the past sessions, and Pete is keen to get some more big fish under his belt, I decide to let him fish my regular swim. There are no more cutouts in the marginal reeds along the bank, but this is no problem if I adjust the Solar Globetrotter Pod to its highest position so that my lines lift over the tops of the reed stems. During the previous two sessions I spotted some very big barbel rolling on the surface, further along the southern arm. I've got a gut feeling about the area; so have been chucking some extra boilies into this precise spot during my baiting campaign. Now is the chance to follow my intuition and cast some hookbaits into this virgin territory.

Earlier this morning, I drove down the track just to top-up the baited swim with more boilies, so we don't need much more out there at the moment. We just flick out a few handfuls with the aid of a

Cobra stick, then cast our hookbaits + PVA stringers. The action to my rods is almost immediate, and I hook, fight and return a nice carp, followed by a double figure barbel. The barbel is only my second ever under 21lb.

The dull grey of twilight rolls like a carpet to engulf the lake in shadow. My swim has quietened down, and Pete's baits remain undisturbed. Dusk deepens into the black of night and still no action except for the odd crash of a feeding fish over our baits. Then at precisely 10:45hrs, Pete gets his first take. The fish makes a powerful run and he is unable to prevent it from ploughing deep inside the weed. This is our chance to use the dingy, and as soon as we drift over the snagged fish, there is a sudden stab at Pete's rod tip as the fish rushes back out to open water. Following a dogged fight beneath the dingy, the 25lb+ barbel surfaces and rolls into the outstretched landing net.

Dawn arrives with a splash of golden light, which scrapes layers of cold fog off the surface of the bay. Soon we are stripping away layers of clothing to bare our fading tans once again to the sun's warming rays. The day draws on, but nothing stirs and we have to wait until darkness once again draws in before the fish start feeding.

By the time a new sun begins to peak over the rugged cliffs to chase away the shadows, black sacks can be seen in the clear, deep margins beneath our rod tips. Inside one sack is Pete's nice upper-double figure Barbel, and the other three sacks contain my fish: a 20lb+ mirror with cherry coloured flanks, a big common with golden scales the size of giant sovereigns, and a superb upper twenty pound barbel.

The daylight hours drift by with their usual monotony, until we eventually enter our final night full of expectant action. But it is not to be, and tiredness finally overcomes our eagerness as we both fall to sleep on the bedchairs beneath a canopy of stars. When eyelids eventually open again, my eyes show me tightly clipped lines and a layer of frost on the rod handles. I drag my body from the warmth of the sleeping bag and boil the kettle for a fresh brew, but just as I am lighting up the stove, two sudden bleeps make me turn my head towards the pod. One of the rod tips is tapping gently so I rush over, and then sweep the rod hard over my right shoulder. The line twangs taught as the hook embeds deeply and the rod arches into its beautiful full curve. Almost immediately the fish buries itself in the thick weed. I know that the power of my rod will dislodge it, but with the dinghy waiting in the margins there is no need to take any chances with a possible light hook hold. We both jump inside the Zodiac and Pete guides the Kota motor to bring us directly above the snagged fish. With a different angle now on the fish, the rod is suddenly almost wrenched out of my hands and the force pulls me onto my knees and dips the fully curved rod tip under the water. Something with immense strength begins to power away from the weed bed and screams line off the spool as it swims through the extremely deep water. My muscles tense and veins begin to rise on the side of my neck as I struggle to keep the rod locked in its parabolic curve, trusting its shock-absorbent fish-sapping power to bring me the goods. And what a lump of goods it turns out to be. A massive back breaks the surface as an extremely long barbel begins to thrash the water to foam and sends sheets of spray over our surprised faces. Then it disappears again and now only the ticking ratchet is left to break the silence. The barbel spends the next five minutes spinning the dinghy slowly around as it swims in wide circles deep beneath us. The rod tip points directly down at the surface and throbs to the constant beat of the barbel's huge tail. Gradually I begin to gain back line, until the fish once again explodes on the surface. Then suddenly it is all over and 30lb

6oz of absolutely awesome looking barbel
turns on its side and I ease it over the big
landing net. We slap each other on the
shoulders in congratulations, and then
head back for shore. But not until I lay the
fish gently onto the big unhooking mat, do
I come to realise just how beautiful it truly
is. Without a doubt, it is the most perfect
barbel I've ever seen.

I originally planned to drive back to
England before 31st December, but during
the Christmas festivities I made a lot of
new friends and received numerous
invitations to parties, so I've now decided
to prolong my stay until at least after the
New Year's Eve celebrations. It is while I'm
in quite a happy, but rather intoxicated state in one of the bars of Ruidera village during the early
hours of New Year, that Jose Luis pleads for me to take him fishing. Jose runs the Hotel Guadiana
in Ruidera and is probably the most successful carp and barbel angler in the area. I tell him that my
plans are to rest for one day after this night of drinking then drive to the UK on 2nd January. He
tops up my glass a few times, and somehow he persuades me to stay an extra day so that we can
fish the next night together.

At precisely 10:00hrs on the morning of January 1st, the sound of a vehicle entering the private
drive of my rented house wakes me from the dead. I silently prey for the van to drive past to enable
me to re-enter my dreams, but the rumbling engine gets louder, until the squeak of breaks and slam
of a car door signals my worst fears. I stare at my watch in the dark gloom of the bedroom then try
to lift my head from the pillow. It feels like a block of lead and only now does a screaming torrent
of blood begin pulsating at my temples. At first I can't figure out the difference between Jose
banging at the front door and the thumping inside my brain, so I try and block it all out and drift
back off to sleep. But the banging and thumping don't go away, so I am forced to drag my body
painfully from the bedcovers. Standing upright is my first mistake, and my stomach suddenly
begins to churn like a washing machine. Opening the window shutters is my second mistake and
the shock of intense, bright sunlight instantly trying to burn the back of my eyeballs makes me
almost fall back on the bed. I stumble downstairs, open the fridge and pour a mouthful of cold milk
down my parched throat, then wish I hadn't.

Plucking up courage, I open the back door and walk across the yard to unlock the gate. Jose looks as fresh as a spring chicken and is raring to get to the lake. He takes one look at me then his lower lip drops in astonishment.

"Oh, Tony, he look not good. Real bad! You not need come fishing today, Tony, I understand. Is OK, me go home, you sleep. Is OK?"

I listen to Jose's broken English spoken with a quaint Spanish charm, and my eyes scan the vehicle packed with his fishing gear, then his sad face. He's been looking forward to this trip and the disappointment is obvious on his demeanour. I haven't the heart to let him down now, no matter how rough I feel.

"It's OK, Jose, I promised to take you and I won't break a promise."

"You sure, Tony?" he replies with a huge grin, and before I can say yes, he is busy at the back of his van sorting out a clear place to fit my own fishing tackle.

We go through the many options available to us on which lake to try. Jose concentrates most of his time on Lagunas del Ray and Laguna Colgada. Most his favourite swims are on the northern shoreline, and he's keen to fish in one of the areas where I have previously tried, so we eventually agree on the southern arm.

Within an hour, we are both set up on the high bank overlooking the big bay. Jose very much wants to learn exactly how I fish, and although his fishing gear is adequate for his normal margin floatfishing during summer days, it isn't quite strong enough to cope with the extremes of this particular swim. For this reason we have decided to share four of my own rods on a single pod. Jose picks the two left hand rods to cover the same area where I have been baiting up heavily, and I choose to fish the two right hand rods so that I can cast the baits to yet another virgin area of territory.

It takes all my willpower to hold back my stomach while I'm setting up, and by the time I collapse on the bedchair in a sweaty heap, my head is spinning like a racing car tire. We have no headache pills to relieve my discomfort, so I just close my eyes and try to relax. But I'm not given the luxury of this, because within seconds of closing my eyelids, the right hand Delkim bursts into song. I instantly jump off the bedchair, which doesn't help my pounding brain, then whack the Globetrotter rod over my shoulder and feel the confident sensation as it meets solid resistance. It turns out to be a carp, which is brought over the weed beds quite easily, but then it roars up the bank and I'm forced to wade through the high marginal reeds to land it. By the time I've got the carp inside the net, my stomach and brains are trying to greet each other, so I quickly release it without photos and climb back up the high bank. All this early morning activity finally becomes too much more for me and I suddenly run back down the slope and spray the grass with half of last night's excesses.

It is like opening the cork on a fizzing champagne bottle. I begin to feel better almost immediately and after ten minutes my headache and stomach cramp is gone. I even begin to feel hungry again! Jose opens the back doors of his van then takes out a box full food and hands me a steaming hot coffee from his flask. I begin to get over my embarrassment at being sick in front of Jose and we both start to laugh and joke about the situation. The tension seems to ease and we both relax and stare out over the water while munching on sandwiches and sipping coffee. Then the left-middle rod bounces on the pod and Jose pours half his coffee over me as he dashes towards the rod and strikes into a fast swimming fish.

Almost 15 minutes pass and Jose is still playing the fish and not making much headway. I've not wanted to say anything to him because I know he's got a lot of experience behind him, but begin to realise that this was gained using very delicate float rods and light line. Many of his past big fish have taken more than an hour to land and judging by the small bend in the rod tip I think he's settled in for another prolonged battle.

"You don't need to be so delicate with Globetrotter rod, Jose, give it some stick! Don't worry about the line, it won't break." I say to Jose, biting my lip as the words leave my mouth in hope that both the line and hookhold are strong.

Jose leans back slightly, but more pleads from me to apply more pressure to the fish gives him more confidence, as I watch the rod begin to keel over into its full battle curve. The fish reacts almost immediately and crashes on the surface several times then goes on a strong run along the margins, but this time Jose holds on hard and stops it in its tracks. Moments later a big, golden-scaled common rolls over my deep sunken landing net. Jose is over the moon and the huge grin on his face tells me that it is the biggest carp he has ever landed in a lifetime of fishing! I take some quick shots of the upper twenty-pound common and Jose's beaming smile then he releases it immediately. From that moment on Jose won't stop telling me how much he loves the rods and spends most of the day badgering me into selling him one on the cheap!

Time races on and the sun moves across a clear blue sky. Soon it begins to dip towards the horizon and as temperatures plummet again the air becomes fresh and crisp. Suddenly I hear a single bleep, then turn my head to catch the sight of a green diode. The Solar Buttbanger indicator is dropping just a fraction so I rush over to the pod and let my hand hover over it in anticipation. Then the same indicator lifts back up to horizontal and begins to quiver, so I lift the rod high over my shoulder in one even stroke and walk back three paces until the line twangs taught. There is a series of heavy thumps on the line, then what ever it is on the other end of the line seems to wake up and speeds off down the lake. Continuous pressure with the full 13ft of carbon locked over in its power curve stops the first mad rush, and I'm able to lift the fish into the upper layers of water and over the dangerous weed bank. But as soon as I ease off pressure just a fraction, the big fish goes ballistic and goes on a series of really gut-wrenching runs up and down the deep water of the margins. Eventually it tires and I begin to lift its heavy bulk out of the deep darkness and up to the surface. An extremely long, dark shadow slowly transforms into a golden-bronze fish as the sunlight cuts through the gin-clear water and dapples off its broad back. It looks absolutely fabulous swimming in this crystal water, but minutes later it looks even more stunning when I unfold the mesh of the landing net and gaze down on 30lb of colossal barbel. For a few precious moments I am reined almost speechless by this wondrous New Year prize. It is only then that I realise that it is my thirtieth monster-sized barbel of the winter. My barbel total for the period between mid-November and New Year's Day is two upper doubles and twenty-eight over 21lb with an average weight around 28lb. The top three of these weighed in at 30lb 6oz, 30lb 8oz, and 31lb+!

Less than 48 hours later, I am driving on the snowbound N1 route north, surrounded on all sides by the snow-capped mountains of the Sierra de Guadarrama; heading for France and onwards to the white cliffs of Dover.

"For a few moments I am reigned almost speechless by this New Year prize." Tony displays a 30lb 8oz barbel caught on New Year's Day (his third barbel over 30lb!).

NORTH AMERICAN

DREAM

The bigger the dream,

the higher you need to climb'

...The distant village church bells have just chimed four times and I'm standing half naked, up to my waist in water, while the solemn grey glow of predawn rises above the distant shoreline. Twelve feet of arched carbon shadows the water, while its slow-throbbing tip points at the horizon. The line is taught as piano wire and gale force winds play a whining tune on its narrow surface.

My skin is covered in goose pimples and I start shivering from a mixture of cold and intense excitement. Hundreds of metres out in deep water, a warrior is battling for freedom and I can feel the strong, powerful strokes of his tail, vibrating like a telephone message along the line and tingling under my palms. The rod is now locked solid, well past its test curve and the whistle from the wind against taught nylon turns into a high-pitched scream. I dare not give the fish any more line, because I can now see the metal showing at the base of the spool. I try to lift the rod up from its horizontal plane, but it doesn't budge an inch and remains almost parallel to the water....

Into The FRENCH-CANADIAN WILDERNESS:

Tonnes of iron and steel rattle the cement and timbers of the bridge as we leave Perrot Island and cross over to Chênes Point. The north-facing window gives me views over the Lake of Two Mountains (Lac des Deux Montagnes) and the islands of Avelle, Hiam, Wight, Harbec, Sunset, and Béique. Beneath us flows the southern arm of the River Ottawa as it squeezes past the bridge pillars and ripples against the islands of Chevirier, Ronde, and Pins, on its way to meet the mighty St Lawrence River and to flow as one into the giant Lake Saint-Louis. It is but a fleeting glance of green islands and brown water, for soon the tarmac and bricks surrounding Dorion Station hide the view. I lift the heavy rucksack onto my back, shoulder the rod tube, and then squeeze out of the train. Dark grey thunderclouds rumble over the rooftops, dropping their heavy loads from the skies until the gutters are filled with rushing water. My leather boots squeak under the strain as they walk along the Boulevard St. Jean-Babtiste and Route de Lotbinière which both cling to the muddy banks of Rivière des Otaouais. Clammy pools of sweat begin to form beneath my clothes as even the breathable capacity of Gore-Tex is overloaded by my constant exertion. Even though the rain still pours from the sky in sheets, I decide to stop to take off my over-trousers and then continue in only shorts. Almost an hour passes by before I finally reach the Riverside Campsite and collapse on the lawns in a soggy heap. As if to signal its gratitude for my hard labour, a gap opens in the clouds and a bright hot sun begins to beat down on the grass. After stripping off my waterproofs, I lay with my back propped up against the rucksack and watch the sparkling waters of the river. Steam rises in clouds as the rising temperatures begin to vaporise raindrops from the grass. Trees stand half-submerged in the rising floodwaters and giant Bullfrogs croak from freshly made pools. I set up my small Gore-Tex Mountain bivvy well back from the rising waters and spend most of the afternoon walking the banks of the river, while my clothes and gear dries in the glorious sunshine.

The day wears on until the twilight hour sees me back at the camp in front of a roaring log fire built from wood kindly provided by the campsite owner. Two rods are set up and I cast boilie hookbaits + PVA stringers past the submerged fringes of reeds, where 2 metre deep water flows over a clear bed of sand and gravel. I am not bothered whether I get a take tonight, just chucking out in hope.

Tomorrow I will have my carping head screwed on and begin some serious fishing. I unfurl the sleeping bag on the self-inflating Thermo-rest mat then climb inside, and within minutes my tired body drifts off into the world of dreams.

The first light of dawn greets me with a continuous melody sung from the hearts of Redwing blackbirds that perch in the branches above my bivvy, or hop across the flooded grasslands in search of worms. I slept quite well last night and only needed to rise from my sleeping bag twice to remove Channel catfish from the hook. On the second occasion I was so tired that I just reeled in both baits so that they wouldn't disturb me again.

There is a vast bed of reeds stretching upriver from the camp and it should provide good spawning grounds for carp at this time of year. With the river so high, there is no way that I can reach any part of it from the campsite area. Yesterday I found a small section of bank that gave me access to the other end of the reed bed about 1km upriver. A few nice carp were spotted during that exploratory walk, so I will head for there first. The end rig is stripped from one of the rods and I grab the small daypack and landing net, and then walk for almost 1km up the road, before eventually turning through an opening in the trees. My footsteps become quieter on the grass and I begin to creep stealthily like an Indian scout, until I am able to peer into the weedy margins. The river now almost covers the tips of rushes and the floodwaters have drowned hundreds of acres of land to form a giant backwater. Many carp hold stationary near the surface with their upright dorsal fins glistening in the sunshine, but they are just too far out to cast to and a profusion of weeds, lilies, half-submerged branches and other debris lie between us. It would be suicide to try and bring a hooked fish back through that lot.

There is a small, narrow and fairly clear channel in the weeds running almost parallel to the bank in front of me. Two carp were basking in this area yesterday evening, but nothing is showing at the moment; so I turn away from the water and my boots retrace my footsteps back to camp in search of food to satisfy a rumbling stomach.

I've just been chatting to Pierre, the campsite owner. He's a French Canadian, but he speaks some English and has agreed to let me borrow one of his boats for free. This will allow me to search throughout the flooded backwaters and bring me much closer to the carp.

A rod, reel, water bottle, and daypack filled with various items including floats, leads, hooks, and a couple of carp sacks are loaded into the boat and pushed off from shore. The boat is made of metal and during the next half an hour I'm taught the lessons of how to avoid clanging the oars against the sides, and just how close I can actually get to basking carp. But despite my efforts, the float-fished sweet corn and floating dog biscuits are ignored completely. Most of my problems are being enhanced by the change in weather. First, layers of clouds drift across the blue sky to hide the sun; then light drizzle lowers air temperatures, and now a strong breeze is blowing across the river. The high stands of thick bull rushes closest to the deep section of the main river are blocking most of the gusts of wind, but the wave action is making it almost impossible for me to keep the boat still and quiet.

Using the oars in the rowlocks just makes too much of a racket and I'm unable to spot carp with my back to the bow, so I am kneeling at the front of the boat and paddling with a single oar. This gives me a better view of the waterscape and allows me to stop the boat before it slides over the carp's heads. To avoid spooking them, I dip the paddle and dig the blade into the bottom silt and let the

boat slowly slide to a halt. The anchor (a large stone tied to a rope instead of a chain to avoid noise) is then gently lowered over the side.

Most of the larger carp seem to be cruising around the inner edges of sheltered rushes in fairly deep water, which is preventing me from touching the bottom with the oar, and the wind is compounding my difficulties.

A nice mirror suddenly crashes out about 100 metres away in the centre of a vast section of arrowhead lilies. The anchor is quickly pulled back up and I paddle across the bay to investigate. When I arrive at the approximate area where the carp leaped, I am confronted by a mass of fizzing bubbles in a small open section in the tangle of lily stems. By the look of the disturbance, there seems to be quite a few carp probing the bottom mud in search of food. As quietly as possible, I lower the anchor stone then open up a can of chickpeas and throw a few handfuls to sink amongst the rolling clouds of disturbed silt. Fresh brown clouds continually kick up to mingle with the clear water and I continue to flick out more chick peas until the water in front of the boat begins to rock with the carps activities.

A float is slid up the line and a single chickpea placed on the hook, then a quick flick of the wrist sends it out across the water to land with a gentle plop. The float cocks with the weight of the pea alone, and then slides under. It must be too heavy for the float, so I lift the rod tip, only to have it wrenched back down! A 26lb 4oz common carp has sucked in the pea as it sank towards the bottom and is now churning the bottom into a cauldron of boiling mud. I increase pressure on the rod and let it curve through its complete progressive power band, and then hold it there. The carp goes berserk beneath the rod tip, constantly showering the boat in sheets of spay with its flapping tail, but I don't give an inch of line and soon engulf it in my landing net.

The commotion has obviously moved the other carp away from the feeding area but I'm sure that the extra layers of disturbed silt still rolling in brown clouds will attract them back. More handfuls of chickpeas are thrown out and I sit back to wait. Eventually the red tipped float rises high and falls flat. A strike meets solid resistance and for three seconds the water just boils beneath the quivering rod tip while the carp tries to fathom out what is happening; then the clutch suddenly begins screaming as the carp explodes on the surface and tries to flatten half the weed bed. Within moments a bow wave has placed 25 metres between the boat and me and I am about to up anchor to chase it, but fortunately the line begins to cut through the soft strands of lily stems. The carp explodes on the surface and I use this opportunity to keep the fish high in the water. With steady and unrelenting pressure I am able to regain line lost, until the big common is circling in a wide figure of eight beneath the rod tip. Soon it is all over and I hoist a fabulous looking 35lb common over the gunwale and lower it onto the inflatable mat. This coincides with the heavens opening again to drop buckets of water on my head. By the time I've managed to sack the carp, heavy rain is pounding the surface so hard that it is difficult to distinguish the river from sky. It is still early afternoon, but I think I'll row back to camp to photograph this carp and then call it a day.

I row out to the same big weed bed on the second day and soon stalk a lovely brace of commons weighing 16lb and 31lb 2oz, but yet again heavy rains stop play and I return to the campsite.

It is now early morning on my third day in Quebec. The grey clouds have at last completely disappeared and the sky is a rich, cloudless blue. The boat is loaded up again as usual, but I have added an extra type of bait to my armoury - big, juicy lobworms! Before the boat has even entered the interior section of the weed bed I begin to spot carp; many of them. These rising temperatures must be moving the fish and this particular reed & lily bed is the largest I know of on the lower Ottawa, and so must therefore be the main spawning grounds for hundreds of fish. Temperatures aren't quite high enough yet for spawning, but shoals of carp will already be attracted to it from their normal haunts of the deeper main river.

The first fish to suck in a wriggling lobworm is a sprightly 20lb+ common, which gobbles up the bait before the bigger carp that it was intended for, can open its mouth! Twenty minutes later, a wonderful 33lb 6oz common gives me a tremendous tussle and tows the boat for 50 metres through the lilies before I can eventually land it. The thirty is quickly sacked and lowered over the left gunwale, which tends to tilt the boat to one side making it very difficult to row the boat properly. Luckily I'm soon able to stabilise the boat by hooking and landing another big common, and filling its 37lb 2oz of weight into a sack and lowering it over the right hand side! The action has been so furious and exciting that I've almost forgotten about eating and drinking. One can easily dehydrate in this strong sun without cover, so I quench my thirst with fluids from the water bottle, then row back slowly to camp for a photo session and a well earned lunch.

It is so hot now that I haven't eaten much for lunch, but my eyes keep wandering back to the big weed bed. It seems that I have a bigger hunger for carp than food, so I'd better row back out on the river before I die of starvation!

Soon I am back inside the densely packed reeds and lilies, hunting for yet another golden torpedo to thrill the senses and make the heart race. Within an hour of intensive stalking I am covered in sweat but manage to hook into my third thirty of the day, an extremely powerful 36lb 9oz common which tests my tackle to the limits in lilies that seem to grow thicker by the hour in the intense afternoon heat.

In the evening, while we watch sparks from the campfire rising towards the stars and extinguishing in the cold night air, Pierre tells me an interesting story. Some years previous, he was travelling with his family in the untamed regions of the vast Vérendrye Fauna Reserve – a landscape of lakes, rivers and forests spreading across thousands of square kilometres of wilderness in northern Quebec. One day, his son was standing on a bridge that crosses just one of the thousands of rivers which criss-cross this forested region, and began excitedly shouting for him to join him. When he reached the bridge and stood beside his son, then looked down to where his son was pointing, his eyes raised in their sockets. There below them on that warm spring day, swimming in the clear rushing waters of a stream that fed one of eastern Canada's largest lake systems, swam a shoal of absolute monster-sized carp.

I place another log on the fire and watch the hot red flames licking for a foothold in the cold night air. Pierre helped photograph my 33lb, 37lb brace of commons, so I have no doubts that he understands what a big carp looks like, but my eyebrows rise in surprise when he tells me that the fish he saw were considerably larger than my 37 pounder. I question him on size, shape and length

A bear takes a cool kip! This brown bear is sleeping in the lake during hot weather in Canada!

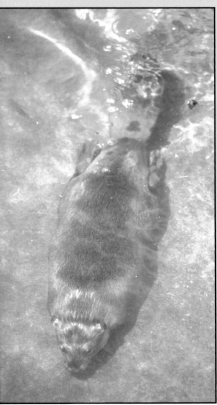

This amazing photo shows carp feeding below Bernie Haines float in the clear waters of the St Lawrence River. Notice the boat anchor in centre of picture, surrounded by big fish!

A wild beaver swims along the bottom of the river, sending up a stream of bubbles.

of the fish he saw and if he had taken into account his height above the river and refraction, etc. The bridge was low over a small and fairly shallow clear river and the carp were near the surface. It soon becomes apparent that the carp he saw at close quarters with his son that day were very special. Indeed, both our estimates put such fish in excess of 60lb. Pierre goes back to his house and brings out a large-scale map of 'Réserve Faunique La Vérendrye. Under the yellow glow of a flashlight my eyes follow his finger as he traces it across the paper until it stops on an almost insignificant junction of thin blue lines in a huge maze of green and blue.

"There, near an outflow of that lake is a bridge over the stream where we saw those carp," explains Pierre as he twists the top off another bottle of beer and hands it to me with a smile.

The stars continue to slowly spiral above our heads as we talk on through the night. By the time the roaring fire is but a small bed of red glowing embers, Pierre is back in his house and I am lying in the darkness of the bivvy, my mind churning over with plans. Tomorrow I will rise before the sun and begin my long journey north into the Canadian wilderness.

I take a train from Dorion to the capital city of Ottawa, book into a cheap hotel and then spend a few days looking around. I had already obtained a special licence to fish for carp throughout the large state of Quebec when I visited the Ministry of Fishing and Hunting in Montreal. While I was there, I was lucky to meet Jacques Bergeron and Michael Letendre, two experienced Biologists who gave me free access to the private books and scientific papers in the Montreal Library of Biology.

Michael also gave me an important contact in Ottawa to gather more details on the history and studies of carp throughout North America, so I go to this address first. With this information plus knowledge gleaned from E.J. Crossman and W.B. Scott of the Department of Ichthyology and Heretology, Royal Ontario Museum, Toronto, I am able to piece together a complex map of carp stockings and natural migrations throughout the vastness of Canada.

As much as I am enjoying my stay in Ottawa, after two days here I am already getting itchy feet to travel north. After obtaining some wonderful large-scale maps of the northern forests and river systems, I head for the Voyageur Colonial Bus Station at 265 Catherine Street and book a ticket. Within two hours the Route 521 bus is whisking me over the Ottawa River Bridge and onwards to its destination of Grand-Remous, near the awesome expanses of Baskatong Reservoir.

It is dark by the time the bus pulls into Maniwaki, so I walk to the small campsite just north of town and erect my tent beside the river. After breakfast I meet Guy Bois, a representative for Environment Haute-Gatineau – a group that fights to protect the environment of the northern Gatineau River system. To a background of rippling waters, we discuss together the problems of keeping this pristine wilderness safe from pollution and giant logging firms. Our conversation is filled with my probing questions concerning the movements of carp. In such pleasant surroundings I am tempted to stay a while, but this section of the Gatineau River does not look the right place for carp, so I take another look at a 1:250 000 Scale map of Mont-Laurier District. The map is covered in green and blue – indicating a thousand square miles of forest and water. The Gatineau is a major tributary of the Ottawa River, so it should hold carp, but the incredible Baskatong that is 25km wide and over 45km long, just pulls at my pioneering spirit.

I decide to head north towards a wilderness camp situated on Lake Fiske, which is connected to the big Sable Bay arm of Baskatong. But during the bus route to Grande Remous, I change my mind and decide to head for the Mercier Dam. My main reason for this is that if carp are swimming up the Gatineau, they will congregate below a major dam holding back the waters of Baskatong. It is still a little too early for the large migrations of carp up fast, oxygenated rivers to reach spawning grounds, but there could be some early arrivals or even possible resident populations.

From the town of Remous, I begin walking north on route 117 in the hope of hitching a lift. Vehicles are sparse in the far northern wastelands, but after an hour of sweating beneath the crippling weight of my rucksack, a pickup van stops beside me. It turns out that he owns a house situated on the banks of the river at Rapides Bitobi. My interest and questions about carp surprise him, but he suddenly seems keen to answer them.

"Carp? Oh you should have been here last week! There were literally thousands of them spawning above the rapids opposite our house. They come upriver to spawn this time every year; most of them have gone back down river now though. It's really beautiful up near the house and there are some Bald Eagles nesting up near Lion Falls. You're welcome to stay at our house if you want, or you can set up a tent beside the river..."

He looks a real wild Hillbilly, as most of them do around these parts, and he doesn't stop talking but I smile and nod my head. How could I possibly refuse such an offer? The van turns down a deserted track that winds for 5kms through evergreen forests, until it reaches a large old wooden building perched only a stones throw from the river. The faint yellow glow of oil lamps brightens the dim interior and as I step inside the doorway, three half-shaven faces stare at me like wolves at

This pristine conditioned 40lb 8oz Canadian carp was caught on float-fished maize in the margins of a major river.

The Author with a 42lb Canadian river carp taken at long range on pop-up maize.

a kill. My mind is filled with apprehension, but their handshakes and warm smiles soon dispel a tinge of fear. Cold beers are handed round and one of the brothers cooks us all a feast fit for kings. Later that evening I erect my tent beside the river and cast two baits into a marginal eddy, and then prop the rods on the Optonics. This is indeed a magical place. All I can hear are the hoots of an Eagle Owl perched in the branches of a giant Fir tree that towers above my head, and the gentle song of water rushing over pebbles. I sit on the lush grass and wait. I sleep inside the bivvy and wait. For two whole days and nights I wait, but nothing comes, not a single bite or a single sight of a carp. I walk the banks and search for signs, but the only fish that I see are Suckerfish and the only crash I hear is when the beautiful Bald Eagles swoops low over the water and crashes sharp talons through crystal waters.

On the second day, after a long talk with one of the brothers, it transpires that the name 'Carp' in this region refers not to our beloved Cyprinus carpio, but to the White Sucker (Castosomus commersoni) or the Quillback (Carpiodes cyprinus) that grow to a maximum of about 5.5kg. Suckers belong to the Family Catostomidae and there are 59 species found in North America. The high arched back of the Quillback looks very similar to a small common carp, except for a snub nose and elongated primary ray of the dorsal fin – like a long 'quill' from which its name is derived. It is a close relative of the Smallmouth Buffalo (Ictiobus bubalus), Bigmouth Buffalo (I. Cyprinellus) and the Black Buffalo that all look like heavy shouldered common carp and can reach more than 50lb in weight (and occasionally 100lb), but these giants are not found in the Ottawa River System.

On the third morning I get a lift to Grand Remous and then catch a bus heading north on route 117 towards Rouyn-Noranda. The road winds for hundreds of kilometres through dense evergreen forests, over rivers and streams, and past endless expanses of shimmering blue waters. I have with me a superb large-scale map of La Vérendrye Reserve, showing all the campsites and canoeing routes. Just looking at this map, with its mind-blowing number of lakes makes the fine hairs on the

Two carp are caught by the author's camera as they leap up a waterfall in Canada.

This superb carp from USA, was caught wade-stalking with a live crayfish hookbait.

back of my neck tingle with anticipation. As I stare out of the window the bus continues to whiz past millions of trees and billions of gallons of water, until the fading light of dusk finally hides my view.

The location on the map where Pierre spotted the monster-sized carp was on a connecting stream to the Lake Camatose system. It is two years since Pierre's sightings of the big fish, so I am obviously not under the assumption that carp are still located in the stream that flows beneath that same bridge! Although they could still use that particular stream as a through-route to other parts of this vast network of interconnecting waterways during spring migrations, it is too early in the year for them to be there now - I think! But the map does show a campsite on the eastern shores of Lac Camatose, so it will be a good place to begin my search.

By the time the bus reaches Grand Rapid, a halo of light rims the outer treetops, leaving the inner forest locked in darkness. I had planned to trek overland through this forest wilderness, but it is obvious now that a canoe or kayak will need to enter my plans. My map indicates 'Accueil Lac-Rapid' - what seems to be a large central visitor centre - so it should provide overnight camping, canoe rentals and further information; but it turns out to be a tiny building and it's closed! I dump my rucksack on the grass and look around me. The red glow of bus taillights, fade into the night, until I'm left at the side of the road in total darkness. An owl hoots at the starlit sky, and away in the distance, a wolf howls at the moon. Yet again, follicles of hair begin to rise involuntary on the back of my neck.

Suddenly, the forest is filled with the sounds of an engine firing into life, and then two headlights beam down a track and almost blind me. It is Paul Morin, one of Quebec's many Range Wardens, and as soon as he spots this mad Englishman standing in the pitch darkness holding a rod tube, he feels

The stunning beauty of Yosemite National Park.

the need to investigate. The screech of rubber on loose stones sends up a dust cloud beside me. Paul soon informs me that Lac-Rapid provides few facilities, no camping and no provisions to buy food. He is heading back down the road to Accueil Le Domain, where there is a place to stay overnight and canoe rentals - would I like a lift? An hour later, I am fast asleep inside the luxury of Domain's rental chalets, planning an early morning assault on Lake Jean-Pére.

As the dawn mist begins to twirl and rise above the giant firs, I am already kneeling in the centre of a canoe and slapping a paddle into the cold, dark waters. The heavy rucksack is counter-balancing my weight and makes it easier to guide the vessel in a smooth, straight course through these tranquil waters. My passport, money and other small items are encased inside an Orloebt waterproof wallet strapped to my waist, and the camera equipment is inside a large waterproof Dry-bag that has also been filled with air to keep it buoyant if it goes overboard.

An eerie, far reaching call carries across the waters and fades into the distance. The beautiful sounds emanate from a Great Northern Diver, or Loon as they are called here, which glides along the surface only 30 metres in front of my canoe. The white band markings on its black neck look like keys on a piano, and a bright ruby eye shines within a glossy head of ebony. Suddenly it slips inside its own mirror image and disappears beneath the depths, to re-emerge about 80 metres further on, with a miniature silver fish wriggling from a black beak. The head jerks back, and instantly the live feast is gone; then it sends another warbling, drawn out cry across the waters of Jean-Pére. My arms stroke the paddle downwards and backwards in a steady rhythm, lifting the excess water and flicking it off a shining blade. The rhythmic slap and splash mingle with the call of the Loon, as the canoe carves a moving 'V' on the lake's surface.

The clear water fades into blackness and I can sense that the canoe is already sliding over extremely deep water. Lake Jean-Pére stretches its wet fingers through 20kms of northern forests, but feeder streams connect it to thousands of other lakes. I could paddle onwards for years.

There are two giant islands located in the southern section of Jean-Pére, but these are surrounded by hundreds of smaller islands. A birds-eye view would reveal each green island in a sea of blue, but sitting here at water level makes everything blend into one. A tree-lined bank seems to stretch completely across the horizon only 500 metres ahead of me, but no matter how much I keep paddling towards it, the bank never gets any nearer. All day, the bow of my canoe chases a constantly retreating horizon, but never seems to catch up with it. An hour before dusk, I've had enough and turn the canoe towards a small island.

By the time I've erected a bivvy and ate some food, the first hungry flying scouts are sniffing for blood in the fading gloom. I begin to set up a single rod but the added heat of exertion brings beads of sweat to my forehead, and when combined with sweat from a day of hard paddling, it gives off a lovely odour for the miniature vampires. Winged friends join their team until a buzzing swarm is dancing above my head then descend like locusts on my face and hands. Soon a moving black cloud formed by a million humming insects blocks the sky out.

There are now so many mosquitoes that even the 100% DEET doesn't seem to deter them from their feast. The bait is cast somewhere or anywhere towards water and as soon as the tiny 'plop' is heard, I chuck the rod in the rest and dive inside the bivvy. Hundreds of individuals dive-bomb the mosquito netting and I watch in horrified fascination as they stab and probe through the minute mesh holes in hope of contacting warm flesh. The drone of a billion wings is so loud that it is giving

Tony cradles a massive common carp caught in very fast, deep waters of a big river.

White-tailed deer in the high mountains above the wild rainforests of Olympic National Park.

Bernie Haines fighting a powerful river carp in scuba gear!

me a headache and the mosquito netting has become so choked with bodies that it blocks out all remaining light and darkness falls inside my bivvy before the red sun has even slipped below the horizon.

These incredible black swarms of mosquitoes often descend on Caribou herds and can drain so much blood from some individuals that they cause a slow and agonising death. I have never in all my travels around the World, ever seen so many mosquitoes at one time. The loud scream that fills the air is incredible and I now understand how some gold prospectors and explorers of the far north have been known to succumb to their onslaughts over a period of days without adequate cover or protection.

For the next few days I paddle onwards through the unending waterscape of La Vérendrye - searching for carp during daylight and camping on wild, mosquito-infested islands during darkness. Not a single big carp is spotted.

Eventually I become tired in my quest and decide to head back to shore and take another detailed look at the maps. The mighty expanses of the Cabonga Reservoir complex spread across 5,000 square kilometres of uncharted wilderness. Just staring at this impressive blotch of blue on the map gives me goose pimples. But looking more closely at the mind-blowing network of waterways snaking through the forests, reveals that the water from Cabonga actually runs SW into Baskatong, which flows into the Gatineau River. I now have my doubts about waters in the southern and eastern sectors of the Vérendrye Reserve holding concentrations of carp, especially outside of the spawning migrations. Some isolated shoals must surely exist, but if I am to find the carp without a motorboat or lifetime of hours at my disposal, I must look elsewhere.

To find the carp I must search closer to the main Outauais watershed, for larger concentrations of fish will be found there. Further investigation of the map reveals that there may be a barrage splitting the huge Dozois Reservoir from the Cabonga Reservoir. If this is so, I should revert my interest from the Cabonga to the Dozois. My big Vérendrye map shows red direction-of-current-arrows as the Ottawa River flows out of Dozois into the impressive 60km long Grand Victoria Lake, then into Granet Lake, Jordan Lake and the northern Carrière Bay of the mighty Decelles Reservoir. I went to try Decelles, but there are no bus routes down the Twin Rapid road, so I opt to take the Rouyn-Noranda bus again, then get off at Accueil Nord - the Vérendrye's northern visitor centre. From there, I shall hopefully be able to thumb a lift to the Granet Lake campsite.

When I hand back my rental canoe at Domain, it transpires that the last bus north on route 117 just went past 5 minutes ago and the next one will not be until tomorrow! A quick change in plans has me crossing to the other side of the road to catch the last bus heading south to Montreal, and then a train back to Dorion. During the long bus journey to Montreal, I start up a conversation with the passenger sitting next to me. It just so happens that he also likes fishing for carp - which is a very unpopular fish with most Canadians! He lives in Val d'Or and is travelling to meet friends in Mont-Laurier. A number of lakes surrounding his hometown contain carp and only one week previous he landed a 20lb+ mirror from Lac Rouillard. This information interests me greatly, because Rouillard is a lake situated on a tributary of the upper Ottawa River between Lac Lemoine and Lac Mourier. The small tributary enters the Ottawa about 80kms upstream of Lac Simard, which must mean that carp have colonised Simard. The tributary junction is only 25kms downstream of the Reservoir Decelles, so I ask him if he's seen carp there and his answer confirms my suspicions. My pioneering spirit is suddenly on the boil again and I feel the urge to explore the vast, open waters of Decelles, but the only problem is that this bus is motoring down the winding forest road in the completely opposite direction!

Two days later, and I finally arrive almost 1,000km downstream of the beautiful Vérendrye Reserve, on the productive stretch of the lower Ottawa River near Dorion. Within hours I am back in a boat, stalking carp in the giant weed beds and soon hook into a 40lb+ common carp....

Why did I spend so much time and trouble searching endless stretches of virgin territory upriver, when I could have stayed near Dorion and caught good fish? The simple answer is because I love to pioneer new and untouched waters and blanks are part and parcel of searching the unknown.

Those first few weeks in Canada were very special and sowed the seeds for more adventure. During the next decade, this strong passion to explore drove me on to search for carp in ever-widening horizons throughout North America. In Canada, this pioneering quest took me again through the untamed marshes and densely forested wilderness of northern Quebec and Ontario, then onwards to the majestic snow-capped spires, placid azure-blue lakes and raging white water rivers of British Columbia. In U.S.A. my search ranged from the arid desert moonscapes of Nevada, Utah and Arizona, to the sweaty, humid heat of alligator-infested swamps in Louisiana and Texas. Through lush rainforests of the Olympic National Park and over jagged peaks of the Cascades, then across sun-baked plateaux of east Washington. Searching reservoirs that nestle amongst rugged valleys of California, and on to the spectacular high altitude waters of the high Sierra Nevada. I was to follow many false avenues, which resulted in the inevitable blanks; but when everything came right, the prizes far exceeded my expectations.

Tony submerges a big North American river
carp back in the clear waters.

DANGEROUS PERSUITS

Fighting a Great African Wedgefish in the Gambia River, West Africa. This monster broke the line just seconds after the photo was taken.

During a lifetime of fishing adventures throughout the globe, I have amassed not only a lot of fish, but also an amazing amount of macabre moments or near death situations. The following true tales are just a small selection from a vast vault of scary memories!

WITCH DOCTORS & AFRICAN MAGIC

The tips of the four carbon-Kevlar rods quivered to the vibrating movements of the big Rapala lures. The engine's constant beat was the only sound that pierced the noonday heat. European bodies stripped of their winter clothes, turned pink under shining layers of suntan oil; their heads grew slack and bobbed in rhythm to the rod tips as the mounting hours of inactivity and heat took their toil, then...Bang! The left-hand rod wrenched round until it was almost pulled out of the gimbals as line screamed from the big Shimano reel.

Hassan, the boatman, instantly moved the throttle to push the boat forward and so help in setting the hooks. There was a bulging of water about 50 metres behind the boat and for split seconds everything went silent, as if we were in a slow motion movie. Then out it came...a solid wall of silver, rising higher and higher, until full 2 metres of shining scales thrashed the water to foam. John tried to manoeuvre the rod to keep the line away from its body, but it was all too late and the huge fish fell back on to the mainline and broke it with a resounding 'crack', before disappearing under the mountain of waves. John stood in dejection as the limp line blew in the breeze...Then out it came again, angry and defiant, shaking a massive head and flaring its gills in a desperate attempt to get rid of the lure. On a third leap, the big Rapala plug flew from its bony, cavernous mouth and the wall of silver once again sank into the white foam; then all was silent. We all stood like statues in open-mouthed awe, until Martin finally broke the spell and uttered-
"WOW!"

The next few minutes were frantic on the boat as lines were reeled in and Tarpon lures were attached. These are the same as the original Magnum Rapala plugs, except that both sets of treble hooks have been removed. Trebles were found to be completely inadequate for hooking big tarpon and time after time the fish had thrown the lures after mangling the trebles beyond recognition. Instead, a 15ft length of 200lb-test nylon rubbing leader is attached to a large, strong single Mustard Tuna hook (in size 4/0 – 6/0). The plug is then attached to the bend of the hook by a few twisted strands of copper wire. When a tarpon hits the bait, its huge mouth completely envelopes both lure and hook. The thin strands of copper then break on impact and leave only the strong, sharp single hook lodged in its iron-hard jaws. If many barracuda are in the area, the single hooks will have to be connected directly to the plugs own hook fitting so as to prevent unnecessary loss of expensive lures. However, this is not so reliable as the copper method because attaching hooks directly to the fittings allows a big tarpon to use the plug as a fulcrum to lever out the hook points as it jumps. Some large plugs such as the Rebel Jawbreaker, which has two sets of self-swivelling treble hooks attached directly to an internal metal spine, gives superb hook holds and can alleviate most of the problems.

Hassan swung the small 20ft Orkney boat around in a large arc as the Rapala-Tarpon lures were let out once more. The rod tips again bounced and vibrated to the pull of the strong action plugs, but this time the whole atmosphere aboard the boat had changed and the air was thick with expectation. Each angler now ignored the inviting cool that the overhead canopy provided from the searing heat of the sun, and instead, sat tight to his or her rods and kept all eyes peeled on every movement of the rod tips.

The first tarpon had hit close to a large rock that lay just inches beneath the surface and it was as we were passing this same area for the third time, that something huge struck again. There was a flash 60 metres behind the boat as it hit one of the middle lures, but missed, then rocketed across and crashed into the outside lure, causing the rod to whack around in a fantastic curve. With some difficulty, Peter lifted the rod from the gimbals, but this time the welcoming sound of a ratchet as line ripped off the spool at an alarming rate, told us that the single hook had found a hold in the bony mouth.

All of a sudden the scream of the ratchet fell silent and the line went slack. Peter couldn't believe his bad luck and almost threw the rod into the water in anger. I immediately screamed for him to take the bow out of the line.

"Reel, Reel, REEL!" I shouted in alarm.

Peter realised what had happened and began to turn the reel handle frantically, but it was not until almost all the line had been replaced on the spool that he again made contact with the fish. The curve of the line suddenly straightened and the rod wrenched down until the tip sank under the surface and Peter was almost pulled overboard.

We were positioned in only 4 metres of water and down below the boat we could see a massive grey submarine moving swiftly under the bow. The line began to slide dangerously against the side of the boat, but Hassan expertly swung the bow round and we watched the big shadow emerge on the other side. I noticed the angle of line cutting sharper and sharper with the surface.

"She's coming up!" I shouted.

Then, only 10 metres from the boat, a gigantic fish broke the surface film and threw itself at the sky. The impact as its heavy body crashed back down through the waves was like thunder, and we were covered in a shower of spray. Shouts of excitement came from all on board as Peter desperately tried to keep in contact with the fish. Again and again, she threw herself from her elements, before screeching line from the ratchet on incredibly powerful runs.

It was not until 1-hour later that the fish was tired enough to bring alongside the boat. I grabbed hold of the thick, nylon rubbing-leader and pulled the tarpon closer, until my hand could grip the edges of its cave of a mouth, then gently dislodge the hook. The huge fish lay quietly in the water beside me and I touched its big armour-plated scales that shone like silver sovereigns in gold dust. What a beautiful fish, and what an incredible fighter! This, my first introduction to the queen of the sea, was my greatest.

The setting was The Gambia, a long, thin strip of country surrounded on all borders by Senegal and caressed by the warm breezes off the western coast of Africa. The huge and mystical River Gambia is its lifeblood and stretches like a snake through impressive tropical forests and deep mangrove swamps until it reaches the Atlantic Ocean.

Always be careful when a big fish is hooked on a large lure – be it plug or spinner. The treble hooks can easily whip out at unexpected moments and lodge deep into your flesh. It happened to one of my guides in the jungles of southern India, and twice to myself during two years of intense fishing in river and coastline of The Gambia. Both incidents were serious, but the second was more so....

'Places of darkness roam the deepest corridors of hell, but the darkest places of all can be found here on earth'

Dolphins swimming up the Gambia River - scene of "African Magic"!

.... I was leaning over the side of the boat and was about to gaff a very lively 8kg Barracuda for one of my guests. The angler was piling on the pressure with a 30lb line-class boat rod on a very short line, and then in his excitement, almost tried to lift the fish out of the water. He was an inexperienced fisherman and I shouted for him to ease up on the pressure; but it was too late. The barracuda shook its head wildly at the surface and threw the hooks. The rod, which was locked over into its full bend, recoiled like a powerful spring and sent the massive Magnum Rapala flying like a bullet, straight into my face!

This particular Rapala lure is one of the largest plugs made, and one of the huge barbed, treble hooks pierced my upper eyelid and became deeply embedded behind the eyeball. I thought at first that the hook point had shredded the pupil and blinded me; but after a terrifying torment of darkness, I slowly peeled the eye open and was glad that sight remained with me. The lure had been catapulted with such dramatic force, that one of the large hooks had sunk well past the bend and the hook point became lodged behind and inside the eyebrow bone, which prevented it from puncturing the delicate eyeball tissue – for the time being!

The four passengers on the boat were all holiday clients and each seemed in more shock than I was. It was then left to my black African boatman to try and pull the gigantic hook out using rusty pliers. A wave crashed against the bow and he almost poked my eye out with the pliers, so I ripped them out of his hands before he caused more damage and continued the job alone. First, the Rapala plug was still hanging on my face and the bottom trebles were dancing free and liable to impale my cheek; so this was removed with great difficulty. One hook was hidden deep within the eye socket, but the remaining two hooks of the treble were pointing outwards, and it was important to get rid of them before they penetrated the skin. There followed a terrible ten minutes of blindly trying to cut quickly through the thick joint of the treble hook with pliers whilst trying to balance steady on the boat in choppy seas.

I tried to feel gently with my fingers to ascertain the damage, but without a mirror I could not see how deeply embedded the hook was and was terrified to find out just how close the point and barb was to the back of the delicate eyeball. All the passengers took a closer look at my eye, and the thick chunk of metal poking out of the eye socket reflected off their pupils. They could not hide their horror at what they saw, which did nothing to stem my own fear. I needed to get urgent medical attention before a sudden jolt moved the hook point and made me blind forever.

We were still 1-hour sailing time from the nearest port, so I decided to leave my boatman to take the boat passengers back, and then dived over the side and swam for 500 metres through shark-infested waves and rolling breakers to reach the shore. Then I ran to the nearest hotel, through the foyer and up to the reception and asked-

"Could you please get the manager; it's urgent."

She was busy browsing through a pamphlet and when she looked up, she saw that I had one hand cupped over my face.

"Urgent? The manager is very busy at the moment; can I help you?"

Alan, the manager was actually a good friend of mine and on a recent fishing trip aboard my boat he had even managed to catch a superb 300lb Stingray – which broke the existing I.G.F.A. World Record. The receptionist continued to inform me that the manager was not available at the moment and asked me to come back later; but when I lowered my hand and stared at her with my one good eye, she let out a loud scream and ran off along the corridor! Moments later, she reappeared at the reception area with Alan. He assessed the urgency of the situation immediately and phoned for a colleague to bring a car round to the front of the hotel, then whisked me off to the nearest medical centre.

A doctor at the medical centre told us that he was unqualified to assist me and then went off looking for someone who was. We sat on a bench in the stifling heat for more than half an hour. No one came back. I was getting slightly annoyed, so Alan's friend walked off to find someone. He returned with the head doctor, but as soon as he took a look at my eye, he said that it was way too serious for him to treat and that I should be rushed immediately to hospital in the city.

Banjul, the capitol and only city of Gambia, was a long and dusty trip over pot-holed roads, and because no ambulance existed at the medical centre, Alan drove me there himself. Most of the city was packed with people and heavy traffic, so it took at least another hour to reach the main hospital. I cursed every time the vehicle jolted my head as it bounced over yet another deep crater in the road. Unbelievably, the doctor at the hospital informed me that I would have to go to a separate emergency unit, which just so happened to be on the opposite side of the city!

Time was ticking away frantically and I knew that it would take too long to reach the emergency unit in the car, so we chose to walk. The directions they gave us, as normal in African countries, were totally wrong, so after walking down a lot of false avenues we finally arrived at the correct address.

A dusty set of steps led up to an old door with half the green paint peeling off the wood. We stepped inside and entered a dark and dingy corridor that led to a single room with two hospital beds. Both beds were empty, but sitting on the floor beside one of the beds was a black African woman. Her left hand held a big spoon that was busily stirring food in a large, iron pot, and in her right arm nestled an infant who at that precise moment was avidly suckling on one of her over-sized naked breasts.

The thought of undergoing major eye surgery in such an unhygienic environment gave me the shivers. I almost stormed straight back out of the door, but Alan calmed me down and persuaded me to follow the nurse into another small room, where she asked me to sit on a metal chair and wait. Thirty minutes later, she returned to inform me that a specialist Eye Surgeon could only treat the wound, but there was none available today so she would have to telephone to try and find one.

I sat quietly losing my patience while the nurse rang several different numbers, until she finally contacted a surgeon who was willing to see me.

"Yes, yes doctor, OK. Yes, he's sitting here now. What? ...Give him an injection...Yes, OK...Intravenous; err, Yes, OK...is that under the skin or in the muscle?"

I almost choked as she said it. She's a nurse and doesn't even know how to administer injections?! I sat fidgeting nervously on the chair while I watched her walk over to a table and begin searching inside the draws. They were so overfilled with papers and junk that she needed to slip her hand into the half open draws and press down on the piles to enable her to open them fully.

"What are you looking for, nurse?"

"Syringes." She replied.

"WHAT the hell?" was all I managed to say as my good eye began searching for a way out of this living nightmare.

All kinds of diseases are rampant in this part of the World and the last thing I needed right now was a needle full of AIDS virus. My throat went dry at the thought of it. She walked over to the sink, opened two doors beneath it and began searching behind the bleach and Vim canisters! 'Sometimes the needles fall behind the sink.' She calmly informed me. By now, I was anything but calm.

The nurse then walked over to another cupboard with over-filled draws and began searching through the detritus. Suddenly she stopped what she was doing and lifted a small package triumphantly in her hands. I walked over to her to take a closer look. It was a needle & syringe heat-sealed inside a sterile package. I could spot no tears in the plastic, so grudgingly allowed her to fill the tube with unknown liquid and jab the needle into my arm. She was unsure how to administer the injection, so I had to show her first. I knew that my years in Veterinary hospital would come in handy one day! I was then told to go back to the room and lie on the spare bed. Thankfully, the woman in the other bed had finished cooking and suckling her child and had been asked to leave the room.

Almost another hour had passed before the nurse re-entered the room with a young half-cast woman in tow. It seemed that this was the long-awaited 'Specialist Eye Surgeon'. I took one look at her and thought 'no way', but as soon as she began speaking and asking intelligent questions, It eased some of my doubts. She was educated and well spoken, with an air of authority – I just hoped that she was an experienced surgeon!

Alan had brought a treble hook off a Rapala plug to show the surgeon exactly what was imbedded behind my eyeball, because only the broken base of the tip now poked out from the eyeball. She took one look at the huge treble hook and raised her eyebrows in surprise.

"You mean to say that the complete hook is hidden inside?"

"Yes, doctor, and look at the size of that barb; you can't just rip it out..." I began to answer in tones of alarm.

After a thorough examination, the surgeon decided to just give me local anaesthetic and proceeded to pierce the skin of my cheek and eye socket with a series of injections. This was followed by a period of waiting for the anaesthetic to take effect.

"Does that hurt?" she asked, as she squeezed around the eye socket with finger and thumb.

"Just a numb sensation, doctor" I replied, and then looked at her with horror as she gripped a pair of long-nosed forceps in one hand and a sharp scalpel with the other, and then leaned over me.

"Good, Mr Davies-Patrick. Then we shall begin..."

The next 30 minutes were nothing short of horrific. First, the upper eyelid was cut open using the scalpel and the forceps were inserted in the opening. Exploratory twists and pulls failed to dislodge the hook point. More and more incisions were made to the internal skin and muscle tissue, but nothing seemed to work. At one point, the doctor actually climbed onto the bed beside me so that she could obtain a better leverage with the forceps. The arms of the metal long-nosed forceps were now pushed so deep inside my head that the finger grips were lodged against the eyeball. She began pulling, twisting and tugging in desperation, until her efforts actually lifted my head off the pillow and Alan was needed to grip both my shoulders just to hold me on the bed.

By now the pain was so intense that I almost lost consciousness. I felt my voice letting out an almighty scream; but the voice was inside my head as my brain fought to keep me from passing out. Never, ever, have I been submitted to so much pain – even when, many years later, someone shot me in the head – and the only thing that prevented me from passing out into oblivion, was the thought of waking up without an eye.

Halfway through the operation, the doctor stopped what she was doing and bluntly told me something that I didn't really want to hear.

"Instead of local injections, I should have giving you a general anaesthetic to put you to sleep. I just didn't realise how bad the situation was. The hook is far deeper than I realised and the barb is too big to pull back through. I want to put you to sleep because I know that I am now hurting you more than I ever wanted to do, but it is too dangerous to do so now and I must continue with you awake."

I was by now in a state of delirium, and the only thing I wanted was for her to stop the immense pain stabbing at my brain each time that she tugged or twisted the forceps behind my eyeball. One incredible hour later, she climbed back off the bed and stood triumphantly beside me with her hand in the air.

"At last, we have got it out. Look! It's the biggest hook I've ever seen! Do you want to keep it as a souvenir?"

She then handed the bloodied hook over to Alan and picked up a giant, curved needle.

"Now then, I suppose we had better close up that gaping wound in your eye before half of Africa's microbes make a home there"

Three days later, I could be seen looking closely at my reflection in the mirror with a pair of sharp scissors in my hand. I was supposed to go back to the hospital in Banjul to have the stitches removed. There was no way I was going to go back to that terrible place, even if a team of wild horses tried to drag me screaming. So, I leaned closer to the reflection of my eyeball and slowly cut the stitches out myself...!

SIERRA ROLL

...It was a cold, dark night, deep within the heart of the wild Spanish mountains. My bedchair clung precariously to the steep-sided slopes, while I slept peacefully beneath a canopy of stars. The heat of the day had already evaporated into the giant vault of cloudless darkness and now a freezing wind blew relentlessly across the lake. To block out the cool air and maintain body temperature, I had pulled up the zip as far as it would go. The wind's icy tendrils continued to search for cracks, so that it could suck out any pockets of warmth, but now only my nose tingled to the breeze as it poked out from a tiny opening in the sleeping bag.

The previous 24 hours had been hectic, and after a day of blistering autumnal Sierra heat, my brain had become numb and I now lay almost comatose within the envelope of cosy duck feathers. So deep was this sleep that it must have been a few seconds before a high-pitched note triggered an alarm to my brain cells. Two eyes blinked open, but I seemed blinded as they tried to focus on the inside of the sleeping bag hood. Instinctively, my body sat bolt upright, which partially pulled the hood back from the right eye and gave me a glimpse of a red Delkim diode. But the view was only fleeting, because the sudden force of my torso lifting into an upright position caused the lower legs of the bedchair to collapse and fold beneath me. With both arms still locked by my sides inside the sleeping bag, I was catapulted straight off the cliff!

Like a piece of tumbleweed blown in the wind, I began tumbling head over heels down the mountain. My arms fought to stretch out and cushion the blows to my body, but they remained clamped to my side as turf, blood and stones flew in all directions. A massive, shoulder-high boulder stood in my path and I head butted it with full force, ripping open the skin in a red gash between tip of nose and scalp. But the impact was not enough to stop my downward flight. Still locked inside the sleeping bag, I spun straight over the rock then plunged into the lake until water closed in around my head.

Darkness, bubbles, and shock threw me into a catalectic state as I sank slowly to the bottom; but a sudden impulse of wild panic electrified my fingers and unlocked them from temporary paralysis. With savage frenzy, I clawed at the zip until somehow it slid down enough to enable me to swim free. After dragging my drenched body back up the shoreline, I collapsed in a soggy heap of exhaustion; but something was still screaming inside my brain and as my eyes focussed on a red light high above me, I suddenly realised that the carp was still on!

Somehow my mind was able to function enough to climb back up the slope, strike the rod and play the fish to the net. It was a lovely common, but I was in no fit state or frame of mind to want to prolong our acquaintance, so let it swim immediately away from my open palms. The waterlogged sleeping bag was dragged out of the deep margins, and then I began to search for a torch but couldn't find it. As I sat on the mountainside and stared down at the inky water, shivering with cold and shock, a cool sensation began to slide down my face and neck. My hand reached up to trace the source of discomfort and found it as a searing pain jerked my head back at the touch. Thick, warm liquid flowed in rivers over my cheeks and fingers. My brains thumped in pounding beats and felt as if half my skull had caved in. 'Oh my God!' I thought to myself; what have I done to my face?

Sid was fishing only 100 metres further along the bank, so I shouted over to him, but received no answer. I began to walk half blind along a narrow goat track that clung to the steep edges of the mountain. My legs were still shaky and I stumbled a few times in the pitch darkness, but eventually managed to locate Sid's bedchair. Quietly I called his name to wake him, but he didn't move a muscle - he always did sleep like the dead! My wet hand reached out to his shoulder and shook gently; then more vigorously.

"Sid...Sid...SSSiiiiiiD! Wake up!"

The sleeping bag began to move, and then a head poked out from the top and a scruffy looking character looked up at me. He coughed out some phlegm and then spoke in a gruff tone - I don't think he was very happy...

"What the f**k do you want? Do you know what bloody time it is!"

"I've fell in, Sid. Have you got a torch? I think I've split my head open."

He reached under his bedchair, then handed me his torch.

"Here, take this, and don't bother me again tonight."

Trying to hide my facial scars from the camera while holding a big, powerful common, caught on the day following the 'Sierra Roll".

And at that, he simply rolled over then went back to sleep!

"Sid!"

"WOT!?"

"Can you take a look at my face?"

"Can I what?"

"Take a look at my face, Sid; I've head-butted a big rock and..."

"You've f**king done what?"

"That stupid old bedchair that you've loaned me has bloody collapsed again...It flung me down the mountain and threw me into the water. I hit a giant boulder with my head on the way down. It feels pretty bad, can you take a look?"

This last sentence persuaded Sid to prop himself on to his elbow and grab the torch from my hands. He pointed it at me and the beam lit up my face. His head jolted back in astonishment, and then he asked me to come nearer. I kneeled down beside him until the torch beam almost blinded me.

"SHIT! Oh my god...Oh my GOD! What the hell have you done to yourself, Tony!?..."

"What? What is it? Does it look bad, Sid?"

The vision that faced Sid in the torchlight must have wakened his deepest nightmares. My complete face was covered in blood and only the whites of my eyes blinked from behind a sea of gushing red liquid. He now shot off his bedchair and began running around like a chicken with its head cut-off.

"I've got a medical kit, but first we need something to clean up all that blood...now where the hell did I put those cloths..."

Finally he came back to my aid, holding a fistful of rags.

"Let's take a closer look at it."

Then he began wiping away the fresh and encrusted blood from my face.

"Oh, it's not as bad as I thought, Tony. I don't think the wounds are too deep. There's a deep gash and a lot of skin is missing from your nose and forehead, but I think you'll survive. You're not going to look such a pretty sight in the morning though."

My face jolted back and I gritted my teeth as the antiseptic solution made contact with the soft, moist lumps of open flesh...

Eventually a red ball of fire lifted above 'Penon de la Cuna' and beamed soft shafts of light down on the clear waters of 'Embalse de la Encinarejo' – Lake Montana. The warming rays began to lift layers of moisture off the calm surface in spiralling columns of white clouds that vanished into a vault of blue. Carpets of mist descended the valleys and crept over my bedchair, depositing moisture on the cool, outer layer of the Gore-Tex sleeping bag cover. I glimpsed half-heartedly at the rodpod, but all seemed normal, so I just pulled the hood back over my eyes and slept on.

A few hours later, rising temperatures began to turn the sleeping bag into a sauna, so I peeled open the bag and opened my eyes, only to be almost blinded by a blazing white-hot sun. My head felt as if it had been squashed in a mangle, and my fingers began to search for moist areas around the cuts, but found only swollen mounds of flesh and scabs. I stumbled along the mountain edge to wake Sid and applied for some sympathy, but only received a bucket full of laughter when he opened his eyes.

"Christ, Tony, it looks as if you've been run over by a truck!"

As mentioned previously, this was not the first time that the old bedchair loaned from Sid had let me down. A few days previous, I had been fishing in another location of the lake opposite the dam wall. Close to the southwestern corner, high, steep banks gave superb views of carp as they fed slowly along the marginal shelf. The sheer wooded cliffs and dense undergrowth gave no comfortable options to set up my gear, so I chose to position the rodpod on a point overlooking the dam and cast diagonally across the lake. This meant that I was further away from the margin patrolling fish and would enable me to relax more without fear of disturbing them. Each of the three hookbaits were cast very tight to overhanging bushes and submerged boulders, then at dusk, I walked around the steep cliffs and dropped handfuls of boilies in accurate baiting patterns around them.

Carp had seldom, if ever, come across baits positioned in this area, so I was not surprised when they fed avidly on the boilies that first night. What did surprise me was the strength – or shall I say lack of strength – of the ratchets on Sid's wonderful old Fox bedchair.

It was during a hectic feeding period about an hour into darkness when it happened. The alarm started bleeping, the Baitrunner began revolving and just as I sat up, I let out a yelp and began screaming! The reason was that I had been sleeping with my right hand close to the cog on the adjustable headrest, and when I sat upright at the first tone of the Delkim, my palm rested in the grooves in the metal ratchet. Somehow, this was a signal for the ratchet to suddenly give up its support and the headrest sprung forward, trapping my hand inside the inter-locking metal teeth. As I wrenched to free myself, the back legs of the bedchair collapsed beneath me as the ratchet simultaneously revolved two cogs and dragged the skin of my palm inside it. With the complete weight of my screaming body now on top of the half collapsed bedchair, I was unable to open the headrest to free my hand.

Eventually, the pain was just too much and I decided to wrench the hand free, pulling a large lump of skin and flesh from the inside of my palm in the process! The Delkim was still screaming at me that a carp was trying to empty the spool, so I ran over to the rod and struck into a fast swimming fish. A lot of line was out, but fifteen minutes later, a wonderful looking common carp slipped inside my landing net. In the commotion, I hadn't had time to find my torch; but when I eventually located it and switched it on, the bright beam lit up a butchers nightmare. Bright red blood was everywhere – my hands, rod, reel, landing net handle, bedchair, sleeping bag, and even the mud around my swim – it looked like a scene from the film -'Interview with a Vampire'!

SHOT IN THE DARK

'No man is safe from trouble in this world'

The beams from the headlights cut a path through the darkness as I swing the car round yet another bend in the road. I've been driving for hours, but still haven't found a place that has good access to the lake. Fatigue is beginning to overwhelm me and I can feel a pain behind the eyes. My knuckles try to wipe away the ache, but they only force tears to well up in blood-red sockets so that it impairs my vision. It is like driving under water. If I don't stop soon there's going to be an accident, so in frustration, I pull off the road to take a rest. Within minutes my eyelids close and I begin to drift into sleep, but the cool night air makes me think about some added comfort, so I walk to the back of the car and open the boot. Just as I am about to take out the sleeping bag, a siren shakes the night's silence and a blue spinning bulb lights up the inside of my car like a jet's cockpit. One of the two uniformed officers jumps out of the patrol car and rushes to my side with his hand hovering over his gun holster.

"Anything wrong? Can we help you?" He asks.

"No, no problem officer; I have just this minute stopped the car. I will be driving off again soon."

He glances inside the boot, just in case I forgot to inform him about a dead body, and after a few questions seems satisfied that I'm not a mass murderer, so he wishes me a pleasant trip before eventually walking back to his companion. The red taillights of the cop car disappear over the ridge, and once again my ears tune into the loud drone of crickets calling from the desert grasses. I climb back inside the car and think what to do. It's getting late and I desperately need some sleep. I don't fancy spending hours looking for a campsite, so I turn the car around and head along the river road that leads to the dam.

A sign points to the Pine Flat Dam Overlook and car park but the road is closed and will not re-open until 07:00hrs. It is worth staying close by so that I can rise at dawn and view the lake from the Dam Overlook, as this will give me a better idea of where to begin my search for carp and spot any likely looking feeding areas. I drive back down the road for half a mile and then pull onto the grass verge, hoping that the cops will not bother me again tonight. It is not wise to sleep in the driver seat because your foot can jam the brake lights on and drain the car battery. So I pull down the backrest of the front passenger seat, then get myself comfortable and soon fall into a deep sleep....

While I sleep in the valley of dreams, it abruptly feels as if someone smashes a sledgehammer with full force across the back of my skull. Instantaneously, my brains and a car window seem to explode within the heart of darkness....

The impact is so sudden and horrific that it jolts my body forward as if struck by lightning, my eyelids spring open, and my face is almost thrown through the windscreen. At the same instant, my ears catch the screaming yells as a vehicle sweeps past my car. I think that some beer-swilling idiots have thrown a rock through my window, so I scream obscenities at them as their car whizzes past...Then silence.

My thoughts and brain patterns shift into overload. I look for my keys but fumble like a child, desperately trying to find the slot in the darkness. Eventually I find contact and start the engine then, with difficulty, slide across into the driver seat. I want to drive after them to vent my rage, but as I twist my head and look through the rear window, I see three pairs of taillights slowly moving up the road. Anger is quickly replaced by panic.

I am about to drive straight down the road in the opposite direction, but I'm sure that when I looked at the map last night it showed that this road leads to a dead end. I certainly don't want to be trapped down there with a group of thugs in the middle of the night, so I grab the steering wheel and turn the car around.

I drive only about 50 metres when I notice a bunch of headlights parked on the brow of the hill on the road ahead. Damn! They are waiting for me! My automatic reaction is to turn off the headlights so that they can't see me. Instantly, night blindness throws the road ahead of me into a black abyss. I slow down and try to keep the car on the road, but it is too late as I feel it skid across the grass then bounce over rocks and boulders before my panic braking eventually brings the car to an abrupt stop. The gear stick is rammed into reverse, but I begin to scent the putrid odour of burnt rubber as the wheels spin madly. I climb out of the car and run to see how bad the situation is. It is worse than I think; the car now sits with two wheels hanging off the edge of a cliff and I've narrowly escaped from driving it straight over the edge....

I now stand alone in the middle of the road. The car lights on the hill have gone. Total silence; except for the blood gushing through my veins and the pounding throb at the back of my head. Panic turns into dread and fear. What if they come back? I am completely alone. A thought suddenly enters my head and I rush to the car to collect the keys so that I can open the boot and remove the expensive camera gear before they return.

As I lean across the front car seats there is a cold, damp sensation at the back of my neck. It urges me to switch on the internal car light. Instantly it lights up my nightmares. Bright red liquid is

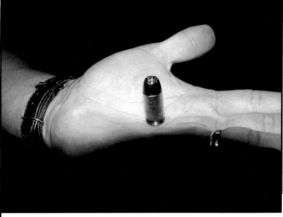

The bullet went through the door like cheese wire.

A sheriff visits Tony in hospital and shows him a massive .45 calibre bullet similar to the one that hit his head!

pouring from my head, and the car seats are splattered with blood. I grab a T-shirt and try to ebb the flow. Strangely all I can think of is to not get too much blood on the upholstery because it is a hired car!

I try to hide my bags of camera equipment, but can't find anywhere in this almost desert landscape, so am forced to tear at clumps of grass in an effort to camouflage them in the open field. I stumble back to the car, then look at my watch - 03:30hrs. It will be a long wait for morning. I lower the T-shirt and feel around the wound with my fingers. It is soggy wet and my hair is caked in dried blood. I begin to worry about how serious the injury is and realise that it may need urgent attention. So I begin to walk down the lonely road in the darkness and say to myself that if the cars come back for me I will roll off the road and lay in the grass until they pass. Luckily they never return.

Eventually on reaching the crest of a hill, my eyes spot the lights from buildings nestled in a valley about another mile in the distance. When I reach them and see the vehicles parked outside, they look vaguely familiar - is it them? Amongst the din of barking dogs, I stand outside the lighted windows trying to listen for drunken men talking inside. My apprehension gradually subsides and I pluck up enough courage to knock on one of the doors.

The occupants are a bit wary of me at first. An old man sticks his head out of the window and says that he will ring the sheriff on my behalf, then he goes back to sleep! Fortunately, his son, Jeffrey, is a bit more concerned and after showing him the gaping wound in my head, I manage to persuade him to drive me back to my car to remove the precious gear before it is all stolen. When we reach my car I immediately begin looking inside for the rock or object that must have been thrown through the window.

"I can't find anything in here", I shout as Jeffrey walks to the other side of the car and shines his torch to assess the damage.

I notice a rip in the upholstery inside one of the doors then rub my finger along the tear.

"Whatever smashed through the window must have made this gash, but its strange how...."

Then Jeffrey interrupts me and quietly says, "They've shot at you!"

The remark fails to register properly and all I can muster to say is "What?!"

Jeffrey moves his torchlight closer to the car door then continues talking.

"I think it's...Yep, it's definitely a bullet hole. The crazy idiots shot at you!"

My mind starts spinning as I quickly change my search and begin desperately hunting for an exit hole through the other side of the car. There isn't one. Neither can I find a bullet. It can only mean one thing, yet my mind still cannot accept it.

"Let me take a closer look at that wound," says Jeffrey, as he walks over and asks me to lower the blood-encrusted T-shirt from the back of my head. The bright torch beam shines a path for Jeffrey's fingers as they pull back the matted clumps of hair to expose the soft, red grunge of my scalp.

"There's definitely a hole in your head, Tony, but I can't see any exit hole..." Jeffrey mutters softly then stops, as his probing fingers suddenly touch a soft spot and I wince away in pain.

"Oh my God...do you know what this means?" and just as I say it, Jeffrey looks into my eyes and his pupils reflect my own desperate fear. There is only one conclusion - the bullet must still be in my head!

The ambulance seems to take forever, but we eventually flag it down as it screams down the country road, followed by no less than three police cars with flashing blue lights and wailing sirens. Cops and paramedics flood the roadside then swoop on my blood-spattered body like vultures. A barrage of stupid questions stream from the cop's tongues as the paramedics strap a blood pressure band to my arm, pierce needles in the other arm, shine lights at my dilated pupils, and stick oxygen tubes up my nostrils. Then someone begins to take photos of the bullet hole in my head with a Polaroid camera... My mind begins to scream at the absurd chaos, and all I can think of to ask the doctor is -

"Is the bullet still in my head?"

On the first night after leaving hospital I am afraid to sleep in a tent and definitely don't fancy sleeping in my car again, so I book into a hotel and try to calm down. But by morning, covered in sweat following a succession of nightmares, I know that if I do not face my fears I will never be able to do the thing I've come to love: - travel to wild and unexplored places of this planet in search of big fish. So I pluck up courage on the second night and erect my tent on the yellow sands of Point Magu - even though I still choose to park my car between my tent and the main road to shield it from possible drive-by shootings!

As the Californian sunshine wakes me on yet another glorious morning, I slowly realise that most of my fears have flown. For the moment though, I still don't feel the urge or confidence to go fishing again, so I take a short drive along the coast road until the smell of the saltwater makes me stop. I grab my camera and tripod from the boot then find a quiet spot and sit cross-legged on the warm sands of Malibou Beach. Crazy memories still haunt my thoughts, but with my eye pinned to the viewfinder of the camera I try to block them out and concentrate on the scene. The giant blue waves of the big Pacific Ocean roll and crash before me, and as the 400mm lens carries me to the sun-tanned surfers riding each fabulous white crest, my confidence begins to soar. I can feel the freedom and wonder of the unknown in the power of nature as each wave thunders against the rocks. I know now that I will always need to face my fears to enable the true spirit of the Globetrotter to continue riding and searching for the perfect wave.

"To keep the Globetrotter spirit free, I needed to keep searching for the perfect wave."

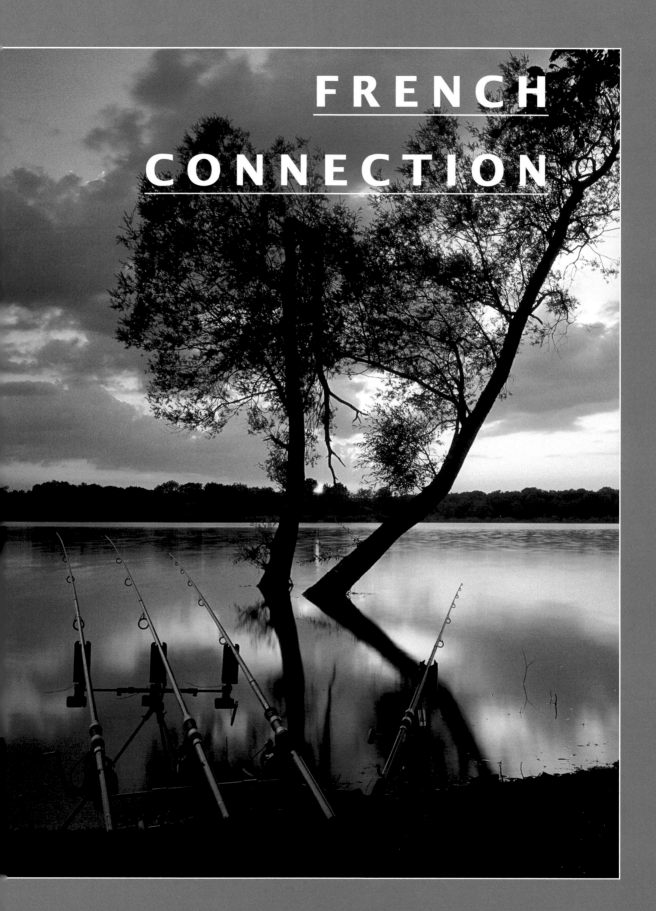

FRENCH
CONNECTION

It's May and I'm on the banks of a large gravel pit in eastern France. I arrived here yesterday following a long drive south from the big Lake Madine, northwest of Nancy, in the 'Parc Regional De Lorraine'. I was due to meet a Dutch friend, Leon Hoogendijk on the banks of Madine, but after a day of looking for him and constantly leaving messages on his mate's mobile, I still couldn't find him. This meant that I would have to fish alone, which was no problem, except that Leon had the boat with him and I wanted to fish from Bois Gérard Island. I detest the noisy, public areas of Lake Madine, so most of the morning was spent searching for a quiet, untouched part of the lake to fish from the bank. After driving down a deserted track and parking beneath the shade of forest canopy a few kilometres north of Montsec, I eventually discovered a wild and overgrown bay. But due to recent heavy rains the water level was still a little high, which would force me to spend most of my time wading back and forward through knee-deep margins to be able to cast beyond the reeds. It was indeed a superb looking area, but swarms of mosquitoes were already dancing over the swampy marshes and I didn't fancy the hassle. I mapped the place in my brain and promised to return when the water level was lower.

'Where shall I go from here?' I thought to myself. Contacting Leon was never easy at the best of times, so I gave up on that job and seriously began thinking of waters beyond Madine. The river Mosselle runs very close to Madine, and the stretches near the town of Pont-à-Mousson have produced carp to 70lb+ in recent years. One of my Dutch friends had shown me a video of carp to 60lb being caught from a secret stretch downstream of the nightfishing area. I visited this stretch the previous year with two pals from Amsterdam, but by that time the normal access road had been blocked off, which prevented us from leaving our cars within sight of the swims, so we drove elsewhere.

Other areas of the river have produced stunning fish and one recent 60lb+ has been landed from the stretch near Pont-St.Vincent. I also know of a small, secret back-arm of the Mosselle near Dieulouard, which has produced plenty of forties. But the 'secret' seems to have got out during the past 18 months, because now the two small swims with beautiful overgrown banks have been torn open and the place looks like a rubbish tip. My heart sank when I saw it again, this time completely devoid of green grass and now replaced by mud, empty cans, paper and human excrement. I drove further downstream and found some wonderful looking areas, especially around Liverdun; but because of the high water levels, I eventually turned away from the Mosselle Valley in search of stillwaters.

So here I am, back on one of my favourite French waters after many hours of driving south on the motorways south from Nancy. This lake holds special memories in my heart since I first visited the overgrown banks almost 15 years ago. Now the forests of trees growing tight to the eastern banks have matured and dip their densely leafed branches into the margins along the entire length of shoreline. The west shoreline, where I now sit, is more open with green meadows and copses of trees set at intervals. The openings in the trees provide natural places to set up a bivvy and I'm glad to see that even though the lake ownership has now switched into new hands, the water still retains its magic.

I have only ever blanked once at this particular lake, and this was during that very first visit during the 1980's. I was forced to give up because of the hungry crayfish and massive swarms of Black Bullheads (Ictalurus melas) that would reduce my large boilies to the size of peas within minutes.

Tony and Leon Hoogendijk look for signs of feeding carp, as the early morning sun rises over a mist-shrouded River Saone.

This Bulhead is a miniature catfish species that was introduced to France during the early 1900's and has now over bred and run riot through most French rivers and lakes. Since that first lesson, I have always carried plenty of rock hard air-dried boilies with me on most foreign expeditions. On my previous visit to this water almost two years ago; I managed to land a stack of good carp, including two mid-forties on extremely hard 20-22mm baits fished at 140 - 180m distance. My baits were placed on top of a wide plateau during that session, and now three of my 20mm double-boilie hookbaits are in position in waist deep water on that same plateau, and a fourth is positioned in deeper water at the edge of the plateau shelf. Maybe they shouldn't be, because just ten seconds ago a big carp rolled tight to the overhanging trees on the far bank, and I didn't get a touch on the plateau baits last night.

There are quite a lot of odd bits of discarded line lying around this swim, so it looks like it has started to receive some hammer since my previous visit. I'm not too perturbed though, because most of this is beginning to rot, and the fresh green grass plus an absence of bare ground or any bank stick holes indicates that it has had plenty of rest during the winter. I spend the next ten minutes gathering up the discarded line and odd bits of paper hidden in the bushes then sit back down on the bedchair. The small road running parallel to the lake used to give direct access to this particular swim, but now this entry is blocked by a high fence that circuits most of the water. The only possible access now is by a singular gate near the lakeside restaurant and then by a muddy dirt track that follows the western margins. When I first saw this fence I was disappointed and thought that it was now completely private, or that expensive fishing licences were enforced. But after speaking to the restaurant owner I realised all my fears were unfounded. The licence is still as cheap as ever, night fishing is still allowed and at this moment not a single other person, let alone angler, is on the water. I know from experience that the weekend periods, especially during summer, can be hectic on this lake and the profusion of boat traffic can drive you mad. But now, in May, the lake looks tranquil and calm with only the sounds of birds singing.

I've got two weeks to spare, but I'm not sure whether to spend the whole period here or move onto another lake next week. You have to really work for your fish on this water. They have seen it all from a number of highly experienced European anglers during the past, and combine this with the low density of carp per acre can make it a very long wait between takes. About 90% of carp anglers tend to blank on this lake and it is mainly the beautiful scenery combined with the odd lump crashing in their swims that keeps them sane. I will stick it out for at least the next three nights before I make the decision to move to different water.

I watch two Marsh Harriers, but then realise that they are Red Kites circling low over the lake in front of me. Occasionally they swoop down and plunge their talons into the water and scoop small prey off the surface. Kites normally hunt over open fields or marshes and it is rare to watch them fishing like Ospreys. The young bullhead catfish form tightly-knit shoals that swarm in living balls just beneath the surface at this time of year, and I'm sure that the Kites are taking advantage of this abundant food source. The large Grey Herons, squawking and fighting as they spiral above the overhanging branches along the opposite shoreline, have also found the larder. I wish they caught more of them, because they don't seem to even make a small dent in the huge numbers of catfish.

The time is now almost 20:00hrs. Dark grey banks of clouds have been moving low over the water for most of the day. It was quite mild at midday, followed by short periods of drizzle that gave a slight chill to the air, but now the rain has stopped it has turned mild again. Evaporation carries with it the lovely odour of fresh leaves. Sudden breezes also waft the scent of Scopex and putrid flesh across my nostrils. I accidentally knocked over a plastic bottle of bait soak an hour ago. Those Nash dips don't half honk quite a bit! I've poured water over it to try and disperse the greasy slick, but now the grass beneath my rodpod shines like an oil refinery and stinks like a skunk's rear regions...

A gentle breeze slowly dies away and turns the surface of the water into a sheet of glass. Faint ripples begin to wrinkle the surface, and within ten minutes the whole lake becomes dimpled by a thousand miniature rings. The line on the right hand rod plucks a few times, then slackens slightly. I'm tempted to hit it, but feel that a cray or catfish is the culprit, so remain seated. Darkness is beginning to creep in. I'll give it another 15 minutes then reel in and check the baits. I cant believe these mild temperatures, because it was absolutely freezing a few days ago in England, yet here in France I've been dressed in T shirt and shorts all day!

A nice carp tops near my right hand hookbait at 20:35hrs. Then another rolls slightly closer in than the tightly baited area. As I haven't got a dingy with me, I've been using the big Cobra throwing stick to chuck out the freebies. During a session here the previous summer I actually swam out with boilies inside a plastic bag, but the water is still too cold at the moment. The only problem with catapults and throwing sticks is that some boilies always go astray during the baiting up. That last carp looked like it was feeding over some of the odd baits that dropped short of target. Judging by the small amount of fizzing bubbles kicked up by the carp each time it disturbs the bottom, it looks like it is moving round picking up single items. Another twinge vibrates on one of the rod tips, but I still think that cats are to blame. I'm using four rods on the Solar Globetrotter Pod.

Another carp gently lifts its head above the surface about 25m closer in than the plateau then slips back down with hardly a ripple. A puff of light brown debris rolls up in a tiny smoke cloud as the carp disturbs the bottom silt. It is unusual to see them feeding so close in. I've had so much past success from the big plateau that I still have bags of confidence in it, but if I don't get any takes tonight I will try one of the hookbaits closer in.

It's just coming up to 23:00hrs on 11th May. I am a bit cheesed off at the moment because I missed a good take about 5 minutes ago. I was sitting in the car, which is parked right next to the bivvy, and listening to the radio with the door open. During the evening, when it is easier to pick up MW bands on the radio, I sometimes tune in to pick up the English news or just to listen to a voice to break up the hours of solitary silence. I had just tuned into BBC radio, when the Delkim suddenly lit up beneath the right hand rod and began emitting a constant high-pitched tone. The fish really screamed off and even though only seconds passed before I reached the rod, already a lot of line had flashed through the rings. The line was whipping through the rings at such incredible speed that I dared not strike hard into it for fear of cracking off. Instead, I just disengaged the Baitrunner lever, and then leaned into the fish. For some reason the hook didn't find a good hold and the line instantly fell slack. Normally I always strike hard into a fish, and curse myself for not doing so with

Sundown on the famous Lake Orient - home of 70lb+ carp.

A deep-bodied 45+lb mirror carp, hooked at dusk on rock-hard air-dried boilies, fished at extreme range.

this one, but there will always be the odd occasion when the hook point only penetrates a thin layer of soft skin tissue and no amount of luck will keep it there. On a lake such as this where 20% of my previous takes have been forties, the chances are quite high that this latest run came from a lunker – which makes me much happier now I think of it!

This take came to a 20mm Crayfish flavoured floater/Spice flavoured sinker combination soaked in Monster Pursuit dip and presented on a very short 2.5 inch bolt rig, cast out to the heavily baited plateau area in chest deep water. I should also mention that I'm pinching some Solar dissolving foam over the hook point prior to casting out so as to prevent from snagging up in the weed. There seems to be a lot more weed than I've seen in previous years. I am trying out this particular foam for the first time and although it seems to be doing a fine job, sometimes it pops to the surface almost instantly after the bait hits the water making me uncertain whether it stayed on until the bait hit bottom. I would prefer that it remained wrapped around the hook for just a few seconds longer.

I cast out a fresh bait to the plateau (I say fresh, but in fact they are ultra hard air-dried boilies which are now 2 years old! Pre-dried boilies can be kept indefinitely as long as they are stored to prevent the re-absorbtion of moisture.), then sit beside the rods until midnight, before climbing into the warmth of the sleeping bag. I'm soon asleep, but around 2 hours later a 15lb common carp picks up the 26mm spice flavoured single bottom bait on my extreme left hand rod. The pristine condition of the fish makes up for its lack in size. Ten minutes later, I get a short drop back on the right hand rod but nothing materialises. Small cats often cause these small drop-backs on the indicator when they continually hammer the boilies until they eventually hook themselves, which happens twice during the rest of the night.

Morning greets me with a very fine layer of windblown rain. A deep layer of grey clouds move with a southwesterly wind that blows crested waves down the lake towards the restaurant. I'm making up my mind whether to move with this wind to another productive area in a small bay near the restaurant. It's always quieter up this end than down the restaurant end. Yesterday there was a jet ski down there making hell of a racket, but it only stayed for one hour and at least it didn't come up this end of the lake. I think I'll reel in the baits and drive down to the restaurant for a quick shower, and also take a look around the bay for signs of carp while I'm there. The hot shower makes me feel good, but the look of the small bay doesn't. I've had some exciting sessions fishing that part of the lake but today it just does not give me the right vibes. The waves are crashing against the far bank and conditions look perfect for these swims, but I don't sense that the big carp have moved with this wind yet.

I get back to the swim and spend some time relaxing reading a good book: Living Dangerously – The Autobiography of Ranulph Fiennes. The book is quite poignant and parallels some of my own lifestyle, especially living dangerously, or should that read: accident-prone? As the day wears on and the sun begins to sink slowly behind the treetops I am soon to make, or should I say feel, my point...

It's 2 hours before dusk and I have just finished baiting up heavily and cast two hookbaits + PVA stringers back on top of the plateau, but the third I have placed closer in where the carp was showing yesterday. With the fourth hookbait I want to try six mini boilies (triple boilies on two separate hairs), and begin to thread them on the hairs with the aid of a needle. The smaller boilies tend to dry out much harder than the big baits, and these 8mm boilies are as hard as diamonds. The needle gets stuck halfway through one of the boilies so I'm forced to exert extra pressure to push it through. Suddenly the bait splits in two, sending the point of the barbed needle straight into my thumb. To make matters worse, the point enters the base of the thumb and is pushed at an angle almost parallel to the hand, right up to the nail and scrapes the bone. I scream in pain and the bag of boilies scatter like marbles around me. The baiting needle that I am using is the Big Fish Adventure dual model that can be crewed off the handle. I gingerly unscrew the handle and now all that's left sticking out of my thumb is the screw thread – the rest is deep inside my thumb from root to tip!

During the next half an hour I try to gingerly pull the baiting needle out of my thumb, but this means also pulling the barb back, which drags half the meat inside my thumb with it. I try to push the point of the needle further so that it will burst through the tip of my thumb, and I then can snip off the barb and pull the needle back through. But the point is lodged right behind the thumbnail and the last thing I want is to break the needle off inside my thumb, so I give up in despair. It looks like I'm going to have to take a trip to the hospital, but I can't leave all my expensive equipment at the lakeside and I'm loath to pack up all my gear with one hand. I'll give it one more try. If I pull very fast and hard in one motion, the barb might come free and hopefully won't cause too much damage. Let's go for it! First I wipe away the sweat formed on my hands during the past 30 minutes of exertion, so that I can secure a firmer grip on the screw thread. Then I close my eyes, count to three, and wrench back with full force. Amazingly, the baiting needle plops completely out of my thumb in one motion, followed by only a small squirt of blood. I lick my wound and go back to threading the larger 20mm boilies onto the hair...

Two French lads walk across the meadow behind me and stop for a chat. I tell them how slow it is here and advise them to fish another lake further along the valley. I suppose I'm being a bit selfish and would like this lake to myself, but the main reason is because many French carp anglers tend to fish very close to each other and I don't fancy them settling in the adjacent swim, which is only 30metres along the bank. Besides, I'm also fishing at an angle to the bank so their rigs would cross my left-hand lines. (I rarely cast straight out because most people do this and the carp quickly learn to associate these areas with danger). Not all French anglers are the same of course, and these two seem OK, but my mind is eased when I see the taillights of their car disappear in the darkness.

I settle in for the night, but don't need to wait for too long because at 22:30hrs I get a screaming take on the left-hand rod to the plateau. It has picked up the same big, spice boilie that produced the common, but judging by the power of this fish it feels like a much larger specimen. This proves to be true and following an exciting fight with the fish ploughing up and down the margins, the brutal power of my fully flexed rod saps its strength until the big carp rolls inside the net. The beam of my head torch lights up an absolutely stunning dark mirror with big silver scales. It looks about 35lb+, but just as I am about to transfer the carp to a sling, the clouds open up and it begins to rain quite hard, so I decide to sack the fish without weighing.

While the carp was tearing up and down the margins during the fight, it picked up two of the other lines. The rain is now coming down in sheets and is turning the swim into a mud bath. Even though the hookbaits hardly moved they could have been dragged into weed, so just to stop my doubt I

Tony with a colossal French carp caught at long range in 1 metre deep water. The fish picked up two 20mm boilies on a very short bolt rig.

put on my Gore-Tex gear and brave the elements. All four baits are checked and recast, this time without added stringers.

It's now 00:50hrs and the rain is still pounding on the outside of my bivvy. It hasn't eased up since I caught the mirror carp, but I'm very happy, even though the area around my rodpod looks like a quagmire.

I'm happy, mainly because there are now two full sacks staked out in the margins. Just before midnight, a big 41lb 8oz Italian mirror carp picked up the far right hand bait that was cast away from the plateau into deeper water. I had been watching this carp crashing out a number of times further out than my right hand bait, but had decided to wait for it to move closer and feed over the heavily baited area. I waited and waited, but two more leaps from the carp showed that it was staying at the same distance, but moving slowly away from the baited area. It was still like a monsoon outside and the sounds of heavy raindrops on my bivvy were deafening, but a gut instinct told me to get off my arse because 'this fish can be caught'. Eventually I could no longer blame the weather for my idleness, so climbed from the lovely warmth of the sleeping bag, donned the cold waterproofs then stepped out into the torrential rain. The right hand bait was reeled in as fast as possible, and then I ducked back under the bivvy canopy with the end rig. A buoyant crayfish and a normal shellfish boilie were removed from the Scopex dip and threaded on to the same hair. My hands were wiped dry as possible using a cloth, and then I picked out a pre-made thick strand PVA stringer from the bag and tied it to the rig. Then quickly before the PVA disintegrated, I picked up the rod and wacked the bait out as accurately as possible to the area where I thought the carp was

An electrical storm sends lightning bolts across a carpwater in eastern France. Notice the ghost image of Tony beside the Globetrotter Pod; this is because he left the picture frame during a long-time exposure of several minutes.

moving towards. Within fifteen minutes the bait was picked up and the Delkim's diode lit up the streaming raindrops in blue light. What a pity that I'd just climbed out of my waterproofs!

A bright sun shining through the open door of the bivvy wakes me from deep slumber. The grey clouds have been swept away by a strong westerly breeze and the sky is now a pure sapphire. Temperatures are rising steeply and everything – the leaves, trees, grass, rods, bivvy, car, - seems to be steaming as litres of water evaporate and rise in clouds of steam. The sound of a car door slamming makes me look down the meadow and I notice the two French lads I met yesterday, setting up their tackle. They must have blanked last night at the other lake (they don't spend long in a swim if they're not catching!), and are now moving in to a swim about 300 metres away from me.

A car drives along the tree line road and stops on the opposite side of the fence behind my swim. A figure steps out of the vehicle and I immediately recognise the face of a good local friend who I haven't seen in ages. Strangely enough, the last time we met was when he helped photograph a French 45lb 8oz carp for me; so now after shaking hands through the fence in greeting, he happily agrees to drive round and help take photos of the 30lb & 40lb brace. While he's driving round, I get my camera gear ready and choose a suitable place in the meadow that is receiving good light for photos. My preparations attract the two French lads fishing along the bank. There's no point in trying to hide anything from them now, so I ask one of them to take some extra photos with my spare camera.

A brace shot would be nice, but the smaller mirror is more spectacular looking than the bigger carp, so I decide to photograph them separately. I didn't weigh the first mirror last night, so I think I'll just quickly check it on the scales to see how close was my guess of 35lb+. I begin to wade out in the margins and untie the cord from the bankstick, but it feels strange as I draw the sack towards me. Then I stare down in disbelief at the half open sack. "Shit! It's empty!" This is one of my older Nash models without a zip and I normally tie an extra knot in the neck of the sack, but obviously forgot during the torrential rain last night. I quickly walk over to the other tethered sack, then feel relieved to feel a heavy moving weight inside. This one is one of Gold Label's big carp zip-sacks with an extra safety clip. I make a decision there and then to throw all my old sacks away and will replace them with new ones from Terry Eustace as soon as I get home.

I'm gutted about losing the opportunity to photograph such a wonderful looking fish, but at least the photo session with the 41lb+ mirror goes smoothly. The shots of the big mirror turn out OK, but I must confess to not having a love for fat-gutted Italian-strain carp and always prefer long, lean fighting machines. However, the two French lads seem quite impressed with the forty, so impressed in fact, that by the following morning they are noisily moving all their paraphernalia of carp gear and dumping it in the vacant swim right next to me!

I sit back on the bedchair in the afternoon sunshine, listening to the noisy French lads and contemplating whether to make a move to another water. Suddenly an English car with two occupants and full to the brim with carp gear comes driving across the meadow and stops behind me. A blond, long-haired guy who I've never met in my life, then sticks his head out of the car window and shouts across to me: "Hey! Globetrotter! Caught anything?"

AUSTRALIAN

GIANTS

The heat grows intense as the sun rises towards its zenith, until it hangs high in a deep blue sky above the Tabon River. Slow-moving 'V' formations are sliding on the surface. Ripples emanating from within a tangle of overhanging branches betray the presence of carp attracted in to the warmer, upper layers of water. Jens landed a 16lb common carp during the grey light of pre-dawn, but since that fish, our indicators have remained as if glued in position. Now is the time to go stalking - so I pick up a rod and landing net, then creep across the meadows.

Three carp are soaking in the warm rays that beat through a gap in the branches of a big willow tree. A network of branches grows almost horizontal to the river, and the lowest of these actually lay completely submerged. The carp cannot be reached from the bank, but one of the half-submerged branches should provide a stable platform for me to fish from, so I edge my sandals quietly along its length. The landing net arms are too wide to fit through the branches, so it is left behind on the bank - I can always shout to Jens if help is needed.

It seems to take forever for me to gently manoeuvre along the branch without disturbing the fish. Eventually, a position is reached on the branch close enough to enable me to present a bait. The three carp hold themselves stationary just beneath the surface. Soft light dapples across their golden backs, and droplets of water sparkle off a solitary, erect dorsal fin. At first, I am sure that they are unaware of my presence and try to refrain from fidgeting as each carp eyeballs the corn hanging beneath a small, Drennan float. But half an hour later, I realise that this was never true, and all three remain unmoving, completely ignoring the hookbait inches from their heads.

When I first slid in to position on the overhanging branch, I noticed that one of the submerged branches beneath my toes had a single black line running along its length. It reminded me of the fin of an eel, but I of course dismissed the thought immediately because this branch was the thickness of a man's thigh! I've grown tired of waiting for one of the carp to take my offering, so decide to try elsewhere; but just as I am about to walk back along the branch, I get a sudden urge to poke the submerged branch very gently with my rod tip.

The rod eye sinks below the surface and rests softly on the edge of the branch. Nothing moves, so I lift the tip back out of the water. Suddenly, the black central line begins to undulate and slowly, ever so slowly, the branch rises until near the surface, then sinks just as slowly back into position. I cannot quite believe what I am seeing - only inches from my toes, is a gigantic eel...and it must weigh at least 50lb!

Not only is this eel awesome to view at such close quarters, but also quite beautiful, with a lovely pattern of light and dark mottle brown across its broad head and back. Without a second thought, I slide the float further up the line, then slowly lower the corn hookbait until it hangs motionless in front the huge head. The eel shows no interest, so I gently lift and drop the rod tip to make the bait twitch in front of it's nose. There is an instant response, as the great eel engulfs the dancing corn within its cavernous mouth, then snaps the lid shut.

I am expecting the eel to explode through the tangled web of twisted snags in a turmoil of churning water; but instead, the rod tip is dragged beneath the surface as the monster simply sinks a few feet deeper, then wedges it's massive body beneath two branches. I lock the rod into it's full battle curve in an attempt to lift the eel back towards the surface, but now a tail the size of a giant's forearm is wrapped around one of the sunken boughs and there is nothing I can do to budge it. Panic forces me to yell out a loud series of cries that carry across the meadow to Jens' tent.

"Jens! JENS! Come and give me a hand...I'm hooked in to a monster!"

Jens shouts back that he's coming, and shortly after I hear his heavy footfalls getting louder and louder as he dashes to my aid.

" How the hell did you get out there? Is it a big carp?" asks Jens, as he pokes his head through the maze of branches, twigs and leaves.

"No, it's a massive eel, Jens. It's got to be well over 50lb...Grab the landing net, quick...It's propped up against the tree beside you."

"50lb!!...You've got to be joking, Tony!" Answers Jens; then I hear a jumble of curses and snapping of twigs as he desperately tries to climb on to the tree branch beside me.

" I can't get the landing net arms through this jungle, Tony!"

"Just collapse the arms, then re-fit them in the spreader block when you get up here beside me; but hurry up Jens, I can't hold on much longer; if it decides to dive deeper, I'm not going to be able to stop it."

There are more snapping sounds and the air heats up with swear words; but eventually Jens is able

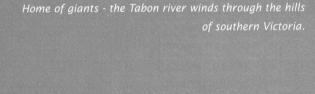

Tony with a massive and powerfully built double-figure freshwater eel.

Home of giants - the Tabon river winds through the hills of southern Victoria.

to climb on to the same tree bough, and then begins to open the net and insert the fibre glass arms back inside the spreader block. I pile on as much pressure as possible in an attempt to loosen the giant's vice-like grip on the submerged branch, but there is nothing I can do to dislodge it. Then the rod tip pulls back slightly, and I watch the eel's broad head lift up through the murky waters like a submarine; as if it wants to take a closer look me.

"Hurry up Jens! It's coming up!"

Jens quickly begins to shuffle along the branch towards me. The eel decides to shake it's massive head from side to side and I have a brief idea about slipping my foot underneath the jaw bone, in an attempt to lift the body higher and persuade it to loosen it's strangle hold of the branch. But the thought of a mouthful of needle sharp teeth piecing through my bear toes makes me quickly forget the idea!

Suddenly the rod tip jerks sharply downwards as the great eel rolls beneath my feet then dives for the bottom. There is a grating sound as the almost tight spool revolves slightly to give off a few centimetres of line, then the rod tip springs back and rattles loudly against the branches above my head.

"It's too late Jens. The line's parted...."

The following minutes are taken up by excited conversation about the lost leviathan, which masks the turmoil inside my brain. But as we walk slowly back across the sun-drenched meadow, the realisation of just how close I'd come to landing a dream eel hits me hard and begins to tighten my stomach in knots.

We had originally come to this part of the Tambo River in search of big carp, but now we couldn't draw our minds away from big eels. Both of us realise that my midday encounter with the monster-sized eel would probably never repeat itself, and that stalking carp through the daylight hours is still our best chance of continued action. Darkness however, is a different ball game, so tonight we would begin our eel safari in earnest!

First, we need to obtain some baits to attract the eels in to our swims. Jens finds a nice looking cow in the field, but I suggest to him that the farmer who has just given us permission to fish on his private land wouldn't be too impressed if we killed his prize milker! In the absence of free meat, we take the next best option and head for the nearest town in search of a supermarket. A few hours later, we return to the Tambo valley with our hired car smelling like a slaughterhouse. Inside a plastic bag on the back seat is an assortment of ox kidneys and sheep hearts...

It's now nearly midnight on a starlit Wednesday night. Ground fog drifts through the valley, leaving moisture on the outside of our tents as it passes, until it finally settles like a white veil over the surface of the Tambo. Suddenly, one of Jens' Fox alarms signals a take, but after a few seconds contact he reels in a slack line. We've had plenty of action tonight, but also have experienced major problems with the end rigs. My first take of the evening came to a piece of ox heart cast next to a large, half-submerged swim in the margins. It felt like a very big eel, but the needle teeth bit through 50lb test wire trace as if it were cotton. An hour later, I eventually manage to land a 6lb+ eel before it brakes the wire, but the majority of the eels are getting free within moments of being hooked. Jens is busy tying up extra double traces, but it seems pointless, because I've already tried platting two 50lb strands of Spiderwire around a double 50lb wire trace but it still didn't stop them biting through. Damn, these Aussie freshwater eels have got sharp teeth! We'll have to shop around

Jens, 'tree-stalking' for carp on the upper Tabon tributary.

A stalked carp is released back to the shallow morass.

for some better wire traces tomorrow.

At the dawn of a gorgeous day without a cloud in sight, we both climb up the steep-sided hill behind our tents towards the farmhouse. John, the owner has kindly allowed us the use of his shower, so after a quick wash, we tell him about the monster eel that I lost and our subsequent problems with wire traces. The farmer's brother looks at me and asks how big the eel looked in the water.

"About as thick as my upper arm, almost 6ft long and..." I start to reply.

His head begins to nod and he interrupts my sentence even before it is finished.

"Oh, that ain't nothing for this place; they grow much bigger than that..." Then his finger points across at a selection of objects hanging on one of the walls.

"See that one in the middle?

I stare at a pitchfork with giant barbs on the three metal arms, as he continues to describe its barbaric use for impaling eels.

"That's my favourite tool for catching the biggest ones. Years back, they used to swarm on mass at the river junction and I'd sometimes get'em as thick as my thigh. But there aren't so many these days, although I've still seen some this last year that would make the one you lost look small in comparison. The best place to fish for them is that giant sunken tree near the river's edge at the bottom of the second field"

My eyebrows lift up as he mentions the place and a huge grin immediately splits Jens' cheeks, for this is the exact part of the river that we have chosen to fish!

I mention to the farmer that we don't want to kill them - only catch them with rod and line, photograph them and then release them back to the river. The brother can't quite understand our notions (neither can I sometimes!) but it seems that John can, and with a wink of his eye, he persuades both Jens and I to follow him into another room. He then opens a draw filled with the paraphernalia of ancient fishing equipment and begins to take out selected items. Amongst the items are a number of different coils of wire and huge, gaff-like trebles. I feel the thickness of the wire between my fingers and have no doubt that it would be useful for Great White Shark fishing. At least they're not as bad as the coils of wire that his brother showed us, because they were just cut strands of thick steel cable! We thank them for the interesting insights into their fishing methods, but tell them that we are looking for a more subtle approach to our own fishing.

The rest of the morning is spent driving around Gippsland district in search of suitable wire traces. It takes a lot of searching, but by chance, we spot a small fishing tackle shop near the town of Lakes Entrance. The shop has a narrow range of medium quality tackle items, but some packets of black-coiled traces catch my eye. They are 80lb wire Marlin traces with plastic coatings that feel quite stiff, but are considerably better than anything we have so far seen and should be able to withstand the giant eels cutting teeth - we hope! Some really nice looking Mustard big game hooks are also bought to try out with the traces. We stop off at a village butcher on the way back to base camp, and manage to secure a large bag of offal to be used for baiting up.

Finally we arrive back at our swims on the Tambo River and set about tying up fresh traces with the new material. Berkley 100lb test swivels are threaded on to the Marlin Wire then the trace is twisted back on itself and sealed by heating the plastic coating over a flame before being left to cool. This forms a neat and secure loop holding the swivel. A large, single hook is threaded on the other end of the trace, then twisted and sealed using the same procedure. We try a selection of different pattern hooks in sizes between 1/0 and 4/0, and the finished traces look very neat and strong.

Most of the afternoon is spent stalking carp on various stretches of the winding river bank, with some success, but by early evening a strong breeze begins to blow upriver. This creates so much havoc with our surface bait presentations that we eventually decide to head back to base camp and set up our tackle for the night ahead.

We are each using two rods apiece. I have a cut piece of ox kidney on the left-hand rod and about a third of a lamb's heart on the right hand rod. Again, the same as last night, I am fishing within a rod's length from the margins and very close to the sunken tree. Some pieces of ox liver and other offal have been scattered around the hookbaits to attract some giant night hunters. It's now 18:00hrs and the light is fading fast, with just a hint of orange glow left on the edges of the horizon. A platypus plops to the surface near the far bank, then slaps it's wide tail like a beaver before disappearing once more into the black depths. The eerie whoosh from a nightjar's wings passes low over my head, and behind me, I hear the heavy muffles and vibrations from a large wombat going on his nightly forage for food. The wind drops to a breeze, then gradually fades away until the surface of the river reflects a canopy of sparkling stars.

There is now a strange 'hush' over the land. Nothing moves or stirs the complete silence of darkness; not even the whirr from a cricket's wings. I walk the few steps across to Jens' tent and sit cross-legged on the unhooking mat to keep my backside off the damp soil. We discuss in quiet whispers about how weird this night is compared to the last, when it seemed like an army of insects, birds, animals and fish were competing with each other to make the loudest noise possible. Now not even the heavy crash of feeding carp disturbs the utter silence.

"It looks like we're going to blank tonight, Jen...."

Then a loud 'BBEEEEEEEeee..' almost gives me a heart attack! I rush over to my right hand rod, then strike into a very fast swimming fish. The rod buckles under incredible power as something big almost finds sanctuary in the outer branches of the sunken tree, but I have my hand clamped over

A black swan glides on the reflections of autumn gold.

the spool and will not give an inch of line. There is a heavy splash on the surface and that unmistakable double judder and thump vibrating down the rod tells that this must be an eel. I begin walking slowly back and gradually ease it away from the snag until it is twisting like a snake in the margins. Instead of using the landing net, Jens grabs the end of the wire trace and drags the eel across the moist grass until it is well away from the margins, then I transfer it onto an unhooking mat.

Writhing like a serpent in the yellow beams of our head torches, the massive eel quickly tries to make it's escape off the mat, so I jump on it with both hands and straddle my legs either side of its back and squeeze. The eel wraps a thick tail over my thigh and begins to slide from my grip, so I squeeze harder.

"Give me a hand, Jens; this thing's as strong as a python!"

Jens grapples with one half of the big eel, while I hold on to its wide head and try to calm the creature down. I manage to turn the eel on to its back and this quickly subdues it enough to allow me to remove the hook using long-nosed forceps. The eel is weighed in a sling and quickly transferred inside a wet sack and lowered into the margins. I re-bait with another half of sheep's heart and chuck it back towards the snag with an underhand swing of the rod. When I finally am able to sit back down, I can still feel the heavy thumping of my excited heartbeat. I look across at the sack slowly waving in the margins to the constant rhythm of a 10lb+ eel and think to myself, 'wow!' these Aussie eels are really something - what is it going to be like if we latch onto a fifty pounder?!

No further action comes to our rods during the night, so shortly after the sun rises high in the eastern skies to provide enough light for a short photo session, we both pack up and make a move to new swims. We fancy the look of a section of river that winds through a lot of submerged bushes with overhanging trees along its banks, but this particular part of the Tambo runs across a neighbouring farmers land; so first we have to ask his permission to camp and fish there. Rob, the owner, turns out to be yet another really pleasant Australian farmer and following a short chat about our intentions to fish, he immediately agrees to give permission and also let us re-fill our water containers.

After driving the car through a gate into the adjoining field, we finally choose another nice looking area of the river about 1km further upstream. It is situated right on a tight bend and where a small tributary joins the main river at the opposite bank. By the time we have re-erected the tents, a hot sun is beginning to bake the cowpats on the grass behind us, so we grab a stalking rod each, then head back down river in search of carp.

Between midday and sundown, we both enjoy tremendous sport, landing plenty of hard fighting commons and the one heavily scaled mirror. I spot the odd 30lb+ carp, and also spend hours trying to tempt a common (estimated to weigh around 37lb) to move out from its security within a tangle of tree branches and suck in freeline bait. But eventually give up when the fading light of dusk makes it impossible to see. Most of the carp landed today have only been in double figures, but their power, speed and fighting stamina have made up for their lack in size and we have both thoroughly enjoyed the stalking session.

Darkness once again cloaks the Tambo River and turns the vibrant colours of the landscape into shapes of monochrome. Carp begin to roll on the surface next to an overhanging tree in Jens' swim and during the next few hours he lands two carp on boilies. Then I am next to experience some action when a 6lb eel picks up a whole sheep's heart! Jens decides to also try a larger hookbait on his eel rod and quickly discards the chunk of liver to replace it with another complete sheep's heart. But the rest of the night is quiet, and it is not until cold dawn mist is skating across the surface that a 7lb eel swims off with the whole heart in its jaws. Half an hour later, I get a screaming run, but the eel drops the bait a fraction of a second before I strike. The sheep heart is completely mashed to pulp and I feel that this is another opportunity missed of landing a giant eel.

Jens is ecstatic after landing his personal best eel, and it gives us confidence to try one more night in pursuit of a monster; but this is to be our last eel. The following dawn greets us with a sheet of white frost covering the meadows. It is the first signs of winter and we now realise that our hopes of landing a 50lb giant freshwater eel have flown. Our flight to New Zealand leaves from Melbourne this afternoon, so we must begin to pack away our gear for the last time.

I am sad to leave Australia because I believe that it has taken me so long to search for the big fish and now that I've finally found all the best places for giant specimens, my trip has come to an end. Late Autumn/early Winter (Spring/early Summer in England) is really a difficult time to catch giant eels, and as the jumbo jet whisks us high across the Tasmanian Sea, I am already making plans for a serious return expedition during the warmer, more favourable conditions of Springtime....

OZZIE OUTBACK

Lake District

Away in the distance, steel-tinged thunderclouds are rising like giant mushrooms against a column of high pressure. Their bases are as black as coal dust and sheets of water begin to fall towards earth in slowly moving grey veils. But their giant formations are rolling gradually along the coastline towards New South Wales, and when I tilt back my head to look high above me, all I can see is an unending backdrop of cobalt blue sky.

I'm fishing on a small wooden bridge crossing a feeder stream that connects a large morass to the lower reaches of the Mitchell River, situated in the Gippsland Lake District near the coast of Victoria. Groups of carp are leaving the main river and moving up this small feeder stream. There is a small pool of fairly clear water near the entrance, and from this high viewpoint I can watch each carp swimming directly beneath the bridge.

Talking of elevated viewpoints, earlier today, in an effort to get a better view of patrolling carp, I decided to climb a huge Gum tree that towers over the main river. After 30 minutes, I still hadn't spotted anything, but then I noticed a group of six very big commons ranging between 32lb-40lb. I was so excited and intent on watching them swimming directly beneath me, that I suddenly lost my footing on the smooth bark and began sliding down the trunk. My arms grasped against the bark in an effort to find some grip, only to have half my chest ripped open as it scraped against the wood. The hot friction was too much for me, so I let go and catapulted out of the tree and almost head-butted the big carp on the way down through 20ft of cold water!

My chest is badly scarred from that episode, but at least I'm warm and dry now. I've already caught and returned two mid-twenties, but am finding it extremely difficult to reach the few larger fish that I've spotted. The main problem has been that there are so many carp below 20lb, that they more often grab the bait before the intended larger specimens manage to suck it in. Most of the carp are also swimming so fast up and down stream that I need to flick a bait well ahead of them in the hope that they will take the bait on the drop. To try to stop them, I've just chucked in a few handfuls of maize, bread and broken boilies. This has immediately attracted hoards of smaller carp, but at least the clouds of silt kicked up by their foraging is enticing the odd larger carp to stop and investigate. Another problem has just entered the scene. A car load of Czechoslovakians, carrying ancient fishing rods, have just exited the car park and are walking straight towards me. They walk down the track and stop on the bridge beside me. I say hello, then turn my head to look back across the hillside in an effort to pull their attention from the groups of carp swimming beneath my feet. Too late, one of them is already pointing his finger excitedly at a 4 pounder and wants to cast a huge pike bung float on its unsuspecting little head!

"Excuse me! I'm fishing here. There are miles of water to fish; could you please not cast from the bridge because it will disturb them." I quietly ask the man who is about to cast his giant projectile. "Ve vont to feesh here! Ve vound deeze fish yesterday and vonted to catch von but couldn't get them to take our hook. Now vee are back vor another time. They taste verry godt, yes? You like to eat the karps also?" Says a big, buxom lady with black-rooted, bleached blonde hair and yellow, misshapen teeth.

I try not to glance at her enormous mammary glands that are trying to escape from a moth-eaten

A big common carp in the margins of the Mitchell River.

A dramatic photo as Jens Bursell battles with a carp, hooked in a shallow bay of Clydbank Morass. I just hope Jens' skinny legs don't break before he lands it!

old jumper, and as my eyes flick away from her ugly face and past those mountains of flesh, they fall upon a frying handle sticking out of her shoulder bag. Damn, these folk mean business! I will have to think of something fast before they scare all the fish away. A quick glance through my Polaroid sunglasses shows me a shoal of small carp tails waving inside the cloud of disturbed silt. No big carp can be seen; so I turn to one of them and say-

"I have been feeding these carp for many hours and am waiting for a large specimen to..."

"Oh, no, doo dont vont to have the beeg fisk. The leetle vons taste much better!" Interrupts one of them, and now begins to grin at me with saliva already forming on his lips.

"Look" I continue with the conversation, while pointing my finger towards the stream. "See those carp down there? They are not difficult to catch. If I catch one now and give you one, will you leave me to fish on in quiet solitude?"

All five of them look at me with strange expressions then one of them tells me that it is very difficult, almost impossible to catch these carp. Looking at their giant treble hooks connected to ultra-thin nylon, I'm not surprised, although I refrain from saying so. Eventually, but with a little scepticism, they agree to my request. So I immediately lower a tiny freeline knob of boilie paste amongst the moving clouds of silt. The line tightens within seconds and soon I have a 5lb common flapping in the margins. They are surprised, but elated by this quick capture and are happy when I hand it to them as a gift.

"Oh please can doo pull up von more karps vor us?" shouts the bleached-blond maiden.

So I oblige, and within seconds a similar sized carp is hooked, landed and handed over to them. But then they ask me for one more, just a little bigger. I begin to get a little angry, but bite my tongue, then lower a fresh offering of bait from the bridge.

"If I catch one more, then you must please promise to leave me in peace." They all turn to each other then look back at me nodding with smiles on their happy cheeks. But before I can look down to spot the bait dangling just under the surface beneath my rod tip, something grabs it and almost wrenches the rod from my grasp. It is a long, Wildie-type carp of around 11lb, and I have to get it in the net fast if I'm to avoid disturbing the area too much. I hurry along the bridge then scramble down the steep, grassy bank towards the water. Halfway down, my foot gets caught in an old railway sleeper hidden in the long grass. I try to prevent from falling headfirst into the margins by stamping my left foot forward, but it only manages to locate a deep hole covered by the overgrowth. The sudden jolt and jarring of bone against metal brings a scream of terror and pain from my lips, as I fall headfirst into a gorse bush. I'm still holding on to the rod and rush the carp, splashing into the landing net and then hand it to one of the Czechs, who has just ran to my aid.

I sit down to take a closer look at my leg. Half the skin has been ripped off my shin and a mound of red, swollen flesh rises from the bone in a throbbing heap. My immediate fear is that the leg is broken, but following an extensive and agonising investigation with my fingers around the wound, I fail to find any protruding bone or splinters. I'm in no fit state to continue fishing, so I hobble back to my car and try to sleep it off without the luxury of painkillers. Before trying to rest however, I must feed my stomach because I haven't eaten anything all day. Sandwiches wrapped in cellophane are found in the boot. They still look fresh; well at least they're not green yet, so I begin chomping through them. On the third bite, something crunches like a nut inside my mouth. Damn! The complete filling has fallen out of one of my teeth! By morning, the swollen mound has subsided and my leg feels sore, but otherwise OK. Although my back molar is aching like mad and I will need to visit the dentist....

Flying Carp

It's just a few minutes after midnight and I'm dozing on the front seat of my car, which is parked next to a small pier at the end of a long spit jutting out into the vast waters of Lake King. I chose this particular place so that I could escape the weekend crowds that ascend on Point Dawson. Another reason is that I have spent the last few days trying to hook into a 30-40lb+ carp on the lower Mitchel River, but without success. It was so difficult to present a bait to the largest specimens amongst a mass of smaller carp, and in the end my largest was a 28lb common. In frustration, I turned to this part of Lake King, because it is where the freshwater from the Mitchel meets the saltwater influence of King. This produces an area of brackish water that fluctuates with the moving tides and rain floods. There are a lot less carp in this area, but that is precisely why I'm here, because I feel that the larger carp are more tolerant to high saline levels. It might mean that I have less takes, but during darkness when I have no chance of seeing which carp will suck in my baits, it will give me a higher chance of hooking the carp that I'm after. I haven't landed a big carp since the superb 35lb+ common from Alexandrina Lake, and I'm now very hungry for another.

There is heck of a lot of weed in this section and this has forced me to use very buoyant pop-ups on sliding helicopter rigs to keep the hook from snagging up. I've only seen one single carp since I arrived, but that looked a decent size, so hopes of success are high. My eyelids begin to droop and the strain of the past days hectic stalking periods finally catch up on me. I slide into the realms of dreams; then a sudden banging on the car window shakes me back into the real World. The beam from a torch cuts through the glass and stabs at the back of my eyeballs. I wind the window down slightly.

" Oh, sorry, didn't realise that you were asleep, Cobber. Did I wake you?" Asks a guy holding the blaring torch.

"Well if I was asleep, I sure am wide awake now!" I answer him, with half a smile.

"What you fishing for, mate?" asks his friend, standing behind him with a big silly grin across his face.

"Carp." is my short answer.

"Carp! Oh...Errr...How long you here for, mate?"

"Two months."

They both then look at each other and aren't sure whether I'm joking or not.

"Caught anything?" One of them finally blurts out.

"Well, I've been here a month, so I certainly hope so!" I say, and try to hide a sheepish smile.

"A month! You mean that you've been here for a whole month?" They both shout out in unison.

"Well, not exactly in this place the whole time; but I've been searching and fishing for carp all over Australia."

" Do you mind if we fish here, mate?" One of them asks.

I'm not in the mood to argue I just want to get back to sleep, so I agree to their request but ask them

Hundreds of carp in the Murray River near Mildura, explode in a sheet of spray as they fight to get at my surface baits!

A pile of dead carp stretches for 50km along the Koorang, following accidental jamming of flood gates, which prevented the fish swimming back into Lake Alexandrina.

not to cast over my lines. For the next ten minutes I'm kept awake by a constant bombardment of noise as they both walk back and forward with rods and other gear from their car. I'm relieved when they plonk their two striped deck chairs on the pier and finally sit down. A few minutes later there is another knock on my window, so I slowly wind it down again.

"Do you want us to watch your rods?" He asks.

"No, it's OK I'll hear them." I answer with nonchalance.

They then look strangely at each other and this is followed by a long, baffled silence while they scratch their heads.

"How can you hear them?" says one of them, eventually. But just as I am about to tell him, he stands on the planks of the mini-pier and cause the Delkims to let out three loud 'bleeps' that light up his face in a multicoloured glow. 'Oh...Wow!' are the only words he can muster on seeing these amazing fishing gadgets. There is another long pause while he studies the rest of my gear. I can almost hear the rusty cogs in his brain slowly moving. Then he finally pokes his head through my window and asks-

"How big are your hooks?"

I look back at him, but am in no mood for a prolonged explanation, so decide not to answer him. He stands admiring my rod set up while waiting for me to speak, but eventually my silence gets to him and he walks back to his mate. They cast out their big bung floats and illuminate them with a gigantic lantern as if it is a warning for ships to avoid the lighthouse. They continue to stomp and barn dance on the rickety wooden rafters of the pier with their metal deck chairs for almost an hour, until they finally get bored and drive off to bother someone else. It is so nice to be left alone in peace again and I quickly drift into deep sleep.

Time passes, until a loud Delkim screams at me through the morning mist and I jump out of the car and strike into something very powerful. This is more like it I think to myself, and already have visions of a monster 30kg carp laying on the unhooking mat. Then all of a sudden, my monster-sized 'carp' takes off and flies upriver! I pull back on the rod to try and stop it, and then a huge white beast comes screaming out of the mist. I'm connected to a bloody great swan!

The adult mute swan has somehow picked up one of my lines and got tangled in it, so I have to bring it completely to the bank before I can free it. The swan splashes off down river unharmed, except for its ego. I am not too pleased with my early morning alarm call; but at least it gave me a good fight!

Cowirra Bay

Both a white-hot sun and the mercury level are rising together to their zeniths. Clouds of morning mist have already vaporised with the rising temperatures and vanished into a blue void. The 'slap, slap' of paddle blades keeps in time with my moving shoulder blades as the kayak glides slowly across the shimmering waters of Cowirra Bay, a giant backwater of the mighty Murray River system. High above my head, thousands of Sulphur Crested cockatoos spiral in a noisy, moving mass of white feathers against a backdrop of endless blue sky.

In front of me, grouped together in the shape of a horseshoe, fourteen white pelicans move in formation. Every fifteen seconds, the outer swimming pelicans will quickly close the gap to form a tight circle. Then fourteen wide-open beaks dip beneath the surface, probing for frightened fish that dart blindly inside the trap. It is wonderful to watch them at such close quarters and their teamwork makes them move together as if a single, giant bird. Small, silver fish are their main prey but occasionally a juvenile carp bolts into one of the traps and a pelican snaps its beak shut. Twice this morning I have already witnessed the amazing sight of a carp sliding down inside the narrow tunnel of a Pelicans throat.

Spread out for almost 2km across the bay, hundreds of carp have formed into smaller groups and hang suspended in vertical positions near the surface. Tight circles of pouting lips suck continually at the warm air. This phenomenon is known as "kissing carp", and on numerous occasions during the past few hours it has allowed me to glide stealthily with the kayak up to some unsuspecting circle of fish, then to lower a freeline bait into the widest pair of lips. But now I've spotted bigger prey. Only ten metres in front of me a long, torpedo-shaped common carp is swimming just beneath the surface. The peak of its dorsal fin scythes through the water as a massive, waving tail propels it onwards. Judging by the width of that bronze-coloured back, it looks to be around 30lbs - an uncommon beast in Australian rivers and a worthy quarry.

I slowly increase the pace of my paddle strokes, until the bow of the kayak is within 5 metres of the moving tail, and then stop paddling. The rod is then lifted from my lap and pushed forward, so that the tip points towards the carp in front of me and the hookbait dangles just above the surface on a short line. The kayak continues to glide onwards without further propulsion, and just before the bait is about to cast a shadow over the carp's eyes, I quickly flick the rod tip. The bait hits the surface film with a quiet 'plop', then slowly sinks in the water and disappears through the murk. That big, orange-tipped caudal fin continues to wave from side to side, propelling the carp forever onwards. Drat! It didn't even notice my offering!

A few turns of the reel handle, brings the bait back upwards and I let it dangle beneath the rod tip as I continue in my pursuit. Three more attempts are completely ignored by the carp, but on the fourth try, my persistence is rewarded. This time the crayfish tail falls perfectly and passes just in front of the eye, almost causing the carp to bolt in alarm. But the carp is inquisitive and follows the bait down. The coils of line still left on the surface, twitch a fraction then suddenly jolt forward like a twisting snake. I lift the rod tip sharply and feel a satisfying thump transmitted up the line and through my fingers. Then the water literally explodes.

The kayak swings violently around amongst the boiling foam, and then jerks forward in the wake of a giant bow-wave that powers across the bay. I let the carp tow me for about 25 metres, then quickly flick open the bail-arm. Line springs off the spool and streaks over the surface; but instead of pursuing the carp, I swing the kayak back round until the bow points to shore, then begin paddling like mad. The rod now lies in my lap with the tip pointing back towards the fast swimming carp, with the line still ripping off the reel. As soon as the kayak slides over the marginal mud, I climb out and grab the rod again. The bail-arm is immediately flicked closed and my right hand begins winding like crazy to place lost line back on the spool. I trust that the first strike found a good hook hold, but it is not until the line suddenly twangs taught again and the rod tip wrenches towards the horizon, that my confidence returns.

Even after swimming halfway across the bay, the carp is still full of power and it is many gut-wrenching long runs before its energy is sapped enough for me to wade slowly out and engulf it within the landing net. At 29lb+, this carp is not a monster, but now, as I look down on those

Four wild pelicans swim past my rods at Salt Creek, a backwater of the Murray River system near Gurra Gurra Lake.

"..A large kangaroo, oblivious to my presence, hops to the edge of the water..."

fabulous golden scales and my eyes sweep along its incredible length, it fills me with utter satisfaction.

Teal Flat

It is now three days later, at 19:10 hrs in the evening and I'm sitting beside my rods, looking out across the windswept waters of Teal Flat. I arrived here after taking the ferry across the Murray River at Panong. This area is quite incredible and a high ridge of sandstone cliffs separate the milk chocolate-coloured river as it winds in a half circle past the gin-clear waters of the marshes. Strong winds are lifting the surface of the lake and blowing white foam off towering waves. They constantly roll and crash against the stone shoreline and swing great tufts of reeds from side to side like Hawaiian Dancers skirts. My Delkims are bleeping in rhythm with the swaying grass, so I'll need to de-sensitise them a little if I'm going to gain some sleep tonight.

This lake is split into two sections and stretches for about 4 square kilometres across a flat area of open marshes. A narrow channel runs along one edge, but I cannot see any direct connections to the main river. However, it is obvious that in times of flood the Murray easily breaks over the small lip that separates them, allowing entry and exit of river carp into Teal Flat.

I've just whacked out a double pop-up boile + 2 bait PVA stringer, about 80 metres amongst the crashing waves, and a double sinking boilie + 3 bait stringer to the margins. Earlier this evening, just before sunset, I had stopped the car on a high buttress of sandstone that towers over this giant backwater. For one hour I sat cross-legged at the cliff edge, scanning the expanse of lake and river system with binoculars while my chest was buffeted by rising winds. In that period I noticed only one carp jump, but it was large enough to give me confidence to try to spend some time there. Carp rarely roll or leap in Australian waters. I don't really understand why this is so, because many

Aussie rivers and lakes are absolutely teeming with carp and waters with high populations generally translate into active surface activity. The absence of crashing carp on most waters does make my job of locating the larger specimens much more difficult, especially when searching long stretches of the Murray River with its murky water and teeming shoals of stunted fish.

There is such a wild feeling in my heart, just sitting here beside the windblown rods with hair flapping around my ear lobes and listening to the heavy slap of waves against the bank. Groups of ducks, chased by the fast-fading light of dusk, are cupping their wings and falling like stones from the cobalt skies. I can hear the roar of wind in their feathers as they glide over the surface then ski across the waves. A large kangaroo, oblivious to my presence, hops to the edge of water and begins to drink. The audible slurp is akin to an old man sucking tea off a saucer. Spray flies off the shoreline waves and lodge as minute droplets amongst fine strands of its fur. I continue watching the kangaroo with quiet fascination, while a black cloak begins to slowly envelop the sky, until suddenly a loud 'bleep' from a Delkim almost gives us both a heart attack! The rod tip bounces once, then line 'pings' out of the clip and a diode lights up the grass in a red glow. A carp has picked up the margin bait and is now swimming as fast as possible in an effort to reach the far bank, while the kangaroo is beating a hasty retreat through the bush in the opposite direction!

My strike instantly cuts off the noisy alarm tone and once again the air is filled only with the sounds of slapping waves. The rod arches towards the unseen horizon, and now a screaming ratchet begins to join its song with the wind. I can feel the handle bending beneath my palms and pushing the butt hard against my right elbow. Already, there are no doubts in my mind that this is by far the biggest carp that I have hooked in the Murray River in almost three weeks of searching. The thump of my heart starts to compete with the thumping of waves pounding against my feet. By looking up at the rod curved against the faded glow from a long lost sunset, I can just make out the slow, easy throb of the tip ring. The incredible power of the fish is slow, steady and constant. This is indeed a special fish.

For five long minutes the carp swims onwards and outwards, pulling line slowly off the ticking spool. A line of half-submerged barbed wire fence stretches out into the lake from the margins about 100 metres to my left. The carp is still well clear of this danger, but if it decides to kite towards it with this amount of line out, I'm in deep trouble. With added finger pressure on the spool the fish suddenly stops and makes an incredible run parallel to the bank. Happily, the direction is away from the fence, so I ease my finger off the spool and continue to lean back on the rod. The fish begins kiting towards the marginal rushes, so I run along the bank, winding and pumping frantically on the reel handle in an effort to keep contact.

Soon I am level with the fish, and in a desperate attempt to prevent it from ploughing through an overhanging gorse bush; I jump into the water and wade out to my hips. The waves crash against my back and the wind begins to whistle against the taught nylon as I fight to stay in control. The rod buckles under the strain when I sink the tip deep under the water to keep the line free of the snags. There is an almighty explosion of water right against the outer branches, then the tip wrenches round in the opposite direction as the carp bolts back out to open water. The ratchet and wind scream in unison as I fight to keep a steady foothold on the lake bottom. My finger once again presses gently against the fast spinning spool. The friction begins to heat up the skin, but there is a sudden splash of foam as the carp rolls on the surface and turns back towards the bank.

This big fish is not yet beaten, but its power is quickly ebbing and soon it will be mine. The rod remains locked completely over, stabbing its tip eye towards the water in time with a constantly beating tail. The waves now pound against my chest and fine spray licks at my face, as the fish battles in the shallow water in front of me. I haven't seen the carp yet, but it won't be long now.

Then all of a sudden my heart misses a beat. The rod tip springs back straight and a bulge of 'V' shaped water rockets towards the centre of the lake then disperses amongst the distant waves. The line flaps in the rings and bows against the buffeting winds. Unseen hands crush my stomach in a vice-like grip and I almost feel the sudden urge to vomit. I turn away from the dark waves and wade back to the bank. A quick glance at the rig shows me that everything seems OK; the hook must have pulled and there is little I could have done to prevent it. But this information doesn't prevent me from throwing the rod at the Australian bush in a sudden fit of childish temper. I sit down on a tussock of grass and stare in silence at the rolling waters hidden in darkness. The constant slap and thump of waves is somehow comforting and calmness slowly eases my raging heart.

No more takes wake me from a fitful sleep, until a cool dawn slowly spreads yellow light over Teal Flat and across my closed eyelids. The first thing I see is a strand of loose line that still hangs limply from one of the rods and swings in the gentle breeze. The sight of it brings a sudden cramp to my throat as reality sweeps across my senses. Strangely, I don't feel the urge to continue fishing here. My instincts tell me that last night's monster carp was an isolated specimen and not part of a shoal of similar-sized beasts. I could be wrong, but my heart isn't in it right now, so I decide to pack up and drive upriver towards Wongulla Lagoon.

Riverland

It is now 20:10 hrs on a warm and sultry evening in the Riverland district of Southern Australia. After finding most of Loveday Swamp already dry, I have moved to the banks of the lower reaches of Cobdogla Swamp. Cobdogla itself is quite an amazing sight, with hundreds of dead trees pointing out of the water, reminiscent of a small backwater at Krung Kra Wia Lake in Thailand. The wonderful Riverland is a portion of the Murray River where it slows its pace as it passes through the marshes, to form complex maize of interconnecting lakes and backwater channels.

For most of the day I have been stalking carp in the intense 35-Centigrade heat of late March. There is no doubt that the temperatures remain much higher here than further south near the coast at Lake Alexandrina. This lagoon is stuffed full of carp and I can actually see most of them because their backs are constantly above the surface in this extremely shallow, muddy water. Yet I'm finding it very difficult to get one to suck in a hookbait. I was at a loss to understand the reasons at first, but following a thorough investigation of an area surrounding an inflow pipe where hundreds of carp were congregating, I think that I've found the answer. The stones and underwater debris are festooned with millions of miniature worms. These are very similar to bloodworms, except that they have transparent bodies. The carp are going crazy about them and seem to become so preoccupied that they aren't interested in anything else. At one time there must have been more than a thousand carp in an area no larger than two tennis courts, and I had problems keeping the line away from their backs in an effort to prevent foul hook-ups. But no matter how much I tried, I could not induce a positive feeding response to the variety of man made baits that I offered to them.

In frustration, I decided to drive to the nearest town to buy some earthworms. These did eventually work, but only after a lot of hard work and persistent concentration. The biggest obstacle has been the profusion of dead trees and the first carp broke the line, then a second carp ripped out the hook when I tried to stop it reaching the snags. Eventually I managed to hook and land a carp, but it barely passed the 10lb barrier. There is an enormous amount of double figure carp in here, but I've clearly seen a few of the better specimens at close quarters and some of them are easily over 30lb. The small carp that I landed was extremely stocky for its length, so it seems that they must be feeding well. The carp here are also very powerful and it takes some effort to stop their initial runs.

I've cast out two rods with boilie stringers + pop up hookbaits to keep them off the soft layer of silt. I've chose to revert to boilies during the dark hours because they will give me a better chance of avoiding the smaller carp. A crescent moon is slowly rising behind the silhouettes of a hundred leafless branches that point at the stars. I am sitting in the car with the door open and listening to a thousand lips sucking at the surface. The noise from so many surface-feeding carp is amazing. But are they actually feeding? They seem to be avoiding the floating baits that I chucked out earlier. They could be sucking at insects on the surface, but I think they may be just going through the rituals of "kissing carp" like I witnessed at Kowirra. It might also be possible that some of the mosquitoes are in transformation stage and are popping to the surface, but judging by the lack of insects seen floating at dusk, I doubt that this is what is attracting the carp.

Some fish have begun crashing deep inside a tangle of almost impenetrable branches. They try to seduce me to cast near them, but I already know by my earlier experiences that to do so is just asking for trouble. So my baits remain in a small clear area, which at least gives me some chance of stopping the fish before they reach a snag. With so many carp feeding, I'm quite amazed that I still haven't had a take yet, especially after catching so many carp on these baits in other parts of the river system. I sit back on the car seat, close my

Tony with one of the largest carp ever caught on rod & line in Australia - a 35lb+ common from the vast, 582 square kilometres of Lake Alexandrina.

'Waiting for a bite is never boring' - a gorgeous Australian Kingfisher perches in the tree beside me.

eyes and try to get some rest after a tiring day, but soon need to wind up the car window to shut out the maddening din of a thousand sucking lips!

When finally a yellow sun rises to chase away the mist that hangs in thin layers over the swamps, all the carp seem to have vanished and the air is held in a grip of silence. I rise out of my sleeping bag and immediately pack up the gear, then begin to drive down the track to a different location on the map. The sight of three big tails wafting above the surface near one of the overflow pipes makes me tread on the brake and wind down the window for a few moments. They have probably just begun their morning feed and it's possible they are not fully pre-occupied on the bloodworm yet. Now might be my best chance of a thirty. Those waving tails are just too enticing, and I'm soon set up with a single rod and quietly creep down the sloping bank towards the margins.

My hopes are quickly fulfilled, and within minutes of casting out a delicate float and fresh worm, the rod becomes fully arced under the pressure of a bolting carp. Unfortunately the hook rips out when I am forced to try and prevent the carp from ploughing through a tangle of tree branches. I'm such a happy man right now! I got a good look at that fish, and I'm almost certain that it topped thirty - around 32-34lb. On afterthought, there is not much I can do to prevent such hook pulls

A beautiful corner of Mulwala Lake on the Victoria/New South Wales border.

because these carp have abnormally soft lips and inner mouth skin tissue. This is a common problem with fish that feed heavily on soft food items in deep silt.

Thirty minutes later, my rod hoops over as another carp explodes on the surface, then storms off with incredible power. It makes a concerted effort to wrap the line around a dead branch poking out of the water, but fortunately both line and hook hold and I soon have a fish splashing inside the landing net. This carp measures more than 3ft between nose and tail, but it possesses only half the body depth compared to the previous carp, so its weight falls well below thirty; in fact it only just scrapes twenty. But looking at its huge orange-tipped caudal fin glistening in the morning sunlight, and that fantastic wildie-shaped body covered in bronze, makes me more than happy to have caught it. I take a quick few portrait shots using the camera on a tripod, then watch it flap from my hands and cover me in spray as a bow wave rockets across Cobdogla Swamp.

These last two takes have given me renewed confidence and I decide to stay a while longer; at least until they become too pre-occupied on their bloodworm larder. But my early stalking session is cut short when the ground suddenly begins to shake as if in an earthquake. The carp seem as shocked as I am and there is a mass exodus from the margins as a hundred bow-waves head for the far edges of the swamps. I stand up and walk a few paces towards the source of the sounds, then raise my eyebrows when a massive digger truck comes rumbling up the track. The huge metal beast comes to a halt beside me, shrouded in a cloud of rolling dust. My eyes look up above the rubber tyres that tower above me and I notice a head peep out from a small cabin window and shout above the din of a noisy engine.

"You'll have to take you car away I'm afraid, because we're about to dig up this track and put down a new layer of gravel...."

Oh, well, I think to myself, the action was fun while it lasted! I suppose I'd better continue my plans to explore other virgin waters dotted in intricate blue maize of blobs and streaks on my map, like some giant unfinished spider web.

Buffeted by winds, Tony sits at the very edges of a 1,000ft cliff above the Colorado River, as the setting sun paints the awesome Grand Canyon in a warm orange glow.

WILD WEST

Carp feeding on surface baits in the clear waters of the Colorado River.

Close-up of surface feeding carp in the Wild West.

Swollen from recent heavy rains, the Okanogan River pushes chocolate-coloured waters deep inside the clear heart of the Columbia. One kilometre upstream of the confluence, I stand up to my knees in the transparent waters; so clear that I can easily see the crisp images of my toes sliding over the bottom silt. A big, slow bend on the lower Okanogan had been my original choice. Its dense beds of lilies often tempted me to wade amongst them during previous visits. Those wade-stalking sessions were kind to me and there are numerous battles with big-scaled mirrors and golden commons stored in my memory banks. They were long, lean specimens with giant tails that propelled them like missiles, and even though they rarely weighed more than 30lb, their strength and beauty made it a pleasure to fish for them. But there were sometimes 40 pounders, and once, a carp so long that its image will remain forever implanted in my brain. My eyes close for a few moments, and I re-live that exciting event on the Okanogan...

'.... Eventually, I am close enough to lower a freeline bait slowly off the rod tip and let it flutter close to where I judge its head to be. I still cannot see the size of the fish, but its large shoulders impress me enough to want to hook it. The offering is completely ignored and the fish drifts out of sight, only to emerge on the far side of another lily patch. I wade closer to get within rod length range again - then suddenly swear between clenched teeth. The fish is head down, feeding, with its massive tail lobes sticking out of the water. I quickly lower the hookbait again through the turbid water close to its head, but the fish immediately straightens and swims onwards. From where I stand, it moves in a large arc, occasionally lifting that big grey hump through the surface scum. At one point, as it swims past a wide opening in the weeds, I catch full sight of it. I am astonished, because this fish is well over 4ft in length.
In my excitement, I fluff the first cast, which almost costs me dearly, but I quickly compose myself and try

*Tony searches for carp in a wild backwater of the
Colorado River at Topock Gorge in Arizona.*

*to wait for it to come closer. Eventually, my patience pays off and the incredible fish moves within a
rod's length of me. It is now or never, and I battle to stop trembling as I try to make the descent of
the corn seem natural as possible. Now I'm able to judge the true length of the fish in the gin-clear
water. This carp is 4 feet 6 inches long!*

*Time seems to speed up in a sudden rush of electric energy as the whole weed bed explodes. A tidal
wave rockets through the lily pads as I race after it, trying to keep contact and almost having heart
attacks every time the line 'pings' out of each clump of tangled weed. To try to stop such a powerful,
fast swimming carp is asking too much of my tackle, so I let it swim onwards. Suddenly, the line pings
out of the last clump of roots at the weed bed's outer edge. It brings a smile to my lips as I watch the
bow-wave moving through safe, open water. Strands of weed dangle off the taught line as it whistles
in the breeze.*

*I quickly wade deeper than my chest, so that mainly open, snag-free water lies between the fish and
me. Now I'm happy and begin to try to slowly sap the gut-wrenching power of this turbo-charged
monster. The rod arches fully over and points at a 'V' shaped ripple that cuts through the surface skin
and heads steadily upstream. All of a sudden, the power stops as the rod tip recoils like a spring to
point at the deep, blue sky. Line sags in the breeze; I reel like mad to try to catch up with a fish
swimming towards me, but no..... the hook has pulled.*

*I wade back through the weeds and throw my rod at the water in temper. A rising flood of anger
squeezes at my stomach and almost makes me vomit.*

Time eventually calms my shaking body, so I pick up the rod and then wade along the knee-deep shoreline, dragging the landing net behind me. Basking carp bolt and scatter in confusion before me, but now I don't give a damn. My rod will make no more casts today...'

INDIAN BAY

I had hoped this return trip would allow me to wade through the waist-deep water of Okanogan's 'Big Bend', and maybe give a chance to hook, or at least see, that amazing common carp again. But the torrential rains have filled the Canadian streams that feed the Okanogan River, so that by the time it has wound its way over the USA border, it is also carrying tonnes of suspended mud, silt and debris. Yesterday, a half-hearted search for carp in the muddy backwaters had eventually led me to a large bay on the main Columbia River. I know this particular bay quite well, having caught numerous 20lb+ commons from its murky corners the previous year. But the millions of gallons of excess water has had an opposite effect on the Columbia, and the open gates of Chief Joseph Dam now spew crystal waters through the valley to flood across green pastures. This raising of the river level also triggered a spawning response from the carp and their gold-plated armies swarmed into Indian Bay. My first short stalking session yesterday afternoon produced a lot of good carp, including many 30lb+ specimens. Now I'm back for more action.

The black rain clouds that cloaked most of the Pacific North West States for the past few weeks have disappeared, and hot rays are beaming down from a clear blue sky to tan my shoulders. It feels so good to feel the warmth of the sun again. The brim of my Australian Bush hat, paints a shadow across my face as I peer through the Polaroid glasses in search of carp. A group of seven commons and a single mirror swim slowly past me. They are all in the 15lb class, so my eyes continue to scan the sparkling waters. A shoal of fish lies close to the surface in a tight group at the centre of this

A 30lb+ carp caught beside the famous Route 66 highway, during a desert heat wave of the lower Colorado valley.

The author clings to a wind-buffeted cliff opposite the towering walls of the Glen Canyon Dam.

The Snoqualmie Falls thunders into a rocky chasm after nightfall. This photo was taken on a long-time exposure covering several minutes during almost complete darkness, and shows detail not seen by the naked eye.

pool, a tiny backwater-connection of Indian Bay. Some individuals amongst the shoal could scrape the 25lb barrier, but still not what I am after, so I resume the quest.

Only footprints remain in the soft silt of the pool, for now my legs carry me across the meadows. I have just heard an almighty splash at the northern fringes of the main bay, so make haste towards the sound. The rising floodwaters have swelled the edges of Indian Bay so that now her excesses stream over the mud and fan out across the meadows. A newly formed river that gushes past cacti plants and gorse bushes, blocks my path, forcing me to circumnavigate a flooded field. The extremely shallow water covering the field is quickly heating up beneath a blinding sun. The warm water of this virgin 20-acre lake has attracted hoards of carp to feed on the rich pastures. Hundreds of dorsal fins scythe through the shallows and gold scales reflect sunlight off their backs. But these carp are all juveniles, because the water covering this field is both too warm and shallow for the adults.

It will be a long walk around this newly formed lake, so I take a short cut by wading across a knee-deep section. A narrow gully at the centre of the field is now a rushing stream, so I must wade chest-deep to navigate it. Carp bodies bang against my legs then form moving ridges of water as they bolt across the flooded meadows.

Just as I am about to wade across a second flooded section, my eyes catch then hold on an unusual form and colour. My feet carry me stealthily across the mud then slide gently beneath the shallow waters, until a closer view reveals the beautiful form of a Bridgelip Suckerfish. The sun cuts through clear water to gleam off the blue fins and glints against miniature azure and gold tinted scales. This

The beautiful barbel-like form of a Bridgelip Sucker in the clear waters of the upper Columbia River in USA. Tony actually caught this fish on worm only moments after the photo was taken.

A mass of pouting lips wait for Tony to chuck more floaters on the surface of Lake Mead!

is indeed a gorgeous looking species of fish and must be recorded on film, so for the next few minutes I work hard with the camera to obtain some good shots. It takes great patience to get close enough for full-frame photos without disturbing the fish in this gin-clear water, but eventually the image in my Pentax viewfinder is the one I want.

I place the camera back inside its waterproof bag, but suddenly get an urge to have a closer look at that wonderful creature holding steady like a Hampshire Avon barbel in the strong flow. A float plops on the surface upstream then drifts downstream with a worm trundling along the bottom behind it. The float passes over the Bridglip's head then dips. Suddenly there is a blue flash in the water and my rod tip keels over - yes, it's on! The fight is short-lived and soon I am looking down into the landing net at a spectacular fish. This species is only meant to grow to 12 inches (30cm) in length, but this particular specimen is twice that size. I take a couple of photos of the fish against the rod, then watch it swim back through the clear, rushing currents.

High rushes rim a small backwater connection of the main bay, and it is while I am walking past their high stems, I get a sudden urge to investigate. My body begins to form an opening in the dense bulrushes and reeds. Noisily at first, then slower and quieter with each tread, until I'm able to peep over the outer stems and peer into the margins.

Wow! What a sight! Tight to the reed stems, as if they are waiting in a bus queue, more than twenty carp bask in the shallows. But it is not this sight that has made me hold my breath and crouch in a rigid position like a stalking heron. For there, only inches from my sandals, is a metre long band of gold. An eye revolves in its socket and seems to look at me, but I remain rigid and hope that this fish doesn't realise what it is actually looking at! I can see every scale along its beautiful flanks and watch in fascination as a huge pair of rubbery lips stretch forward and back in constant motion. Small particles are sucked inside a cavernous mouth then blown back out again, as if they are dancing in time with the slowly flapping gill covers.

Ten minutes later, my hand is resting on those same gill covers and my fingers are probing inside that giant mouth; for I am removing a size 2 hook from its rubbery bottom lip. The carp had shot off like a bat out of hell as soon as it realised that the worm it had sucked in, was also attached to some wild animal that burst out of the reeds holding a bent rod!

I admire row upon row of golden scales as I slip the golden creature inside a carp sack, then lower it into the margins. At a weight of 36lb+, I am well pleased with my first common carp of the day. Although there are still some fish milling about in this small pool, the disturbance has caused most of the larger carp to disappear. A thudding sound reaches my ears once again, as an almighty carp crashes beyond the marginal reeds about 150 metres away. I quickly make my way back through the rushes and head towards the sound. A few minutes later a clearing in the reads reveals a feeder stream that opens out into the northern part of Indian Bay. I stop in my tracks and slowly drop to my knees. The sight is mind-blowing. In front of me, packed like sardines in a can, are hundreds of carp.

I spend the next 30 minutes watching the water through Polaroid lenses. As always, there seems to be a hierarchy at play here. The shallow, upper reaches of the stream inlet are choc-a-bloc with carp in the 3lb-9lb classes. The central section holds fish mainly in the 10lb-18lb, and the lower section contains fish in the region of 18lb- 25lb+.

As my eyes scan this multitude of fins and scales, they gradually begin to hold on a particular area on the outer fringes of the inlet, where it gradually widens and shelves down into deep water. Beyond the basking bodies of 30lb+ commons, I can see slowly moving shapes. Like sharks at the edges of a Pacific coral reef, their shadows drift past, and then softly fade into the deep blue void. They seem to linger in the cooler layers of water, but occasionally a fleeting glimpse of a moving shadow catches the sunlight, and reflects solid gold. There is no doubt in my mind that many of these carp exceed 40lb.

For the next two hours, I brave the sweltering heat and cast a delicate 'crystal waggler' float at slowly moving shadows. I try to tempt them with a hook covered in maize kernels, then prawn tails, then fat, wriggling worms. The clear water gives perfect views as each offering gradually descends towards the bottom. But following the quick capture and return of two commons weighing 27lb and 28lb 12oz, I come to realise that I must change tactics. My casts are not only falling short of the mark, but the hookbait is also not getting down quickly enough to reach the deeper water.

I begin to creep quietly through the thick stands of rushes until my sandals slip through an opening at the very edge of the Bay. It is like standing at the edge of a cliff and the knee-deep, clear margins quickly change to sky blue, blue green, dark green, then deep black water. A mass of smaller carp is now behind me, and only the shark-like shadows of the reef move silently past me.

By the time the sun is vanishing behind the Wenatchee Mountains, I am tired, hungry and dripping in sweat. But I am happy, for my rod has been flexed to the limit by the explosive power of fish weighing 34lb+, 36lb+, 37lb 2oz, 38lb+, 39lb 4oz and two over 40lb - all golden-scaled, fabulous Columbia River commons.

These two short days of stalking amongst the clear waters of Indian Bay have been the most exhausting, yet most exciting period of a lifetime filled with wonderful carp fishing moments. But the party is over; this brief stalking session has been just a short detour while I waited for the flooded water levels to drop. At the crack of dawn, I must pack up the tent and head hundreds of kilometres downriver - in search of White Giants....

Tony returns a broad-shouldered 40lb+ common to the clear waters of the Columbia River; just part of a single day catch of carp, which included two upper twenties, five 30lb+ and two 40lb+.

IN SEARCH OF

WHITE GIANTS

"..It becomes the most awesome moment in a lifetime of fishing.." Tony bends down to kiss the shoulders of a
700lb+ Great white Sturgeon as it swims back into the depths of the Columbia River.

Watching a storm rolling down the Columbia Gorge towards us.
Beacon rock, the Worlds largest monolith, can be seen at the
centre of background.

First Encounter:

For the fourth time that day, we up anchor and move the boat to a new position. One hundred and fifty metres in front of us, a bellowing white column of water drops from the dam gates and pound the river below it. Bob opens the throttle on the 200HP engine and waits until we are dangerously close to the massive cauldron of white foam and spray, before giving me a signal to lower the anchor. As I let out the rope, a thundering roar begins to shake my eardrums and I can feel the cold, fine spray licking at my exposed skin. The engine cuts, and within seconds the fast current grabs hold of us again, and catapults the boat downstream. The anchor rope seems to go on forever, but eventually Bob signals to lower the buoy, so I quickly chuck it overboard then tie off the rope. Immediately, the strong flow whips the rope tight as piano wire and then swings the boat round in a bow wave until it settles in mid-river.

We are positioned just at the edge of a steep drop-off that leads into a 26 metre deep hole. Up until now, Bob has insisted that we use fillets of fish for bait, but after many bite-less hours I am keen to try something different. It is clear in my mind that the bulk of food for the big specimens at this time of year must be the Shad. Many of these small, silver fish swimming in huge shoals numbering many thousands, are snapped up as they swim up river on their way to the spawning grounds. It is obvious that live shad would be the most natural bait, but because live fish baits are banned in Washington State, I take the next best option – a whole dead shad.

The shad is mounted with the hook showing proud, and an extra coil of braid is threaded through with a needle to prevent the strong currents from ripping off the bait. Like a gigantic version of pike fishing, I cast the 2kg bait into the river, then control the speed of the decent with my finger over the spool. As soon as the heavy lead hits bottom, I lift the rod tip a fraction and feel the lead bounce up, before settling again a few metres downstream. I continue to trundle the bait for thirty metres until I can sense that the lead is dropping into deeper water, then lock the drag-arm of the reel. The rod is then set in the gimbal and I'm now confident that the bait is positioned perfectly on the edge of the steep slope that leads into the hole.

Evergreen trees cling to majestic cliffs that swoop down to the edges of the river. Cotton wool clouds race and roll along the crags until they crash against the jagged rocks, then lift and vaporise into a sea of blue. I am fishing for the Great White Sturgeon, North America's largest freshwater fish, and have picked the premier place to begin my search for them – the fantastic Columbia River Gorge. As I sit here, swallowing the beauty of the landscape around me, I can sense the big sturgeon swimming in the dark depths below the boat in their constant search for food.

The tip of the rod taps very gently and I immediately stand up then leave my hand quivering like a mosquito over the reel handle. There is another gentle tap, so I smoothly slide the butt from the gimbal. The third tap is more positive, as the rod tip plucks down sharply. I need no further indication, and without hesitation lift the rod in a strong, powerful sweep. The 'Ugly Stick' whacks round until it forms an incredible curve, then locks solid. I'm snagged on the bottom; but slowly, ever so slowly the bottom begins to move...Tick, tick, tick, tick, sounds come from the ratchet until they speed up and turn into a constant whine, as I watch the line cut sharper and sharper with the surface.

"It's coming out!" I scream.

But before the words have left my lips, the fish is airborne. A gigantic creature hangs in the air as if I've pressed 'stop' on the video. Thrashing its mighty head from side to side, it tries to free the hook; then more than 3 metres of fins and flesh fall back into the foam.

"Wahooo!" I scream.

"A 10 footer" Shouts Bob, as the ticking of the ratchet begins to once again turn into a constant tone. The fish bolts down river like an express train. 100, 150, 200 metres of line strip off the spool in one single rush. Then out it comes again, way down river, flaying its gills and raging like a Marlin, before finally crashing again through the white foam.

Meanwhile, Bob has thrown over the anchor buoy so that we can drift downstream, and now, 20 minutes later, the line is cutting straight down beneath the boat. Suddenly, the fish makes a long, powerful run towards the navigation channel. I can do nothing to slow the fish down, and Frank is forced to start the small outboard motor so that we can follow the fish.

Five minutes later, we have caught up with the fish and it is here that the real battle begins. This channel is where the giant ocean-going barges enter the lock gates of the canal, so that they can by-pass the main dam. I just hope that a large barge doesn't come through right now...

Frank tells me that there is a large snag close to where the fish is swimming, and that it was at this very place that he managed to lose a monster the previous week. It's not quite what I need to hear at the moment! I double the strain on the rod, and begin to hear the creaking of fibreglass and grinding of line being forced against the rod rings.

The sturgeon wakes up again and makes a fantastic run back towards the fast current. I'm terrified of it reaching the turbulent flow that boils and swirls 80 metres away, so I lock the butt firmly into the fighting belt and dig in my heels. The sun beats down on the back of my neck, forcing sweat to drip in rivulets all over my body. The line starts to twang and whistle in the wind as I cram down tighter on the reel and lean back.

Then, as if in defiance, right at the junction between fast and slack water, the sturgeon comes out again. With gills flaring, it shakes the heavy lead as if it's a Ping-Pong ball, and then finally crashes back through the waves. The thud of skin hitting water sounds like a hippo belly-flopping into the Zambezi.

The sturgeon just keeps on fighting; but eventually, 1 hour 25 minutes after first hooking it, I manage to grab hold of the trace. I pull the great beast close to the side of the boat, then lean over and place my hand inside its huge, extended mouth. Now the fun begins!

Because Bob is scared of damaging his boat on the rocks, he refuses to go into shore so that I can obtain some decent photographs. With only two of us on board, Bob is forced to take pictures of me, with one of his hands holding the camera while his other hand controls the steering wheel connected to the outboard motor. The boat swings and sways as the camera clicks, while I strain to hold on to more than 3 metres (10ft+) of fish whilst hanging over the side of the boat in rushing currents! I hate to let this fantastic creature go before I've obtained decent photos, but I must eventually let go of the tail and watch it sink into the depths...

Of course, the photographs turn out dreadful! For the next two weeks, I toss and turn in my sleep, depressed with the thought of having no decent photographs of my biggest freshwater fish ever.

One day, I wake up from another nightmare, determined to catch another monster, and this time take some proper photographs. So I pick up a phone and ring another guide, Frank Russum and ask him if he will take the boat into shore so that I can obtain good photos of any large fish that I may catch. He agrees! So I also persuade a good friend, Vern Westerdahl from Brewster, to accompany and help take some decent photographs with my cameras.

To catch a sturgeon over 10ft long just once in a lifetime is indeed rare, but to catch two of this size is indeed a miracle – but I'm going to try! Less than 24 hours later, I am back on the amazing Columbia River....

Second Attempt:

The boat swings gently against the powerful flow. Thirty metres below us, three baits bounce over the bottom in the darkness. The three rods lay gripped in gimbals, waiting for the tug of some primeval force. Clouds charge like black stallions across the peaks of rugged cliffs. Their snorting breaths vaporise on contact with ancient volcanic rock. A crystal stream rushes forth through the velvet green of Mt. Hood National Forest, where wild Lynx roam, and tumbles over Horsetail Falls. The giant monolith of Beacon Rock rises out of the Columbia's boiling currents and dominates the landscape. Ospreys wheel above our heads on thermal currents, scanning the water for shad. Time spent waiting for monsters is never boring in places such as this.

Vern's rod is the first to bounce in its gimbal and, as soon as the hook is set, the fish strips more than 200 metres of line in one long rush. Way downstream, we watch a wall of flesh and fins crashing out of the water. Jessica immediately throws the anchor buoy overboard and the boat begins to drift down river as Vern pumps wildly on the reel handle.

We are soon level with the fish and Frank starts the small outboard motor so that we can manoeuvre the boat. I fit a fighting belt to Vern's waist to relieve some of the pressure from his aching shoulders, but 1 hour and 30 minutes later, the boat is 3 miles downstream and Vern is almost collapsing under the strain.

Eventually, the 8ft 6 inches long fish is landed. As Vern holds the fish in the water, I cannot believe the size of its pectoral fins. They are massive, like tyre rims and Frank comments that he's never seen fins so big – any wonder it fought so well! 288lb+ is the average weight for this length, but this sturgeon is also very stocky for its length and we estimate it at 300lb before releasing it.

We steam back to the anchor buoy and recast into the same deep hole. My bait is immediately taken and, after a hard battle, I am grinning at the camera with a 9ft fish, weighing around 350lb. Vern cannot believe how quickly I have beaten such a fish. I make a light-hearted joke about why it took so long with Vern's fish and Jessica giggles, but I know that it was not just physical strength alone that beat the fish, but more a combination of technique and years of experience.

Jessica, Frank's 14 years old daughter, is next to fight a tail-walking 400 pounder. I forgive her for sitting down and resting the rod against the gunnels during the fight, for I know of many full grown men who would have given up against the onslaught of constant pressure. She grits her teeth and I watch in admiration as her stubborn nature gives strength to her Tomboy weakness.

"..I managed to capture some shots with the camera as the sturgeon spat the shad high in the air.."

Close quarters battle with a 700lb monster! - in the final stages of a long, tiring shoreline fight with a sturgeon measuring10ft 9_inches. Notice the heavy ball lead on the line, needed to hold large baits down in the deep, strong currents.

Within minutes of recasting, I hook into yet another massive fish. Four 300lb+ fish are enough to make any group of anglers happy, so we don't mind if there is no further action today – but it is not to be...

I mount a very large shad onto the No. 7/0 Mustard hook and cast it, with great difficulty, across the river. 1.5lb of lead is needed to keep the 4lb+(2kg) bait down in the ripping currents. I'm using a multiplier filled with 100lb test high-tech braid. By lifting the rod tip and releasing the spool under finger pressure, I trundle the bait downstream until I am sure it is in the right position. Twenty minutes pass by without action. Jessica and Frank get to work and cook up a sumptuous feast of prime steak and the sizzling aromas drifting over my nostrils begin to make my mouth water.

Jessica passes around the wonderful plates of food and I mentally hope that the next fish can wait until we've finished eating. Suddenly 500lb of sturgeon lifts its body out of the water, only a rod's length from where I sit. I gulp down the rest of the steak and move to one of the rods – I am sure the tip just quivered slightly. My stomach rumbles with undigested food and expectation...

Ten minutes pass then the rod is wrenched out of the gimbal and then straightens again. I pick up the rod and strike, but fail to connect. The line is bowing against the thousands of gallons of water rushing over it. Quickly, I wind like mad until the line starts to straighten again, then heave back on the rod. The tip abruptly stops halfway through the sweep and wrenches down to the river's surface, almost pulling me overboard.

Deep, deep down below the boat, a colossal fish swims slowly on with primeval force. It doesn't even realise that it's hooked. A tick, tick, tick breaks the silence. Vern quickly fits the fighting belt to my waist and, once the rod butt slips into place, I lean back with the full strength of my legs. The slow moving submarine gradually grasps the fact that someone is trying to stop it swimming!

Like a desert wind, there is a sudden rush of activity on board the boat; a screaming 'WHEEeeeee' emits from a smoking reel as some unseen express train almost empties the big spool in one fantastic run. Frank begins shouting at Jessica to hurry up with the anchor rope and, with fantastic speed, the motor is fired up then we chase the fish down-river.

Pumping on the handle like some demented piston, I eventually place line back on the reel. As soon as I catch up with the fish, it powers off like a rocket across river.

"She's coming out!" I shout to Vern but, each time, the fish stops within inches of the surface, sending vortices against the flow.

Even without seeing the fish I know that it is larger than anything so far hooked today, so I ask for Frank to start manoeuvring the boat closer to shore.

"If you want some pictures we'll have to put the boat in before we reach those bank anglers", shouts Frank.

I look over at the tight lines shining in the sunlight as they span out from the rods propped up on the high Washington bank. Another option would be to stay in mid-river, ease off a little on the pressure, and allow the fish to swim downstream past the bank anglers, where the battle could be resumed. This might prolong the fight an extra hour, with a big chance of the hook-hold working loose, so I grit my teeth and hold on. The rod, reel and line begin to whine and creak as the expanded veins in my muscles almost explode through the skin. Never have I placed so much pressure on any fish in my life; I work like a mad animal, fighting back every foot of line that I am forced to give.

The line begins to cut sharper and sharper with the surface. Suddenly, a massive fish breaks the surface. Sharp intakes of breath are followed by whoops of " Wow! Look at the size of that monster!" The bow of the boat bumps gently to shore and I manage to jump to the bank, still gripping the rod. But the sturgeon isn't ready, and with a sudden surge of power it drags me into the water up to my waist and almost wrenches the rod from my grasp. The margins drop steeply into deep water and I'm forced to dig my boots into the grooves between the rocks to prevent being dragged into the depths. My white fingertips begin to open with the incredible strain and I fear of letting go and losing everything.

"You bas...d!" I shout in rage then, through bloodshot eyes, I tense every straining muscle in a do-or-die attempt to stop the fish.

The stalemate seems to go on forever but, in reality, only a few minutes pass before the mighty fish breaks the surface again and rolls onto its side. As soon as the head is close to shore I move quickly, handing the rod to Frank and grabbing hold of the trace. Once I'm sure the fish is safe, I jump into the river and try to get my arms around it – I can't! I try to roll the sturgeon upright in the water but its massive bulk make it almost impossible. I'm forced to wrap my arms around the tail section as I shout instructions to Vern, who scrambles around the rocks, clicking away with my two cameras.

Frank hands me a tape measure and I measure the fish at a fantastic 10ft 9 inches. Frank is probably one of the most experienced professional sturgeon anglers in North America, so I ask his opinion on the weight of this monster.

"I've seen many 10ft+ fish Tony but never, in a lifetime of fishing this river, have I seen such a fat and massively built sturgeon. I'd put it at 750lb", replies Frank.

Using my own judgement, backed up by seeing many official big sturgeon photos and having weighed many large sharks, I also place the fish in the 750lb+ region. The official White Sturgeon Length for Weight Chart gives 657lb for an average fish of 130 inches, yet this is no average built sturgeon. However, there is no way I'm going to kill such a wonderful fish then hang it over a gantry just to prove my point.

We all agree on a weight of 700lb+ as I spend a few moments straining to hold the great fish upright against the current and let the oxygenated water flow through its gills. As the great white giant begins to wave its caudal fin, I bend down to kiss the massive shoulders before feeling its whale-like body brush slowly past my chest and sink into the depths. It becomes the most emotional, yet mind-blowing moment in a lifetime of fishing.

Shoreline Attempts:

The 700lb sturgeon made a special impact on my life. Only a few months before the capture, my father – the kindest, wisest, proudest and most incredible man who has ever touched my heart – died after six long and terrible weeks of fighting. When I loosened my grasp and opened my arms to watch that huge fish swim away from me, and gradually fade into the deep darkness of the river, a sudden overwhelming presence of my father filled the air. We are all free to believe or disbelieve what we can't or don't understand as rational, but during those very special moments I truly believe that my father was with me. I have always striven to follow my heart and turn away from artificial goals set up by society; but since that amazing day on the Columbia, I have realised more than ever

"..Then out it comes again, way down river.." A huge sturgeon strips off hundreds of metres of line and jumps clear of the water

that the quality of life is purely governed by the precious and magical moments that we experience. In the end, all material wealth crumbles into insignificance, and the only true valuables are our golden memories.

I was still hungry for magical memories, so, following a glorious day of boat fishing, I turned towards the shoreline in search of a battle from the banks. I already knew how difficult it was to hook and land a big sturgeon entirely from shore, but I now needed to add a touch of difficulty to my pursuit if I was to truly gain from my experiences – and add spice to my life!

There were of course numerous exciting battles with monster-sized fish from the glorious banks of the Columbia River during my expeditions over the following years. But none hold such strong cords in my memory than a trip with my good friend Jens Bursell to the river while it was in raging flood...

Final Pursuit

It took us most of the following day to drive up to the dry, desert location – only to find it amidst torrential rain! We camped in my mate, Vern's, back garden over the next three nights and thankfully the weather improved to allow us to try some stalking. We eventually found big carp and over two short, sunny days enjoyed carp fishing beyond our wildest hopes.

Jens and I, spent one more night in our tents and rose with the dawn so that we would have plenty of daylight for a long drive south, back to the gorge. On route to Bonneville Dam, we stopped to take in the awe-inspiring vistas at Dry Falls and Vantage Canyon; so by the time we finally reached

The Dalles it was late afternoon.

We had booked to go out in the boat with my good friend Frank Russum the following morning, but Jens was keen to spend these last few hours of today in pursuit of a bank-caught monster from our favourite cliff-edge perch. The car was still full to the brim with our rucksacks and carp fishing gear, but we only needed to use Sturgeon rods, so we grabbed these, locked the car and strolled down the steep path that clung to the rocky brim of the gorge.

It was good to be back on this awesome eyrie that gave superb vistas of the Columbia River Gorge. The soft yellow light beaming through white clouds that sped across the cliff tops indicated that time was waning fast. It did not take us long to rig up a half section of bloodied lamprey each, and cast them into the rolling currents. The river level had dropped dramatically since our visit four days previous, but it was still in flood and we still needed our heaviest leads to hold bottom in the raging flow.

With both rod butts lodged in the rest, we sat back and sucked in the ever-changing moods of the landscape; and waited. Both tips remained unmoving except for their gentle, swaying dance in time with the river's flowing currents. Two hours passed us by, and then something massive grabbed hold of Jens' lamprey section and almost tore the rod in two before he could lift it out of the rest. Within seconds, this fish nearly emptied the big Abu multiplier spool then catapulted Jens back against the rocks as the 80lb braid parted.

Jens finally stopped shaking and calmed down enough to be able to re-tackle and place fresh bait on the hook. I sat on the ground with my back propped against a rock, and watched him make a cast. The lamprey dangled on a short length of line from the rod tip as he lowered it behind him. Then he whipped the tip forward with force and waited until the carbon had flexed into its full arc, before releasing thumb pressure on the spool and catapulting the bait skyward. The lamprey followed the heavy lead as it flew across the river and exploded through a crease in the rolling currents. He waited for the lead to hit bottom, then bounced the rod tip a few times and controlled the spinning reel drum with a thumb as the bait kited back towards the bank. Soon the lead stopped rolling as it wedged against some stones on the river bottom, and Jens pushed the drag control lever forward, then walked back and propped the rod butt in the rest. This rod rest held both our rods firmly and was but a simple natural wedge formed by the entwined limbs of a small, stunted tree.

It was at this point that a man came strolling down the path that wound its way down the steep sides of the gorge, across a railway line and then snaked between giant boulders, before finally reaching our isolated cliff-edge swim. His abrupt entrance into our wild domain at first startled us, for we both didn't realise that he was standing behind us until his shouts lifted above the roar of water.

"Caught anything?" was his primary question.

We knew that if we gave but a hint of even getting some bites, let alone actually hooking fish, it would not be long before our sacred haven was swarming with other anglers, eager to receive their share.

"Not a touch. The river is too high and this current is just too strong" We both answered almost in unison.

At least the second sentence was close to the truth. We shrugged our shoulders, but our negative responses still didn't seem to deter him.

"How long are you staying here?" He asked.

Dusk was fast descending on the lower cliffs of the gorge and we had just been discussing whether to pack up, but his question seemed to make up our minds to stay a little longer.

"Oh, we'll probably stay for another half hour." Was my reply as I gestured a response from Jens, and he nodded in approval.

Our uninvited guest stood chatting to us for another ten minutes while a train rumbled down the track, screeching wheels and hooting loudly as it screamed past, until its echoes bounced off the canyon walls and faded in the distance. The guy seemed forever to be flicking his head nervously back up the track while he chatted to us. He seemed a little strange, and we were glad when he finally said goodbye, turned his back on us and walked back up the steep, winding path.

We fished for another 25 minutes until the sun disappeared behind the ridges and cast dark, cool shadows across the river. Jens began to shiver in the fast falling temperatures, and I was getting hungry, so we quickly reeled in our baits and shouldered our small daypacks.

It took us only about 5 minutes to reach the tree line that separated us from the road, and before I walked through a gap in the trees, I stopped to take a leak, while Jens carried on walking to the car. Necessities finished, I continued up the muddy track. Suddenly Jens came rushing through the trees and almost bumped into me, babbling so fast that his words were hard to grasp. But as soon as my eyes fell on the car I needed no further explanation from Jens.

"Oh no.... Oh no!" The words seemed to stumble out of dry lips as my legs propelled my body towards the half open door.

The window had been smashed into a million pieces and glass fragments were scattered everywhere. It was a hired car, so our expensive and precious gear was my first concern. I climbed inside to check what was missing. Both rod tubes were gone, along with the eight new carp rods inside them. My new Swedish rucksack, packed full with most of my clothes and other important gear, had also vanished. I scrambled around under the seat in a frantic search for a padded bag containing vital electronic cables, flash units, camera prism and other important equipment - but in vain. Outside the car, all I could hear from Jens was a constant stream of "Shit...Shit...SHIT!!"

My own four letter words began to echo his own as I climbed back out of the car and rushed to open the car boot. For moments I just stood in a daze, trembling and unable to turn the key in the lock. 'What if it has all gone?' I thought to myself. I had taken two camera bodies and two wide-angle lenses with me down to the fishing spot. But all the rest of gear – including another camera, and a special big-pocketed photo vest that held all my extremely expensive ED/APO high quality long telephoto lenses – had been locked in the boot.

Finally, I plucked up courage to lift up the lid. My heart lifted back off the floor as my eyes scanned the trunk and my fingers rummaged through all the pockets, to find everything still in its place. The lost carp rods and other items were worth thousands of pounds, but the lenses were worth 10 times that sum and I felt more than slightly relieved that they remained where I'd left them. I never insure all my professional camera gear because the insurance premiums for global cover are astronomical, so touching the lovely expensive glass lenses again prevented a heart attack!

For some reason the thieves took both our rod tubes and my big rucksack, yet they left Jens' rucksack. It still was lodged behind the back seat, covered in dirty washing. His rucksack was filled

Tony strains to hold onto the smallest sturgeon caught during his second trip!

11ft long sturgeon leaps free of the river in an attempt to throw the hook.

to the brim like mine was, but looking at it again – covered in grime, with all the straps and material frayed and stinking like Jens' old socks – it is no wonder that the thieves left it where it was!

We both spent the next fifteen minutes cleaning up the glass inside the car. It was during this period when my mind started sorting through all the items that were missing. Included amongst the missing items were my three Delkim alarms, three new Shimano 6500 Baitrunners and an expensive Penn Multiplier loaned from Frank. The list of items continued to mount in my head and my heart began to plummet back to the ground....

Apart from a broken window, the car itself was unaffected, so we drove back along route 84 to the Toll Bridge restaurant to find a telephone. The police department said that they would send a sheriff to take statements and that he would arrive in about half an hour, so we chose this opportunity to have a meal at the restaurant. When the sheriff arrived, he told us that a group of guys had been driving along route 84 between Portland and Hermiston, breaking into parked cars along the river, and that they had already 'smashed & grabbed' from three other cars before they broke into ours!

Over the evening meal, we discussed whether to call off our plans to fish with Frank in the morning. Although the loss of most of our prized fishing tackle had hit us a heavy blow, we realised that in some ways we had been lucky. The equipment had received extensive use over recent months to enable us to enjoy wonderful fishing in Australia and New Zealand. We had also just arrived back from an incredible two days of stalking carp on the upper Columbia, in which we landed many thirties and I even caught two 40lb commons in the same afternoon. At least we had enjoyed a superb carping session before the carp gear drove off in someone else's car!

I was due to fly to New York State later that week to meet Bernie Haines for an intensive search for big carp on the St Lawrence River. Although all my carp gear was now gone, I was sure that Bernie would loan some of his gear to allow me to continue the expedition. Jens was due to fly back to Denmark in five days time, but the main reason he had joined me on this expedition was to catch a giant sturgeon, so it would seem pointless to turn away now when he was so close to achieving his ambition. I assured Jens that Frank would help us catch plenty of monster Great White sturgeon from his boat, so it didn't take much convincing to continue our fishing as planned. I had booked Frank's boat for two days, so I phoned the car hire office at Se-Tac airport and arranged to drive to their Portland headquarters in three days time so that I could exchange our vehicle for another car. It was dark by the time we reached the riverside campsite and began to erect our tents. The campsite owner, a good friend and experienced angler who had loaned me one of his hand-built Sturgeon rods for bank fishing, was surprised when he noticed the smashed car door window. I told him about the incident, but said that because we were travelling, we had to store all our equipment somewhere, and the locked car was our only choice.

"Why didn't you tell me?" He shouted. "I've got a big empty garage on site. You could have stored all your equipment in there – no problem, and for as long as you want!"

Jens then looked at me and we both raised our eyebrows in mock disgust – 'Now he tells us!'

We rose from the warmth of our sleeping bags to meet the twilight of dawn as a cold mist swept low over the river. Frank soon arrived and following our happy reunion, I introduced him to Jens. Then Jens and I walked down to the edge of the pier while Frank reversed the trailer and let the boat slip into the sheltered waters of the quay. The motor was fired up as we stepped on board to join him, then within moments the boat was in midstream, battling against the mighty currents of the Columbia.

Since I had fished with Frank the previous year, there had been a major change in the rules for fishing boats within the gorge. Although rules for bank anglers remained unchanged and they could still fish anywhere downstream of the first set of marker buoys below Bonneville Dam, the new rules for boats forbid them to anchor upstream of the second set of marker buoys. This second line of markers stretched across the width of the river about 3 miles downstream of the dam, an in effect, prevented us from covering the prime hotspots for big sturgeon on the river. The new rules only applied for the following few months of spring and early summer, and would be lifted again in July, but this didn't help our wishes to fish in the same areas where I'd enjoyed so much success in previous years.

I discussed the problem with Frank, but he was already pointing the bow towards a section of river below the second buoy line, as he turned to answer my barrage of questions with a confident smile. "Don't worry, Tony, I know plenty of other places for us to fish. There is no doubt that some of the best areas lie upriver of us, but I have caught hundreds of big sturgeon downstream of the second markers. In fact, I actually prefer it because far fewer boats fish that particular stretch and even fewer skippers know exactly where to fish - but I do!"

He then gave me a knowing wink and another smile as the motor sounds lifted an octave and pushed the boat at speed towards the very last marker positioned next to an island close to the Washington bank. I climbed onto the bow and dropped the anchor, and then Frank cut the engines and let the boat drift downstream with the current. The anchor rope uncoiled off the edge and I waited until Frank gave a signal, then clipped on the large orange bubble-buoy and chucked it overboard. Within seconds, the rope twanged taught as a crossbow and swung the boat sideways in the strong currents, until we finally settled in mid-stream.

"Perfect!" Uttered Frank, with satisfaction.

The first hour was spent fishing with light spinning tackle for small fish to use for bait. American Shad (Alosa sapidissma), a small fish of the herring family, was our prime target as it is one of the best baits to use for White Sturgeon. Shad can grow to 76cm (30") in length and weigh up to 4.2kg (9lbs+), but average between 1 – 2.3 kg, which is a perfect size to use as hook bait.

Apart from the odd tiny plucks at our miniature metal spinners, nothing seemed interested in our offerings. Frank couldn't understand it, because two days previous he had caught 50 shad in an hour from this very spot! Shad are an inshore saltwater species that migrates into freshwater for a brief spawning period, before returning back to saltwater. This seasonal migration was still a long way from its late spring peak, when they swarm in a silver mass. Now they navigated upstream in small isolated shoals, so there could be days between sudden surges of fish. We now enjoyed one of those quiet days and the river seemed completely empty of Shad.

The shad need to swim hundreds of kilometres upriver before reaching their spawning beds, and many of the fish become weak and die. Many more are killed in their desperate attempts to navigate up the difficult fish ladders or are churned through the dam turbines. While we fished, Frank's eagle eyes constantly scanned the river's surface in a search for these dead fish as they floated downstream. Suddenly he spotted something, then rushed to the back of the boat with a small landing net in hand and scooped something silver off the surface as it swept passed. Another shad whizzed passed him in the fast flow, but he failed to catch it in the mesh.

"Up anchor, Tony!" Frank called back to me, and within minutes we were speeding down river in a desperate chase after the floating shad. It may seem strange that we should have spent so much of our valuable time in an attempt to catch shad, when Frank had some frozen shad in the cooler box, but Frank had already shown me on his earlier trips just how crucial a fresh bait could be. When the going got tough, a fresh shad would produce 10 times as many takes as a frozen shad.

After 15 minutes, we had scooped five more shad off the surface as they sped past and had enough to begin a serious search for big sturgeon. Frank cranked back the accelerator lever and pointed the boat downstream to one of the many 'hot spots' mapped out in his memory.

The area he chose was quite unusual in that it was far from the main volume of fast current that I'd come to expect to find large sturgeon. It was at the entrance to a carpy-looking backwater and near the edge of a giant eddy that moved millions of litres against the flow. I must admit that this was not my idea of a 'sturgeon hotspot', but my faith in Frank's immense knowledge of this river made me follow his predictions.

"We're now circling above a very deep hole, Tony. I know that there doesn't seem to be much flow up here, but I can assure you that 40ft down, there is quite a ripping current sliding beneath it in the opposite direction. It is about 55ft deep here but there is a huge ledge running diagonally along the eddy where it drops to about 90ft. Some large snags are wedged at the edge of this hole, so we'll need to be careful, but if you want big fish you'll have to place a bait where they are."

I couldn't agree more with the workings of Frank's mind and his words gave me confidence as, with an underhand swing of the rod, I flung the whole dead shad towards a crease in the eddy. Jens had a lot more problems trying to cast a whole shad using the short boat rods combined with multipliers, so Frank filleted one of the shad and mounted half on the hook. This still was too much weight for Jens, and his second cast almost took my ear off as the bait crashed into the river, just inches behind the outboard motor.

A 500lb+ Great White Sturgeon breaks surface during a long fight. Notice the heavy ball lead, needed to hold the large fish bait close to the bottom in strong river currents.

"Great cast, Jens! You'd better let Frank chuck it out for you." I remarked.

Frank grabbed hold of Jens' rod in his massive hands then flicked the short, stubby rod with a quick twist of his bulging biceps. The cast seemed so insignificant, yet the heavy ball of lead and bait went flying 50 metres past where my own bait had landed.

"There you are, Jens. Just leave it there, its right in the hole." Frank said with a smile as he turned to Jens and handed him the rod. It looked like Goliath handing a stick to David.

Jens cast out a small slither of cut bait on another rod, but I was keen on contacting only monsters, so also mounted a whole dead shad on my second rod. We then sat back in the comfy chairs to wait. Within ten minutes, there came a series of gentle taps on the small piece of fish bait, followed by a more aggressive pull down of the rod tip. Jens was already standing holding the rod in excited anticipation of landing his first big sturgeon. A strike met solid resistance, which lessened in pressure as the fish was brought nearer the surface, until a 5lb sturgeon spiralled beneath his rod in the turbulent water. The expression on Jens face said it all. He released the fish then turned to me and asked:

"How big a bait did your 700lb sturgeon take, Tony?"

"Oh, around about the same size as the last sturgeon you just chucked back." I replied with a wry smile.

Jens turned to Frank to ask him to put on bigger bait, but Frank was ahead of him and had already removed the largest shad from his cool-box and began mounting it on the hook. He then cast it back out and set the rod butt firmly in the gimbal. We waited for another thirty minutes, and then something whacked one of my rod tips down hard and then straightened again. I stood up with my hand quivering over the butt, but the rod remained rigid in the rest. I waited for a further twenty minutes for something to happen, but nothing came back to the bait, so I reeled it in for inspection. The hook was bare. I was about to take another whole shad from the cooler, when Frank stopped me and began slicing through two fresh shad on the cutting board with expert precision. The resulting four large fillets were then mounted on the No 7/0 Mustard hook and he handed the rod back to me. Rivulets of blood trickled down the sides of the fillets.

"That was a big sturgeon and I'm sure he's still down there sniffing around the bottom. He might be a bit wary of the whole bait or the scent from our hands may be tainting it, but they usually can't resist a big bundle of fresh fillets. It does tend to also attract the smaller sturgeon and catfish, but if the big one is still in the area he should snap it up first." Frank said as I chucked the bait back out to the same spot.

His words could not have been truer, because even before I had lowered the rod back into the gimbal, something heavy pulled the rod tip down towards the water and it stayed there.

"Don't strike yet, Tony. Just leave it for a few moments" Whispered Frank.

It felt as if a dead body was hanging off the rod tip, unmoving, except for the line quivering in the spiralling currents. Then there were three sudden jabs on the rod tip and the line began to change angle as something deep down below the boat started swimming upstream.

"Now!" Shouted Frank.

I lifted the rod with slow and deliberate force, and at the same time wound down on the reel handle until taught and solid pressure could be felt beneath my palms; then I hit into it more violently a second time. The rod became a living thing in my hands as a huge caudal fin pushed 8.5ft of fish at turbo speed along the riverbed. Pure adrenalin injected into my veins and a racing heartbeat pumped blood faster through my body. I could feel my biceps and calves begin to tense and bulge as they fought to counter balance the immense and mounting pressure.

A loud and continuous sound screamed from within the bowels of the big metal spool as it span at an alarming rate. The noise filled the air and ricocheted off the canyon walls. It was a terrifying, yet beautiful sound.

Frank started up the motor then went to the bow of the boat, unclipped the buoy and threw it overboard. He quickly climbed back to the controls and swung the craft in a wide arc until we were again level with the fast moving fish. My left hand pumped wildly in an effort to wind all the lost line back on the reel, and at the same time keep constant pressure on the hook-hold. The rod buckled under the incredible strain, as the decreased length of line between boat and fish allowed me to apply more direct pressure. But the fish was far from ready and suddenly sped across the width of the river, and then raced down stream. Frank spun the steering wheel and the boat carved a path through our own bow waves as we gave hot pursuit.

Five minutes later, the boat caught up with the fish and once again the more direct contact made it change direction. But this time it didn't go on a long run; instead, the big sturgeon swam directly upwards. Within seconds the incredible creature was airborne, shaking its mighty cranium from side to side in anger, before crashing back through the waves.

"Wow!" cried Jens in utter excitement and wonder.

The sturgeon that he'd hooked from the bank earlier that week had jumped just before he lost it, but he was so engrossed in his own battle that he didn't see it clearly. This time his eyes were wide open as the fish heaved its bulk towards the heavens, and I understood his joy at seeing such a monster fish at close quarters. I began to tighten up the slack following the jump, but as soon as the line twanged taught, the sturgeon was airborne again, breaching like an Orca Whale and tail-walking across the surface. Its heavy body slapped sideways through the waves, but it was only seconds before the water began bulging yet again. The great fish rose out of the commotion until half of its bulk hung in the air, and then almost without a sound, it slid back down and disappeared beneath the foam.

There was an eerie silence, as we all stood rigid with our eyes transfixed to a vacant space amongst the waves. It was as if we all expected the sturgeon to crash out for a fourth time, but it was not to be, and the sound of a screaming ratchet eventually shook us from our trance. The jumps had sapped most of the power from the great fish, and now it only went on short runs or rolled near the surface. Eventually it erupted in a cascade of fizzing bubbles, before turning on its side to show us an enormous white flank.

Frank expertly manoeuvred the boat closer into shore, to enable me to climb into the waist deep water with the rod and then gently pull the tired fish across to the shallow margins. Jens quickly jumped in beside me and clicked off a series of photos. The motor driven cameras whizzed through the film, and it was soon time to release the fish. I lifted the Great White Sturgeon upright, until I could see the massive gill flaps pumping through oxygenated water to its exhausted muscles. Then as the huge fish began to slowly flex its powerful body in my grasp, I opened my arms and watched it swim like an undulating crocodile through the turbulent waters.

Another hour flew by without action, so without hesitation Frank stoked up the engine and powered us further down river. When he reached a certain area, he began to make the boat zigzag across the flow; always keeping an eye on landmarks along the margins, until he was entirely satisfied that it was the exact spot. Then he cut the engines and called for me to drop anchor. This part of the river was completely different from the last. The river was much wider and the flow seemed less powerful, but this was deceptive, and we soon found out that there was plenty of force beneath the spiralling vortexes that buffeted against the taut anchor rope.

Jens' whole shad bait was the first to be taken this time, and it turned out to be a very acrobatic fish. On it's second jump, I managed to capture some shots on my camera as the sturgeon spat the shad high in the air in a desperate attempt to rid itself of the hook; but the strong hook held firm, and Jens was finally able to land his first giant sturgeon, weighing around 275lb. The nearest shoreline turned out to be a series of high, muddy banks with deep-edged margins. But Jens was desperate to obtain photos of this fish, so he jumped in the water beside it. However, bandy-legged Jens was no match for even a tired sturgeon, and I spent the next few minutes photographing him being smacked in the face or thrown against the bank by a huge caudal fin, until he was caked from head to toe with glutinous brown mud!

I was next to hook up with a very powerful fish, which turned out to be a stunning looking specimen with glorious skin colours and perfect conditioned fins the size of tractor tires. Because this fight had taken us out to mid-river, we decided to pull into the opposite bank, which had no mud and gradual-sloping margins. Jens did some fine work with my cameras, until I eventually said goodbye to the beautiful 350lb+ fish.

Soon after clipping back up to the anchor buoy, Jens yet again hooked into a high jumping fish that gave us a spectacular display of strength and agility – which is more than can be said about Jens! This sturgeon was also over 300lb, and by the look on Jens' face I'm sure he thought that he'd finally reached seventh heaven!

We still had time to catch one more fish, so we steamed back to the same position and waited in expectation of more exciting action. Our good luck was by now attracting the attention of other anglers. Frank is well known in these parts, and unsavoury characters, who don't seem to have a clue how to fish, never mind find them, seem to spend most of their time spying us with binoculars and following our boat. One such boat had been trailing us since my very first fish upriver, and now it was anchored very close to our boat. Frank got on well with most of the experienced crews that worked the river, but seemed to detest the guys who always tried to take advantage of other people's hard work. They had been fishing all day, but had yet to hook up to a fish.

Time dragged on as a bright white sun arched through the skies and finally disappeared behind the majestic Beacon rock. It cast a gigantic shadow across the river, and the last rays of sunshine beamed over our heads to strike the opposite cliffs of the gorge and turn them into gold. I knew we had about 45 minutes left before we'd have to fire up and race back to the docking bay. Suddenly Frank stood up from his seat and rushed to the side of the boat and leaned over the side until he was almost falling in. Two seconds later, his outstretched hand plunged into the cold waters.

"I've got it! I've got it", He shouted triumphantly. "Quick, pull in one of the baits and cut off the rig. Quick!"

We weren't quite sure what the hell he was on about at first, but another bellowing scream from Frank soon had me winding in one of the rods like mad. The rig was quickly cut off and I could now see that Frank was holding on to a length of line that was trailing on the surface. The two ends were then expertly tied together and another shout from Frank had me winding hard on the reel handle like a man demented.

"Quick Tony, climb to the front of the boat. I saw someone hook into something earlier and then they lost it. Maybe this line is still attached to the fish that broke them."

All of a sudden my right hand jerked to a halt on the revolving reel handle and the rod was almost ripped out of my hands as it keeled over and crashed against the gunwale.

"Hold onto it, Tony. Hold on to it!" Screamed Frank.

The line was now fully taut and rubbing the underside of the anchor rope. The rod & reel clattered against the metal bow as I grappled with all my strength to swing it underneath without letting go or toppling into the river. Just as I was halfway underneath the anchor rope and holding on like a trapeze artist, a sudden jerk on the rod almost pulled it out of my grip. Then way downstream, something massive heaved its body clear of the river and shook its head in anger. I didn't see the jump, but Frank did.

"Yes! He's still on, Tony. Don't let go of that rod!"

Frank's shouts spurred me on and I tightened my grip on the butt as I swung it under the rope, then clambered back like a monkey to the back of the vessel. The battle continued, but now that I was in full control the fish soon became tired and swam closer to the boat. Two more jumps sapped all the energy from the fish and eventually it rolled near the gunnels and showed me a huge white underside.

"It's a big one, Tony. Do you want me to take the boat in so we can take some pictures?" asked Frank.

It was indeed a lovely fish, but it wasn't exactly my capture, even though the event had been full of excitement.

"No, mate; it's OK I'll let it go."

I quickly removed the hook from the gigantic funnel mouth, then let go of the sturgeon's rubbery lip and watched its massive body sink back into darkness.

"Give me that hook," asked Frank.

He looked closely at the offending rig and line, and his huff told us just what he thought of it as he wrapped it all in a neat ball. Then we quickly up anchored and motored back upriver towards the other boat. Frank manoeuvred us close to their boat then he asked them politely if they'd lost anything. They looked puzzled, but after a few moments they shook their heads. They'd seen our sturgeon jumping during the fight, so asked us how big it was and what bait we used to catch it! Frank tried to suppress a grin as he expertly guided our boat a little closer in the treacherous currents, then handed their rig back to them.

" You ought to use stronger line if you want to land those big fish. That last one you hooked put up a nice fight though. We've just let it go. About 480lb, I'd say – wouldn't you lads?" said Frank with a confident grin, as he turned to face us.

Jens and myself nodded in agreement. The occupants of the other boat glanced down again at the rig, and they looked astonished as the realisation that the sturgeon that they had hooked and lost, was the very same fish that we had just caught. I'll never forget the gormless look on their faces! Then Frank slipped our boat away from them and opened up the engine to power us upriver. The three of us were laughing so loud that it almost drowned out the sound of the engine...

Tony holds onto a gigantic White Sturgeon from one of his recent expeditions.

Fishing the wild heart of Devils Rock Canyon.

RETURN TO THE

VALLEY OF MISTS

Tony fishes the expanses of Savanna during the sweltering heat of a
Spanish summer. The castle in the background is normally under
water during winter!

Tony's underwater camera
captures the release of a big
mirror carp.

At the edges of the dry open plateaux of La Mancha in central Spain, a ribbon of shimmering blue-green waters snakes for 10km through a valley of the upper Guadiana River. The lake reflects upturned images of a forest of firs that line the eastern bank and an unending band of golden brown cliffs that grip the western shore. I stare out of the passenger window and my eyes easily penetrate the gin-clear waters, to reveal an army of red-claw soldiers clambering slowly across the rocky, sand-coloured bottom. The thousands of crayfish are like spots on the flanks of a giant wild trout. A stream of cool breeze wafts from the air-con system as the big 4WD Pajero continues to roll and bounce over the pot-holed track that clings to the rim of Embalse de Peñarroya - Lake Cambarosso in the Valley of Mists.

My eyes continue to scan the magical waters, but suddenly the vehicle begins to lean to one side as Peter slams on the brakes to prevent us from sliding off the cliff. A dust cloud envelopes the car, then rises and disperses into a sapphire sky. I swing open the door and a wall of heat hits my body and sucks out the pocket of cool air from the cabin.

" Drat! We've got a puncture," shouts Pete, as he walks to the rear of the vehicle and begins to remove the big spare wheel.

The Pajaero is crammed full of tackle, bait, food and drink, so we spend the next 15 minutes unloading most of the gear to ease the load off the axle. The vehicle is jacked up, the wheel removed and the spare wheel tightened in its place. As Pete slowly cranks on the handle I watch in silent interest, then hope, then horror as the vehicle gradually sinks back on to its side. The tyre on the spare wheel is also flat! Pete has also forgotten to pack the foot pump! It's nice to know that we are in the middle of a Spanish heat wave; 3 hours walk from the nearest garage....

Luckily, once the jack has been lowered completely, there still seems to be some air left in the tyre, so we unload the rest of the gear from the vehicle, then Pete drives slowly and delicately back along the track in search of oxygen. I spend the next hour moving all the iceboxes and other gear into the shade, then collapse in a soggy heap of sweat.

A fast moving dust cloud on the horizon signals the triumphant return of Pete, screeching back up the desolate dirt track with five tyres full of air. The mountain of equipment is loaded back inside the vehicle and we are soon in motion again, searching for a place to fish and set up camp. It takes a further 2 hours of searching along the shoreline, before we eventually arrive back where we started. The problem is that the lake level is still very high and most of the marginal thorn bushes are beneath water. There are only a couple of open stretches to cast from along the next 4 kms of bank, but even in these swims the deeper water hides a profusion of submerged bushes and other snags. The sun is sinking fast, so we need to find a place soon before darkness falls over Cambarosso.

Following a lot of discussion, we eventually decide to head back towards the Double Tree swim.

An extremely long common caught from Devils Rock Canyon.

Pete battles with a hard-fighting carp in the clear waters of Cambarosso

An American Crayfish (Procambarus clarki) shows its aggression as it captures a young pike in the gin-clear margins of Camborroso, and settles down for dinner!

With daylight quickly fading, we scan the bottom with an echo sounder and then drop two marker floats at a depth of 9 metres, around 85 metres from shore. I bait up heavily with carp pellets and Nash Scopex air-dried 20mm boilies. Three semi-balanced double-boilie hookbaits are cast out to the baited area. Pete chooses not to bait so heavily on his marker, and then casts out 3 single crab-flavoured boilie hookbaits.

The area looks quiet as we set up the rest of our gear (no tents or bivvies allowed in this area), then sit back on the bedchairs and watch the changing light over the water. The odd small carp tops beyond the baited area, then one rolls in the margins directly in front of Pete. A strong breeze began to blow while we baited up, but it died down as soon as the sun crept below the horizon and now the surface is as smooth as glass. A second fish crashes out in front of Pete, but his buzzers remain silent as the valley becomes cloaked in darkness.

The intermittent daytime chirp of grasshoppers hiding in the dry grasses behind us is gradually replaced by the whirr of cicada and cricket wings, until their sounds blur into a constant scream. Swarms of mosquitoes dancing above our heads bring out hundreds of Mouse-eared bats that dive-bomb the insects and catch them in flight. The clicking sounds of their sonic high-frequency calls tingle the inside of my eardrums as they swoop like miniature Kamikaze pilots. A moth flutters nearby, and I suddenly duck and almost fall off the bedchair as one of the bats expertly snaps it up only inches from my nose!

The World spins and soon the hum of cicadas is joined by the grinding sounds emitted from Pete's flaring nostrils. At 01:30 hrs, the snoring abruptly stops as a 12lb mirror carp swimming off with a crab boilie causes a Delkim to scream at us. Our sleep remains undisturbed for the rest of the night, until the first shafts of light from a rising sun, signals another low double figure carp to pick up a Scopex hookbait.

A group of small carp begin topping over our baits during the early part of the morning, but by the time the sun is high and bleached in a cloudless sky I am restless from inactivity. The cord clips are connected to the 12V battery and soon the MinnKota motor is silently pushing the Zodiac across the smooth surface of the lake. I am heading for a large group of half-submerged bushes situated in the eastern corner of the bay, about 50 metres out from shore. Within moments of reaching the outer lying bushes I begin to spot carp, and by the time I am in the centre of the snags, the Zodiac is surrounded by hundreds of fish.

I quietly manoeuvre the craft close to a bush then tie it to one of the branches. The disturbance has unsettled some of the fish, but soon they regain confidence and continue to circle the snags. Many of the carp are swimming directly beneath the dinghy and this crystal clear water is allowing me to see every scale and marking on their bodies. The clarity however is also working against me and some of the larger specimens are becoming disturbed by the shadow of the dinghy. A slight breeze that has suddenly picked up is also producing a slight choppy wave that transmits minute movements and subsequent noise of rubber brushing against branches. Most of the carp range from 15lb - 25lb, but there are a sprinkling of good 30lb+ commons amongst them. It is noticeable that the largest specimens are keeping to particular routes through the maize of snags, and these tend to be amongst the densest tangles of branches covered by the deepest water.

As I watch in fascination at this wondrous sight of hundreds of carp milling beneath the dinghy, I fail to notice a dark cloud creeping silently over La Mancha. Suddenly my body is surrounded by cool air as the cloud blocks out the blinding sun and casts Cambarosso in shadow. A wind whips up the surface of the lake,

Pete fights a common carp and Tony captures the exact moment with his camera as the fish leaps clear of the water!

sending most of the carp scuttling for deeper water. I can still see some of the carp drifting in and out of the maize of sunken bushes, but this wind is making it very difficult to keep the dinghy from rocking and scaring carp within casting distance, so I untie the cord and head straight back for shore.

We open up our umbrellas and wait for the storm to hit us, but the rumbling black cloud skirts around the edges of the mountains and refrain from dropping their heavy loads of water. A few spots of rain strike against the dust near our rodpods, but soon the heavens open up again and we are bathed in brilliant sunshine.

Pete drives to town to buy some more large bags of maize, and by the time he returns I've already decided on a move. I want to fish close to the sunken bushes where I tied the dinghy earlier. I did fish the northern edges of this particular line of bushes during my first trip to this lake, but although I had plenty of action I also lost most of the fish due to unseen snags. The southern fringes of the submerged bushes flank a small bay. A steep cliff skirts the margins and although most of the bay contains shallow, snag-infested water, one section opens into deep, fairly snag-free water.

Pete chooses to try where the lake begins to narrow towards the river. A steep cliff drops steeply towards the shores of the far bank, but the near bank is very flat and will provide a stable platform for him to fish from. My chosen swim however, is like the north face of the Matterhorn and there is only just enough space to fit a pod + bedchair level with the water.

The big move begins, and following hours of sweaty toil lugging heavy gear down the steep cliffs, I finally collapse in a heap next to my rods. A short trip out in the dinghy has revealed a few extra 'blips' on the echo sounder, which unfortunately are big, prickly bushes submerged under 6 metres of water. This will entail some extra care when playing hard-fighting fish, but the area is clear compared to the other swims I've so far tried. A 3 metre-wide belt of dense, green weed (similar but stronger than Canadian pondweed) grows along the margins. It is stuffed full of crayfish, so I decide to cast one bait in the margins. I want to place the other two baits as tight as possible to the line of submerged bushes, but my miniature platform is a long way from it, and with the heavy line I am using it will make it hard to reach. I could take the baits out with the dinghy, but I expect frequent takes, which will not only make it a chore to replace rigs in position, it will also disturb the area too much. In the end, I find that if I wade 30 metres along the shoreline and then cast towards the bushes, I'm able to accurately get my hookbaits in place.

By sunset there is a grin on my face due to a hectic period of action. It was not long after I had heavily baited the bushes area with the aid of a dinghy and settled back behind my rods, that the indicators began rattling. I've had a stack of fish now, some beautiful commons, but also a sprinkling of spectacular fully-scaled mirrors. Nothing really big has shown up yet and most of the carp are between 15 - 25lb. The best fish hooked was a stocky built fully-scaled mirror of around 28lb+, which fought like a demon in the gin-clear water. I brought this particular carp right to the edge of the weed belt and although it tried three times to get inside some marginal sunken trees, a fully arced rod managed to stop it from entering the branches. The net was ready to scoop up my fully-scaled gem, when it decided to power off on a final run, and the hook pulled. The air went blue with my four-letter words following that incident, but a stream of other good fish has brought a smile back to my face.

Pete's also had a number of carp up to low twenties. As usual, we've both had our share of hook pulls. This we have discovered is mainly due to very delicate skin membranes of the inner mouth of most of these carp. With so many snags to pull the strong fish away from, it is inevitable that we lose some fish. Pete has no sunken trees or bushes in his swim, but a shallow plateau stretches for 60 metres from his margins, then the bottom shelves sharply into the deep water of the old river channel. Pete is finding it a chore to bring carp across the apex of this shelve and the best of his fish have torn the hook free after jamming in clumps of weed growing on top of the shelf. It is quite strange that these carp have soft inner mouths, because all the other lakes in this valley have similar type bottoms, yet the carp that occupy them possess thick, rubbery mouths.

One incident of note occurred shortly after I lost the big fully-scaled mirror. Pete had forgot to buy something from town, so while he was gone, I reeled in my own, then walked round to his swim to make a brew and watch his rods. His car had only just disappeared down the track, when his right hand rod shook on the pod! My strike met a wall of slowly moving resistance. This fish just went on and on. Only when I began to notice the base of the spool beginning to show beneath the line, did I realise that something had to be done fast. Extra thumb pressure on the revolving spool made not a jot of difference. Eventually, and with hardly a slowing of pace, the fish reached within a few coils of the spool knot, then the line fell slack. I reeled in like mad, just in case the fish had abruptly changed direction, but no, the hook had just pulled.

When Pete returned, he couldn't believe that he'd missed a golden opportunity to fight a biggie. At first I thought the fish was maybe a monster barbel, but after a few minutes fight the sensations down the line told me that it was more likely a big carp in the 40lb+ region. I was angry at losing such a powerful fish; Pete was merely gutted!

A strong wind has begun to blow since the sun disappeared behind the ridge. Within an hour, the grey dusk has been replaced by pitch black as an angry sky sweeps a giant, rumbling cloud above our heads. Heavy raindrops spit against the dry earth and lightning bolts stab at the mountaintops. Then suddenly the wind and rain stops, as

Lean, fighting machine!

A muscular Cambarosso common carp with a pink-tinted underside, typical of a fish that has fed heavily on red crayfish.

if someone has flicked a switch on a giant fan.

There is an unearthly silence as the massive cloudbank directly above our heads begins to spin. Every few seconds the clouds turn a luminous green, as sheet lightning rips through the clouds. I can actually feel the electricity in the air and the hair begins to lift on the back of my neck. The air begins to smell like the sulphur on burnt matches. I look up at the amazing, slowly spinning black mass of vapour and a quiet "Wow!" falls from my open lips. We are in the eye of the storm.

It suddenly dawns on me that the rods on my rodpod have been left pointing at the sky like a rocket launcher, and the umbrella is till up, so I rush back to my swim. One conducted bolt of lightning could turn the whole lot into a dust pile. But I am too late, and within fifty metres of the cliff edge, the first lightning bolt strikes through the trees and reflects off the water. A raging wind funnels down the valley and begins to bend the big trees back as if they are made of rubber. I reach the pod just as the heavens open and pour gallons of cold water over my head. Forked tongues rip from gaps in the clouds and search for a foothold on earth. They find it. Stab, stab, POW! - As a tree on the far bank splits in two and bursts into flames. I am wary to touch those fishing rods, but in a sudden urge of desperado, I grab all three rods and place them horizontally on the ground. The pounding raindrops chase me all the way back up the cliff and down the muddy track towards Pete. I slip and slide in my sandals and only prevent myself from head-butting a tree by the guiding light from the electrified sky.

I reach Pete's bedchair, only to find it empty. He is sitting inside the big Pajero, hiding from the rain and shielded by rubber tyres. A vehicle is both the driest and safest place to be during a storm, so I fling open the passenger door and jump in to join him.

The next hour is absolutely fantastic - both awesome and frightening at the same time. The wind increases in strength and begins to rock the big 4WD vehicle and we feel like we're on the high seas. Strike after strike rips out of the sky and probes against the spires of lofty trees. The ground shakes and rumbles, followed by incredibly loud claps of thunder. Suddenly the whole lake lights up as if it is a mid-summer afternoon - then again, and again. We can actually see so clearly that the bottom weed is showing beneath 5 metres of green waters! Never have I witnessed such an amazing sight. Then a small red light shines at us through the waters that stream in rivers down the windscreen. It is one of Pete's Delkims; he's got a run!

At first, Pete just sits staring out of the window, his eyes transfixed by the glowing diode, yet seemingly glued to his seat. He doesn't want to go near those lightning conductors! Then all of a sudden he swings open the door and runs towards the spinning spool. He doesn't strike, but just begins reeling in like mad. In fact, he's so scared of lifting up his rod towards the sky, that he almost reels the carp straight out of the water and along the grassy bank. Luckily (!) the line breaks and the carp flaps off the grass and bow-waves back out to open water. A sudden flash of lightning, lights up the lake again and I can actually see the carp swimming through the clear water. It also lights up Pete's face and the fear shines in his eyes like some macabre horror film.

I can see that he urgently wants to get back to the safety of the car, but the thought of another run gives him a boost of bravado as he gets down to the task of reeling in the other two rods and chucking them down on the grass. I wind down the window just a fraction and then shout if he's OK. Five almost continuous lightning strikes then light up Pete's body like a Christmas tree to reveal him reeling like mad with the rod tips wedged in the mud in front of him!

Pete jumps back into the rain-lashed vehicle and we spend most of the hours of darkness sheltering from the storm. The wind dies down again, but the phenomenal smell of electricity in the air caused by strike after strike of white-hot bolts stabbing at earth, makes us continually uneasy. Our ears ring to the constant explosive claps of thunder and no matter how tired we become we cannot sleep tonight.

Dawn eventually breaks over a tranquil scene of calm blue-green waters. The black clouds have blown over, but the morning news on the radio tells of a country blasted by the storm. This night has been the worst storm in living memory and Spain recorded more than 1,000 lightning bolts hitting various objects around the country!

I row out in the dinghy and drop a lot of maize and boilies over the sunken bushes area. This gets the swim boiling with activity again, and the first carp soon come rolling in over my landing net. The fish feed intermittently throughout the day, so I keep the boilies going in with the aid of a throwing stick, just to keep them interested.

The day wears on and the heat grows in intensity, until the sun reaches its peak, then falls slowly back towards earth. The scenery is quite beautiful now. An orange-tinted sky hangs above a sheet of water seemingly made of glass.

The silhouette of a Sparrowhawk hovers over me, then I realise that it is a Nightjar catching flies and mosquitoes. It's quite amazing to watch these birds every evening flying so low over my head that you can hear the air rushing through their wings. The sky turns red and mauve then fades into black, as a giant crimson moon begins to peep over the mountain crest. An hour later, the moon has seemingly diminished to half its original size, yet its luminosity is now so strong that it paints shadows across the landscape. I'm sitting here perched on a big rock behind my three rods that point out across the water. This is a lovely swim. The air is completely still, except for the hum of cicadas in the background and the odd whine from mosquitoes and midges. The mosquitoes are not so bad, because it is now August and the intense daytime heat has killed most of them off.

The carp have been on my baits for most of the daylight hours and I've experienced a lot of action. Many superb

Tony's camera captures a 'golden moment' as Pete releases a big common.

looking carp have already been caught and returned, but the slap of skin and fins on the surface above my baited area foretells of more action. I can feel it in my blood that one of the reels is about to spin again. It's a lovely feeling of excitement.

Pete has driven into town to pick up Miguel, a young mad-keen carper who has driven hundreds of kilometres from the Deep South, just to spend a few days fishing with us. But at the moment I'm left alone to watch the changing light spread across this tranquil scene. It's so beautiful here and now I'm the only angler on the whole 10km of lake. Where in England could I repeat that phrase? I continue to stare out across the fabulous waters of Cambarosso, waiting patiently for an unseen giant to pick up one of my hookbaits.

A thump, then another thump and crash break me out of my trance. A group of big carp have moved in on my baits. They are attacking the crayfish that have crept out from the protection of the weed beds at dusk to scrape their claws on my pile of free bait. The carp must be chomping on the crays like crazy down there, because every few seconds I can hear the strange sounds like a dog barking as a carp surfaces. The reason for this behaviour is that the crayfish are crushed inside the mouth and then ground by the pharyngeal teeth. During a bout of heavy feeding, claws and broken shell fragments soon clog up the passageway and the carp are forced to periodically clear out the shells. To do this, they swim fast directly upwards and spit the shell fragments out as they break through the surface, then roll like porpoises and dive back to the bottom.

The noise of the 'barking' carp reaches a crescendo. There must be more than a hundred carp crashing out over my baited area. The air is tense with expectation. A rod suddenly taps, and then is almost wrenched off the pod as one of the carp, now full from a banquet of fresh crayfish, decides to suck in a boilie for desert!

SIAMESE GIANTS

The wild waters of Jungle Mere in northern Thailand.

JUNGLEMERE

Yesterday we were fishing the superb looking Mae Reservoir that holds 60kg Siamese carp and 100kg Mekong catfish. The Delkims remained silent for 24 hours and with no signs of fish, we decided to follow up a lead on a nearby lake reputed to hold many common carp. Our first recognisance of this water proved that the reports were genuine. A local angler lifted his keepnet and inside, amongst many exotic species, was three fish that we immediately recognized as common carp – Cyprinus carpio. The three carp were only small but at least it showed that this particular lake held them.

A short talk with the bailiff confirmed that the lake was a disused reservoir more than 30 years old and had been stocked with about 2000 carp 13 years previous. More good news – this water had never been netted, one of the very few lakes in Thailand that strictly stuck to this rule. Just how big were the carp in this water? One of the local lads said that he'd landed an 18lb common carp, but many bigger fish had broken his line. Which, looking at his feeble tackle, did not say very much, but at least it indicated that big carp might exist. Was this virtually unfished water holding big carp, or was it water full of stunted, miniature commons? We were keen to find out, so our recognizance ended with plans to return the following morning for a full day session.

So here we sit Stuart and I, fishing a promontory of ancient granite rock that juts out from the margins of Jungle Mere. My two Globetrotter Mega rods are propped on the titanium pod and their tips point towards the far bank. But I cannot actually see the solid ground of the shoreline, for it is completely covered in dense jungle and this thick carpet rolls like a river, swallowing everything in its path, until it swoops like a waterfall into the fringes of the lake.

Behind us, creeping vines as thick as a man's torso twist around giant trees that reach for the heavens. Thousands of different plants fight for space in this dark jungle, home of a million unseen creepy crawlies. I wouldn't fancy fishing this swim during the night; I might get carried away on the back of something big and hairy – and I'm not talking about Stuart!

I have cast a popped-up peanut/maize combination hookbait to the near margins beneath a tree branch that droops towards the water. Vines wrap around the branch like snakes and a bouquet of beautiful red flowers hang like a candelabrum in the breeze. The second hookbait is a pop-up crayfish flavoured boilie combined with a PVA stringer of Shellfish boilies, and this has been cast about 80 metres out in deep water.

Stuart has cast one bottom-bait out for carp and a second rod has been set up with light float tackle and paste hookbait for anything that comes along. A splash in the margins indicates another ball of groundbait hitting the water, and as the crumb ball explodes, the particles attract thousands of young Threadfin catfish and Tapia fish that dart exited inside the cloud. Stuart's delicate antenna float bobs under the surface a few times during the next few hours, but each strike fails to connect. At about 10:00hrs a noise, like a million leaves rustling in the wind, reaches our ears. The noise gets louder and louder until it is a bellowing roar of thunder. It sounds as if a thousand trees are rocking their trunks against each other; then we suddenly realize what it actually is - the sound is drops of rain falling through the thick jungle canopy on the distant mountains.

Fifteen minutes later, the rain hits us. Like a giant moving mountain, it sweeps slowly across Jungle Mere until it crashes against our bodies. We have no time or space to raise the tent, so we rush to erect a makeshift shelter with the flysheet. I tie two ends to two trees and prop the rest up using

A monk looks down towards the rushing torrents of the Ping River.

my tripod and landing net. Stuart props up one corner with a spare rod.

Already after two minutes the raindrops have found a way through the tent cover stitching and cold water begins to trickle down my neck. The rain thumps the cover harder and harder until it pierces the material and cascades over our bodies as fine spray. Every few minutes a giant puddle forms above our heads and Stuart gives regular pokes with the rod to send buckets of water over our feet. For almost an hour we sit huddled under the makeshift shelter, wearing only our shorts, as the torrential rain pours out of the skies. We begin to get hungry and open a packet of crisps, then eat our feast as a sea of water surrounds us.

Suddenly it stops and we choose this opportunity to erect the complete tent properly on the grassy slope of the dam wall, which is the only place free of thick jungle.

We are just in time, for soon another wall of water begins to fall from the skies and sends us both running for the tent and zipping up. We are still hungry, so Stuart braves the rain to fetch the gas cooker. He lights it inside the tent and once the water is boiled, we happily sip down our Pot Noodles.

For four solid hours the rain pounds the tent and by the time it eventually stops, big puddles have formed inside. So much for buying a cheap Thai tent from the market, hey Stuart?!

The short time we have left before darkness is spent trying to extract a carp from the lake. As we sit amongst the mud-splattered fishing gear, water constantly drips from the jungle canopy. Rising temperatures causes clouds to form inside the green forest on the far bank and they begin to drift through the trees, until they vaporize beneath the sun's rays.

Eventually Haiman Nangkam, affectionately known to us by the nickname "Odd", arrives with the car. So we hurry to load the gear before the armies of mosquitoes and other insects swarm at us from the darkening jungle.

"...I'd already held a 50kg carp in my arms..."

That evening, Stuart and I discuss our plans of where to try next. Some of the lakes around Chiang Mai are wonderful, and Jungle Mere is simply stunning, but I think the deluge of rains that have flooded most of Thailand for the past weeks has put many fish off the feed. Even the locals are complaining that no fish are being caught.

I desperately want to catch a Giant Siamese carp. I had planned to try to fit in an extra day at Lake Kahore, located on the outskirts of Bangkok. I'd already held a 50kg carp in my arms from Lake Kahore, but this was because a local angler couldn't lift it off the ground for photos! Stuart flew to Thailand a few weeks before me and, using the two new Globetrotter Mega rods, had landed two incredible Siamese carp from this lake. I will let Stuart take up the story...

'...I had some customers arriving from England on Sunday, so I thought I'd better go down to the lake to obtain some information on what's been caught and also to try some fishing myself. I went to the same swim as I fished earlier in the year, because I'd caught some big catfish from there. A big half-sunken tree is in this particular swim, so it seemed a likely place for Kahore (this is the Thai name for Siamese Carp). I bought a couple of big bags of bread – known locally as Knom Pang, which is a combination groundbait of different coloured bread flakes. This I mashed up with coconut milk then formed a large grapefruit-sized ball of the bread mix on a method feeder and placed a white pop-up boilie hookbait inside the ball. I cast the large bait close to the snags near a bridge that crosses the lake, then fed five similar sized balls of bread over the hookbait. While I waited for a carp, I occupied my time by floatfishing with a second rod in the margins using breadflake as hookbait.

Underwater photo of an incredible 150lb carp.

During the following 5 hours, I caught several small Pla Buk catfish up to 10kg (known locally as Sulawie – a different species; but Tony reckons Sulawie are sometimes young Pla Buk).

At 18:45 hrs, just as it was getting dark, the bait near the bridge screamed off. I was more than surprised, because I didn't expect a take on my first session. The fight felt different from a big catfish, but I still wasn't sure what it was. When the fish first rolled under my rod tip then shot off again, my heart almost stopped because I'd clearly seen that it was a Kahore. I'd been trying to catch one for the past 2 years and I'd finally hooked one!

After about 10 – 15 minutes, the fish rolled inside the landing net. I still wasn't sure how big the fish was, but it took two of us to lift it out of the water.... after three attempts! We weighed the monster immediately and it banged the Nash scales needle round to 41kg (91lb+). To say that I was delighted at catching my first Giant Siamese Carp is an understatement!

The next day was a Saturday, and it's normally very busy on this lake during weekends, so, because I arrived very late in the morning I didn't expect to get in the same swim, but luckily it was still free. At 14:00 hrs in the afternoon, using the same tactics in exactly the same place as before, I had another screaming take. The moment it took off across the lake at a wild rate of knots, Lung Dam – the lake's most experienced angler with a number of giant fish captures under his belt – immediately shouted "Kahore!"

Twenty or more people came running when they heard Lung's first shouts. My wife, Tune, ran to me with the video and proceeded to tape the fight sequence. After about 10 minutes I thought I was winning the battle as the fish began to roll under the rod top. Suddenly a huge, white pair of lips came to the surface and I lifted the rod high to lift the fish's body over the net. Then the hook 'pinged' out and the fish was gone. I was gutted, because the carp was clearly as big or bigger than my first fish. Everybody sighed and gave comments that I should have played it gentler because the carp have very soft mouth tissue. That is easy to say after the event, but at least I could cry when I watched the playback on the videotape...!

I just couldn't believe it – 2 takes in 2 days, when normally people fish for weeks or months without a carp. These facts quickly brought me back to earth with a bang, because I proceeded to blank for the next 7 days!

On some friendly advice from the old fisherman Lung Dam (translated to English as Uncle Black), I tried a swim at the opposite corner to the tree swim. The English customers fished with me during the week, and although I say 'blanked' as far as carp are concerned, we did all manage to land a stack of big, hard-fighting catfish to 25kg. The English guys (a father and son team) managed to land 40 cats between them in the first 3 days. The unbelievable power of the Pla Buk eventually burnt them out and they spent the final 2 days trying to catch a 200lb Arapaima that constantly began rolling in their swim.

I organised a farewell meal with the English duo at the small restaurant close to my swim. Nearby, my hookbait – a giant-sized ball of Lam (rice kernel flour) paste that had been lowered slowly down the edge of the wooden platform and the line wedged under an elastic band wrapped around a board so that ball of paste hung suspended at mid water – suddenly screamed off! This fish put up a very strong fight and a crowd slowly gathered. When it first surfaced in the darkness, everybody shouted "Pla Buk" and proceeded to walk away uninterested. I was left alone to fight this catfish, but somehow

Stuart Brewster bends fully into the Globetrotter Supreme rod to prevent a catfish from swimming beneath the platform.

Golden splendour of a Thailand monastery.

I knew by the fight that it was not a catfish. The English duo also thought that it was a catfish, but I continued to voice my own opinions.

At one point during the fight, the fish made a long 80 metre run along the bank close to the platforms. I tried to slow the fish down by tightening the clutch lever on my multiplier, but turned it the wrong way and fell on my backside! I thought I'd lost it at this point, but luckily the birds-nest of line on my reel slowly peeled off smoothly.

Suddenly the fish surfaced in the margins and a shout came from behind my shoulder – "Kahore! And it's a big one!"

My bottle went once again because I'd already had this fish on for 25 minutes and didn't want to lose another carp. The shouts of "Kahore!" attracted a big crowd around me once again, and Tune already had the videotape rolling.

The carp went in the net held by Lung at the fist attempt. Everybody shouted "80kg!" Everything was a blur after that. My wife was so excited that she forgot to film the fish and left the video on the platform so that all it taped was people's legs and feet! She then picked up my 35mm camera for some still shots but it wouldn't work – there was no film left in the camera! Luckily, a couple of other people had cameras with them and they proceeded to take pictures of me trying to lift the beast off the floor. This carp was too heavy for my 112lb Nash scales, so we estimated the weight at 80kg, which is around 180lb; but after closely examining the photos I don't think it was as heavy as that. Lung Dam said the photos do not do my carp justice, which I have to agree – because they are crap photos! – But I would place the weight more in the 60–70kg class. This would place the weight between 130–150lb. I've settled for the lower weight, because a gigantic 130lb carp is plenty big enough for me!'

FINAL COUNTDOWN

It is 13.10hrs on Monday 25th September. We are fishing at Lake Kahore from the second to last rented platform hut, situated in the far northeastern corner between the long bridge and a big bed of lilies. Two local Thais are fishing from the hut beside us. This cuts out our options for the lily bed, but at least their extra baits going in will make the catfish more active. They've been hooking catfish about every 20 minutes and have lost a couple of good ones. Stuart hooked into a good catfish first cast, but this broke his 30lb line soon after setting the hook. Just now, he had a take on a big ball of bread paste with a hair-rigged pop-up boilie on a short hooklength suspended above it. The rod whacked round, but the hook only pricked the fish – possibly a carp.

One of my rigs has been set up with a big paste ball and a Tigernut buoyed up using a cork ball cut to size so that it just floats. I've engaged the Baitrunner and walked this around to the bridge, then lowered it by hand tight against the rafters, followed by a few handfuls of pre-soaked corn and peanuts. I hooked a big Siamese carp close to the wooden posts during my previous session, so hopefully it will work again. I've had one take so far to the float & method-feeder rig at long distance. This turned out to be a chub-like fish with red fins – probably a White Lady carp or a Small Scale Mud carp.

When I first arrived at the lake this morning, I stopped to watch an angler fighting what I thought was a big fish. I placed my rucksack on the platform and proceeded to take out my camera for a few action-shots. Something caught the clip of the camera bag as I pulled it free of the rucksack and the object bounced on the platform then fell through a crack in the wooden rafters. The 'plop' sounded insignificant as it hit the water and sunk like a stone. I immediately checked the contents of my rucksack...the object on the lake bottom was my mobile phone! I swore at my stupidity and Stuart didn't think that I had any hope of retrieving it, and thought it too dangerous to attempt a dive under the platform. Luckily, Odd found a local guy to swim to the bottom for a search in the green gloom amongst a spider web of old lines and hooks. On his second attempt, he managed to surface with a big grin, holding the dripping mobile aloft in one hand. The phone worked after drying out, but clapped out again 24 hours later. At least I still have my SIM card!

I've just had another take on the float & method feeder. This fish stormed off to the far bank, then my 46lb line parted. There wasn't enough pressure on the line to break it with a straight pull, and a close inspection reveals a breakage above the float. Possibly the line is cutting against the fish's body or fin grooves. If this is the case, maybe it is worthwhile using a heavy braid leader.

The time now is 16:50 hrs. Storm clouds have brought with it a fine spray of rain. We've both had cats to 30lb+, but Stuart has already snapped off on 3 catfish.

At 18:40 hrs, one of the Globetrotter Supreme rods whacks over and Stuart hooks into a wild beast of a catfish. This fish puts up an incredible fight and keeps the rod locked from tip to butt throughout the battle, until the arms of my big Terry Eustace landing net finally swallow my prize. It is a wonderful 'Pla Buk' or Mekong Giant catfish, and whizzes the scales past 62lb. Stuart is over the moon with his personal best catfish. It is a very long specimen, but at 28kg+ it is still a baby as far as Pla Buk go - there are catfish over 100kg in this lake! We pack up shortly after landing the sixty, and then return to the same swim the following day.

THE WAR ZONE

Already, shortly after our arrival, we have both lost fish; so have tied 45lb Kryston Quiksilver leaders above the feeder in an attempt to prevent further breakages. At just before 16:00 hrs, I attach a very heavy self-loading bung float so as to achieve extra casting distance. This achieves my aims and as soon as the missile splashes on the surface a big fish crashes into the feeder and

The muscular form of a big Mekong Catfish. Tony rates these as one the World's hardest fighting fish.

instantly grabs the hookbait. The rod is almost dragged out of my hands as the fish tears across the lake and screams 100 metres off my spool in an attempt to get under the bridge platform. The Mega rod remains locked in its full 6lb test battle curve, until the fish decides to tear along the edge of the bridge supports for 150 metres, then tries again to get beneath the bridge section. This time the fish wins and parts the line as it rubs on the edges of one of the wooden, nail-encrusted supports. I am gutted and throw my rod down in a fit of anger, for I know that this was a big Mekong catfish, possibly over 100lb.

Ten minutes later I hook into another much smaller but faster catfish that goes under the adjacent platform, through all the fishermen's lines of the nearby hut, under a tree, through a boat jetty, then round a wooden post! I am forced to follow the fish and almost break my leg and open an old wound when I fall off the jetty. (I'd accidentally whacked a spinning, red-hot circular saw into my knee and cut it to the bone while I was trying to saw an iron bath in half just 2 days before I flew out to Thailand!) Finally I manage to land the fish, a perfect conditioned Pla Buk.

Ten minutes later, I land a very long 18kg specimen, followed shortly after by yet another straight pull breakage on a very heavy fish. To the accompanied drone of heavy rain, I curse as I strip off all the nylon and spool up with 85lb Kryston braid straight through and an 80lb Spiderwire Spectra hooklength. The next fish tests this heavier gear out by going straight beneath my feet, under the platform and I have to ask one of the locals to help me pass the rod beneath it. The line grates and grinds against the wooden supports as I strain to stop the fish getting back underneath. Amongst thunder claps and torrential rain, I stand alone in the darkness with the Mega rod creaking under constant strain, trying to hold a wild fish in an area no bigger than a bath tub. The tackle stands the test and eventually an awesome looking catfish rolls in my net.

During the next few hours I get 5 abortive dropped runs on the live goldfish rig. It could be a Snakehead fish or a big Barramundi, but shortly after the second dropped run I witnessed a colossal fish surface where the goldfish had been. It rose up and lifted its body high above the water, thrashing it into foam. The lights on the bridge and fishing hut lit up its giant silver scales and I could clearly see the red-tinged scales along its tail section. With no exaggeration, I could easily have rode on its back – it was as broad as a horse! But this is not my first sighting of this absolute mind-blowing and beautiful fish. I'd seen this Arapaima nine times today, and there is no doubt that it weighs in excess of 400lb.

Eight small Arapaima were originally introduced to this lake (from South America) and now each one weighs in excess of 70kg, with a few over the 140kg barrier. At least 2,000 Siamese carp were introduced to this lake (although I'm sure there are now less), with the biggest landed so far weighing an incredible 182kg! In the past year alone, at least seventeen catfish over 50kg have been caught and one bottomed the 100kg scales! How does such a small lake maintain such a massive head of awesome fish?

A Thai lad has just delivered a hot meal of garlic chicken with cashew nuts and rice, plus a couple of Chang beers to wash it down. Now that's what I call service – and he brought it to me on the handlebar of his pushbike!

The rain starts again, but this time it is so torrential that I refrain from re-casting the method feeder rig and leave only the livebait out.

At 19.15 hrs the weather gets really rough. A constant stream of water pours from the skies, accompanied by buffeting winds. By 20.30 hrs the wind is so strong that it pushes water off the lake's surface and begins to tear part of the roof above me. All my tackle is now inside the little wooden hut perched on stilts above the lake. I crouch in the corner to avoid the sheets of blowing spray, and then try my mobile phone – it lights up, so I make a quick call to Stuart.

"Hi Tony! We're confined to the hotel because of the storm. I'm looking out of the window now and the road is beneath 3 feet of water! Are you OK?

"Yes, Stuart. I can't do anything either because there is nowhere to go but huddle under this shelter; I just hope it holds...."

Just then there is a loud crack behind me as a tree explodes in half. The timbers of the platform and hut begin to warp and bend like rubber. A quick phone call to my girlfriend in Germany is abruptly cut-off as the wind almost reaches hurricane force. Giant trees are snapping in half all around me and heavy objects are being thrown across the lake. One tree snaps and crashes through the roof of the workers hut – and they're still inside! I now begin to fear for my own life. If this roof comes down I'll be crushed, but if I go outside I'll be blown across the lake. I glance upwards and watch in morbid interest as the thick, strong timbers twist and roll as if they are made of cardboard.

Now I can't see the difference between water and sky. Sheets of rain blow horizontally past me as my ears ring with the constant claps of thunder. Lightning strikes are poking earth like a pitchfork and incredible winds are snapping almost every tree in half and some are falling into the lake. I sit crouched in the corner for many hours of dark hell. All of a sudden the wind stops, then, eventually, also the rain. It is all over.

30 minutes later, the lake surface is like glass. Well, it would be except for the 500 rings and splashes. The fish have suddenly begun feeding like crazy out there. I take this opportunity to cast out a catfish rig again (sliding bung float, method feeder filled with bread mix, three large, thin pieces of crust on a size 4/0 Gold Label Carp & Catfish hook). The rod is almost wrenched out of my hands before the float settles and a fantastic fight ensues. These ultra sharp hooks are simply brilliant.

Four hours later, I have landed eleven catfish, with ten over 20kg. I wind in and collapse in a tired heap. I can take no more fighting tonight...

When Odd and Stuart arrive in the morning, the lake and surroundings look like a scene from a Vietnam War zone.

Footnote:

As I write these lines accompanied by the background hum of an air-con system in my Bangkok hotel room, it is hard to believe such bad weather can exist in hot and steamy Thailand. To be fair, these rains have been way beyond the norm and most of the North East is completely flooded with thousands homeless. But it hasn't been all bad weather. This week has been mostly dry and sunny in Bangkok. It only rained once in Chiang Mai during our stay, the rest of the week saw sun and blue skies. On hindsight, we picked the wrong time of year. Stuart's information pointed towards this September period as being the best time to catch Giant Siamese Carp. Now we know different and realise that it can be just as good for carp during the dry season. This is why Stuart is planning to fish through the months – December, January and February.

During my fishing time in Thailand, I met an angler called Francois fishing at a Thai lake, and once photographed one of his young customers holding a giant catfish almost as big as the boy himself! Little was I to realise what a tremendous influence Francois was going to make on the world carp scene. I can think of no better introduction to this great angler than to let him tell his own story by the banks of the famous Bung Sam Lan near Bangkok...

ARDUOUS QUEST

By Jean-Francois Helias
(Translated and edited from extended French version)

In the course of operating my guiding service, I often get the chance to meet anglers from around the world. I love listening to them telling me stories and anecdotes from their various trips. Some of those guys bring me to the banks of the Amazon fishing for big size Peacock Bass, I cast with them lures for huge Nile Perch on the lake Nasser in Egypt, boat with them on the Frazer River targeting giant Sturgeon, or walk through the French Guyana jungle in search for the mighty Amaira. I travel a lot in my head. But when I need a break from my guiding work, when I really feel it is time to have a vacation, you won't see me going that far around the globe with rod in my hand. I'd love to; but I have not enough free time for travelling in search of those adventures. The demand from visiting anglers to fish with us here in Thailand is such that it is impossible to have a long break from guiding. So my needs for fishing adventures have always to be much closer to Thailand. I'll be somewhere near the Burmese border, or in Boleh territory, beautiful Malaysia, hunting for one of my favourite fish species of all time: the Giant Snakehead. But there is one other species that has really captured my imagination: the Saimese Giant Carp (Catlo carpio siamensis) – A wonderful fish known locally as 'Caho' (pronounced 'Cahore') and often referred by me fondly as the " mother of all carps". Without a doubt it is the world's biggest carp species.

How big? It is known some Caho specimens can reach exceptional weights in the wild river systems – some specimens exceeding 100 kg. It is a rare fish at this kind of weight, but they do exist. I talked once to Khun Somchai, the Bung Sam Lan owner, about the fish population at its lake. He confirmed to me he released five specimens close to 100 kg that had been netted in the wild from the Chaophraya River, in Singhburi province.

Being a professional fishing guide makes it of course so much easier to get more opportunities than any other fellow angler to catch fish all year long of all sizes and weights. But we are not speaking here of any other fish. We are speaking about the Catlo carpio siamensis! Some of you readers might not know anything about that fish. But if asked, any Thai angler would tell you how shy and cautious that particular carp species is, how difficult it is to induce the fish to bite, and how frustrating the fishing can sometimes be.

I am joking with my Swiss and French clients on the fishing pontoon by this beautiful afternoon of the 12th August 2001. All of a sudden, the screeching sound of my reel suddenly breaks our talking. Come to Papa, baby! I run like crazy to my rod, strike gently to set the hook better, my heart already pounding in my chest like the drumming tempo in a Joe Jones Trio record... The fish run seems like

Lung Dam displays his fantastic 242lb Siamese Carp!

A massive 300lb+ Arapaima caught by Lung Dam.

it will never end and meters of line are rushing out of the spool full speed. Nothing to do yet, just feeling through my fingers on my rod butt each move of that giant carp in the water. Those sensations from the Siamese carp are most of the time unmistakable for a Caho angler. I know what I have been waiting for is at the other end of the line. And it is big.

"Is that a carp?" asks my friend Dominique.

"Yes, I hope so 'mon ami'! And I think not a small one buddy!" I answer him with a smile.

At last now the carp has stopped running – maybe only because it has almost reached the other end of the lake! I start slowly pumping – (I've learnt the lesson that fighting the big carp too brutally and hard can cause just too much stress in oxygen-starved waters. This is especially true with the added tropical heat of Thailand and heavily stocked waters such as Bung Sam Lan). Following a few unfortunate Caho deaths during the early years, we were quick to change our methods. A man called Khun Siddhichai provided me with some helpful advice, and since that day we have never had a fish death.

Everyone on the pontoon is watching me but I am with them no more - I am somewhere else in my mind, talking to myself:

" Be patient my man. Be smooth and easy with the lady. Don't fight her hard but let her do the fighting. Let her get tired herself step by step. Just control her moves. Only if this 'bitch' starts to play some dirty tricks on me, then I will have to put some more pressure on her to counter her moves!"

The fish is now getting closer to the pontoon. I've got to be extra careful now, to stay more in focus. I know very soon she's going to go for the wooden pillars supporting our bungalow. She's got to give it a try. It is so hot. I'm sweating like butter under the sun. I wipe quickly with one hand, the stinging drops of sweat that are sliding down my forehead and burning my eyes. In my head I hear a second voice telling me:

"You should quit smoking man. You're not in shape like you used to be. See this fight is lasting and you're puffing badly now!"

All of a sudden the big Caho appears for the first time at the surface in an enormous boil and splash. Whooaah! It looks like almost everyone on the pontoon has shouted this "whooaah" at the same time. They have seen for a split second the huge size of the carp. Me too. So impressive! No way now will I lose such a huge fish. Underwater the giant carp has seen the pontoon pillars and goes for them. I reel in full speed to shorten the amount of line I have out, dip the tip of my rod in the water, forcing her to make a turn.

"Sorry baby, nice try but not this time!"

I have to stop her several times again. She still has enough strength to display in these everlasting minutes, a combination of appearances at the surface in giant boils, big splashes of her tail, and vicious last chance runs underwater to the pontoon's pillars. Then she appears in front of us, so wonderful in her black-blue dress of scales, quite exhausted and almost not moving, it's over. She must know by now she lost the fight and lets me slip the net beneath her. I open the bale arm and put my rod down on the pontoon then sit and look now below me - Oh what a splendid carp in the landing net! My heart is pounding heavily and I just cannot stop the shaking of my hands. I feel my friend's hands touching my back, congratulating me. I don't listen. I'm exhausted myself and before anything else…I feel I really need now a cigarette (smile).

An electrical storm rages above globetrotters Tony's bamboo hut on stilts, at a lake near Three Pagodas Pass.

I don't hesitate a second after that. This splendid 46 kg Siamese carp that has given me such an unforgettable fight is looking exhausted. I am too. Even though she is to me the one really worth entering for the All Tackle World Record list, I am not going to take the risk of ending her life because of the stupidity of pleasing my ego. Saving the life of such a beautiful fish is ten million times more important to me than any certificate made of paper saying in golden letters I was a world record holder again. That fragile carp could eventually die later if she has to be kept too long out of the water. I take the decision right away to release her fast. We go in the water, weigh her quickly at a satisfying 46kg, but don't take any of her measurements. Then I take that huge carp out of the landing net, trying hard to keep her calm in my arms, just the time for my visitors to take a few pictures of us. Then I swim with her, kiss the Siamese Carp on her head for a last "au revoir" and let her go back to her true life.

After this 46 kg catch, it took another 2 long months to get another chance! Four visitors from the UK we were guiding had 7 bites from carp in 3 days. Four Caho were landed, three others lost, including a real big one we estimated being well over 50 kg. The best souvenir of these 7 bites was an unforgettable catch hat trick, an exploit in itself: one of the UK anglers, Kevin Vass, landing on the very same day 3 specimens weighing 34 kg, 24 kg, and 20 kg.

At the beginning of October, we had our 4th opportunity to make the Catlocarpio siamensis species entry into the IGFA record list. This time with another record catch landed by a UK client named Bruce Dale. I call Bruce a "lucky Caho angler". He showed us during his 2 stays with us here in Thailand that Lady Luck has apparently a close eye on him. Bruce had previously the chance to have 3 takes from carp on the same day during his first stay with us, landing a 20 kg Caho and losing 2 very big fish. He is back with us a few months later, asking me to fish for carp for a single day, and this time lands a huge Caho specimen. Fighting that kind of big size specimen took some time. The carp looked tired and Bruce a dedicated carp angler and a gentleman decided himself to release the fish promptly rather than going for a record. We didn't even weigh the catch. By experience we estimated his carp weighing around 45 kg.

On the 4th November, we had to guide for a day a Singaporean angler by the name of Francis Chia Hung Meng. When I arrived at the lake with him, Kik – my faithful and extremely experienced guide - was already waiting for us. I noticed he had brought one of his custom built rods. A thing he has never done before. While guiding, Kik would only take care of our guests but never fished himself. Curious, I asked him:

" Hey luk pee wan nee koon yak tok pla la? " (Hey brother, are you going to fish today?).

Giving me a big smile he answered:

" Kap! Pom may day tok pla caho nan " (Yes! I haven't done any fishing for the giant carp for a long time). And smiling even more, he added on a joking tone: " Wan nee pom tja dai toa yai " (And today, I'm going to get a big one).

I knew he was teasing. But a couple of hours later I could have said then he had been in fact deadly serious, if he hadn't admitted himself what happened on that day was just pure luck. That day Francis, the Singaporean angler, was fishing only for the Pla Buk and was having a ball fighting these mean Cats. While taking care of him, Kik and myself set up our rods for the giant carp next to each other on the side of our bungalow, a part of Francis' 'Catfish battlefield'. Who knows? Any of us could have smiled at lady luck that day. This time the luck was with Kik. A Caho took his bait. Playing that fish on light tackle was a pure lesson of angling skills. Kik was using a custom built rod of 7 ft he built himself for Snakehead fishing with surface lures. The rod was coupled to a small reel loaded with 20 lb braided line. Of course it is not really the best fishing gear to fight those giant carp....

On the first run, the carp was already far away on the other side of the lake. It took him 20 long minutes to bring the fish close to our pontoon. And once the giant carp came up for the first time to the surface level in a huge boil, we knew immediately that fish was much bigger than any other fish we fought before. We even had to use 2 nets to land that giant fish. Lucky catch, unlucky day! We had the record fish but we didn't have the scales - except for my 50 kg portable scales, which would have not been of any use for that monster fish anyway. I had purchased from England a few months before 100 kg portable scales. Too bad that we didn't have them with us! They were at the institute still awaiting official calibration. Hon, one of the lake employees was there to witness the catch. He has seen it all after so many years working there and can guess quite accurately the weight of any fish without using scales. He looked at the netted fish and said it was over 80 kg but couldn't be 90 kg. To be fair, Kik and myself agreed to give that carp an estimated weight of over 80 kg.

What a frustration! His catch was the biggest carp caught at the lake during the past two years. It would have been such a hell of a giant carp to make a first entry with the IGFA! I guess that record would have lasted for some years before being broken by any other angler. What a pity! I would have loved so much that Kik, a gifted angler, skilful guide and my fishing soul mate, could hold for the Siamese giant carp species such a well-deserved IGFA world record.

The 11th November, I landed a 22 kg and lost a much bigger one. But it was the 12th that was going to be at last our lucky day – a bigger carp took my bait. It is impossible to estimate an approximate weight of a fish while fighting it but I had no doubt the carp I was playing was another good size fish. Using Kik's custom rod, the same light tackle gear he had fought his 80 kg carp with, I knew I had really to play it smart or I would lose it. On 20 lb line I couldn't afford to do a single mistake. At the last moments of the fight, I was tense when the fish came close to our pontoon, played on me the usual dirty tricks, trying several times to snag me. I remember motivating myself, staying in focus and thinking to myself: " That one will be the one for sure to enter the IGFA list. There is no way I am going to let that potential record go away this time! "

We had everything ready: cameras, scales and meter, to proceed to the required weighing and measurements session. At last we had done it. The fish weighed exactly 45 kg. One kilo less than my best personal catch, but still good enough for me to end that long wait of several months for a first record with the IGFA. That carp had a length of 117 cm, 99 cm from its mouth to the beginning of its tail, and a girth of 96 cm.

Can you believe it? We had been waiting 9 long months before setting that record.... and it lasted only 7 days. Fishing can be such an amazing sport full of unexpected surprises! During those long months I was having a permanent exchange of mail with European carp fanatics keeping them posted about our experiences with the giant carp. One guy in particular was a real Siamese Carp lover: my Dutch angling globetrotter friend Arnout Terlouw, himself an experienced carp angler. Being in charge of Karper, a magazine dedicated to carp fishing, Arnout was of course very attentive to any information about Siamese carp fishing. He had heard of our very good results not only from my mail but also at the same time from other well-known European carpers. Apparently, through mouth to ear, our reputation was spreading fast in the European carp-angling world. I already spent a week in December 2000 guiding him and 8 other European legendary anglers for the shooting of a movie. That film was done for "Seasons", a European TV fishing program, and was about the Mekong Giant Catfish and Bung Sam Lan Lake. Of course, apart from the Pla buk (Mekong Catfish), Arnout and two other legendary European carpers - Belgium's Ronnie De Groote and Danish Doctor Jens Bursell – also gave a try for the Siamese Giant Carp during their stay.

I know how much they would have loved to add the Caho to the long list of their personal numerous fish species catches around the world, especially in front of the camera. Unfortunately fishing conditions for the carp were difficult. December in Thailand is the fresh season. On some days, the water temperature at that period is too cold. Carp still bite sometimes but only on very sunny days, once the water has been warmed. They didn't succeed. They had a few bites but missed. It was impossible anyway to be certain those had been carp bites. It could have been any other fish species, pla buk or pla sawai. Apart from the difficult conditions, I believe we had another handicap. We were not using yet the bait formula we use today for the carp. We were using at that time the usual based rice husk bait called locally "lam" that the best local carp anglers still use nowadays. It works OK on the carp, and even better on big size pla buk with the bottom fishing method. They were catching carp of course... but too few. And their average of bites was not good enough in my opinion to say it is the best bait to be used for that species. Arnout didn't catch a carp but did so much better. I wanted him to try the Arapaima and he landed one in front of the camera. An estimated 110 kg Arapaima gigas that made him the first foreign angler to have landed one of the 5 Arapaima specimens ever caught at Bung Sam Lan Lake. Arnout wanted to be back in Thailand. He was still very much interested in a giant carp catch but there was another fish that was even more important to him. He had been researching about the Jullien's Golden Price Carp or Probarbus jullieni for 4 years and wanted me to organize for him an expedition in the wild for that rare fish.

Jean-Francois with an incredible-looking 46kg carp caught in June.

The main problem with the Probarbus expedition was to set months in advance dates. I had previously a destination in mind for that species here in Thailand and I knew the best guide I could think of for such an expedition had to be another brilliant local angler, my lovable friend Oot from Ban Phong. But we had to fish around August if we wanted to have the best fishing conditions. Arnout couldn't make it. He already had fishing commitments in some other part of the globe. He could only travel to Southeast Asia in November. Knowing the water level would be at its highest at that period, I advised him to forget about the Probarbus for a while. If he wanted to have a real fishing adventure in Thailand then I would be glad to take care of him. We could eventually fish for the Siamese Carp and then live upcountry in the jungle for Giant Snakeheads and Transverse Bar Barb, species he had never fished for.

Arnout accepted the offer. He had a week vacation and wanted now to experience a 5 days jungle fishing expedition. He had heard how exciting was "Snakehead hunting" with surface lures from fellow writers and had to give it a try. Before leaving for 'upcountry', being a carp fanatic, he couldn't resist to ask me to pay a visit to Bung Sam Lan Lake. I knew how much a Catlocarpio catch was important to him and both of us knew too that fishing for the giant carp for a single day was going to be pure gambling. It was going to be again - all or nothing. The night before our fishing day I told Arnout I was very confident. I had caught a 22.00 Kg two days before his arrival and got snagged the next day by a fish well over 40.00 kg. The carp were biting well. He just had to cross his fingers.

We were together again by the water on the 19th November. We were using only one rod each, fishing together the very same spot. Will "sweet Lady Luck" show up again today? Yes! It didn't take long. Arnout had a first bite around 11.00 am. Unfortunately he will loose the very first Caho he had the chance to hook. There was absolutely nothing he could do about it. The way that carp was moving in the water meant without a doubt he had at the other end of his line a very serious big "submarine with fins". 60.00 Kg? 70.00 Kg? 80.00 Kg? Who knows? It is often impossible to estimate the weight of a fish while fighting it. But it was huge. At that weight, there is no way you can stop such a fish when it has decided to run to an obstacle for cover. Often, carp act the same way, escaping through the same pattern.

Arnout's line got snagged several times around the wooden bridge pillars as the tricky carp had run all along the inside of the bridge. Once again we had to do some teamwork to eventually save the catch. Kik and myself swam to retrieve the line underwater, found it, and as usual started to cut, tie again, repeating many times the operation to free it from snags. Too late! We had worked hard for nothing. When we reached the last piece of snagged line, we found out it was already broken. We were of course a bit frustrated and disappointed but that is what fishing is about, isn't it? I could only repeat to cheer Arnout's mood a few words I heard many times from Joe Taylor, who would say in that kind of situation: "At the end of the day, it is only a fish!".

The funny thing about it was that everyone on the two fishing pontoons had been hooting, screaming and cheering like crazy once Arnout had taken his rod in his hands to start playing the fish. Most people would wait for the fish to be surely landed before expressing their joy - never before a fight, as superstitious anglers would hate that. It could bring bad luck and disappointment. But Arnout's friends were of course so happy for him and very excited too to have the chance to see for the first time a Siamese giant carp. I still wonder today why Kik, Lek and myself joined in the cheering too. Maybe we should have kept quiet. But at least we had a bite. For Arnout who has seen so much through his fishing years that miss was no big deal anyways. I told him the day was not over yet. We had already experienced in the past a few "crazy days" with carp bites. We only had now to cast our baits... and to wait to see if it could happen again.

It happened. Beginning of the afternoon it came, again on Arnout's rod. This time it was a very good one. The Siamese Giant Carp was landed after a long 20 minutes tough fight observed by 8 witnesses. Eight "very mute" people who didn't dare to speak a single world this time, until the carp reached the landing net. Each of us helped to organize the weighing and measurements session on land. That Caho was weighed exactly at 47 kg. The fish had a total length of 137 cm and a girth of 106 cm. We went into the water again for a short photo session before releasing the carp. The day was still not over. I had myself a bite a couple of hours later but the carp didn't get hooked properly. She runs a few meters and then a heavy silence took over the sweet screeching sound of my reel. The carp got unhooked before I could even take the rod in my hands. I didn't care. We were glad to have experienced again 3 carp bites in a single day. It made that day such a very successful one.

Just 7 days after my 45 kg Caho catch, Arnout had already broken my pending IGFA All Tackle World Record with a bigger catch. I was delighted "to have my ass friendly kicked" not only by a legendary angler, but a lovable buddy too. I knew Arnout was not going to submit his catch with the IGFA. He is not the kind of angler interested in any record. But I advised him to do a special exception this time. To submit his 47 kg giant carp as a new IGFA record would certainly help reveal better the Catlocarpio siamensis to anglers worldwide. Arnout was kind to accept. I know he did it mostly for me as a token of his friendship and coming from him I sincerely appreciate his gesture.

In the carp fishing season for the year 2002, we already had a good start, experiencing 26 bites and landing 10 fish. Records are made to be broken! I firmly believe it is only a matter of luck and time now before we break Arnout's IGFA record. Of course it would be a kind of miracle if we could land a fish the size of Lung Dam's super biggie. I am not asking for that much. Any "smaller" one (70/80 kg) of those giant fish will do!

Elephant trekking through the jungle.

ARCTIC SPAIN
&
SPANISH HEATWAVE

Snow in Mequinenza

As I sit here in a centrally heated apartment, tapping the keyboard on a computer and stopping often to sip hot drinks in an effort to ward off my flu symptoms, one could be forgiven for thinking that I am somewhere in England, but you would be wrong... I am in 'sunny Spain'! Colin has just phoned, informing me that our trip to visit a friend, living on the Ebro Delta, has unfortunately been cancelled due to hazardous driving conditions on the winding mountain roads. I look out of the window towards Mt. Montenegre, but it is almost completely masked behind a blanket of flakes streaming from whitewashed skies. The few cars attempting to drive along the streets are skidding round in circles, and my turbo-charged Rover parked outside is now almost hidden beneath a deep layer of snow. It is the heaviest fall of snow in Spain in living history.

Before the snow began to fall, Gary and Peter (who work at the Bavarian Catfish Guiding Service) were enjoying daily action near the junction of the Segre and Ebro rivers. In fact, Gary managed to land a superb 30lb+ common four days ago and as this had been his last session prior to driving home to England for Christmas, he decided it would be a great opportunity to celebrate the capture of his thirty. "Just one pint in the bar" said Gary. Two hours later, Peter had drunk enough 'one-pints', leaving Gary and myself to continue downing San Miguel lagers until sun-up. It took at least

Tony with a rare 30lb 8oz 'black-gold' Spanish carp.

another 48 hours for my head to recuperate from that 'one pint'!

I arrived in the small riverside town of Mequinenza last week and have been so busy writing and editing final photos for the book, that I haven't had much time to go fishing – but some spare hours cropped up a few days ago, so I finally managed to fill the car with tackle and drove along the shore road.

I found Peter fishing alone in Gary's vacated swim. He'd been there a couple of hours and had already landed quite a lot of carp, but mainly low doubles. The previous evening I'd spent some time driving along the roads that skirt the reservoir, searching for likely-looking swims to fish for carp during future sessions. Plenty of good locations were observed, and I intended to seriously give these a try at a later date, but today I fancied fishing downstream from Peter. The main reason was that a few days prior, I'd observed a lot of bubbling and activity on the edge of where both currents of the Ebro and

A rare big Spanish carp in the snow

Cinca rivers meet. Here the chocolate coloured waters of the Cinca are pushed back by the clearer waters of the Ebro that rush downstream of the Mequinenza Dam. This meeting of two different coloured currents can be seen as a straight line stretching from the bank diagonally across the main Ebro. More interesting was the fact that these colour changes in water coincided with a vast change in depths where the fairly flat plateau met the steep downward slope of the old riverbed. Also, an old submerged road with a parallel high wall ran diagonally along the crease of meeting currents.

I had quizzed Gary why he wasn't casting hookbaits on to this steep-sloping shelf, but his reply was that it was at least 10-15 metres deep and he had more confidence in 6 metres or shallower water. I can well understand this belief and once held the same doubts about fishing regularly in deep water, but many successful sessions fishing in 10-35 metres depth has drastically altered those notions.

I parked the car downstream of Peter and set up my gear opposite the junction. Here the margins have been cut away by years of floods to leave a steep cliff overhanging the water. A narrow strip of waterline bank allowed me to fish from water level, but I chose to set the rod pod at the edge of the cliff so as to keep as much line as possible out of the drag of forceful currents. Only two rods are allowed per angler on the Ebro, so I cast a Nash Shellfish double 20mm boilies hookbait, and a Scopex double 20mm boilies hookbait to the exact crease of meeting currents in approximately 30ft of water. Both short 3inch long rigs were pinned to the bottom by 3 oz Korda flat leads, and at the sharp end was a size No2 Continental Penatrator. The Shellfish boilies were heavy sinking baits, but the Scopex sinker was balanced with a pop-up – ala 'snowman' style.

Peter had already been enjoying action, and continued to reel in a decent high double or low twenty during the next few hours. Meanwhile my hookbaits only received the odd knocks and plucks. This was a sure sign that medium-sized carp were picking up the outer boilie in their lips, but not taking the complete hookbait in far enough to be pricked by the pin-sharp hook point. This did not perturb me, because it was in fact what I wanted. The bigger specimens needed just a little more patience – my time would come.

The biting winds began to increase in strength and howl down the valley until it cut like a knife at any exposed part of the body. Temperatures plummeted and clouds of water vapour steamed off waters of the Ebro like some immense Swedish sauna. Yet this was not warm steam but strange phenomena caused by the mixing of ice-cold waters of varying temperatures that were continually sucked off the river's surface. These freezing fog banks rolled up the edges of the valley like gigantic clouds until howling winds eventually scraped them off the surrounding mountain peaks.

Three hours passed, until a small tap came to the right-hand rod tip, shortly before the complete rod suddenly vibrated and the spool began spinning at an alarming rate. The culprit was a lovely, thick shouldered, white/gold common carp weighing 28lb 8oz.

The temperatures continued to plummet well below freezing until the wind-chill factor chased me inside my car for regular bouts of finger and toe warming over the heater fans. An hour later, and just as the sun had dipped beneath the crest of Mt. Punta Plana, sending a shivering veil of dusk to slide like a vampires cloak through the reeds, it happened again. The rod bounced in the rest, a single bleep from the Delkim, followed by a continuous

Gary lands a big common for Peter Ölschläger.

Tony cradles a stunning white-
gold common.

Snow on the Ebro – the deepest snow covering Spain in living
memory.

high note as the white diode lit up the pod. This time the fish came in quite easily at first, until it woke up just twenty metres from shore, then hugged the deep rocky margins for the rest of the fight. I could continually feel the line rasping against the sharp rocks and stones at the edges of the submerged road, or felt it 'pinging' against rough edges as I leaned hard into the fish to lift it over the sunken wall. The wonderful braid did its job again admirably and soon another hunk of scales rolled inside the net. This time the fish looked different – it was a stunning 30lb 8oz black/gold-scaled common carp in perfect condition. I was over the moon – a thirty on my first short session; and a rare black common put icing on the cake.

The snow continues to pile outside my window, until 24 hours later it is 4ft deep in places and still the flakes continue to stream from whitewashed skies. Jens Bursell makes contact via mobile phone from Denmark, asking me when the photo package for the book will arrive at the scanners. He seems amazed by my reply – 'I cannot send it yet, because the post van is unable to reach the village!' not only that, but the borders between Spain and France are suddenly closed to prevent more horrendous lorry crashes on the motorways.
For almost a week, I bide my time, re-editing photos, editing text, reading books, watching television (without understanding hardly a word of Spanish!), washing clothes, writing letters, eating, drinking, and extended periods of staring out the windows, until I can take no more of behaving like a caged animal, and decide to brave the weather and take a long walk along the riverbank. The deep snow makes luscious sounds as my boots crunch through the white powder and each lungful of air is like sucking mint lozenges. It feels so good to be out in the fresh air again. By the time I return to the apartment, my face is flushed red with oxygenated blood, and my fingers soon begin winding new

line on the spools and tying fresh rigs. A hasty call is made to Colin 'I'm going carping for a few hours tomorrow – do you fancy joining me?'

The following afternoon we are both set up on the confluence of the two rivers. Six hours fly by in mind-numbing cold temperatures. A lonely Snipe hunts amongst pebbles. Two Grey Herons glide through freezing fog. Behind us, gaps in fast-moving ice clouds give short glimpses of the ancient castle perched on the lip of a craggy mountain. Kingfishers hunt on ice-blue wings beneath our frost-covered rod tips.

Darkness eventually descends and the temperatures cut like a knife. We stamp our cold toes, and the duty of packing away fishing gear forces us to cry out in pain as numb fingers stick to metal reels, pods, carbon, ice-covered net and frost covered carp mat.

The roaring sound of the car heater on full blast begins to painfully jolt blood back into our extremities. But we are laughing and joking and our spirits are high – for inside both cameras are images of Colin, grinning like a Cheshire cat, holding a 27lb 12oz golden-scaled carp, in front of a stunning white backdrop.

Two days later, I am back alone at the same swim for a short 5-hour session. By the time comes to pack up in the freezing temperatures of dusk, I've returned four common carp to 34lb 4oz, and a superb 100lb+ catfish – (all taken on boilies) to the wonderful Ebro River, surrounded by a Spanish landscape covered in snow...

Heatwave in Mequinenza

A white-hot ball gradually turns yellow, before it slowly sinks behind the silhouettes of mountain peaks. As the earth spins away from the setting sun it races towards darkness, but not before the last sparks of daylight send crimson fingers to scrape across the sky.

Warm breezes waft down from the mountains then channel through the Segre valley, pushing against the river's flow and forming crested waves that crash against the shoreline. Cream-coloured foam rides each wave, until it is lifted like candyfloss to spiral in the wind, and eventually ends up as a white band along the shoreline. This constant action of waves against current produces bubbles of oxygen that churns and rolls in the green soup of the river, until it eventually reaches the deep darkness of sunken trees and passes over the gills of sleeping giants...

Six rods stand vertical in their rests, like rockets waiting for a launch. Lines, as taught as piano wire, span out from each rod towards the swaying rows of high reeds that flank the island. I can hear the warm winds playing a high-pitched tune as it whistles past the braided lines.

Colin and Lee have driven towards town to pick up our extravagant order from the Chinese restaurant. On the far side of the river, I notice their red taillights sweeping round the tight bends towards Torrente de Cinca. I sit back on the comfort of the bedchair, watching the red lights fade slowly in the distance and begin to feel the saliva form under my tongue at the thought of eating all that greasy Chinese food!

Suddenly, a rod tip jerks back and a tiny bell begins to shake like a desert rattlesnake. The line falls slack, making the rod lean back on a contact inside the rod rest and emits a loud note from the electronic alarm. The noise is abruptly cut short as I lift the rod out of the rest and begin winding in the slack. It takes a few turns on the handle of the Shimano 6500 Baitrunner before the braid tightens again, and I lean back hard to set the hooks. The rod bends over, but there is only a token resistance, so I shout back to Ron that this is only a small one.

A large, flat-topped rock juts out into the main flow of the river, so I edge my sandals

Spectacular action as a carp crashes over the landing net, during a fishing session at the Ebro junction near Mequinenza.

along the rocky shoreline until I am standing on the stable platform. From this position, I can easily keep the line clear of the other rods, so I begin to relax and continue winding the fish in. It doesn't fight much, and feels about 20-40lb, so I relay this message back to Ron. I should have kept my mouth shut...for moments later, the rod tip wrenches downwards and slaps against the river surface.

Deep, deep down in the darkness, a huge creature almost twice as long as a man and built like a 4-wheel-drive truck, shakes it's head then begins to swim violently over the gravel bottom like a runaway train. This sudden surge of power from the fish almost drags me to my knees, but I manage to remain upright, clenching my calf muscles and straining my biceps against this incredible force. The rod curves over as if made of rubber, and I begin to hear tiny splintering sounds as varnish creaks all along the blank.

"Grab the fighting belt!" I shout back to Ron, and he quickly jumps over to the flat rock then fits the belt around my waist.

I wedge the rod butt in the groove of the fighting belt then begin to lean back. This added pressure makes not a jot of difference...because the steam train on the other end now decides to shift into top gear! Within seconds, more than 150 metres of PowerPro braid rips off the spool and I am left in no doubt that this fish is very special.

I clamp my hand over the madly spinning spool to try and slow the beast down, until the friction forces me to wince in pain at the build up in heat. The fish eventually stops, but only to change direction and rush back across the river towards the island. All along the fringes of the island, 3 metre high reeds are rooted deep in the mud, and hidden beneath the depths are a mass of sunken

Tony (helped by Lee Woodward) prepares to release the 7ft monster back to the Segre River.

Tony (helped by Ron) displays his golden 125½lb specimen.

timber and tree roots. Many of the tree roots still harbour a profusion of branches and their fingers form a web of danger. The catfish rushes head first into this spider's web as I clamp down on the reel and fight to keep my sandals from sliding along the rock face. The taught braid sends signals like a telephone line and I can 'feel' the leviathan shaking its head in the deep darkness of the river. I grit my teeth and hang on, feeling my eyes swelling in their sockets and my veins rising in long ridges under the skin of my neck. The tackle is about to 'explode' but I trust the incredible strength of this high-tech braid, and maintain constant pressure. Within a hair's breadth of sanctuary, the fish turns away from the web of sunken trees and begins to swim at even greater pace along the rim of the deep shelf that flanks the edges of the main riverbed.

For the next ten minutes I stand alone on the rock, winding and pumping, until eventually a long pair of whiskers breaks the surface.

"It's ready for the net...go steady, it's a big one..." I say to Ron, as he slips into the river and wades towards a massive, dark head floating directly in front of me.

Ron stretches his arm towards the hook length, and then grips his fingers over the lower lip of a cavernous mouth. On feeling Ron's touch, the beast wakes up again and suddenly churns the water at our feet into a cauldron of swirling mud and vortices.

"Steady, steady!! Let it go, it's not ready!" I scream at Ron, as the fish bolts back into the sanctuary of deep darkness.

The Shimano reel quickly heats up again and the skin begins to peel off my fingertips as some crazy beast repeatedly strips off almost all the line in its constant attempts to reach the hidden snags.

I'd already landed some nice fish up to 125lb 8oz during the week, but I know this is something bigger, so I ask Ron to use the landing net (this is a special ultra-large net specially hand built for the landing of giant-sized catfish). Ron makes two attempts to slip the mighty beast inside the net, but each time the fish rolls back over and flicks its mighty tail then heads back towards the depths of the riverbed.

A pair of white beams cut through the fading light of dusk on the opposite bank, but I am too engrossed in my battle with the giant to notice that the lads are returning with the takeaway meal. Five minutes later, a car grinds to a halt inside a dust cloud behind us. Quickly, and without panic, Colin slips up to his waist in the water. By now, I can sense that the fish is fully tired and almost ready, so I increase pressure on the rod tip and lift a colossal-sized head back towards the surface. Colin slips on a single glove then gently grips the lower lip of the fish. He tries to lift part of the fish to reveal it's full length, but on feeling the heavy bulk, stops and turns to me then smiles.

"It's a big one, Tony...over 150lb..."

At that, I shake my fist in the air then watch in amazement as Colin begins to drag the monster out of the water. Ron has already laid down ground sheets to protect the fish from a stone-covered ground, so he immediately rushes to the margins to assist Colin. There is a steep, high slope to encounter before the catfish is on level ground, so it takes four of us to eventually drag the big catfish into position on the mega-sized weigh sling.

The bar is slipped through the hook of the weighing scales and both Ron and Colin lift the full sling off the ground. A needle spins round on the scales and I switch on my Lucido Cool light torch to read the dial.

"100...120...150,158,165...." I call out, as the needle swings round. The pointer bounces then settles back to rest just above 160...so we all agree on a weight of over 160lb, before lowering the monster back to the ground.

"Yahoooooo!!" I scream out loud and handshakes are shared all round. We then quickly remove the hook from inside that cavernous mouth; measure its length at 7ft 5inches, before tying a long length of cord and slipping the huge fish back into the water.

It should be noted that on the previous evening when I caught the 125lb+ fish, I decided to take some photographs straight away following capture. This was with the intention of returning the fish quickly without the need of attaching it to a stringer overnight. On reflection, this was a mistake and almost caused the loss of a wonderful fish. The continued stress (no matter how short in duration) on a huge fish when taking photos immediately after a long, hard fight can be too much for the fish. A lot of air also tends to hold in the swim bladder, and grappling around on the bank or even in water tends to increase this retention of excess air. It took me half an hour of 'walking' the catfish through the water so as to pass extra-oxygenated water over its gills. This eventually worked and happily the catfish perked up. I then attached a stringer to let it rest on the bottom and fully recuperate before releasing back to the river. Try to remember that sustained high temperatures in hot, or tropical countries can drastically lower dissolved oxygen levels in water, so it is imperative that you let big fish rest immediately after capture and also refrain from sacking them as this prevents the adequate flow of oxygenated water across the gills.

The final tally of catfish caught between three of us (Colin, who operates the superb – Catmaster Tours, did not fish on this occasion) in 5 days of fishing, was sixteen, with two over 90lb, and seven over 100lb. No less than five of the catfish exceeded 150lb! The majority of catfish were caught on live eels, but the largest (my 160 pounder) took a small koi carp presented at mid-depth.

Tony with an incredible 160lb+ catfish.

RAGING WATERS

'For years I had dreamt of places of immeasurable beauty and grandeur where great fish swam. And now, having found one at last, I began to shake' Paul Boote – Initiation

'With the vision of the massive golden fish still swimming through my rum-sodden brain I am tearfully overwhelmed to be in such a place at such a time' Jeremy Wade – A Season in the South

It seems very strange that almost 25 years after the actual event, and a decade after Paul published the account of his first introduction to Mahseer in 'Somewhere down the Crazy River', I find myself re-reading the book while at the same time, seemingly soaring above the skies, follow Paul's adventures with the aid of a Microsoft Encarta Interactive World Atlas. The wonder of a modern computer! A slight movement of the 'mouse' passports me across the globe to another realm in Paul's quest, and almost helps me believe that I'm there fishing beside him – but not quite, for reality is the only road to travel. You just have to be there to truly experience – view, scent and touch – the passion. I had travelled to India and fished for the mighty Mahseer on two separate expeditions prior to Geremy and Paul's book – and also shared with them my experiences of a recent epic battle with a fish hooked on a plug in the rock-strewn rapids of a wild Indian river, during their book release at the 1992 Carp Society Conference.

I believe that 'Somewhere down the Crazy River' is one of best ever published works on fishing – an epic of our time. The book excites my mind just as much now as I re-read it for the fifth occasion, as it did on that cold November day 10 years ago (my only small critic is that there were not enough colour photos to match the inspiring words).

I have had a number of written accounts covering past Mahseer expeditions published in various magazines (and two chapters in my first book: Big Fish In Foreign Waters, 1991), but one particular narrative covering my second expedition to the Kaveri River has always remained one of my favourites – so I've chosen (without regret) to re-tell the events in this chapter. Forgive me if you've ever read this before, but like my own feelings on recounting the events, they never fail to rekindle memories and the thrill of adventure...

The old tin bus rattles and hums over the potholes as it kicks up clouds of brown dust that seems to suck the last drops of moisture from my breath. 'At least the bus isn't crowded', I think to myself as the tin can screams to a halt at yet another fly-infested village. Sun-baked cowpats mingle with the soft scents of multicoloured spring flowers that drip from whitewashed walls. A swarm of squabbling school kids stand in an orderly rabble, seemingly waiting for something to happen. I suddenly realise with horror that they are going to board this very bus, and within seconds they spill forth like a swarm of ants and fill every space and crack – on top of, between and under every seat.

The old bus chugs off in a cloud of black diesel fumes, as I try to balance the rucksack on my knees to make room for a grizzly old man who squeezes up so tight that I can smell the spiders on his breath. Every deep, wind-cracked furrow in his skin is filled with dried mud and his earth-encrusted fingernails scratch repeatedly at matted clumps of hair that stink like a bears armpits. I console

Portrait of a 'master of the jungle'.

myself with the comforting thought that I only have another hour to wait before he gets off the bus...

The bus bounces and rattles on through the dust cloud as it swings around the 'S' bends on two wheels with regular ten second bursts on the horn that threaten to burst my ear drums. A greasy urchin leans out of a window, picking his nose and breathing in the diesel fumes while his tie flaps against the nose of a goat that watches him with contempt from the next window. Suddenly, the boy belches and spews out a stream of vomit that seems to hang for seconds in the hot air outside the bus, before being blown back through the window that I just happen to be sitting next to. The old man turns and gives me a toothless grin, no doubt happy that I now smell as sweet as he does....

The bus finally comes out of a tight bend that grips the edges of Kanayatana Kallu hillside and my heart jumps at seeing an old friend – there, far below us, snakes the blue-green Kaveri River that shimmers under a heat wave.

Five minutes later, the tin can coughs to a halt and a swarm of screaming locusts in school ties, invade a tranquil Sangam village. To the east, the Arkavati stream trickles through the drying wadi, before reaching a wide pool at the Kaveri confluence, where village women slap their husband's shirts against smooth rocks, while standing knee deep in the rivers warm currents.

I pick up my rods then shoulder my pack, before setting off on the desolate dust track that weaves its lonely path through dense scrubland and bamboo forest. Every fifteen minutes I stop to quench my rising thirst from the bottle, but within minutes the water is pouring out again as salt-filled sweat from my open pores. I walk on, with the grass crackling underfoot and black vultures circling overhead on warm thermal currents. Within an hour, I reach the base of Mari Kallu and glimpse the huge boulder called Crocodile rock. I take five minutes break and sit beneath the shade of a tree, watching the river swirl through the deep pools. A 15ft Mugger crocodile lies sprawled out on a flat rock on the opposite bank, eyeing me with interest. I quickly attach a telephoto to the Pentax and creep down behind a thorn bush, but only manage one shot before a ton of prehistoric reptile gently slips off the rock and disappears below the Kaveri's currents – to swim in the very area where Steve Harper fought with 104lb of gold.

My eyes scan the water and way upriver, just below Galibori Pool I can see a long-haired, pink fleshed man fishing with two W.A.S.I. guides – Bula and Suban. 'It must be Matt', I think to myself, so quickly make my way towards Galibori camp.

This night, amongst a chorus of a thousand crickets, we both lie on camp beds talking of the mighty Mahseer that we will hook tomorrow, while the hot sparks drift up above the warm glow of the campfire and vanish in a galaxy of stars.

The soft tones of conversation continue deep into the night, but it is abruptly cut short when a low, deep growl comes from behind the tent. We both look at each other in silence, and the fear shows on Matt's face when another deep, hair tingling growl wrenches the night's stillness.

"Leopard", I whisper, and we listen with heartbeats thumping in our eardrums as the big cat passes within feet of the tent flap, pads heavily over the dry leaves and through the thick brush, then is swallowed into the dark heart of the jungle...

"..A 15ft crocodile...slides off the rock and disappears below the Cauvery's currents.."

The orange cloak of dawn sweeps over the bow of the coracle, as Karya expertly guides the craft across Galibrai Pool with strong, even strokes. Our destination is to be the far end of the middle rocks at the head of a long, deep pool that stretches to Crocodile Rock. Within five minutes we are clambering out of the coracle and pulling it up onto a submerged rock, so that it balances steadily in mid-stream.

Two rods are set up with livebaits from the bucket. The end rig consists of a 5ft long, 45lb Quicksilver trace with size 4/0 'Mahseer hook', attached to the 40lb Berkley Big Game mainline by 100lb Berkley swivel. (I now prefer to use the tougher 50lb PowerPro line straight through to the hook knot). Just below the swivel, a spiral lead is wrapped around a short length of rubber tubing, that protects the line when the lead has to be forced down to the hook to free it from a rock on the bottom (a frequent occurrence). A much lighter-action Downrigger rod is fitted with a 25lb Kryston Silkworm trace and size 4 Drennan Boilie hook, then baited up with a small knob of paste.

I am fishing in the same place where I hooked and lost two very big Mahseer the previous year on livebait. One of the fish had snatched up a 2lb Saran (Barbus sarana) and sizzled off more than 200 metres of line before pulling free. This time however, the livebaits remain untouched and at 11:00hrs I reel in the rods and head back to camp for a late breakfast. The small rod has been quite active during this period and I have landed four barbel and five small mahseer up to 12lb. Although the mahseer is a very powerful fish, it is noticeable that, size for size, the Pink Barbel put up a far better fight and I long to latch on to one of the rare 40lb+ barbel that swim in the Kaveri's strong currents.

I discuss with Matt over breakfast about the complete lack of action from the big mahseer. Matt spent his first 10 days at Ontu Gundu without a single fish. He then moved to Galibori camp, and after one successful session at Moseli Halla (Crocodile Stream) where he landed two mahseer of 40lb and 60lb in quick succession, it was followed by yet another long period of inactivity. The two fish that Matt landed put up a poor fight (not ALL mahseer fight like crazy) and he is now keen to hit into one that fights like a runaway train. Matt has only one day left before the 4-man team consisting of Lez Chudzici, Hugo Luczyc-Wyhowski, Dave Goy and Mick Jefferies arrive from England. He will then be flying back to the cold, soggy banks of his beloved salmon rivers in Scotland.

The hours fly by and the river remains quiet. Eventually the solitude of the jungle is broken by the arrival of a vehicle carrying four 'mad dogs and Englishmen', headed by a one-legged paparazzi. Warm greetings are made to the team, and sad goodbyes to Matt who has proved to be a great fishing companion and friend.

The four 'mad dogs' settle into their allotted tents and every evening we gather around the table under a huge parachute, drinking beers and playing Yatzi. After a further ten days without a single big mahseer, we look forward to those Yatzi matches and I have now become the fifth mad dog!

Lez's team rent a jeep during the second week that enables them to drive down to fish Onto Gundu every morning. One afternoon, I am sitting under the shade of the parachute when the jeep returns from yet another fruitless trip. Everyone is wearing the same glum face as they wore on the return from every previous trip, - all except one... Mick carries the hint of a glint in his eye. I ask Mick what he has caught and then suddenly everyone's faces turns into huge grins. Lez shoves a video camera in front of my eyeball and then the spool starts spinning – the fight is on! After ten minutes of me glued to the video eyepiece, Mick then suddenly lifts 92lb of golden mahseer from

Mick Jefferies (centre).. ' lifts up 92lb of spectacular Mahseer and begins grinning at me!'

the water and begins grinning at me!! What a fantastic fish, and a great moral booster for all of us. Later in the afternoon, I decide to take the coracle way down past Crocodile Rock and fish the entrance to the third pool. I am rewarded for the effort. Within a few minutes of casting out a small livebait, the ratchet starts ticking and gives out line steadily. I lift the rod, pull back the Baitrunner lever then sweep the rod back sharply. The strike is stopped halfway as the rod keels over into a slow, heavy fish that moves so steadily that I am not convinced that this is a mahseer. I turn to Karya and say –

"Maybe big catfish?"

Karya shakes his head and answers " No sir, big, big mahseer! Coracle sir, coracle!"

We drift downstream about 200 metres with the big fish keeping a strong and steady course. After half an hour, I begin to have visions of a monster grandfather mahseer pulling with slow, powerful strokes of its huge tail, deep down below the coracle. Then suddenly the fish comes off the bottom and the line cuts sharper and sharper to the surface. I am determined to see this monster, so I keep up the pressure with the rod buckled over in its full curve. A long branch emerges from the depths and my heart sinks at the thought of being connected to a tree branch.

"Talao!" shouts Karya.

At that moment the branch moves and I see that it is connected to a shell the size of a tabletop. The 'creature' dives in alarm and the rod is almost torn from my hands as the line screams off the spinning spool again.

Now realising that it is not a fish, I become angry and fight it like a madman; but it takes another 30 minutes before I finally manage to beach it. The huge animal turns out to be an Indian pond terrapin with a long red, yellow and blue striped neck and scaly feet with bear-like claws. It is later identified as being a Sail Terrapin (latin: Kachuga kachuga) and must have weighed close to 80lb. I remove the hook with longnosed forceps (almost losing my hand in the terrapin's jaws in the process), and watch the big shell scramble over the sand then disappear into the depths of the Kaveri River, leaving only waves lapping at our toes.

The following morning, as the hot glow of the sun bakes the sand and rocks beneath our feet, we walk along the goat-track leading to Haira. I carry with me a light 9' long Daiwa Eliminator rod and a small backpack. Haira is a long walk upriver from the camp and it is a good half hour before we reach the first set of rapids. We both wade out up to our chests through freezing water that has still to be touched by the sun's warming rays, and reach a large set of boulders that slows down the river's flow, before it crashes through a maze of rocks in a series of raging white-water. A large Rebel 'Jaw Breaker' plug is already attached to the line, and I begin casting across the pool, letting the lure swing enticingly behind every submerged rock and break in the flow that might harbour a waiting fish. I systematically cover the complete area of the lower end of the pool, making sure that my shadow never touches the water's surface.

On the second cast, just after the plug has wobbled behind and past a submerged rock only inches from my feet, a streak of lightning speeds through the aqua-blue water and the rod hoops over as a wall of silver scales crashes into the lure. Within seconds the mahseer rips 25 metres off the spool and holds station behind a large rock in midstream. Following a ten second pause, the fish tears off downstream, ripping another 80 metres from the spool before resting behind another rock. The line is still caught around the first rock in midstream, so I can do nothing to control the fish and Karya is forced to run to the head of the pool, jump in and swim through the strong currents until he is level with the rock.

The coracle balanced on a rock in midstream, above the famous Crocodile Pool.

"..No sir, big, big mahseer!" – the long neck of a large freshwater terrapin breaks surface...

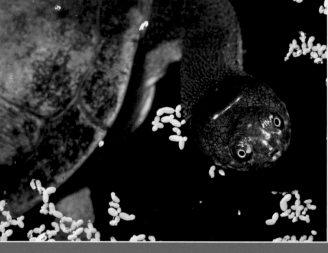

The force of water glues the line under the rock like a limpet, and every time Karya tries to get nearer to the rock he is swept off his feet by the incredible flow. Just at this moment, the fish decides to take a look further downstream and the spool begins revolving at an alarming rate. There are only about 20 metres of line left on the spool and I shout over to Karya that I'm going to run out of line. He motions for me to swim over to him, so I rip off my boots and run over to the rocks where Karya jumped in. The spool is still revolving but I am loath to try and swim across using only one hand, with the other holding the rod. I look down at the spool and with terror; begin to see black carbon appearing underneath the line. Within moments of reaching the spool knot, I stick the rod handle between my teeth and dive in.... Somehow I manage to reach a large rock close to Karya in midstream and am able to reel a few yards back onto the empty reel. Kaya eventually whips the line off the rock and I begin to wind the bow out of the line, but as soon as I regain contact with the fish, the rod is wrenched down to the water and the remaining line sizzles off the spool. Below me is an incredible set of rapids and ragged rocks, but without thinking, I bite into the rod handle and dive once more into the maelstrom of raging whitewater.

For the next half hour I swim for my life, often being completely submerged under water. Sometimes I am forced to swim back upstream because the fish chooses to take an awkward route through the tangle of rocks. Even though I rate myself as a strong swimmer, I eventually begin to tire and as I am swept past a rock in the full force of the flow, I reach out and grab hold of it. But the fish will not let me rest. With a violent wrench, it almost drags the rod from my teeth and I am forced to let go of the rock then follow the fish downstream. All this time, Karya is swimming with me, working frantically every 50 metres to pull line free of the rocks.

Before I realise it, we reach the last pool before the Big Rapids. These rapids lie just above Moseli Halla and it is the most powerful stretch of water on the upper Kaveri. I am reluctant to follow the fish down those next rapids and now that I am in full contact again, I am able to stop the onward rushes of the fish by locking the rod in its full power curve and keep the mahseer within the pool.

A tiger watches me through the foliage of a south Indian jungle.

A number of scorpions visited our camp beside the river, including this friendly beast (notice the sting protruding from tip of tail!); which just happens to be one of the deadliest species of scorpion known to man...

I can see the line is now badly frayed, but the amazing Berkley Big Game doesn't let me down and my heart sighs with relief as Karya finally gets a firm grip of the fish. But we still have a problem – we are latched to a small rock in the middle of the rapids and the stringer cord is still in my rucksack over one kilometre upstream!

Karya swims back across then runs back for the cord; all the time I hold onto the mahseer with the water pounding at my legs and trying to pull the fish from my grasp. With some difficulty, he swims back across to the rock and attaches the stringer. But we still have a problem! – How can we photograph the fish out here in mid river? Karya grabs the rod and starts to swim back across. He heads for a sandbank that lies 150 metres away and I jump in after him with the stringer cord wrapped around my wrist. The mahseer decides to power off towards the rapids while I furiously try to swim to shore. With a last gasp effort, I drag myself onto the sandbank, still holding the fish, one hour after first hooking it.

"...Still holding the fish, one hour after hooking it."

Maybe the saddest reflections of my courtship with the WASI stretch of the fabled Kaveri, is that at the end of my last expedition I knew that I would probably never return. Like a stunningly beautiful and soft-hearted women who had gradually grown hard and ill-tempered with age, so had the soul of Kaveri. The outside pressures of the human race for land and riches were already crushing at the borders of that sacred place in southern India. The plans to build a tarmac road along the river and the constant, daily explosions from illegal poachers that ripped fish to shreds, also ripped at my heart. The most vivid memory of Kaveri is when I sat beside Bula and watched in unbelieving awe as a mighty mahseer leaped clean out of the water in front of us. I immediately asked Bula – in my opinion, one of the most experienced guides on the river – what he estimated the monster could have weighed. His answer mirrored the thoughts I was afraid to shout out – that this mighty golden-scaled fish must have weighed close to 200lb.

My deepest regret is that during the sweltering heat of that afternoon, and in the very same place where Bula and I had previously stood in awe, an unstoppable fish grabbed the largest livebait that I'd ever used as bait on the Kaveri. The monster stripped line off my reel almost to the spool knot, but unfortunately the hook-hold was not good enough to hold it. The slow, mind-blowing strength and power of that fish, had left me shaking, and I was certain that it was the very same monster we had just seen.

Final Reflections

Bula and I sit cross-legged on a pancake-flat rock at the fringes of a rippling current. The water sings tunes as it glides over smooth pebbles, but then falls silent when it floods into the deep, long trench known as Crocodile Pool. Behind us an orange ball speeds towards the peaks of Eastern Ghats, while we continue talking softly in the fading light. The fingers of shadows creep slowly over us and sweep silently across the waters, until it touches the forest canopy, painting its heart in darkness. Bula gives me a nod, and I know without asking what he means…it is time to pack up.

Yet another complete day has passed without a take from a big mahseer. I walk back along the goat track towards the coracle with my head hung a little lower than usual – not through misery, but more perhaps through sadness, for there will be only one more such night to dwell in the depths of the jungle. As I listen to the droplets of water spinning off Bula's paddle, and gaze in silence at the reflections from flickering camp lights dancing on the inky river, a droplet begins to slide across my cheek…and I wander whether it is from a splash of the paddle blade…or from the rivers of my soul…

If you rub Aladdin's lamp, he will grant you four wishes, but don't get greedy, for often one of those wishes is best kept for another rainy day...

RED BREEZE

Soon after the big '2001 A Fish Odyssey' awards ceremony at Earl W Brydges State Artpark in Niagara Falls, Flip Scheggetman drove me to Buffalo International Airport so that I could pick up my hired car. We booked into a nearby hotel for the night, and then the following morning Flip began his long drive south to his home in Pennsylvania. His homecoming would be a short one, for Flip's 2-year USA naval posting had come to an end and he was soon due to fly back to his original homeland of Holland. His wife and family were already busy packing before their long flight, but Flip would not be staying long in his new Netherlands house; for within weeks he would be sent off to for a 6-month Navy tour in Bosnia!

It was a sad goodbye, for Flip and I had become great friends during the past few weeks, which had culminated in our first and second placing in the Carp tournament. A 36lb common carp caught by Flip won him $2,000.00 and my largest carp of the tournament meant that I was awarded with a hefty $ 10,000.00 cheque! Flip's blue Chevy van disappeared over the brow of a hill, and I climbed inside my car then sat for a while staring at the map contemplating where to go next. I had 2-weeks at my disposal before I too would be climbing on board a plane for Europe. With the recent Terrorist attack on the New York twin Trade Towers still strong in my memory, the thought of stepping on a plane did not transmit positive vibes.

I'd already searched numerous inland lakes, but none had so far looked productive. The best so far was Bond Lake, situated east of Tuscarora Indian Reservation, which had been stocked with Grasscarp to help stem the profusion of weed growth. This lake looks nice, but it is extremely shallow and didn't seem to hold many big common carp.

I began to drive, first heading east through Genesee County, then north towards Oak Orchard Swamp. This vast acreage of lakes and marshlands stretches for 15 miles either side of the Orleans and Genesee County borders, and is cradled within the protective wings of Iroquois National Wildlife Refuge. It is a quiet, wild and stunningly beautiful area full of reed-filled lagoons and waterways that attracts huge flocks of birds. Standing outside my car and scanning the vistas before me, there were no doubts in my mind that numbers of carp, and probably big ones, travelled these interlocking waterways, but without a boat or canoe I'd be very restricted in choice of swims. Most of the water is fairly shallow, and although big female carp would move into these areas during spring spawning migrations, now that it was autumn and fast approaching winter, I preferred to look for deeper water.

My next port of call was Glenwood Lake, situated 10 miles downstream. The car crunched to a halt on the gravel road beside the lake just as a dark cloud began to release her load from the heavens. I donned a Gore-Tex jacket, and then slowly walked around the shoreline while the sky spat silver raindrops on a mirror-like surface. Not a breath of wind stirred the orange leaves. Within minutes I was standing on a peninsular near the dam overflow, staring into the water while a carp fed in the margins. It was only a small mirror of about 12lb, but watching it sucking and blowing out detritus in a constant search for food items on the gravel bottom was fascinating.

A lone Cormorant sat motionless a few feet from the margins. On closer inspection I could see that it had serious wounds and a broken wing. Judging by its sad condition, it hadn't fed for a long time, so I walked back to the car and brought back some food. It was not long before this wild creature fed happily from my hands. I understood that there was little that could be done to help the bird, and probably my feeding it was actually prolonging its slow death, but I felt compelled to satisfy its hunger. In Europe the cormorant has bred to plague proportions, but not here in USA, so I held no grudge for this species, and besides, I'm a soft touch for any type of wildlife.

As I sat feeding the bird, my ears picked up the occasional distant splash. Within the next half hour my eyes caught brief visions of golden-scaled flanks as carp after carp began hurling themselves form the water and crashing back in sheets of spray. Some carp exceeded 20lb, but most were around 15lb. There was just one other car parked beside the lake, and I struck up a conversation with the occupant. He was able to provide me with some information about the lake and felt that the maximum was about 35 – 40lb. Glenwood is a lovely looking stretch of water, and judging by this short visit, it held promise. I was tempted to try to fish it for at least 24 hours, but other blotches of blue on the map tempted me to investigate, so I climbed back in the car and headed east on route 31, and later pulled off north on the Long Bridge Road, and then finally east on Presbyterian Road.

This long, hard-fighting 41lb 2oz common won Tony $10,000.00!

Soon I was staring out the window at a big pool of water that screamed 'carp'. It reminded me of many big turning bays on the great canals of Europe.

This particular backwater was connected to the Erie Canal, but as far as similarities with European canals were concerned, this was where they ended – for in front of me was, for the most part, a wild, overgrown lake that had hardly ever seen a fishing rod.

Without a doubt, the junction of lake and canal – a narrow gap between a line of trees – would be the obvious place to fish, but it would take a great deal of 'jungle trekking' to reach the desired location. Again I realised that most of the larger carp would use this backwater more during spring and early summer. A second more serious slice of information was that the Erie Canal was often drained during winter and the possibilities that carp in this location were a seasonal occurrence, so I opted to look elsewhere.

My searching finally brought me to a bridge crossing Waterport Lake, just as the slate grey skies again unloaded their heavy burden and began to pound the surface. Beneath this manmade

The raging waters of Niagara plummet over the precipice in a plume of white spray and foam. The Niagara River is home to many big carp.

construction swam pods of carp ranging from 3-5 in number. More interesting was the fact that at least two specimens (commons) exceeded 30lb, and one big mirror must have weighed at least 45lb. For the next half hour I watched them swimming in large figure-of-eight circles either side of the bridge, their dorsal spines cutting the surface and broad backs deflecting raindrops (they ignored my offerings of floaters). A local fisherman stood on the bridge, casting a delicate line to entice small fish for his supper. He wore only a thin T-shirt and rain streamed in mini rivers down his ebony arms – yet he stood unflinching, like a heron. I pulled up the hood on my EMS Gore-Tex jacket and began to marvel the tenacity of black-Americans.

The bridge area looked promising, but I wanted to camp and fish over several days, and erecting a tent near such an obvious crossing point for people and traffic would attract too much attention.

The remainder of the day was spent driving along the roads skirting Waterport, until finally a few hours before dusk; I found a secluded campsite called Redbreeze. 'Seclusion' is an apt word to describe this location because the place seemed completely deserted. I began walking over the well-kept lawns surrounding a lovely bungalow perched on a hilltop that provided stunning views across the northeastern bay. A vehicle eventually drove down the gravel road and Fran, the campsite owner, greeted me with a warm friendly handshake. I introduced myself as a photojournalist and mad carp-freak. 'Carp? There's plenty in this lake. Nobody intentionally fishes for them, although I've heard that you Europeans adore them. Sure, you can set up your tent anywhere you like. Let me know if there's anything you want. Enjoy your stay...'

I didn't actually stay that night because I had organised to meet a good friend, Neil Derisley, who lived nearby. But the following afternoon I drove back to Redbreeze and set up my lightweight mountain tent on a brow of the hill, at the edge of

Flip Scheggetman lands one of his many carp caught during the New York carp tournament – '2001 A Fish Odyssey'.

Flip with his second place USA Tournament carp that won a price of $ 2.000,00.

some steps leading down to Fran's private boat jetty. The reason I'd chosen this particular spot was because a thick band of weed stretched along the margins and the boat dock provided a narrow opening for playing and landing fish. The water was about 15ft deep off the point of the jetty, and although the old disused boat dock had silted up, the area adjacent to it was a 30ft deep basin. Beyond this, the bottom shelved steeply into 60ft, and eventually 100ft depths towards the dam.

The night brought with it a layer of dense cloud cover and bouts of wind-blown rain. Darkness signalled a period of heavy feeding and I had intermittent action until dawn, landing no less than fifteen superb fighting commons. All of the carp had picked up hookbaits presented over a large bed of freebies in 30ft of water, only two rod-lengths out from the jetty. By the time the first yellow sparks of sunshine reappeared over the opposite horizon, I was tired but happy.

Even though I managed to land a lot of carp, a number of the biggest specimens were lost due to them kiting into the 18ft high walls of weed that grew in profusion all along the marginal shelf. Often the fish would bury their heads inside the densest areas and I would be forced to hand-line great clumps of weed fronds to shore, only to watch the hook ping out of a thick pair of rubbery lips right at the last moment. At the end of the most hectic period of action, the whole marginal area surrounding the jetty became piled high with steaming heaps of weed. Each slowly drying heap seamed to almost 'move' with millions of freshwater shrimp, snails, and a million different tiny aquatic species – a banquet for hungry carp.

Fran came down to the jetty late that morning to stop for a chat and bring a welcome plate of hot breakfast. So impressed was he with the talk about my obsession with carp and my recent success in the USA Carp Tournament, that he was soon on the phone to inform newspapers of my exploits. It was not long before two journalists from rival newspapers were parked outside Fran's house, pen and notepad in hands, busily interviewing me about my own work as a global photojournalist, my fishing life, and especially the recent events in the '2001 A Fish Odyssey'. Less than 24 hours later, Fran brought me yet another welcoming breakfast cooked by his lovely wife Cindy, along with two copies of different New York newspapers. Splattered across the front pages in full colour, were photos of myself at Redbreeze, and me cradling the winning 41lb 2oz common carp, along with full two-page written features about my life's exploits photographing wildlife and searching for big carp around the world. Apart from the good promotion, it was nice to at last see positive recognition in the USA press for the much-aligned carp, which they often refer to as a 'trash fish'.

That afternoon I packed up the tent and headed for Neil's house, for he had invited me to share a meal with friends. It was my plan to spend the next week fishing the mighty Lake Ontario. Although I'd already caught a stack of big carp to 40lb+ at Point Breeze – where Oak Orchard River flows into the lake – I was keen on finding a secluded place far from the hustle and bustle of the harbour. Luckily, a friend had helped me obtain permission to fish from the garden of a private house situated on a point where the Johnson Creek is swallowed in the vastness of Lake Ontario. He also was kind enough to loan me his boat with outboard motor, so I could transport my gear to the swim and also make it easier to bait up. My only fear was if there were adequate depths of water near the creek mouth, because the recent droughts of summer had lowered the level of the lake by several feet.

Neil drove with me to Johnson Point the following morning. When we arrived, Lake Ontario was still

Battling with a carp at Red Breeze.

*Just one of many carp caught from the
wonderful location of Red Breeze.*

getting over the wild fury of a stormy night. The water had been shook into a chocolate-coloured tempest, and we stood in awe as huge waves rolled in repetitive cycles to crash against the rocks. Autumn was in full swing, but I could smell the crisp bite of a fast-approaching winter.

This place was a wonderfully secluded vantage point to fish for the big carp of Ontario – a place of solitude, where the only sounds were cries of seagulls and thumping of waves along the beach.

This quiet was enhanced because even though the main part of Johnson Creek has numerous deep glides and salmon holes, the narrow entrance does not provide ample depth for large boats such as those that navigate up the Oak Orchard or Niagara rivers.

I quickly set up a rod, tied on a lead, and then began casting into the rolling breakers of Ontario, searching for the snake-like route of the creek as it swept through a deep salmon pool then wound past sandbanks. Thirty minutes later I gave up in frustration, for according to my calculations, the water was only inches deep over the sandbanks and only dropped to a couple of feet inside the creek trench. Even the first 'salmon pool' was barely 9ft deep.

The waves looked dangerously high, but I was determined to obtain a more precise calculation of depth, so quickly fired up the outboard and guided the boat away from the haven of Johnson Creek, and then straight towards the maelstrom of Lake Ontario. Within minutes the boat had been struck by a series of white-foamed breakers that promised to swamp and sink it if I dared to challenge them. Suddenly the propeller jarred on the edges of a sandbank, and without propulsion I was powerless to control the boat. A huge wave lifted the stern until it almost overturned. Miraculously, I managed to steer the rudder in time to manoeuvre the boat so that it lifted on the next wave, and we rode on its crest like a Hawaiian surfer until it carried us back to the safety of tranquil waters. Back on dry land, I stood beside Neil and discussed the situation. My short surfboard ride had been enough to ascertain that although the 2ft water at the creek mouth was deep enough during springtime to attract big females that navigate up its length for spawning rituals, it raised serious doubts that they would do the same during autumn. I desperately wanted to fish for the monsters that inhabit the mighty ocean of Lake Ontario, but I knew that most of the carp would be patrolling the deep shelves in the 30ft-90ft zones that lay more than a mile offshore. Only the depths and flow of major feeder-rivers would attract big fish at this time of year, and all of these also attracted too many people and noise – a noise that I needed to escape from.

So where would I go from here? Redbreeze had entered my mind on a number of occasions during the past hour, but now it was pushed to the forefront. Fran and Cindy Perry maintained an immaculate, yet secluded waterfront campsite. The fishing was action-packed, and apart from the serious problem with marginal weeds, it certainly held the 'lunkers' I was searching for – indeed, during the first night I'd watched a 50lb+ mirror heave its shoulders at the stars. My mind was quickly made up, I would return to Redbreeze.

Fran and Cindy were glad to see me back and even invited me to join them for a wonderful meal that evening. This time I set up camp at the base of the steps, with the rodpod positioned directly on the pier so that I could quickly walk to the edge once a carp was hooked, and hopefully help keep the line clear of the weeds. The meal, along with a few bottles of red wine and good company, kept me longer than intended so it was dark by the time I returned to camp. Reflections of stars were flickering on a black carpet and a crescent moon danced gently on the waves. Even under the moonlight, I could still make out thousands of open zebra muscle shells scattered in the margins, or dotted amongst the heaps of decaying weed. The carp in this water would not go hungry if they avoided my boilies – but another night of almost constant action to rigs cast over the heavily pre-baited marginal shelf proved that small round 'sweets' were very attractive – like children walking inside a candy store after eating a Sunday dinner.

The following day I had to drive to Lockport to collect my Carp Tournament winners-cheque. I didn't want to cash such a large amount of money into dollars, so had the bank covert it to an international cheque that could be placed in my bank on return to England. It was indeed a strange feeling that afternoon sitting outside the tent, dressed like some penniless vagabond, with $10,000.00 in my back pocket, but I must admit there was a smile on my face!

For the next 24-hours, I was blessed with a succession of immaculate carp caught during darkness from my pre-baited 30ft deep area, but the daylight hours were punctuated by large carp rolling at about 100 metres away. At this distance the water seemed to be fairly deep, because even when I cast short of the active area, a 4oz lead took a full 15 seconds to touch bottom!

While I was still contemplating whether to cast out to the distant zone, yet another golden beast heaved its shoulders above the surface and crashed back in a sheet of spray. The left-hand rod was quickly reeled in; a 25mm boilie was removed from the pre-soak jar of Scopex dip, and then threaded on the short hair. While I was doing this, yet another fish crashed on the surface in exactly the same area, so I quickly thumped out the rig, satisfied to watch the lead disappear in the concentric ripples left by the leaping carp.

It was not long before the distant bait was picked up, but shortly after hooking the fish, the line became snagged, so I pulled for a break. Just on breaking point, the braid tugged back, and I reeled in a two-foot section of tree branch. The rig was quickly dispatched to the same deep-water zone, but it was not lying on the bottom in darkness for long before something once again decided to suck in the big, smelly round ball. An intense struggle followed, with some scary moments at the edge of the weed, but eventually an immaculate-scaled big common was engulfed inside the landing net. During the next few days, the single boilie cast into 65ft deep water (with no baiting) produced only about half the number of carp caught to the rod cast in the heavily pre-baited 20-30ft zone. Yet all of the carp caught from the deep water were almost twice the weight of those caught in the marginal area! A couple of times I reeled in fragments of tree branch from the deep zone, so I had no doubts that a large sunken tree was the main factor attracting the carp.

Neil had been visiting me regularly during past days, and even though essentially a salmon angler, he became interested in carp. So keen was his interest, that shortly after catching a nice carp at Point Breeze, he ordered a heap of new carp tackle – including buzzers and a rodpod! A few days prior to my flight back to Gatwick, Neil visited my camp with a flask of coffee and invited me to join him later for a steak meal at his favourite restaurant. I looked across the lake and sat contemplating for a few minutes. I'd come to USA with the intention of trying to win the main 'roving' carp competition and hopefully also land a forty from 'virgin' water – and eventually managed to fulfil both wishes. My third wish was to spend some time after the tournament, searching for a carp to beat my old North American record of 52lb 2oz, and possibly land that true monster that had slipped my hooks on several occasions during the past. My fourth and greatest wish was to find a secluded big-carp-water in stunning surroundings far from the maddening crowds. Redbreeze had provided that last wish, and even though the elusive third wish had still to be granted, I was more than happy to wait until a return visit in the future.

With my heart full and Aladdin back in the lamp, I packed up the gear, said a tearful farewell to Fran and Cindy, and then drove back with Neil to wash and spruce-up prior to our meal in town. The food was as Neil had promised – absolutely delicious. We eventually drove back to his house, and though

A vulture soars through the canyon.

A huge Canadian grizzly bear stands on its hind feet to sniff the air, as it stares directly at Tony's camera lens!

The amazing 'Fall' colours of October in Upstate New York.

I hate long spells indoors in front of a TV, the odd evenings following days facing a cold wind are more than welcome. Neil had become a great friend during past weeks, and our long talks about carp fishing must have caused some havoc inside his brain, because now he was a confirmed 'carp-freak' So much had his passion for carp grown, that Neil even bought my two Globetrotter Supreme rods and landing net!

Time passed quickly and soon I was strapped in the seat of a jet heading skyward. The apprehension - that I was about to be blown out of the skies by a terrorist's remote-operated bomb - gradually faded and I began to relax as the plane levelled out on its flight path. I stared through the double-glass window beyond the big turbine wing engine, until my eyes rested on a green carpet scattered with spots and ribbons of blue. The waters shimmered in the sunlight and pulled at my heartstrings. I was homeward bound, but I knew then that I would need to return to Redbreeze for a crack at that third wish...

'Globetrotter' fishing at the confluence where Oak Orchard River flows into the vast expanses of Lake Ontario.

Carp fishing at Lake Kawagchiko, with the stunning snow-capped Mount Fuji volcano as a backdrop.

By Steven Sands

LAND OF THE
RISING SUN

"Aouo, Aouo!" came an excited shout from the car which had just pulled up beside me in my swim. Frantically gesturing to follow him, my wife and I quickly jumped into our car and proceeded to pursue him further down the river. We approached a small group of Japanese anglers, one of them obviously into a very large fish judging by the violent bending and jerking actions his rod was making. We hurriedly got out of the car and I had already prepped my camcorder for some recording, hoping to obtain my first action footage of a very special fish. The fish had been hooked for some 30 minutes and was very soon to make an appearance on the surface. I quickly focused my lens into where the line was zigzagging through the dark slow flowing water in front of us. By now one of his friends had slipped into a pair of chest waders and was carefully making his way out towards the step drop-off, which was around 10 feet from the bank. Meanwhile the locals were all having a good giggle about the strange Western person filming their actions but at the same time they were extremely friendly and polite while I tried communicating to them in my limited Japanese. The net was now under the fish; it was not until I zoomed back out from just a headshot of the fish that I realized the true size and proportions of the fish. As the fish came into contact with the net, the water exploded in front of us as if someone had chucked in several sticks of dynamite. The Japanese guy holding the net nearly followed head first as the fish tried to make one last attempt at escaping. The fish was quickly transferred into a large folded plastic sheet and hauled up the bank by three guys. It was then placed on a measuring board. Japanese anglers very rarely record weight, but take great care and precision into measuring the length of their catch. The fish was then manoeuvred until its lips were just touching one end of the board and the tail was smoothed and stretched out at the other. After a few minutes of deliberating, very much in the same way as we do over a couple of ounces, the group of guys surrounding the board agreed on a length of 140cm. More sniggering and pointing soon followed as I produced my scales and weigh sling from the car. With its head and tail poking from either end of the weigh sling, the fish pulled the needle around to 55lb. I had just witnessed a capture of a Black Carp and it was there, at that time I fell in love with a fish I knew I just had to capture.

The habitual heavily congested roads in Japan had me on my mobile ordering suitable terminal tackle from a shop back in England while I sat in the never ending traffic jams on my way back home to central Tokyo. I also placed an order for some 120lb scales, you just never know. I came to know about the existence of the Black Carp in Japan a month prior. I was fishing for carp in one of the immense inland seas north of Tokyo, when one weekend I found myself in the middle of a weekend long Carp match. As was the norm, many of the local "Koi" fishermen (common carp are referred to as Koi in Japan) found my methods and approach very interesting and sometimes very amusing, especially the small black boxes which made loud variable noises, usually not enough noise for my liking though! The president of the club was pegged a few swims away further along the bank. As with most of the locals, his friendliness and curiosity soon had us exchanging information and stories while sipping hot green tea and eating Yakatori (meat on sticks). He suggested that I give a short speech at the weigh in ceremony on the Sunday evening, albeit in my broken Japanese.

As I packed away my six rods (no restrictions on the number of rods you can use, six rods per angler is the average in Japan!), the President of the club pulled up and informed me the weigh in was about to commence. While I was listening and trying to translate in my head what he was telling me, there was a strange banging noise coming from the plastic carrying case attached to the roof

Steve Sands strains to hold up a colossal 110lb Black Carp!

of his car. As he drove away, my wife and I looked at each other thinking the same, had he kidnapped someone and stashed them in the box? A couple of miles drive further around the lake soon had us at the presentations and some thirty members of the club greeting us. They had been fishing three locations that weekend, Kasumigawa Lake, Kitaura Lake and Tonegawa River, which feed both of these immense lakes. We soon discovered what was causing the banging noises from inside the boxes. Several decent size commons were in the process of being transferred from the carrying case and were being placed into a small paddling pool with many other Carp wrapped in blue plastic bags. We watched carp after carp being measured and the length and captors names being recorded. The haul was mainly made up of high doubles, a few twenty pound plus commons and a couple of well proportioned thirties. We sensed the crowd becoming excited as the largest looking plastic bag was hauled out of the paddling pool and it's contents released onto the measuring board. This was my first encounter with an "Ao", which translates into English as Blue. In Japan, Black Carp are referred to as Blue Carp. Certainly the Japanese description is far more accurate than referring to this fish as being black. The large silver scales, tinged with blue and purple glittered in the sun light as the crowd eagerly awaited the announcement of its length. A small specimen, 120cm long but a clear winner of the competition. A meter long "Koi" in Japan is considered to be a good fish. I have weighed several Carp of this length for the locals and usually this length would represent a fish in the high thirties.

The prize giving and my speech went well, but my wife and I were a little disappointed on the way the fish were released. Some of the carp had been in these plastic bags now for a few hours and some were clearly showing signs of stress as they were quickly tipped back into the lake and left to recover on their own, including the Black Carp which was now doing backstroke some 20 feet from the bank. The next 45 minutes had me in my best underwear reviving this fish while my wife, in her not so best bra and undies, doing the same for the carp, which were not strong enough to stabilize themselves in the strong waves crashing into the bank. One of the local fishermen helped me revive the distressed Black Carp as he sensed my annoyance of the situation. The fish swam off strongly as so did the majority of the Carp my wife revived. A small group who had been watching applauded our attempts as we clambered back up the steep bank; either that or they were applauding my wife for entering a wet T-shirt competition. My disappointment was relayed back to the President and I hoped that a few locals had seen and learnt a lesson here. I have witnessed Carp succumbing to three fates in Japan, taken away and consumed, being placed in the captor's garden pond or being released. Thankfully the latter being the most practiced these days. The Black Carp on the other hand is treated with the utmost respect by the anglers who pursue this species, unless that is, it is caught during a carp match.

After some research and advice from the locals, I decided to concentrate my Black Carp efforts on the Tonegawa River. From the mountains of the Gunma prefecture, some 1,840m up, this river begins its journey, winding it's way through many prefectures including Tokyo. It is an awesome river, covering 16,840 square kilometres if you were to include all of the tributaries and smaller rivers that branch away. The river flows for 322km until it reaches Choshi and eventually joins the Pacific Ocean. As mentioned earlier, the river feeds Kasumigaura Lake, which is the second largest freshwater lake in Japan, with a surface area of 220 square kilometers and over 70 km in length. It is home to many species of fish and can produce Common's of 50lb+. Unfortunately, due to it's sheer size and low population of carp, location can be difficult and therefore good results are few and far between. Tonegawa river also holds many species of fish, Common Carp (Koi), Grass Carp (Sougyo), Silver Carp (Rengyo) and of course the Black Carp (Ao) to mention a few, all of which exceed 50lb+ in size.

The prime fishing season for Black Carp in this river runs from April to November. It was now October and the weather was cooling after the stifling hot summer, so this left me little time to seriously get involved with my quarry this year. Additionally my wife was due to give birth to our first child in November, you can imagine the grievously bodily harm my ears were receiving every time I loaded the jeep up with a mountain of gear. Most weekends found me on the riverbank (but not all), waiting patiently for this elusive fish to formally introduce itself to my hook. I say "elusive" because I had also discovered that even the small group of locals, who concentrate on catching the Black Carp, have limited success. These guys, apart from being some of the most warmest, friendliest people that you could ever wish to meet, are extremely capable anglers. Their knowledge of the fish is second to none and their technical expertise is also of the highest standard. Many regard a guy named Kataoka-san, myself included, as being one of the most capable and successful. This year had seen him capture 11 fish so far and his largest to date was a whacker of 158 cm in length. On the other hand, most of the other anglers may have been lucky to capture one or two that year. I heard of one guy who had been trying for five years to bank a fish and had just succeeded in doing so this year. With these statistics in mind, I knew I had to have patience and spend as much time as possible on the riverbank if I was going to be successful in the capture of a Black Carp that season. I also knew that I had to invest in some ear protection, due to the wife, now uncomfortably large, verbally assaulting me due to her displeasure of this theory. Luckily for me, Kataoka-san decided to take me under his wing and show me the ropes.

The first few weekends proved unsuccessful for all, apart from of course Kataoka-san, who managed to notch up two more fish around the 50lb mark. Even though I was desperate to capture one for myself, seeing this fish on the bank filled me with great excitement and fuelled my desires to capture a Black Carp even more so. The fishing was also turning out to be a very sociable event. Kataoka-san's wife, known by all as Oksan (simply means someone's wife in Japanese), took it upon herself to ensure everyone fishing in the nearby vicinity was well fed and watered. This included breakfast, lunch and dinner, with a few smaller snacks thrown in throughout the weekend. Some of the food which was enthusiastically offered to me, sometimes looked totally unrecognisable, but in Japan it is custom to accept and try. I must say though, the food was always delicious and I am still here to tell the tale, I also invariably went back for seconds.

At night, when the action was even slower than in the daytime, we all sat around a large flickering smoky campfire, drinking Asahi beer, swapping funny stories and swatting the annoying persistent

A huge 158cm Black Carp weighing 116lb.

hordes of bloodthirsty mosquitoes. The more alcohol I consumed the better my Japanese language skills became, more often than not I was able to get my stories across.

Helen my wife, agreed to accompany me for a long weekend fishing before the baby was born. I cannot remember off the top of my head what I had used to bribe her into this, most likely a promise of a nice holiday next year or something along those lines. The jeep was loaded to 100% capacity with fishing and camping equipment, I could just barely squeeze a couple of novels in for Helen to read over the four day session. The morning was spent setting up the seven rods and our home for the next few days. The standard approach was pretty much straight forward. Water snails were impaled or hair rigged on to large strong hooks, mine being some catfish hooks purchased from the U.K. Line also had to be up for the job, apart from the size that some of these fish can reach, this particular stretch of the river was littered with all sorts of snags. The large sharp boulders and rocks that made up the steep margin drop off shelf proved to be the most hazardous. I began using 35lb mono, coupled with Quick Silver snag leaders, anything less was suicidal as baits had to be positioned at the bottom of this shelf in amongst the rocks, this is where the snails lived, this is where the Blue Carp fed.

It was now midday and for late October it was a particularly hot day. The sky was clear and the sun was blazing down on us as we both sat under the awning, soaking up the peaceful surroundings and trying to put the hustle and bustle of Tokyo to the back of our minds.
"Why's that rod tip bouncing", said Helen as she awoke me from a light doze.
"Just floating rubbish flowing down the river", I replied.
At that moment all hell broke lose. The rods had been positioned up at a 45-degree angle to clear the edge of the shelf as much as possible. As the alarm violently screeched into action, the butt of the rod sharply pivoted up into the air as the baitrunner tried to supply line to what seemed to be a Bullet train! I just managed to grab the butt as it was about to be pulled down the steep bank. As I lent into the fish I knew it was something special. The fish slowed and began to swim slowly to my left, parallel to the bank. The sun was fierce and Helen applied sun cream to my dripping head and my already burnt shoulders. After around 30 minutes had passed, a young local guy pulled up beside me in his car.

 "Blue fish, Blue fish! It took me 2 hours to get big fish like this before", he said in his broken English. The guy stood around for another 30 minutes before telling me his lunch break was over. He took off his large straw hat and placed it on my red sweaty head, slapped me on the back and wished me good luck before driving off. The fish was doing very little, even though I exerted as much pressure as the 3.5 lb T.C rod would allow. Everything was creaking under the strain. It had been over 1 hour now and I had still yet to even have a glimpse of what was on the end of my arcing rod. For the first time I began gaining line as the fish became obviously very tired. I gradually worked the fish up into the middle depths of the river as the fish came in slowly towards the shelf. Then a sickening feeling hit me like a Samurai's sword as everything went solid. The fish had become firmly snagged. Whatever I tried failed to move the fish and I eventually decided to go out in the dingy to apply pressure directly above the fish. The line had taken a beating during the 1 hour-long battle and had been damaged on the numerous rocks. It was not much longer until the line finally parted and I was left with nothing apart from my worst-ever fishing experience.

The remainder of the session proved to be fruitless. The weather quickly turned for the worst and we spent much of the remaining time watching spectacular electrical storms in the distance while repeatedly restructuring our tent and awning to avoid getting drenched. Saturday and Sunday saw the arrival of the locals and they were all genuinely as disappointed as me that I had lost my dream fish. Oksan performed her regular duties and provided us all with plenty of food and drink.

My bad luck continued for the next few sessions. I hooked and played very briefly three fish, all of which became quickly snagged and lost, though none of which felt anywhere near as big as the first one. The baby was due anytime now and the weather was cooling down rapidly. I had literally one weekend remaining before putting my rods away until the following year. The Saturday was uneventful, no fish caught or seen by any of the anglers dotted along the bank. I had promised that I would pack away by noon and be home early thus avoiding the heavy Sunday afternoon traffic. As I disappointedly stared out across the wide river I saw a shark like dorsal fin appear as a Black Carp rose in my swim. These fish do not crash broad side like Commons do, instead they gracefully show themselves very much in the same way as dolphins do when they arch their backs out of the water. Within minutes the bite indicator smashed into the rod and the rod tip was being wrenched down as the bait runner went into full speed. Around 7 locals appeared quickly in my swim, their attention being drawn by the wailing alarm. These guys had become good friends over the last several weeks and they all wanted to help and shout advice. These streamlined fish have an amazing turn of speed and use their sharp forked shaped tail to relentlessly test the tackle and the angler to their limits. The fight only lasted for 15 minutes before the net surrounded my first Black Carp. The fish was not going to beat the Japanese record, which currently stands just short of 170cm, but was measured to be 120cm and 38lb in weight. A mere baby but it was a start. I think the locals were even more jubilant than I was, as they all congratulated the strange Westerner who turned up at their river wishing to capture this truly magnificent fish.

With the arrival of baby Zara, and with winter setting in, albeit mild compared to England, I did not see myself on the riverbanks until the following January. My first session of the year coincide with New Years party on a pretty little stretch of the Arakawa River in Tokyo. All the wonderful friends I had made during the previous year turned up, along with the rest of the club members who controlled this stretch of bank. It had been billed as the first carp competition of the year, but it took me all of about 5 minutes to realize that it was going to be a serious drinking and eating weekend, not that the Japanese needed an excuse to consume large quantities of alcohol and enjoy themselves!

The next clear recollection of the weekend was being awoken in the middle of the night by a small common which had taken a fancy to my Whisky flavoured boilie. The bright clear morning revealed a Christmas card picture. It had snowed heavily during the night creating a spectacular winter wonderland. The majestic Mount Fuji, a notoriously reclusive mountain, often hidden by cloud, stood tall across the snow-covered paddy fields. Japan's highest mountain stands 3776 meters high, and with a covering of snow in winter, it transforms in to a majestic and almost perfect volcanic cone.

The research about the Black Carp continued at every opportunity, any fisherman I came across was subject to intense interrogation on their experiences and knowledge of the species. I had already decided the previous season to concentrate my efforts closer to home so as to hopefully avoid spending a large portion of the weekend sitting in the horrific traffic jams, seen every weekend in and around Tokyo. Many weekends were spent searching for accessible and likely holding areas along the Edogawa, Tonegawa and Arakawa rivers. Likely holding areas would usually require a suitable habitat for their main food source, water snails. Many of the riverbanks had been constructed or reinforced with large concrete blocks or stone boulders, these areas provided a good home to the snails and crayfish and a welcoming restaurant to the Black Carp.

A wet weekend in March saw me for the first time that year awakening a few of my "mollusc" friends from their deep winter hibernation ecstasies. For the past 5 months I had been meticulously attending to a few hundred water snails, which were going to be my supply of hook baits for the coming season. I have never been one who gets pleasure or usually the time to roll vast quantities of boilies, but compared to the collection of water snails, then I would certainly choose the boilie option. Basically, if you want to fish for Black Carp from the onset of Spring using snails as bait, then you have to collect them during the previous October before they disappear below the surface to hibernate. This annual snail collecting weekend(s) is usually attended by the whole group and is a social affair with everyone bringing food and drink to consume throughout the days activities. Paddy fields, small brooks and rivers, drainage channels and such are all extensively searched until you feel you have enough bait to get you through most of the following season. The snails are then

A Japanese angler releases a giant black Carp to the water.

Stuart about to return another heavyweight Black Carp.

aired to dry the shells to avoid them perishing, placed in damp moss and sealed in polystyrene boxes where they will fall into hibernation during the coming colder months. I had been living in Hong Kong for three years prior to my assignment in Japan and had therefore not been doing much fishing or buying any new equipment. I made up for this inactivity on the buying front with lots of new purchases, which included a set of Globetrotter Supreme 3.5 T.C rods, and some Daiwa Infinity reels. As mentioned previously, terminal tackle had to be up for the job and readily available to me. For this reason I chose to use items easily purchased from my local tackle shop, Varivas 55lb test copolymer monofilament line, a strong and super sharp Gamakatsu hook pattern and an extremely abrasive resistant Dyneema hook link of 80lbs. Sounds very excessive, but anything less was snapped like cotton on the large razor sharp underwater obstructions that littered the river bed. Hooks where spliced and then whipped with a silk thread onto the Dyneema hook length and then finished off with a coating of Kryston Bondage rig glue. Various main line braids were experimented with over the season but none came close to the exceptional abrasion resistance and overall strength of the Varivas mono. This year PVA bags were going to play a large part in my pursuit of the Black Carp. A strong bag, the Nash variety I found to be the best, allowed me to place my hook bait safely in between the rocks surrounded by a handful of free offerings. So, on this miserably rainy day, sitting alone on the riverbank, I opened the account with a small 25lb specimen that had me grinning like a Cheshire cat as a passer-by took a few snaps for me. A call to Kataoka-san soon had the other members of the group ringing my mobile as the news filtered around about my capture. This grapevine of information proved invaluable during the coming season as everyone reported where fish were seen or captured from and the condition of the river.

A few mandatory blank sessions followed along with the witnessing of a 107 pounder, the biggest fresh water fish I had ever seen, which was captured by one of my friends. A night-caught immaculate, scale perfect, 55lb fish was to be the first of five personal best records set that season. I had set myself a goal of four fish that year along with an optimistic 70lb lump - everyone needs a goal and that was mine!
The end of April saw me on my first long session, this one being four days. The weather was by now, warming up as the first signs of spring began to show. The locals had already explained where the fish should be during this period and they were not wrong. The first night saw me again break my PB with a 57lb carp. Darkness was proving to be very productive but was also very treacherous. The steep banks, deep drop-offs, and the immense power of a 50lb+ Black Carp fighting for its life in a deep and strong flowing river was not something you wanted to do alone, so I was very grateful to a few of the locals who had also decided to fish the session with me.

A ferocious, powerful take and a distressed sounding bite alarm had me awake early the following morning. The tip of the Globetrotter rod was wrenched around to the butt within seconds of me picking it up. Now bearing in mind that I had purchased these rods and chose them from a wide range of other suitable rods from a large market, when I say that their performance is awesome, you will have to accept that I am not just saying it because they were designed by the author of this book. The amount of power that can be exerted on a powerful and colossal fish such as the Black Carp is amazing. Initially you think that you do not have enough power to bring the fish under

Look at the massive tail on this 96lb
Black Carp caught by George Grimes.
No wonder they fight so hard!

control, as the top third of the rod is extremely soft, then the power kicks in right down to the butt cap. The performance of the rod coupled with the power and smoothness of the Infinity reel soon had this lump under control, the only place where it was heading was to my waiting submerged 52 inch landing net. Thirty minutes of arm and back pain had the fish in a 2 meter long unhooking / weigh sling specially made for me by Tracker. The fish looked a real brute as it lay on the matt starring up at me, its dustbin-lid-sized tail, a mouth that could easily engulf a coconut surrounded by large tough lips that were used to vacuum up any crustaceans that were unlucky to be in its path. My friends enthusiastically measured the fish to be 149cm, and I hardly could contain my excitement as the needle of the scales span round around to 76lb. My excitement continued as I dived into the river after returning the fish safely back to its home, much to the bewilderment and amusement to the crowd that had amassed on the bank.

The Asahi beer flowed for much of the day, and soon Kataoka-san and his wife had arrived for the weekend. Oksan was soon providing delicious food for us all, and the party continued late into the night, which incidentally was usually the norm. With the pleasant weekend weather, it was not long before the riverbank filled with day-trippers who were having picnics and playing games. Open space is a premium in Tokyo and the riverbanks provide the perfect refuge for many Japanese people and their children looking to get out of the hustle and bustle of the city. Many people camp overnight, play baseball and have BBQ's during the day, so there is always something happening around you when fishing. The afternoon saw me take my third fish of the session and again set a new PB. This time it weighed in at 80lbs and measured 153cm in length. Again the tackle performed well under the immense power that the fish exerted on every part of my tackle and every inch of my body. It was becoming a dream session, though the three round bruises made from digging the butt into my groin area proved to me that this was no dream. Black Carp measuring over 150cm are considered truly special by the local fisherman and very few have had the pleasure of capturing one that length. The closest comparison would be of a true English fifty-pound carp, so I knew how lucky I had been with this capture. The next day I capped this truly amazing session with a 44lb carp. Four carp for a total of over 250lb in just four days! The locals were certainly impressed, and my extensive research, effort and application were certainly paying off. Kataoka-san was the only person to also catch, his being one of around 50lb.

My main session of the year was planned for late May or early June. A friend from England and I had been planning a weeklong session all year. Ian was obviously eager to arrive, as I had been feeding him with all the details of my current triumphs. The long drive from the airport to where the fish were hopefully going to be was a good chance to catch up on old times, as we had not seen each other for a couple of years. The first day was spent unpacking a mountain of tackle, camping equipment, food wine and beer from the car and trailer - this was intended to be a social as well as a serious fishing trip. While still setting up camp we had our first take. I decided to take the first hit, to give Ian an idea of what to expect once one of these fish decides to pick up your bait. It turned out to be a good lesson, as a 70lb Black Carp did its best impression of a fish high on steroids. Ian netted and photographed the fish and was in obvious shock and excitement to what he had just witnessed. Before the trip, he had made a comment that just seeing one of these beautiful creatures would be more than enough to make his holiday. That wish had already been granted, and now the time had come to make a serious impression on the crate of wine that was waiting to be drunk!

The Optonic screamed into life at around 3am the following morning. Ian was out of his sleeping bag and tent and hanging onto the rod before I could even get my boots on. The adrenalin was pumping for the both of us, Ian because it was his first run and mine because I knew what was swimming around on the other end. An epic battle was to follow, Ian not being the biggest person in the world, had to put all of his strength into getting the fish to the surface. It was still dark and there were some nasty snags directly in front of us, which we had earlier seen on the fish-finder while viewing the riverbed from the dingy. Finally I netted his prize, 70-pound of Black Carp measuring 140cm. Standing at dawn, in the icy cold river did not seem to bother Ian, as he proudly displayed the fish for the camera, before eventually watching another huge fish swim away and back into the dark depths.

It was Friday morning, and a day that I will always clearly remember. The day started clear and warm with a gentle breeze buffering the bank we were camped on. I had been detailing the action so far, in my ever-improving Japanese language skills to a friend who had turned up for the weekend, when one of the rods suddenly had a slow take. The line grated through a snag some 100 yards from the bank for the first 10 minutes of the fight, and to be perfectly honest, I felt that this was going to be the first lost fish of the session. To my delight the line pinged free as I applied as much pressure as I dared to the fish. The carp then proceeded to stay deep for another 10 minutes or so at the bottom of the shelf, just a few yards from where I was know standing. The river is tidal, and during low tide it is possible to stand on the edge of the shelf, thus obtaining better control and pressure of a hooked fish. I was by no means an authority on the capture of these fish, but this particular specimen felt much more like the fish I had hooked last year, but had eventually lost after an hour of fighting. History was not to repeat itself as Daichan - the angler who had helped me to resuscitate the Black Carp that was showing signs of distress following a carp match the previous year - scooped this monster of a fish into the net, with Ian capturing all of it on video. It needed the three of us to haul it up the slippery steep bank before we could truly appreciate its size. The fish was lifted off the floor in the weigh sling, and we watched in mounting excitement as the needle span past the magical 100lb mark until it finally settled at 110lb. This beast measured 155cm and it's condition, proportions and colour were indeed the marks of a truly exceptional example of this species, and certainly a fish of a lifetime. Safely the fish was returned, and we all watched it swim away strongly. News of our captures travelled far and wide, bringing groups of onlookers who were amazed at our continued success. We were certainly on a roll and it continued during the weekend, with Ian taking two fish over 40-pound and me capturing a 73-pounder. That weekend the beer and the wine flowed, and it will certainly go down as an all time high point in my list of fishing experiences.

Sunday evening, as everyone said their goodbyes, the weather began to get cooler and it started to rain heavily. The weather remained like this all week and the fish went off the feed. A few fish were hooked and lost in snags, along with the capture of a few small commons that took a fancy to our snail hook baits. We had to wait until Friday to bank our next fish. Ian took a fish of 67lb and I finished the session off with another stunning looking fish of 65lb. The long drive back seemed to fly by as we added up our results for the week, - 543lb of carp in 8 fish - an average of over 67lb. After talking to my local friends and reflecting back on this session, it was indeed a truly remarkable, and probably one of the most productive, weeks fishing for Black Carp ever seen. To this day, my Japanese friends refer to Ian as 'the lucky one' because most of them would not achieve four fish in a whole season. And in some cases even longer. As for me, they all maintain that I am probably the only "gaijin" (foreigner) to capture an "Aouo" of over 100lb in weight. This probably holds true due to them only (as far as I know) being found at this size in Japan and China. Unfortunately they are still caught for food in China, making it very difficult for the fish to grow to these immense proportions.

As for the remainder of the year, I saw my tally rise to twelve fish, with a 30lb and a 47lb being captured amongst the numerous blanks. The number and size of my carp firmly put me at the top of the season's big-fish list. My first full season had turned out to be a spectacular one, and the most enjoyable in my entire fishing career. The high percentage of blanks soon get lost and forgotten about when I flick through my photo album. The snails have already been collected, and are safely tucked up for a long sleep in preparation for my assault next year on this truly wonderful fish...

REWARD FOR

EFFORT

By "Phippo" Andreas Philipp

Translated by Stuart Sharpe

'The more intense the effort - the bigger the prize'

There's this big lake that I know. It's deep in the countryside, surrounded by jungle-like vegetation, willows, giant reed beds and lilies as far as the eye can see. There's an island in the middle, and the shallow water is teaming with small fish, mussels, snails, and other insects; in fact often when you turn a stone over you find a crayfish or two. "Pure nature"- in fact its a paradise; for anglers and carp alike.

During reconnaissance trips at weekends I often observed many big fish. Especially in a large bay where the prevailing westerly winds blows. Here there are always carp to be seen on the surface, and when I had a bit of time I would often sit and just watch them for hours. Towards dusk they would often betray themselves by rolling and jumping.

Anyway this is the perfect water for my tastes. But there is one slight problem. The lake and particularly the bay are nearly unfishable, due to the massive reed beds, swamp like banks; in fact its virtually impossible to quietly get near the water with rods, and a bivvy would vanish into the bog like banks. The question was, what now?

The only real choice was the island, but of course you're not allowed to set foot on it let alone fish. But sometimes you've got to do what it takes and I knew with the right preparation and equipment a few days on the island without being caught would be possible. So then I began to plan, the lake, its island and its enormous prizes were never far from my thoughts. I wanted to fish for at least five days otherwise the distance and effort wouldn't be worth it. And because you never know what's going to happen I decided to involve my mate Middy, who was of course, after numerous telephone calls, as exited as me. We planned the assault with the precision of a military exercise. Because we needed the cover of darkness and the natural vegetation to camouflage our tracks, our efforts would take place in September. The days would be slowly shortening and most of all the leaves would still be on the trees, and of course its one of the best months to catch, as the fish begin to get their appetites back after a long hot summer.

About two weeks before our planned assault on the lake, found us paddling about with our boat, not only to prepare the fishes dinner table but of course to deposit some important supplies on the island. The moment we thought nobody was looking we disappeared in to the reeds surrounding the island, and then the hard work began. Our drinks (20 litres of beer, 10 litres of coke and juice, and 15 litre of water) and our food (all sorts of noodles and sweet things; Middy is addicted to Haribo's!) - which had been packed into watertight plastic bags at home - had to be hidden in the undergrowth. We wanted to do this early, so that on the day of our start we could sneak in to position under the cover of darkness, with far less to carry.

Because we planned to start at night we also wanted to prepare our pitch. We removed just enough reeds so as we could fish, but left enough to keep us hidden from any passing boats and prying eyes. We were just as careful with the trees; we removed just enough branches so we could just get a two-man dome in place. We were like commandos crawling around on all fours and removing every twig that could break under foot and give us away. At last we were finished, returned to the boat and baited our chosen spots with boilies and tigers. In all we were well knackered; it had been

Middy lays the wonderful deep-bodied 47lb 6oz common carp on the unhooking mat.

over 25°c as we had crawled to and fro, but it was two very happy anglers who went home that night knowing it was a mission well carried out.

In the following days I visited the water twice more, finishing work at lunchtime and then making the long journey to the lake. Even though I rushed, I always arrived after dark but still paddled my little boat round to the bay to deposit a handful of boilies every two or three metres - about a kilo of tigers and five kilos of boilies each time. It was a fantastic atmosphere, alone there on the water in near silence carefully spreading my bait around. It was a mild autumn evening; I could hear fish rolling in the distance and the ducks chattering in the reed beds. My excitement was rising - I could hardly wait to begin.

It was important for me to spread our bait around the whole bay, and not just tip them in one place, so the fish would be confronted with so many baits in different places that they would be more likely to accept them as an extra food source.

Shortly before the start of the session I received an SMS from Tony Davies-Patrick. I'd told him a few days previously about our planned trip, and so he wanted to wish me luck and knew I would catch a fish between 25 and 30 kilos! I was chuffed by his prophecy but thought the weight was in cloud cuckoo land.

Time flew by and at last the great day arrived. I met Middy after work as planned and we set off together. We were on top of the world, but then it happened, enter Mr Murphy; I'd left the valve for the boat at home! Shit! What could we do? There was only one thing for it, we had to turn round and go home and fetch it, as without the boat there would be no island utopia. This cost us a lot of time, and with the many trips backwards and forwards carrying the gear to the water and then inflating the boat, and rowing round to the island, it was about 6am by the time we'd finished putting up the bivvy!

We were both absolutely knackered; in fact we were so tired we didn't have the energy to put up the rods. Besides that it was getting slowly light and we wanted to row the baits out, and the risk was increasing that we would be seen from the bank. So we decided to get some shuteye and both instantly fell in to a deep, satisfied sleep. We woke at 1pm. First a snack and a small beer, then we slowly put our rods together and skilfully hid our buzzers in the reeds. At dusk I began to row the first baits out; Middy waited on the bank and poked the rod tips through the reeds. The atmosphere was electric. We had that indescribable feeling - you know, the one you get as you sit on a new water and wait for the first action?

What would happen? What would we catch? Little did we know it was to be the session of our lives. In the first 24 hours we had eighteen takes!!! We landed sixteen fish and lost two when our lines broke. They just weren't any old fish - they had never seen a hook and hardly any were less than 10 kilos! The high point of the first day was when Middy caught a fantastic common of 21.5 kilos! An absolute beast of a fish, big fat and round! It was a new personal best for Middy so he was over the moon, and because I always expect a personal best on such "trips" I had packed two small bottles of champagne, so naturally we drank the first to celebrate our success.

For the record, the bait was a 20mm boilie - which " the Godfather of baits" Middy had put together following one of his proven recipes - a mixture of birdfoods, fish and meatmeals. Middy was totally responsible for the bait production while my job was to prebait. So we both played our part and that's really important if a team plan is to work well. Rigs were very simple: 25lbs silkworm hooklink, 12lbs Berkley Big Game mainline and 4oz leads. The hooklink was connected with a tube covered swivel to make it easier to disconnect it in the net, and also to make it possible to leave the rod in the reeds whilst carrying the fish through the narrow reed path to the unhooking mat. The hooks I used were size 4 Pro Gold Penetrators (Terry Eustace) tied with a "sliding hair" and thin tube on the shank.

After that truly fantastic first day, the action slowed a bit, but we were still catching well, albeit with increased waits between takes. It wasn't at all boring; there was enough to see in our surroundings. When you're as well hidden as we were and keep really quite, you become at one with the world, see things like foxes or deer coming to drink in the evenings; as well as all sorts of really strange insects and creepy crawlies!

We thoroughly enjoyed our time there, just to be on such a special water and to catch fantastic fish on our terms was unbelievable. What we didn't realise, was that my own special time was soon to come...

At about 6.30pm the following day, I got a "normal" run on a rod that I had cast into the island margins; a distance of no more than 5 or 6 metres. This was only because it wasn't possible to row the baits out to their normal spots during the day.

The fish swam strongly to the right, out towards the main lake, and what was really strange was the fish was taking line from the reel yet at the same time it appeared to be swimming towards me!!! I'd never experienced any thing like that before.

I shouted to Middy, but I could see from his reaction he didn't believe me. At last he got his waders on and was standing next to me in the thick bed of reeds. I pumped the fish a few metres towards me then it obligingly repeated this manoeuvre for a second time! Weird!

We think that the fish had simply swum straight down, and had the line some where round its flank. We could only make guesses as to how big it was, because the whole battle took place no more than 30 metres from the bank, and all we could see were great big swirls on the surface of the lake, that appeared to be some metres away from where the fish was currently swimming!! Had I perhaps a giant catfish on the end?

It was clear to us by now that it was definitely a very big fish! I'd caught hundreds of fish on my trusty (Drennan) carbons, but I'd never had a fish that made the line grate in the rings like it was doing during that fight. The rod was constantly groaning and my arms were trembling. The fish kited to the right and then swam strongly towards the reeds. As I thought it was going to enter it suddenly turned and swam parallel to the bank, directly towards where we were standing. We stared in to the water and tried to see what was causing us such a problem. That first sighting stunned us - the fish was not just big, it was enormous!

It seemed to take a lifetime; first I saw a massive head, body and finally the tail of a giant mirror carp in the shallow water. My knees were suddenly weak and my hands began to shake. What a fish! Middy was standing to the left of me so he couldn't see it. Once again the leviathan swam straight away from me into the deep water close by, but after some further give and take, and prayers from me - "Oh God please don't let the hook pull out" - I had it once again at my feet, and then eventually on the surface. Middy netted it first time. I let the rod fall and couldn't believe what I saw in the net.

Middys first words were "Phippo its a fifty!" With trembling hands I removed the hook and pulled the arms of the net from the spreader block so we could safely bring my prize to the shore. I can tell you, I had collected a 25kg sack of tiger nuts from my tackle dealer a few days before, and it felt about the same weight!

As we put the fish on the mat, and saw for the first time how big it was. I was suddenly filled with mixed feelings, of shock, excitement, and respect. First we measured her, and the tape showed 101cms. We had to both hold the zeroed scales together, so that the needle would remain steady, and we could get the proper weight - exactly 26 kilos. I could now drink that second bottle of champagne!

Then followed the most comprehensive photo session of my angling career. After the first 5 or 6 photos my hands hurt like hell, it's really difficult to hold such a big fish in the correct position for long periods of time.

Luckily there was still enough daylight to get some good photos, and we could avoid keeping the magnificent fish in a sack overnight. After the photo shooting, I carried her back to the lake and kneeled with the fish in the shallow water. We got a few final shots of her there. I gently cradled her so she could regain her strength after the stress of the long fight and the following photo session. As I knelt there in the lake with the fish in my arms, the wind dropped to leave a mirror calm surface on the lake. There was a period of utter still all around the lake, "the calm after the storm". In the clearing opposite, a deer came once again to drink at the waters edge, and even a fox showed its self for a few fleeting seconds. It was an unbelievable atmosphere - a moment that will stay in my thoughts forever.

The great fish slowly became restless and tried to swim away, and after a few moments I gave into her will and looked on as she slowly swam off into the depths of that special place.

Phippo about to return his huge 57lb 5oz mirror carp.

In the remaining two days we caught three more carp up to about 16kgs. In total we had caught 28 carp. The exact weights in lbs of carp caught were, by Middy: mirrors of 30lb 5oz, 31lb 15oz, 36lb 6oz, 36lb 10oz, and commons of 30lb 5oz and 47lb 6oz, plus one double and seven twenties; and caught by me – all mirror carp: 31lb 8oz, 31lb 12oz, 33lb 1oz, 34lb 3oz, 37lb 1oz, 38lb, and 57lb 5oz, plus seven twenties. What a brilliant session!! All our planning and patience had paid off with all those wonderful fish, but of course even though there are many more big fish in the lake to be caught my thoughts will always stay with my biggest fish!

As we fished on, we were already making plans for our next session on the forbidden island, and next time we'll be taking two more bottles of champagne with us, because who knows! I had also to think of Tony's SMS, he hadn't been far out with his estimation of the size of my prize!
Yes, sometimes you've go to do what it takes!

'A crescent moon lifts off the dark silhouettes of mountains and takes its place beside the South Pole star. Lions living in a nearby reserve begin to give a series of deep, throaty roars and a bull elephant trumpets an earth trembling note. On the far bank, a lone Hyena lets out a long and eerie cry that carries across the waters of Snagmere, until it reaches the pricked ears of a pack of jackals scampering over the rocks behind me. They snigger and whimper like puppies as their shadows move briskly through the trees. A single jackal stops and replies with a sharp gruff, that suddenly sets off the wails and barks of almost every domestic dog chained outside the houses of farms throughout the valley. Another Brown Hyena answers with a shrieking laugh that sends shivers down my spine, but all chaos of sounds are suddenly muted in my brain as my own ears tune into a shrieking Delkim....'

DREAMBREAKER

'Snagmere covers an area of more than 250 acres. The water in front of me is about 260 metres across, and widens to 400 metres in front of Tom, then over 500 metres at the main lake area. To my right the lake narrows gradually for a distance of 750 metres until it enters the thin and winding section of river inflow. The riverbed is 10ft deep at the inflow section, but deepens to 28ft in front of my chosen swim, then to over 40ft in front of Tom (I like to use the electronic depth finder in 'feet' mode – just a personal preference carried on from my pre-metric days!). The old riverbed crosses tight to my own margins and this looks a 'carpy' area to place a bait, but so does the far marginal area where grasslands sweep into red-mud shallows. These silt shallows gradually slope to 12ft deep at about 30 metres from the far shore, before continuing to slope into the main river valley. The complete section between far bank and 12ft depths, is littered by a flooded maze of trees – the water is 8ft on the outside edge of these trees. This section of trees poking out of the water stretches for as far as the eye can see in each direction. In the deep margins in front of me, a 20 meter-wide forest of trees juts their pronged tips above the surface all along the waterline!

I decide to canoe out three double tigernut hookbaits for 200-300 metres to three markers (red & yellow inflated armbands wedged on the prongs) and cast the fourth bait – a double 20mm red Granadilla flavoured boilie inside a Gold Label PVA Carp Sox filled with more boilies – to the edges of the tree prongs in the deep margins.

My first run comes during the middle of the first night to the margin rod. It gives the old ticker a racing at first, but unfortunately it turns out to be a small catfish.

At 10:30 on Tuesday 1st October, while I'm basking in the morning sunshine, the line of the left-hand rod pulls out of the clip and I hit it before a few metres are taken off a revolving spool. It's picked up one of the long-distance baits and on striking I shout for assistance and Tom comes running. We both immediately climb into the canoe to get clear of the marginal tree prongs then gradually make are way out towards 'safer' open water. At first the fish feels small – as they often do when hooked at extreme range, and I assume maybe a young catfish is hooked - but it is not until I manage to get close enough that the rod suddenly wrenches down and a nice battle commences in deep water. Eventually a 28lb 12oz common disappears inside the confines of my outstretched landing net. We have some initial problems paddling back, because my particular canoe has a leak in it and the added weight of two people and a carp doesn't help matters!

It's 12:25 and Dean and Gary have gone to the market shops for supplies, and at this moment Austin is sawing off treetops in the margins trying to clear our swims. The catfish action on boilies in the margins has made me decide to change to tigers and row a fourth bait out to the far trees. The wind has increased in strength, so I think I'll wait until it dies down a little or I'll have problems with bows in the line.

Eventually I paddle across and look more closely at the rows of tree prongs sticking out of the water. At one section the trees seem denser, so I lower a pair of popped up tigernuts, pinned down with Kryston putty on a 4-inch hooklink. The hookbait sits tight to one of the outer stems where a slight break in the submerged trees leaves a wide gap. Behind this gap is a shallow mud flat where the first signs of a bed of weeds are growing. I imagine the carp use this gap as a passageway to feed on the items in the weed bed.

The shade of this overhanging tree is a big bonus, because it's really scorching hot again. The main problem at the moment is that I've got my rods pointing high on the pod to lift line away from

A huge common swimming across the wild waters of Snagmere.

marginal tree prongs, but this also keeps a lot of line near the surface and only a few hours ago a Bass angler went straight through them with his outboard motor. Luckily I managed to free them quickly before disaster struck. I'm using the superb Power Pro Braid that tends to slowly absorb water and helps sink it a bit. Dean is using the extremely buoyant Fireline, which is really giving him major headaches – not only with passing boats, but making giant bows in the wind, causing eventual dragging of the 5oz leads along the bottom. Such is his consternation that he's just reeled them in and is waiting for the wind to die down before paddling them out again.

09:20 on Wednesday 2nd October. The big Shimano spool is really spinning on the repositioned right-hand rod. I'm sitting on the chair beside the rods, so I just stand up and lift into the fish. Even at this extreme distance the braid is relaying that I'm attached to a powerful carp. I can feel the line twanging against the far bank trees, so I step back a few paces and increase pressure. The Globetrotter Supreme bends round into its full parabolic curve until I feel a few thumps, then the line is free again. I continue pumping on the reel handle to drag the fish further into open water, before I climb into the canoe with Gary. Once again, the carp puts up a dramatic fight at close quarters beneath the canoe, even though it turns out be only 19lb+. What it lacks in weight it more than compensates with its huge caudal fin. Not only that, but the carp is a stunning mirror with lovely scale pattern.

I'm soon paddling out with another hookbait locked beneath the bait bucket lid, and keep a taught line over my shoulder until in position. The wind is still blowing slightly, but by holding on to the tree prong with one hand and lowering down the rig to the bottom, it prevents the lightweight canoe drifting out of position. I then drop three handfuls of maize chips/tigernut/peanut/chickpea/hemp mix directly over the hookbait and scatter a few more handfuls in a wider arc. Five White-breasted Cormorants and a single Darter bird – all with their webbed feet wrapped round tree prongs poking above the surface – watch me with interest. I also paddle to the other markers and scatter some more freebie mix over the other three hookbaits.

The day passes quietly, with the monotonous sounds of waves lapping against the canoe and dinghy, giving an almost hypnotic affect. Behind me a vibrant-coloured Crested Barbet gives out a short trilling "Trrrrrr, Trrrrrrr", and a drabber coloured female answers. I can also hear in the distance a far-reaching call of "kiow-kiw-kiw" and look up from reading my book to see a large white-headed bird – it is a magnificent Fish Eagle - drifting high above the lake with outstretched broad wings, and circling in wide figure of eights as it is carried on spiralling thermal air currents.

Just as a giant orange sun slides behind the horizon, a distant shout from Gary signifies that the steaks are ready. I'm hungry, but a strange feeling fills my mind and I'm suddenly loath to leave my rods unattended. This feeling had flooded my brain on several occasions on Klaserie Lake, so I should have learnt by now to follow those gut feelings. I walk quickly along the rocky path to base camp and begin gulping down the delicious steak that really demands smaller bites, when a distant sound trills my ears – the Delkim! I scamper back across the rocks balancing a plateful of food and manage to get 20 metres from the pod before the sound stops; then it suddenly sounds again.

This time I put the plate down and rush to the offending noise, crashing my knee on a rock as I go, before finally lifting the rod into a satisfying curve. The fish has pulled a lot of line from the spool and I can feel the braid dragging against tree branches, but luck is with me and constant pressure pulls it free. Once in open water the carp really powers off and I'm forced to give line again on its initial rush. Suddenly I feel the line against yet another snag, and then the hook pulls.

I'm soon out in the canoe again, placing a fresh hookbait and re-topping the other markers with more freebies from the bait bucket.

Just before the first rays of sun sends sparks across Snagmere to signify a new dawn, the left-hand Delkim lights up and lets out two single bleeps. I sit up in the sleeping bag, but before my feet have time to slip into the sandals the Blue diode suddenly blazes bright and the spool begins spinning wildly. So I scamper across the rocks barefooted and immediately attempt to lift the rod high above my shoulder, but the rod is stopped in its upward flight then brutally wrenched back downwards. I'm forced to give line to an extremely powerful fish, but my minds eye can see it swimming through the dangerous snags, so I place my palm on the spool to slow down the revolutions. It stops, so I begin to regain lost line, but am suddenly prevented from winding as the fish powers off on a frightening second run. This time I lock the reel solid and bend the rod into its full 5lb lock, but am almost dragged off the rocks by brute force. Just before I feel the 50lb braid about to part, I grudgingly partially lift my palm off the spool. The carp takes this opportunity to power away again, but I'm ahead of it and this time a full power-lock on the rod again turns the fish from danger. I run back three paces to higher rocks and begin pumping. All seems well as at least thirty yards are placed back on the spool, then suddenly my heart skips a beat – that sickening tremor of braid against solid timber. All goes tight and I'm about to shout for someone to assist with the canoe, but within moments the line parts.

A quick retying of rig then paddle back across 400 metres of water to drop another bait. One hour

Deans fantastic 46lb 12oz Goldmire carp

later I have a drop-back to the same rod. A strike fails to connect, so I'm forced yet again to labour the 400-metre paddle. Up until now the left-central rod has remained quiet. The marker is positioned tight to a single tree-prong pointing out of 23ft deep water. A quick change of plans has me moving this marker to the far tree line at about 280 metres distance, close to where I caught the last mirror carp. I paddle back to the pod, reel in the second bait and change it from chickpea/tigernut combination to three tigernuts on separate hairs buoyed up by a small piece of shaped cork; paddle out and drop it against re-positioned marker, paddle back to land and tighten up bow in line as wind is beginning to strengthen, then paddle back out to drop a few extra handfuls of freebies over the other markers – about a 1,700 metre round trip!

I notice during my paddling that a tree prong almost pokes through the surface about two thirds out to my right marker. I've had no problems so far, but I'm worried about controlling a much larger carp. Shall I give a fairly loose line immediately after hooking, and hope the fish goes doggo on the bottom then slowly paddle in the slack, and hope it hasn't gone through too many snags? – Or should I lock up solid and try to pull the carp clear with the added risks of the hook tearing out?

'Wild eyes' – a beautiful cheetah rests beneath the shade of a tree at midday.

Martin Davidson has also suggested clipping a large bucket to the line on the surface above the rig, because at least then you can follow the bucket as the carp weaves a spider's web through the sunken trees. This method does sometimes work when you are fishing short range, but trying to keep a rig on the bottom and a bucket on the surface at 200-300 metres ranges during heavy winds at night is almost impossible!

Above me is an overcast sky. The wind is on the change yet again, swinging round from north to south. The waves begin rolling down the lake towards the dam. This tends to be a much cooler wind from the south. I've noticed a long spell of mild wind pushing from the dam, and upriver, tends to increase carp activity over my markers. A prolonged spell of wind pushing cool deep water from the dam area, upriver, tends to change the normally muddy-coloured stretch in front of me to gin-clear. Wind in the opposite direction quickly clouds the water.

Dean and Tom have gone shopping again this afternoon. I've been regularly baiting with a small grain and nut mix since arrival, but now I've dropped the miniature particles and 'bits' and have begun baiting solely with a simple peanut/tigernut/large maize mix. Soft micro particles tend to attract all sizes of fish and I feel that a more bulky mix made up from larger items helps avoid the smaller carp. I would much prefer to bait up with large boilies alone, but the abundance of catfish prevents you from using them effectively at Snagmere, except maybe during cold winter periods when the cats are inactive.

A big carp has just crashed out about 30-metres past my right-hand marker. There's been quite a lot of carp rolling activity during first dusk and dawn, but it's quietened down of late and that recent crash was the first sighting in a long while. Tom did experience some action during the first night with two catfish caught and one carp lost. Last night he had a good take about 2-hours after dark. He played the carp back from the distant 300-metre marker, only to lose it barely a rod's length out from the bank - when he decided to try and manoeuvre it through a narrow 5ft gap between two tree prongs sticking out of the water!

I've been sitting here behind my rods all day without a single blip from the Delkims. Dean however has been down by the base camp for most of the morning, lounging in a deck chair and turning pinker in the sun while trying to digest a huge, greasy breakfast of bacon, sausages, egg and beans served up by Gary. He then decides to go to town on yet another shopping spree – leaving me to 'watch his rods' of course.

Dean arrives back from the shops, walks behind his bivvy to relieve himself, walks back to the front of the bivvy then stands beside his rods whilst letting out a few timely belches and farts. His eyes stare closely at the indicators to check if anything has moved since he last looked at them – then suddenly one of the indicators jumps and the Fox alarm begins screaming!

I just cannot believe what's happening – it's as if that carp has begun running on 'Q'! Unfortunately the carp soon becomes snagged up, so we both paddle out in the dinghy the few hundred metres. The wind increases in strength making it very difficult to control the dinghy. Dean is unable to free the line using brute rod pressure, so I'm forced to wrap the Fireline round the paddle, but the line eventually breaks at the 25lb Kryston Silkworm hooklink. I advise Dean to tie on much stronger hooklinks to match his mainline.

At 16:20, he gets yet another storming take, but this time his mainline snaps! Shortly after this episode, Dean announces that he's had enough of fishing and just wants to relax and see some

South African sites for the rest of his holiday. I think to myself, that's what he's been doing for the past few days anyway! Two of his rigs are still far out near his markers, so to save the excess energy of reeling them in, he decides to leave them there for the time being...

Martin Lowe and Henning visit me for a chat – Henning lets it be known that he once lost 76 carp (landing only three) in one session in a swim just a little further along the bank from where I'm now fishing. Henning then tells me that he's doesn't fish this area anymore, because of what happened during that session! They're going to bait up heavily in a relatively snag-free area of the main lake towards the dam, with the aim of fishing there the following week. I've been invited to join them if I wish.

At 22:00hrs my rod begins bouncing above a fast-spinning spool. Half asleep I try to fit my left foot into the wrong sandal, and then groggily search for the tent zip – because at dusk I'd zipped up the mosquito netting to keep out swarms of flying insects. By the time I am rushing headlong towards the white diode, the bleeps have become a constant tone. A strike meets solid resistance, then suddenly the line parts – obviously rubbed against a sharp object. At 01:10 I have another run. At first I'm not sure which rod it is on, because a powerful wind has been blowing that has pushed big bows in the lines, and three are crossed. Eventually I sort it out and paddle one-handed out into the darkness; but twenty minutes later I return half-drenched and minus a hooklink.

Dean wakes early to relieve himself at dawn, only to notice that he's had a take during the windy night, but the Fox alarm has remained silent. One rod is half submerged in the margins, with the only thing that has prevented the lot being dragged into the depths being the reel lodged behind the front rod rest!

This morning we're packing up and moving over to the Beach swim near the guesthouse. I've packed all the heavy gear (even my rod pod) and carried it to the vehicle, and the rest is inside the big dinghy ready for ferrying across the lake to the new swim. The rods are lying on the rocks, with the baits still out on the markers – in my usual desperate attempt to squeeze that last possible second out in the hope of a take! My mind is in a bit of a quandary over the change of swims, because the moment we began packing up this morning, many carp suddenly began crashing out over my markers – as if to say to themselves 'hey guys, they're moving. Let's get our heads down!' That's why I've left all four rods on the rocks. I know I'm going to get a take soon – I can feel it in my bones. But luck is not with me, so I eventually begin winding in the rods.

A few minutes later, when three rods are packed way in the dinghy, I am just about to bend down to pick up the last remaining rod, when I hear the audible click of line 'pinging' out the clip, and the spool begins spinning wildly! A shout to Tom brings him running to my aid and we both climb in the half-full dinghy then make our way out towards the fast-moving fish. At one point I find my line caught around a tree prong, but by snapping off the rotten branch it suddenly breaks free and I'm soon back in direct contact with the carp. Tom does a good job of paddling us out into deep water, and following a good fight a heavily scaled mirror weighing 30lb 4oz. rolls inside the landing net.

Our first view of the new 'Beach swim' does not look good. The large section of gently sloping sandy beach will make it a very nice change from the uncomfortable rocky terrain offered by our previous swim, but out in front of the beach a forest of trees poke out their tips above the water.

Tom and I spend the next hour exploring the big bay opposite the beach with the aid of an echo sounder, while Austin gets down to the task of cutting the tips off all the half-submerged trees in front of the beach. By the time we arrive back, Austin has done a superb job. We have plenty of clear space to fit two separate rod pods on the sand and fan out four rods apiece. The swim now looks quite inviting and definitely fishable. The only problem is that although it 'looks' nice and clear - as if a wide channel has been cut through the trees - the bulk of large trees remain underwater. A short glide in the dinghy reveals a mass of black objects just inches under the surface – the tips of a hundred trees still rooted to the bottom. There is no way we can remove the trees properly without a tractor and long chain, or maybe even an underwater chainsaw with sub aqua gear, so we're stuck with the problem.

A small seasonal stream flows in through lowland marshes from our left to form this large bay. The mouth of the stream is filled with reeds, before it opens out into the main bay for a few hundred metres then eventually joins the main open section of lake – with one arm leading towards the main river entrance and the other section leading towards the dam. The bottom in front of the beach slopes gradually from bare inches until 12ft deep at 60 metres out, where it begins to drop sharper towards the old

Tony releases a big carp back to Snagmere.

streambed. At 100 meters from the beach it is around 23ft, but the stream channel drops to 30ft, with two troughs of 40ft deep water towards the stream entrance, and also where the old streambed joins the old riverbed at about 250 metres from the beach. It is easy to interpret from the echo recordings that a large and deep underwater bowl has been formed hundreds of metres upstream of the stream and river intersections. This was obviously made during hundreds of years of flood conditions, prior to the dam being built. On the far side of the bay, directly opposite the beach, is a wide band of half submerged trees standing in 4 -12ft of water, and increase in their numbers until they eventually peter out near the deep trough at the old riverbed junctions. A very 'carpy' looking stretch of water; but also extremely snaggy!

It is mid-afternoon on our first full day at the Beach. Last night was quiet, and now only a brisk breeze softens the relentless beat of rays from a white-hot sun. A sudden scream from one of Tom's alarms has us all running towards the offending noise! A strike from Tom places a nice bend in his rod, but soon the fish finds a snag. I immediately rush down to the canoe and we both squeeze in (the strengthening wind make us choose the canoe over the dinghy, because it is easier to manoeuvre). Once I have paddled us directly over the snag, no amount of rod bending will free the fish, which lays still on the bottom in 38ft of water, so I grab the mainline and wrap it round the paddle then pull. All of a sudden something releases its hold on the bottom and I quickly let go of the braid as a seemingly heavy fish chugs off. Tom leans hard into the fish, but suddenly half a tree emerges from the depths! I grab back hold of the line; manhandle the tree trunk beside the canoe to untangle it, then the line twangs free once again. The rod hoops back over, but we are both suddenly disappointed when not a big carp, but a catfish flaps on the surface....

The specimen is Tom's largest catfish, so he relays his wish to take it back to shore for photos. I relay back my disgust, look hesitantly at the big waves hitting us due to a strengthening wind, unhook the fish inside the mesh, and then hold the landing net close to the canoe as Tom begins paddling. The wind gets stronger and the waves get bigger, causing white breakers to crash over the sides and cover us in spray. By the time we are only halfway back to the beach, the canoe is already half-filled with water. The waves just get bigger and I can see a wave twice as big rolling amongst them... until it slaps against the fibreglass and almost swamps us. I try to use my leg muscles to negate the wave action, but Tom in his fright seems to be twisting his hips and just rocking us harder.

In the distance I notice a powerful ski-boat do a sharp turn near the distant marker buoys and watch in fascination as the large backwash pushes a huge wave towards us. By now we are almost full with water and it will only take one more wave to hit us side on to sink us. I scream at Tom to stop rocking, but he tries to confirm that he's not... then suddenly gets up on his knees and begins swaying like some Hawaiian dancer! The waves crash and slap, sending spray flying in all directions, but both our heads are turned in the direction of the huge Tsunami-type wave rolling darkly towards us, until it smashes against the canoe and engulfs us. The wave passes by and rolls on towards the reeds, leaving us up to our waist in water. I look straight into Tom's eyes and his terrifying fear is almost comical as we float for two more seconds, then the canoe goes down....

We sink up to our necks, and I fear for Tom's safety because we are in almost 40ft deep water amongst crashing waves - without lifejackets! I'm a strong swimmer, so I try to stay calm. Tom desperately clings onto the last remaining section of canoe bobbing only inches above the pounding waves. I'm loath to drop the expensive rod, reel and net, so I hang on to everything and begin

A tranquil evening at Snagmere, as Tony sits between Tom's and his own rodpods, looking for signs of feeding carp.

treading water, but manage to release the catfish from the net before it is torn from my grasp.

Gary comes storming to our aid in the dinghy, bouncing on the waves like a Navy Seal officer on a combat mission. After a lot of commotion and almost loosing the canoe to the dark depths, we are finally hoisted aboard the dinghy. We motor back towards shore with the canoe being towed on a rope behind us, while I continue to bail out the water with a scoop. As the water gradually empties out of the canoe, I'm suddenly aware of a long dark object swimming around in circles inside...it's the catfish! Obviously after swimming out of my hands it went straight inside the submerged canoe, but was unable to swim over the rim.

The night eventually draws in again and we all sit down beside a roaring campfire, while a delectable aroma passes over our nostrils from the huge steaks being cooked on the grill.

Dawn greets us with due drops shining in the sunlight on spider webs draped across the rod pods. Today we will give the fishing a rest and go on a safari at one of the big Game Reserves.

On arrival back from the safari, we're greeted with the news that a local who moved last night into a swim on the opposite bank, caught a 43lb+ common.

Charmaine Coetzee, who runs the stunningly beautiful Twin Scales guesthouse overlooking the lake, comes down to the beach with a large bottle of champagne to celebrate the facts that Dean is the first foreigner to stay at the guesthouse, and that it is also Tom and Dean's last night at Snagmere.

Two days have quickly passed, and now that Gary, Austin, Dean and Tom have all gone, I am left to savour the pure beauty of Snagmere in solitude. I've enjoyed their company very much, but sometimes one has to fish completely alone to appreciate the quietest moments of nature. Within hours of being left alone, the birds and wildlife seem to sense the absence of noise around the camp, and soon come very close. While I sit quietly reading a book, five white cattle egrets drift over my rod tops and alight on the sand close by. A multitude of vibrant coloured birds hop and sing all around me, and even the Fish Eagle lands on a branch of the tree directly above my head then begins calling across the waters.

The carp are quite active in the bay for about 1-hour each morning, but I don't get a touch. I start to have doubts about the effectiveness of tiger nuts – because this is the only bait used by carp anglers on this lake – so I try boilies combined with PVA Sox tube for a while, but soon give up when the big catfish home in on them!

An amazing thing is happening as I sit here scanning the bay with my binoculars. I've spotted a snake writhing across the surface – not an unusual occurrence in Africa – but what is strange is that five Little Grebes (dabchicks) are surrounding the snake trying to impede its progress. Within moments, their calls attract many other grebes from near and far – and even some Great Crested grebes join the commotion. By the time that the snake has twisted an extra 100 metres, more than 20 dabchicks are surrounding the snake, occasionally pecking and trying to impede its progress. This is a poisonous species, so they dart and jab and dive all around that dangerous flicking tongue – but never give up in their quest to annoy the snake. It is obvious that a snake is an unwelcome guest during this the height of breeding season, but I've never witnessed such a gathering of grebes in the sole pursuit of keeping a snake away from nesting sites – indeed, the whole of the lake!

Cloud and wind rise up throughout the day then peter out by mid-afternoon. Now as I look up at the sky again during the last waning light of sunset, I notice a foreboding black cloak on the horizon. A strong breeze begins to flap the sides of the bivvy, and occasional gusts make the guide ropes whisper and the braided lines in my rod rings sing. Others are also singing tonight – the voices of African natives dancing to the beat of a single drum, carries on the rising winds.

Yet another team of voices begins to fill the air – the vibrating throats of a million bullfrogs. Soon their song is so loud that it makes the ground 'hum' like ten thousand rattle snakes. The frogs must be able to sense the storm clouds gathering on the horizon...

The storm hits me like a tidal wave – almost wiping out my little camp with its fury. Fork tongues of white-hot lightening flick from the black sky like a viper tasting for prey – probing and licking highpoints jutting out of the horizon. Rumbles of distant thunder make a hyena, which is hunting at the base of the mountain behind me, call out a series of horrific cries. There is a weird silence between each lightning strike and rumble of thunder – moments when I can almost smell the static electricity in the air. But soon the moments between hot strike and rumble of thunder cannot be counted in seconds, but mere heartbeat – until wham! A white cord of power rips out of the night and hits one of the trees and my eyes see it almost explode on impact. Simultaneously an incredible clap of thunder almost bursts my inner eardrums and shakes every grain of sand on the beach. Sheet lightening spreads throughout the low-lying clouds directly above my head, turning night into day. I can now even see the sawn-off stumps of trees beneath the water! The air has become still, and I can almost taste the burnt scent of raw power...then the winds hit me like a sledgehammer.

'Globetrotter' with his hands full of 'African Gold'... a spectacular common carp from Goldmire.

I cannot make out the difference between heaven and earth as I fight to stay upright against the full force of buffeting winds. Tent pegs are torn from deep inside the sand and are flung like matchsticks. I rush around, frantically trying to push bedchair, fridge, rucksack and any other heavy objects I can find, against the inner sides of the bivvy. The four rod-butts remain clamped tightly in the rubber Mangrove rear rests, but the Delkims are lit up like a Christmas tree. Objects all around my camp are being picked off the sand and thrown like confetti. And just as my bivvy is fully open and flapping to the elements, sheets of stabbing rain finally join the incredible winds. Each raindrop spins off the lake's surface until all I can see is a massive sheet of water sweeping through the darkness.

At last; the storm has past and the lake is now calm once more, accept of course for the incessant drone from countless bullfrogs that seem to relish the fresh scent of moisture in the air. The rain stopped for an hour, but now it's started again – a fine spray being blown by gentle winds. A fish eagle appears through the grey light of dawn, circling over my head, until eventually landing on a tree close by. The normal short bout of morning carp activity is noticeable by its absence from the bay today – except for a couple of big lumps crashing out over the area where I moved my marker from a few days ago. Typical! Another one has just crashed out in the same place, so I decide to reel in one of the rods and paddle the bait back out then drop it over the action – but no more action – typical!

At 09:10 the left-hand rod tip suddenly whacks round and the line literally fizzes off the spinning spool. The line is going directly over a snag and the line breaks almost as soon as I engage the Baitrunner. It shouldn't have snapped so quickly, so I check the drag and notice that it's slightly over tight. I pulled for a break in a snag last night and had obviously not reset the drag correctly before recasting the new end rig - a stupid and fatal mistake. A fresh trio of maize, peanut and tigernut are threaded onto a hair and I recast to the same spot next to a marker only 25-metres out. At 10:20 the inside left rod bounces on the rests and the Delkim sounds. I'm busy bailing out rainwater from the dinghy, so it takes a few extra seconds to run across the sand and pick up the rod. The strike pricks something, but the fish drops off immediately. A catfish is the suspected culprit.

I've not experienced the expected action from the middle bait placed tight to submerged trees on the far bank in 8ft of water, so I paddle out and lower the bait onto the edge of the old stream bed in 18-20ft of water.

Carp begin crashing behind the trees near the stream entrance, and a few roll close to my marker in the old streambed. The clouds have long departed and the intense rays are really starting to bake my shoulders, so I've coated liberally with cream to ease the pain of my sunburn and donned a T-shirt. I decide to boil some more nuts in the big pot, then sit down to read Shaun Harrison's enjoyable article in Carworld magazine No.134. I'm just getting to the part where Shaun catches a big common from the Mangrove and has forgotten his camera, when suddenly I hear a noise beside the bivvy. The gas burner has collapsed, making the big pot roll on its side and empty its contents of nuts all over the sand. Although Austin had placed the big stove burner nicely in place before he left, he's somehow forgotten to mention that two of the legs are broken and a stone wedged beneath it precariously balanced the heavy stove!

Just when I'm beginning to get used to a blue sky and blazing sunshine, another black cloud creeps over the mountains and chucks rain at me for the next two hours!

A blue hole in the sky eventually shows amongst the clouds and I finally get a run. The fish soon becomes snagged somewhere deep in the old streambed, so I try to go out in the dinghy but the motor will not start! I begin to paddle just as a strong wind begins to gust down the valley. It spins the big dinghy like a cork in a whirlpool. The fish turns out to be a big catfish. I'm completely gutted! The paddle back against rising gusts of wind seems to take forever, until I'm finally able to reach the beach, strip off my waterlogged fleece jacket then collapse on the bedchair.

At 13.05, while I'm cooking some tasty-looking steaks, a take comes to the left-hand margin rod. As soon as I make contact I know that it is a powerful carp, but after managing to pull it clear of most of the dangerous trees it suddenly locks solid. It feels like the lead is jammed down there somewhere, but I'm unable to free the line and eventually pull for a break. By now, the steaks are shrivelled up like the soles of old boots....

Two hours later, the same rod bounces on the pod and I'm soon fighting another carp – although initial feedback tells me that this carp has a lot less power than the previous one. The carp manages to wrap itself around a series of half sunken trees, but eventually brute force gives me the upper hand and it is swallowed in the landing net. At a shade over 20lb, it is not quite the size of carp I'm after, and I begin to seriously doubt my chances of landing a 60lb+ specimen from this type of swim unless I'm extremely lucky. Martin Davidson managed to land two 50lb+ commons from this swim, but that was when there was at least 10ft more water depth covering the dangerous trees.

I've just received news that the two anglers who moved into my vacated swim last night were fishing directly over my pre-baited marker positions. Not only that, but they've had some action

A long and powerful Snagmere mirror carp   *"almost a koi" – Gary's beautiful pale common.*

and landed two common carp weighing 30lb and 50lb+. That's lovely news...maybe I should have left some more bait for them!

It's 06:30 and I'm sitting and watching the vibrant array of birds feeding and singing all around me, when suddenly one of the Delkims bursts into life. Unfortunately the run stops before I'm able to pick up the rod. A detailed look at the rig and a short drag across my nail reveals that the hook point is very slightly turned over. A quick change of hook and out it goes again to the same spot. A dramatic splash next to the left-hand margin marker adds a feeling of excitement. I know it is a big carp even though I only caught a fleeting glimpse of the fish. Just as I'm contemplating whether the fish is feeding on my bait, the fish suddenly crashes clear of the water again. This time I'm able to judge the true size of this heavily-scaled mirror carp and estimate a weight of 55lb+. I just know I'm going to get a take from this fish, and just as my eyes spot a circle of bubbles fizzing and popping above the marker float, one of the rod tips sharply taps down, then line begins screaming off a spinning spool. The fight is electric as the big carp rockets across the bay then turns left around a submerged tree and cuts me off!

Gary is driving back to Snagmere today, so if I need a hand moving to a new area, now is the time to decide where to. The binoculars reveal that the two lads have now vacated my old swim, so I decide to make a move back across the lake. As much as I like this bay area, the very low water conditions are giving me no confidence on landing anything really big amongst the horrendous forest of half-sunken trees. Gary eventually arrives and transports the heavy gear by road. It takes quite a few hours to paddle everything else across the lake and set up new markers, but finally I'm able to relax on the chair. It feels good to be back.

Not a breath of wind – completely opposite to the severe storms of previous evenings. Not even a single sighting of a carp crashing out this evening – very strange. Slowly, a large yacht drifts across the lake until it glides past my first marker float then decides to drop anchor! A quick paddle out in my canoe to ask them if they 'will be staying very long?' - receives the reply 'no, they will not stay long'. So I paddle back to shore and wait...and wait.

I-hour later, the yacht is still anchored over my lines. A second paddle out to them reveals that they misunderstood my question and thought I had asked 'have you been here long?' - Their intentions are to stay anchored all weekend – and this is only Thursday! Passing on the knowledge that their anchor rope is trailing over my lines and their position will entail me losing any fish hooked, plus a series of desperate pleas for them to 'sleep elsewhere on this big lake' gradually persuades them to up anchor and move to a different location.

A crescent moon rises above the horizon and slowly slides past a bright shining star. A screaming run on the left-hand far marker results in me pricking a fish. It could have been a catfish, but you can never tell when fishing at these extreme distances. I immediately paddle back out to the marker float. It's a strange feeling paddling out across a vast African lake at night. Your mind often dwells on what might be lurking under your canoe – at least there aren't the possibilities of hippo or crocodiles like at Klaserie Lake! The main difficulty is judging where your markers are during pitch-black nights. Fortunately I can use the silhouettes of trees on the horizon, and the red light of a radio mast on the crest of the mountain, to help guide me across 400 meters of inky water.

A strong breeze picks up through Sunday night, until it is a howling gale by morning. Finally the winds ease off and I paddle out to check if the baits have moved. They have, and even the 5oz leads were not enough to prevent them dragging in the strong undercurrents. The rigs have rolled about 15-20 metres off the baited areas. Often in these situations one can visualise that the freebies would also roll along the bottom, but this is rarely the case. More often it is only the moving upper layers of lake water that causes a taught bow in the mainline, which eventually pulls the heavy leads along the bottom – whereas the back current is moving at mid-depth in the opposite direction, causing the bottom few inches of water close to the lakebed to be almost still – and therefore the un-tethered baits stay where they are, even during storms.

There is still quite a chop on the water, so I'll need to wait a while before I reset the rigs. Both Gary and I discuss why the carp seem to be so inactive, and my only conclusion is that the carp are waiting to spawn. I've seen groups of carp following each other in the shallows on the far side all this past week, but no actual spawning activity. The water levels have fallen drastically during past weeks and normally carp prefer to spawn during rising levels or floods, because this not only provides abundant reeds and grasses to lay eggs, but also an abundant supply of fresh food for the hatching fry. The carp's bio-functions are telling them to spawn, but they are receiving negative impulses from low water conditions – which must also have a knock-on effect with their appetite to feed. However, they cannot withhold the spawning urge forever, and if the expectant rains and floodwaters don't arrive soon, they'll just have to begin spawning in not-so ideal conditions.

I awake at almost 12-midnight to sounds on the surface of the lake. At first my half-asleep brain tells me that it's only the waves slapping against the rocks, so I lay my head back on the pillow. But another series of distant splashes awaken me again, so I sit up on the bedchair and stare at the moonlight reflecting off the dark waters. Once my ears tune in to the noises they quickly begin to hear many crashes and splashes emanating from the distant submerged tree line. The carp have begun spawning! A sudden urge to investigate has me donning the safety vest and paddling out to the far shoreline.

For the next two hours I paddle amongst hundreds of spawning carp. An awesome and fascinating sight unfolds inside my torch beam. Huge tails and flanks from heavily scaled mirrors and golden-scaled commons roll and thrash as one at the surface. They are not alone, for following each group of spawning carp are hoards of catfish – spinning and winding like snakes in their wake. There are literally thousands of catfish enjoying a feast of carp-caviar tonight!

The weekend brings with it the expectant crowds and flotilla of boats and noisy jet skis. Apart from the odd catfish, the carp are noticeable by their absence. I hate to do so, but I decide to paddle halfway out across the lake and slide back-leads down each line. This will at least prevent the boats going through my braid.

Before first light on Monday morning I get a flying take and I'm soon out in the dinghy trying to keep a tight line to the fast-moving fish. Suddenly I hear something plop over the side and I'm unable to paddle the dinghy. It seems that the somehow the sonar on the depth-finder has become loose and lodged in a rock crevice, so now the rangefinder cord is connected between rock and dinghy! It is too dark for me to see all this at the moment, so I just continue paddling hard until something plops over the side and sinks to the bottom – it is Gary's Eagle depthfinder! The fish also turns out to be yet another catfish! Luckily I'm able to retrieve Gary's prized and expensive electronic items from the lakebed....

At 06:30 there is a sudden 'one-noter' on a Delkim and I'm quick to scuffle out of the sleeping bag and hit the fish. I'm soon out in the middle of the lake in the dinghy with Gary, and I'm certain that it's a decent-sized carp, but unfortunately it becomes snagged in deep water and I eventually pull for a break. At 09:30 another take from a big carp, but yet again it becomes snagged in a similar area to the last and I loose the fish.

Gary has just returned from a chat with Hennie, who moved into a swim in the main lake section on Sunday night. Hennie has a marginal bed of weeds in front of him and completely open water beyond that with no sunken trees. Gary relays to me that he's already caught fourteen carp! All his carp are between 22lb and 25lb. His fishing companion, Lowe, has only banked one 7lb carp, so he's moved to a different swim closer to the dam wall. Gary laughs as he talks to me and says that he's a bit sceptical of Hennie's claims, because Gary is fishing just round the corner from him and has yet to get a take!

Gaz gets his first run at 06:30 in the morning but he loses that one. Soon he gets another take and after going out in the dinghy with him we are able to keep it clear of the snags and land it in deep water. This turns out to be a beautiful pale common carp (almost a koi) that weighs 31lb 8oz. This is followed an hour later by a 25lb scattered-scaled mirror.

Later in the day my curiosity gets the better of me, and I decide to reel in the rigs and take a long walk round the lake to Hennie's swim. He has one take during the hour I spend sipping cold drinks on deckchairs outside his bivvy. This turns out to be an old emaciated-looking deformed common carp of 23lb 12oz. He mentions to me that the carp have been spawning heavily in the weed bed in front of him during Saturday night. Now I do not doubt the amount of takes he's had. The lack of snags in this area is also a positive advantage, and he only needs to wade out beyond the weeds to land them safely.

I've also had action today, but with three takes and none landed I'm getting very cheesed off!

At around midnight, I'm awoken by one of the Delkims and pounce on the rod, pumping and reeling like mad to keep the fish clear of the far tree line. My efforts are rewarded and I soon have the carp in deep water. Immediately I rush to the canoe and begin paddling out with the rod until halfway out – well away from danger, or so I think. Suddenly I feel something crawling in the darkness over my bare left foot. My first thoughts are that it's either a big scorpion or a tarantula, and I stop paddling then involuntarily freeze. The 'thing' then decides to crawl over to my right foot and slowly up my leg! I spread my legs slightly in terror and am about to try to flick it off my thigh, but before I can spot what it is in the light of my head torch, the dark and hairy creature jumps off my thigh and scampers quickly along the canoe rim towards me, and under my arm! I almost topple the canoe over in my panic not to be bitten by this venomous monster...but suddenly I realise that it is only a large mouse! With its grey hairs shining in the torchlight, it looks harmless gripping to the rim of the fibreglass, but I'm not about to let it hide back inside my canoe while I continue fighting the fish, so a gentle flip tosses it overboard and I watch it swimming back to shore. I pick the rod back up and tighten up, but by now the carp has found a snag. Great!

Martin Lowe moved swims again yesterday and set-up on the point between Gary and Henning. To say that Gary is displeased is an understatement, because immediately Lowe paddled straight out and dropped a massive marker only a few rod's lengths away from Gary's own marker! He might be even more disgruntled soon, because Martin is standing holding a bent rod, and judging by the action it looks a good fish. I grab my binoculars for a closer look and they eventually show Martin

engulfing a hefty carp inside his landing net. Friends are there to help him carry it to the unhooking mat and they struggle under the weight of the net.

I decide to run round with the camera, and just as I arrive they are hoisting the weigh sling on the scales. The dial shudders then points at 47lb 8oz! A wonderful stocky built common carp and soon I am in the water with Martin snapping off a series of photos.

The sun is high in a blue sky and the sun beats relentlessly on my shoulders as I paddle out to the markers. Gary has gone to the shops, but left me to watch his rods. A sound reaches my ears, a sound of a distant alarm. My head swivels back towards my rods, but then I realise that it is one of Gary's! I paddle like mad towards shore, but the run has now stopped. Quickly I flash my eyes over each rod then decide to strike the one with an almost empty spool. The rod keels over and kicks a few times – I'm in! I go out in the canoe, fight and land the carp, weigh it, take a few pictures and Gary arrives just at the moment I'm releasing a nice-looking extremely long 27lb common. Gary looks well pleased!

Following three more lost carp in my own swim, I decide to spend a few extra hours slowly and rigorously zigzagging with the echo-finder along the complete section of water between my camp and markers. What I eventually find is horrifying. What I thought to be fairly snag-free areas 30 metres out from the submerged trees turns out to be riddled with more trees and branches stretching from the bottom in 20ft of water. A closer look at the scrubland beyond the far dry bank shows groups of trees pepper-potted at intervals all over the valley. The scanner's display reveals that this also continues under water. I drift all along the deepest slopes of old riverbed, only to be gutted by the continued presence of snags. In fact, there is literally a forest of trees rooted to the bottom all along the riverbed – an area I had thought was almost completely free of snags! No wonder our backleads are getting caught-up!

The highest waters have obviously been a factor in helping me land carp during the first few days, but now that the level has dropped so drastically I'm not able to bully the carp into the upper layers of water clear of the uppermost branches, because the branches now almost reach the surface all across this section of lake. I'm loathe to carry on fishing in this situation, but with only one more day to go and with so much pre-bating carried out on my markers, I decide to stick it out and hope for a miracle. I also decide to not use backleads and hope for no wind or speedboats!

Gary has just landed a 20lb+ common from a bait positioned on his farthest marker (next to Lowe's marker). Something suddenly sucks in the tigernuts positioned near my left-hand distant marker. A quick strike and constant pressure while walking backwards keeps the fish clear of trees and Gary is soon beside me getting the dinghy ready. The carp fights well, but this time luck is with me and finally a gorgeous, long and wild-looking common is engulfed inside the landing net. The scales

37lb 4oz of gold

reveal a weight of 37lb 4oz. Soon after I manage to land another carp, but this time it's only a mirror carp around upper doubles.

Friday arrives and its time to say goodbye to Snagmere. I've arranged to relax at Martin Davidson's house over the weekend, then to fish together with Martin for a few days prior to flying back to UK. It seems to take forever to pack up all the gear and ferry it to the van. I stop on the hillside and take one last look at the shimmering blue waters of Snagmere. The levels are still dropping. During the past week almost every take has come from my left-hand marker – obviously a good feeding area. The sad realisation is that I lost on average 2-3 carp every 24-hours! Some of these losses have really shaken me, for I know they were real beasts and I sorely would like to have landed one. A 60lb+ was my goal during this session, but I now realise that unless you fish the fairly open and snag-free water nearer the main dam you are not likely to land one of that size. The only problem is that most of the 50lb+ carp spend most of their time feeding in amongst the densest snags....

Three days later, and after enjoying the relaxed comforts of Martin Davidson's beautiful villa-type home, Martin and I decide to visit a new lake. After a few hours without sightings of fish, we drive around to another area of this large and reed-rimmed reservoir. The water is gin-clear and within moments of stepping out of the car I spot a large fish in the water. I quietly call Martin over and when he sees the fish, he asks my judgement on its weight.

"About 90lb." I whisper quietly.

Martin just cannot believe his eyes – it is a massive grass carp. The fish looks stunning in the crystal water. We stare in awe for a few minutes until it swims behind a wall of densely packed weeds growing up from the bottom. Martin treads lightly along the bank and stops to peer into a gap between high rushes. He stops abruptly, as if hit by a bullet, and I almost bump into him.

"Oh my god...look at the size of that!" whispers Martin through clenched teeth.

"JEEEEZ!!" I squeal quietly and in utter amazement.

There in front of us swims a gigantic carp well in excess of 100lb!

Our excitement is difficult to contain, and after sighting more giant-sized carp, we make up our minds to fish here for the last two days prior to my flight back to UK. During these first sightings, I realise that not all the big fish are grass carp (Amur), but about 50% of them (mainly the largest) are actually Black carp.

It's 18:45 in the evening of the first day. I've already seen a lot of huge grass carp and a few smaller common carp swimming under my rod tops. The carp range from 45lb to 100lb+, with a seemingly average weight of around 80lb! It is surely an incredible sight for any eyes. I'm fishing in a tiny gap made in high reeds, with just enough room to place a rodpod. Due to the underwater wall of entangled weed growth at only 15 meters out, I'm dropping the hookbaits in the margins and chucking a few handfuls of freebies over them. The water is so clear that when I stand up I can easily see each boilie lying on the bottom.

My first take turns out to be a small and energetic common carp of low doubles. Another bionic common of around 18lb gets me out of my sleeping bag during the night, but no more action comes to our rods and we all sleep well, until a bright sun chases away the cold mist. Very few fish show until around 10:00, when dark shadows appear from the weeds like submarines. Within two hours, at least eighty carp have swum beneath my rod tips, and not one has shown a single interest in the bait. That is until now...I've just reeled in a rig, removed the lead, mounted a small tube-shaped

"... It moves into the clearing, like a Tiger shark looking for prey... A guess any lower than 150lb would do this fish an injustice..."

boile then cast it across an overhanging reed stem. By slowly giving some line from the reel, I'm able to lower the hookbait until it dangles just inches beneath the surface. It is bright orange, so it can easily be observed.

Three huge submarines drift by, and one slides beneath the overhanging reed stems then stops only a hairs breadth from the dangling bait. I'm physically trembling all over, with hand poised over the rod. The carp noses the bait gently, seems about to engulf it inside a cavernous mouth, but then changes its mind and slowly swims onwards until it disappears from view. That carp was at least 95lb!

Hardly letting me catch my breath from this close encounter, another group of large shadows drift out of the darkness and enter the crystal clear aquarium-like pool of water in front of me. Bright sunshine now cuts through the water and shows up every detail on the scales of each carp. I cannot breath; for in front of me is an incredible sight. No less than seven carp glide beneath my rod tops, until they are all hanging motionless in the sunlight. Two common carp – the largest around 25lb, swim at the very edge of the underwater wall of weed. Just in front of the two commons, is a thickset Black carp of about 85lb. Two grass carp – one 45lb and the other around 60lb are almost hidden beneath the reed fronds just past my overhanging bait. A trio of Black carp ranging between 80lb and 100lb+ drift slowly through the clearing and follow behind the grass carp. But these massive fish barely hold my attention for seconds, because another Black carp has entered the scene. It moves into the clearing like a tiger shark looking for prey. Gliding silently past, it suddenly stops, pivots clockwise towards me, and then hangs motionless beneath the surface directly underneath my rods. My jaw is agape yet no sounds are expelled except a trembling murmur from my lips. I want to shout, but I cannot – for I do not want to scare this beast of a fish. The Black carp in front of me is built like Mike Tyson, and as it spins quietly round and shows me its full girth and impressive shoulders, I am able to place an approximate weight. A guess any lower than 150lb would do this fish an injustice. It eventually tires of showing me its colossal size, and eventually follows the others and glides beneath my bait – stopping for a brief second, enough to start my heart racing – until it disappears beneath the sanctuary off rushes. It is almost like watching a full-grown man swimming past. My ears begin to notice a heavy thumping, but it is only the pounding of my own heart.

During the next 24-hours Martin, Gary and myself try almost every technique and every type of bait at our disposal – all to no avail. Gary and Martin even try a long episode of 'night stalking' in canoes. They witness hundreds of huge carp basking in the moonlight, yet not one fish is interested in their offerings. In 48-hours intense fishing, the only reaction I have is when a 70lb+ Black carp sucks in a piece of floating bread flake, then blows it out again.

Finally it is time to pack up. I've only managed to land four carp, but not one was the species I'm after – the impressive Black Carp. I now realise that large water snails and other molluscs are the preferred food of these gigantic fish. I take a last look at the crystal waters where giant blue-backed monsters swim, then turn and walk away. But I'll be back someday - for I'm already deeply sick with fever...'Black Carp Fever'!

STAIRWAY TO

HEAVEN

"Pure, gut-wrenching excitement!"

A kayaker battles through rapid 9 - called 'Commercial Suicide'. This is the most dangerous rapid on the mighty Zambezi River.

A blue wall of water falls from the skies and roars into the deep abyss. It crashes into the maelstrom of white foam then boils in the cauldron of a thousand whirlpools. Millions of airborne droplets catch the sunlight to form a giant rainbow. Luxuriant green foliage hangs from the steep rock faces to drink from the spray. I can hear a pounding roar as the mighty Zambezi is sucked to the bottom of the gorge, and then spat out in a rolling wave, to smash its way through the narrow canyon. My eyes scan through the veil of mist and suck in this awesome sight of the Mos-oa-Tunya: "The Smoke that Thunders".

As well as awesome Fishing amongst spectacular scenery, the Victoria Falls area offers more exciting opportunities for the adventurous traveller than almost any other area in Africa. Canoeing, Kayaking, Whitewater Rafting, Trekking, Game viewing, Horse Trails, Bungi Jumping, Absaling, Gorge Swinging, Rock Climbing, High Wiring, Cable Slide, River Cruises, Fishing, and an unending list of photographic wonders are all available within a short distance of the spectacular Falls. It is also the gateway to some of Africa's most impressive National Parks - including Hwange, Kafue, Sidma Ngwezi, Chobe, Mudumo, and Mamili, as well as the incredible Okavango Delta.

21st Century travellers require a host of facilities, such as bars, restaurants, arcades, shopping malls, booking agents, campsites, and hotels. Over the past decade, the small town of Victoria Falls has grown rapidly to meet these demands from modern tourism. This influx of money and trade has also attracted the inevitable troops of street sellers, hawkers and beggars. To that end, the town is fast becoming what many people try to avoid - the dreaded "tourist trap". The cheapest and quietest accommodation at Victoria Falls is the Iyati campsite situated a few kilometres south of town; but if you plan to stay any length of time in this area, the small town of Livingstone is a much better option.

Tony displays an immaculate African upper forty mirror carp.

A stunningly-scaled carp is captured on film by Tony's Pentax, as Martin Davidson lowers it back into the waters of Rushmere.

Livingstone is situated on the Zambia side of the mighty Zambezi River and just a few kilometres north of the waterfall. The town was named after David Livingstone, who was the first white explorer to reach the famous Victoria Falls in 1855. Even though it is classed as the "tourist centre" of Zambia, Livingstone has yet to be fully consumed by the greedy tourist industry, so it still retains a certain charm and laid-back feel to it. Although the majority of booking agents for adventurous activities on the Zambezi River are situated in the busy town of Victoria Falls, almost all the adventure companies operate from the Zambian side of the river.

If you bring a tent, Grubby's Grotto in Livingstone provides safe and pleasant surroundings for camping in their private gardens. This large and spacious house is the home of a likeable, English eccentric called "Grubby". He runs one of Africa's most famous extreme sport companies, called African Extreme Bungi. Grubby's business partner, the equally likeable and eccentric Englishman called Murray Trail, runs the whitewater rafting company - Raft Extreme. Together, they have built up an impressive record of offering the safest, most professionally run Extreme Sport business in Africa. Murray will also be offering new and exciting weekly expeditions down river through the wildest and virtually unexplored areas of the canyons. This will be a combined Whitewater Rafting and Fishing expedition concentrating on searching for the big Tigerfish that have never seen a hook. These fish live in quiet pools between raging sections of some of the World's most dangerous rapids. For the adventurous rafter or angler, it sounds like something not to be missed!

If you prefer to base yourself in the comfort of a wilderness Lodge, the best three close to Livingstone are: Cundukwa Tree Lodge; The River Club; and my own favourite, the spectacular Taita Falcon Lodge. It is built in complete isolation amongst Africa's wildest scenery, at the very edge of the Zambezi River gorge.

For more information, contact addresses and telephone numbers of Lodges, Safaris, and Adventure Activities surrounding Vic' Falls, see the special Contacts list at back of book.

To give the reader a small insight in to the varied and exciting adventures on offer in the Victoria Falls area, I will take an extract from my diary that follows a memorable whitewater rafting trip down the mighty Zambezi River, the home of crocodiles, Barbel and giant Tigerfish...

...I am mesmerised by the Falls, but the mighty river gives me no time to ponder. Wellington flicks his wrist and the long, wooden oar cuts into the crease of water at the edge of this giant eddy. For five minutes we have been drifting around in gentle circles, but now, our yellow craft seems to come alive. Thousands of tonnes of liquid ripples beneath the rubber and we begin to spin, as if someone has pulled the plug in a monster-sized bath. The other oar slaps the water and we immediately stop revolving, but a white-crested wave catches the bow and drags us backwards. It is my last glimpse of the Falls, before Wellington drags deeply with the left oar and we spin once more until the bow faces downstream.

One hundred and eleven metres above us, a young woman stands on a bridge that spans the gorge. I can see her golden hair blowing in the wind. I cannot see her eyes, but sense the tension in her body, as she stands rigid, with her toes flexing at the edge of a platform. Opposite her, a troop of wild Baboons clamber over the rocks and one solitary animal seems to watch her with interest as it clings to the very edge of a precipice. The girl now raises her arms like a crucifix; a long pause.... then she jumps!

Gravity drags her stiff body downwards, like a missile to dive into oblivion. Her flowing locks seem glued to her back as she hurtles headfirst through the air. Screams fill the gorge, as her body is about to slam into the water; but the elastic around her feet has reached full stretch, and within inches of impact, she is catapulted skywards.

A shout from Sai brings my eyes back to water level as the raft races towards Rapid 1, named "Against The Wall". I can once again hear a thundering roar and watch in silent fear at the mountain of water, which is lifting like a carpet and bulging against the rock face.

Shouts begin to ring out from Sai's lips "Pull, pull, pull!".

Sweat already drips off Wellington's brow as the powerful muscles in his dark arms twitch and pulse. His arms are like tree branches carved from ebony and they lift the heavy oars in slow, deliberate strokes. A wave catches the raft and lifts us on to its crest, only to drop us again into a deep trench. The walls of water surround us and are about to envelope us, but suddenly we are lifted again and riding another crest. My left hand grips

A wild elephant blows a cooling layer of dust over its head.

tightly to the safety rope; while at the same time my right hand holds on to a Nikonos camera. A strap to my safety vest connects the underwater camera, and I frantically try to take action photos, winding on the film using finger and thumb, as we bounce on down river. Eventually, Wellington's right arm digs deep with the oar, making the raft spin off the wave and glide across the ripples, as we again enter the relative safety of a giant eddy.

Shouts once again echo through the canyon and my head wrenches round, just in time to witness Kulu Bunda's raft flip over and hurl its occupants at the waves. For seconds, all I can see is the big, grey raft spinning upside down in a corkscrew; but suddenly the yellow helmet of Kulu bobs up through the foam. One by one, other helmets appear, until the water is dotted with pink and blue helmets. Kulu grabs hold of a rope, pulls himself on to the overturned raft then expertly flips it back into the upright position. Safety kayaks are already amongst the bobbing helmets, and Wellington quickly manoeuvres our raft back upstream so that we can give a helping hand.

Soon, our two rafts and all their occupants are back inside the relative safety of a spiralling eddy of calm water. I look around at everyone and can see a combination of exhilaration and fear etched on their wet faces. We all watch in anticipation as Kevin brings the third raft down river, but a gasp fills the air as "Up Against the Wall" takes it's second casualty and flips the dingy over. Once again,

"...As close to committing suicide as possible!" The amazing Gorge Swing. A man, seemingly walking on air, jumps directly towards the canyon floor a thousand feet below!

the safety kayaks are quick to react in helping people back in to the raft.

Murray Trail, nicknamed "Buzzer", who operates the rafting company 'RAFT EXTREME' is running a very slick operation on this extremely dangerous section of river. Today, Buzzer and his six other professional guides are making sure that the 47 paying clients reach their destination in one piece. Most of the rafts will be negotiating all 20 major rapids, but because I have booked to fly a Microlight over Victoria Falls at sunset, I will get out at Rapid 10.

This is my first ever whitewater trip down the mighty Zambezi River, but because I am the official photographer I have been assigned to the lead boat. This is also the first accent of the year between rapids 1-10, which contain some of the most dangerous whitewater sections in the World. Normally there are 5 to 9 people per raft, but to ensure manoeuvrability, my raft has been assigned only 3 members - myself, and the ultra experienced duo of Sai Sakala and Wellington Boot (nicknamed due to his massive black feet that look like gum boots!).

Before all the rafts are assembled together in the quiet eddy, Wellington grips the oars again and rows our raft down river. After 500 metres, he points the raft towards a calmer section of water close to shore, until it glides gently and wedges it's bow between two rocks. Quickly, we untie the straps around the waterproof Pelican case, which holds all my dry camera bodies and lenses, and then scamper over the rocks. I need to reach a location directly opposite Rapid 2 - "In Between Worlds" before the main flotilla of rafts come through. I manage to get in position just in time, and try to calm my racing heartbeat before pressing the shutter, as the first raft and kayaks come hurtling past me. All craft negotiate this big rapid without flipping, so we hurry back to our raft and chase them down river.

Finally, we are able to overtake everybody and I position myself on a cleft of high rocks overlooking Rapid 4 - "Morning Glory". This section provides me with plenty of good action shots as four different rafts steered by Garreth, Neville, Leonard and Kudu are chucked on their backs by the raging whitewater. At the next rapid - "Stairway to Heaven", all except Neville's raft makes it safely through the massive, tumbling wall of 15ft high waves. Through the viewfinder, I watch the fear grooved on everyone's faces as each raft plunges into a deep trough, then rides up the liquid stairway, before being spat out like champagne corks. With each group of passengers safely through the rapids, their fear reverts to excitement as clenched fists reach for the sky in signs of utter exultation. Then I watch Neville and his companions disappear in a white maelstrom of raging foam. The river in front of me now looks empty, as if no one has ever passed through this lonely place.

The roar of the rapids rings in both ears as my eyes scan wildly for signs of life; but all I can see is dark water and white foam. My heart seems to miss a beat and time stands still, but suddenly a grey dinghy pops to the surface, followed by a sequence of brightly coloured vests and helmets. Happy that they are all safe, I quickly re-pack the camera gear and follow Sai and Wellington, as they run bear foot over the rocks back to our raft.

We make our way slowly towards the thundering sound that is the "Stairway to Heaven". Our smooth negotiation of the first four sets of rapids has given me a massive boost of confidence, and now I stand up in the raft and wave my fist in excitement at the distant, puny waves.

"Take no prisoners!" I shout in excitement.

The yellow raft slides quietly onwards. Our speed increases and the soft, rippling sound of moving water beneath the rubber begins to rise in frequency, until it reaches a high-pitched squeal. The 'bump' in the waves down river begins to grow and grow, until it is a dark grey moving mountain. Positioned at the bow of the boat, I now turn and face both Sai and Wellington. My feet wriggle into the cleft of rubber between sides and floor of the craft so as to form a wedge for my body. The fingers of my left hand curl around the safety cord while my other hand fights to hold the camera tight to my eye. With my

An African guide looks for signs of wildlife at sunset.

'The united colours of Africa'.

back facing downstream, I fly blindly into the mouth of hell.

Sai and Wellington rise up above me and climb to heavens door. Behind them I can see only blue. Then they are suddenly plucked from the skies and sink into a grey trench that has opened beneath us. For an instant, I stare vertically down on to their helmets; then my stomach is wrenched against my throat. As if in slow motion, my body falls to the very bottom of the trench. The grey walls of water climb all around me...then topple on my head and cloak the world in darkness.

It is like being locked inside a giant champagne bottle and someone is shaking it vigorously. All I can hear are the millions of fizzing bubbles and strangely, my own thumping heartbeat. I feel my body being spun in cartwheels through the water, until I cannot tell which way is up or down, just complete and utter darkness. The seconds tick past and I begin to feel a heavy weight on my chest. When I first went under, the breath was knocked out of my lungs, and now they desperately need oxygen. Inside the black void, I can just make out a faint light, so my feet kick hard and send me towards the light. Blue slowly appears above me; but within 12 inches of the surface, a huge wave blocks out the sky and crashes down on my face. A tremendous weight of water drags me back in to darkness until I feel my sandals bang against the rocks of the riverbed....

The pain inside my chest is so intense that I almost pass out, but my legs make one last effort to thrust my body to the surface. Suddenly, the pressure of water is released and my mouth opens involuntary as two lungs suck in copious amounts of sweet oxygen. But the sky is not blue it is yellow! I have surfaced directly beneath the upturned raft. I try to reach my arm around the outside of the raft to grab on to the safety rope, but just as my fingers touch the cord, a giant wave impacts against my chest and catapults my body from under the raft. For a brief second I am flying through the air; then crash headfirst back in to the maelstrom of foam and bubbles. When my helmet pops to the surface again, there is already 50 metres between the raft and me. The safety kayaks are with the main group of rafts, way downstream at Rapid 6, so they don't realise that we've flipped over. I try to swim towards Sai and Wellington, who now cling to our yellow raft, but the current is just too powerful and it sweeps me down river. My only chance is to swim to one of the whirlpools that churn water around like a washing machine. With luck, I eventually reach one, and this allows the raft to catch up with me. As it hurtles past, Sai grabs hold of my arm to pluck me from the waves. Immediately we combine our strength to flip the raft back over, and within seconds we are back in control. This time, the more experienced Sai takes hold of the oars and quickly brings the raft expertly back in line for our assault on the next rapid. A bump is swelling on my forehead where the camera must have smashed against it as I was flung overboard. As I kneel in the bow and watch the next set of rapids growing in stature as we hurtle towards it, I can feel my heart racing. But this time my blood is filled with pure adrenaline, and it brushes aside the fear to replace it with wild excitement...

A beautiful and pristine-conditioned 48lb+ mirror carp.

I spent an on-and-off period of 15 years in Scandinavia. Learned their languages, drank barrels of their tasty larger, and once was so seduced by the charms of one of their women, that I married her...So I suppose the 'Lands of the Vikings' must surely be planted deep inside my memory banks! That is no doubt true, but each time I think back on my times spent in this beautiful, often cold, often gentle, sometimes wild region of Europe, it is the carp fishing sessions that most often jump to the forefront of my dreams.

The fondest memories are carp expeditions to the big lakes hidden in wild, forested regions of Sweden, or to the cluster of atmospheric 'Redmire-type' carp waters, hidden amongst ancient woods that surrounded my home, on the picturesque island of Fyn in Denmark...or maybe I should also include my many connections with silky Danish maidens...!

Maybe I will divulge some of those secrets next time...until then, I will offer a selection of special photos that highlight my long list of wonderful 'Scandinavian Memories'.

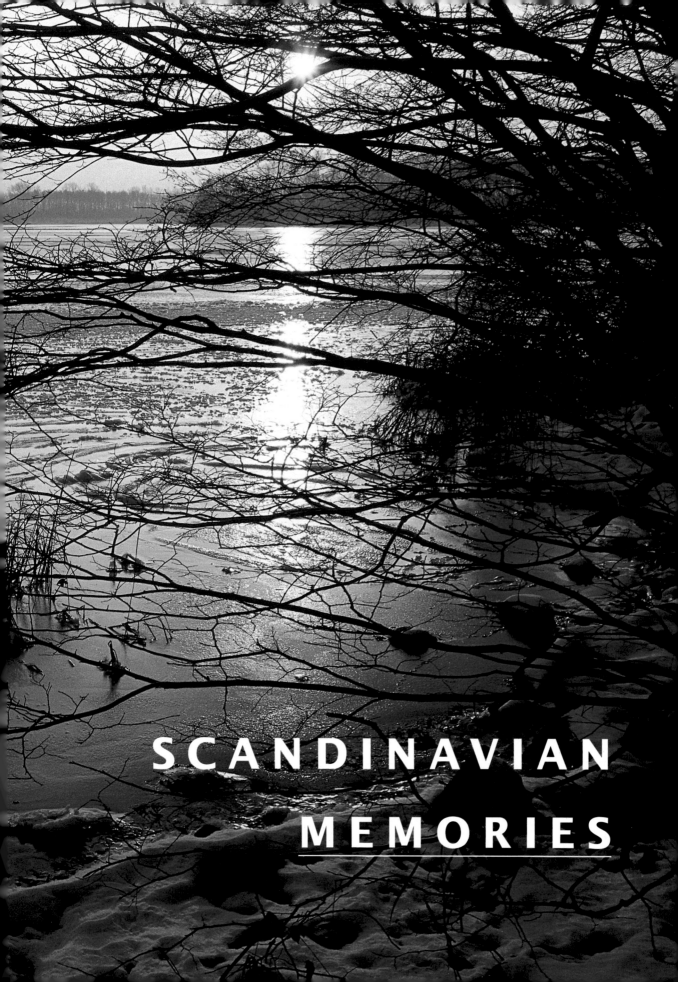

SCANDINAVIAN

MEMORIES

A mirror carp confidently sucks down floaters at a lake on the island of Fyn in central Denmark.

Margin fishing at Springpool in Denmark. 'The less the carp know of your presence, the more you will catch'; is Tony's motto.

Searching for signs of carp on a large Swedish lake.

Tony displays a stunning
Danish mirror carp.

SERGEANTS &

SILVER GEMS

'I am a part of all who I have met,
and all that I have touched'

Tony with his third roach over 4lb!

The red bus pulls away and leaves me holding my breath inside a cloud of diesel fumes. A cold wind pushes whitecaps along the crests of waves as it races across 500 acres of green-tinged waters and tries to blow my cap off. It quickly disperses the diesel smoke so that I can at least draw in a deep breath of oxygen. Now the sweet smell of fish and foam wafting off the lake begins to drown my senses. A pair of chestnut-headed Goosander bob on the waves in front of me. Spread out across the lake, more than twenty different pairs of Great Crested Grebes dive in search of fish. Thousands of Scaup, Tufted ducks, Pochards, Shovelers, Pintails, Eider, Mallards, Teal, Goldenye and Shelducks crowd together in the calmer sections of water behind the islands. Black 'V' formations of Cormorants wing across the darkening skies on their unending journeys between lake and Baltic Sea. Numerous Grey herons stand like rigid sentinels along the margins and Buzzards soar above the forest's highest branches.

I shoulder my rucksack and begin walking along the meadow and through a forest that skirts the great lake. My footsteps send up a black hoard of white-beaked Coots that try to walk on water, until they find sanctuary within the dense reed beds, then cluck out their alarms. A single Grey Heron rises up from the bulrushes and screams at me as he wings with great beats across the surface.

A short climb down a cliff brings me to the water's edge, where ocean-like waves spray mares' tails off the whitecaps and a thick line of foam rocks along the shoreline. I erect a lightweight mountain bivouac close to the water and position the rod rests so that the cork butts of the rods are tight enough to the tent opening to allow an instant strike.

From the shallow margins, a hard bottomed plateau stretches for 50 metres, before gradually sloping down into deeper water. It is at the leading edge of this slope that I intend to fish. The lake holds numerous different species of fish: carp of unknown size, eels to 10lb+, bream to 20lb, roach to 4lb+, rudd to 5lb+, and perch to over 5lb....Yes, it is indeed a special lake!

I soak two loaves of bread in a plastic bag and then squeeze out the remaining water, before adding a few handfuls of tinned corn and chopped lobworms. This is then left open to the winds so that the mixture can dry off enough to enable me to roll it into palm-sized balls. Half of these bait balls are hurled into the area of the underwater slope. I then begin wading in the shallow margins in search of live mussels. Due to it being so cold, most of these have moved back into deeper water, but I manage to find enough remaining in the shallows to use as hookbaits.

Even though my main target today is to be large roach and perch, I am not set up with ultra light tackle. A 50lb carp or 20lb bream could also pick up the bait that I am about to use for these two species, so I want tackle strong enough to cope with such fish. I've never found roach or perch to fight extremely hard on even the finest tackle, so to me, the more important

A spectacular 4lb 2oz roach.

aspects of these two fish are to look at their silver scales at close quarters or to admire their striped flanks and proud dorsal fin. It is not the fight that impresses me with roach and perch, but more their outstanding beauty. Even so, I don't want to land such glorious fish on stiff pokers! My heavy-duty carp rods are left at home and instead, I have brought with me a pair of 1.5lb test curve 11ft Conoflex glass fibre Jack Hilton replicas, bought from Alan Brown way back in 1979. The varnish is well chipped and chunks are missing off the well worn cork handles, but they have landed everything from chub to barbel to carp, and have formed an important stepping stone to my most fondest of memories.

A large Swan mussel is prised open and the complete inner 'foot' is placed on the hook. The longest pieces of flesh are trimmed off to avoid twitches or missed bites. A small plastic tub is then opened which contains hard maize that has been left soaking in water for one week. A small touch of sugar and Scopex flavouring has also been added. Although the softer tinned corn undoubtedly attracts more roach, as a hookbait I prefer the much harder pre-soaked maize because it puts off most small roach, is more difficult for the fish to remove from the hook, and also allows repeated casts.

I often prefer to use large antenna floats in this particular swim, but the strong winds combined with the fact that it will be dark soon, has swayed me to attach free-running ledger rigs.

From a nearby field, a large gaggle of Canadian geese stop feeding, then lift into the sky and sweep over my head. Their constant, hoarse, disyllabic 'aah-honk' almost drowns out the sounds of their heavy wing beats. Then, like one living animal, the calling stops as each cup its wings and glides low over the water. I can hear the great rush of wind whistling through a thousand flight feathers. Like miniature Jumbo jets, the under carriages swing down, then they water ski on outstretched webbed feet and crash through their own shadows. As if in defiance of this noisy spectacle, a Mute swan unfolds a pair of great white wings and begins to pound the air with drumbeats.

The earth spins more and forces the sun to change into a mound of molten lava as it gradually slips behind the horizon. A grey, brooding sky turns orange, then vibrant red and eventually fades into the purple velvet of twilight. Waves lose their whitecaps as the wind slowly dies and transforms the water into a sheet of unmoving glass. Cold mist creeps out of the reed beds and skates across the

On this occasion the needle swings around until it stops on 4lb 8oz!'

'A swan unfolds a pair of great white wings and begins to pound the air with drumbeats'.

Glorious 4lb+ perch in wonderful condition.

A Grey Heron flying above the lake.

surface. Thousands of heads tuck back into down quilts and the cacophony of sounds echoing across the lake slowly ebb away.

I turn off the bite alarms and spend the last hour of dusk just sitting in silence, with my back propped up against a willow tree and gazing at the water lapping gently on the base of the indicator needles. Time seems to stand still, until a rustle breaks my trance. It is the indicator bobbin, ever so slowly moving up the needle...so loud as to make it almost eerie. It is strange how acutely tuned the human ear can become to certain sounds.

I lift the rod off the rests and pull back sharply in one flowing movement. A dull, heavy thumping of the rod tip tells me straight away that this is a good bream. And so it turns out to be, as a bronze plate eventually slides over the landing net. I quickly weigh it at just over 11lb, and then let it swim gently from my fingers. Just as I returning the bream, the other indicator jerks upwards then rattles against the rod as line pours off the spool. A 3lb 12oz perch has picked up the corn/lobworm cocktail.

Gradually, a grey sky fades into an inky blackness and the freezing, moist air forces me to retreat into the small mountain tent. First, I switch back on the bite alarms then snuggle inside the duck-down sleeping bag, thankful of the warmth that all my feathered friends have provided....

Dawn finds me once again sitting beneath the willow, pouring steaming hot coffee from the Zojirushi flask and watching cold mist being chased off the water by a slowly rising orb of yellow warmth. Although another big perch and a glorious 4lb+ roach have taken a liking to my swan mussel and worm baits during the night, it is the dawn hours that have brought on the heaviest bout of feeding.

The sun continues to climb until it reaches its peak in an azure sky and signals all feeding to abruptly stop. I don't mind in the least, because I've already landed a string of good fish, including

a second monster roach. On this occasion the needle swings around until it stops at 4lb 8oz!

As I walk back across the fields, weighed down with heavy tackle, I suddenly stop then slip the rucksack from my shoulders. I sit down in the grass that blows in the wind on a hill overlooking the majestic waters. This time the bus can wait. It is a sad moment for me, for I know that this is probably my very last fishing trip to this glorious lake. After 15 years living in Denmark, I will soon be moving back to my homeland, England. Over the past decade, this particular lake has become a living part of me but it has waited until now, on my very last visit, to eventually open her heart and reward me with the biggest prize - monster sergeants and silver gems. So I take these moments to savour the memories and stare across the green waters, while behind me on the country road, a red bus whizzes past....

A misty dawn as I wait for 'sergeants & silver gems'.

Tony with a brace of big 'sergeants'.

BEHIND

THE WALL

*A quiet corner of a lake
in wildest China.*

by Jens Bursell

In articles on exotic fishing expeditions you may easily get the impression that the monsters virtually are begging to take your bait. Nothing is further from the truth. This is the story of Jens Bursell's first black carp and about a gigantic temple fish...

Many, many generations ago - somewhere in Manchuria - a bewitched king reigned. Every single week he sent his minister out into the countryside to find a beautiful young girl to be his queen.... Since the beauties were not to his liking, he had them killed in a bestial manner. One day a travelling Buddhist monk passed the royal palace. In order to facilitate the king's best choice of a wife, the monk gave the king his magic mirror.

"This mirror retains the mirror image of a true beauty - even when her back is turned", said the monk. The minister took the mirror and went down to the nearest lake, where he found an exceptionally beautiful girl. It was soon evident, that the mirror worked as the monk had claimed. The reflection of the wondrously lovely face of the fisherman's daughter was frozen in the mirror, and it was a joy to behold. The king was immediately summoned, and before long he proposed to the beautiful girl.

"What is the most precious thing in this world ", the girl asked the king.

The king did not hesitate a second before answering: "Power". When the girl heard this, she threw the mirror into the lake. A violent storm arose, and in a few moments all perished in the foaming waves.

Butterflies sucking up moisture during the first warming rays of dawn.

Marinated dogs and deep-fried carp

Mudandjang 3/7-98: "China, here I come". Yesterday I ate a dog with raw chilli and oceans of garlic. Today I am trying to contain a flux of diarrhoea and vomit. My urine is orange from a profusion of suspicious Northeast Chinese herb extracts. One could be tempted to believe that the bordello lighting in the toilet is the cause, but alas! My mouth said yes, but my body said no....

After a whole week in Mudandjang, which is a smallish Chinese provincial town of about 1 million inhabitants (!), I at long last manage to get a lift to Jingbo Hu - the lake where the magical mirror disappeared many thousands of years ago. The object is to make an old dream come true: To catch a Chinese carp.

10/7: Time for departure - I thought. On the way to the lake I was taken to the home of Feng Chang to meet all his family. There was no escaping putting on a show of politeness. Not until after another 24 hours does it finally happen... We are off. Not alone, but with his two spoilt and podgy sons. Feng is the local construction matador. It does not take long before he, like so many other well to do Chinese, gives way to his irrepressible urge to demonstrate that he has a lot of money. After a few hours drive, he contrives in a most indiscreet manner to get us settled into the absolutely most expensive luxury hotel in Manchuria. Following a hot bath in a gigantic bathroom, we are invited to dine with the owner of the hotel, who, of course, is one of Chengs in-crowd friends. I have never before seen so much food at one time; there is simply nothing edible that is not to be found on the table. Dog (not again...), deep-fried carp, meat cakes of crucian carp, glass kelp, carp in garlic, dry fried red-tailed carp, sweet and sour pork, strips of fillet of beef, sugared cocks-combs, crispy fried thighs of chicken, stuffed grasscarp, boiled catfish, rice porridge, noodles, crispy rice, rice cakes, tons of raw chilli, beer and lots of rice-brandy.

When toasting a person in China you say "Ganbei", and this word the Chinese like to hear uttered again and again, whenever they meet foreigners. Ganbei means something like "down with.... and the rest in the hair". Follow the custom or flee the country as we Danes say! Since home is far away, I decide to demonstrate my goodwill with regard to the project. The rice brandy tastes like a mixture of spirits, vinegar and stale cloying white wine that has been left for a couple of weeks in the heat of the summer. Nobody understands English, but after countless Ganbei I no longer seem to have any difficulty in speaking Chinese or Manchurian, or whatever language we were speaking. The conversation is loud and rapid and finally I succeed in making it understood that the goal of my trip is a Chinese wild carp, or Black Carp, as they are also called. This type of carp is in fact nothing but a subspecies of the carp (Cyprinus carpio hameopterus).

I quickly realize that it is impolite not to burp, belch, fart, hawk and spit at table. If you throw scraps of food on the tablecloth or cigarette buts on the floor, you are really behaving like one of the locals! Being a carp-junkie these things don't take long to learn. When the night is over, I have become bosom pals with several of the partygoers and blow me if I didn't manage to get a promise of a lift to a remote Manchurian village, where I can hope to get into some fishing.

Jingbo Hu

11/7 - After the small detour to the luxury hotel I arrive at Jingbo Hu. Already after a couple of hours, I succeed in hiring a slim rowing punt. I must confess, I have seldom experienced a boat that

Jens fishing beside a campfire in a remote region of northern China.

wobbly, except possibly the dugout canoe I used for carp fishing in Uganda. The boat was loaded with 40 kilos of gear, and subject to close scrutiny from half the village, I rowed out onto the lake. Luckily I managed to avoid capsizing while the locals were watching. After half an hour's going, I was getting a sense of balance and was gaining a little more confidence in the project. The whole of the day was spent in making echo-soundings and in finding a suitable quiet spot on the opposite shore to that of the village - some 3 kilometres away.

When the sun began setting, I was finally ready. I had seen fish on my portable echo sounder, the baiting had been done and the rigs were placed to perfection. Not a Chinaman within miles - I thought. Suddenly, I heard something that reminded me of a Chinese band with the most strident singer in the world. The notes rang across the lake so much out of tune, that you thought it must be a joke. It soon turned out that what I had taken to be an abandoned boat, in the evenings was transformed into a Karaoke-Bar. All through the night I was entertained by the latest Chinese hits, rudely manhandled. Not as much as a single run.

The next morning I decided to find an isolated cove - even if I had to row halfway around the lake. Back in the village I tanked up with sundry foodstuffs, and chicken pellets and rice, which served admirably as carp-fodder.

A ferry lift

13/7 - I am now ready for "Operation Far Away". A strong wind has risen, and in these conditions the lake seems boundless. It is more than 45 kilometres in length, covers an area of 90 square kilometres and is one of the most impressive sights in Heilong Jiang - whatever the wind. A couple of kilometres out and the winds now are so strong, that I must fight for all I am worth to avoid drifting back to where I came from. After half an hour with copious amounts of sweat on my brow, I see a ferry drawing nearer. Mostly as a joke I make the thumb sign to get a lift. To my immense

A first-class taxi transports Jens to his swim!

surprise, the ferry, which is empty, stops. After some sign language and gesticulation the captain, whose name is Liy, understands that I am on my way to an isolated cove with good chances of catching some carp. Soon both my gear and the boat are hoisted onto the ferry, and we sail easily through the mounting waves. About 10 kilometres further on the ferry stops in a perfect little bay. Since we are only two persons on the ferry, Liy invites me to dine with some friends, who have a small ragged hut at the entrance to the cove.

After loads of crucian carp soup and equal amounts of rice brandy, the local fisherman's tales are told around the table. The carp in this part of the Amur-river-system are rather small. If you catch a fish of more than 2 kilos, you have actually got yourself a good one... On the other hand it turns out, that a 40-kilo grasscarp was caught in the cove a couple of years ago. So that is definitely worth taking into account... The fishermen owned the cove, but since I soon became regarded as one of their own, I had no difficulty getting permission to fish.

14/7. After some hour's of echo sounding, I find a wonderful spot - and this time perfectly isolated, far away from everything. Owing to 15 meters of rushes in the margins, it is very difficult to get the place ready. The solution is to cut a couple of narrow tracks through the rushes, and then fish a bait at the edge of the 2-meter curve. In the hope of getting a monster grasscarp, I fish one rod with giant maize and the other with a KN squid-boilie.

Black Carp

For the first 2 days absolutely nothing happens. The fishermen come every day to invite me for dinner, but I had firmly decided to catch a Chinese carp, so I didn't budge from the place. Rarely have I felt more at ease - the time was spent tending the fire, staring in to the glowing embers, eating noodles and looking at mystical butterflies and spiders. Finally, in the evening of 16/7, the run comes. Overwhelmed by the sudden activity I rush to the rod and make my strike. The fish fights well on the rather light gear. Flustered at the thought of loosing my first Chinese carp, I jump into the boat to avoid the fish getting snagged. As soon as I am out of the rushes, I quickly realize that the fish is absolutely not of the heaviest calibre. After a short fight the carp is in the net. In spite of the fish weighing no more than 4 kilos I am in seventh carp-heaven. My first black carp was a reality, and maybe because I had struggled so hard to get it, I was at least as pleased with this fish as I had been a few months back, when I caught a fish 6 times the size in Sarulesti. When the fishermen saw the fish in the morning their mouths started watering, and they started to peel garlic... Seeing that I had graciously been given permission to fish in their private waters, I omitted - for diplomatic reasons - to release the wonder. As a matter of fact it tasted absolutely delicious. Carp in garlic sauce is not to be sneered at - The thing is, if sufficient garlic has been used, you can't taste the otherwise distinctly muddy flavour.

New waters

In the hope of landing a giant grasscarp, I continue fishing for a couple of days; but unfortunately without result. The grasscarp has its origin in Heilongjiang - River of the Black Dragon. This river is better known in Western countries as the Amur. In it's natural habitat the grasscarp is a migrant, which travels thousands of kilometres up and down the river, in order to spawn in the area between the confluence of Heilongjiang and Sounghua, and downstream to Fuyan/Ussuri. Determined to fish the main river, I decided to travel the 500 kilometres northwards to Tongliang, a fishing village at the confluence. The plan was at the same time to investigate the possibilities for catching one the world's largest sturgeon species - the Kaluga Sturgeon. The sturgeon family Huso contains two species - one is the Beluga and the other is the Kaluga. The fish of both species attain approximately the same weight - say no more... The largest documented specimen was caught at Leninskoya and measured 420 centimeters in length. A good guess at its weight would be around 700-800 kilos.... I already knew, however, that the stocks had been heavily depleted due to over fishing during a long period of years. But that sort of information you have, of course, to check out for yourself before you believe it.

The River of the Black Dragon

20/7: After a long and troublesome bus journey I have finally reached Tongliang. That, which from all accounts should have been an idyllic fishing village, had in the course of a few years grown to become a reeking provincial town with several hundreds of thousands of inhabitants.... Things happen fast in China. According to the local fishermen there were unbelievably few sturgeon left in this area. When I came down to the river, it dawned upon me what I am up against. The river is at this point about 10 kilometres in width, and the current was so strong that you had to have 5 kilos of lead at the end of the line to hold the bottom. When I heard rumours of solitary Kaluga sturgeon catches a couple of hundred kilometres downstream, I packed my gear and travelled up to Fuyan in the furthest north-easterly corner of China on the border to Siberia.

After a couple of hour's effort in sign language, I succeeded in hiring a couple of local fishermen and their boat for a couple of days. The current was at this place considerably weaker than at Tongliang, in fact now it only required a 2-kilo stone to hold the bottom.... Large areas were investigated with the echo sounder, and since the few kalugas that had been caught were taken at the edge of the main current, I anchored here hoping for a monster-run. The bait was a half-kilo bream mounted on a double-hook set-up with size 8 Owner Gorilla. - If any hook can hold a fish the size of a cow, this must be it. Unfortunately the result was a blank for three days.

During a reconnaissance-trip with the echo sounder I had found an island about 3 kilometres out into the river, where I had seen a number of grass-carp in the 15-25 kilo range. For several days I mulled over the possibility of having myself sailed out onto the island and go for these fish instead. One evening at the hotel, however, I had seen a Chinese TV-news-cast, where all you saw was children and others drowned in floods. As I could of course not understand a word of what was said, I had no idea of where these floods were occurring. I realized that Yangtze and large parts of the Wuhan area were inundated, but whether the dangerous conditions were expected to spread further to the North, I was not certain. For once I decided not to take any chances and left the Amur-region. A very short time later the flood-wave came and the river rose 5-8 meters... Imagine me sitting on a 2-meter high island 3 kilometers out on the river. I might have ended up washed out into the Sea of Okhotsk!

Rumours of 2-meter long grasscarp

After the somewhat abortive trip to the Amur, I went back to Mudadjang, where I came into contact with Fan Weng Chang, who owned the local tackle shop. When I enquired for large gasscarp, he told me that he knew a chap whose wife had been bathing in a small mountain lake 100 kilometres from the town. When she had squatted to pee at the water's edge, she had been shocked to see a grasscarp 2 meters long staring at her without modesty. As rumour had it, most grasscarp in the lake were of 1 meters length with, many up to 1_ meter...Although you should always beware of old wives' tales, I simply had to check these rumours.

3 days later, I succeeded in getting a lift to the lake, which according to accounts was private, 2-3 kilometres long and desolate. When we got there, it turned out to be 200 meters long, 30 fishermen were sitting around the shores, and at least 200 meters of net were put out daily. It didn't call for a large measure of intelligence to work out that this was going to be another blank. Having taken the trouble to make my way to the lake, I decided nevertheless to try my luck. The result was, that I had a run - and lost an 8-9 kilo grasscarp at the edge of the net, possibly due to too many 'ganbei' salutes with the other anglers.

Thoroughly disgusted with all the hard work and blanks, I decided to travel by way of The Yellow River and Inner Mongolia, up to the Tibetan Plateau to do some riding. After a couple of weeks in this land of grassy plains, I hitched 600 kilometres on the back of an open pick-up to Chengdu, where I was lucky enough to catch 3 Chinese goldfish averaging one ounce and a huge temple-fish. The groundbait was pulverized lotus-flowers and as hookbait, I used a stick of incense.

Moral: *Large fish don't grow on trees – even in China.*

Should you, even after this story, feel inclined to try your luck in China, the best plan is clearly to bet on the larger rivers and lakes - that is if they do not happen to be inundated or in flood. I have in several Chinese magazines seen photos of grasscarp weighing in the order of 35-45 kilos... It can be done, but they are few and far between. Try to avoid small waters - the Chinese love to eat carp, and the average weight is low as a result of this.

MAGICAL ITALY

*'A photograph is the vision of your soul; a fleeting, magic
moment locked in time'*

This region of Europe is truly magical; and so are the wonderful lakes and rivers that stretch in a pepper pot of blue across a map of Italy - From the huge lakes nestled in the Alpine passes of the north – to the mystical southern reservoirs of Calabria - From the productive regions of Lazio and Umbria – to the wild waters of Sicily and Sardinia. I have travelled north-south-east-west, and always I have enjoyed success in my quest.

It is sometimes expressed that 'a photo can say more than a thousand words'. I try to always put my heart and soul into my photography. I hope the photographs displayed on these few pages relay to the viewer more than words can express about the magic of Italian carp fishing.

'Castle of the Lake' - Trassimeno, in central Italy. This huge, open water has a circumference of 56.3km, and holds carp to 50lb+.

An unusual photo of two swans swimming behind Tony's rods in Lake Endine.

Tony cradles a massive common caught on two 20mm rock-hard air-dried Nash Scopex boilies.

A 29lb 8oz common carp caught in cold,
November conditions from Lake Trassimeno.

A fantastic shot of the famous Stromboli Volcano as it
hurls molten lava at the moonlit sky.

SOUTH ISLAND

ADVENTURE

By Jens Bursell

After having spent an exciting week stalking Koi-carp on light gear in Waikato River, it was super to move on – out to experience the true soul of New Zealand – forests, mountains and crystal-clear rivers. The destination was the South Island, which still supports a large population of the fabled Longfin eel.

On the trip down the North Island we chose a tortuous detour to get in some sightseeing. The rugged coastal range on Coromandel, merely half an hour's drive from Waikato, is a fantastic sight, with its dense growth of tree ferns and huge trees. Further south, we pass Lake Taupo, a famous destination for trout-fisherman that flock here from around the Globe, and the Tongariro vulcano, which rises majestically over the gently undulating and parched plateau.

South Island

After a stupendous passage from Wellington across the Cook Strait and through Marlborough Sounds, we finally arrive at Picton on the Northern part of the South Island. At this point in time we have not quite decided where we are going to fish, and a quick look at the map reveals hundreds of

Jens with a stunning New Zealand Koi carp from his second trip to the North Island.

thousands of kilometres of streams, that only wait to be explored. It is a fantastic feeling, but also one of enormity.

Circle Hooks

We start off by trying to fish a couple of lakes in the central part of the South Island. After a few nights' fishing it turns out, however, that eels of just tolerable size are few and far between. One of the nights we caught more than 100 eels, of which only one weighed in excess of 3 kilos. A slimy hell in which we do, nevertheless, gain much valuable experience, which later turns out to stand us in good stead. The most important of this is, no doubt, that circle hooks make the fishing of eel unbelievably much easier - For the angler as well as for the eel. Already by the time we had passed the first 10-15 eels that were deep-hooked, did we realize that something had to be done if we were to accept releasing the fish. In spite of instantaneous strikes, it turned out that 90% of the fish were hooked so deeply that it involved a major operation freeing them - Frequently with the result that the eel had suffered considerable damage during the struggle. Once having unhooked a deep-hooked eel of 500 grams, you can imagine the task of unhooking tons of fish much larger and more difficult to handle. Here we are talking about every square-centimetre of our clothes covered with eel-slime....

We quickly found that Octopus Circle Hooks in size 6/0 (Gamakatzu) were perfect for the job. With this size we avoided hooking many much too small eels in the 1-2 kilo class, whilst anything above this size would be perfectly hooked – as a rule in the corner of the mouth or in the lip. With this technique we could suddenly release practically all the fish caught. Aided by a homemade un-hooker of the type used to unhook conger-eels we could, with a bit of practice, land and unhook the eels with lightning speed. A Circle hook gives a really good hold, once the point has caught. The technique with these hooks is, that although the fish swallows the bait, the inward pointing tip has the effect when the line is tightened, that the fish is not "pricked" until the hook is on the way out and catches on the jaw or the corner of the mouth. If you want to increase the chance of the hook getting a correct hold, you should not make a strike in the normal way. Instead, you allow the line to tighten gradually, so the fish gets time to "turn", whereby the hook more readily gets a hold.

The stocks of eel in New Zealand have in the course of the last 20 years been heavily fished commercially to the extent that fish weighing more than 5 kilos are more and more difficult to come by. It is therefore a good idea to fish waters that are as inaccessible as possible, if the objective is to catch large fish. For the same reason the next destination of our trip - a river in the Northwestern part of the South Island – entailed 3_ days trekking from the nearest access road.

Sand-flies and damaged knees

According to some reliable sources, eels of good size were to be found in some large pools created by tectonic faults located in the central part of this river system. As is the case with any rumour about big fish, there is only one way to verify.... Unfortunately the necessary kit was not confined to an AFTM 5-6 fly rod and 20-30 dry flies, but consisted of approximately 2 x 30 kilos of smelly gear. On top of each of these reeking backpacks was tied a nosebag filled with bloody pieces of lambs-hearts, ox-liver and shinbones of lamb!

Having trekked for 2_ days through the most wonderful forests of Beech festooned with moss and

A monster eel glides into the landing net.

lichen and interspersed with tree ferns; we found that the path had petered out. To carry on to reach our goal we had to cross the river and make our way off-track for about 10 kilometres. Bearing in mind that we had to force our way through well-nigh impenetrable forest up and down steep rocks and over rotting tree trunks, where we constantly had to struggle to get a footing, we had to exert ourselves tremendously to cover one kilometre per hour. Already before we crossed the river the heavy going had taken its toll on my companion Søren's knees - Particularly the descent from a high defile, which had placed an overly heavy strain on him. However, it was the off-track trekking that broke the camel's back. After a few hours of this, Søren's knee had to capitulate.

When the knee finally packed up, it unfortunately happened at the top of a ridge where there was no space to pitch a tent, and what was worse; there was no fishing to be done.... The solution we decided upon was for me to perform a shuttle-service with both backpacks until we reached a suitable campsite with fishing possibilities. After 5 hours of hard work, during which we twice had to make a descent down vertical cliffs hanging on to roots and branches, we finally found a good campsite next to a small tributary.

Below the tent there was a small waterfall and immediately downstream of this there was a perfect little pool. We just managed to unpack the rods before dark. The hook was baited with half a heart of lamb, and even before the bait reached the water I got at bite from a nice brown trout of 2 kilos, that fought like mad. To hold such a fish on a 3 lbs "Siluris" rod of the type used for smaller catfish was of course like taking candy from small children. The trout had a giant head – clearly an old cannibalistic male that had terrorized the pool and devoured every living thing there for quite a while.

In the next cast it is Søren's turn, and this time it is the biggest fish of the trip – an eel of 4.6 kilos (10lb). All things considered, we are well satisfied with having upped our record by 1.2 kilos, bearing in mind that to a pair of beer-burping Danes like us a fish like this still seems like a monster when compared to our home grown knitting needles. The next day Søren gives his bad knee a rest, whilst I make a recognisance downstream. However, I do not get further than halfway to the pools that were the intended goal of the trip. Since this took 1_ hour without pack and involved quite a bit of climbing, it left no room for discussion – we had to give up the idea of proceeding downstream. Instead we decided to live for a few days entirely on fish, since our rations of spaghetti and soup cubes had to last for the duration of the return trip. In this way we could prolong the trip somewhat, so that we at least would have had some gratification for all our labour. That night we catch quite a few eels up to 4,3 kilos, and we feed on boiled eel and fish-soup to the point of being about to puke.... Constant stings from hordes of hungry sand flies (a sabre tiger version of the black-fly) makes any further stay an abomination, and since the whole object of the journey from the start has been to catch considerably larger eels, we decide to start the return trip so that we can get on with our search for the big ones, preferably in a place where there are fewer sand flies.

Eels during dishwashing

Halfway back towards the river where we crossed a few days earlier, we find a super pool where brown trout of 2-4 kilos circle enticingly in the crystal-clear water. Although we are not trout-fishermen, we can't help ourselves – we are human beings, after all. After a few casts with a small spoon we both land a couple of trout of 2,2 and 2,3 kilos, which go directly on to the frying pan to be fried in a discreet mixture of curry powder and pepper. A lot can be said about boiled eel, but fried trout definitely gets a much higher culinary ranking. The night only yields a few runts, which firms up our decision to seek other waters.

In the morning as I wash the dishes, two pairs of penetrating eyes appear from under a submerged tree trunk. The eels slowly wind closer until they lie no more than a meter away malevolently eying my fingers, which are surreptitiously withdrawn from the water. For fear of scaring the fish I get Søren to hand me one of the rods. The largest of the fish appears to weigh about 6 kilos (around 14lb), and with shaky hands I manage to present a piece of lambs heart, freeline right in front of the fish. For several seconds the fish lie without stirring, as if their favourite hunting technique is to stare at their prey until it dies from fright.... Suddenly both the eels move the last 10 centimetres to the bait whilst mutually entwining. When finally one of the eels bites it is unfortunately the smaller one, which later turned out to weigh 4,2 kilos. In the hope that the larger fish would come back, we stay on at the campsite. When nothing has happened after half an hour, we decide to start on the long trek back. 3 days later - having burnt off a lot of calories - we arrive at the place we had parked our car and make our way towards Nelson, there to celebrate the Millennium in a suitable fashion.

West coast eels

A week of the new Millennium has passed by. Having made a few short trips to various indifferent waters, we realize that some changes have got to be made if we are going to succeed in catching the eel of our dreams. We have already spent 14 days on the South Island, and in spite of having caught lots of fish; we have not yet managed to catch a single eel in excess of 5 kilos

Having heard rumours of large eels from the wilds of the Fiord land, we decide to make a drastic move southwards. En route we pass the West coast, where we spend a fair amount of time checking various more or less convincing waters. After quite a bit of research combined with a certain dose of coincidence, we finally come across some waters that smell of big fish.

The sphagnum-man

One of these waters is a small stream that winds through fields of Fermium, the flax of New Zealand, and forests of tree ferns and Silver Beech. We are told by the local eel-fisherman, that the upper reaches of the stream have not been commercially fished within memory.... With high expectations we decide to make our way to the upper reaches. On the way, we have to cross a small tributary stream in our battered Civic Shuttle. Since the stream is too deep, we have to spend an hour or so filling the worst holes with the stones lying about. Finally we succeed in getting the car across in one piece, and after driving about on out-back dirt roads we eventually find an approach-road that leads towards our stream. At the end of the road is a ramshackle corrugated iron shed, which most of all resembles some corrugated iron sheets leaning onto piles of old rubbish.

To our great surprise, an old toothless greybeard emerges from the shed. Our first thought is that he is going for his shotgun.... It soon turns out however, that he is the friendliest person on earth. Since his wife died 20 years ago, he has lived here with a couple of sheep and made a living by collecting peat moss in the impenetrable bogs around the stream. Far out! When we have disclosed our intensions, he escorts us to the stream and takes his leave with a subtle smile.

The water in the stream is uncomfortably shallow and even in the deepest pools the depth is no more than 1m. There is now no more than an hour of daylight left, so we decide to stalk with freeline lambs hearts in the upstream pools, after which we will spend the night at an oblong pool a little way downstream; in this way to explore as much of the stream as possible. Already in the third pool I get a run, and after a fierce battle in an area no more than 2x2 meters, I am able to land our first eel exceeding 5 kilos. It is a magnificent fish with the broad neck of a bull. The night offers only tiddlers up to 4 kilos. In the light of dawn we go stalking for eel. Already in the first pool I hook and lose an eel of 6-7 kilos (16 lb), but in spite of this, we decide to spend the next night trying out another extremely promising water.

The Gold Pits

During the gold rush on the West coast of New Zealand in the 1860's, the going was awesome. Panning for gold was done in the traditional manner, but in some areas the digging was done the way one excavates gravel in a gravel-pit. The result was, that large areas of the West coast is perforated like a Swiss cheese with gold pits, into which ground water has gradually percolated. Many of these are covered with re-growth of impenetrable forest around the edges and have for years remained as forgotten pearls in the raw and untended West coast landscape. Many of the pits are emitting an aura of oblivion and eels thick as a man's thigh.

The next afternoon we are ready for action at the pits. To attract the eels, we had filled a rubby-dubby net with pieces of ox-liver oozing blood, and hung it where we earlier in the day had seen some quite nice fish. While the lure did its job, we went across to another pit merely 50 meters away. Søren gets a good run from a 4-kilo fish in a small bay, and in the heat of the struggle a lot of other eels are attracted. At nearly every cast the eels bite - frequently on the drop - and the hectic action culminates with my landing an unbelievably strong fish of 6,2 kilos (14lb+). We are all out of breath and blissfully happy over the many large fish. Had we at that time known what the night would bring, we would probably not have been so over-geared.

Jens stands beside a stream sign, during his first expedition to the north island with Tony Davies-Patrick in search of giant eels. The 'Die Hard' reflects our difficulties in finding them during the trip!

'Sometimes the hardships make it worthwhile'- Jens slogs through the dense forested slopes in search of wild waters.

At nightfall we make our preparations near the rubby-dubby trail. The bait is quartered lamb's hearts that are fished loose-line merely 3 meters from the edge of the pit. We use the classical touch-ledgering tactics – holding the line loosely by the fingers. No more than 30 seconds have elapsed before we get the first run and so it goes on. During the next four hours one large eel after the other takes the bait. Never before have I experienced so much but-cracking non-stop action. Since we are fishing right next to a snag, the fish are held hard and every time we hook one of the big ones, the rod thumps heavily - bending completely right down to the butt. Before the night is over we have caught at least 90 eels, of which about 50 exceed 5 kilos. A number of fish weighed in at 6-7 kilos. The two largest went to Søren and weighed no less than 7,7 (17lb 10oz) and 8,8 kilos (19lb 12oz!). It's a super feeling finally to wallow in large fish after having driven thousands of kilometres in our search for the ultimate eel-water.

The monster
The next 5-6 nights we live through the eel fishing of our lives with lots of fish weighing in at 5-7 kilos. As for me, the fishing culminates after about a week. For several weeks it has been virtually cloudless weather on the West coast, but this night in question a wild storm crosses the coastal area. The storm warning envisages a rainfall of up to 20 centimetres during the night.... It is a well-known phenomenon that a sudden drop in the barometric pressure can cause any fishing to run amuck, so I decide to go the whole hog. Søren drives with me to the pit, but after a couple of hours in pelting rain a steady runnel of rainwater starts to find it's way down the back of his neck. Since he is well satisfied with the fish he has caught so far, he decides to pack it in and go back to the

camp. At this time I am still completely dry, and since the storm has by no means spent itself, I decide to stay on,

The rain gets wilder and so does the fishing – Constantly I pull in eels of 4-7 kilos. After a couple of hours all hell breaks loose with thunder and lightning over the old gold pit. Suddenly there are no more strikes, and several minutes pass without as much as a nibble. Relieved by the let-up, I can't help speculating whether the fishing is ebbing out or possibly the opposite - that an outsize dominant eel has turned up and has chased the smaller ones out of the way.... At the same moment the line runs out, and I hammer into a fish that feels much larger and more violent than any eel I have caught until now. Knowing full well that the beast is lost if I do not hold it firm as a rock, I lean back on the rod and block the brake. The fish thrusts heavy as lead, but with a supreme effort I get its head to the surface. The fish slides reluctantly a tad closer to the net. When I switch on the headlamp on my forehead, a shudder runs down my back. The animal is much wider across the back than any other eel I have seen - about 18-20 cm in diameter across the neck. Since only parts of the fish are visible on the surface, it is difficult to judge its length, but about 140-150 centimetres is probably not far off the mark. The fish is by no means ready for the net and bashes back and forth just outside the frame of the net. The thunder is on the increase and some bolts of lightning are so close, that they illuminate both the water and the head of the fish, which throws heavily from side to side on the surface.

Heaven and earth is all one, and in spite of the clutch being nearly blocked - both mechanically and manually – the fish manages to make a heavy run in under a nearby floating island of weed and debris. In a miraculous way, I succeed in again pressing the head of the fish to the surface, but unfortunately only half a meter from the edge of the island, so the fish has approximately one meter of it's tail in amongst the roots... After a short while I can feel that the eel gets a firm hold of one of the roots, so I have no alternative but to play my last card. The rod gets loaded to the limit, and suddenly the wire breaks and the large Owner swivel whips like a bullet past my head. The battle is lost, and as I sit there in the pelting rain, it suddenly dawns on me the extent to which the storm has worsened. The eyeglasses are misting, all the gear is soaked, and thunderbolts constantly rip the sky. Completely broken, I pack up. To continue fishing and end up grilled by lightning would after all be more than the biggest eel is worth.

One of Those Nights...

The next couple of nights we get a fair amount of 5-7 kilo fish and decide to explore some new waters in order to find some bigger fish. One of these is an old gold pit in the middle of a deserted forest area. We have lent an inflatable rubber dinghy from our local friend and as night falls, we disappear out onto the water, which is bathed in moonlight. As it would be impossible to land a big eel from the dinghy, we spend some time finding a place where we can fish from the shore. The water is black as coal, and as we glide across the dead calm of the water we can't help fantasizing over the meter-long eels, perhaps swimming under the dinghy on the lookout for a solid meal, a human corpse for example.... Finally we find a piece of shore free of growth and make for it in order to land there. The bottom drops nearly vertically and the bank, which is quite steep, consists of large boulders. With some difficulty I manage to climb ashore. I am about to suggest to my friend Søren that he hands up the gear, when the boulders suddenly start to slide under me. One of my

'Paradise on earth' - a beautiful waterfall in the south NZ island wilderness.

feet is about to get caught under a falling boulder, when I luckily manage to catch hold of a half-rotten root. Shocked, I remain sitting on the root; until Søren can manoeuvre the dinghy close enough for me to be able to jump back into safety. Merely the thought of ending ones days squashed under a big boulder under 6 meters of water, whilst large hungry eels gradually eat your cold decomposing body was enough to provoke a methodical retreat.

The next day we make our last trip to our favourite pit, where I wound up with a PB eel of 8,4 kilos (almost 19lb). Actually, there are many waters worth exploring in the former gold-mining area, but since we also would like to see other parts of New Zealand, we decide to follow the original plan - to explore Fiord land and the central parts of Otago. During the following two weeks we are able to enjoy some of the most marvellous scenery of nature on the island – fiords, lakes, mist-forests and snow clad mountains. We also catch eels, but far from the quantities we caught in the gold-area. The last place we manage to test is a promising bay in a large lake. A couple of night's fishing yields quite a fair number of eels, but relatively few exceed the 6-kilo mark. The top-fish – a pair of massive fish of 8,3 and 8,5 kilos – go to Søren. Unfortunately, the days of fishing passed all too fast.... Although it took a lot of hard work to find the right waters, we can hardly complain about the results – at least 100 eels over 5 kilo, have made it an unforgettable and action packed fishing adventure of a lifetime.

Myths and facts

For the indigenous people of New Zealand – the Maoris – the large eels have for more than a thousand years been of great importance, nutritionally as well as in their mythology. Since the tasty fish in many areas was the primary source of food, the fishing rights have frequently been the cause of tribal wars.

According to Maori-legend, the eels hail from the celestial waters – Puna-kaurariki – and are the progeny of the rain –Te Ihorangi. As the first fish on earth, the eels were regarded as the forefathers of all other fish. When some eel-clans left the fresh waters to convert into saltwater fish, the clan Tuna was ordered to remain in the revolting waters of the swamps for the purpose of providing food for man.... Divine creatures demand respect – and to have assured success when fishing for eel, the Maoris sang the following homage to the elongated beings:

Hei kai mau te tangata
Makutu mau, mahara mai
Kei reira to hara
Harahara aitua, harahara a tai
I pakia ai koe, i rahua ai koe
Niniko, koi tara, kia u o niho
Niniko koi tara koe
Kei te tai temu, kei te tai pari kei Rangiriri
Hau kumea, hau toia
Nau ka anga atu, anga atu
Nau ka anga mai, anga mai

Check it out, if the fishing starts to drop off a bit....

Different species of eel

In New Zealand there were originally two different species of eel, short finned eel (Anguilla australis), which as the scientific name indicates also lives in Australia, and the long finned eel (Anguilla dieffenbachii), which is exclusively to be found in New Zealand. The former species are in New Zealand primarily to be found in the low country, and is dominant in many waters on the North Island. The average size is 0,5-1 kilo and absolute maximal weight is 7 - 9 kilos. The long finned eel attains a considerably larger size and is distinguished from it's smaller cousin in that the dorsal part of the tailfin continues much further up the length of the back of the fish. This species is dominant on the South Island and in the water systems in the higher altitudes. Although there have been dubious rumours of fish of more than 40 kilos, the largest well-documented fish caught by commercial fishermen weighed in at 20 kilos. The largest fish caught by sports-fishers, which I have heard about, are said to have weighed 12-14 kilos. The accompanying photos suggested, however, that the master of the scales had a blurred view – if you subtract 50 - 75 %, the weight sounds more realistic. There is no doubt however that fish up to 10-12 kilo have been caught on sports fishing gear.

Many years of intensive commercial fishing has left it's mark on the stock of large long finned eels.

In by far the most waters the average fish weighs 1-3 kilos. If you put in some effort you may, nevertheless, find waters where fish of 5-6 kilos are reasonably common. Fish of the order of 10-15 kilos do exist, but you would have to arm yourself with extraordinary patience, you may have to land hundreds of thousands of smaller fish before you catch one. Luckily it was decreed 3 years ago, that all eels caught commercially on the South Island and weighing in excess of 4 kilos must be released. That the protection came in the nick of time is amply corroborated by the 1999-logbook of a local commercial eel-fisherman: Out of 5 tons of eels caught, only 12 individuals weighed more than 4 kilos! The same year 250 tons of eel were delivered to a local fish processing plant – only one eel weighed more than 10 kilos, and this one tipped the scales at 13,5 kilos.... The monsters

still exist, but for sure you have to work hard to get at them. Since the decree does not pertain to the North Island, soon the plight of the stocks there will be a sad one - Many of the large eels take 60-80 years to attain a weight of 8-10 kilos, according to the biologists. The maximal age is said to be more than 100 years.

The sexually mature long-fins at the age of 23-30 years head for salt water to migrate to spawning areas that are thought to be situated around the Samoa Islands in the Pacific Ocean. At this time they typically weigh 4-5 kilos. Fish that exceed this weight often are therefore old females that are sterile, or are unable to leave their water on account of too steep or shallow an exit.

During the last 10 years the Australian species - mottled long fin eel (Anguilla reinhardti) has migrated to a few places on the North Island. Under subtropical conditions in its land of origin, Australia, this species is supposed to reach a weight of up to 45 kilos...!

Jens with another huge New Zealand river eel.

Tips for catching long-finned eels:

If you are seriously considering a bid for the long-finned eels of New Zealand, you will be in trouble without a car. Used cars in OK condition can be purchased from other travellers at most of the larger back-packer hostels in Auckland and Christchurch. With a couple of day's patience it is an easy matter to pick up a well-functioning car for 400-800 US-dollars. The change of ownership is easily arranged at any post-office, and the car can as a rule, if it hasn't been dented much more than it was or covered in eel-slime, be sold for nearly the same amount you paid for it.

The best gear for eels in the 3-10 kilo-class is a full-action 12ft 2-3lbs TC carp-rod, or the 3 piece, 13ft Globetrotter Supreme travel rod used by Tony. With a solid fixed-spool reel such as the Shimano Baitrunner 6500, you are geared for the worst imaginable situation. If there are not too many large fish, you can manage okay with a smaller reel without a metal spool, for example, the Shimano Baitrunner 6010 or 8010. As the fish frequently stand close to a snag, a 0,50-0,60 main line of elastic nylon – such as Big Game or Gold Label - is clearly preferable. If there are many rocks it may be necessary with a snag-leader of 80 lbs Spiderwire. The fish frequently swim close to the margins and here you will get the best results fishing loose-line. The teeth of the eels are much like those of catfish and are not nearly as sharp as those of a pike. Nevertheless, it is necessary to use wire, in order to avoid the trace breaking when the fish starts to twist round itself. If you are going for the somewhat larger fish, you will find, that Drennan's 28 lbs Green Wire seems to be made for the purpose. If the wire is much more rigid, it will affect the rate of bites. The best hooks are, as mentioned elsewhere in this text, Circle Hooks, f.ex. Gamakatzu Octopus Circle Hooks in sizes 4/0-6/0.

Bait and baiting

The hook is best baited with halves or quarters of lamb's hearts, whole hearts of chicken or other bloody pieces of meat. Pieces of mackerel are another super bait. Kidney and liver of ox and lamb attract the fish allright, but are not retained well on the hook. For the same reason the latter are best suited for creating a scent trail – either cut into small pieces then placed in a swimfeeder or in a rubby-dubby net, which is tossed out in the swim. Another hyper-effective way of enticing the fish is by pouring blood directly into the water. However, blood may be difficult to come by and a good alternative is to put a half kilo ground meat of ox into a container with half a litre of water + flavour. Shake well and pour the tempting soup into the water. If there are eels around they are guaranteed to come. If there is no butcher in the area, you can collect road-kills en route. Most road-kills are possums. Fresh road-kills - which are the best – are most easily found night and morning, before the carcasses dry out in the sun. The carcass is tied to a suitable stone and thrown into the water at the feeding site. If you remember to pierce the carcass thoroughly, a tempting scent will soon ooze into the water.

Landing and sacking

A large catfish landing net of the type produced by The Catfish Conservation Group (UK) is absolutely ideal if you are fishing for big fish. With such a net you have a good chance of landing a monster-eel of 10-15 kilos. Even for 7-9 kilo fish, it is with this type of net considerably easier to handle the eels. The advantages are self-evident, in that there is ample space when the beast is being unhooked. The eels can be most conveniently kept in a quite ordinary large carp sack. If the fish is on the wild side, it may help the proceedings to take the sack up 10 minutes before taking your photos. If it is too lively it may be difficult to hold in photogenic poses...

Waters and times of day

Large eels can be found in all types of water from tiny drainage ditches to large lakes and rivers. Since commercial fishing is the main reason for the large fish having been fished out, the trick is to find waters that haven't been fished commercially for many years - which will typically be areas with extremely poor conditions of access. Other obvious waters for big fish are isolated small lakes – for example: old gold pits, where the eels will have difficulties migrating once they have reached maturity. The more isolated, the better. It is worth your while keeping your ears cocked, should you happen to come across local commercial eel-fishermen. - Frequently they will be able to give you a lot of valuable hints on which waters could be expected to yield large eels.

The fishing is clearly the best during evening - night - morning. As with so many other forms of eel fishing I find the period leading up to a full moon the worst period to go for. Overcast nights or the time before the moon rises is the best bid for something approaching acceptable conditions, if you have to fish during this period.

'*Toitu he Kainga, whatunga rongaro he tangata*' – The land and the water will remain long after the people have vanished from the earth – *old Maori proverb.*

WILD GEMS

I have always admired, and often dreamed of fishing for, a wild version of the vibrant coloured Koi carp, and often lusted to wander the wild and rugged contours of New Zealand – so when both these wishes were offered in one travel package, I packed my bags and jumped on a plane!

The 'Koi' version of the common carp is more often connected with decorative garden ponds, or as expensive objects of Japanese desire – but in New Zealand, the tables are turned. This amazingly vibrant coloured fish has been introduced to wild rivers of the North Island, and it has now become truly established in the eco-system. My travels across that sparsely populated and beautiful part of the world filled my senses with joy – but none more so than when I fished for the amazing 'Wild Gems'.

The wildlife in New Zealand and Australia is unique in its variety. Tony photographed this mother climbing a tree, with its young clinging to her back, at night during a carpfishing session.

The incredible beauty to be found in wilderness areas of the North Island.

A superb wild Koi carp from the Waikato River in New Zealand, caught on long-trotting a float along the margins, with a chunk of banana for hookbait!

Tony caught these superb Waikato River Koi carp on pop-up maize and short bolt rig. The carp were feeding so close to the margins, that Tony did not cast out the rig, but instead, quietly lowered it into position by hand! Koi carp have now spread throughout the river & lake systems of the North Island of New Zealand. They come in a variety of colours, including orange, orange with black flecks, white with black flecks, and pure white.

by Jens Bursell

KASAKHSTAN

ADVENTURE

I am standing up to my waist in the freezing margins of the Ural River, near the border area between Kazakhstan and Russia. Nearly two weeks with unusually cold and stormy weather, has meant a delay in the spawning run of Nase (Chondrostoma nasus). This small, silver herring-like fish is the preferred prey of another species of fish travelling upriver to spawn – the massive Beluga Sturgeon. Out of the few Belugas that were landed during the past seven days, most were caught in the main reaches, no more than 5 -10 meters from land. If you try to fish any further out, the current is so strong that even with a heavy 2-300 gram flat lead, you have great difficulty holding bottom.

In spite of energetic attempts to catch bait by dragging a landing net along the border of the rushes, we have now laboured for more than half an hour to catch only a single bream. Even though the wind has begun to subside, it is still so cold that we can see our own breath as clouds of vapour in the cold, afternoon air - it does not bode well for the fishing during the next few days. Following futile efforts along the edges of the rushes in the windy main reaches of the Ural River; we finally succeed in landing enough bait for our next quest in search of giants.

After 10 minutes sailing we find a good place 30 meters downstream from the mouth of a minor side-channel. In order to create maximum attraction, half a bream is thoroughly cut up, and then mounted on a size 12/0 single hook. I make a short cast near the margins and see a splash as the 200-gram sliding flat-inline lead drags the bait to the river bottom. I can now imagine the strong currents spreading an enticing scent-cone of blood and odours through the water.

On account of the difficult conditions I have only succeeded in landing a single sturgeon of 120 kilos during the course of the last few days, and the prospect of another blank is not really inspiring. Just as I sit and contemplate, watching the tip of my rod bobbing in time with the river's flow, a 15 centimeter beluga-nose appears above the surface only 10 meters downstream from the boat. The water is so murky; that the only thing I see is the tip of the nose, which most of all reminds me of a semi-thawed icicle. Unbelievable, that behind such a small snowman's nose lurks a sturgeon of more than 100 kilos. In seconds the dejection is transformed into intense excitement, since already at this point the fish must have caught the scent from my thoroughly pierced bream a mere 3 meters upstream.

Jens Bursell with a wonderful Beluga Sturgeon estimated to weigh over 150kg (330lbs).

The next minute feels like an eternity. As the seconds slowly tick past, I constantly fiddle with the adjustment of my fighting belt, and repeatedly check that the drag lever is set properly on the multiplier. Finally it happens. A few gentle taps on the tip of the rod is a signal that the fish has taken the bait. There is a short pause, before the line begins to run evenly from the disengaged Ambassadeur 9000. After a solid series of strikes the hook is firmly set, causing the fish to rocket to the surface like a Russian missile. The extreme force as the giant sturgeon explodes in a sheet of spray, is transmitted mercilessly through the inelastic Spiderwire. In an attempt to stop the fish before it succeeds in accelerating, I lean fully back on the rod and place my thumb on the already fully tightened drag; but it is to no avail. As if made of rubber, the rod bends completely over, right through to the last reserves of the butt cap. Suddenly the fish starts to run, and makes the reel spin so fast that my thumb gets thoroughly scorched.

When 100 meters has run off the reel, I consider giving a sign to my boatman, Ruslan, to free the boat from the rushes; but at the same moment the fish slows down, stops and retraces its course.

Suddenly the situation is reversed, and I must race the line back on the spool in order to keep in contact with the fish. The mouth of the Beluga is relatively hard, and it does not take much slack on a spun line before there is the risk that the hook loses its grip. Not until the fish is nearly level with the boat does it stop, but however much force I apply to the rod; it is impossible to raise it from the bottom. For nearly 10 minutes the fish moves slowly back and forth along the bottom without budging as much as a centimetre upwards.

Finally, with a single pumping of the rod, I succeed in winding about 1 meter of line onto the spool; but in the same moment the fish turns in a violent cauldron of swirls and vortices, then ploughs leadenly downstream. The line begins to rise quickly towards the surface, until the fish flaps in a forceful horizontal jump above the river, and at the same time the bait gets thrown out of the fishes mouth in a cascade of water. Luckily, the hook is solidly planted in the lower lip of the fish, and after another quarter of a hour's tug-of-war, the mighty back of the fish appears on the surface next to the boat.

The first three times Ruslan gets a hold of the fish, he ends up losing his grip, which with violent splashes frees itself from his experienced hands. Finally, however, he succeeds in threading a stringer through the gill-cover and out through the mouth. The fish is anchored safely to the side of the boat, and at approximately 150 kilos, it is my largest freshwater fish ever. It is a fantastic feeling having finally caught a decent Beluga. To make certain that we get a good photo, we sail the fish to the edge of the rushes, pull it on land, and take some photos with tripod and automatic release. A few minutes later, the fish lies ready to be set free, and with a thrash of its large tail, it disappears in the murky brown water.

When we get back to our original anchorage place, no more than 5 minutes elapse before the next beluga strikes, and after a good heavy fight I can land a fine beluga of about 110 kilos. For several hours I nourish a hope that the beluga run is getting going, but as it happens, there is not a single run all the rest of the day.

The laguna - a pike paradise

On the western bank of the main arm of the river, there are a couple of subsidiary canals connecting to a gigantic freshwater luguna that stretches along the edge of the Caspian Sea. The area is choc-a-bloc with hungry and willing pike, and the next day we decide to take two boats and try our luck with this exiting opportunity.

I share a boat with the German Dietmar Rittscher; in the other boat are two Austrian predator specialists, Kurt Macacheck and Josef Gebhart. During the course of the day we experience hectic pike fishing in amongst small islands of rushes. Contrary to the water in the main river and the canals, the water here is crystal clear, and with Polaroid glasses you can spot pike all over the place. At one point the boat is afloat in about 1 meter of water and we have about 10 pike in sight - the largest of about 8 kilos. The pike strike as if possessed - on spinners, spoons and rubber fish alike. The fishing is fit to cause you heart failure, for in nearly every throw you can see pike follow the spoon, and observe their reactions to various forms of spin-stop and in-spinning variations. Frequently the strike occurs when you spin in extra fast. The feeling when you see a good pike accelerate violently and clamp its jaws solidly together over the spoon, followed by the angry pulls on the rod, is enough to make even an incarnate carp-fan into a predator-freak. The largest fish in this area falls to Dietmar's lure – a wobbled plug, but a couple of hours later, Kurt and Josef land a fish of about 10 kilos. At one time Josef's spoon gets snagged on the bottom, and while the boatman is trying to wrest the lure free, a pike of about 5 kilos attempts to snatch the spoon - quite wild, no less! If you are for pike spinning, this area will make your wildest dreams come alive. Catches of 30-50 pike after a couple of hours punting and spinning is quite normal....

The Laguna is a true jungle of rushes, flats and canals - and after a short while I have lost my orientation completely. All islands and clumps of rushes look exactly alike, but luckily the boatmen have a sixth sense, which enables them without compass or GPS, in an unexplained manner to unerringly find their way through 30 kilometres of featureless rush forests- an amazing experience.

New swims

On the last day the fishing loosens up a bit and on a new site we experience an, in the circumstances, action-filled morning. The game opens with Dietmar landing a fine fish of approximately 120 kilos, whereupon I land two fish of approximately 90 and 100 kilos respectively, then foul hook another fish of about 120 kilos. Annoyed with having wasted valuable time on a foul hooked fish, I loose no time in getting my line out again. The fish are still around, and after a quarter of an hour, the line runs off the reel with a speed that leaves no doubt about the authenticity of the bite.

As I hook the fish, I can feel that it is a good one, and after a violent run the Beluga comes to the surface and throws its broadside above the waves. Line races off the reel, and soon after we let go of the mooring, so that we can follow the fish. This beast is a bit bigger than my previous largest, so it is with sweat on my brow, and after some hard work, that I finally manage to press the fish closer to the boat.

About 15 minutes later, a broad neck and an enormous mouth appears on the surface, just one meter from the boat. The fish has been hooked at the corner of the mouth, but the lead has wrapped itself around the pectoral fins, so it proves very difficult to pull the big mouth up to the surface. Two or three times the boatman manages to get a grip on the lower lip, but each time the fish shakes loose and makes a short run. The fish appears to weigh in the neighbourhood of 170-180 kilos.

The last time the fish comes up, it makes an unstoppable run at an angle under the boat, and so the tip of the rod is about to be crushed over the gunwale. Luckily, in spite of the violent pressure on

This photo (taken by Tony) of Jens with a Great White Sturgeon from the Columbia river in USA, shows the difference in colouration,

flank markings and broad nose when compared to the Beluga.

the rod, I manage to hold the tip clear. After another quarter of a hour's heavy fight the line suddenly goes slack. I reel in like mad in order to obtain contact, but it soon becomes evident, that the hook has lost its hold on the fish. The lead has been broken off at the swivel, probably by the pectoral fin.

During the afternoon, most of the boats try their luck a few kilometres from the mouth of the Ural, where it spills into the Caspian Sea; but only a single fish, which goes for the bait of Josef, is landed. Last year at the same time he caught no less than 200 Beluga in a mere two weeks of fishing; but because of the weather conditions this year he has been confined to this one fish - the result of 6 days of intensive fishing. In May of last year the record for a weeks fishing was beaten by Thomis Seewitz with an unbelievable 156 fish in one week, so when the conditions are optimal you can fairly walk on the water and roll around in big fish. A Hungarian landed the largest fish caught by rod in the Ural 2 years ago. The beast measured 3,4 meters, equivalent to a weight around 350-400 kilos. Even this fish is a dwarf compared to the maximum weight of the species - off the delta of the Volga, commercial fishermen a few years back, caught a photographically documented fish of 1500 kilos. I have seen a copy of the photo in a Russian newspaper, and the monster is about the size of a fully-grown cow!

Unfortunately, our week fell in the wrong place in the calendar - with the result that the major part of the 20 participants on the trip only landed 0-2 fish during the 6 days. A few landed 5-6 fish, and the top rod managed 7 fish. Under normal weather conditions, the average catch would be 3-5 fish per man each day. We might of course have hoped for more action, but it has, in spite of the difficult conditions, been a fantastically exciting week.

As we return from the Caspian Sea, the outermost canals lie washed in a glowing golden afternoon sun, and in the East, raises a wall of heavy black storm clouds. As I get ready for my last cast, a flock of beautiful Sooty Terns pass the boat in a gracious undulating flight. I have only a single wishy-washy piece of bait left, but what does that matter? The mere sight of these expanses of rushes and the landing of just one single Beluga is ample reward for the long journey to Kazakstan. Hopefully it is not the last time that I pit myself against this mysterious, primeval fish.

Beluga fishing can exclusively be arranged through "Husky Tours", which is a very professional outfit based in Germany. The fishing is done from small boats with two fishermen and a guide to each boat. A large modern houseboat, situated a mere 10 minutes sailing from the best fishing spots, is used as a base for the fishing. Service and food is tip-top. Accommodation is in small cabins, and there are very good bathing facilities with hot water. The best fishing normally occurs during the month of May.

Fishing over the sandbank at Lake Austin on the Colorado River system.

LONE STAR CARP

In March 2003, I flew across the mighty expanses of the Atlantic Ocean to take part in the CAG Carp Championships held at Town Lake in Austin, Texas USA. Carp matches or championships have never been at the forefront of my agenda, even though I actually won the USA Carp Tournament top prize of $10,000 during my previous expedition! That particular competition was special in that it allowed the competitors to 'roam' in search of big fish across a massive area of lakes and rivers covering thousands of square miles. This CAG event however was like most other 'matches' and was a pre-pegged day-only competition over Friday and Saturday. I had decided to enter the event more for the social side of things as it allowed me to meet old friends and to hopefully make new ones. The main goal of this trip was to begin soon after the CAG competition, and I'd already made plans to spend the remaining two weeks searching for carp and buffalo carp on the Colorado River system. It should be noted that this river winds through Texas and is not the main Colorado River of Grand Canyon fame. Many of my expeditions in search of carp in new locations are spent in my own company, but this time I was to be joined by Dean Gay from UK, and two German friends – Andreas "Phippo" Philip and Stuart "Middy" Sharpe.

With only two short weeks at our disposal, it was not possible to travel and search the complete river from mountain to sea, so we decided to search upstream of Austin in the area known as the 'Hill Country'. Like its bigger brother in Arizona, the Texas Colorado is dammed to form many reservoirs throughout its journey towards the sea. In the section we had chosen to explore, there were seven main reservoirs: Lake Buchanan, Inks Lake, Lake L.B. Johnson, Lake Marble Falls, Lake Travis and Lake Austin.

The following are extracts from my notes on a micro cassette recorder.

Friday 28th March 2003

At the gathering of sleepy-eyed anglers inside the cosy interior of the hotel lobby, I manage to extract an ominous No.1 peg out of the hat held out by CAG competition organiser, Dave Moore. Dean and I drive through the gloom of dawn to find our chosen swim on the map. Within minutes of tackling up, I notice a carp crash out, cast a popped-up maize rig to it, have an instant blinding run, weigh and return the 17lb common, then remain bite-less for the rest of the day. Not a single ripple from a single carp, except for a biting icy cold wind cutting at our fleece jackets. Middy, who is sitting beside team Germany partner Phippo, manages to land a 26lb common, but sadly also loses a big fish halfway through the day.

Day two finally arrives and Phippo strangely manages to pull No.1 peg again out of the hat this morning! Dean manages to pull No.12 out of the hat, and our first sighting of this non-descript peg does not warm our souls against the freezing winds. At around 09:30 I have a slow run on the long distance rod rigged with a large 28mm shrimp-meal boilie. The rod keels over and it feels that I am latched onto a competition-winning big carp. Following a long and powerful fight, the 'beast' is in the deep margins sending up boiling vortexes and masses of swirling mud with fizzing bubbles. Suddenly I catch sight of a large brown moving object and I at first think that it may be a big catfish...but it turns out to be a huge Snapping turtle with a massive shell the size of a round table top!

The wind is again biting cold and by 11.00 (only a few hours into the contest) both Dean and I decide to pack up. Our first port of call is to unload the equipment at the hotel, drown in glorious

hot showers, and then head for a shopping spree on the outskirts of town. Now warmed up and relaxed, although with lighter wallets, we decide to drive through town and visit Phippo and Middy's peg beneath the noisy railway bridge. They too are not enjoying themselves, as they fight to remain warm on this bite-less day. It takes just a few seconds for both of them to decide to stop fishing. All four of us quickly help pack away the gear and then drive direct to Hooters restaurant for a hot meal, cool beers and a bit of eyeball excitement from the half-naked waitresses!

To fly halfway around the Globe just to sit beneath a car-infested dual carriageway, facing skyscrapers and stinking garbage was not our intention!

Town Lake is as its name implies, slap bang in the centre of town - or more exact, in the centre of a bustling city - with its added baggage of noise and pollution. In all honesty, Town Lake (at 1,830 acres, the smallest of the lakes we will fish) does probably offer the best chances of catching big carp in the short time we have available. It holds the highest number of 30lb+ carp per acre of any body of water in Texas, and a fair few 40lb+ specimens. There is no 'night fishing' allowed on Town Lake (although I'm sure this could be done in some 'quiet' areas), but the main downfall for this lake is its location. We discuss the matter and all quickly agree that we do not want to spend another moment fishing in the centre of town!

We all decide to move on to Lake Austin, which is a far more beautiful location than Town Lake. None of us have particularly enjoyed fishing during the competition, although we did enjoy meeting other carp anglers from around the world.

Sunday March 30th

Once we leave the cement madness of Austin – a town that sprawls for many miles in each direction – the landscape begins to change. I gently touch the power steering on the big 4WD vehicle and we smoothly exit Ranch Road and drive up the steep City Park Road that climbs over the lovely Grey Mountains. The foliage either side of us becomes more green and dense as the road winds like a snake through the rolling hills, before finally descending sharply into the Colorado valley. Soon we are at the main entrance to Emma Long Metropolitan Park. The park warden allows just myself to view the park campsite areas, while the others wait at the entrance in their two vehicles. My first view of the boat-ramp area looks promising, but a large open section of meadow with short-cut grass sweeping gently onto a sandy beach looks a superb place to fish. I quickly scout the whole river section within the large park, including the night-camping zone where most previous carp anglers have fished at the northern end, but nothing takes my fancy. I've already made my mind up – I want to fish the 'Beach'.

Back at the park entrance, I relay my thoughts to the warden, who then suddenly points at the red marked areas of the map declaring that the Beach area is 'Day-only' and strictly no camping. I do a little smooth talking, and within a few minutes I'm back with the lads relaying our plan of action. The Park warden has been kind enough to offer us special permission to camp at the Beach! Not only that, but I manage to clinch an extremely cheap deal for us all.

All the lads are happy with my choice of location, and following a quick pulling of long & short straws to pick our swims, we unload the vehicles and begin to tackle up and set up the tents. Middy inflates his mini one-man dinghy while I inflate the 3-man dinghy recently bought by Dean at a local sports equipment store.

16:00

I've just caught and returned a 16lb common carp. It picked up a popped-up maize & Tigernut rig cast 140 meters from shore in 25ft deep water along the original riverbed.

Dean and I are fishing from the central areas of the beach, with Middy to my left, and Phippo to Dean's right. With my 13ft Globetrotter rods matched with Big Pit Shimano Baitrunner LC reels spooled to the rim with 50lb PowerPro braided line, I'm able to thump two baits out to the maximum distances where the old riverbed skirts the far cliff face. Two other baits are cast out to another marker set about two thirds of the way across the lake. My fourth hookbait is cast about 30 meters out at the very edge of the marginal shelf.

The sandy beach extends from the shallow margins and slopes very gradually into knee-deep water, rises in a hump to ankle deep, before descending gradually to chest-deep water. This sandbank abruptly stops at about 25 meters out in a line horizontal with the shoreline. At the very edge of the sandbank, the depth drops very sharply to 14ft deep. Hidden from view, but not far beyond this drop-off is a long series of dense and extremely strong-stranded weed growth.

Dean places most of his baits on a marker halfway across the lake, while both the German lads place baits in an arc from margins to halfway across. We've all gone out to our markers and baited up heavily with pre-soaked maize and boilies. If any big shoals of carp move past, they are bound to intercept our baits.

One major difference with this lake when compared to Town Lake is the boat traffic. Town Lake has no motor-powered boats, but there are no such restrictions at Austin Lake. From mid-afternoon until sunset, high-powered speedboats, bass boats, jet skis and speedboats dragging water skiers, plough a furrow through the narrow channel of water in front of us.

Eventually, the constant slap of rolling waves caused from the onslaught of waterborne traffic slowly ebbs away to leave the valley in tranquil calm - Time to breathe in the true atmosphere and beauty of this place. The water is actually almost gin-clear, with the far bank consisting of a steep rocky cliff face overgrown with trees and green foliage. Hawks and buzzards sweep through the green canopy, herons stalk the far shoreline, and the deep blue sky is dotted with vultures spiralling on thermal currents. It is truly a beautiful section of the lake to fish and now that the boats are gone, we enter an almost forgotten timeframe.

I can scent the lovely aroma of prime steaks and hamburgers cooking on the grill tended by Phippo, and as soon as he calls over that all is ready, we all gather around the feast. While we sit staring at our rodpods in the fading light, happily munching on Texan meat, and listening to the hoot of owl and shrill of nightingale song, Phippo mentions that this section of the lake reminds him of the wilder sections of the River lot in France. Now he mentions it, I'm inclined to agree. We are situated

This photo of Tony holding a superb 37lb 12oz Black Buffalo carp and Phippo holding a gorgeous golden common carp shows the marked differences in colouration of each species.

on a long curving bend in the lake where it narrows and enters a natural gorge cut by the old Colorado River. It is the awesome backdrop of green foliage clinging to steep cliffs that remind us of that lovely corner of central France.

The extremely shallow sandbank in front of us will mean that we have to wade out to land each fish, but at least this same obstacle can prevent the boats and skiers from coming too close into shore and ripping our rods off their rests. The deep incline at the edges of the sandbank also means that our braided lines remain fairly deep, and so the initial fears that the lines cast at long-distance will be picked up by propellers are unfounded.

The action following nightfall is hectic. I manage to catch a number of carp both on maize and Nash boilies. I also hook a good fish on a single Eurobait 28mm shrimp-meal boile, but lose it in the weedbeds (these particular flavoured boilies tend to expand in water, so it was probably in excess of 30mm in size by the time the take came). A recast of the same bait results in a 25lb+common which I only manage to land with the aid of the dinghy. The weeds are becoming a major problem, especially for Middy and Phippo, because neither has spooled up with braid. Unlike the PowerPro, which tends to give more direct contact and cuts through the weed, the nylon lines either allow the fish to bury their heads inside the weed until they become bogged down, or the lines snap under mounting pressure. Apart from the very odd fish that need the help of the dinghy, I am able to keep most of the carp moving with heavy and constant pressure on my rods. The two Germans are having nightmares though, and they seem to spend more time in the dinghy than on their bedchairs! The areas in front of Dean are relatively weed-free and he manages to land a number of doubles topped by a 21lb 8oz fish. Phippo's total so far is: first 8kg, second one lost in weed, and a third at 10.5kg (which needs the help of the dinghy to extract from the weed). Darkness brings on a steady stream of takes from all the rods, but mainly from baits cast at around 100 meters.

Dawn eventually breaks in the valley, sending sparks of warm sunshine to chase away the freezing temperatures. Jack Frost visited us last night and all our tents and gear are covered in a sprinkling of white icy dust. In the two hours after dawn, I get four more blinding takes, three from carp, with the largest a superb, streamlined torpedo weighing 29lb 12oz. The most productive method seems to be a double 20mm Nash Maple flavoured bottom boilie hookbait with around 5-8 extra boilies in a Terry Eustace PVA bag.

The third take of the morning turns out to be something very special. Once again the maple-flavoured boilies are sucked in, as the 5.oz flat Korda lead helps the large SS. Penatrator No.2 hook to prick a lip, causing the PowerPro braid to tighten against the rod tip. Three single Delkim bleeps shake me from sleep, and by the time the braid 'pings' clear of the line clip I am already hovering over the rod. The big spool almost bounces as a second jerk forces the big metal spool to suddenly begin spinning widely. I lift the rod sharply at the blue sky, halting the offending noise of the Delkim, but not the onward rush of the fish, for it jets off like a rocket across river.

The first mad rush of the fish is soon stopped, and for the next few minutes it moves very slowly upriver. I lean back on the rod and begin to feel that wonderful, slow and heavy progress that tells me that this is a big fish. My legs automatically carry me into the water until I am waist deep. I am aware of the danger of the deepwater weed beds hidden beneath 15ft of water, but my memory of where they are growing (learnt from previous carp heading straight for them!) helps me steer it clear of danger. Soon a big fish surfaces in front of me and the high first ray of a big dorsal fin slicing through the water makes my heart leap – for this indicates not a common carp, but a prized Buffalo carp! I drag the big 52-inch landing net into position at the very edges of the submerged sandbank, but the fight is not over, for the carp suddenly wakes up. With awesome power, the fish wrenches the rod tip into the water and many meters of line scream off the spool. Again and again the fish finds strength to go on short but explosive runs. Eventually a big mound of bronze rolls into the landing net. I wade happily back to shore with my prize, lower it onto the green padded mat, and then unfurl the mesh. What a fabulous fish! It is my very first Buffalo carp, and at a weight of 37lb 12oz, although lighter than its deep and broad frame would indicate, it is an extremely welcome sight. I slip the broad-backed fish inside a big zip sack (noting that orange boilie particles and mussel shell fragments are oozing from its vent) and position it in deep water while we organise the photo gear.

I can't believe that we have experienced such a sharp frost in the heart of sultry Texas! But there is no need to worry, because before long a white ball of fire is beating down from a cloudless blue sky, forcing us to shed our layers of thermal clothing and don shorts and T-shirts, and then rub on the sun-cream.

I noticed last night that the water level fluctuated quite a lot (due to opening the dam gates or distant rains filling tributaries), and now at this moment it is on the rise, causing my marker floats to dip beneath the surface. A strong breeze begins to blow diagonally down the valley and soon the ripples and undertow cause all our marker floats to disappear. In the end I decide to dispense with the need for markers, due to them either being moved by waves from daily boat traffic, or the varying water levels – but this is not a great problem, for by now I know exactly where to cast to by remembering prominent bushes on the far bank. Even though I can judge the places to cast my hookbaits, they will never be quite as accurate as actually casting towards a marker float, so to compensate for this, when rowing out in the dinghy I've began to widen my baiting area by scattering the freebies in a larger arc.

Some of the carp caught seem to be holding some pre-spawn, but the Buffalo carp had a slightly extended and red anal cavity. The Buffalo carp is actually a member of the American Suckerfish family, which tend to spawn well before Cyprinus carpio, and my specimen may have recently spawned.

I've only caught one carp on popped-up maize cast long distance to the old riverbed, and one on double boilie 'snowman style' at the edge of the sandbank shelf at 14ft depth. All other carp have come from the central channel at 90-110 meters ranges. I've had a few doubles, with the majority exceeding 20lb, and only one under 10lb. Middy has caught four twenties, but he's also landed a lot more smaller fish, and this is mainly because he's been using maize hookbaits and baiting the marginal shelf very heavily with particle mix. Phippo has managed around 4-5 twenties up to 27lb, and Dean landed a few twenties amongst a lot of doubles.

The carp have been periodically crashing out all night, and now even at midday they are still topping, although not quite so regularly. The strong wind is keeping down temperatures, although it gets very warm when you sit out of the wind. Martin has just arrived, saying he spent some hours fishing a swim at the northern end of Emma Long Park, catching a couple of carp. He drops off an empty rod tube (he bought two of my Globetrotter Supreme rods a few years back, and is buying

It is stunning carp like this powerful Colorado River specimen, which makes Texas such a great destination for pioneering new waters.

two more) so that I can send the rods to his California home before I fly back to UK. We have a short chat, and then Martin drives off for a look at the big Lake Travis during his long journey homebound.

Dusk once again descends on the river, and the tasty aromas drifting up from the barbeque are attracting a number of black vultures to swoop down from the skies to hopefully join in our feast. Dean, Phippo, Middy and I are all too hungry to share our succulent meat, so the vultures just perch in the trees around us, hunchbacked and sulking, like a comical scene from Jungle Book.

18:30 Tuesday 2nd April

The fishing itself has been very good up to now, and I've landed fifteen 20lb+ carp, including a glorious-looking 31lb 12oz common. Middy has caught at least five twenties, but he's also lost some nice fish in the emerging weed beds. Phippo has not caught so many fish, although he's managed at least four exceeding 20lb up to 27lb+.

It has been another windy day, although clouds are now scudding across the sky – our first since we arrived. Middy, Phippo and myself have just recently enjoyed yet another tasty grilled meal. Earlier today we had a bit of an upset when Dean suddenly announced that he intended flying home. I must admit that the news shocked me, but I could understand a little better when he gave some of his reasons - problems developing with his company business at home that needed him 'in person' to properly sought out, and this combined with the fact that his wife was expecting their second child. I drove him to the Austin International airport and waved him a very sad goodbye. Driving back again, alone towards the Colorado River, brought a tight knot to my stomach as my mind raced over the sudden change of plans.

19:55

The clouds are becoming heavier and denser by the hour as a stiff breeze pushes them at speed above our heads. Carp activity has been absent for most of the afternoon, but I've just noticed the first one crash out. They begin to top and roll mainly in front of Phippo, but within an hour some carp start to show over both Middy's and my own baited areas.

As dusk settles, dogs begin barking in the fading light. Successions of lights switch on in the huge houses built into the hillside on the opposite bank. Each home is the size of a castle, probably costing millions of dollars and owned by rich and famous Americans. Each 'mansion' has its very own road, or even steps cut into the cliffs, leading to individual boathouses harbouring sumptuous white boats or yachts, each costing a king's ransom. My eyes sweep across the far bank from right to left until they settle on the steep cliffs directly opposite Middy. Here the rocky outcrops, clothed in a green carpet of trees and foliage, are far too steep to build luxury homes. This area is wild and untouched, and now as the last sparks of sunset show in the sky, it is as dark as the Congo.

10:10 Wednesday 3rd

I pull my rods in sometime during the night. An extremely hectic bout of feeding has me in and out of the sleeping bag like a yo-yo. I've already landed twenty two carp, with twenty over 20lb, so the only way to gain some much needed rest is to reel in the baits and dive back into the Bolivian of dreams. Most of the carp are 22lb-25lb, with the largest at 27lb. Phippo's had around ten carp, and Middy about fifteen, but again nothing exceeding 30lb.

Thursday morning

We've decided to pack up our mountain of gear and move on. Last night was extremely quiet compared to previous nights. I only managed to land one double and a mid-twenty during the early hours of dawn. The other lads also only managed a couple of carp each, although Phippo's catch included three catfish. The catfish seem to love the homemade boilies made by Middy, yet I haven't caught a single catfish on either the Eurobait or Nash boilies.

Our first port of call is to drive to REI (a large Outdoors & Adventure sports shop) to buy top-grade, but very cheap, Gore-Tex boots, LED headlamps, etc, and then visit a supermarket to stock up on supplies of food and drink, plus ice for the cooler. We drive on north following the snaking route upriver along the Colorado valley. The wheels continue to roll fast along route 620 until suddenly our two vehicles crest the edges of a hillside and a wide vista opens before us. The tyres screech to a halt and clutching our cameras, we all walk in the blistering heat down a dirt track until it peters out at the very edges of a cliff. The shimmering blue vastness of Lake Travis spreads out before us. This impressive reservoir, built in 1942, floods over 18,930 acres, with depths exceeding 190ft.

Our first option is to visit the first main campsite and this is choc-a-bloc and requires bookings a week in advance! We drive to the big main Dam-overlook to take in the awesome views. The sights of heavy boat traffic, even crowding such a vast acreage of water as this, do not impress us. I phone Bernie Haines - who has lived and fished in Texas for many years but now lives on the USA/Canadian border near the St Lawrence - for some guidance on our best options for big carp on the Colorado system. Like I had thought, Town Lake offers the easiest chance to catch a big carp in a short time frame. The big Lake Amistrad (67,000 acres, with maximum depths to 200ft!) offers the best chances of a really big carp, but not only is it too far to drive, it needs a powerboat to explore properly, and as Bernie mentions, most of the big carp are on the Mexican side of the lake at this time of the year. Marble Falls and L.B. Johnson (6,375 acres) tend to get quite crowded with boats, so this leaves Buchanan as our main option. Bernie confirms my thoughts that it is Lake Buchanan that will probably provide us with the best chances of catching some very big carp, although his advice that the shoals of bigger-sized specimens are difficult to locate on this particular lake, and really need a motor-powered boat + echo-sounder, is duly noted. The large Granger Lake is an option away from the Colorado valley and maybe also the boat traffic, but Bernie squashes these thoughts by mentioning that it holds a profusion of small carp. So we drive on northwards.

We stop off for a drink beside the 780 acre Lake Marble Falls. It looks nice, and I'd heard of a CAG member caching a 39lb common near the bridge where we stand, but we all decide to drive onwards. To vary the type of terrain we drive through, I decide to turn off the main Route 281 along Route P4. Almost immediately the heavy traffic is left far behind as our two cars travel along the narrow road that winds through rolling hills smothered with flowers. The views on either side of the road are spellbinding by a carpet of red and mauve that fills the verges. The sun beats down from a glorious cloudless sky as our vehicles snake through the colourful landscape until we are forced to stamp on our brakes at an even lovelier site. It is a backwater of the impressive Inks Lake, nestled like a jewel amongst red-rock and cactus, and a profusion of flowers. Some time is added to our journey by a brief walk around and taking photographs. We also stop to visit the campsite area – set within the borders of Inks Lake State Nature Park. A warden lets us know that there are definitely carp in this lake. The Park is naturally a little crowded because of weekend, but we make a note to return during the week if we decide to not fish Buchanan.

Our first site of Lake Buchanan takes our breaths away as our eyes squint in the glaring sunshine glistening off the surface as it spreads across 23,200 acres (885,507 acre ft!). We stop for lunch (whopping great burgers + tons of chips!) at a restaurant overlooking the lake, before driving onwards on route 261 that skirts the western shoreline. Black Rock Park looks quite nice, but further north the Cedar Point Park offers free camping and some good fishing options. Just as I am driving around the dirt road looking for decent places to fish and camp, I suddenly loose all forward drive...it feels like the accelerator cable has snapped! Jeeeez! Thankfully a Park Warden gives helpful advice and another camper offers a spanner as we look under the bonnet and hope. I could phone for breakdown assistance, but because we are far from civilisation it could take a long time to arrive! Thankfully, we find that a tiny piece of plastic has come loose and all it needs is for Phippo to push it back into position. Hey Presto! – The car is 100% working again! None of us can believe that such a new and expensive vehicle could possibly stop dead on the track due to a simple chunk of plastic slipping off the accelerator cable!

During the time spent working on the car, the free spaces for camping have suddenly been filled with vehicles and campers! Oh well, we might as well spend the night camping back at Black Rock and come back to Cedar Point on a weekday.

We set up our three tents beside the lake and sit on the benches sipping down cool beers while slapping hoards of biting mosquitoes. Darkness brings on a bout of other slapping, but this time it is the sounds of carp crashing all over the big bay. Most of the carp can easily be distinguished as being small, but sometimes the heavy 'thud' indicates there are bigger 'lumps' feeding. Soon the long, hot day sends us all into our dreams and all that can be heard is the slap of water on the beach and the distant crashes of leaping carp.

Dawn greets us with bright sunshine and clear blue sky. Canyon Of The Eagles is situated on the opposite shoreline to Cedar Point Park and also contains some free 'Primitive Camping' spots, so following breakfast we begin our long drive round the Buchanan dam and then northwards on route 2341 that skirts the eastern shoreline. On arrival, our hearts sink because the few primitive camping places are not only full of Scout group tents, but are also quite expensive per night. The actual bank fishing options don't look too good either, and judging by the hundreds of boats gathered together just offshore, filled with anglers fishing a Striper Bass Tournament, we wouldn't get much peace and quiet this weekend. Hardly needing to discuss our mutual thoughts about this place, we turn our cars around and head back south again. There are no doubts that most regions will be packed with people during this holiday weekend, but most should be leaving by tomorrow afternoon, so we decide to fish Inks Lake.

It doesn't take us long to reach the Inks State Park, but our hopes of obtaining primitive campsite number 346 are thwarted and most other camping places next to the lake are also filled with tents. The good news is that the people in number 346 will be going home Sunday afternoon. We go back to the office to book that spot

Globetrotter releases yet another carp to the gin-clear waters at the 'Beach' swim of Lake Austin.

*A truly awesome-looking carp
caught by Tony on two Nash
20mm Maple flavoured boilies.*

for Sunday night, but we are then told that you cannot pre-book campsites and must arrive early next morning on a first come first served basis. Luckily, Dave, who is camping with his family at 346 site, turns out to be an extremely friendly guy and not only allows us to set up or tents beside him, but also knows one of the Wardens and manages to obtain our bookings for this site for the next two days!

The number 346 site is probably the very best camping spot at Inks Lake State Park. Not only is its position at the very point of a peninsular one of the prime places to fish, but also the camp area itself is one of the largest. Dave's family tents are gathered close to the main barbeque grill area beneath a towering old tree. There is one main open swim close to this area, which Middy chooses to fish, but Phippo and I decide to fish 'in the wilds' at the peninsular point. The peninsular is completely overgrown and it takes Phippo some time to clear a path through the undergrowth between his bivvy and rodpod. My swim is slightly more open, except for overhanging trees and a high rock face! Before we actually set up the rods, I decide to wade around the edges of the peninsular. Just as I am about to step into the open, I see a pile of bones in the undergrowth and lean down to pick one up. A slight movement catches my eye, and I am suddenly paralysed as my eyes focus on a snake coiled beneath my outstretched fingers. Later identification shows that it is actually a Western Diamond Rattlesnake. Here is what the Field Guidebook says about it:

Due to its large size, potent venom, aggressive disposition and widespread range, the Western Diamondback Rattlesnake easily rates as one of the most dangerous snakes in the world. It is responsible for more serious snakebites and fatalities in Texas than any other species.

I gingerly retract my hand to a safer distance and watch the snake slither through the underbrush. During the next few days we are to witness many other snakes, mainly twisting across the water surface beneath our rod tops, but the majority of these turn out to be Cottonmouths or Water

Moccasins. Here is what the book says about this species of reptile:

The cottonmouth, or water moccasin, rarely strays far from water and can be found in marshes, swamps, ponds, lakes, ditches, and canals in East and Central Texas and along the Gulf coast. It is a stubby, muscular snake and can grow to nearly six feet. Moccasins can bite underwater. These snakes can be very defensive and sometimes aggressive. Swimmers, bathers and anglers on riverbanks should always keep an eye open for these snakes.

Needless to say, we keep our eyes open, especially while wading, or stepping through deep underbrush in our open sandals...

Later, a massive Texas Redhead (Scolopendra) centipede is caught and placed in a box for photos before being released. Here is what the book has to say about this ugly-looking beastie:

Scolopendra can inflict a painful bite with a pair of poison claws located directly under the head. These poison claws, once a pair of walking legs, have undergone a drastic change over thousands of years and are now used for capturing and killing their prey instead of walking. It can harm a person with the sharp claws of its many walking legs. Each walking leg is tipped with a sharp claw capable of making tiny cuts in human skin. A poison produced from the attachment point of each leg may be dropped into the wounds resulting in an inflamed and irritated condition. The best rule of thumb is NEVER HANDLE CENTIPEDES.

As Jim Klinger, better known as "Jungle Jim" from Texas so mildly put it -

"I grew up in Indiana where I could run through the field and catch butterflies. In Texas if you run through the field you're going to get nailed by something!"

We decide to not fish this first night, but to relax and enjoy Dave's family and friends company at the barbeque. Tomorrow morning we will take out the dinghy for a more detailed look at our swims. Darkness descends on our tents, as all manner of creepy-crawlers exit from underneath every leaf, stone and black hole of the forest. A series of trill hoots sound directly above our heads, making us look up at a small owl perched on a bow of the big tree. Firelight flickers orange light over our tanned faces and burnt noses, as we swig on bottles of cold larger and tuck into the feast of freshly grilled meat served up by Dave. Dusk blends into the black of night, as we all sit in front of the campfire and talk for hours while the stars slowly spin above our heads. By the time the Great Plough has tilted to touch the horizon, we have all departed to snore in our separate tents.

We all sleep-in quite late, but eventually the dinghy is pumped up and then Phippo and I paddle out past the peninsular. A small reed-fringed island almost forms an extension of the peninsular, with a narrow channel of water between them. Most of the water on either side of the peninsular is only ankle deep with stony bottom. A large rocky outcrop sits high out of the water and extends a shallow arm to connect to the island. The water deepens gradually, but then sharply to about 4metres off this big pile of rocks, so it becomes the first place for my marker float. A second marker float is placed at around 120-meters from shore in 6.5metre deep water at the transition zone between weed-filled bottom and clean silt. I bait heavily over each marker with pre-soaked maize and boilies. Handfuls of maize are also scattered around a large submerged tree stump in the margins.

The water depth near the edges of reeds at the apex of the peninsular drop much more sharply, and would certainly be the ideal area to place a bait, but it is blind to Phippo's position. I could possibly wade out and cast to this area, but decide not to because there is too much ankle-deep water littered with rocks between the point and me.

Phippo's Delkim is the first to sound, as a fish sucks in his maize hookbait, but he is far from his rods and I'm forced to strike for him. He eventually arrives, and although the carp manages to get round a tree stump and halfway round the island, it turns out to be a very small carp. Soon Phippo is in action again and this time it turns out to be a catfish (Phippo is fast becoming the 'catfish king'!).

Later in the day, I walk back to Middy's swim to witness some huge fish showing over his markers. At first sight - due to a small upright dorsal fin similar to a Grass carp showing each time they surface - I'm almost convinced that they are Black carp (introduced species to USA), but eventually realise that they are the dorsal fins of a group of huge native buffalo carp. When buffalo carp porpoise through the surface film, the majority of their long dorsal fin is held flat to their backs, but the high first ray of the dorsal is held upright as it scythes a path through the water.

At 19:30, just as the yellow sun begins to change orange and dips its golden reflection in the lake, something sucks in a single 28mm freshwater shrimp-based boilie (all the 28mm size are made for me by Eurobaits of Germany). The right-hand rod taps sharply, and then shudders as line is suddenly ripped off the spinning spool. Due to the overhanging trees, I'm unable to strike, so just lift into the fish and then scramble down the rock face towards the margins. By the time Phippo runs round to assist with the landing, I am already waist deep near the rocky outcrop, battling with a powerful fish. A high dorsal fin cutting through the water lets me know that it is the species I'm after, but the fish still unleashes a few more heart-stopping bursts of power before Phippo is able to slip it inside the landing net. I wade back to shore with my prize, noting that it's body shape is far less robust than the buffalo carp from Lake Austin, and although very deep in body shape, its narrow back (very similar to a giant European bream) causes it to weigh light on the scales. At 27lb 12oz this Smallmouth buffalo carp is still a wonderful fish to catch. The body colouring is beautiful with a bluish-purple iridescent tint to the scales, which may indicate that this is a male in spawning colour.

A strong wind begins to blow from the north, pushing back the warm, moist Gulf air and carrying with it a blast of cooler, dryer air. Waves buffet against the rocky peninsular for the next 12-hours, enticing the carp to feed on our scatterings of pre-bait.

By afternoon on the second day of fishing, we have all caught carp to 20lb+, but no hoped for giant buffalo, although Middy does have a powerful take and then witnesses a very large buffalo carp's back parting the waves, but he soon loses it in a submerged tree stump.

At sunset, while standing next to my rodpod on the rocky outcrop high above the water, I notice a dark shadow drift beneath my rod tips. During the following thirty minutes, hundreds of carp swim past in extremely shallow water. I decide to try and entice some of them to feed on floating crust. Before long I have groups of carp slurping on the surface. I wait patiently for my chance to hook a big specimen, because although most are between 15lb-25lb, a few well over 30lb are spotted. Unfortunately, a pair of ducks spot my feeding activity and bulldoze their way across the backs of the carp to reach the bread. I manage to scare the offending ducks away, but soon the fading light makes it too difficult to spot which size fish are taking my freeline bait - until the sudden hooking of a 20lb carp destroys any further chances of landing a biggie.

By the third night, we all begin discussing our future at Inks Lake. None of us have yet landed a carp over 25lb, and even though the number of carp per acre seems to be quite low, the average weight is also. Our final agreement is that if none of us land anything exceptional by tomorrow morning, we'll pack up and spend the last days fishing at Lake Austin.

Snow has fallen on the distant Rockies, and this cold air is being sucked southwards across the Hill Country of Texas. The wind increases to almost gale force and blasts our positions throughout the night. Dawn eventually arrives, but our packing up is made extremely difficult due to the continuous freezing cold winds biting at our exposed skins.

It is good to be back at Emma Long. I'm fishing the southern end of the Beach, Middy is central, and Phippo is back in his original swim at the northern end of the Beach. The lads decide not to bait up with maize, but I feel that now that a week has passed without baiting it needs something substantial to stop a shoal of big fish, so I paddle out in the dinghy and bait very heavily with most of the remainder of the maize, and then scatter about 5kg of boilies over it. I choose to bait one area at 120-meters out, and another in the margins just past the sandbank. Two rigs are baited with double 20mm Maple boilies and two are baited with 28mm White Chocolate flavoured boilies. To my right, I flick out a large bait beyond the sandbank, and whack out the others long distance, then sit back to wait.

An hour passes, when suddenly the solitude of the valley is abruptly shattered as the right-hand Delkim bursts into song. I am sitting beside the pod, so hit the run instantly and the rod thumps completely round into its parabolic curve. The braid twangs taught, and where it enters the water a 'V' shape cuts steady and slow through the surface film. I am in no doubt that this is a good fish,

"...A backwater of the impressive Inks Lake, nestled like a jewel amongst red-rock and cactus, and a profusion of flowers."

so I wade out to my waist and lean hard to the right in an attempt to prevent it from reaching the weed. But I am too late, and I curse as I feel that the rod top has stopped throbbing. With stubborn anger, I lean hard into the rod to gain as much line onto the big Shimano LC spool, and then slowly lift. Stalemate, as nothing budges, so I increase pressure on the rod, forcing its 13ft of carbon to creak with pain – but trusting it's strength - until suddenly the tip judders back a few inches. I am quick to pump on the reel handle and then continue the process. Seconds later the fish comes free

*A white-headed Bald Eagle –
proud symbol of USA.*

of the weed and without pause goes on an incredible run across the lake towards the old riverbed. Finger pressure on the spool slow its onward rush, but the fish makes five more awesome short rushes before finally crashing on the surface in a shower of spray. A high-pointed dorsal fin cuts through the water like a shark, and I instantly recognise that I'm latched to another big Buffalo carp. Middy wades out to join me, but the carp has still plenty of strength left and once again rips line off the madly spinning spool. Constant pressure brings it back towards the big landing net held by Middy. A broad back covered with shining silver-grey scales glides through the gin clear water, and once its nose almost touches the spreader block I ease off the pressure so that the fish sinks inside the net. Middy is slower than expected in lifting the net arms, and with amazing speed the carp twists completely round and almost swims straight back out of the net, but luckily ploughs into the mesh just beneath the tension cord! Holding the 52-inch carbon net arms, I peek inside. There below me swims an absolutely stunning fish. I slap Middy triumphantly on the back as we slowly wade back to shore dragging our prize through the glistening waters…

Two more nights pass and it's finally time to leave the Colorado. We all pack up and head for a shopping spree at the huge Fishing World store just outside Houston, and then the following day we visit the NASA Space Centre, before finally flying back to our destinations in Germany and England. During the 9-hour flight back to Gatwick, I reflect on the past two weeks. I'd landed almost 100 carp, with eighty in excess of 20lb. The hoped for 60lb+ carp never made an appearance, but the three beautiful Buffalo carp to over 40lb truly made this a very worthwhile and enjoyable expedition to one of America's largest States – the 'Lone Star' of Texas.

WORLD CARP LIST

Global introductions of Cyprinus carpio

During the rise of water levels in spring, many carp will try to reach virgin areas or adjacent lakes to spawn and colonise feeding grounds.

Native Countries:

The CARP (Cyprinus carpio) is native to a band of countries stretching from central Europe to Far East Asia. This includes: Holland, Belgium, Germany, Luxembourg, Liechtenstein, Romania, Poland, Austria, Czech Republic, Bulgaria, Hungary, Albania, Yugoslavia, Bosnia & Herzegovina, Croatia, Slovenia, Fyro Macedonia, Greece, Turkey, Syria, Iraq, Iran, Armenia, Moldavia, Belarus, Estonia, Latvia, Lithuania, Azerbaijan, Georgia, Ukraine, Russia, Kazakhstan, Uzbekistan, Turkmenistan, Mongolia, China, Vietnam, and Japan.

Introductions within Europe:

Historical introductions were made to the following European countries prior to 1500's. : United Kingdom, Ireland, Switzerland, Spain (including Baleares Islands), France - including Corsica, Portugal, Italy - including Sardinia and Sicily.

In 1560, carp were first introduced to Denmark, with later introductions from France and Germany in 1879. The late 1800's also saw the first introductions to Swedish waters. The first introductions of carp to Finland were from Germany in 1955, with later introductions from neighbouring Sweden in 1959, and from USSR in 1961.

Worldwide Introductions:

Outside of Europe, carp have been introduced on a massive scale throughout the far-flung reaches of the Globe.

The first of these major movements of carp stock began during the 1800's. Some introductions were recorded but exact dates are unknown, such as the introductions to:

French Polynesia, Ecuador, Togo, New Caledonia, Afghanistan, Cambodia, Guam, Hong Kong island, Myanmar (Burma), West Irian, New Caledonia, Pakistan, Tahiti, Tanzania, Togo, and Uruguay.

China introduced carp to Malaysia and Indonesia during the 1800's; to Singapore in the early 1900's; to the Philippines in 1910 and 1915 (from Hong Kong); to Thailand in 1913; to Peru in 1960; and to Afghanistan during the 1970's.

Brazil introduced carp to Uruguay in 1850.

Germany, at the forefront of fish distribution during the 19th Century, introduced carp to South Africa in 1859; to Northern USA in 1872; to Chile in 1875; to Thailand during 1900's; to Finland in 1955; and to Tunisia in 1965.

The UK first introduced carp to New Zealand in 1864, and continued to make further introductions until they ceased in 1911; they introduced carp to Australia during 1900's (possibly also in 1872).

France brought carp to southern USA in 1872; to Mexico in 1872 and 1911; to Morocco in 1925; and Tunisia in 1967.

The USA moved some of their second-generation carp stocks to Canada in 1880 and 1885; to Brazil in 1898 and 1977; and to Panama in 1976.

The Hawaiian Islands were stocked with carp around 1900.

The island of Madagascar received its first stocks of carp in 1914.

The island of Sri Lanka (Ceylon) received carp from Europe in 1915.

South Africa introduced carp to Swaziland during the late 1800's; then to Zimbabwe in 1925; and to Zambia in 1946.

The first introductions to Cuba came from USA in 1927, but they received further stocks from USSR in 1983.

Israel began serious carp farming after the Second World War, but their first carp came from Europe in 1931. Israel's first exports of carp were to Germany, Thailand and Haiti; then to Nigeria in 1954; Rwanda in 1960; Uganda in 1962; Cyprus, and Central African Rep. in 1966; Cameroon in 1970, Korea in 1973; Panama in 1976; Malawi in 1977; and Zambia in 1980.

Indonesia (Java) introduced carp to Egypt in 1934.

New Zealand transported carp for introduction to the Pacific Fiji islands in 1936.

Ethiopia also received their first carp during 1936.

Sri Lanka moved some of their stock carp (which had originated in Europe) to India during 1939.

India was to later receive more carp from Thailand in 1957.

Both Columbia and Venezuela received introductions of carp during 1940.

Bolivia received carp from Mexico in 1945.

Japan exported carp to Peru in 1946, but they had already sent shipments to Thailand and Taiwan prior to this date. Japan also sent carp to Surinam in 1968.

'Globetrotter' with a huge African mirror carp. Although still looked on upon as 'vermin' in some countries, the joy and happiness that this wonderful species has brought to millions of anglers, makes sure that its popularity will continue to grow as we travel through the uncertain future of the 21st Century.

A consignment of carp from Mexico reached the Dominican Republic in 1953. Part of this DR consignment also reached Puerto Rico in the same year.

The first carp to be stocked to Guatemalan waters were during 1954.

Also in 1954, Austria sent a consignment of carp for introduction to waters in Nigeria.

In 1956, carp were introduced to Honduras from Nicaragua.

Australia introduced carp to the incredible, wild island of Papua New Guinea in 1959. Subsequent breakouts due to frequent flooding of stock ponds gave them later access to the magical Sepik River system.

Carp were introduced to Ghana and Uganda from Israel during 1962.

Mexico replenished fresh bloodline stocks to Nicaragua in 1964.

Guatemala introduced carp to El Salvador in 1965.

Uganda transported carp across the neighbouring borders of Uganda in 1969.

Hungary has an ancient history of exporting carp to neighbouring European countries, but they also reached the far-flung Himalayan valleys of Nepal during the 1970's.

Carp from India were introduced to Sudan in 1975, and Mauritius in 1976

In the same year, Taiwan introduced carp to Cost Rica, and Italy introduced carp to Côte d'Ivoire in West Africa.

India and Thailand introduced carp to Laos during 1977.

Tony releases a true 'wildcarp' to the Vorskla River, a tributary of the Dnepr, in a wild and remote region of the Ukraine.

Today, re-introductions of carp are being made to many waters, especially within Europe, but these are mainly to reinforce fresh or new bloodlines to existing stocks. One of the final countries in the World for carp to be introduced by man was the exotic, semi-secret Himalayan kingdom of Bhutan in 1984.

This means that carp (Cyprinus carpio) have been introduced to at least 80 different countries, and have a Worldwide distribution of 110 different countries, covering an incredible latitude range around this planet of 60° North to 65° South!

WORLD'S LARGEST CARP caught on Rod & Line

82lb 3oz: Sarulasti Lake, Rumania. Mirror carp. Christian Balamair. 1998.
81lb 5oz: Yonne River, France. Mirror carp. Marcel Rouviere. 1981.
78lb: Sarulaesti Lake, Rumania. Mirror carp. Robert Raduta. 1997.
77lb 15oz: Sarulasti Lake, Rumania. Mirror Carp. Henk von Dorn. 1999.
77lb 9oz: River Mossell, France. Mirror carp. Emmanuelle Walt. 1998
77lb 8oz: St Cassien Lake, France. Mirror carp. Dave Walker. 1998.
76lb 2oz: Kempisch Canal, Belgium. Mirror carp. Philip Cottenier. 1995.
76lb: St Cassien Lake, France. Mirror carp. Kevin Ellis. 1986.
75lb 11oz: St Cassien lake, France. Mirror carp. Leo Vender Gugten. 1987
75lb 6oz: Sarulesti Lake, Rumania. Common carp. Erich Ungar. 2003
75lb 5oz: Orient Lake, France. Common carp. Jerome Gigault. 1996.
75lb: Orient Lake, France. Mirror carp. Michael Brechtmann. 1995
74lb 6oz: Kempisch Canal, Belgium. Mirrror Carp. Ronny de Groote. 1995
70lb 2oz: Orient Lake, France. Common carp. Leon Hoogendijk. 1993

MONSTER

FRESHWATER FISH

OF THE WORLD

This reference list details all major fish species, Worldwide, capable of growing in excess of 25kg (50lb+). Covering maximum lengths & weights, habitats, feeding habits, prime fishing periods and other important facts, it is one of the most detailed and comprehensive chapters ever compiled for the big fish angler.

SOUTH AMERICA

ARAIPAIMA (*Araipaima gigas*). Maximum length: 4m. (13ft). Maximum weight: 200kg (400lb+). Predatory.

Reports of specimens in excess of 4.5m., but not verified. Fish longer than 3 metres are quite rare and 2 - 2.5m.(7-8ft) is more frequently encountered.

Found in the great Amazon River system in Brazil, Peru, Bolivia and Columbia and the Araguaia River and its tributaries in Guyana.

Although this beautiful silver-scaled fish lives in some of the wildest river locations on this planet, it is showing alarming signs of extinction in many areas due to over fishing and poorly enforced size limits, especially in Peru.

Local names: Guyana - Araipaima; Peru - Paiche; Brazil - Pirarucú.

DOURADO (*Salminus maxillosus*). Max length: 1m+. (36inches+). Max weight: 30kg (66lb). Predatory.

Found in the fast flowing, well-oxygenated stretches of the Paraná/Paraguay river system in Brazil, Paraguay, and Argentina; the Uruguay River system in Uruguay, Brazil and Paraguay.

One of South America's most sought after fish. Caught mainly on fish baits, spinners, plugs, large flies or other lures. A wonderful golden-yellow body colouration gives the Dourado its name, meaning 'the gilded one'. Both a nocturnal and diurnal feeder and the best fishing period is August until late December. Migrates upriver during high floods around end of December, and in 1-2 months of active swimming through rapids and cataracts, can often cover distances of 4,000 kilometres.

PIRAIBA Catfish (*Brachyplatstoma filamentosum*) Max length: 3m. Max weight 200kg (440lb+), but more normal at 2 metres and 110kg. Predatory.

Found in large rivers of Brazil, Paraguay and Argentina.

Like most catfish species, it is most active nocturnally. Lives for most of the day in deep trenches of the main river at depths between 10 - 30 metres and sometimes even deeper, but this giant of South American catfish moves into shallower water during darkness to feed on prey fish.

Best fishing time (like all S.A. cats) occurs between early September and late March. The three prime feeding periods are: during the low water period, when the shrinking flood plains concentrates shoals of prey fish in the narrow river channels; during the initial rise of floodwaters, when they migrate to tributary mouths to wait for the thousands of shoals of small fish descending to spawn in the muddier rivers of the flood basin; or during the migration of characin fish species as they move between upstream tributaries at the peak of the floods.

Jens, looking like 'Dr Livingstone' as he lies beside his fantastic 200lb+ Nile Perch, caught from the Murchinson Falls area of the Nile, in Uganda.

PINTADO (spotted) Catfish & SURIBIM (striped) Catfish (*Sorubimichthys planiceps*). Max length; 2.5m. Max weight: 90kg+ (200lb+). Predatory.

Found in major rivers of central S. America, especially the Pantanal and Corrientes regions of Brazil and Paraguay.

Both are attractively marked big cats with streamline body shapes. The Suribim is also known as the Firewood Catfish or Roundhead Shovelnose Catfish. Local name: Peixe Lenha. They inhabit a very wide range of waters spreading throughout the Orinoco and Amazon basins.

Best fishing times are Sept - March. A cautious feeder compared to the smaller (max.8kg) Barbado catfish species.

CAPARARI or TIGER SHOVELNOSE Catfish (*Pseudoplatystoma tigrinum*) Max length: 1.3m. Max-weight: 20-25kg.

Similar to Sorubim, but much smaller and is just one of many medium-sized shovelnose catfish (such as P. faciatum) that attain 15-25kg maximum weights, and are identified by their slightly differing striped patterns along the flanks.

PLATED CATFISH (*Pseudodoras niger*) Max length: 1.2m. Max weight: 20-25kg.

The largest of the Doradidae family of catfish. Inhabits a wide variety of waters. Mainly in lakes and rivers of the flood plain, but can also be found in waters up to an altitude of 300m.

BANDED CATFISH (*Phractocephalus hemiopterus*) Max length: 1.3m. Max weight: 80kg.
Found in waters of the Amazon basin. One of the most spectacular S.A. catfish. Brightly coloured with counter-shaded dark brown/black, with a thick, brilliant white band along the central body and red/orange tipped fins. Sometimes completely white albino specimens are encountered.

JAU Catfish. Max length: 1.5m+. Max weight: 90kg+. Predatory.
Found in similar rivers as the Pintado. Minimum legal retaining size is 90cm.
A shorter and far stockier bodied fish than either the Suribim or Pintado. Best fishing times are evenings and after darkness, year round. Livebaits such as Pirambóia (a type of eel), or Lamburari are best for tempting these enormous catfish.

TAMBAQUI Max length: 1m+. Max weight: 30kg (66lb+). Fruit and seed eater.
Found in major rivers and tributaries of the Amazon flood plain in Brazil.
A wonderful looking, heavily built fish with a black back and black to moss green or greenish yellow ventrally. This stunning creature (a member of the characin group, of which the piranhas also belong) is often seen in large aquariums around the globe.
Best fishing times are when the rising river levels flood the surrounding forests, during December and January. The Tambaqui's favourite foods are certain fruits, and the seeds of the Spruce rubber tree. The nut capsules of the rubber tree 'pop' open during the brief, but very hot, sunny spells of the rainy season. The seeds scatter across the water's surface, sending the Tambaqui (pronounced: tam-bah-key) into a feeding frenzy. A supreme candidate for stalking with floaters!

Introduced Species to South America:

CARP (*Cyprinus Carpio*). Carp have been in Central and South American waters for almost 200 years (longer in fact than in North America!). Some of the earliest introductions of carp were to Brazil in the 1800's. Offspring of these were introduced to Uruguay in 1850. Between 1875 and 1981 carp were introduced to many waters all over South America. See carp in the North American section and the Worldwide Carp Introductions chapter for further information.

NORTH AMERICA

INCONNU (*Stenodus leucichthys*). Max length: 125cm (49inches). Max weight: 25kg (50lb+). Predatory.
Found in the arctic drainages of Canada, Alaska and Siberia.
Anadromous near coastal areas. West - East range stretches from Kuskokwin River in Alaska, to the Anderson river in North West Territories. Abundant in the upstream reaches of Yukon and Mackenzie rivers. Landlocked in large inland lakes such as Great Slave Lake and Bear Lake. A streamlined, powerful fish with small silver scales. Similar to the Asp (Aspius aspius) in apearance. Migrates far upstream to spawn. A strong taker of lures, such as plugs and shiny spinners.

GREEN STURGEON (*Acipencer medirostris*). Max length: 2.13m (7ft). 100kg+ (220lb+). Predatory. Range stretches from northern tip of Alaska to central California; but abundant only in the Pacific coastal rivers of Alaska, the Klamath River and the Sacramento River. Also found in north Japan, China, and north to Amur River.

LAKE STURGEON (*Acipencer fulvescens*). Max length: 2.4m. (8ft). Max weight: 140.6kg (310lb). May reach 274cm (9ft). The N.A. rod caught record measured 7' 11" (2.4m). A 208 pounder (94.3kg) caught in 1953 in Lake of the Woods, was calculated to be 154 years old! Canadian rod caught record - 168lb from Georgian Bay, Ontario on 29/05/83, was also a line class record.
Found in St.Lawrence River & Great Lakes system, Ottawa River system (especially Baskatong Reservoir), and Hudson Bay. Now very rare and nearing extinction in Coosa, Missouri, Ohio, and Mississippi river systems.

ATLANTIC STURGEON (*Acipencer oxyrhynchus*). Max length: 4.3m (14ft). Max weight: 500kg+.
Range stretches from Hamilton River in Newfoundland, to rivers draining into Gulf of Mexico. Now uncommon and severely depleted throughout its normal range; which is also reflected in the sturgeon's European range. Two subspecies exist: A. o. oxyrhynchus of the Atlantic coast and A. o. desotai of the Gulf Coast.

WHITE STURGEON (*Acipencer transmontanus*). Max length: 3.8m (12'6"). Max weight: 630kg (1,387lb). Earlier records indicate that it may reach 20ft and 2,000lb+. The White Surgeon is U.S.A.'s largest freshwater fish.
Found in Pacific coastal rivers from Gulf of Alaska to Sacramento River, California. Introduced into lower Colorado river, Arizona/Mexico. Ascends coastal rivers to spawn. Landlocked throughout most of Columbia River in Oregon, Washington and British Columbia. A high death rate in the Frazer River during 1995-96 caused by unknown source depleted stocks. Strict fishing rules are now enforced on Frazer system. A Spring - early Summer boat fishing ban began to be enforced on the lower Columbia River from 1996 onwards. Livebaits are banned throughout the sturgeon's range. No dead fish baits (except squid) allowed in B.C. Canada. Dead fish baits are still allowed in Washington/Oregon, USA.
In 1996, Tony Davies-Patrick landed a Great White Sturgeon from the Columbia River estimated to weigh in excess of 700lb (the fish was returned to the river). This is believed to be the World's largest freshwater fish landed on rod & line.

PADDLEFISH (*Polyodon spathula*). Max length: 2.2m (7'1") Max weight: 90.7kg (200lb). Predatory.
Early range extended to Great Lakes system, but present range stretches only from Mississippi River system, through Mobile Bay drainage, Alabama, to eastern Texas.
These unusual looking fish are caught by snag fishing below dams during the spawning season from April - June; which, along with pollution, has helped speed their decline. Large specimens can be up to 30 years old. Generally they inhabit slow moving stretches of major rivers in depths below 4ft (1.3m).

LONGNOSE GAR (*Lepisosteus osseus*). Max length: 183cm (6ft+). Max weight 25kg (50lb+). Predatory. Range stretches from lower Great Lakes and St Lawrence/Ottawa rivers, south to Florida; west to lower Mississippi and Rio Grande river systems.

Prefers heavily vegetated bays, pools, oxbows and swampy areas of rivers with sluggish flow. Often seen near surface during late May - early July.

Related species (all under 25kg): Shortnose Gar; Spotted Gar; Florida Gar.

ALIGATOR GAR (*Lapisosteus spatula*). Max length: 3m (10ft). Max weight: 137kg (302lb). Predatory. A more confined range than the Longnose Gar. Found in Ohio River, Mississippi River (downstream from Illinois), and Gulf Coast rivers from Enconfina River, Florida, to Cordoba River, Mexico.

Inhabits sluggish backwaters, lakes and bayous of large rivers. In the extreme south USA/Mexico coast, it often enters brackish waters and sometimes even salt-marine waters. It is a very streamlined, hardy species with pike-like form and crocodile-like teeth and armoured scales.

Best periods for fishing are during late spring - early summer, using livebaits, deadbaits or lures. Boats are sometimes essential to reach the backs of the largest bayous.

GIANT GARFISH (*Lapisosteous tristoechius*) Max length: 3m (10ft). Max weight: 135kg (300lb). Predatory. Found in S.E. Mexican, Central American and Cuban fresh and brackish waters. Very similar to Alligator Gar. Caught commercially in many areas.

LAKE TROUT (*Salvelinus namaycush*). Max length: 1.3m (4ft 2in). Max weight: 46.3kg (102lb). Predatory.

Found in a wide range of waters spreading across eastern Alaska and throughout Canada, including the Great Lakes system. Introduced outside its native range to various parts of North America; also to South America, New Zealand and Sweden.

This huge trout inhabits both deep and shallow lakes of the far north, but it is restricted to cold, deeper lakes in the southern part of its range. Great Lakes population is low, except in isolated areas where they are artificially introduced.

The 'Siscowet' is a very robust form that occupies the deep, cold and wild waters of Lake Superior.

CHINOOK SALMON (*Omcorhynchus tshawytscha*). Max length: 1.6m (4ft 10in). Max weight: 57.2kg (126lb). Predatory. Although this, the largest of North America's salmon can reach 100lb+, it rarely exceeds 25kg(50lb+). Canadian rod caught records: Inland - 45.83lb, Credit River, Ontario, on 04/11/80. Sea-Run - 92lb in Skeena River, British Columbia on 19/7/59.

An extremely rare Golden Carp (Probarbus julieni) caught in Thailand.

Found in a large range of Pacific coastal rivers, spreading from Alaska in the north to Ventura River, California. An anadromous fish that has been successfully introduced outside its native range, including the Great Lakes; also introduced to parts of Asia.

This is a very sought after fish that can be found in freshwater during most months of the year, although its major spawning runs occur in either Spring or Autumn months.

ATLANTIC SALMON (*Salar salar*). Max length: 1.3m.(4ft 5in). Max weight: 35.9kg (79lb+). Predatory. Found in rivers of northern Quebec, Newfoundland, New Brunswick, Nova Scotia and Maine. Landlocked in lakes of New England states. Also present in European coastal rivers ranging from Arctic Circle to Portugal. Introduced to many waters, but rarely successful. Becoming increasingly uncommon throughout range. Specimens over 25kg are now very rare.

Unlike Pacific Salmon, the Atlantic Salmon returns to the sea after spawning.

Canadian record: 47lb in Cascapedia River, Quebec on 16/6/82.

Some Canadian populations are landlocked in lakes and only migrate within the inland river/lake system (local name: Ouananaiche). Another form is the American Sebago Salmon.

MUSKELLUNGE (*Essox masquinongy*). Max length: 1.8m (6ft). Max weight: 45.4kg (100lb). Predatory. Native range is Hudson Bay drainage, Great Lakes/St Lawrence system, and upper Mississippi River system. Introduced to many states, but not always successfully. Inhabits slow, thickly vegetated areas of river. Also frequents the edges of deep, rocky drop-offs of boiling eddies formed below large dams. This is especially valid on the St. Lawrence, where numerous 25kg+ specimens have been landed. Widespread, but rarely numerous. This species has been crossed with the Northern Pike and is then known as the 'Tiger Muskie.

Canadian records: Tiger - 34lb in Eagle Lake, Ontario on 06/08/81. Natural form - 65lb in Georgian Bay, Ontario on 16/10/88.

COLORADO SQUAWFISH (*Ptychocheilus lucius*). Max length: 1.8m (6ft). Max weight: 45kg (100lb). Predatory.

Native range covers complete Colorado River Basin. 100 years of water pollution, Dam construction, water diversions for irrigation etc., has placed a massive toll on this giant of the carp family. Now extinct in the lower half of its range below Lake Mead, the Colorado Squawfish's present range is confined to the upper reaches in Utah and Colorado, and possibly in wild areas of the Grand Canyon, Arizona. Even in most of these sections of the river, I believe that this fantastic fish has become extinct due to a dramatic fall in water temperatures below major dams. Some specimens possibly still exist in the warmer waters within Lake Mead and Lake Powell.

During the late 1800's and early 1900's, 5ft long specimens weighing 80lb+ (36kg+) were quite common. Now, sadly this wonderful fish is on the U.S. Endangered Species List.

Inhabits bays and eddies off main river flow. The largest individuals tend to move into the deepest parts of strong runs at the edges of rocky or sandy pools.

SACRAMENTO SQUAWFISH (*Ptychocheilus grandis*). Max length: 1.4m (4.5ft). Max weight: 25kg (50lb+). Predatory.

Found in the Russian, San Joaquin, Sacramento, Salinas, Pajero rivers and Clear Lake system in California.

Habitat is similar to that of the Colorado Squawfish, and although its present population is not endangered, specimens longer than 3ft (9cm) are now very rare.

SMALLMOUTH BUFFALO Carp (*Ictiobus bubalus*). Max length: 1.2 m. (48in). Max weight: 55kg (120lb+). Omnivorous.

Natural range spreads south to Texas and Mexico, with isolated populations in Rio Grande. Has also been introduced to some reservoirs in Arizona.

BLACK BUFFALO Carp (*Ictiobus niger*). Max length: 1.2 m. (48in). Max weight: 55kg (120lb+). Omnivorous.

Confined mainly to lower Great Lakes area and Mississippi river system. Natural range spreads to Mexico, but now only found in Sabine Lake, Texas (possibly isolated populations in Rio Grande. Has also been introduced to some reservoirs in Arizona).

BIGMOUTH BUFFALO Carp (*Ictiobus cyprinellus*). Max length: 1m+ (40in+). Max weight: 40kg+ (90lb+). Omnivorous.

Found in Nelson River drainage, Manitoba; South Saskatchewan, Canada; southern Great Lakes; Mississippi River system. Has also been introduced to numerous other waters in USA.

All three Buffalo species have a strong physical resemblance to the common carp (Cyprinus carpio). The Bigmouth has the most robust body shape of the three. A particularly interesting species for the 'carp addicts' amongst us.

BLUE CATFISH (*Ictalurus furcatus*). Max length: 1.65m (5ft 5in). Max weight: 60kg (132lb+). Predatory/Omnivorous.

Found in Mississippi system, rivers draining into Gulf, including Rio Grande and other rivers in Mexico. Also has been introduced to other lakes and rivers in Minnesota, as well as some Eastern U.S. and Western U.S. States.

Inhabits deep water in lakes and main channels of rivers, or backwaters. Like most catfish species of the World, the 'Blue' feeds more heavily at night or during days of low light intensity. During these periods, they will often move on to shallow shelves to search for prey fish or other food.

Has a distinctive pale blue to olive upper body colour. This tends to darken to a blue/black in larger individuals.

CHANNEL CATFISH (*Ictalurus punctatus*). Max length: 1.27m.(50 in). Max weight: 26.5kg (60lb). Predatory/Omnivorous.

Original range was Hudson Bay drainage (Nelson & Red rivers), Great Lakes system, St. Lawrence/Ottawa river system, Mississippi/Missouri river system, and Rio Grande River. It has been introduced to most States of the U.S., so today it is widespread and fairly common.

Prefers middle and lower stretches of main rivers. Large specimens seek out deep runs or holes during daylight hours. Large specimens often feed in powerful, but steady flows below large dams.

This is a very popular food fish in U.S., and is the principal catfish reared in aquaculture. The Red River in Manitoba, Canada, produces some of the largest specimens in North America every year.

FLATHEAD CATFISH (*Pylodictus olivaris*). Max length: 1.4m (4ft 5in). Max weight: 41.4kg (91lb+). Reports also of 100lb+ specimens. Predatory/Omnivorous.
Range stretches throughout Mississippi, White/Little Missouri and Rio Grande river systems, including Gulf Slope drainages. Introduced to numerous lakes and rivers throughout U.S., and now fairly common.
This catfish prefers to be close to or inside snags, such as sunken trees, rock piles and other debris - so heavy gear and strong, abrasive resistant lines are needed to land the larger specimens.
A similar sub-species, the 'Opelousas' catfish is found in Texas and other Gulf State waters, with the largest, a 67lb specimen caught from Sam Rayburn Reservoir.

STRIPED BASS (*Morane saxatilis*). Max. length: 1.8m (6ft). Max. weight: 56.7kg (125lb). Some reported over 2 metres long. Predatory.
Found in east coastal rivers flowing into Atlantic and Gulf - from St Lawrence River, Quebec, to St.John River, Florida. Also introduced to many Pacific coast drainages and some lakes/reservoirs far inland. Marine habitat, but mature fish swim far upriver to spawn during spring. Some populations are landlocked and so remain in freshwater habitat.
A strong fish that actively takes lures, which has resulted in it becoming a very popular sportfishing species in America. Locally known as 'Stripers', and can hybrid with the smaller White Bass if introduced to same environment.
Fairly common, but is under constant threat due to pollution of river spawning grounds.

FRESHWATER DRUM (*Aplodinotus grunniens*). Max length: 89cm (35 in). Max. weight: 24.7kg (54_lb). Predatory.
Distributed across a wide latitude range, spreading from the Nelson, Saskatchewan and Red River drainages in Canada; the Great Lakes/St Lawrence system; throughout Mississippi River system and other Gulf drainages south to Rio Grande, Mexico and Usumacinta River, Guatemala.
Very similar in appearance to the saltwater Croakers, and also has the same ability to make strong 'drumming' sounds. This is the only North American fish that produces buoyant eggs that float to the surface. Large specimens possess a beautiful iridescent scale colouring.
In stillwaters, it tends to keep to deep drop-offs. Roams to more variable depths in rivers, but is more common below dams or waterfalls.

Introduced species to North America:

GRASS CARP: (*Ctenopharyngodon idella*). Max length: 1,25m (4ft+). Max weight: 45.5kg+ (100lb+). Aquatic plant eater/Omnivorous.
Native to eastern Asia (especially Amur River system), this fish species was introduced to ponds in Alabama and Arkansas during 1963, in an attempt to control aquatic weed growth. Since then, it has

been introduced to at least 35 different U.S. States, as well as some parts of Canada, including lakes in the Frazer River valley, British Columbia. Further introduction is now banned in some states.

COMMON/MIRROR/LEATHER CARP (*Cyprinus carpio*). Max length: 1,25m+. (4.5ft). Max weight: 38kg (85lb+). Omnivorous.

Maximum length to weight ratios varies dramatically between different populations and even within the same shoal. A 3ft carp may sometimes weigh as much as a 4ft carp, even though both may be healthy individuals. Official Canadian record: 35lb 4oz, from Lake of the Prairies, Manitoba.

Note: On my first fishing session ever in Canada, I smashed the official record and now have lost count of how many 35lb+ fish that I've landed over recent years. My best carp from Canada are: Ottawa River - 37lb 2oz (Quebec); St Lawrence River - 52lb 2oz (Ontario), including 42lb 10oz, 42lb; 40lb+, and many 35lb+ specimens. My best carp from U.S.A. include: St Lawrence River - 39lb+ (New York State), including many 35lb+ specimens; Oak Orchard River – 42lb 2oz (Upstate New York); Columbia River - a brace of 40lb+ commons (Washington State), including numerous 30lb+ fish; Colorado River – 35lb+ (Arizona).

The U.S.A. record stands at 59_lb (4ft long), caught back in 1955 in Iowa State.

The carp was first brought from Europe and introduced to North America in the late 1800's. After initial introductions were established, the carp spread further naturally throughout the massive network of river & lake systems. Today, the carp is the most widespread freshwater fish in North America. From glass-smooth lakes to raging whitewaters, it has spread like wildflower and now is well established in Canada, U.S.A., and Mexico. By mid-1960's the most northerly limit of its range was already the lower Nelson River near Hudson Bay, Manitoba and the upper Frazer River, British Columbia. At the dawn of the 21st Century the carp's range may be even further north, possibly into the Churchill, N. Athabasca or Peace River systems. The opportunities for the pioneering carp angler are mind-boggling!

EUROPE

MIRROR/LEATHER/COMMON CARP. Native in mainland central Europe (Danube & Rhine river systems) from at least before the last Ice Age. Thought to have been transported south of the Alps by Romans; although it is also possible that carp may have reached Italy by natural migration throughout Europe's network of rivers, streams, canals, and drainage ditches. Introduced to England around the 1400's. The first recorded date being 1462. These were the original long, lean 'Wildie' strain. Successions of genetically manipulated varieties of fast-growing strains were introduced to the British Isles at later dates. Natural northerly movements of carp may have reached southern Jutland (Denmark) before the 1500's, but the first recorded introduction to Danish waters was to Faurholm, in 1560. Peder Oxe was instrumental in stocking faster growing stockfish to selected carp farms throughout Denmark and Sweden, from 1566 onwards. Carp were first stocked by man into Finnish waters with consignments from Germany in 1955, from Sweden in 1959, and USSR in 1961. But carp have also spread naturally into the southeastern corners of Finland, probably from natural migration movements up Vuoksa River from Ladosjskoje Lake in Russia.

30kg is approaching the maximum weight limit for carp in both Britain and Scandinavian waters.

Numerous 27kg+ (60lb+) carp have been caught all over mainland Europe (Hungary, Poland, Greece, Italy, Rumania, etc.,) but French waters probably hold the largest percentage of carp in excess of 25kg. A few 35kg carp have been landed in France, topped by a 37kg (81lb+) mirror from Montereau, in 1981. The largest French common carp ever landed on rod & line was a wonderful 32kg (70lb 6oz) specimen caught by my good friend Leon Hoogendijk, from Orient Lake. This particular fish was caught at a later date when it reached its maximum-recorded weight of 34kg.

A 34.6kg (76lb) mirror carp was caught by Philip Cottener from the Kempisch Kannal(canal) in Belguim and held the Benelux record (this specimen was caught and returned on numerous different occasions before its final death). A 90lb carp was reported caught in nets from Lake Volvi, Greece. A huge 35.5kg (78lb+) mirror carp was caught from Sarulesti Lake (Raduta) in 1996. The same lake produced the largest rod caught carp in Europe (also a World Record), an incredible 82lb 4oz mirror carp caught by Christian Baldemair on May 27, 1998. More recently, Tim Paisley landed a colossal 73lb 13oz common carp from Raduta. A huge 34.2kg common was also caught from Saurlesti in 2003 – the world's largest ever rod-caught common carp.

See North America section for further details on Cyprinus carpio.

WELS or EUROPEAN CATFISH (*Silurus glanis*). Max length: 5.5 m. (18ft). Max weight: 437kg (959lb). Predatory/Omnivorous.

Two large Grasscarp above a dense bed of Canadian pondweed enjoy the sun on their backs during a warm, summer afternoon in Denmark.

A 900lb+ specimen was caught in nets and witnessed in the Maritsa River (Greece/Turkey border) by an experienced Greek fisherman living in Alexandropolis. The largest officially recorded specimen was caught from the River Dnepr, Ukraine, at 5m. (16ft) in length, and weighed 306kg (674lb). The largest catfish that I have seen is a 560lb+ specimen from the Donau River. Today, specimens in excess of 200kg (440lb) are very rare.

Native to most large river systems of central & Eastern Europe; especially Ural, Volga, Dnepr, Donau, and Kizil Irmak. Introduced to France (Seille-Saone rivers, Lake Cassien etc.), Spain (Ebro River system), Sweden (Em River, Mälaren etc.), and Italy (Po River system etc.). It also has been introduced to England - Bedfordshire lakes and the Great Ouse River originally, but now more widespread in various lakes, although still uncommon.

The most northerly limit is the southern lakes system of Finland. The easterly limit of its range is the Amu-Darja and Syr-Darja rivers that flow into the Aral Sea basin.

Sometimes enters brackish waters, but prefers freshwater habitats with plenty of shelter - such as submerged trees or tangled debris. Gathers into large groups in deep hollows of the river bed during Winter or cold weather. Most active at night or during days of low light intensity.

NORTHERN PIKE (*Essox lucius*). Max length: 183cm (6ft). Max weight: 34kg (75lb). Predatory.

Distributed throughout European rivers and lakes. Native range spreads throughout northern latitudes (except Greenland & Iceland), across Asia and North America. Tends to reach smaller maximum size in Canada/Alaska where 25lb+ is rare, although a few 40lb+ specimens have been landed (Canadian record: 42lb 13 oz from Delaney Lake, Ontario). Most 27kg+ (60lb+) specimens have come from Russia or Siberian waters. The largest official European Northern Pike was landed from the brackish, but prolific coastal waters off Sweden and weighed 57lb 4oz. Old reports of pike weighing 65kg (143lb) from the previous USSR seem to be doubtful, although they may possibly refer to an extinct sub-species.

Prefers fairly shallow waters or marginal shelves. All very large specimens tend to be females, and these are sighted most often during spring spawning periods when they enter margin bays or backwaters. A very popular sport fish throughout its range, especially in Europe.

GREEK CATFISH (*Siluris aristotelis*). Max weight: 45kg+ (100lb).
Sub-species of the Wels, that resides in the lower Achelós River and surrounding lakes.

HUCHEN or DANUBE SALMON (*Hucho Hucho*). Max length: 1.5m. (5ft+). Max weight: 52kg (114lb). Predatory.

Restricted to the Danube River system. Attempts have been made to introduce it to various rivers and lakes throughout Europe, although France seems to be the only country where introductions have been fairly successful. Heavy industrial pollution on the middle/lower Danube has taken a heavy toll on the population. Tributaries in Austria, and some parts of Eastern Europe, seem to be its last stronghold.

This salmon does not migrate to saltwater, but it does migrate within the river system and after spawning runs.

Best fishing normally occurs during the cold, winter months or early spring.

ATLANTIC SALMON. European range stretches throughout coastal waters and rivers. Today the population is largely decimated - with Iceland, Scotland, and Scandinavia being its last stronghold. Norwegian re-stocking programs with artificially reared fish have caused major problems with the surviving population's defences against parasites and diseases.

Anadromous, eg: migrates from the sea, far upriver to spawn, before returning to saltwater. A very popular sportfish.

See North America section for further information.

BROWN TROUT (*Salmo trutta*). Max length: 1.5m (5ft). Max weight: 42kg (94lb+). Predatory.

Three separate forms exist: the stationary river-form, the lake-form and the migratory-form. A 2-3kg river-form (Brown Trout) is a large specimen. The migratory-form (Sea Trout) often reaches 15kg+. The lake-form can sometimes exceed 20kg. The largest reported lake-form 'Brownie' was reported by a Swiss fisheries biologist at 42kg. A 1.4m. (4ft 7in) long, 31kg specimen was caught from Walshensee (lake) in Bayern. Lake-form Brown Trout exceeding 20kg are now very rare.

Brown trout are common throughout Europe, and have been introduced to waters around the World, mainly in their smaller river-form.

ATLANTIC STURGEON (*Acipenser sturio*). Max length: 3m.(10ft). Max weight: 214kg (470lb). Predatory/bottom living invertebrates.

Related and more likely identical species as the N. American Sturgeon (Acipencer oxyrinchus); see North America section.

Range covers most of European coastline, from Norway and Baltic, to Spain; including Mediterranean and Black Sea.

Anadromous, ascending large rivers to spawn during Spring.

Exploited by man from at least Mesolithic period. Now this wonderful fish is rare and faces extinction throughout its range. Isolated pockets of breeding fish still remain in the Gironde River, France; Quadalquiver River, Spain; and Lake Ladosjskoje, Russia.

Possibly already extinct from British rivers. Alec Allens's amazing catch of a 9ft 2in long (59in girth), 388lb Atlantic Sturgeon from the River Towy at Nantgaredig on July 28, 1933, was quite incredible. The account of this capture was written by Byron Rogers, and published in The Sunday Telegraph (with photo), and later re-published in 'The Fisherman's Bedside Book, by David & Gareth Pownall.

SEVRUGA or STELLATE STURGEON (*Acipencer stellatus*). Max length: 2m. (6ft 6 inches) Max weight: 77kg (170lb). Predatory.

Range is confined to the Caspian and Black Sea basins. Anadromous, ascending major rivers, such as the Volga, Ural, and Araks. Two migrating forms exist: some move upriver during autumn, and over-winter in freshwater. A second group that ascend the rivers in springtime joins them. Both forms spawn in late May-June.

The Black Sea population is still facing decline; but the decline of the Caspian population was halted by conversation measures and now seems to be recovering in numbers.

Two other large acipencer species inhabit the Black Sea and Caspain Sea: the SHIP STURGEON (Acipenser nudiventris) Max length: 2m. (6ft+); and the RUSSIAN STURGEON (Acipenser gueldenstaeti). Max length: 2.4m. (8ft). Both species ascend the rivers to spawn during April-May. The Ship Sturgeon is the only species of European sturgeon that normally inhabits the Aral Sea. Over-irrigation of feeder rivers has now caused the Aral Sea to shrink drastically and raised saline levels. This possibly has caused the extinction of that lake's population.

BELUGA (*Huo huso*). Max length: 5m. (16ft). Max weight: 1,524kg. Predatory.
Europe's largest freshwater fish, and a candidate (together with the Chinese Kaluga) for the World's largest freshwater fish; although the Chinese Paddlefish gets my vote for this supreme accolade!
A Beluga of 1,228kg (2,707lb) was caught in the Volga river mouth in 1924 (246kg of her weight was eggs!). Another giant of 1,220kg (2,690lb) caught in 1922, was carrying 146kg of eggs, and its head alone weighed 288kg (635lb)!
Found in the Caspian and Black Sea basins. Ascends the rivers in spring to spawn, although some groups enter during late autumn and over-winter in freshwater. More predatory than other European sturgeons, and large specimens will even attack and eat young Caspian seals.
Populations have been depleted throughout its range, with the Ural River being its last stronghold.

Introduced Species to Europe:

GRASS CARP. Native of Amur River system. Fish taken from the Amur River were first introduced to European Russia in 1939. The first artificial fertilisation of Russian Grass Carp stockfish took place in 1961, and these were later transported to North America (see N. America section). In 1963, Hungary received the first batches of stockfish. Two years later, some of these Hungarian fish were introduced into Germany. It was later introduced to lakes and rivers throughout Europe, and other countries Worldwide. It seems unable to reach weights in excess of 15kg when introduced to northern latitude waters of Scandinavia or Great Britain. Sometimes reaches weights in excess of 35kg in central-southern European countries. 100lb+ specimens have been reported from Italy, Germany and Yugoslavia.
Another Amur River species, the SILVER CARP (Hypophthalmichthys moltrix) Max length: 1m. (39in). Max weight: 20kg, has also been introduced to Germany and a few other European countries, but is less common than the Grass Carp.

MARMOR CARP (*Aristichthys Noblis*). Max length: 1.5m Max weight: 58kg (130lb). Aquatic plant eater/Omnivorous (also predatory at certain times).
Native range is Chinese and S.E. Asian rivers and lakes. It has been introduced to numerous European countries, but German waters seem to have had the greatest success.
It was first thought that the above 3 forms of 'grass carp' could not breed in European waters. This has later been proved incorrect and many lakes and rivers now have breeding populations.
At least two 100lb+ Marmor carp have been landed on rod & line from German waters; the first in 1993, and another from the Havel, near Berlin, in 1996. A 129lb Silver Carp was reported caught from Lake Valence in 1995, but this more probably was the large-headed Marmor species.

WEST, N.CENTRAL & EAST ASIA

TIGRIS BARBEL (*Barbus seich*). Max length: 2.4m (8ft). Max weight: 100kg (220lb+). Predatory/Omnivorous.

Range is restricted to the Tigris and Euphrates river systems that flow through S.E. Turkey, Syria, W. Iran, and Iraq.

The largest of all Barbel, and a close relative of the Indian 'Mahseer' species. Records of two 50kg+ specimens caught on rod & line in 1915 and 1918. Specimens weighing 167lb and 123lb were recorded from the Euphrates River in 1918 on hand-lines (mentioned by Lt.Col. R.B.Praye).

Typical of the large barbel species, it is a very powerful and exciting fighter on rod & line. Past writings on this magnificent fish detail feeding habits similar to that of the S. Indian Mahseer.

Recent information is almost non-existent on this species, due mainly to the constant conflicts in its complete native range. How much damage has the last 70 years of bombs and pollution inflicted upon the fragile environment of the mighty Tigris Barbel? I hazard to guess, but I still hope that there are some wild areas left which hold numbers of this wonderful fish.

USATCH (*Barbus brachycephalus*). Max length: 1.3m (4ft+). Max weight: 25kg (50lb+). Predatory/Omnivorous.

It comes in two forms: One resides in both the Anu-Darja and Syr Darja rivers that flow from the N.W. Pamir and Tien Shan mountain ranges, then flow west over the Mujon & Kara Plains to feed the (shrinking) Aral Sea. The other form is native of the northern brackish waters of the Caspian inland sea, and migrates up the Volga, Ural, and Terak rivers to spawn. Again, pollution and over-irrigation rears its ugly head, causing the Usatch Barbel to decline rapidly in recent years.

TAIMEN (*Hucho taimen*). Max length: 2m. (6_ft). Max weight: 70kg (154lb). Predatory.

This Siberian form of the European Huchen is found in medium to large rivers throughout northern Asia. A range stretching from N.E. Finland to N.E. Siberia. There have been past reports of massive specimens over 200lb, but catastrophic pollution and uncontrolled destruction of the environment over much of its range during the past 60 years, would rule out such sizes. Major rivers like the Ob, still receive tons of toxic waste from industrial & chemical plants that line its banks. However, Siberia is a huge area and there still is a slow trickle of reports of 100lb+ fish being caught from rivers that flow through the wildest areas of Siberia's vastness. Most of such rivers can only be reached by helicopter, or weeks of overland travel.

CHINESE PADDLEFISH (*Psephurus gladius*). Max length: 7m (23ft). Predatory.

Found only in the lower reaches of the Yangtze Kiang River in E. China. Possibly the World's largest freshwater fish. Scant information exisits on this 'giant of the giants', but it is known to be primarily a predator on small fish, unlike its relative in N.America which is a plankton eater. The size of its present population is unknown, but because the banks of its entire range are crowded by large cities and heavy industry, I fear that not many large specimens remain. The flesh of the paddlefish is highly regarded by the Chinese. These facts, combined with China's obsession about killing any large or rare living creature on this planet, just to satisfy their thirst for "cures from all evils" found in glass bottles or powdered potions, does not paint a rosy future for the survival of monsters such as the Paddlefish.

KALUGA (*Huso dauricus*). Max length: 5.5m (18ft). Max weight: 1,200kg+ (2,645lb+). Predatory. Found only in the Argun/Amur river system.

Another candidate for the World's largest freshwater fish. This monster migrates within the river system, but does not enter the sea. Like the White Sturgeon (Acipencer transmontanus), the Kaluga over-winters in very deep holes or channels of the main river or estuary (although the White Sturgeon does also enter coastal waters). Fish of all species - from carp to migrating salmon - predominate in the great Kaluga's diet.

Almost faced with extinction from over exploitation, but recent intervention has slowed down its decline. Even so, very large females (which like most sturgeon species, can be more than 100 years old) are still a rare sight. It is hard for a 5 metre long fish to escape the hands of man for more than 100 years!

NORTHERN PIKE. Inhabits a large range, including northern Asia. See European section for further information.

AMUR PIKE (*Essox reicherti*). Max length: 1.25m (4ft). Max weight: 25kg (50lb+). Rare over 15kg. Predatory.

Found only in the Amur River system (and connecting lakes), that flows from the Mongolian mountains east of Ulaanbaatar, to the delta at Nikolayevsk.

Overwinters in main channels of rivers and migrates to shallow back-bays or weedy inlets to spawn during spring. Otherwise it is much less restricted to margin habitats than that of its relative the Northern Pike, and the Amur Pike much prefers the open-water habitat of large lakes or rivers.

GRASS CARP. Native of the Amur, Lia Ho, Hwang Ho, Yangtze Kiang and Si Kiang river systems of lowland China. Introduced throughout Asia and Worldwide. See other sections for more information.

SILVER CARP & MARMOR CARP. Native to lowland rivers and lakes in China, especially Amur,Yangtze Klang and Hwang Ho lower river basins. Introduced to numerous other countries, especially in S.E. Asia and Europe. See 'Introduced Species - Europe' for more information.

BLACK CARP (*Mylopharyngodon piceus*). 1.5m. (5ft). Max. weight: 75kg (150lb+). Omnivorous. Native to the Amur River system, this huge carp has a long history of introductions across China, and other countries in South East Asia. Introduced worldwide to at least 26 different countries during the past century. Most of these introductions failed to establish the Black Carp, but countries such as Cuba, Costa Rica, Vietnam, South Africa and Uzbekistan now have reproductive populations. Very similar in shape to the grass carp (Ctenopharyngodon idellus), except for slight differences in shape and size of fins, position of eyes and size of mouth. The most noticeable difference is a

bluish-slate colouration to the scales, which is why it is called 'Blue' carp in some regions. In Bangladesh, this carp is referred to as the 'Snail' carp due to its ferocious appetite for snails. Large snails are the main hook bait used to catch this species in Japan, where it is known as 'Ao-uo'.

This fish feeds mainly on crustaceans and aquatic insects, but its main diet is muscles and snails. First brought to USA during the early 1970's. Approximately thirty Black carp, including thousands of Bighead carp escaped from a fish farm in Missouri, USA and entered into the Osage River in April 1994.

The Black carp is a beautiful species and its torpedo-like shape and great size gives it superb fighting qualities. Read the 'Land of the Rising Sun' chapter for more detailed information on this relatively unknown carp.

MIRROR/LEATHER/COMMON CARP. Native range stretches from central Europe to China. Clay models of ponds containing common carp were excavated in the suburbs of Hanzong County, Shanxi Province that dated from the Han Dynasty 25-220 AD.

Introduced into many countries throughout the World and has also expanded its range by natural migration over vast distances. Today, the carp is the most widespread freshwater fish in the World, covering a total of 110 different countries. Some notable waters (just part of a list of thousands) include: rivers running into the Caspain Sea - Volga & Ural river systems; Balkhash Lake in Kazhskaya; Issyk Kul Lake in Kirgizskaya; Amur, Hwang Ho, Yangtze Kiang, and Liaho Ho river/canal/lake systems in China.

See other sections for further information.

INDIA & SOUTHEAST ASIA

HIMALAYAN MAHSEER (*Tor putitora*). Max length: 2.7m (9ft). Max weight: 65kg (140lb). Predatory/Omnivorous.

Note: the latin name of Barbus to classify Mahseer has been dropped, and all Mahseer species are under the genus - Tor.

This long, slim but muscular-built fish is native of most rivers draining the southern Himalayan mountain chain, from Pakistan to Yunnan province, China.

Severely depleted through pollution, irrigation, dams and over-fishing throughout its range. Today, 45kg+ specimens are unheard of, and 25kg is approaching maximum weight. A few monster specimens may still exist in the main Ganges River, but I would hedge my bets on the big rivers draining the eastern Himalayas to be the last stronghold of this magnificent fish - such as the Tsangpo/Bramaputra River where it falls thousands of feet off the cold Tibetan Plateau, then plunges through the sultry heat of the N.E. Assam jungle; or the upper sections of the Naku Chu (Salween), Lan Tsang Kiang (Mekong), and Yangtze Kiang in N.E. Yunnan province of China.

These areas are either strictly out-of-bounds for foreigners, or very difficult to reach. The best prospects with easier access, is either the upper Ganges above Hardwar Dam, or the Lubit River, which is a tributary of the Brahmaputra.

The best periods of the year to tackle the snow-fed rivers of the majestic Himalayas are shortly after the monsoon seasons, when the weather becomes hot and the gray-slate coloured flood waters begin to drop and clear. Large plugs or spinners seem to be the most chosen method, but live or dead baits might also be worth a try.

In 1882, Hamilton stated that the Mahseer of the Brahmaputra River system was a completely different species than the mahseer found in the Ganges River system. In his later published report (Day and Buchanan, 1877) he states that the Brahmaputra species grows to 9ft in length, with 6ft being a common size. He also stated that although the Ganges mahseer may attain 4-5ft (1.5m+) in length, it grows nowhere near as large as the Brahmaputra mahseer. He actually placed the Brahmaputra mahseer under the latin name Tor putitora and the Ganges mahseer under Tor mosal. With all the confusion over latin names for the mahseer over the past 100 years, I have chosen to use the more accepted placing for Tor mosal, which is now only used for the south Indian mahseer that resides in the Cauvery (Kaveri) River.

HUMPBACKED MAHSEER (*Tor mosal*). Max length: 2m+ (7ft). Max weight: 70kg+ (150lb+). Predatory/Omnivorous.

Definite sightings of 150lb+ specimens. Fish up to 200lb may still exist. Largest rod caught specimen was landed by J. de Wet Van Ingen, in 1946 from the Cubbany River, south India. Most of the rod-caught 100lb+ mahseer were taken 1870 - 1950. Since 1950, 45kg+ fish tend to fall to experienced handline techniques of local Indian villagers. Apart from two very recent exceptions: a 104lb specimen falling to Steve Harper's ball of Ragi paste cast into the head of 'Crocodile Pool' on the W.A.S.I. stretch of the famous Cauvery River; and yet another 104lb monster (which turned out to be the same fish that had swam miles upriver) caught from the Cauvery Fishing Camp stretch near Bhimeswari.

Native range is the Coleroon River system of South India. Although tributaries such as the Bhavani, Shimsha, Hemavati and Amaravati hold dwindling numbers of mahseer, it is only the Cauvery and to a lesser extent, the Kabbani tributaries which are left as their true strongholds. This mahseer comes in a variety of colours, ranging from black, green, silver or gold. A black mahseer of 75lb is indeed a rare fish, but quite common in the gold/silver variety.

JUNGLE MAHSEER (*Tor progeneius*). Max length: 1.5m (4ft 6 inches). Max weight: 31.7kg (70lb). Predatory/Omnivorous.

Range stretches across Burma and northern Thailand. Over fishing and netting, rising population levels, pollution levels, tree-felling etc., have placed pressures on this mahseer. Only the wildest, jungle-fringed rivers of northern or N.E. Burma are likely to still hold specimens over 25kg.

THAILAND MAHSEER. (*Tor tambroides*). Max length: 1.5m (4ft+). Max weight: 32kg (70lb+). Predatory/Omnivorous.
Slightly more robust and deeper bodied than Tor putitora, and its range covers the Ping/Chao Phraya and Mekong river systems.

GOONCH CATFISH (*Bagarius yarelli*). Max length: 2m+(7ft). Max weight: 113kg (250lb+). Predatory/Omnivorous.
Found throughout India, Burma, Vietnam, and the large islands of Sumatra, Borneo and Java.
In the middle reaches of large rivers, it frequents areas with bottom debris such as dead or sunken log piles, or beneath floating houses. In fast, boulder-strewn stretches of the upper river, the Goonch will often be found side-by-side in areas frequented by the large Mahseer. During spawning time, this huge catfish forms large groups or shoals and enters depressions or large eddies at the edge of rapids.
Its body is long and slender with many colour variations, from deep olive-green, to deep brown or bi-coloured. The head is sometimes striped with blue, which may indicate a colour change associated with the spawning period, like that of the south Indian barbel species. In India, it seems to be much more common in the Ganges River system than in southern rivers.

SILOND CATFISH (*Silondia gangetica*). Max length: 1.85m. (6ft+) Max weight: 60kg+ (132lb+). Becomes almost solely predatory when fully grown.
Confined mainly to the lower or tidal stretches of the Ganges. Unconfirmed reports of this fish also from rivers in Burma. Migrates to upstream stretches to spawn at the end of the rainy season. Like the Boalli, the Silond is sometimes termed by locals as a fresh-water shark.

BOALLI CATFISH (*Wallago attu*). Max length: 2m. (6ft+). Max weight: 55kg (120lb+). Predatory/Omnivorous.
Range extends throughout most of mainland South-eastern Asia, including large islands such as Sumatra and Java.
A very active and ferocious predator, hunting at all depths, but also prone to attack prey fish at the surface in a commotion of froth and spray - Reports of massive specimens in excess of 2.4m (8ft) in Bengal. Sometimes referred to as the "freshwater Shark" by natives, because of body-parts sometimes being found in stomach contents. This is more likely to stem from eating bodies offered to the river during ceremonial offerings. In some areas, the Boalli is as much feared as the crocodiles!
It is valued as a good food source by many, but in some areas it may be avoided because of its allegedly unclean feeding habits.
Large spoons, plugs, livebaits, deadbaits, or pungent smelling pastes will attract this goliath Asian catfish.

SEENGHALLA CATFISH (*Aorichthys seenghala*). Max length: 2m. (6ft+). Max weight: 120kg (265lb). Predatory/Omnivorous.

Range spreads across Pakistan, India, Bangladesh, and Burma. A very similar catfish in the same genus, Aorichthys aor, also grows to at least 2 metres in length. Both of these massive catfishes have a similar elongated body shape as the Goonch, but slightly more robust. They are differentiated from the Goonch by their plainer colouration, smaller pectoral fins, more pronounced lateral-line groove, and much larger fins.

MEKONG CATFISH (*Pangasianodon gigas*). Max length: 2.5m. (8ft). Max weight: 150kg+ (230lb+). Vegetarian.

Range is restricted to the Mekong River and its tributaries in Thailand, Laos, Cambodia and Vietnam. During constant downpours of the rainy season, these gigantic catfish spend most of their time in the lower reaches of the Mekong. As soon as the floodwaters subside, they begin to move upstream on their long and arduous journey. Some large specimens even reach the Yunnan province of China, thousands of kilometres upriver. Other groups enter the large backwaters or lakes that connect to the main river. The largest individuals have no teeth and this has given rise to the belief that Pangasionodon is not actually a separate species after all, but merely one of the Pangasius species that has grown very old and lost its teeth - and therefore has adapted to an almost predominately vegetarian diet. Not a single juvenile Mekong catfish has ever been captured, and because Pangasianodon is differentiated from certain small Pangasius specimens solely by lack of teeth, this may confirm that belief.

PUNGAS CATFISH (*Pangasius sanitwongsei*). Max length: 3m.(9.75ft). Max weight: 200kg (440lb+). Predatory/Omnivrous.

Restricted mainly to the Chao Phraya River and its tributaries, which include the Ping, Yam, Nan and Pa Sak in western/central Thailand.

The young fish can be found in small tributaries, but the larger adults tend to inhabit deeper channels of the main river. Although not poisonous, monster-sized specimens should be handled with care, as their lethal-looking pectoral fin spines can inflict deep - and sometimes fatal - wounds. Is reputed to scavenge on dead animal carcasses and other refuse, which has made it unpopular for eating in some locations. However, it is valued as a food source in most localities, although the market selling size is generally around _ - 1 metre long.

As with most large Asian catfish species, over-fishing has severely depleted the current population and it is now a very rare sight to view a specimen Pungas over 2.5m long. In the past, fish of this size were relatively common, and one 3m long monster was reported to require the strength of eight grown men to carry it!

GREEN CATFISH (*Plotosus canius*). Max length: 1.6m (5ft). Max weight: 25kg+ (55lb+). Predatory.
Found in rivers and lakes of India. A long and slender eel-like body with a dark olive colouration tinged with violet. A much sought after food source by the natives.

INDIAN LONGFINNED & AFRICAN MOTTLED EEL (*Anguilla nebulosa*). Max length: 1.8m (6ft). Max weight: 25kg (55lb+). Predatory.

The two subspecies A. nebulosa nebulosa from the Indian sub-continent, and A.n. labiata from East Africa and Madagascar are almost identical in features and also have similar colouration and body form to the Australian Mottled Eel.

The Indian form breeds in the Indian Ocean and the African form is believed to breed in the deeps off the Madagascar coast. Like its relatives found in Australia and New Zealand, these big eels often travel many miles upriver. One specimen was found in Zimbabwe, 1,610km (over 1,000 miles) from the coast.

INDIAN CARP (*Catla buchanani*). Max length: 1.3m (4ft 2in). Max weight: 45kg+ (100lb+). Omnivorous.

Found mainly in rivers and lakes of northern India, but has also been introduced to various south Indian waters. Has a very large head and pronounced, upturned mouth. It has a very fast growth rate and is often contained in breeding tanks because of its high food value amongst the Indian population. Reports of 100lb+ carp from various Indian waters and one documented 89lb specimen from Race Course Lake, Calcutta.

SIAMESE CARP (*Catlocarpio siamensis*). Max length: 3m. (10ft). Max weight: 200kg+ (440lb+). Omnivorous.

Found in the rivers & lakes systems of Thailand, Laos, Cambodia and southern Vietnam.

This, the World's largest member of the carp family, inhabits the largest and deepest of S.E. Asian rivers - but 100 years of waste products being dumped into the water, combined with construction of irrigation channels and reservoirs has attracted this colossal fish into artificial storage areas, lakes and populated environments.

It is thought to migrate within the river systems. A very strong fish, with reports of large specimens that have towed fishermen's boats for hours before being landed. The Siamese Carp will take various baits, such as balls of cooked rice and no doubt also flavoured pastes or boilies. See special chapter on this species.

GOLDEN CARP (*Probarbus julieni*). Max length: 1.6m (5ft). Max weight: 75kg (160lb+). Omnivourous. Although the Golden Carp is scientifically classed under the 'barbus' family, it is definitely more of a carp – and must rate, along with the Black carp, as World's second largest species of carp. Sometimes referred to as 'Julien's Golden Price Carp', this must surely be one of the most spectacular looking fish in the world. Similar to a massive common carp in body shape (except for shorter dorsal fin), with large golden scales and black diagonal stripe markings (similar to the Dorado's), makes this carp an absolute stunner! A rare and much sought-after carp in its native Thailand.

Introduced Species to India & Southeast Asia:

MIRROR/LEATHER/COMMON CARP. Introduced into selected waters throughout India & S.E. Asia and

also spread naturally through many river/lake systems. It seems very patchy in its distribution and is more numerous within man-made stock ponds, canals or reservoirs. Unfortunately, in these environments the carp often becomes over populated and has stunted growth. This may also be due to constant warm temperatures combined with competition from numerous other large Cyprinidae species.

AUSTRALIA, NEW GUINEA & NEW ZEALAND

GIANT PERCH or MURRAY COD (*Maccullochella macquariensis*). Max length: 1.85m (6ft). Max weight: 90kg (198lb). Predatory.
Found throughout the Murray/Darling river system in Australia. Smaller populations exist in the Dawson and Mary rivers of New South Wales, including the Clarence and Richmond rivers in Queensland. It has also been introduced to various other waters, such as the 25-mile long Eildon Lake in Victoria.

Intense fishing, dams, irrigation, etc., has placed a heavy toll on the native population. Large 40kg+ specimens are now a very rare occurrence and a maximum of 25kg is now more normal in most waters. Some stretches of the Murray River & lake system still hold dwindling numbers of monster-sized fish. The best areas are: Mulwala Lake near Yarrawonga; the Barmah Island (part of the State forest area); the Boundary Bend State forest area; the Riverland District in South Australia; and upstream of Alexandrina Lake.

Medium large plugs, livebaits, crayfish, grubs or worms are favourite baits for the Murray Cod. The fish is not actually a "cod", but more related the large perch or bass species. It resembles the Nile Perch in body shape, except it has a much smaller head, with beautiful green-mottled markings along the back and flanks.

It prefers dense, overgrown habitat - such as submerged trees and tangled branches - so heavy gear is a must in most areas; although it is not a particularly strong fighter in relation to its size. The Mulwala Lake holds the fastest growing stock of Murray Cod in Australia.

QUEENSLAND LUNGFISH (*Neoceratodus forsteri*). Max length: 1.5m(5ft).   Predatory/Omnivorous.

Natural range is restricted to the Burnett and Mary rivers in Queensland, but it has also been introduced to numerous other waters, including: the Enoggara Reservoir and the Albert, Coomera and Brisbane rivers.

Unlike its African relative, this species does not aestivate in drying mud-burrows during summer, but is confined to permanent waters (although it is able to breathe air).

The Lungfish is one of Australia's most threatened freshwater fish. Some conversation measures have been taken, but large, mature specimens of this species still remain very rare.

GOLDEN PERCH or CALLOP (*Plectroplites ambiguus*). Max length: 91cm (3ft). Max weight: 25kg (55lb+). Predatory.

Found throughout the Murray/Darling river system, including muddy backwaters and farm pools. It has also been introduced to numerous waters in S.W. Australia.

It has a very deep, bream-like body shape with striking gold-coloured flanks. Sought after for eating and as a sportfish. Over-fishing has caused a scarcity of older specimens exceeding 18kg (40lb). Most Golden Perch caught are under 10lb.

GIANT PERCH or PALMER (*Lates calcarifer*). Max length: 1.8m (6ft). Max weight: 60kg (134lb). Predatory.

Often referred to in Australia as 'Barramundi', but this confuses matters because the only true species by that name is the Spotted Barramundi (Scleropages leichardti) that rarely reaches lengths in excess of 90cm (35.5 inches) and weight over 5kg. Therefore, any 'Barramundi' weighing much over 10kg is almost certainly a Giant Perch.

Found in both fresh and brackish/salt waters. Its wide range spreads across most of the Indian Ocean's coastal waters from the Persian Gulf to Indonesia, the Philippines and China. In Australia it is confined to the northern rivers and shallow coastal bays, especially those rivers running into the Gulf of Carpentaria, which include: the Leichhadt, Flinders, Norman, Roper, Gilbert, Mitchell and Coleman rivers.

It is very closely related to the Nile Perch of Africa and has similar external features, except that the Palmer is not so robust and has a more gradual slope from dorsal to gape. It is an impressive looking fish with strange forward dorsal fin spines, bright red eyes, and flanks covered with silver scales.

This fish is sought after for both food and for sport throughout its range. In northern Australia it ranks as the most popular sporting fish. The best fishing times are when the large adults move upriver to spawn, or during April/May.

The Palmer also inhabits the southern rivers of Papua New Guinea, especially the lower reaches of the Fly River.

Australian MOTTLED EEL (*Anguilla Rheinhardti*). Max length: 2m. (7ft). Max weight: 45kg (100lb). Predatory.

I first found this huge eel by accident whilst fishing for carp in Victoria, Australia. Very little information has been written about this very interesting species. Two smaller species of eel: Anguilla bicolor pacifica and Anguillla marmorata are found in northern Australian and Papua New Guinean rivers, but it is only Anguilla nebulosa (both African and Indian forms) that closely resembles A. Reinhardti, so it is possibly closely related.

Abundant in most rivers and their tributaries in South Australia, Victoria and Queensland.

It has olive-tan to light brown colouration with darker mottling along the back, especially pronounced around the head; with yellow or cream underside.

It prefers dense, overhead cover, especially sunken trees and tangled roots. Like its neighbour the New Zealand Longfin, it is a very ferocious predator and will attack and eat all types of fish or animals in the water, including animal carcasses. Its sharp teeth can cut through any thickness of nylon, so it is imperative that you fish with heavy wire traces. Sheep or Ox organs, especially kidney or heart, prove to be a superb bait. Like most eels, it is most active at dusk or during warm nights. See special 'Australian Giants' chapter for further information on this, the World's largest freshwater eel.

New Zealand LONGFINNED EEL (*Anguilla dieffenbachi*). Max length: 1.8m. (6ft). Max weight: 25kg (55lb+). Predatory.

Found in most river systems of both the north and south islands. Enters reservoirs and lakes, and will often travel many miles up small creeks or tributaries. In warm months it will enter minute streams and ditches at fairly high altitudes.

Colouration is black/dark grey to dark brown, and is more similar to the European eel than it is to the more robust Australian species. Grows to a much larger size than the other NZ eel - the Shortfinned Eel (A. australis).

The longfinned Eel has been under pressure from over fishing, especially commercial fisheries over the past 30 years. Massive specimens up to 50lb were quite common at one time and were often caught by Maori tribe fishermen, but now a 30lb+ eel is very rare. The south island gives a better chance of monster specimens today.

See special chapters on NZ eels for further information.

A giant Perch (Murray Cod) caught by Simon Channing from Australia.

Introduced Species to Australia, NG. & NZ:

MIRROR/LEATHER/COMMON CARP. Introduced into mountain lakes of Maokari Province in Irian Jaya. Introduced into Papua New Guinea from Australia in 1959 for aquaculture. Breakouts from holding ponds due to floods, gave the carp initial access to the Sepik River system in 1980. Now carp have spread throughout river drainages of the lowland reaches of the Sepik and Ramu rivers. Although weights of 60kg have been reported, these have proved to be almost certainly false. David Coate has been studying the Sepik fish species for many years and has yet to encounter carp much in excess of 10kg. However, with little competition from other species, it may be possible that the Sepik could produce some outstanding carp in the near future.

Introduced to Australia in the late 1800's, although there is some confusion to whether these dates actually refer to the Crucian Carp (Carassius carassius). The first introductions of true carp (Cyprinus carpio) were obviously the 'wildie' strain and faster growing strains came from England in the early 1900's. However, it is only during the past 50 years that carp have become widely established. Two separate isolated reports of carp caught near Perth in Western Australia and in Tasmania during 1996; otherwise, the carp is mainly confined to the Murray/Darling River & lakes system and the Gippsland Lakes & rivers system in S.E. Queensland. Because of over population and slow growth genetics, most areas hold few carp over 15kg. Specimens in excess of 20-25kg are best sought after in Lake Alexandrina or the Gipppsland District.

The largest recorded rod & line caught carp in Australia was a 35lb+ common, caught by Tony Davies-Patrick on boilies from Lake Alexandrina. See 'Ozzie Carp' chapter for more information.

KOI CARP (*Cyprinus carpio*). An exotic variety of carp that comes in a fantastic array of different colour body patterns. Originally produced in Japan for ornamental ponds, it has become a favourite and sometimes very expensive aquarium or pond pet for many collectors Worldwide.

Smuggled into New Zealand from Singapore in 1950. It was then distributed to various private customers around the country. Some years later, a flash flood caused some holding pools to overflow on a private Koi breeder's farm situated at Parrongia, near Hamilton. They naturally reproduced and spread to the larger Waikato River. Today the Koi Carp is well established in many rivers and lakes throughout the north island. It is believed that these fish are the only true 'wild' breeding population in a major river system in the World. I have seen specimens of at least 15kg (30lb+) and one resident carp angler living in New Zealand has told me of fish seen in excess of 23kg (50lb). Average size tends to be between 3 - 8kg. Varied shades of orange are the most common colours, often speckled with black fleks, but they may also have white with black fleks, or sometimes a pure white or cream. Mirror Koi Carp is also present, although these are very rare.

Wild Koi Carp tend to be much more timid in their feeding habits than common carp, so to be successful, a different approach to normal fishing techniques is needed.

See special photos in this book of the spectacular wild Koi Carp from New Zealand.

AFRICA

BARBEL-CATFISH (Clarius gareipinus). Max length: 1.4m. (4ft 6inches). Max weight: 60kg (132lb). Predatory/Omnivorous.

C. gariepinus is sometimes referred to as the South African form and C. mossambicus is given to the East African form, but both of these are generally recognised as the same species. Body colouration is usually grey/brown mottling with a distinct dark stripe either side of the lower head and cream-white underside.

This catfish has a wide distribution in lakes and river systems across eastern and southern Africa, including: Orange River system, Natal River drainage, Zambezi River, Lake Victoria, Blue Nile, etc.

Although it is sometimes found in deep, open water, it prefers to hunt in relatively shallow areas or marginal shelves. It can survive in poorly oxygenated water and may even leave the water at night to search for land-based food, by using its strong pectoral fin spines for "walking". It is generally a freshwater fish, but sometimes it can be found in fairly brackish waters of the upper estuaries. It migrates upriver in large numbers to spawn during floods. Most of the spawning takes place at night in the swollen tributaries or inlets. Hatchlings remain upstream for about six months before they are large enough to migrate downstream. In Lake Victoria, spawning takes place inside the flooded papyrus swamps shortly after the rains. Growth is very rapid as they are partial to a wide variety of foods, although as they grow older they become more predatory.

This catfish is very sought after for its good tasting flesh. Over-fishing has vastly reduced the number of adult catfish over 1 metre long.

VUNDU Catfish (*Heterobranchus lonfilis*). Max length: 1.5m(4ft+). Max weight: 60kg (130lb+). Predatory/Omnivorous.

Widespread throughout Africa, including: the Niger, Nile, Congo and Zambezi river systems.

It prefers lakes or slow-moving waters of creeks or swamps, but may also be found in more turbulent waters, such as the fabulous Murchison Falls area in Uganda.

Body colouration can vary considerably according to location, but is usually olive brown with white underside and cream-yellowish fins. Its flesh is not as popular for eating as the Clarius species and large specimens are more frequent. Even so, it is still rare to come across a 30kg+ specimen. This large catfish also undertakes breeding migrations upriver during floods.

Note: A number of other species of catfish set under the genus Dinotopterus (such as D. cunningtoni...sounds like me!) occupy the Malawi and Tanganyika lakes and are almost identical to the Vundu, except for slight variations in adipose fin length or head shield length, etc.

TANGANYIKA CATFISH (*Chrysichthys grandis*). Max length: 2m+ (7ft). Max weight: 190kg (420lb). Possibly 600lb specimens. Predatory/Omnivorous.

This is the largest species of catfish in Africa. A stockier and more robust body form than either the Barbel-Catfish or the Vundu. Little is known about this monster fish and I would therefore conclude that it is quite rare. Another monster catfish inhabits the Congo River and although I cannot find reference to that species, (although Jeremy Wade has indicated at it being Heterobranchus) it may possibly be the same species as the Tanganyika, or at least in the same genus.

AFRICAN CATFISH (*Auchenoglanis occidentalis*). Max length: 1m+.(3.5ft) Max weight: 20-25kg.

Widespread across West Africa, Sudan, Egypt, central Africa, Kenya and Lake Tanganyika. This catfish is the most common species of the genus Auchenoglanis that is kept for aquarium use (first imported in 1909), although it has never been so popular as some of the smaller species because it can attain such a large size.

LONGFINNED CATFISH (*Bagrus docmac*). Max length: 1m+(3.5ft). Max weight: 34kg (75lb) Predatory.

Widely distributed throughout the Nile River system, Great Lakes, Ghana and Nigeria. A valued food fish in most areas. Small specimens are quite omnivorous in their feeding habits, but large individuals are almost solely predatory on smaller fish species.

ORANGE RIVER BARBEL (*Barbus kimbeleyensis*). Max length: 1m+(3.5ft). Max weight: 25kg (55lb). Predatory/Omnivorous.

Found in the Vaal and Orange rivers of South Africa, and adapts well to large manmade reservoirs. Referred locally by the name 'Yellowfish'. It is the largest of South Africa's indigenous scale-bearing species. Like most barbel species, this fish is a very powerful fighter. Takes a variety of baits, but large specimens prefer live fish or crayfish. The rod-caught record is 48lb 13oz.

NILE PERCH (*Lates niloticus*). Max length: 2m.(6ft+). Max weight: 115kg+ (250lb+). Predatory.

Found in Lake Victoria, and the Nile, Congo, Niger, Volta and Chari river/lake systems.

Worshiped from the time of the Egyptians and mummified in their burial grounds, and is still highly regarded today as a food source or sporting fish. This giant fish (which is closely related to the Palmer) is a voracious hunter and will often leap clear of the water when hooked. Even so, it is not generally regarded as a particularly 'strong' fighter in relation to its size. It has been re-introduced to some waters, such as Lake Nasser, to replenish waning stocks and on this particular water the fish are growing very well, with a few now reaching 200lb.

LAKE ALBERT PERCH (*Lates albertianus*). Max length: 2m+ (6ft+). Predatory.
Sub-species of the Nile Perch that is confined to Lake Albert and drainage (Albert & Murchison Niles).
Although sometimes found in deep water, it prefers the shallower inshore areas or margins of the rivers. This is a very important food fish to locals in the area. One of the best places to fish for specimens exceeding 200lb is below the spectacular Murchison Falls in Uganda.

GOLIATH TIGERFISH (*Hydrocynus goliath*). Max length: 2m+ (6ft+). Max weight: 115kg (250lb+). Predatory.

Catfish often grow to Monster sizes.

Found in the great Zaire River basin (Congo), including lakes Tumba, Mai-Ndombe, Tanganyika, Mweru, Upmemba, and Bangweulu. A giant version of the common Tigerfish, but with huge, razor sharp dog-like teeth that can cut through wire as if cotton. Often found near snag-ridden areas, at edges of deep drop-offs and river junctions or major tributaries. Will take most lures, livebaits and wobbled deadbaits. Tends to jump when hooked and often throws hooks if there is not a strong hookhold in the bone-hard mouth.

Introduced Species to Africa:

MIRROR/LEATHER/COMMON CARP. First shipments of carp came form Germany in 1859, and were introduced to lakes in the Cape Province; then later to other waters around South Africa until around 1879. A large amount of natural colonization and spread has also occurred throughout the river & lake systems. Now well established throughout the Vaal/Oranje (Orange) River system. Large reservoirs tend to hold some of the biggest specimens, such as: Vaal Dam, Gariep Dam, PK le Roux Dam, Raubenheimer Dam, Bloemhof Dam, Hartbeespoort Dam, Bram Raubenheimer Dam, Allemanskraal Dam, etc.

Numerous 40lb+ carp have been caught from many different waters in recent years. Most of these have come from Goldmire Lake (Donaldsons), Rushmere Lake, and Klaserie Reservoir. The last of these two waters have produced carp topping 50lb, and are controlled by the superb South African carpfishing holiday company - African Gold. The current S.A. rod & line Record for carp is a 66lb+ from Klaserie.

Earlier recordings of large carp include: a 48lb specimen from Hartbeespoort Dam; a 55lb fish from Bon Accord Dam, and a massive 37.72kg specimen from the same water, which was beached then killed by a local African fisherman. (74lb carp – now dead and mounted - was also caught from an African Gold venue near Johannesburg).

Consignments of carp from South Africa were transported across the northern border into Zimbabwe in 1925 and introduced into selected waters. The largest carp caught on rod & line in Zimbabwe was a 53lb 12oz specimen from Mazoe Dam. Two other very large carp were reported from the same water: a 62lb caught on hand line in 1965, and a 72lb 12oz giant that was snagged by a bass angler who eventually dragged in the dead fish.

The large dams receive the heaviest pressure from local fishermen, but the smaller waters also hold some very good carp and have the added advantage of being less crowded. Generally the more remote the water is and more difficult the access, the better the fishing and more spectacular the scenery.

Between 1925 and 1977, numerous introductions of carp were made to waters all over Africa. Wherever the British have travelled or colonised in the past, you can be almost certain that some Cyprinus carpio have been introduced. Many African countries hold isolated populations, even in very remote mountain lakes.

BLACK CARP & GRASS CARP: Both species introduced (as far as I know) to only one special lake in South Africa – where the Grass carp reach 100lb, and the Back carp now exceeds 150lb in weight! See 'Dreambreaker' chapter for more information.

'Globetrotter' with a beautiful Smallmouth Buffalo carp caught in Texas.

CONTACTS LIST

GLOBAL FISHING & ADVENTURE TRAVEL:

Globetrotterworld Adventure Fishing (Special guided trips to Big-Fish locations with Tony Davies-Patrick. Email: globetrotterworld@hotmail.com, Internet: www.globetrotterworld.co.uk

PHOTOGRAPHY:

Globetrotter-World Photography (Fishing, Nature, Travel & Adventure Sports):
Email: globetrotterworld@hotmail.com
Pentax: http://www.mir.com.my/rb/photography/hardwares/classics/pentaxlx/
Nikon: http://www.nikonians.org/

PUBLISHERS & PRINTERS:

Drukkerij Westerlaan, v.d. Meer de Walcherenstraat 1, 7131 EN Lichtenvoorde, Holland. Postbus 84, 7130 AB Lichtenvoorde, Holland. Tel: +31(0)544371207. Email: info@drukkerij-westerlaan.nl
Westerlaan Publisher, Postbus 84, internet: www.westerlaan-publisher.com

FISHING HOLIDAYS to:

France:
European River Tours, 2 Brougham Close, Great Wakering, Essex SS3 OHS. Tel: 01702218965. Mobile: 07969132773.

Spain-catfish & carp:
Bavarian Guiding Service, CTR Fraga S-N, E50170 Mequinenza, Zargoza, Spain.
Tel: +34-974465032. fax: 0034-974465403. Mobile: Gary – +34-67455863.
Email: Bavarian@worldonline.es

Spain – carp & barbel:
Peter Staggs, Avenida España,Edificio Zamora VI-1-A, 29680 Estepona, Malaga
Tel. 00-34-952-798018   Mobile 00-34-608-452861. Email: pstaggs@wanadoo.es

Spain -catfish & carp:
Catmaster Tours, Colin Bunn, Siluro House, 37 Marsh End, Kings Norton, Birmingham B38 9BB, England. Tel/Fax: +44-(0)1214511861. Mobile: +34-620605113.   Email: catmaster@telinco.co.uk
Website: www.catmaster.co.uk

USA/Canada – St Lawrence River:
The Complete Angler, 5630 Valerie, Houston, Texas 77081, U.S.A Tel: +1-713 777 22 55 or 315-7641324. Email: bernieh@carp.net

Upstate New York, USA:
Redbreeze, 13645 Waterport-Carlton Road, Waterport, NY 14571, USA. Tel:+1-716-682-3156. Internet: www.redbreeze.com Email: redbreeze@worldnet.att.net

Thailand:
Fishing Adventures Thailand, Jean Francois Helias. Tel/Fax : (662) 651 21 39.
Mobile :(661) 846 98 94. Website: www.anglingthailand.com Email: info@fishingasia.com

Kazakhstan:
Husky Tours & Trading GmbH, Bahnhofstrasse 3, Bäumenheim, Germany. Tel: (0045)-0906 9062. Fax: 0906 91001. E-mail: info@husky-tours.de Internet: www.husky-tours.de

South Africa:
African Gold, Martin Davidson, PO Box 722, Walkerville, 1876 Johannesburg, South Africa. Tel/Fax: +27119491958. Mobile: 0824 447139. Email: inpipe@mweb.co.za
Worldwide:
Ultimate Angling. Email:andy@ultimateangling.com Website:www.ultimateangling.com

ADVENTURES in AFRICA:
Accommodation:
Camping - GRUBBY'S GROTTO in Livingstone. Email: muzza@outpost.co.zm
Lodges - TAITA FALCON LODGE, run by Faan & Anmarie Fourie and Andre Malan: P.O. Box 60012, Livingstone, Zambia. Tel/Fax:(+260)3321850. Mobile: (+263) 11 208387.
Email: taita.falcon@outpost.co.zm
THE RIVER CLUB: Wilderness Safaris, P.O. Box 288, Victoria Falls, Zimbabwe.
Email: wildlodges@telconet.co.zm
CHUNDUKWA TREE LODGE: Cundukwa Adventure Trails P.O.Box 61160, Livingstone, Zambia.
Tel: 260 03324452. E-mail: chunduka@zamnet.za
Cundukwa also have the Nanzhila Bush Lodge and Tented Camp at Kafue National Park. They even organise 1-3 days Horse Trails with qualified guides and 1-3 days Canoeing Safaris on approximately 90 km of the upper Zambezi River.
Flights over the River & Game parks:
BATOKA SKY - operate a 15-minute "Feel The Freedom" flight over the Falls and Zambezi River); or a 30 minute "Great African Air Safari" flight over the falls, Batoka Gorge, Zambezi River and the Mosi-oa-Tunya National Park.
Microlight Flights with Batoka Sky: Maramba Aerodrome, Sichango Rd., Livingstone, Zambia. Tel: +2603320058 or Fax: +2603323095. Mobile: +26311407573. E-Mail: reservations@batokasky.co.za
Internet: www.batokasky.co.za
Del-Air also operates from the same airport. They offer 15 minute or 30 minute Helicopter flights, or longer trips in a Fixed Wing - Cessna 206.
River Cruises:
TAOMGA SAFARIS - This is probably the best of all the Zambezi River cruises. They have been established for 6 years, and run Morning, Lunchtime, and Sunset Cruises. They also provide special Champagne Cruises, Booze Cruises, or Tailor-Made Cruises on request; including camping on the beautiful islands in mid-river. The 'Small' boat holds maximum 40 people; the 'Large' boat max 70 passengers.
The launch site is near 10km peg on River Road from Victoria Falls. The Cruise runs 2km upriver and around the island to the deepwater channel, that divides Zimbabwe and Zambia; which takes about 2 hours. The upriver section of the journey takes you beside the National Park, with chances of viewing wildlife, such as Elephants, Giraffe, Rhino, and other Game. For bookings, contact: P.O. Box 60760 Livingstone, Zambia. Tel: 324081 or 322508. Fax: 324081. Email: taonga@zamnet.zm
Extreme Sports:
AFRICAN EXTREME BUNGI - P.O. Box 60353, Livingstone, Zambia. Tel: +260 3 324231 or fax: +260 3 324238. Mobile: +263 11 405868. E.Mail: bridge@zamnet.zm

Bookings can be made with your agent or directly on the Victoria Falls Bridge (If entering from the Zimbabwe side of the river, you must get a ticket from the Border Post before walking to the bridge). Jumping hours are 09:00 - 17:00 daily.

RAFT EXTREME - P.O. Box 6110577 Zambia. Tel: 3 3324024 Fax: 5260 3322370 Email: Grotto@zamnet.zm

ABSEIL ZAMBIA - This Company offers Abseiling, Highwiring, Rock Climbing, Cable Slide, or the amazing Gorge Swing. Leon Joubert is the originator and designer of this cliff jump, which has been operating since 1995 and is the only one of it's kind in the World. They have secured their own private part of the gorge, set amongst stunning scenery. This must be the closest possible way of committing suicide and surviving! In my view, it surpasses even the Bungi jump for sheer, gut-wrenching thrills! You stand at the very edge of a fantastic 145 metre wide gorge, then literally jump straight off the cliff and free-fall 51 metres directly downwards, until the rope tightens and then swings you like a swooping eagle straight across and in to the 95 metre deep canyon. For bookings or more information, contact: P.O. Box 61023, Livingstone, Zambia. Tel: Livingstone -(03) 323454. Office hours are: 07:00 - 18:00. E-Mail: nidebele@mweb.co.za

TACKLE & BAIT:
Globetrotter Supreme carp & Globetrotter Mega fishing rods:
Email: globetrotterworld@hotmail.com
Gold Label Tackle (High quality carp & big-fish equipment):
Tel: +44-(0)121 3734523. Trade order, Tel: +44-(0)121 3737533
Delkim (Premium quality electronic bite-indicators):
Delkim Limited, 82 St.Andrews Road, Warminster, Wiltshire BA12 8EU, England.
Tel or Fax: +44(0)1234721116
Globetrotter Pod + indicators:
Solar Tackle, PO box 22, Orpington, Kent BR6 7XF, England. Tel: +44-(0)1689-827489
Internet: www.solartackle.co.uk
Carpo Extreme Pod:
Amiud Peche, 346 Rue du Petite bourbon, 85140 Saint-Martin Des Noyers, France.
Tel: +33-0251 078267. Fax: 0033-0251 078429. Internet: www.amiaud-peche.com
Email: info@amiaud-peche.com
Chub Tackle:
www.chubleisure.co.uk
Husar Carp Tackle:
Szczurek Piotr, Buderricherstr.27, 46487 Wesel, Germany. Tel: +49-2803802535.
Mobile: +49-1725482434. Email: info@angel-husar.de Internet: www.angel-husar.de
Nashbait(Carp boilies, mixes, & full range of ingredients & flavours):
PO Box 2061 Rayleigh, Essex, SS69 WQ, England. Tel: +44-(0)1702233232.
Internet: www.nashtackle.co.uk
www.nashteam.net

Eurobaits(carp boilies, mixes & flavours):
Eden Baits GmbH, 46414 Rhede, Holtkamp 1, Germany. Tel: +49-(0)28728225.
Email: info@eurobaits.de
Weighing Scales:
Reuben Heaton Ltd. Tel: +44(0)1455 230241. Fax: +44(0)1455616869
Internet: www.reubenheaton.co.uk Email: info@reubenheaton.co.uk

MAGAZINES:
International Carper: Email: info@internationalcarper.co.uk
Carpworld (UK): Email: info@carpworld.uk.com
Karper(Holland): Email: redactie.karper@vipmedia.nl
Blinker (Germany): Internet: www.blinker.de
Carpe Mirror (Germany): Email: achim@carpmirror.de
Media Carpe (France): Email: media.carpe@wanadoo.fr
Top Carpe (France): Email: tope.carpe@wanadoo.fr
Carpa Tutti (Italy): carpaxtutti@inwind.it
Kapri Svet (Czech Republic): Email: redakce@kaprisvet.czInternet:www.kaprisvet.cz
North American Carp Angler (USA): Email: berntzen-mckenzie@prodigy.net
Trofea Pesca (Spain): Internet: www.cotosdepesca.com
Sportsfiskeren (Denmark): Internet: www.sportsfikeren.dk

CARP & FISHING WEBSITES:
www.globetrotters-quest.com
www.globetrotterworld.co.uk
www.westerlaan-publisher.com
www.carp.com
www.carpforum.com
www.carpanglersgroup.com
www.carpfishing.it
www.anglersnet.co.uk
www.sportfisker.nl
www.magazine-peche.com
www.vbk.be
www.carpmirror.de
www.carphunters.com
www.carp.dk
www.carp.de

A full moon rises over the pinnacle peaks of the Cascades in USA.

Fighting a big carp in the freezing temperatures of a South African winter.

*Globetrotter' releases a big mirror
carp to the tranquil waters.*

A dramatic scene as the sun sets during the final stages of a long battle with a big carp, at the St Lawrence River on the USA/Canadian borders.

The Quest is never over, for the best journeys have no endings, only new beginnings...

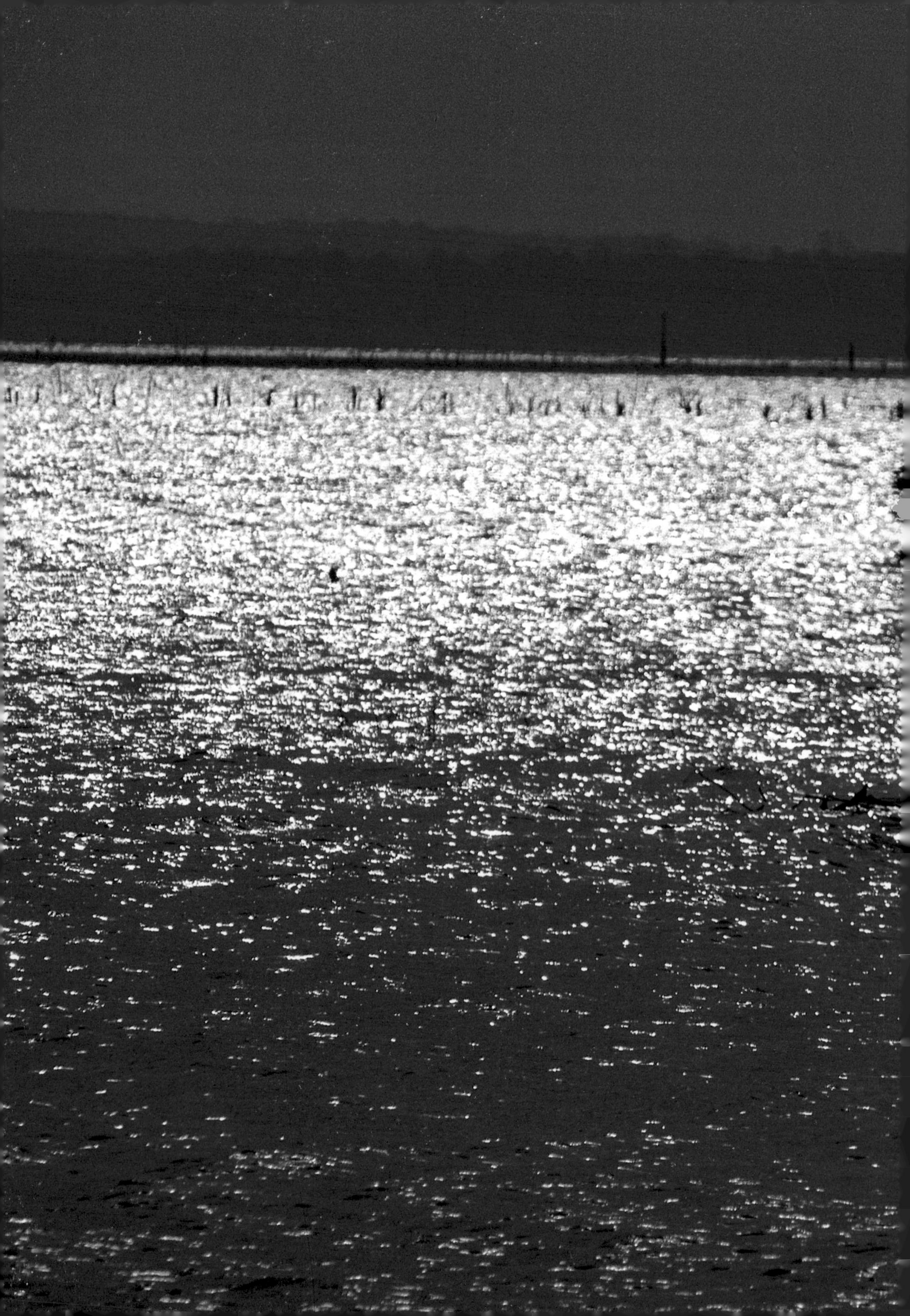